DISCARDED
Mead Public Library

AD Ref Ready Reference
Ready Reference 813.08762 H3511
2010
Heaphy, Maura, 1953– 100 most popular
science fiction authors : biographical sketches
and bibliographies   9001030717

RR

100 Most Popular Science Fiction Authors

Recent Titles in the Popular Authors Series

The 100 Most Popular Young Adult Authors: Biographical Sketches and Bibliographies, Revised First Edition
Bernard A. Drew

Popular Nonfiction Authors for Children: A Biographical and Thematic Guide
Flora R. Wyatt, Margaret Coggins, and Jane Hunter Imber

100 Most Popular Children's Authors: Biographical Sketches and Bibliographies
Sharron McElmeel

100 Most Popular Picture Book Authors and Illustrators: Biographical Sketches and Bibliographies
Sharron McElmeel

100 More Popular Young Adult Authors: Biographical Sketches and Bibliographies
Bernard A. Drew

Winning Authors: Profiles of the Newbery Medalists
Kathleen L. Bostrom

Children's Authors and Illustrators Too Good to Miss: Biographical Sketches and Bibliographies
Sharron McElmeel

100 Most Popular Genre Fiction Authors: Biographical Sketches and Bibliographies
Bernard A. Drew

100 Most Popular African American Authors: Biographical Sketches and Bibliographies
Bernard A. Drew

100 Most Popular Nonfiction Authors: Biographical Sketches and Bibliographies
Bernard A. Drew

100 Most Popular Thriller and Suspense Authors: Biographical Sketches and Bibliographies
Bernard A. Drew

100 Most Popular
Science Fiction Authors

Biographical Sketches and Bibliographies

Maura Heaphy

Popular Authors Series

Libraries Unlimited
An Imprint of ABC-CLIO, LLC

A B C · C L I O

Santa Barbara, California • Denver, Colorado • Oxford, England

Copyright 2010 by Maura Heaphy

All rights reserved. No part of this publication may be reproduced, stored in a retrieval system, or transmitted, in any form or by any means, electronic, mechanical, photocopying, recording, or otherwise, except for the inclusion of brief quotations in a review, without prior permission in writing from the publisher.

Library of Congress Cataloging-in-Publication Data

Heaphy, Maura, 1953-
  100 most popular science fiction authors : biographical sketches and bibliographies / Maura Heaphy.
    p. cm. — (Popular authors series)
  Includes bibliographical references and index.
  ISBN 978-1-59158-746-0 (acid-free paper) 1. Science fiction, American—Bio-bibliography—Dictionaries. 2. Science fiction, English—Bio-bibliography—Dictionaries. 3. Authors, American—20th century—Biography—Dictionaries. 4. Authors, English—20th century—Biography—Dictionaries. I. Title. II. Title: One hundred most popular science fiction authors.
PS374.S35H43 2010
813'.0876209—dc22   2009045693

14 13 12 11 10   1 2 3 4 5

This book is also available on the World Wide Web as an eBook.
Visit www.abc-clio.com for details.

ABC-CLIO, LLC
130 Cremona Drive, P.O. Box 1911
Santa Barbara, California 93116-1911

This book is printed on acid-free paper ∞
Manufactured in the United States of America

For Tom

Contents

Acknowledgments.......................................xi
Introduction..xiii

Douglas Adams..1
Brian W. Aldiss..5
Poul Anderson...12
Catherine Asaro.......................................19
Isaac Asimov..23
Margaret Atwood.......................................30
Kage Baker..34
J. G. Ballard...37
Iain M. Banks...42
Stephen Baxter..46
Greg Bear...51
Alfred Bester...56
Michael Bishop..60
James Blish...65
Ben Bova..70
Leigh Brackett..76
Ray Bradbury..81
Marion Zimmer Bradley.................................87
David Brin..93
John Brunner..97
Lois McMaster Bujold.................................101
Anthony Burgess......................................105
Edgar Rice Burroughs.................................109
Octavia E. Butler....................................114
Pat Cadigan..119
Orson Scott Card.....................................123
Suzy McKee Charnas...................................129
C. J. Cherryh..133
Ted Chiang...139
Arthur C. Clarke (Sir)...............................142
Samuel R. Delany.....................................148
Philip K. Dick.......................................154
Thomas M. Disch......................................160
Cory Doctorow..166
Harlan Ellison.......................................171
Philip José Farmer...................................178
Jack Finney..185

William Gibson	189
Kathleen Ann Goonan	194
Colin Greenland	198
Joe Haldeman	201
Harry Harrison	207
M. John Harrison	213
Robert Heinlein	218
Frank Herbert	224
Russell Hoban	229
Nalo Hopkinson	233
Aldous Huxley	237
Gwyneth Jones	242
James Patrick Kelly	247
Ursula K. Le Guin	252
Stanislaw Lem	258
Madeleine L'Engle	262
Jonathan Lethem	267
Ken MacLeod	272
Anne McCaffrey	276
Maureen F. McHugh	282
Vonda N. McIntyre	286
Frank Miller	291
Walter M. Miller	296
Elizabeth Moon	299
Michael Moorcock	303
Alan Moore	311
Larry Niven	316
George Orwell	322
Marge Piercy	327
Frederik Pohl	331
Mike Resnick	339
Kim Stanley Robinson	347
Spider Robinson	352
Joanna Russ	357
Pamela Sargent	361
Robert J. Sawyer	366
Robert Sheckley	371
Mary Wollstonecraft Shelley	377
Lucius Shepard	381
Robert Silverberg	386
Dan Simmons	394
Cordwainer Smith	398
E. E. "Doc" Smith	402
Neal Stephenson	406
Bruce Sterling	410
Charles Stross	415

The Brothers Strugatsky 419
Theodore Sturgeon 423
Michael Swanwick 428
Sheri S. Tepper 433
James P. Tiptree Jr. 438
A. E. Van Vogt 443
John Varley 448
Jules Verne 452
Vernor Vinge 458
Kurt Vonnegut 462
David Weber 467
H. G. Wells 472
Kate Wilhelm 478
Connie Willis 483
Gene Wolfe 488
John Wyndham 495
Roger Zelazny 499

    References 505
    Author/Title Index 511
    Subject Index 565

Acknowledgments

For their kind help with this volume, I would like to thank

Bernard Drew

Jenz Kjelberg of *The Douglas Adams Continuum* (http://www.douglasadams.se/)

Chris Ogle

Rebecca Testerman and Jeff Tolliver

I would like to thank photographer Beth Gwinn for her permission to use her photographs of great SF writers, taken over her 29-year career as a freelance photographer, to illustrate some author entries. Her talent, enthusiasm and generosity have helped to make this a better, more attractive book. For more information about Beth's photographs, visit her Web site (http://www.cybersecretary.com/bethgwinn/).

I would like to thank the authors, and their assistants and agents, who responded so helpfully to my requests for a picture.

I would also like to thank General Editor Barbara Ittner for her feedback, her patience—and her encouragement.

And, as always, thank you to Richard (for his good advice), and to Kate and Claire—my personal links to a future full of wonders.

Introduction

> *People are walking around the streets with phones to their heads talking to someone ten feet away. . . . We're surrounded by technology and the problems created by technology, and science fiction isn't important?*
> —Ray Bradbury

We live in a science fiction world.

It's a truism, but stated as simply and dramatically as it is by Ray Bradbury, a recognized Master of the Future and the Fantastic, we can see just how true it is. At the end of the first decade of the twenty-first century, we may not have antigravity boots and flying cars, but our days are filled, and our lives made lazier, with gadgets and concepts that only forty—thirty—even ten!—years ago would have seemed like "the stuff of science fiction." Like characters from *Star Trek*, doors whisper open as we approach them, we talk to our computers, and we flip open our "communicators" to speak to someone a few yards—or thousands of miles—away. We pump music straight into our brains, "nuke" our food, and clone sheep. We are cyborgs—our bodies saved from deterioration and disease by hi-tech implants and secondhand replacement parts. We have triumphed over the lowly germ, although periodically we have scares that suggest maybe, just maybe, the germs are getting smarter, and fighting back. We fold up our personal computers, which are smaller than a good dictionary, and slip them into our carryalls—toting more computational power than the mainframes that put one of our number on the moon only forty years ago. We pore over photographs taken on the planet Mars—which are better focused and clearer than the holiday snaps taken at the shore last summer; abandoned hardware, frozen in rustless sleep, whirls in orbit over our heads.

So, presumably, it isn't necessary to justify or explain why science fiction means so much to a great number of passionate readers and viewers. If anything, as the twentieth century came to its close, the writers of science fiction faced a challenge to keep ahead of the discoveries and developments that we could all read about by just picking up a newspaper or a pop science magazine. But rise to the challenge they have, as even the strictest of the hard SF writers have pushed at the boundaries of what might be, and used the "science" as a leaping-off point to consider deep questions of ethics, psychology, community and the very essence of what it means to be human. Meanwhile the writers of "soft" SF—the fabulists, the modern mythologists, and the slipstream artists—have been using the tropes of SF like kids locked in the toy store overnight; boldly going where the story, and particularly the SF story, has never gone before.

Scope and Selection Criteria

This reference book, *100 Most Popular Science Fiction Authors*—the latest volume in Libraries Unlimited's Popular Authors Series—provides an overview of these authors: the hard and the soft, the fabulists and science-grounded, the classic and the cutting-edge contemporary. And while it may be unnecessary to justify the existence of a science fiction volume in this series, it is almost certainly necessary to say a few words of explanation and justification about those authors who have been included and (even more delicate) excluded. For although SF may be a "broad church," covering eons of history, myriad styles, and whole volumes of human achievement and ambition, it is also a genre made up of "territories"—subgenres that have their passionate devotees, who know their stuff, and may not take the exclusion of a favorite lightly.

Other genres of popular fiction have their own special interests, their own splinter groups: detective fiction varies from the hard-boiled to the cozy, romance from the sweetly sentimental to the hard core. But I would argue that science fiction is even more fractured than most popular genres. Hard SF, cyberpunk, slipstream, pulp, gothic, mundane, technothriller, fabulation, steampunk, speculative, New Wave, space opera, golden age. Those who ought to know can't even agree on a baseline definition of the genre: the Web site *Definitions of Science Fiction*, compiled by Neyir Cenk Gökçe, had cataloged fifty-two definitions of "science fiction" duking it out for supremacy when it was last updated in August 1998.

Working with SF and its subgenres can be a minefield. Hard SF—what Robert A. Heinlein called, in a 1952 essay, "legitimate—and often very tightly reasoned—speculation about the possibilities of the real world"—sneers at the New Wave of the 1960s and 1970s for being soft, too character driven and unscientific. Authors such as the late J. G. Ballard, or Margaret Atwood, who for many years has fought the description of her classic *The Handmaid's Tale* as "scifi," may refuse to be bracketed with such simplistic, "unliterary" stuff, preferring to operate under the cover of aliases such as "speculative fiction," "magical realism," or "fabulation." And some of the very latest subgenres of SF, such as slipstream and mundane, seem so different from anything that has gone before that it may be a struggle to identify them as "science fiction" at all.

It would take hardly any effort at all to recruit 100 popular authors to fill volumes devoted to any one of the subgenres of SF. *100 Most Popular Hard SF Authors*? Easy. *100 Most Popular Military SF Authors*? Very easy. *100 Most Popular New Wave SF Authors*? Give me ten minutes. *100 Most Popular Time Travel Authors*? I think I have that list right here. *100 Most Popular Slipstream Authors?* Perhaps a little more challenging, because the subgenre is so new, and the boundaries, appropriately enough, keep shifting. But, with an open mind and a fast broadband connection, it could probably be done.

The fact is, each and every keen reader of SF will have his or her own *100 Most Popular* list, hardwired in personal random access memory. But the remit of this volume is "science fiction," and the 100 authors here must, of necessity, cover a wide spectrum; as well as having interesting and entertaining turf wars, SF readers also have long memories. Writers who would have been read by our grandparents (e.g., E. E. "Doc" Smith or Edgar Rice Burroughs) or even our great-grandparents (Jules Verne, or H. G. Wells) are today still held in fond esteem. There are writers like Robert A. Heinlein, who was doing his best work between 1939 and about 1970. Giving young readers work by Heinlein, Isaac Asimov, Arthur C. Clarke—even Ursula Le Guin, whose classic *The Left Hand of Darkness* was published in 1969—could be seen as the equivalent of giving them an iPod filled with the greatest hits of Frank Sinatra, Bing Crosby, and Perry Como. It's difficult to interest your average undergraduate in classic movies that were made more than a few years ago. ("But . . . it's *black & white*.") And yet—try teaching an undergraduate SF class that leaves Heinlein, Asimov, Clarke, or Le Guin off the syllabus. Cue howls of protest and long (quite intelligent) arguments.

Certain SF writers, and certain works, have unique staying power: not only do they transcend subgenres and narrative fashions, but they can define the kind of SF reader you are, as well as providing a portal to other writers and other works. Others, although not necessarily "best sellers" are recognized as originals who shaped the styles and ideas of countless generations of their literary heirs. The selection in this volume has been based on these various criteria, and not only the "best-seller" label:

- longevity, measured by the timelessness of an author's work and the influence it has had on those who followed;

- critical respect, based on prizes awarded by critics, peers, and readers, and special commendations awarded to living Masters for their lifetime achievement;

- the special niche, for authors who have developed a particular aspect of the SF genre, such as Vonda N. McIntyre, who has done so much with her Star Trek novels to bring respect and narrative weight to what could be a neglected area of the genre; and

- the future, representatives of new print media, like Alan Moore and Frank Miller, who have opened up SF narrative to a whole new dimension with their graphic novels.

Purpose of the Book, Its Intended Audience, and How to Use It

Finding reliable, accurate information about contemporary science fiction authors can be a challenge, particularly for newer authors. Web sites may bury the desired information in pages cluttered with "special effects" and amateur enthusiasm. Reference texts tend to limit their scope to the "usual suspects" (the acknowledged historical and literary giants) and do not take a gamble on the people who are writing the best-selling stories *today*.

The purpose of this guide is to give users a one-stop resource to SF writers who are most popular with today's readers. It is hoped it will be especially useful to smaller public and school libraries that don't have access to online databases. It will be a solid resource for college-level SF classes and for high school students wishing to do reports on SF authors.

Organization and What's Included

Authors are listed in alphabetical order, under the name most likely to be familiar to a reader or bookstore browser (thus, James Tiptree Jr. *not* Alice Bradley Sheldon, Cordwainer Smith *not* Paul Linebarger).

About Pen Names

Many SF authors, particularly those of the golden age of SF pulp magazines, wrote under *multiple* pen names to give themselves the chance to score more than one short story sale per issue. Authors of all periods have adopted pen names as "escape mechanisms," to allow them to try different styles and subgenres rather than being pegged to one particular type of story by their loyal fans. And authors writing as teams sometimes use a pen name for a collaborative "persona." Important pen names are mentioned in the biographical details and listed with the titles linked to those names.

Format

The opening of each entry includes key information to locate the writer in time and in the genre and, where possible, a picture of the author.

- **Writing Types:** The subgenre(s) of SF that the author is best known for writing, listed below the author's name.
- **Benchmark Title:** A possible starting point for a reader new to this author. The title given is not necessarily the author's most famous work or the one most lauded by critics and award committees, but simply a good place to start to get a taste of the author's writing style and an introduction to the author's favorite themes.
- Date and place of **birth** and (if applicable) **death**.
- **Epigraph:** A quotation from the author that says something about the writer's attitude to his or her craft or to science fiction in general. The quotations have been chosen—with a few exceptions—from authors' interviews or nonfiction work.
- **About the Author and the Author's Writing:** A brief biography. This information comes from the sources listed as "Further Information" for each author; direct quotations are cited to the sources listed.
- **Awards:** A tally of major awards won by each author, both for lifetime achievement and for specific works. The following major awards are noted for each author as applicable:

    ACC—Arthur C. Clarke Award

    BSF—British Science Fiction Association

    Campbell—John W. Campbell Memorial Award. Not to be confused with the John W. Campbell Award for Best New Writer, which is listed with lifetime achievement awards.

    Dick—Philip K. Dick Award

Hugo—Science Fiction Achievement Award

> **Retro-Hugos**—awards given retroactively to works and individuals eligible fifty years prior to a current World SF Convention.

Locus Poll—*Locus* magazine's annual readers' poll

Nebula—Award of the Science Fiction Writers of America; presented by professionals to professionals

Prometheus—The Libertarian Futurist Society award; also "Hall of Fame" award for classic fiction

Sturgeon—Theodore Sturgeon Memorial Award

For full information about these awards, awards in other categories and genres, and international SF awards, see http://www.locusmag.com/SFAwards/index.html.

- **Works by the Author:** Beginning with novel-length fiction, grouped together by series, and listed in order of date of publication. Within this section are also

    notable mainstream and other genre fiction,

    other notable short fiction,

    collections, and

    works done "as editor"

    This section is not intended as a complete and comprehensive bibliography. (References and links to comprehensive bibliographies, text and online, are listed wherever possible—see below.) Many SF writers are extremely prolific, and "notable" is always a matter of taste. I have based my selection on

    titles and series with which the author is most closely identified;

    award-winning fiction and collections;

    work that is currently in print; and

    short fiction, novel excerpts, and nonfiction available (observing copyright) online.

- **In Other Media, Nonfiction Books**, and **Articles and Essays:** Listed alphabetically, these items include critical essays and other nonfiction, as well as versions of the author's work in other media (film, television, and radio). **In Other Media** doesn't include every single movie or TV program that the author was ever credited with—instead, it lists movie and TV spin-offs with interesting SF connections, or a "how about that?!" quality. **Nonfiction Books** and **Articles and Essays** are usually limited to items of particular SF interest, but occasionally stretches a point to include books and essays that offer a valuable insight into the author and his or her extracurricular interests, such as Iain M. Banks's guide to whiskey distilleries of Scotland, or Paul Linebarger's ("Cordwainer Smith") volumes on counterespionage and Chinese history.

- **Bibliographies:** Lists of works by and/or about a given author, including bibliographic Web sites. Fiction (novels and stories, poetry, drama, screenplays, etc), nonfiction and criticism, interviews and autobiographical work by the author are *primary* sources; articles and essays that have been written about the author and his or her work or life are *secondary* sources. Authors' official Web sites usually include a comprehensive bibliography of primary sources, and some include lists of or links to key essays and reviews.

- **For Further Information:** This section may include biographies and profiles, interviews, critical work (monographs and essays), and Web sites devoted to a particular author or an author's particular novel or series.

    If there is an official Web site for the author, that will be noted first. An official Web site usually includes biographical and bibliographical information and current author news. Some bonus features may be samples of the author's work (full text of short stories and short articles, excerpts from longer work), FAQs, links to interviews, and photo galleries. Author Web sites are usually professionally designed, up-to-date, and easy to navigate.

    In general, the more current an author, the more likely you are to find information about him or her via the Web. Thus, it is much easier to find online information on Neal Stephenson than on Alfred Bester. However, this isn't always the case. For various reasons—a proactive, technologically savvy estate; dedicated fans; or a revival of interest because of movie or TV tie-ins—there are a number of attractive, well-organized Web sites about classic SF writers (e.g., Edgar Rice Burroughs, Robert A. Heinlein, Philip K. Dick, Cordwainer Smith, and H. G. Wells).

    All URLs for Web sites cited in this volume were checked during October 2009.

The entries in this volume concentrate on the most current interviews available. Sources range from "monographs" (books on a single subject, whether that is the author's career as a whole or a specific novel or story) to collections of essays. Individual essays and articles appear in scholarly journals and magazines or may be posted, or self-published, online.

What distinguishes scholarly essays from popular criticism, or self-published opinion, is not who writes it or where it appears. Essays that appear in scholarly journals are subject to "peer review"; that is, before the essay can be published, it is read by experts in the field, who comment on accuracy and the rigor of the scholarly method. Articles submitted for publication in popular magazines are subject to review by the editor or editorial staff. Articles that are self-published, or posted online, are not necessarily checked by anyone.

What's Not Included

Individual book reviews are not included. There are so many reviews available, online and in print, and they tend to be easy to find, particularly if you consult the home page of online journals and magazines (see the General Bibliography). You can also use indexes such as *Book Review Digest* or *Mostly Fiction*: *Beyond Reality* (mostlyfiction.com/scifi.htm). The exceptions to this are occasional reviews that use the volume under consideration as a launching point to survey the author's entire career.

In Summary

Science fiction is the genre that grew up asking the hard questions about what it means to be human and how we adapt to a world of change. Science fiction does feminism and hard-core military adventure. It does breezy humor, surreal absurdity, and tightly plotted noir thrillers; SF can just as easily turn its sights inward, on the inner workings of the mind and the soul, as well as outward, on the farthest reaches of the universe.

And somewhere in this volume, you will find authors who do exactly what you want SF to do for you.

Sources Cited

Gökçe, Neyir Cenk. *Definitions of Science Fiction.* NCG's Science Fiction Page, May 25, 1996. www.gokce.net/SF/sf_defn.html.

Guardian.co.uk. "Science Fact: The Tech Predicted by *Star Trek.*" *Photogallery Report* (May 15, 2009). www.guardian.co.uk/technology/gallery/2009/may/15/ star-trek-technology?picture=347323502.

Heinlein, Robert A. "Ray Guns and Rocket Ships." In *Expanded Universe,* 372–79. New York: Ace, 1981. (Originally published by the Bulletin of the School Library Association of California, 1952.)

Mesic, Penelope. "Cosmic Ray." *Book Magazine* (December 1998/January 1999). www.raybradbury.com/articles_book_mag.html.

Douglas Adams

Humor and Satire; Science Fantasy

Benchmark Title: *The Hitchhiker's Guide to the Galaxy* (Radio Premier, March 1978)

b. 1951 (England: Cambridge);
d. 2001 (Santa Barbara, California)

I may not have gone where I intended to go, but I think I have ended up where I intended to be.
—The Long, Dark Tea-Time of the Soul (1988)

Photo credit: Chris Ogle

About the Author and the Author's Writing

By the late 1970s, Douglas Adams had acquired a solid background in comedy broadcasting and theater: At St John's College, Cambridge, where he studied English literature, he wrote and performed with the Footlights Club, mixing with various greats and soon-to-be greats of British comedy. After graduation, with the encouragement of Graham Chapman of *Monty Python's Flying Circus*, he embarked on a career as a scriptwriter for the stage, radio, and television. Although success was not immediate —Adams had to take odd jobs as a hospital porter, barn builder, chicken shed cleaner, and bodyguard to make ends meet—his work gradually began to appear on BBC radio and television. By the late 1970s he was regularly writing episodes of various comedy series, writing and appearing in *Monty Python* sketches, and in a position to pitch (usually unsuccessful) ideas for comedy series of his own. In 1977, with producer Simon Brett, he presented an idea for a SF comedy radio program, inspired (as he later told the story) by a cheap vacation he had taken in Europe, where he realized how utterly reliant he was on his handy tourist guidebook.

The Hitchhiker's Guide to the Galaxy first appeared as a BBC Radio 4 series in March 1978. Success was immediate:

> In 1979, soon after publication of the Hitchhiker's Guide, author Douglas Adams was invited to a book signing at a small science fiction shop in Soho. As he drove he was held up by what he assumed to be a demonstration. It was only on arrival that he realised the massive crowds were there to meet him. Rarely has a book, particularly a sci-fi comedy novel, created a following of such scale. (Hope 2007)

Adams's idea—a ragtag group roaming the universe on a ship powered by an Infinite Improbability Drive, relying on the idiosyncratic advice of the *Guide* of the title—has been the driving force behind a series of best-selling novels, a TV series, a record album, computer games, several stage adaptations, and a Hollywood movie. Over 15 million books were sold in the United Kingdom, the United States, and Australia, and it was also a best seller in German, Swedish, and many other languages. Although there may be other writers (Vonnegut, Sheckley, and Sladek, for example) whose SF humor is deeper, more consistent, or even more surreal, *The Hitchhiker's Guide to the Galaxy* is still arguably the funniest thing ever written, because of Adams's sharp, clever prose style, and the way it uses the recognizable absurdities of life, popular culture, and classic SF to construct a looking-glass universe of bad Vogon poetry, depressed androids, and planet designers named Slartibartfast—a universe where it is of supreme importance to know where your towel is at all times, and the meaning of life is 42.

Given that Adams found writing to order an ordeal, it is amazing how much he wrote and accomplished. (Famously, in an interview during the early days of *h2g2* fame, he is supposed to have said, "I love deadlines. I like the whooshing sound they make as they go by." There are apocryphal tales of Adams, deadlines long past, being locked in hotel rooms by his agents and publishers.) The success of *Hitchhikers Guide* and its follow-ups gave him a ready-made audience for his real passions—the environment and the protection of rare and endangered animals. Adams was also fascinated by the real-life possibilities and implications of the infant Internet. He had a personal Web site, adopted a very early version of e-mail, and ran a newsgroup for corresponding with fans, long before most people had heard of such things.

Douglas Noel Adams was born in Cambridge, England, and grew up in Brentwood, Middlesex, in the suburban outskirts of London. After the success of the first radio series of *The Hitchhiker's Guide*, he became a BBC radio producer and then script editor for *Doctor Who*. In 1999 he moved from London to Santa Barbara, California, with his wife Jane Belson and their young daughter, Polly. There, he worked on the screenplay of the long-awaited movie version of *Hitchhikers Guide*, lectured, developed new projects, and made friends. In an interview with *The Daily Nexus* in April 2001, he said, "My books tend to use up ideas at a ferocious rate.... I have a huge backlog of story ideas, and now the sort of panic is, 'Can I do them all in the rest of my career, given the speed at which they're arriving at the moment?'"

Douglas Adams died, suddenly and unexpectedly, of a heart attack on May 11, 2001. Shortly before his death, the Minor Planet Center announced that they had named an asteroid "Arthurdent," in honor of *h2g2*. In January 2005 another asteroid—preliminary designation "2001 DA_{42}"—was named "Douglasadams."

 Works by the Author

The Hitchhiker's Guide "Trilogy"

The Hitchhiker's Guide to the Galaxy (1979)
The Restaurant at the End of the Universe (1980)
Life, the Universe and Everything (1982)
So Long, and Thanks for All the Fish (1984)
Mostly Harmless (1992)

Dirk Gently

Dirk Gently's Holistic Detective Agency (1987)
The Long, Dark Tea-Time of the Soul (1988)

Collections

Douglas Adams at the BBC (BBC Audiobooks, 2004)
The Original Hitchhiker Radio Scripts (1995)
The Salmon of Doubt: Hitchhiking the Galaxy One Last Time (2003)

In Other Media

The Hitchhiker's Guide to the Galaxy:
>Radio series: BBC Radio 4. First broadcast March 8, 1978.
>Television series: BBC, 1981. Directed by Alan J.W. Bell; starring Simon Jones, Peter Jones, and David Dixon.
>Motion picture: Touchstone Pictures, 2005. Directed by Garth Jennings; starring Martin Freeman, Mos Def, and Zooey Deschanel.

Hyperland. Documentary. BBC, 1990.
Starship Titanic. Computer game. http://www.douglasadams.com/creations/

Nonfiction Books

Last Chance to See (1992, with Mark Carwardine)

Articles and Essays

"The Internet: The Last Battleground of the 20th Century" (interview, September 1, 1999). BBC Radio 4. http://www.bbc.co.uk/radio4/douglas_adams/

"Parrots, the Universe and Everything" (lecture, May 2001). *Voices—A University of California Santa Barbara Television Series.* http://www.uctv.tv/search-details.aspx?showID=5779

For Further Information

Official Web site: http://www.douglasadams.com/

Botti, Nicolas. *Life, DNA and H2G2.* June 2006. http://douglasadams.info/. A comprehensive fan Web site covering biographical information about DNA and his work, *H2G2,* in all of its incarnations, from radio to movie.

Buhler, Brendan. *The Daily Nexus* (University of California Santa Barbara), April 5, 2001. http://www.dailynexus.com/article.php?a=678

Gaiman, Neil. *Don't Panic: Douglas Adams &* The Hitchhiker's Guide to the Galaxy. London: Titan, 2005.

Hope, Simon. "DNA—The Source of Life, the Universe and Everything." *SciFiUK.com* (February 2007). http://scifi.uk.com/2007/02/18/douglas-adams-dna-the- source-of-life-the-universe-and-everything/

Kjellberg, Jenz. *The Douglas Adams Continuum* (April 23, 2009). http://www.douglasadams.se/

Lee, Jay. Interview. KPFT Radio, 1988. http://www.baldheretic.com/2005/07/15/125

Shircore, Ian. "Douglas Adams: The First and Last Tapes (Full transcript of a 1979 interview for *Penthouse Magazine*). *Protospace* (April 3, 2007). http://www.protospace.com/2007/04/03/douglas-adams-interview-part-i/

Simpson, M. J. *Hitchhiker: A Biography of Douglas Adams.* Boston: Justin Charles, 2005.

Swaim, Don. "Audio Interviews with Douglas Adams: 1983 and 1989" (interviews from 1983 and 1989). *Wired for Books* (March 7, 2009). http://wiredforbooks.org/douglasadams/

Webb, Nick. *Wish You Were Here: The Official Biography of Douglas Adams.* New York: Ballantine, 2005.

Yeffeth, Glenn, ed. *The Anthology at the End of the Universe: Leading Science Fiction Authors on Douglas Adams'* The Hitchhiker's Guide to the Galaxy. Dallas, TX: Benbella, 2005.

ZZ9 Plural Z Alpha. Official Web site of the *Hitchhiker's Guide to the Galaxy* Appreciation Society. http://www.zz9.org/

Brian W. Aldiss

Myth and Legend; New Wave

Benchmark Title: *Helliconia Spring* (1982)

b. 1925 (England: East Dereham, Norfolk)

I love SF for its surrealist verve, its loony non-reality, its piercing truths, its wit, its masked melancholy, its nose for damnation, its bunkum, its contempt for home comforts, its slewed astronomy, its xenophilia, its hip, its classlessness, its mysterious machines, its gaudy backdrops, its tragic insecurity.
—"The Glass Forest: An Attempt at Autobiography" (1986)

Photo credit: © Studio Edmark.
Courtesy of Brian Aldiss, OBE

About the Author and the Author's Writing

If Brian Aldiss had only written the SF novels and many stories that he has to his credit, he would have been guaranteed a place on any respectable list of 100 SF Greats. If he had only written his many essays, reviews, and histories of SF, he would be considered one of the great scholars of the genre. The many anthologies he has edited, and his important role in SF's New Wave of the late 1950s and 1960s, would guarantee that he be remembered as one who helped to shape the genre as it exists at the beginning of the twenty-first century. But the fact is that Brian Aldiss has done all of these things. In a genre that is generously endowed with prolific authors, insightful critics, and writers with strong opinions and big ideas, he is a figure to be reckoned with. After sixty years in the business, Brian Aldiss remains SF's "Renaissance Man."

Brian Wilson Aldiss was born in East Dereham, in the county of Norfolk, England. His father worked in the draper's shop established by his grandfather; his family lived above the shop. Upon the birth of a baby sister, when he was age six, he was banished—there is no other word for it—to boarding school, because his mother could not cope with a new baby and a lively little boy. At eighteen he (as he puts it in the 1987 biographical notes for *Trillion Year Spree*) "escaped to the Far East for some years," joining the Royal Signals Corps and serving in Burma and Sumatra.

But at some point in this sad childhood, which he has chronicled in volumes of autobiography and semiautobiographical novels, such as *The Hand-Reared Boy* (1970), Aldiss discovered SF and pulp magazines such as *Astounding Science Fiction*: "Destiny led my tiny if palsied hands to buy that. I felt this was the real world: that it was much more important than anything I knew before" (Brown 2001). On his return from the Far East he began writing—his first published work was a collection of amusing stories based on his experience of working in an Oxford bookshop.

Given Aldiss's lifetime experiences—as a powerless member of a family in meltdown; as an isolated and lonely child in boarding school; as a young man in the military, surrounded by the alien entropy of the Sumatran jungle; and even as a professional writer whose career has seen highs and lows, and who in the early 1980s saw all of his accomplishments swept away due to the mistakes of an accountant—it is not surprising that some of his finest work deals with extremes and the way humankind's better nature survives—or fails—under fantastic pressures. Unlike some New Wave writers, Aldiss had no problem adapting the classic tropes of SF to accommodate sophisticated psychology and plausible characters. His first SF title, *Non-Stop* (1958), concerns a primitive society struggling to survive in a strange landscape of bulkheads and corridors and riotous vegetation—the U.S. title, *Starship*, gives away the forgotten secret at the heart of this strange society. *Hothouse* (1962) deals with a far-future Earth that has been overrun by enormous baobab trees; the unimaginably evolved descendants of the human race play out their drama of survival in the trees' nooks and crannies. The Helliconia Trilogy is set on a planet that has such an eccentric orbit around a binary star system that one "year" takes 1,000 Earth years; in the course of its "Great Year," the seasons consume whole generations, and civilization itself is forgotten in the struggle for survival.

Back then, I thought two things: one, that the future would be highly technical, without superfluous fat, cockroaches or famine. And, on the other hand, that we would all go to Hell in a bucket.
—Auden (2005)

Brian Aldiss has written mainstream realistic fiction (the Horatio Stubbs saga), fantasy (*The Malacia Tapestry, Dracula Unbound*), historical fiction (*Jocasta*), thrillers (*The Cretan Teat,* The Squire Quartet), memoirs, travel books, science fiction of the near future and the far future, space opera, surrealism, and planetary romance. He has been the recipient of some of SF's most prestigious awards, for lifetime achievement as well as for his individual works. In the 2005 Birthday Honours list of HM Queen Elizabeth II, Brian Aldiss was awarded the title Officer of the Order of the British Empire (OBE) for services to literature. In July 2008 he was awarded an honorary doctorate by the University of Liverpool in recognition of his contribution to literature. Over a literary career that spans six decades, Brian W. Aldiss has been the inspiration and good conscience of whole generations of SF readers and writers. Long may he continue to surprise and delight us.

Awards

Most Promising New Author, World Science Fiction Convention (1958)
International Association for the Fantastic in the Arts Distinguished Scholar (1986) and "Permanent Special Guest" at the annual IAFC conference
Grand Master, Science Fiction and Fantasy Writers of America (1999)
Prix Utopia (1999)

SF Hall of Fame and First Fandom Hall of Fame (2004)
Officer of the Order of the British Empire (2005)

Novels
Helliconia Spring (1982) **BSF, Campbell**
Helliconia Winter (1985) **BSF**

Short Fiction
"Hothouse" (1962) **Hugo**
"The Saliva Tree" (1965) **Nebula**

Collections
Moment of Eclipse (1970) **BSF**

Nonfiction
Billion Year Spree (1973) **BSF, Hugo**
Trillion Year Spree (1986, with David Wingrove) **Hugo, Locus Poll**
The Twinkling of an Eye: My Life as an Englishman (1999) **Hugo, Locus Poll**

Works by the Author
Non-Stop (1958)
Equator (1959; orig. *Vanguard from Alpha*)
The Interpreter (1960; orig. *Bow Down to Nul*)
The Primal Urge (1961)
Hothouse (1962; US, abridged: *The Long Afternoon of Earth*)
The Dark Light Years (1964)
Greybeard (1964)
Earthworks (1965)
An Age (1967; US: *Cryptozoic!*)
Report on Probability A (1968)
Barefoot in the Head (1969)
Frankenstein Unbound (1973)
The 80 Minute Hour (1974)
Brothers of the Head (1977, illustrated by Ian Pollock)
Moreau's Other Island (1980)
The Year Before Yesterday (1987). A fix-up of *Equator* (1958) and *The Impossible Smile* (1965).
Somewhere East of Life: Another European Fantasia (1994)
White Mars Or, The Mind Set Free (2000, with Roger Penrose)
Super-State (2002)

Sanity and the Lady (2005)
HARM (2007)

The Helliconia Trilogy

Helliconia Spring (1982)
Helliconia Summer (1983)
Helliconia Winter (1985)

Notable Mainstream and Other Genre Fiction

The Brightfount Diaries (1955)
The Malacia Tapestry (1977)
Dracula Unbound (1991)
The Cretan Teat (2002)
Affairs at Hampden Ferrers (2004)
Jocasta (2005)

The Horatio Stubbs Trilogy

The Hand-Reared Boy (1970)
A Soldier Erect (1970)
A Rude Awakening (1978)

The Squire Quartet

Life in the West (1980)
Forgotten Life (1988)
Remembrance Day (1993)
Somewhere East of Life (1994)

Other Notable Short Fiction

"But Who Can Replace a Man?" (1958)
"Man in His Time" (1965)
"Total Environment" (1968)
"Super-Toys Last All Summer Long" (1969)
"The Secret of Holman Hunt and the Crude Death Rate" (1975)
"Enemies of the System" (1978)
"A Chinese Perspective" (2000)
"The Hibernators" (2003)

Collections

Space, Time and Nathaniel (1957)
The Canopy of Time (1959; US: *Galaxies like Grains of Sand*)
The Airs of Earth (1963; US: *Starswarm*)

Best SF Stories of Brian Aldiss (1965; US: *But Who Can Replace a Man?*)
The Saliva Tree, and Other Strange Growths (1966)
Neanderthal Planet (1969; orig. *Intangibles, Inc. and Other Stories*)
The Moment of Eclipse (1971)
The Comic Inferno (1972; orig. *The Book of Brian Aldiss*)
Last Orders and Other Stories (1977)
New Arrivals, Old Encounters (1979)
Seasons in Flight (1984)
A Tupolev Too Far (1994)
The Secret of This Book (1995, US: *Common Clay: 20-Odd Stories*)
A Romance of the Equator (1989)
Super-Toys Last All Summer Long and Other Stories of Future Time (2001)
Cultural Breaks (2005)

As Editor

Penguin Science Fiction (1961)
Introducing Science Fiction (1967)
Space Opera (1974)
Evil Earths (1975)
Galactic Empires 1 (1976)
Galactic Empires 2 (1977)
The Penguin World Omnibus of Science Fiction (1977, with Sam J. Lundwall)
Perilous Planets (1978)
A Science Fiction Omnibus (2007)

With Harry Harrison

Farewell Fantastic Venus (1968)
Decade the 1940's (1975)
Hell's Cartographers: Some Personal Histories of Science Fiction Writers (1975)
Decade the 1950's (1976)
Decade the 1960's (1977)

In Other Media

Frankenstein Unbound. The Mount Corporation, Twentieth Century Fox, 1991. Directed by Roger Corman; starring John Hurt and Raul Julia.

A.I.: Artificial Intelligence. Warner Brothers Pictures, 2001. Directed by Steven Spielberg; starring Haley Joel Osment and Jude Law. Screenplay by Ian Watson and Steven Spielberg, from an idea by Stanley Kubrick; based on Aldiss's short story "Super-Toys Last All Summer Long."

Brothers of the Head. Potboiler Productions, 2005. Directed by Keith Fulton and Louis Pepe; starring Jonathan Pryce.

Nonfiction Books

Cities and Stones—A Traveller's Yugoslavia (1966)
The Shape of Further Things (1970)
Billion Year Spree: The History of Science Fiction (1973). Revised and expanded as *Trillion Year Spree: The History of Science Fiction* (1986, with David Wingrove).
Science Fiction Art (1975)
This World and Nearer Ones (1981)
The Pale Shadow of Science (1985)
. . . And the Lurid Glare of the Comet (1986)
The Pale Shadow of Science (1986)
Bury My Heart at W. H. Smith's (1990)
The Detached Retina: Aspects of SF and Fantasy (1995)
The Twinkling of an Eye: My Life as an Englishman (1998)
When the Feast Is Finished (1999, with Margaret Aldiss)
Art After Apogee: The Relationships Between an Idea, a Story, a Painting (2000, with Rosemary Phipps)

Articles and Essays

"The Glass Forest: An Attempt at Autobiography." In *. . . And the Lurid Glare of the Comet.* Seattle: Serconia Press, 1986. http://www.solaris-books.co.uk/aldiss/html/glassforest.htm. Previously appeared in a shorter version in *Contemporary Authors—Autobiography Series* Vol. 2 (1985).

"The Sky's No Limit." *The Guardian* (London), July 8, 2006. http://books.guardian.co.uk/departments/sciencefiction/story/0,,1815451,00.html

Bibliographies

Aldiss, Margaret. *The Work of Brian W. Aldiss: An Annotated Bibliography and Guide*, ed. Boden Clarke. San Bernardino, CA: Borgo, 1992.

For Further Information

Official Web site. http://www.brianwaldiss.co.uk/

Auden, Sandy. "Aldiss and More: An Interview with Brian Aldiss." *SF Site* (2005). http://www.sfsite.com/08b/saba206.htm

Blish, James. "In Conversation: James Blish Talks to Brian Aldiss." In *The Tale That Wags the God,* ed. Cy Chauvin, 170–84. Chicago: Advent, 1987.

"Brian W. Aldiss comes to HARM. (Interview)" *SF Crowsnest.com*, August 1, 2007. http://www.sfcrowsnest.com

Brown, Andrew. "Master of the Universes." *The Guardian* (UK), June 16, 2001. http://www.guardian.co.uk/Archive/Article/0,4273,4204853,00.html

Collings, Michael R. *Brian W. Aldiss*. Starmont Reader's Guide No. 28. Mercer Island, WA: Starmont, 1987.

Griffin, Brian, and David Wingrove. *Apertures: A Study of the Writings of Brian W. Aldiss*. Westport, CT: Greenwood, 1984.

Henighan, Tom. *Brian W. Aldiss*. New York: Twayne, 1999.

Hunt, Stephen. "Brian Aldiss: The Master of Glacial Heliconia." *SF Crowsnest* (January 2003). http://www.sfcrowsnest.com

Swaim, Don. Audio Interview. *Wired for Books* (1984 and 1986). http:// wiredforbooks.org/brianaldiss/

Poul Anderson

Hard SF; Myth and Legend; Time Travel

Benchmark Title: *Tau Zero* (1970)

b. 1926 (Bristol, Pennsylvania);
d. 2001 (Orinda, California)

As for the value of the individual, I'm quite consciously in the Heinleinian tradition there. It's partly an emotional matter—a libertarian predilection, a prejudice in favor of individual freedom—and partly an intellectual distrust based on looking at the historical record . . . a distrust of large, encompassing systems.
—Interview in *Locus* (1997)

Photo credit: Beth Gwinn

About the Author and the Author's Writing

Poul Anderson was a scientist, a historian, and a romantic. All of the characters in Anderson's stories, in their distinctive ways, are fighting to hold back entropy—the tendency for all things in life and in the universe to crumble and fail. His characters struggle for survival against the forces of physics (*Tau Zero*); they guard the integrity of the past against those who would corrupt it (the <u>Time Patrol</u> series); and, as immortals (*The Boat of a Million Years*), they face up to every wound and indignity that entropy can inflict upon them. In a career that encompassed over 50 novels, and 200-plus short works, Anderson wrote space opera, hard SF, romantic and historical fantasy, sociopolitical drama, horror, adventure comedy, and broad farce; what links them all is that his characters are always, in their ways, "special people, slowly wise, [who] meet their universe head-on and prevail. Courage accomplishes deeds entropy cannot mar" (Miesel 1978).

Anderson's larger-than-life adventure stories achieve their impact through a skillful interweaving of history, mythology, and a solid, believable grounding in science; meticulous astrophysics, according to *Anatomy of Wonder* (2004), blended with brooding romanticism. Anderson is an acknowledged master of world-building, offering lush (but believable, and scientifically sound) alien settings, and vivid and carefully imagined alien life-forms, all presented with an awareness of the way that a story's detail can reinforce its themes. This was all enhanced by his knowledge of myth and legend, especially Scandinavian languages, literature, and history; according to *The Encyclopedia of Science Fiction* (1999), his novels are "peopled by solid, canny stock (frequently . . . of Scandinavian descent) whose politics and social views often register as conservative . . . although perhaps this cultural style could more fruitfully be regarded as a form of romantic, Midwestern libertarian individualism."

Anderson was fascinated by the fate of empires, and his romantic pessimism is borne out by the Earth empires that he replicated in space—the Roman, Scandinavian, American, and Soviet—all great powers mightily striving and forging forward to the inevitable Dark Ages that await them all. He was unashamedly conservative, but his libertarian ideals were as rigorously thought out as his science, and in his stories there are no easy "good guy/bad guy" face-offs—there are complicated issues, with two sides and hard consequences for all involved. Horrified by the prospect of a Soviet hegemony over Earth, Anderson was still wise enough to see that putting America in that role could just as easily result in the destruction of American democracy. He has more faith in the individual; for example, his larger-than-life character Prince Nicholas van Rijn of the Technic History stories, the "entrepreneur as hero," swashbuckling capitalist, cast in the mold of seventeenth-century merchant-adventurers, who were in it for the sheer joy of the adventure.

Poul William Anderson was born in Bristol, Pennsylvania, and grew up in Texas, Denmark, and Minnesota. His first story in a long, prolific career was published in 1947, while he was studying physics at the University of Minnesota. Upon graduation he moved to San Francisco, where he met Karen Kruse. They were married in 1953, and they made their home in the Bay area for the rest of his life; husband and wife often collaborated on writing projects. Their daughter, Astrid, is married to SF writer Greg Bear.

Anderson was called "the enduring explosion" by fellow writer James Blish; a true reflection of his work would take many pages. He was a widely respected member of the SF community, much loved for his good humor and hard work. In addition to the many awards he received during his life, both for individual work and lifetime achievement, Anderson was president of Science Fiction and Fantasy Writers of America and a member of the Swordsmen and Sorcerers' Guild of America; he was a founding member of the Society for Creative Anachronism. Anderson was a great believer in the personal and historical advantage of humankind's expansion into space, and throughout his life he was a tireless proponent of the space program. He also served on the Advisory Board of the SETI League, the organization devoted to the search for intelligent life in the universe, from its inception in 1995.

Poul Anderson died July 31, 2001, in Orinda, California. His work is a testimony to his observation, "Life can be cruel, and it is ultimately tragic, but mostly it is wonderful, or would be if we'd allow it to be."

Awards

Edward E. Smith Memorial Award for Imaginative Fiction ("Skylark award") (1982)
SFWA Grand Master (1998)
SF Hall of Fame (2000)
Prometheus Lifetime Achievement (2001)

Novels

The Star Fox (1965) **Prometheus Hall of Fame 1995**

Trader to the Stars (1969) **Prometheus Hall of Fame 1985**
The Stars Are Also Fire (1995) **Prometheus**
Genesis (2000) **Campbell**

Short Fiction

"The Longest Voyage" (1960) **Hugo**
"No Truce with Kings" (1964) **Hugo**
"The Sharing of Flesh" (1969) **Hugo**
"The Queen of Air and Darkness" (1971) **Hugo, Nebula, Locus Poll**
"Goat Song" (1972) **Hugo, Nebula**
"Hunter's Moon" (1979) **Hugo**
"The Saturn Game" (1981) **Hugo, Nebula**

Works by the Author

Tomorrow's Children (1947, with F. N. Waldrop)
Chain of Logic (1947)
Vault of the Ages (1952)
The Broken Sword (1954)
Brain Wave (1954)
Question and Answer (1954; aka *Planet of No Return*)
No World of Their Own (1955)
The Long Way Home (1958)
Perish by the Sword (1959)
War of Two Worlds (1959)
The Enemy Stars (1959; aka *We Have Fed Our Sea*)
The High Crusade (1961)
Murder in Black Letter (1960)
Orbit Unlimited (1961)
Twilight World (1961)
After Doomsday (1962)
The Makeshift Rocket (1962)
Murder Bound (1962)
Shield (1963)
Three Worlds to Conquer (1964)
The Corridors of Time (1965)
There Will Be Time (1972)
The Star Fox (1965)
World without Stars (1966)
Tau Zero (1970)
The Byworlder (1971)

The Dancer from Atlantis (1971)
There Will Be Time (1973)
Fire Time (1974)
Inheritors of Earth (1974, with Gordon Eklund)
The Winter of the World (1975)
The Avatar (1978)
The Demon of Scattery (1979, with Mildred Downey Broxon)
The Devil's Game (1980)
New America (1982)
Orion Shall Rise (1983)
The Boat of a Million Years (1979)
The Saturn Game (1989)
The Longest Voyage (1991)
War of the Gods (1997)
Starfarers (1998)
Genesis (2000)
Mother of Kings (2001)
For Love and Glory (2003)

Harvest of Stars

Harvest of Stars (1993)
The Stars Are Also Fire (1994)
Harvest the Fire (1995)
The Fleet of Stars (1997)

Hoka (with Gordon R. Dickson)

Earthman's Burden (1957)
Star Prince Charlie (1975)
Hoka! (1983)

The Psychotechnic League

Star Ways (1956; aka *The Peregrine*)
The Snows of Ganymede (1958)
Virgin Planet (1959)
The Psychotechnic League (1981)
Cold Victory (1982)
Starship (1982)

Technic History, Terran Empire: Dominic Flandry

We Claim These Stars (1959)
Earthman, Go Home! (1960)

Let the Spacemen Beware (1963; aka *The Night Face*)
Agent of the Terran Empire (1965)
Flandry of Terra (1965)
Ensign Flandry (1966)
The Rebel Worlds (1969)
A Circus of Hells (1970)
The Day of Their Return (1973)
A Knight of Ghosts and Shadows (1974)
A Stone in Heaven (1979)
The Long Night (1983)
The Game of Empire (1985)
Flandry (1993)

Technic History, Polesotechnic League: Nicholas Van Rijn

War of the Wing-Men (1958; later revised and reissued as *The Man Who Counts*)
Hiding Place (1961)
The Trouble Twisters (1966)
Satan's World (1969)
Trader to the Stars (1969)
The People of the Wind (1973)
Mirkheim (1977)
The Earth Book of Stormgate (1978)

Time Patrol

Time Patrol (1955)
Brave to Be a King (1959)
Gibraltar Falls (1975)
The Year of the Ransom (1988)
The Shield of Time (1990)

Other Notable Short Fiction

"The Helping Hand" (1950)
"The Man Who Came Early" (1956)
"The Life of Your Time" (1965, as Michael Karageorge)
"Marque and Reprisal" (1965)
"Kyrie" (1968)
"The Fatal Fulfillment" (1970)
"The Ways of Love" (1979)
"Star of the Sea" (1991)
"The Lady of the Winds" (2001)

Collections

Orbit Unlimited (1961)
Un-Man and Other Novellas (1962)
Time and Stars (1964)
The Many Worlds of Poul Anderson (1974)
The Night Face & Other Stories (1979)
The Dark Between the Stars (1981)
The Guardians of Time (1981)
Winners (1981) (collection of Anderson's Hugo-winning stories)
Maurai and Kith (1982)
The Long Night (1983)
Past Times (1984)
The Unicorn Trade (1984, with Karen Anderson)
Dialogue with Darkness (1985)
Space Folk (1989)
The Shield of Time (1990)
Alight in the Void (1991)
Kinship with the Stars (1991)
All One Universe (1996)
Hoka! Hoka! Hoka! (1998)
Hokas Pokas! (2000)
Going for Infinity (2003)
Time Patrol (2006)
To Outlive Eternity and Other Stories (2007)

As Editor

Nebula Award Stories Four (1969)
A World Named Cleopatra (1977)
No Truce with Kings/Ship of Shadows (1989, with Fritz Leiber)
The Saturn Game/Iceborn (1989, with Paul A. Carter and Gregory Benford)
The Longest Voyage/Slow Lightning (1991, with Steven Popkes)
The Night Fantastic (1991, with Karen Anderson)

With Martin H. Greenberg and Charles G. Waugh

Mercenaries of Tomorrow (1985)
Time Wars (1986)
Terrorists of Tomorrow (1986)
Space Wars (1988)

In Other Media
The High Crusade. Centropolis Film Production, 1994. Directed by Klaus Knoesel and Holger Neuhäuser; starring John Rhys-Davies.

Nonfiction Books
Is There Life on Other Worlds? (1968)

Articles and Essays
"How to Build a Planet." In *Turning Points: Essays on the Art of Science Fiction,* ed. Damon Knight. New York: Harper & Row, 1977.

"On Thud and Blunder." In *Articles on Writing.* Science Fiction and Fantasy Writers of America, January 4, 2005. http://www.sfwa.org/2005/01/on-thud-and-blunder

The Staff of *Analog & Isaac Asimov's Science Fiction Magazine.* "The Creation of Imaginary Worlds: The World Builder's Handbook and Pocket Companion." In *Writing Science Fiction & Fantasy.* New York: St. Martin's Griffin, 1993.

Bibliographies
Benson, Gordon, Jr., and Phil Stephensen-Payne. *Poul Anderson, Myth-master and Wonder-weaver: A Working Bibliography.* San Bernardino, CA: Borgo, 1990.

For Further Information
Barrett, David V. Obituary. *Guardian Online,* August 6, 2001. http://books.guardian.co.uk/news/articles/0,,532151,00.html

Blish, James. "Poul Anderson: The Enduring Explosion." In *The Tale That Wags the God,* ed. Cy Chauvin, 86–92. Chicago: Advent, 1987.

Interview. *Locus* (April 1997). http://www.locusmag.com/1997/Issues/04/Anderson.html

Miesel, Sandra. *Against Time's Arrow: The High Crusade of Poul Anderson.* San Bernardino, CA: Borgo, 1978.

———. "Poul Anderson." In *St. James Guide to Science Fiction Writers*, ed. Jay Pedersen. Detroit, MI: St. James, 1996.

Tenn, William. "Poul Anderson." In *Dancing Naked: The Unexpurgated William Tenn.* Framingham, MA: New England Science Fiction Association, 2004. http://dpsinfo.com/williamtenn/poulanderson.html

Catherine Asaro

Hard SF; SF Romance

Benchmark Title: *The Quantum Rose* (2000)

b. 1955 (Oakland, California)

Traditionally, you couldn't write intimate scenes in science fiction. You just turned the lights out. Well, you don't have to turn the lights out anymore.
—Interview at *Physics Central* (2001)

Photo credit: Stephen Baranovics.
Permission of Catherine Asaro.

About the Author and the Author's Writing

There have been SF mysteries, SF thrillers, and SF horror; with a little thought, and a little generosity with subgenre boundaries, it would probably be possible to find examples of the "scientification" of any and all fiction subgenres you might care to name. Every subgenre, that is, except romance. Romance is generally a sideshow, marginalized by either the science of hard SF or the formulaic chivalry of science fantasy. Dr. Catherine Asaro, holder of a master's degree in physics and a Ph.D. in chemical physics from Harvard University, saw the gap in the market, and to the delight of her fans, filled it with her thoughtful, sexy, and firmly science-grounded tales, eleven of which are based on the convoluted political and personal relationships that fuel the galactic wars of the Skolian Empire. Asaro's current total of twenty-three novels includes hard science fiction; near-future thrillers such as *Sunrise* and *Alpha*; and science fantasy and romance, the <u>Lost Continent</u> series.

Araso's SF is a lively mix of space adventure, romance, and erotica; although her stories deal with the larger-than-life politics and intrigue that beset the ruling families of the warring Skolian Empire and their sworn enemies, the neighboring Eubian Concord, they are usually anchored firmly in the convincing relationships of men and woman who are struggling to find fulfillment in situations much bigger then themselves, "with detailed and plausible explanations of the physics behind the technologies she describes" (Harman 2000). Her debut novel, *Primary Inversion* (1995), introduced the Skolian empire with a familiar story of star- (and war-) crossed lovers, whose attempt to find happiness sets in motion events that will disrupt the status quo between the warring dynasties for generations.

One of the hallmarks of Asaro's fiction is the way she challenges gender boundaries and faces up to difficult issues in the relationships between her characters. In *Primary Inversion*, Sauscony Valdoria is a warrior, biomechanically enhanced to be a fighter and pilot. She is the dominant partner in her relationship with the hero, Jaibriol Qox—dominant in every way, as she is physically bigger, stronger, and almost twice his age. When Asaro's novel *The Quantum Rose* was first serialized in 2000, it shocked some readers with its uncompromising depiction of the abuse—physical, verbal, and sexual—that the central character Kamoj Quanta Argali has to endure in a relationship. Asaro's is not your grandmother's romance. *The Quantum Rose* won the Nebula Award for best novel of 2001. Asaro is also a three-time winner of the Prism Award for best novel, Analog Readers' Poll, and the Romantic Times Book Club award for "Best Science Fiction Novel."

Catherine Asaro was born in Oakland, California, and grew up in El Cerrito, just north of Berkeley. As well as her MA and PhD from Harvard, she also earned a BS with highest honors in chemistry from UCLA. Her research involved using quantum theory to describe the behavior of atoms and molecules, and her paper, "Complex Speeds and Special Relativity," which appeared in the April 1996 issue of *The American Journal of Physics*, forms the basis for the faster-than-light capability of the societies in her novels. She was a professor of physics until 1990, when she established Molecudyne Research. In addition to her fiction, she has also published essays and scientific papers in distinguished academic journals.

A former ballerina, Asaro was principal dancer and artistic director of the Mainly Jazz Dancers and the Harvard University Ballet. Recently she managed to combine her interest in music and the performing arts with her fiction, with the *Diamond Star* project: in April 2009, the indy rock group Point Valid released a CD of music that serves as a soundtrack to Asaro's novel of the same name, the story of an aristocratic refugee from the Skolian Empire who tries to buck his violent heritage by becoming a rock star on Earth.

Asaro is the founder of Molecudyne Research and a member of the board of directors of The Lifeboat Association, a group of scientists and futurists from other disciplines who are dedicated to encouraging research on possible ways that humankind might survive an extinction level event, such as an asteroid strike. She recently completed two terms as president of Science Fiction and Fantasy Writers of America, Inc. (SFWA). Catherine Asaro lives in Maryland with her husband, who is an astrophysicist with NASA, and their daughter, Catherine.

Awards

Novels

The Quantum Rose (2000) **Nebula**

Short Fiction

"The Space-Time Pool" (2008) **Nebula**

Works by the Author

The Veiled Web (1999)
The Phoenix Code (2000)
Sunrise Alley (2004)
Alpha (2006)

Saga of the Skolian Empire

Primary Inversion (1995)
Catch the Lightning (1996)
The Last Hawk (1997)
The Radiant Seas (1998)
Skyfall (2003)
Schism (2004)
The Final Key (2005)
The Ruby Dice (2008)
Diamond Star (2009)

Radiant War Aftermath

Ascendant Sun (2000)
The Quantum Rose (2000)
Spherical Harmonic (2001)
The Moon's Shadow (2003)

Other Notable Genre Fiction

Lost Continent (aka Aronsdale) series

The Charmed Sphere (2004)
The Misted Cliffs (2005)
The Dawn Star (2006)
The Fire Opal (2007)
The Night Bird (2008)

Other Notable Short Fiction

"Dance in Blue" (1993)
"Light and Shadow" (1994)
"Aurora in Four Voices" (1998)
"Boot Hill" (2000, with Mike Resnick)
"Soul of Light" (2001)
"The City of Cries" (2005)
"The Shadowed Heart" (2005)

As Editor

Irresistible Forces (2004)

In Other Media

Diamond Star. Starflight Music. Performed by Point Valid, April 2009. Music CD, "soundtrack" for Ansaro's book, *Diamond Star*.

Articles and Essays

"A Luminous Future." In *Year Million: Science at the Far Edge of Knowledge*, ed. Damien Broderick. New York: Atlas, 2008.

With John Cannizzo. "Through the Apple." In *Stepping Through the Stargate: Science, Archaeology and the Military in* Stargate, ed. P. N. Elrod and Roxanne Conrad. Dallas, TX: Benbella Books, 2004.

For Further Information

Official Web site: http://www.catherineasaro.net/

Aylott, Chris. "Catherine Asaro: Space Opera = Physics + Romance." *Space.com,* February 6, 2000. http://www.space.com/sciencefiction/books/asaro_000204.html

"Catherine Asaro." In *Authors & Artists for Young Adults*, Volume 47, 1–8. Farmington Hills, MI: Gale Group, 2003.

Gannon, Charles E. "When Music Arises from the Fusion of Binary Stars." *SF Site* (April 2009). http://www.sfsite.com/05a/ca295.htm

Harman, J. Alexander. Interview. *Strange Horizons,* October 2, 2000. http://www.strangehorizons.com/2000/20001002/Article_Asaro_JAHarman.shtml

Heermann, Travis. Interview. *Blogging the Muse,* August 12, 2008. http://travisheermann.com/blog/?p=50

Interview. *Fast Forward: Contemporary Science Fiction* (April 2008). http://fast-forward.tv/blog/?p=53

Interview. *Mike Hodel's Hour 25,* September 29, 2001. http://www.hour25online.com/Hour25_Previous_Shows_2001-9.html

Interview. *Physics Central* (2001?). http://www.physicscentral.com/explore/people/asaro.cfm

Interviews. *The Future and You,* February 13, 2008 and June 25, 2008. http://www.thefutureandyou.libsyn.com/?search_string=asaro&Submit=Search&search=1

Lifeboat Association. *Biography.* n.d. http://lifeboat.com/ex/bios.catherine.asaro

Metherell-Smith, Stephen J. "Catherine Asaro: Fictional Fusion." *Crescent Blues* (April 2000). http://www.crescentblues.com/3_2issue/asaro.shtml

"Sophrosyne's Saturday Salon: Catherine Asaro." *Events in Extropia,* August 9, 2008. http://eventsinextropia.wordpress.com/asaro/. Second lifestyle virtual interview.

Tan, Charles. Interview. *Nebula Awards,* April 22, 2009. http://www.nebulaawards.com/index.php/interview/catherine_asaro_2009/

Isaac Asimov

Hard SF; Sense of Wonder; Space Opera

Benchmark Title: *Foundation* (1951)

b. 1920 (USSR: Petrovichi); d. 1992 (New York)

> *What I* will *be remembered for are the Foundation Trilogy and the Three Laws of Robotics. What I* want *to be remembered for is no one book, or no dozen books. . . . [M]y total corpus for quantity, quality and* variety *can be duplicated by no one else. That is what I want to be remembered for.*
> —Personal letter, 1973, In *Yours, Isaac Asimov* (1995)

About the Author and the Author's Writing

To the end of his life, Isaac Asimov was unsure of the exact date of his birth. Born in Petrovichi, Russia (near Smolensk), his family emigrated to the United States in 1923, when he was approximately three years old. In the course of the fantastic upheaval of this move and the clashing perspectives of the Russian, Julian, and Hebrew calendars, the precise birth date of little Isaac was "mislaid": "[I]t might have been as early as October 4, 1919. There is, however, no way of finding out. My parents were always uncertain and it really doesn't matter. I celebrate January 2, 1920, so let it be" (*In Memory Yet Green*).

But there is no doubt that, from the age of three, Isaac Asimov grew up in Brooklyn, New York, where his parents ran a candy store. He was a remarkably bright child, with an extraordinary memory, his nose perpetually in a book. He discovered SF on the magazine rack in the family store, and by age eleven he had started writing novels of his own. It was an appropriate start for someone who would one day describe himself as a "compulsive" writer, who would end his career with nearly 500 books to his credit, as author or editor, in an astonishingly broad array of genres and subjects: mystery, poetry, science, humor, horror, literary criticism, mythology—even guides to the Bible and Shakespeare. In fact, the career that began in a candy store in Brooklyn ended with Isaac Asimov's work being represented in every single category of the Dewey Decimal System, except philosophy.

In 1939 Asimov graduated from Columbia University with a BA in chemistry and had his first three short stories published: "Trends" in *Astounding* and "Marooned Off Vesta" and "The Weapon Too Dreadful to Use" in *Amazing Stories*. During World War II he moved to Philadelphia to work as a junior chemist at the U.S. Naval Air Experimental Station, where he worked with Robert A. Heinlein and L. Sprague de Camp and still managed to publish eight to ten stories per year. By 1948 he had earned his doctorate in chemistry. Asimov then joined the faculty of the Boston University School of Medicine; he remained associated with that university for the rest of his life.

Although his position was nonteaching after 1958 (when his writing income had already exceeded his academic salary), he retained the title of associate professor; in 1979 the university honored his writing by promoting him to full professor of biochemistry. Asimov's personal papers from 1965 on are archived at the University's Mugar Memorial Library. The collection fills 464 boxes, on 232 feet of shelf space.

There is also no doubt that Isaac Asimov was a great intelligence and a tireless and entertaining writer, beloved of both established fans of SF and the novice readers who discover a portal to a new world through his work. Of his many short stories, "Night Fall" (1941) has been acclaimed as the "best SF short story ever written" (by a poll of the Science Fiction Writers of America in 1968). In the 1942 story "Runaround," Asimov made a permanent mark on the conventions of the genre with his "Three Laws of Robotics":

1. A robot may not injure a human being or, through inaction, allow a human being to come to harm.
2. A robot must obey orders given to it by human beings, except where such orders would conflict with the First Law.
3. A robot must protect its own existence as long as such protection does not conflict with the First or Second Laws.

With these Laws, Asimov defined the territory of the artificial intelligence story, setting parameters that every subsequent author who wanted to write a robot story had to defer to, challenge, or redefine. In a sense, Asimov's Three Laws set the stage for what fifty years later would become a new trope of SF—the singularity and the possibilities of a post-human existence.

Isaac Asimov died on April 6, 1992. He was survived by his second wife, Janet, and his children from his first marriage. Ten years after his death, in the revised and updated edition of his autobiographies, Janet Asimov revealed that Asimov's death was due to AIDS. He had been infected with HIV from a blood transfusion received during a heart bypass operation in 1983.

Carl Sagan described Isaac Asimov as one of " the master explainers of the age." Asimov was the recipient of any number of prestigious science and SF awards; he received fourteen honorary doctoral degrees from various universities. The Honda Corporation named its prototype anthropoid robot ASIMO for him. But perhaps the honor that he would have enjoyed most—the one that might have best pleased the little boy from Petrovichi, who didn't know the date of his own birth—was the asteroid, 5020 Asimov, discovered in 1981 and named in his honor.

Awards

WorldCon Special Convention Awards (1963)

Astounding/Analog, Best All-Time Series (1966): The Foundation series

Edward E. Smith Memorial Award for Imaginative Fiction ("Skylark award") (1967)

SFWA Grand Master (1987)

SF Hall of Fame (1997—posthumous)

First Fandom Hall of Fame (2008)

Novels
The Gods Themselves (1972) **Hugo, Locus Poll**, **Nebula**
Foundation's Edge (1982) **Hugo, Locus Poll**

Short Fiction
"The Mule" (1945) **Retro Hugo 1996**
"The Bicentennial Man" (1976) **Hugo, Locus Poll**, **Nebula**
"Robot Dreams" (1986) **Locus Poll**
"Gold" (1991) **Hugo**

Nonfiction
In Joy Still Felt (1980) **Locus Poll**
I, Asimov: A Memoir (1994) **Hugo, Locus Poll**

As Editor
Before the Golden Age (1975) **Locus Poll**

Works by the Author
The End of Eternity (1955)
Fantastic Voyage (1966)
The Gods Themselves (1972)
Fantastic Voyage II: Destination Brain (1987)
Nemesis (1989)
Nightfall (1990, with Robert Silverberg)
The Ugly Little Boy (1992, with Robert Silverberg; aka *Child of Time*)
The Positronic Man (1993, with Robert Silverberg)

Foundation Trilogy
Foundation (1951)
Foundation and Empire (1952)
Second Foundation (1953)

Extended Foundation Series
Foundation's Edge (1982)
Foundation and Earth (1986)
Prelude to Foundation (1988)
Forward the Foundation (1993)

Robot Novels
The Caves of Steel (1954)

The Naked Sun (1957)
The Robots of Dawn (1983)
Robots and Empire (1985)

Trantorian Empire

Pebble in the Sky (1950)
The Stars, Like Dust (1951)
The Currents of Space (1952)

Other Notable Genre Fiction

The Death Dealers (1958)
Murder at the ABA (1976)
More Tales of the Black Widowers (1976)
The Key Word and Other Mysteries (1977)
The Union Club Mysteries (1983)

Children's and Young Adult Series

Lucky Starr (as Paul French)

From *David Starr, Space Ranger* (1952) to *Lucky Starr and the Rings of Saturn* (1958)

Norby Chronicles (with Janet Asimov)

From *Norby, the Mixed-Up Robot* (1983) to *Norby and the Court Jester* (1991)

Other Notable Short Fiction

"Marooned Off Vesta" (1939)
"Robbie" (1940)
"Nightfall" (1941)
"Runaround" (1942)
". . . And Now You Don't" (1950)
"The Ugly Little Boy" (1958)
"Eyes Do More than See" (1964)
"Founding Father" (1965)
"That Thou Art Mindful of Him!" (1974)
"Robot Dreams" (1986)

Collections

The Martian Way and Other Stories (1955)
Earth Is Room Enough (1957)
Nine Tomorrows (1959)
Triangle (1961; aka *The Empire Novels*)
Through a Glass, Clearly (1967)

Nightfall and Other Stories (1969)
Opus 100 (1969)
The Early Asimov (1972)
The Best of Isaac Asimov (1973)
Buy Jupiter and Other Stories (1975)
The Bicentennial Man and Other Stories (1976)
Opus 200 (1979)
The Winds of Change and Other Stories (1983)
Opus 300 (1984
The Alternate Asimovs (1986)
The Best Science Fiction of Isaac Asimov (1986)
Azazel (1988)
The Asimov Chronicles: Fifty Years of Isaac Asimov! (1989)
Gold: The Final Science Fiction Collection (1995)
Magic (1995)

The Positronic Robot Stories

I, Robot (1950)
The Rest of the Robots (1964)
The Complete Robot (1982)
Robot Dreams (1986)
Robot Visions (1990)

As Editor

Fifty Short Science Fiction Tales (1963, with Groff Conklin)
Tomorrow's Children (1966)
Where Do We Go from Here? (1971)
Before the Golden Age (1974)
Laughing Space (1982, with Janet Asimov)
Science Fiction Masterpieces (1986)
The Dark Void (1987)
Beyond the Stars (1987)

With Martin H. Greenberg

Isaac Asimov Presents the Best Science Fiction of the 19th Century (1981, and with Charles G. Waugh)
Science Fiction A to Z (1982, and with Charles G. Waugh)
Caught in the Organ Draft: Biology in Science Fiction (1983, and with Charles G. Waugh)
Hallucination Orbit: Psychology in Science Fiction (1983, and with Charles G. Waugh)
Election Day 2084: Science Fiction Stories About the Future of Politics (1984)
Machines That Think: The Best Science Fiction Stories about Robots and Computers (1984, and with Patricia S. Warrick)

Cosmic Critiques: How & Why Ten Science Fiction Stories Work (1990, and with Ansen Dibell)

In Other Media

Bicentennial Man. 1492 Pictures, 1999. Directed by Chris Columbus; starring Robin Williams and Sam Neill.

I, Robot. Twentieth Century Fox, 2004. Directed by Alex Proyas; starring Will Smith, Alan Tudyk, and James Cromwell.

Nonfiction Books

Fantasy & Science Fiction Magazine science essay collections:
- *Fact and Fancy* (1962)
- *View from a Height* (1963)
- *Adding a Dimension* (1964)
- *Of Time and Space and Other Things* (1965)
- *From Earth to Heaven* (1966)
- *Science, Numbers, and I* (1968)
- *The Solar System and Back* (1970)
- *The Stars in Their Courses* (1971)
- *The Tragedy of the Moon* (1973)
- *The Left Hand of the Electron* (1974)
- *Of Matters Great and Small* (1975)
- *The Planet That Wasn't* (1976)
- *Quasar, Quasar, Burning Bright* (1978)
- *The Road to Infinity* (1979)
- *The Sun Shines Bright* (1981)
- *Counting the Eons* (1983)
- *X Stands for Unknown* (1984)
- *The Subatomic Monster* (1985)
- *Far as Human Eye Could See* (1987)
- *The Relativity of Wrong* (1988)
- *Out of the Everywhere* (1990)
- *The Secret of the Universe* (1991)

Asimov's New Guide to Science (1960)

In Memory Yet Green (1979)

In Joy Still Felt (1980)

Asimov on Science Fiction. (1981)

Asimov's Galaxy: Reflections on Science Fiction (1989)

I, Asimov: A Memoir (1994)

Our Angry Earth (1991, with Frederik Pohl)

Yours, Isaac Asimov: A Life in Letters (1995, edited by Stanley Asimov)

It's Been a Good Life. (2002, edited by Judith Jeppsom Asimov). Condensed and re-edited version of three previous volumes of autobiography.

Articles and Essays

"Social Science Fiction." In *Turning Points: Essays on the Art of Science Fiction,* ed. Damon Knight. New York: Harper & Row, 1977. Also in this volume, "There's Nothing Like a Good Foundation."

"The 'Threat' of Creationism." in *Science and Creationism,* ed. Ashley Montagu. New York: Oxford University Press, 1984. http://www.stephenjaygould.org/ctrl/azimov_creationism.html

For Further Information

Official Web site: http://www.asimovonline.com/

Boerst, William J. *Isaac Asimov: Writer of the Future.* Greensboro, NC: Morgan Reynolds, 1997.

Freedman, Carl Howard. *Conversations with Isaac Asimov.* Jackson: University Press of Mississippi, 2005.

Gunn, James. *Isaac Asimov: The Foundations of Science Fiction.* New York: Oxford University Press, 1996.

Hassler, Donald M. *Isaac Asimov.* Mercer Island, WA: Starmont, 1991.

Ingersoll, Earl G. "A Conversation with Isaac Asimov." *Science Fiction Studies* 14 (1987). http://www.depauw.edu/sfs/interviews/asimov41interview.htm

National Public Radio ."Robot Maker: A Talk with the Late Isaac Asimov." *Fresh Air from WHYY,* September 9, 1987. http://www.npr.org/templates/story/story.php?storyId=3461066

Saekow, Roland. *Asimov Vault.* April 2007. http://homepage.mac.com/pockyrevolution/asimov/index.htm

Schaer, Sidney C. Obituary. *Newsday,* April 7, 1992. http://tech.mit.edu/V112/N18/asimov.18w.html

Swaim, Don. Audio Interview. In *Wired for Books.* Ohio University, 1987. http://wiredforbooks.org/isaacasimov/

Touponce, William F. *Isaac Asimov.* Boston: Twayne, 1991.

White, Michael. *Isaac Asimov: A Life of the Grand Master of Science Fiction.* New York: Carroll & Graf, 2005.

Margaret Atwood

Feminist SF; Near Future

Benchmark Title: *The Handmaid's Tale* (1986)

b. 1939 (Canada: Ottawa)

Literature is an uttering, or outering, of the human imagination. It lets the shadowy forms of thought and feeling—heaven, hell, monsters, angels and all—out into the light, where we can take a good look at them.

—"'Aliens Have Taken the Place of Angels': Why We Need Science Fiction" (2005)

Photo credit: George Whiteside.
Permission of Margaret Atwood.

About the Author and the Author's Writing

Margaret Atwood is the author of more than thirty books—novels, short stories, poetry, literary criticism, social history, and books for children. She has been awarded honorary degrees from universities all over the world, including Oxford, Harvard, the Sorbonne, and University College Dublin. In addition to *The Handmaid's Tale*, she has written two other novels that make use of SF conventions: the postapocalyptic *Oryx and Crake* (2003); *The Blind Assassin* (2000), which features, as a story within a story, an old-fashioned pulp space opera; and her most recent work, *The Year of the Flood* (2009). But *The Handmaid's Tale* remains, according to *The Encyclopedia of Science Fiction* (1999), "the best SF novel ever produced by a Canadian." It was adapted for the screen by Harold Pinter in 1990; it has been staged as an opera, performed by English National Opera in London, in April 2003. Appropriately, it has stirred much controversy: it is one of the American Library Association's 10 Most Challenged Books of 1999 and was Number 37 on "The 100 Most Frequently Challenged Books of 1990–2000."

Margaret Eleanor Atwood was born in Ottawa, Canada. Her father was an entomologist at the University of Toronto, and much of her childhood was spent living in the backwoods of northern Quebec, where her father conducted his research. She did not complete a full year of traditional school until the eighth grade. However, she did become a voracious reader: classic literature, mysteries, Grimm's fairy tales, Canadian animal stories, and comic books. Shortly after Atwood graduated from Victoria University in the University of Toronto in 1961, with a bachelor of arts in English, she won the E.J. Pratt Medal for her privately printed book of poems, *Double Persephone*. She did her graduate studies at Harvard's Radcliffe College, with a Woodrow Wilson fellowship, and during the late 1960s and early 1970s taught at various universities in Canada and at NYU in New York City, where she was Berg Professor of English. In the early 1980s Atwood noted with some alarm that the automatic response of friends and colleagues to stories of misogynistic religious fanaticism in places like Iran and Afghanistan was to shrug and say, "It can't happen here." *The Handmaid's Tale* set out to show them exactly how it could.

The Handmaid's Tale is a dystopian novel, in the honorable tradition of speculative fiction that teaches us lessons about the present by showing us just how terrible the future could be. But according to Joyce Carol Oates, in a review to mark the twentieth anniversary of its publication, *The Handmaid's Tale* "differs from its classic dystopian predecessors in the intimacy of the protagonist's voice and in the convincing domestic background Atwood has established for her." The narrator, who is called "Offred" —that is, "of Fred" (even her own name has been taken away from her)—is a prisoner of "Gilead," a totalitarian theocracy that has come to power in what was formerly the United States. Among other policies inspired by expediency and a narrow, repressive reading of the Bible, the masters of Gilead force fertile women to be their concubines, in order to produce babies for their barren wives. These "handmaids" are property, beaten if they are uncooperative, killed if they rebel, and cast aside when they are unable to get pregnant. Oates describes Offred's voice as "distinct and individual, with sharp, painful memories of what she has lost (husband, daughter, radical feminist mother, college roommate)." Like the best dystopias, *The Handmaid's Tale* has layer upon layer of horrors, and complications that make it more relevant, and frightening, on every reading.

Today, Margaret Atwood lives in Canada with her husband and daughter, dividing her time between Toronto and Pelee Island, Ontario. For some time she was very resistant to the labeling of her great speculative work as "science fiction." In an interview posted on the Doubleday Book Group Corner Web page, she said, "No, it certainly isn't science fiction. Science fiction is filled with Martians and space travel to other planets, and things like that. That isn't this book at all."

But in 2005 she wrote an essay entitled "Why We Need Science Fiction" for the English newspaper *The Guardian,* and another called "My Life in Science Fiction," for the October 2006 issue of the French SF journal *Cycnos*. SF has always recognized *The Handmaid's Tale* as one of its own—perhaps Atwood has made her peace with SF.

Awards

Novels

The Handmaid's Tale (1986) **ACC**

Works by the Author

The Handmaid's Tale (1986)
The Blind Assassin (2000)
Oryx and Crake (2003)
The Year of the Flood (2009)

Notable Mainstream Fiction

The Edible Woman (1969)
Surfacing (1972)
Lady Oracle (1976)
Life Before Man (1979)
Bodily Harm (1981)
Cat's Eye (1989)
The Robber Bride (1993)
Alias Grace (1996)
The Penelopiad (2005)

In Other Media

The Handmaid's Tale. Bioskop Film,1990. Directed by Volker Schlöndorff; screenplay by Harold Pinter; starring Natasha Richardson, Faye Dunaway, and Robert Duvall.

In addition, *The Handmaid's Tale* has been adapted as an opera (Paul Ruders, 2000), a radio play (BBC, 2000), and for the stage (Brendan Burns, 2002).

Nonfiction Books

Survival: A Thematic Guide to Canadian Literature (1972)
Second Words: Selected Critical Prose (1984)
Strange Things: The Malevolent North in Canadian Literature (1995)
Negotiating with the Dead: A Writer on Writing (2002)
Curious Pursuits—Occasional Writing 1970–2005 (2005)

Articles and Essays

"'Aliens Have Taken the Place of Angels': Why We Need Science Fiction." *The Guardian,* July 17, 2005. http://arts.guardian.co.uk/fridayreview/story/0,,1507718,00.html

"For God and Gilead." *The Guardian,* March 22, 2003. http://arts.guardian.co.uk/features/story/0,,919211,00.html

"My Life in Science Fiction/Ma Vie et la Science-Fiction." *Cycnos* 22 (2005). http://revel.unice.fr/cycnos/document.html?id=616

Bibliographies

Alexander, Lynn. "A Working Bibliography." *Women Writers: Magic Mysticism and Mayhem* (Spring 1999). University of Tennessee, Martin. http://www.utm.edu/staff/lalexand/350/talebib.htm

For Further Information

Margaret Atwood Reference Site. http://www.owtoad.com/

The Margaret Atwood Society. http://themargaretatwoodsociety.wordpress.com/

Bloom, Harold, ed. *Margaret Atwood*: The Handmaid's Tale. Philadelphia: Chelsea House, 2003.

Cooke, Nathalie. *Margaret Atwood: A Critical Companion.* Westport, CT: Greenwood, 2004.

Doubleday. "The Handmaid's Tale." *Book Group Corner*, May 17, 2006. http://www.randomhouse.com/resources/bookgroup/handmaidstale_bgc.html

Howells, Coral Ann, ed. *The Cambridge Companion to Margaret Atwood.* Cambridge, UK: Cambridge University Press, 2006.

Ingersoll, Earl G., ed. *Waltzing Again: New & Selected Conversations with Margaret Atwood.* Princeton, NJ: Ontario Review, 2006.

Jokinen, Anniina. *Contemporary Women Writers* (January 2007). http://www.luminarium.org/contemporary/atwood/atwoodnovels.htm. The Margaret Atwood entry of this resource Web site makes sense of the chaos of Web links available; this extensive and extremely well-designed Web site contains biographical information and links to excerpts, synopses, essays, and reviews.

Nischik, Reingard M., ed. *Margaret Atwood: Works and Impact.* Rochester, NY: Camden House, 2000.

Oates, Joyce Carol. "Margaret Atwood's Tale." *The New York Review of Books,* November 2, 2006. http://www.nybooks.com/articles/19495

Potts, Robert. "Light in the Wilderness." *The Guardian,* April 26, 2003. http://books.guardian.co.uk/departments/generalfiction/story/0,6000,943485,00.html

Stein, Karen F. *Margaret Atwood Revisited.* New York: Twayne, 1999.

Wilson, Sharon R. "Margaret Atwood and Popular Culture: *The Blind Assassin* and Other Novels." *Journal of American Culture* 25, nos. 3/4 (2002): 270–75.

Kage Baker

SF Romance; Time Travel

Benchmark Title: *In the Garden of Iden* (1997)

b. 1952 (Hollywood, California)

Photo credit: Tom Westlake.
Permission of Kage Baker.

People love California because they love hope, and they detest it because no real place can ever match their dreams. . . . Anything is possible here. And, at any given moment and without warning, the earth may move and the solid world shatter like a pane of glass. Nice metaphor for life itself, eh? Which is, perhaps, why I use it as a setting as often as I do.
—Gevers, Interview at *Sf Site* (2002)

About the Author and the Author's Writing

First, about the name: it's pronounced "cage," and it's a combination of the first syllables of the names of her two grandmothers, Kate and Genevieve. And according to Michael M. Levy, writing in *Anatomy of Wonder* (2004) about her 1997 novel *In the Garden of Iden*, "[t]here are few original ideas in science fiction, but Baker has found a good one."

This good idea involves a mysterious consortium, The Company, which exists in a future when time travel is possible, but prohibitively expensive. The Company, or Doctor Zeus Inc., as it is also known, optimizes its time-travel resources by recruiting individuals from various times in the past and turning them into cyborgs—immortal constructs who operate in deep cover over the centuries, doing the Company's business. And what business is that? As the series begins, it seems straightforward, and benign, enough: the Company is dedicated to retrieving and saving the natural and artificial treasures of Earth's past—lost artifacts and extinct species. But over eight novels and many well-regarded short stories, that question becomes darker and more complicated, as Baker develops a fascinating story arc that combines romance, black humor, and dark possibilities for the future of humankind.

Kage Baker was born in Hollywood, California, in 1952. She grew up in a large, artistic family—her mother was the painter Katherine C. Baker—and her childhood was shaped by the expectation that, as the daughter and granddaughter of artists, writers, and teachers, she *would* grow up to become a writer. But the young Kage decided to resist expectations: "And I more or less ran away with the circus for the next twenty years" (Gevers 2002).

Since then she has worked as a mural painter, insurance claims processor, actor, director, and stage manager. She has taught Elizabethan English as a Second Language. In the 1970s she became active with the Living History Centre (now known as As You Like It Productions), the organization that produced the first Renaissance Faire, "[a]nd this was what really shaped my craft, because it gave me a tremendous education in both theatre and history" (Gevers 2002).

In spite of her misgivings about writing, or what one might call her reluctance to embrace her destiny, she began submitting stories (some of which developed into that "good idea," the saga of the Company) to various SF magazines as long ago as the mid-1980s. Her first story sale was a Company story, "Noble Mold," in 1997. This was followed closely by *In the Garden of Iden*, which was first published in England. Her subsequent work has been translated into Spanish, French, Italian, Hebrew, and German.

In the Company novels, Baker draws upon her background in the theater and her love of history. "I find the pageant of history more interesting than rocket ships blasting off to other planets. And, at the end of the day, people are more entertaining than technology" (Gevers 2002). In 2007 she ended the Company series with *The Sons of Heaven* (2007), a novel that promised to explain all and tie up all the loose ends, although she promises that there may be more short stories to fill in gaps in the long and convoluted history of Dr. Zeus Inc. and its operatives, "as I find historical incidents that intrigue me" (VanderMeer 2008). In the meantime, Baker has been writing straight fantasy (*The Anvil of the World,* 2003) and historical romance (*Or Else My Lady Keeps the Key*, 2008), as well as a new foray into pure SF, *The Empress of Mars* (2009), a planetary romance in which Edgar Rice Burroughs's Barsoom meets the terraformed Mars of Kim Stanley Robinson and Ben Bova.

Kage Baker currently writes ad copy part-time for a San Luis Obispo newspaper and resides in a tiny cottage in Pismo Beach, California, with a lilac-crowned Amazon parrot who has learned to say, "Hello" and "Shut up, Harry" (Brown 2003). She is a great fan of Jethro Tull, and at least one of her stories ("Leaving His Cares Behind") draws its inspiration from one of their songs. She gardens and continues to write; sometimes families get it right.

Awards

Short Fiction

"The Empress of Mars" (2003) **Sturgeon**

Works by the Author

The Company

In the Garden of Iden (1997)
Sky Coyote (1999)
Mendoza in Hollywood (2000)
The Graveyard Game (2001)
The Life of the World to Come (2004)
The Children of the Company (2005)
The Machine's Child (2006)
The Sons of Heaven (2007)

Other Notable Genre Fiction

The Anvil of the World (2003)
The House of the Stag (2008)
Or Else My Lady Keeps the Key (2008)
The Empress of Mars (2009)

Other Notable Short Fiction

"Noble Mold" (1997)
"The Dust Enclosed Here" (2001). http://www.infinityplus.co.uk/stories/dustenclosed.htm
"The Angel in the Darkness" (2003)
"The Empress of Mars" (2003). http://www.asimovs.com/_issue_0406/empressofmars.shtml
"Rude Mechanicals" (2007). Online audiobook: http://subterraneanpress.com/index.php/magazine/spring2007/audio-rude-mechanicals-by-kage-baker/
"Speed, Speed the Cable" (2008).

Collections

Black Projects, White Knights: The Company Dossiers (2002)
Mother Ægypt and Other Stories (2004)
Dark Mondays (2006)
Gods and Pawns (2007)

Articles and Essays

"Introduction." In *From the Files of the Time Ranger*, by Richard Bowes. Urbana, IL: Golden Gryphon Press, 2005.

For Further Information

Official Web site: http://www.kagebaker.com/

Blaschke, Jayme L. "An Interview with Kage Baker." *Postscripts* : (Summer 2004): 82–92.

Brown, Charles N. "Kage Baker: Company Time." *Locus* 50 (June 2003): 92–94. http://www.locusmag.com/2003/Issue06/Baker.html

Gevers, Nick. Interview. *SF Site* (August 2002). http://www.sfsite.com/08b/kb134.htm

Martini, Adrienne. "An Interview with Kage Baker." *Bookslut* (June 2006). http://www.bookslut.com/features/2004_06_002632.php

VanderMeer, Jeff. "An Interview with Kage Baker." *Clarkesworld Magazine* (March 2008). http://clarkesworldmagazine.com/baker_interview/

J. G. Ballard

Apocalyptic SF; Near Future; New Wave

Benchmark Title: *The Atrocity Exhibition* (1969)

b. 1930 (China: Shanghai); d. 2009 (England: London)

There are shifts in the unseen tectonic plates that make up our national consciousness. I've tried to nail down a certain kind of nihilism that people may embrace, and which politicians may embrace, which is much more terrifying; all tapping into this vast, untouched resource as big as the Arabian oilfields called psychopathology.

—Hall, "J.G. Ballard," *Spike Magazine* (2004)

About the Author and the Author's Writing

James Graham Ballard grew up surrounded by luxury. Born in Shanghai, China, the son of a director of a British-owned fabric finishing and printing company, Ballard's world was one of swimming pools, servants, and chauffer-driven cars—and a sharp divide between the local population and the expatriate community. But this comfortable childhood came to an abrupt end in 1942 when the Japanese invaded and occupied Shanghai. With other "enemy aliens," Ballard and his family were interned in Lunghua Civilian Assembly Centre from 1942 to 1945. These years of uncertainty and danger—but also a kind of excitement and freedom—form the basis of Ballard's semiautobiographical novel *Empire of the Sun* (1984).

The war over, the Japanese vanquished, the status quo restored (perhaps), Ballard returned to England in 1946. Once again he found himself a sort of "enemy alien"—a teenager who had seen terrible things, a stranger among so-called family, a foreigner in his nominal homeland. He struggled through private boarding school and did a couple of years of pre-med at King's College, Cambridge; he spent an aimless year at the University of London studying English. Instead of attending classes, he immersed himself in avant-garde cinema (everything from German Expressionist films of the 1920s to Hollywood noir thrillers), surrealist art, and the psychological theories of Sigmund Freud and Carl Jung. He began to write, and, during hours of boredom doing his National Service in the RAF at an airbase in Moosejaw, Saskatchewan, Canada, he discovered American science fiction. Something clicked: James Ballard became J. G. Ballard and found his milieu.

Ballard began with deliberate pastiches of that American SF, but before long he was doing something very different. "[G]one are the alien races, the flying saucers and mutated atomic monsters . . . . Instead we are treated to a poet's vision of a haunted world" (Behrens 2003). Even in its very earliest incarnations, Ballard's SF is challenging: the novels known as the <u>Global Disaster Quartet</u> move sharply from conventional disaster narrative to something altogether more rich and strange. The editor of the magazine *New Worlds*, Edward J. Carnell, was a great supporter of Ballard's work at this time, publishing almost all of his early short fiction, even as Ballard was struggling with the determination of SF to hold fast to the wooden characters and ironclad plotting of the pulps. In 1962 Ballard nailed his colors to the mast: he wrote an editorial essay for *New Worlds* entitled "Which Way to Inner Space?," in which he proposed a thematic and stylistic overhaul of the entire genre. Ballard was more interested in the psychology of the modern world than the gadgets; he encouraged experimentation, in form and content, flirted with popular culture, and demonstrated a willingness to push the boundaries and challenge taboos. Ballard's "manifesto" placed him firmly at the center of the New Wave, which shaped the SF of the 1960s and 1970s and still resonates today.

The works that followed "derive[d] their startling power from the contemporary world viewed sideways" (Brigg 1996). *The Atrocity Exhibition* (1970) and *Crash* (1973) were calculated to shock—Ballard was exploring the violence of the modern world using extreme, graphic violence itself to test and probe what he described as the "death of affect," the loss of the ability to feel or empathize, which haunts modern consciousness. One publisher's reader returned Ballard's manuscript for *Crash* with the warning: "This author is beyond psychiatric help. Do not publish!" (Reynolds 2009). Ballard's work is challenging, and not for the squeamish, but the effect he had—on the popular imagination in general, and SF in particular—cannot be overestimated. In his review of Ballard's 1987 novel *The Day of Creation*, British novelist Martin Amis said, "Ballard is quite unlike anyone else; indeed, he seems to address a different—a disused—part of the reader's brain."

Ballard tried to juggle the demands of regular work and writing, but in the early 1960s he made the decision to rely on his income as a writer, and it was as a professional writer—a sharp critic, and observer of modern trends—that he earned his living for the rest of his life. This decision can only have been made more challenging when the sudden death of his young wife, of pneumonia in 1964, left him to raise their three children alone. (The semiautobiographical novel *The Kindness of Women* is based on this period of his life.) In 2006, in an interview in the *Times* of London, Ballard revealed that he had been diagnosed with metastasized prostrate cancer; he died in London on April 19, 2009. At the end of this long, amazingly productive, and influential writing career, it may seem as if he had moved away from the tropes of SF. However, it is more correct to say that wherever he went, he took the perspectives of SF with him, however mundane their settings and scenarios might appear. For J. G. Ballard, after all, the only alien planet is Earth.

Awards

Novels

The Unlimited Dream Company (1979) **BSF**

Works by the Author

The Atrocity Exhibition (1969)
Vermilion Sands (1971)
Crash (1973)
Concrete Island (1974)
High-Rise (1975)
The Unlimited Dream Company (1979)
Hello America (1981)

The Classical Elements (aka, the Global Disaster Quartet)

The Wind from Nowhere (1962)
The Drowned World (1962)
The Burning World (1965)
The Crystal World (1966)

Notable Mainstream Fiction

Empire of the Sun (1984)
The Kindness of Women (1991)
The Day of Creation (1987)
Rushing to Paradise (1994)
Cocaine Nights (1996)
Super-Cannes (2000)
Millennium People (2003)
Kingdom Come (2006)

Notable Short Fiction

"Billenium" (1961)
"The Drowned Giant" (1964)
"The Terminal Beach" (1964)
"The Assassination of John F. Kennedy Considered as a Downhill Motor Race" (1973)
"Myths of the Near Future" (1982)
"Running Wild" (1988)
"The Dying Fall" (1996) http://www.guardian.co.uk/books/2009/apr/25/dying-fall-jg-ballard

Collections

The Voices of Time and Other Stories (1962)
Billenium (1962)
Passport to Eternity (1963)
The Four-Dimensional Nightmare (1963)

The Terminal Beach (1964)
The Impossible Man (1966)
The Venus Hunters (1967)
The Overloaded Man (1967)
The Disaster Area (1967)
The Day of Forever (1967)
Chronopolis and Other Stories (1971)
Low-Flying Aircraft and Other Stories (1976)
The Best Short Stories of J. G. Ballard (1978)
Myths of the Near Future (1982)
The Voices of Time (1985)
Memories of the Space Age (1988)
War Fever (1990)
The Complete Short Stories of J. G. Ballard: Volume 1 (2006)
The Complete Short Stories of J. G. Ballard: Volume 2 (2006)

In Other Media

The Atrocity Exhibition. The Business (New York), 2000. Directed by Jonathan Weiss.

Crash. Alliance Communications, 1996. Directed by David Cronenberg; starring James Spader and Holly Hunter.

Empire of the Sun. Amblin Entertainment, 1987. Directed by Steven Spielberg; starring Christian Bale, John Malkovich, and Miranda Richardson.

Home. BBC Four, 2003. Directed by Richard Curson Smith; starring Antony Sher and Keith Allen. Based on Ballard's story "The Enormous Space" (1989).

"Thirteen to Centaurus." *Out of the Unknown.* BBC Two, 1965. Directed by Peter Potter. Based on the 1962 story of the same name.

When Dinosaurs Ruled the Earth. Hammer Film Productions, 1970. Directed by Val Guest; starring Victoria Ventri. Ballard is credited with the story for this retro-delight of claymation dinosaurs and scantily clad cave ladies, from the House of Hammer.

Nonfiction Books

Miracles of Life: Shanghai to Shepperton, an Autobiography (2008)
A User's Guide to the Millennium (1997)

Articles and Essays

"Which Way to Inner Space?" *New Worlds* (May 1962)

For Further Information

J. G. Ballard.com. *Spike Magazine*. http://www.jgballard.com/. Not an official Web site, but authorized by Ballard and a portal to a wide array of articles, reviews, and criticism.

Obituary and Tributes. *The Guardian* (UK), April 20, 2009. http://www.guardian.co.uk/books/jgballard

Behrens, Richard. "J. G. Ballard." *The Scriptorum* (December 2003). The Modern Word. http://www.themodernword.com/scriptorium/ballard.html

Brigg, Peter. "J.G. Ballard." In *St. James Guide to Science Fiction Writers*, ed. Jay Pedersen. Detroit, MI: St. James, 1996.

Campbell, James. "Strange Fiction." *The Guardian* (UK), June 14, 2008. http://www.guardian.co.uk/books/2008/jun/14/saturdayreviewsfeatres.guardianreview10

Clute, John. "J.G. Ballard: Writer Whose Dystopian Visions Helped Shape Our View of the Modern World (Obituary)." *The Independent* (UK), April 21, 2009. http://www.independent.co.uk/news/obituaries/jg-ballard-writer-whose-dystopian-visions-helped-shape-our-view-of-the-modern-world-1671634.html

Dalrymple, Theodore. "The Marriage of Reason and Nightmare: Novelist J. G. Ballard Exposes the Fragility of the Affluent Society." *City Journal* (The Manhattan Institute) (Winter 2008). http://www.city-journal.org/2008/18_1_otbie-ballard.html

Frick, Thomas. Interview. *The Paris Review* (Winter 1984). http://www.theparisreview.com/viewinterview.php/prmMID/2929

Hall, Chris. "J.G. Ballard: Millennium People: Entertaining Violence." *Spike Magazine* (January 2004). http://www.spikemagazine.com/0104jgballard.php

Luckhurst, Roger. *"The Angle Between Two Walls": The Fiction of J. G. Ballard*. Liverpool (UK): Liverpool University Press, 1998.

McGrath, Rick. *The Terminal Collection*. May 2007. http://www.jgballard.ca/

Moorcock, Michael. "The Atrocity Exhibition." *Fantastic Metropolis,* October 15, 2001. http://www.fantasticmetropolis.com/i/atrocity/

Pringle, David. *Earth Is the Alien Planet: J. G. Ballard's Four-Dimensional Nightmare*. San Bernardino, CA: Borgo, 1979.

Reynolds, Simon. "The Unlimited Dreams of J.G. Ballard." *Salon,* April 22, 2009. http://www.salon.com/books/feature/2009/04/23/ballard/index.html

Self, Will. "The Ballard Tradition." *Prospect* (September 2003). http://www.prospect-magazine.co.uk/article_details.php?id=5696

Sellars, Simon. *The Ballardian* (August 2007). Sleepy Brain Online Magazine. http://www.ballardian.com. Extremely thorough archive of online resources by and about Ballard, including links to articles and interviews available nowhere else.

Vale, V., ed. *J. G. Ballard: Conversations*. San Francisco: RE/Search, 2005.

Iain M. Banks

Space Opera; Utopias

Benchmark Title: *Consider Phlebas* (1987)

b. 1954 (Scotland: Dunfermline)

> *[I]in SF you can design a setting, set of circumstances, society, civilization or even meta-civilization to highlight whatever message or point you want to make, sweeping away all the clutter.... Most fiction is not engaged in this sense, and as I've discovered to my dismay, I'm not particularly good at crafting stuff that is. Still, a chap can dream.*
> —Wilson, "Culture Shock," *One Magazine* (2008)

Photo credit: John Foley. Permission of Orbit, The Hatchette Book Group.

About the Author and the Author's Writing

Iain Menzies Banks is another writer who has cleverly managed to blur the boundaries between SF and mainstream. As "Iain M. Banks" he writes popular and respected SF novels that play with the conventions of space opera, the "big story" that juggles the demands of complicated plot and galactic setting against the fine detail of character and complicated themes. As "Iain Banks" he has published many popular and respected mainstream novels, including *The Wasp Factory* (1984), *The Bridge* (1989), *The Crow Road* (1992), and *The Steep Approach to Garbadale* (2007). The recent British comedy *Hot Fuzz* made a droll reference to the "two Iain Banks"; throughout the film, a character is shown alternately reading the mainstream novel *Complicity* and the SF anthology *The State of the Art*. Later, the "character" is revealed to be identical twins.

But in the real world, the joke is on anyone who blindly assumes that the split between mainstream and SF writer is quite so simple and clear-cut. Banks's mainstream fiction often plays with the sensibilities of genre: horror, fantasy, and, yes, even science fiction. But although his SF is drawn on a suitably larger-than-life canvas, " at the heart of all this vastness is often a small domestic story. In fact, the violent, fast-paced action is often interrupted by flashbacks to scenes of childhood which would not be out of place in a contemporary novel, were it not for the scenery" (Kincaid 1996).

And what scenery! Many of Banks's SF novels are set in the far future universe of the "Culture," a powerful, multi-species civilization that has spread across our galaxy. In the Culture, AI has achieved self-awareness, equal rights with their humanoid fellow citizens, and a pretty biting sense of irony. Limitless material wealth has all but abolished the concept of possessions; peace and comfort are available to everyone who plays according to the Culture's rules. "The Culture is my utopia, my personal image of exactly the place I would like to live. . . . There's nothing to hate about it apart from its smugness. It knows it's smug. The price of perfection, I'm afraid" ("Iain Banks" 2002).

Banks offsets the smugness by creating an interesting dynamic between this postscarcity society and the characters who are most often at the center of his violent, complicated dramas—the mercenaries, the special envoys, the spies, and the go-betweens who do the Culture's dirty work. The perspective is that of the marginalized and disposable, characters who may not be admirable or pretty, but who have good reason to mistrust this perfect society's methods and motives. In spite of his modest claims to the contrary, the world-building in Banks's novels is fully realized and tremendously engaging: he has the knack of blending the fantastic "big idea" (the Lazy Gun of *Against a Dark Background*, the utterly alien worlds of the mysterious gas giants in *The Algebraist*) with the relatively ordinary—lives lived on a recognizably human scale. Banks's SF novels offer a richly imagined technology, although he claims, in an article written for *New Scientist* in 1993, that "there is probably more science in the mainstream books. Well, more reliable science, anyway."

Iain M. Banks was born in Dunfermline, Scotland. His father was an Admiralty official; his mother a former professional ice-skater. He studied English, philosophy, and psychology at the University of Stirling in Scotland. At the beginning of his writing career he lived for a while in London, but in the late 1980s he returned to Scotland, to North Queensferry on the Firth of Forth, near Edinburgh, where he lives today. Banks is famous for having worked out a very civilized work schedule for his writing: he writes fast, producing a novel in about three months, and then takes nine months off to do as he pleases. In his leisure time he writes and records his own rock music, and he has taken flying lessons. Another sideline he has recently found to engage his downtime is "quiz king": in 2006 Banks led a team of writers to victory in a special "Professionals" series of the popular BBC2 quiz show *University Challenge*. He also won his round of *Celebrity Mastermind*, triumphing with his specialist subject, "Malt Whisky and the Distilleries of Scotland."

Banks's fiction (both SF and mainstream) is a clear expression of his own political views; he is a lifelong supporter of Scottish independence, and he has been vocal in his condemnation of Prime Minister Tony Blair and Britain's involvement in the 2003 invasion of Iraq. He is a member of both the National Secular Society and the Humanist Society of Scotland; he is a recent, and very public, convert to the Green Party. As a mark of his seriousness, he sold the impressive collection of vintage sports cars that he had acquired over the years, bought a hybrid car, and vowed henceforth to fly only in case of emergency.

Awards

Novels

Feersum Endjinn (1994) **BSF**
Excession (1996) **BSF**

Works by the Author

Against a Dark Background (1993)
Feersum Endjinn (1994)
The Algebraist (2004)

The Culture

Consider Phlebas (1987)
The Player of Games (1988)
Use of Weapons (1990)
Excession (1996)
Inversions (1998)
Look to Windward (2000)
Matter (2008)

Notable Mainstream Fiction

The Wasp Factory (1984)
Walking on Glass (1985)
The Bridge (1986)
Canal Dreams (1989)
The Crow Road (1992)
Complicity (1993)
Dead Air (2002)
The Steep Approach to Garbadale (2007)

Collections

The State of the Art (1989)

Nonfiction Books

Raw Spirit: In Search of the Perfect Dram (2004)

Articles and Essays

"A Few Notes on the Culture." *Culture Shock,* August 10, 1994. Future Hi. http://www.futurehi.net/phlebas/text/cultnote.html
"Science and Fiction: Escape from the Laws of Physics." *New Scientist,* March 20, 1993, 38–39.

For Further Information

Official Web site: http://www.iainbanks.net/

The Banksoniain: An Iain (M.) Banks Fanzine, February 23, 2007. http://banksoniain.netfirms.com/

Hoggard, Liz. "Iain Banks: The Novel Factory." *The Independent* (London), February 18, 2007. http://www.independent.co.uk/news/people/iain-banks-the-novel-factory-436865.html.

Horwich, David. "Culture Clash: Ambivalent Heroes and the Ambiguous Utopia in the Work of Iain M. Banks." *Strange Horizons,* January 21, 2002. http://www. strangehorizons.com/2002/20020121/culture_clash.shtml.

"Iain Banks: A Quick Chat." *Richmond Review,* May 1, 2002. http://www.pwf.cz/en/archives/interviews/2085.html

Jeffries, Stuart. "A Man of Culture." *The Guardian* (UK), May 25, 2007. http://www.guardian.co.uk/books/2007/may/25/hayfestival2007.hayfestival

Keogh, Robert. *Culture Shock* (September 2006). Future Hi. http://www.futurehi.net/phlebas/

Kincaid, Paul. "Iain. M. Banks." In *St. James Guide to Science Fiction Writers*, ed. Jay Pedersen. Detroit, MI: St. James, 1996.

Kinson, Sarah. Interview. *The Guardian* (UK), February 2, 2008. http://www.guardian.co.uk/books/2008/feb/07/iainbanks

Leonard, Andrew. "The Future Perfect." *Salon.com,* February 17, 2005. http://dir.salon.com/story/books/int/2005/02/17/banks/index.html?source=search&aim=/books/int

Mitchell, Chris. "Iain Banks: Whit and Excession: Getting Used to Being God." *Spike Magazine* (September 1999). http://www.spikemagazine.com/0996bank.php

Walker, Maxton. "Iain Banks: Even at My Age I Have Something to Prove." *The Guardian* (UK), September 8, 2009. htpp://www.guardian.co.uk/global/2009/sep/08/iain-banks-transition

Wilson, Andrew J. "Culture Shock: An Interview with Iain M. Banks." *One Magazine* (n.d.). http://www.iamone.co.uk/index.php?option=com_content&view= article&id=185

Stephen Baxter

Apocalyptic SF; Hard SF; Sense of Wonder

Benchmark Title: *Moonseed* (1998)

b. 1957 (England: Liverpool)

I always loved the big cosmic sweep. . . . My favorite author in my late teens, before he was fashionable, was Dick; I think I write about Dick characters, with doggedness and endurance, in Clarke universes.
—Palmer, Interview in *Strange Horizons* (2005)

Photo credit: Sandra Shepherd.
Courtesy of Stephen Baxter.

About the Author and the Author's Writing

In 1991 Stephen Baxter applied to become a cosmonaut on the Soviet orbital research station Mir. For Stephen Baxter, teacher of math and physics, IT consultant for National Westminster Bank, and a trained engineer who took a first-class honors degree in mathematics at Cambridge University, this might have seemed a bit extreme. But it is exactly what one might expect from a character in a novel by Stephen Baxter, the author of tales based on the plausible scientific speculation of authors like Heinlein and Clarke, but doggedly alive to the possibilities of transcendence and the "big cosmic sweep" in all our lives.

Stephen Michael Baxter was born in Liverpool, England. As well as his degree in mathematics from Cambridge, he has a BA in business administration and a doctorate in aeroengineering research from Southampton University. Since 1989, when his first short stories started to appear in Britain in the magazine *Interzone*, he has written an incredible thirty novels. With a few stand-alone exceptions, Baxter's novels slot into one of several story sequences, which deal with themes such as evolution, geological change, space exploration, parallel universes, and the destiny of life. He has also written more than 100 short stories that complement and expand upon these ideas. The novels and stories in his sequences are not necessarily direct sequels to one another, but instead are linked by concepts, "Big Ideas," and sometimes characters. According to Adam Roberts in *The History of Science Fiction*, he is "better than almost any current writer at creating the 'sense of wonder;' billions of years of cosmic history, and immeasurable spread of possible alternative realities blooming like a fantastically complex flower from the nubbin of the Big Bang."

Baxter's scientific background enables him to shift effortlessly from plausible alternative history, to frighteningly realistic, near future possibilities, to the wildest sort of hard-science speculation. The novels and stories of the Xeelee Sequence describes humankind's survival in a dangerous universe, a story arc consisting of billions of years spent braving natural phenomena and the antagonism of unimaginably advanced alien races, such as the godlike Xeelee. *Moonseed* begins with the spectacular destruction of the planet Venus—exploding as its structure is fatally compromised by rock-eating, tenth-dimensional nano-life forms. And thanks to the carelessness and foolishness of Man, these nano-life forms have been unleashed on planet Earth: by the end of *Moonseed*, Scotland and the Pacific Northwest of the United States are swallowed whole, and the remnants of humankind are facing the necessity of fleeing to the moon. In *Evolution*, Baxter traces the course of evolutionary forces from 65 million years ago, when primitive mammals witnessed the extinction of the dinosaurs, to 500 million years in the future, right up to the end of planet Earth and all life on it, and the rebirth of life on another planet.

And the amazing thing is—he makes it all seem plausible. Perhaps it is his firm grasp of the science and the technology, such as in *Voyage*, in which the American space program is about to send a manned mission to Mars in Baxter's reimagined 1986. He not only invents a credible mission to Mars, but also the technical, political, and personal history that might logically have brought us to that moment; his relentless realism makes clear the perils as well as the possibilities of what awaits us in space.

Baxter acknowledges the early influence of Sir Arthur C. Clarke, with whom he did three collaborations, and H. G. Wells. With the blessing of Wells's literary estate, Baxter wrote *The Time Ships* (1995), a sequel to Wells's *The Time Machine,* which picks up where it left off, as the Traveller embarks on a new journey to save Weena and the gentle Eloi from the Morlocks. Stephen Baxter became a full-time writer in 1995 and has been a Distinguished Vice-President of the international H. G. Wells Society since 2006. He is a Fellow of the British Interplanetary Society. He currently lives in Northumberland, England, and is a lifetime supporter of Liverpool FC, the English Premiership football team.

Awards

Novels

The Time Ships (1995) **BSF, PKD, Campbell**
Vacuum Diagrams (1997), **PKD**

Short Fiction

"The War Birds" (1997) **BSF**
"Huddle" (1999) **Locus Poll**
"Mayflower II" (2005) **BSF**

Nonfiction

Omegatropic (2001) **BSF**

Works by the Author

Anti-Ice (1993)
The Time Ships (1995)
The Light of Other Days (2000, with Arthur C. Clarke)
Evolution (2002)
Flood (2008)

Destiny's Children

Coalescent (2003)
Exultant (2004)
Transcendent (2005)
Resplendent (2006)

NASA Trilogy

Voyage (1996)
Titan (1997)
Moonseed (1998)

Manifold Trilogy

Manifold: Time (1999)
Manifold: Space (2001)
Manifold: Origin (2001)

Time Odyssey (with Sir Arthur C. Clarke)

Time's Eye (2003)
Sunstorm (2005)
Firstborn (2007)

The Xeelee Sequence

Raft (1991)
Timelike Infinity (1992)
Flux (1993)
Ring (1994)
Vacuum Diagrams (1997)
Reality Dust (2000)
Riding the Rock (2002)

Other Notable Genre Fiction

Time's Tapestry
Emperor (2006)
Conqueror (2007)
Navigator (2007)
Weaver (2008)

Young Adult
The H-Bomb Girl (2007)

The Web
Gulliverzone (1997)
Webcrash (1998)

Mammoth
Silverhair (1999; aka *Mammoth*)
Longtusk (2000)
Icebones (2001)

Other Notable Short Fiction

"The Xeelee Flower" (1987, as S. M. Baxter)
"Brigantia's Angels" (1995)
"Moon Six" (1997). http://www.infinityplus.co.uk/stories/moon6.htm
"The Gravity Mine" (2000). http://www.infinityplus.co.uk/stories/gravitymine.htm
"On the Orion Line" (2000)
"Sheena 5" (2000)
"First to the Moon" (2001, with Simon Bradshaw)
"The Ghost Pit" (2001)
"The Children of Time" (2005)
"Mayflower II" (2004)
"Last Contact" (2007)

Collections

Traces (1998)
Omegatropic: Non-Fiction & Fiction (2001)
Phase Space: Stories from the Manifold and Elsewhere (2002)
The Hunters of Pangaea (2004)

Nonfiction Books

Reengineering Information Technology: Success Through Empowerment (1994, with David Lisburn)

Deep Future (2001)

Revolutions in the Earth: James Hutton and the True Age of the World (2004; aka *Ages in Chaos: James Hutton and the Discovery of Deep Time*)

Articles and Essays

"Autobiographical Essay." In *Contemporary Authors,* Volume 204. Detroit, MI: Gale Group, 2003.

"H.G. Wells's Enduring Mythos of Mars." In *The War of the Worlds: Fresh Perspectives on the H.G. Wells Classic,* ed. Glenn Yeffeth. Dallas, TX: BenBella, 2005.

"Lunching at the Eschaton: Douglas Adams and the End of the Universe in Science Fiction." In *The Anthology at the End of the Universe: Leading Science Fiction Authors on Douglas Adams' The Hitchhiker's Guide to the Galaxy,* ed. Glenn Yeffeth. Dallas: Benbella, 2005.

"The Real Matrix." In *Exploring the Matrix: Visions of the Cyber Present,* ed. Karen Haber. New York: St. Martin's, 2003.

For Further Information

Official Web site: www.stephen-baxter.com

Auden, Sandy. "A Man in Shorts: An Interview with Stephen Baxter." *SF Site* (2005). http://www.sfsite.com/06a/sasb201.htm.

Bradshaw, Simon. *The Baxterium* (February 2007). http://www.baxterium.org.uk/

Brialey, Claire. "Visions of the Far Future World: Human Constants and Cosmic Change in Stephen Baxter's Xeelee Sequence." In *Earth Is But a Star: Excursions Through Science Fiction to the Far Future,* ed. Damien Broderick, 401–11. Crawley, WA: University of Western Australia Press, 2001.

Gevers, Nick. "A Painter of Immensities." *Interzone* (February 2001). http://www.infinityplus.co.uk/nonfiction/intsb.htm

Lilley, Ernest. Interview. *SFRevu* (January 2004). http://www.sfrevu.com/php/Review-id.php?id=1257

Palmer, James. Interview. *Strange Horizons,* April 18, 2005. http://www.strangehorizons.com/2005/20050418/1int-baxter-a.shtml

"Stephen Baxter: The Cusp of Transcendence." *Locus Online* (August 2004). http://www.locusmag.com/2004/Issues/08Baxter.html

Greg Bear

Hard SF; Post-human SF

Benchmark Title: *Blood Music* (1985)

b. 1951 (San Diego, California)

Big changes generate big emotions, and big emotions make for exciting and compelling stories. When everything is on the line, we strip ourselves to our bare essentials and examine our lives—and possibly our deaths—with an incredible clarity we never get when we lock ourselves into drawing rooms and garden parties.

—Levy, "The Shape of Kids to Come,"
Publishers Weekly (2003)

Photo credit: Astrid Anderson Bear. Courtesy of Greg Bear and Astrid Anderson Bear.

About the Author and the Author's Writing

Greg Bear sold his first short story, "Destroyers," to *Famous Science Fiction* when he was fifteen years old. It was five years before he sold another story, and another twelve years before his first novel, *Hegira*, was published. But this early promise was eventually made good in spectacular fashion with *Blood Music* (published first as a short story in 1983, and expanded to novel length in 1985), the novel that established Bear as a major name of "hard" SF. In *Blood Music*, a scientist who is researching intelligent, adaptable microorganisms injects himself with his discovery in order to continue his research, and, as he sees it, protect it from small minds who wanted to stop him. This does not work out well.

Bear's breakthrough in the mid-1980s is that he recognized that the fear humankind had hitherto reserved for alien invaders and fantastic weapons of mass destruction should perhaps be turned inward, that the real threat to the survival of the human race could just as easily come from unwise genetic manipulation and thoughtless experimentation with the smallest citizens of planet Earth, unseen organisms and viruses. Bear was, of course, doing exactly what good SF has always done—building on what has gone before: the scientist who doesn't stop to think comes straight out of *Frankenstein*, while we have seen the microorganisms that are the undoing of a proud, heedless race before, in *War of the Worlds*. But what Bear did in *Blood Music* was to make it clear that the old tropes are neither out-of-date nor melodramatic; *Blood Music* is often cited as the moment when the enemy within became a real, understandable trope of current SF; it has also been credited as being the first account of nanotechnology in science fiction.

Although Bear has, from time to time, revisited this theme—*Queen of Angels* and its sequel, *Slant*, are a detailed description of a near-future nanotechnological society—his thirty novels (at last count) tackle themes as diverse as artificial universes (*Eon*), consciousness and cultural practices (*Queen of Angels*), and accelerated evolution (*Darwin's Radio*). In one of his most recent novels, *Quantico*, Bear has been moving his sights a little closer to the terrors of the here and now—searching immediately behind today's headlines, in a near-future thriller about politics and terror, both domestic and religious. *Forge of God*, with its painful, shocking denouement, does not dodge the true, painful cost of galactic conflict.

> When I wrote *The Forge of God*, it was my goal to go *Star Wars* one better and show how long it would take for a planet to actually blow up, and how heart rending it would be. . . . if you are going to lose an entire planet, Princess Leia is going to lose a lot more than her record collection. (Cabot 2007).

According to *The Encyclopedia of Science Fiction,* Bear's significance "lies in the fact that his human beings are more difficult to describe than his physics."

Gregory Dale Bear was born in San Diego, California. His father was in the U.S. Navy and, during his childhood, the family traveled widely around the United States, to Japan, and to the Philippines. After graduating from San Diego State University, Bear worked in a bookstore for a number of years; he also acted as "roving lecturer" for the San Diego school system, speaking on ancient history, the history of science, and science fiction. Since the 1980s he has been a full-time writer, including stints as a freelance journalist; he has written about film for the *Los Angeles Times* and his opinion and nonfiction pieces have been published in *Nature*, *Newsday*, and the *San Diego Union*. He is also a talented artist: his artwork has appeared in magazines such as *Galaxy*, *Fantasy and Science Fiction*, and *Vertex*, as well as on the covers of his own fiction.

Greg Bear acts as a futurism consultant, advising (among others) Microsoft, the U.S. Army, the CIA, and Sandia National Laboratories, and serving on a number of political and scientific action committees. Together with Gregory Benford and David Brin, he was authorized by the estate of the late Isaac Asimov to contribute a volume to a trilogy of prequel novels to the Foundation series. He is one of two authors to win a Nebula in every category. Greg Bear is married to Astrid Anderson, the daughter of science fiction author Poul Anderson; they have two children. "All in all," as he says in his biography on his official Web site, "we're quite a team." They live outside of Seattle, Washington.

Awards

Robert A. Heinlein Award (2006)

Novels

Moving Mars (1993) **Nebula**
Darwin's Radio (1999) **Nebula**

Short Fiction

"Blood Music" (1983) **Hugo, Nebula**
"Hardfought" (1983) **Nebula**
"Tangents" (1987) **Hugo, Nebula**

Works by the Author

Hegira (1979)
Beyond Heaven's River (1980)
Strength of Stones (1981)
Corona (1984; Star Trek Universe)
Blood Music (1985)
Foundation and Chaos (1998; Second Foundation Trilogy)
Country of the Mind (1998)
Dinosaur Summer (1998)
Rogue Planet (2000; Star Wars Universe)
Vitals (2002)
Quantico (2007)
City at the End of Time (2008)

Darwin

Darwin's Radio (1999)
Darwin's Children (2003)

Eon Trilogy

Eon (1985)
Eternity (1988)
Legacy (1995)

Forge of God

The Forge of God (1987)
Anvil of Stars (1992)

Queen of Angels

Queen of Angels (1990)
Heads (1990)
Moving Mars (1993)
/ (aka *Slant*) (1997). Excerpt from *Slant*, "Autopoiesis and the Grand Scheme" (pages 138–46), http://www.goodreads.ca/gregbear/autopoiesis.html

Other Notable Genre Fiction

Psychlone (1979; aka *Lost Souls*)
Dead Lines (2004)

Songs of Earth and Power

The Infinity Concerto (1984)
The Serpent Mage (1986)

Other Notable Short Fiction

"Petra" (1982)
"Sisters" (1989)
"Heads" (1990)

Collections

The Wind from a Burning Woman (1983; aka *The Venging*)
Early Harvest (1988)
Tangents (1989)
Bear's Fantasies: Six Stories in Old Paradigms (1992)
The Collected Stories of Greg Bear (2002)
W3: Women in Deep Time (2003)
Sleepside: The Collected Fantasies (2004)

As Editor

Hardfought/Cascade Point (1988, with Timothy Zahn)
New Legends (1995, with Martin H. Greenberg)

In Other Media

"Dead Run." *The Twilight Zone* (Season 1, Episode 19) Original air date February 21, 1986. Starring John de Lancie and Brent Spiner. Based on short story of the same name.

Articles and Essays

"All the Robots and Isaac Asimov." *3 Laws Unsafe*. July 2004. Singularity Institute for Artificial Intelligence, Inc. http://www.gregbear.com/other/

"Doctors of the Mind: Effective Mental Therapy and Its Implications." In *No Cure for the Future: Disease and Medicine in Science Fiction and Fantasy*, ed. Gary Westfahl and George Slusser. Westport, CT: Greenwood, 2002.

For Further Information

Official Web site: http://www.gregbear.com/

Brin, David. "Greg Bear." *St. James Guide to Science Fiction Writers*, ed. Jay Pedersen. Detroit, MI: St. James, 1996.

Cabot, Myles. Interview. *Aberrant Dreams: Speculative Fiction*, January 2, 2007. http://www.hd-image.com/interviews/myles_cabot_09.htm.

Gambuto, Damon. "Science Fiction Friday: Greg Bear." *Wired Science: Correlations,* December 21, 2007. http://www.pbs.org/kcet/wiredscience/blogs/2007/12/science-fiction-friday-greg-be.html

Gevers, Nick. "The Opener of the Way: An Interview with Greg Bear." *Infinity Plus* (February 2006). http://www.infinityplus.co.uk/nonfiction/intgb.htm

Levy, Michael. "The Shape of Kids to Come: PW Talks with Greg Bear." *Publishers Weekly,* March 3, 2003. http://www.publishersweekly.com/article/CA280993.html

Means, Loren. "Interview with Greg Bear." *YLEM Journal* 24, no. 4 (2004): 4–7. http://www.ylem.org/Journal/2004Iss04vol24.pdf. Includes Greg Bear's cover artwork, "My Conception of Paul Anderson's Tao Zero."

Alfred Bester

Post-human SF; Space Opera

Benchmark Title: *The Stars My Destination* (1956)

b. 1913 (New York City); d. 1987 (Doylestown, Pennsylvania)

> *I've been a writer and editor all my professional life, and SF is only one of the many media in which I've worked. But I love it most because it's the last frontier of complete creative freedom, prose vers libre, as it were, in which the artist is allowed any and all wild experiments with people and places.*
> —Patti Peret, *The Faces of Science Fiction* (1984)

About the Author and the Author's Writing

Unlike some of his contemporaries, who were churning out so many stories for the pulps that they had to have a quiverful of pen names to disguise the fact that whole issues of the magazines were filled with their work, Alfred Bester wrote precisely five SF novels and about three dozen short stories. Two of those novels changed the face of science fiction and paved the way for the revolution in SF that was to follow and continues today.

Alfred Bester was born in New York City in 1913. His father owned a shoe store and was the son of immigrants from Austria; his mother was born in Russia. Bester graduated in 1935 from the University of Pennsylvania; he went on, briefly, to do graduate studies in law at Columbia Law School and then in protozoology at NYU. However, he dropped out of both programs before completing a degree. In 1936 he married Rolly Goulko, a Broadway actress.

Bester's first story, "The Broken Axiom," won an amateur story competition and was published in *Thrilling Wonder Stories* in 1939. In the years that followed, Bester had about a dozen SF short stories published, including the classic "Adam and No Eve" (1941). In 1942 he started working at DC Comics, as a writer on titles such as *Superman* and *Green Lantern*. Later, he became a scriptwriter for radio and television, after Rolly—who had become a busy radio actress—alerted him to opportunities with series like *The Shadow*, *Charlie Chan*, and *Nero Wolfe*.

As Bester established himself as a writer for the comics and the airwaves, the SF dried up. In the early 1950s he was ready to try again. Again there was a mild rush of short fiction, and then there was *The Demolished Man*, published in 1953. "Lightning-paced, hard and glittering, like the multiple facets of a cut diamond.... Bester's disciplined, taut prose had no equal in the early fifties" (Andrews and Rennison 2006).

The Demolished Man is a murder mystery with a twist: in the future, murder is almost impossible because of the development of telepathy as a means of surveillance and social control. But Ben Reich, power-hungry industrialist, thinks he has found a way to get around the telepaths and murder his archrival. *The Demolished Man* was followed by a novel which, if possible, is even more assured and interesting: the SF "revenge tragedy" *The Stars My Destination*. In these two novels Bester demonstrated the power of two stylistic choices that changed the face of science fiction forever: first, the gritty realistic setting, and second, the reliance on an antihero who dares us to sympathize with him and cheer him on, the murderous Reich, and the vengeance-obsessed Gully Foyle. The work that Bester had put in on the comics and radio can be seen in the themes and action of both novels—they chart the development of an unlikely "superhero" and the idea that one man really can create a new reality for the world. *The Demolished Man* was awarded the first Hugo Award, in 1953.

From the mid-1950s Bester was writer and chief literary editor of *Holiday*, a travel/lifestyle magazine, and again, he seems to have found it difficult to multitask. He managed to introduce occasional SF elements to the magazine, for example commissioning an article by Arthur C. Clarke that described a tourist flight to the moon, but he wrote little SF. When *Holiday* folded in the early 1970s, Bester tried to pick up where he had left off, but he found himself left behind. He contributed a treatment for the 1978 *Superman* movie and was devastated when the producer declined to hire an "unknown" writer.

It is tempting to skim over the sad final years of Alfred Bester. Rolly, his wife of forty-eight years, died in early 1984, not long after they left New York and retired to their summer home in Ottsville, Pennsylvania. Bester's own health was not good and was made worse by the loss of Rolly, drinking, disappointment, and, perhaps, an awareness of opportunities missed. He was also stony broke: "Alfred Bester died alone and with little money, all of which he left to his favorite bartender, who was surprised to receive the meager inheritance and could not even remember who Bester was" (Delaney 2008).

Bester died in 1987 in Doylestown, Pennsylvania; but, by a small grace, his death came shortly after he learned that he had been named 1988 Grand Master by the Science Fiction Writers of America.

And although he may not have had all of the recognition he deserves, Alfred Bester is hardly forgotten. He is in the illustrious company of SF giants like H. G. Wells, Mary Shelley, and Philip K. Dick in having a lively "afterlife": characters named after Bester appeared in the TV series *Babylon 5* and *Firefly*, and in a Callahan novel by Spider Robinson. Readers have never entirely forgotten that Bester at his best is fresh and modern—the New Wave and the cyberpunks are proud to call him an inspiration. Without his style, his slang, and his richly imagined future, there might not have been (among many others) a Harlan Ellison, a James Tiptree, or a William Gibson. Bester demonstrated that it was possible to combine action with insights, and he single-handedly moved the genre away from the cardboard characterizations of earlier SF. As Harlan Ellison put it so well, in his introduction to *The Deceivers*, "Alfred Bester was, and remains long after his passing, the preeminent Class Act of imaginative literature. Bester was the mountain, all the rest of us merely climbers toward that peak."

Awards

SFWA Grand Master (1988)
SF Hall of Fame (2001, Posthumous)

Novels

The Demolished Man (1951) **Hugo**
The Stars My Destination (1956) **Prometheus Hall of Fame 1988**

Works by the Author

The Demolished Man (1951)
The Stars My Destination (1956; aka *Tiger, Tiger*)
The Computer Connection (1975; aka *Extro*)
Golem^{100} (1980)
The Deceivers (1981)

Other Notable Genre Fiction

Who He? (1953; aka *The Rat Race*)
Tender Loving Rage (1991)
Psychoshop (1998, with Roger Zelazny)

Notable Short Fiction

"Adam and No Eve" (1941)
"Of Time and Third Avenue" (1951)
"Star Light, Star Bright." (1953)
"Time Is the Traitor" (1953)
"Fondly Fahrenheit" (1954)
"The Men Who Murdered Mohammed" (1958)
"The Pi Man" (1959)
"The Four Hour Fugue" (1974)

Collections

Starburst (1958)
The Dark Side of the Earth (1964)
The Light Fantastic (1976)
Star Light, Star Bright (1976)
Starlight: The Great Short Fiction of Alfred Bester (1976)
Virtual Unrealities (1997) (introduction by Robert Silverberg)
Alfred Bester Redemolished (2001)

Nonfiction Books

The Life and Death of a Satellite: A Biography of the Men and Machines at War with Space (1966)

Articles and Essays

"A Diatribe against Science Fiction" (1961). In *Alfred Bester Redemolished,* ed. Richard Raucci. New York: Ibooks, 2001.

"Gourmet Dining in Outer Space." In *Turning Points: Essays on the Art of Science Fiction,* ed. Damon Knight, 259–66. New York: Harper & Row, 1977.

"My Affair with Science Fiction." In *Hell's Cartographers*, ed. Brian W. Aldiss and Harry Harrison, 46–75. New York: Harper & Row, 1975.

"Science Fiction and the Renaissance Man." In *The Science Fiction Novel: Imagination and Social Criticism,* ed. Basil Davenport. Chicago: Advent, 1959.

"Writing and *The Demolished Man.*" In *Experiment Perilous.* New York: Algol, 1976.

For Further Information

Andrews, Stephen E., and Nick Rennison. "Alfred Bester." In *100 Must-Read Science Fiction Novels*. London: A. & C. Black, 2006.

Cramer, Kathryn. 'Introduction to 'The Pi Man'." In *The Ascent of Wonder,* ed. David G. Hartwell and Kathryn Cramer. New York: Tor, 1994. http://ebbs.english.vt.edu/exper/kcramer/anth/Pi.html

Delaney, Ryan. *Biography and Brief Bibliography.* Pennsylvania Center for the Book, The Pennsylvania State University, Spring 2008. http://www.pabook.libraries.psu.edu/palitmap/bios/Bester__Alfred.html

Langford, David. "On Alfred Bester." *Ansible* (March 2005). http://www.ansible.co.uk/writing/bester.html

Platt, Charles. "Alfred Bester's Tender Loving Rage." In *Loose Canon,* 82–91. Holicong, PA: Wildside, 2001. (Obituary, 92–94).

Schweitzer, Darrell. "Alfred Bester." In *Science Fiction Voices No. 1,* 18–25. San Bernardino, CA: Borgo, 1979.

Wendell, Carolyn. *Alfred Bester.* Mercer Island, WA: Starmont House, 1980.

Michael Bishop

Science Fantasy; Time Travel

Benchmark Title: *No Enemy But Time* (1982)

b. 1945 (Lincoln, Nebraska)

[W]riters ought to write the most vivid, risk-taking books they can—... no writer deserves rebuke for sounding like the Prophet of Annihilation in one novel and the Angel of Annunciation in the next. The more voices the better.
—"On Reviewing and Being Reviewed" (1977)

Photo credit: Beth Gwinn

About the Author and the Author's Writing

Michael Lawson Bishop was born in Lincoln, Nebraska. His parents divorced when he was five and, as a child, he divided his year between his mother's home near Wichita, Kansas, and summers in the various U.S. cities where his father, an officer in the U.S. Air Force, was stationed: "Mcmphis, Tennessee; Cheyenne, Wyoming; St. Louis, Missouri; Denver, Colorado . . . And, yes, this exposure to so many different places as a crewcut kid shaped my outlook and consequently my writing" (Gevers 2000).

Bishop received his BA with Phi Beta Kappa honors from the University of Georgia in 1967, followed by a master's degree in English. He taught at the United States Air Force Academy Preparatory School in Colorado Springs from 1968 to 1972, and later at the University of Georgia. He left teaching in 1974 to become a full-time writer.

Michael Bishop has been nominated for many Hugo awards, and has twice won Nebulas. His work has been translated into more than a dozen languages. But readers who pick up a Michael Bishop novel or short story expecting conventional SF, or even a comfortable clone of the last Michael Bishop novel or short story, will be sadly disappointed—or pleasantly surprised. Over four decades and thirty books, he has refused to be pinned down and "branded"; instead he has shaped his career according to the ideals he stated in the 1977 essay quoted above, trying everything and stopping at nothing to tell the story as he thinks it needs to be told. His early novels of the 1970s are sophisticated planetary romances: transcendent mysteries, in which Bishop uses anthropology to illuminate the mysteries of alien and futuristic societies. *A Funeral for the Eyes of Fire* (1975), *And Strange at Ecbatan the Trees* (1976; later retitled *Beneath the Shattered Moons*), and *Stolen Faces* (1977) are set on strange worlds, where the outsiders who are there on a mission must first understand the locals' customs and taboos, and in doing so transform themselves. In the two volumes of the Urban Nucleus, *A Little Knowledge* (1977) and *Catacomb Years* (1978), Bishop turns that anthropological analysis to our own strange planet. In 2071, Atlanta is a domed city, with its own customers and hierarchies, and a society dominated by the Orth-Urban Church. The status quo is disrupted when aliens from a distant star system profess their belief in the Church, and the certainties of this rigid society begin to crumble.

In the 1980s, in novels like the Nebula award-winning *No Enemy But Time* (1982) and *Ancient of Days*, Bishop shifted his anthropological focus even closer, using the distant past of humanity to say something about the here and now. In *No Enemy But Time*, widely agreed to be Bishop's SF masterpiece, a modern African American man is torn between two worlds—the Early Pleistocene Africa of his dreams and the twentieth-century reality of his waking life. No less a critic than Roger Zelazny said of *No Enemy But Time* that Bishop "exercises a poet's control of his imagery and possesses an admirable sense of the grotesque."

As well as SF, Bishop's output includes fantasy, speculative fiction, and magic realism, or as he himself puts it, "historical narratives, satire, Biblical and/or Borgesian parables, Southern gothic stuff, and, yes, even unadulterated contemporary fiction" ("Writing Science Fiction as If It Mattered"). His Locus award-winning novel *Brittle Innings* is a baseball story—and a consideration of the possibility that Frankenstein's Monster survived the confrontation with his creator in the Arctic wastes . . . and went on to become a Minor League first baseman. With Paul Di Filippo, writing as "Philip Lawson," Bishop has written a series of humorous detective novels. In addition to his fiction, Bishop has published poetry, and in 1979 he won a Rhysling Award for his poem "For the Lady of a Physicist." In 2005 the collection *A Reverie for Mister Ray* brought together his essays, reviews, and general criticism. Bishop has edited six anthologies, displaying what the *St. James Guide to Science Fiction Writers* calls "marvelous taste."

Michael Bishop makes his home with his wife Jeri, in Pine Mountain, Georgia. In recent years he has returned to teaching and is writer-in-residence at nearby LaGrange College. The warmth and esteem in which he is held by the SF community—fans, fellow writers, critics, and academics—comes across in every interview, every review and response to the man and his work, never more so than in the aftermath of the cruel events of April 16, 2007, when Mr. Bishop's son, Christopher James ("Jamie") Bishop, a professor of German language and a talented artist, was one of the victims of the Virginia Tech college shootings.

Awards

Novels

No Enemy But Time (1982) **Nebula**
Brittle Innings (1994) **Locus Poll**

Short Fiction

"The Samurai and the Willows" (1976) **Locus Poll**
"The Quickening" (1981) **Nebula**
"Her Habiline Husband" (1983) **Locus Poll**
"Dogs' Lives" (1984) **Best American Short Stories, 1985**

As Editor

Light Years and Dark (1984) **Locus Poll**

Works by the Author

A Funeral for the Eyes of Fire (1975)
And Strange at Ecbatan the Trees (1976; aka *Beneath the Shattered Moons*)
Stolen Faces (1977)
Eyes of Fire (1979; radically rev. version of *A Funeral for the Eyes of Fire*)
Transfigurations (1979)
No Enemy But Time (1982)
Ancient of Days (1985)
Philip K. Dick Is Dead, Alas (1987; aka *The Secret Ascension*)

Urban Nucleus

A Little Knowledge (1977)
Catacomb Years (1978)
Under Heaven's Bridge (1981, with Ian Watson)

Other Notable Mainstream and Genre Fiction

Unicorn Mountain (1988)
Who Made Stevie Crye? (1984)
Count Geiger's Blues (1992)
Brittle Innings (1994)

As "Philip Lawson" (with Paul Di Filippo)

Would It Kill You to Smile? (1994)
Muskrat Courage (2000)

Other Notable Short Fiction

"If a Flower Could Eclipse" (1970)
"Death and Designation Among the Asadi" (1973)
"The White Otters of Childhood" (1973)
"Blooded on Arachne" (1982)
"Rogue Tomato" (1975)

"Vernalfest Morning" (1978)
"The Gospel According to Gamaliel Crucis" (1983)
"Apartheid, Superstrings and Mordecai Thubana" (1989)
"The Ommatidium Miniatures" (1989)
"*Cri de Coeur*" (1994)
"How Beautiful with Banners" (2000)
"The Door Gunner" (2003)
"Bears Discover Smut" (2005)
"Vinegar Peace" (2009). Available online, narrated by the author, http://www.starshipsofa.com/

Collections

Windows & Mirrors (1977)
Blooded on Archane (1982)
One Winter in Eden (1984) (introduction by Thomas M. Disch)
Close Encounters with the Deity: Stories (1986) (introduction by Isaac Asimov)
Emphatically Not SF, Almost (1990)
At the City Limits of Fate (1996)
Time Pieces (1998)
Blue Kansas Sky (2000) (introduction by James Morrow). Extract: http://www.infinityplus.co.uk/stories/kansas.htm
Brighten to Incandescence: 17 Stories (2003) (introduction by Lucius Shepard)

As Editor

Changes (1983, with Ian Watson)
Light Years and Dark (1984)
Nebula Awards 23 (1989)
Nebula Awards 24 (1990)
Nebula Awards 25 (1991)
A Cross of Centuries: Twenty-five Imaginative Tales about the Christ (2007)
Passing for Human (2009, with Steven Utley)

Nonfiction Books

A Reverie for Mister Ray: Reflections on Life, Death, and Speculative Fiction. Ed. Michael H. Hutchins. Hornsea, UK: PS Publishing, 2005.

Articles and Essays

"Bringing It All Back Home (Introduction)." In *Byte Beautiful,* by James Tiptree Jr. Garden City, NY: Doubleday, 1985.
"On Reviewing and Being Reviewed (1977)." In *A Reverie for Mister Ray: Reflections on Life, Death, and Speculative Fiction,* ed. Michael H. Hutchins. Hornsea, UK: PS Publishing, 2005.

"Writing Science Fiction as If It Mattered: A Self-Interview." Georgia State University, September 23, 2002. http://bellsouthpwp.net/m/i/michaelbishop-writer/bismattered.htm

Poetry

"Jamie's Hair." *Virginia Quarterly Review* (Spring 2008): 251. http://www.vqronline.org/articles/2008/spring/bishop-jamies-hair/

Bibliographies

Stephensen-Payne, Phil. *Michael Bishop: A Transfigured Talent, a Working Bibliography*. Albuquerque, NM: Galactic Central, 1992.

For Further Information

Official Web site: http://www.michaelbishop-writer.com/

Brooke, Keith. Review—*A Reverie for Mister Ray*. *Infinity Plus*. May 13, 2006. http://www.infinityplus.co.uk/nonfiction/reverie.htm

Brown, Charles N. "Michael Bishop: The Blessing and the Curse" *Locus* (November 2004). http://www.locusmag.com/2004/Issues/11Bishop.html

Gevers, Nick. "Michael Bishop: In Prayer the Whisper of the Void." *Infinity Plus* (October 2000). http://www.infinityplus.co.uk/nonfiction/intmb.htm

Hunter, Barry. Interview. *Cybling* (January 2001). www.cybling.com

Melloy, Killian. Interview. *Infinity Plus* (June 2003). http://www.infinityplus.co.uk/nonfiction/intmb2.htm

Morrow, James. "'Such Guileless Beauty in Debris': The Moral Universe of Michael Bishop." *New York Review of Science Fiction* 151, no. 1 (March 2001): 4–6. http://community.livejournal.com/theinferior4/96397.html

Senior, W. A. "Silence and Disaster in the Novels of Michael Bishop." *New York Review of Science Fiction* 8, no. 12 (1999): 12+.

VanderMeer, Jeff. "Introduction." *A Reverie for Mister Ray: Reflections on Life, Death, and Speculative Fiction* (2005). http://www.sfsite.com/12b/mr214.htm

James Blish

Post-human SF; Sense of Wonder

Benchmark Title: *A Case of Conscience* (1953)

b. 1921 (East Orange, New Jersey); d. 1975 (England: Henley-on-Thames, Oxfordshire)

> [W]e have a lot of hardware ... on the moon right now, to show us what can be done with repeated suggestion. . . . It seems to me that the most important scientific content in modern science fiction are the impossibilities.
> —"The Science in Science Fiction" (1971)

About the Author and the Author's Writing

James Benjamin Blish was born in East Orange, New Jersey. His parents divorced when he was very young, and he grew up in Chicago, where he and his mother lived with his maternal grandparents. His life-long love affair with SF followed a time-honored pattern—he became an enthusiastic reader of SF at age ten, when he was given a copy of *Astounding Stories*; he became an enthusiastic writer of SF in high school, where he created his own fanzines. However, two influences not available to every little boy shaped young James Blish as a writer and set him on the path to become a Master of SF. One was his family's regular pilgrimages to the 1933 Chicago World's Fair. The Fair's theme was technological innovation (motto, "Science Finds, Industry Applies, Man Conforms"), and the style and futuristic exhibits had a great influence on young Blish. The other was that while studying microbiology at Rutgers University in New Jersey, he became involved with the influential New York SF fan group called the Futurians. The Futurians included young Isaac Asimov and Frederick Pohl, among others equally keen and equally talented.

Blish graduated from Rutgers University just in time to serve as a medical technician in World War II. When the war ended he began, but didn't finish, postgraduate work in zoology and literature, and worked as an in-house editor for a pharmaceutical company for many years. His first SF story was published as early as 1940.

According to the *Encyclopedia of Science Fiction* (1999), Blish was "an interesting example of a writer with an enquiring mind and a strong literary bent . . . who turned his attention to fundamentally pulp genre- SF materials and in so doing transformed them." Blish had the big ideas, but he developed them to reflect his concerns with the big, eternal questions. In the Cities in Flight series, cities such as New York, and their entire populations, escape from the political chaos of a far-future Earth; powered by antigravity devices called "spin-dizzies," they set off across the galaxy looking for work and a new life. The Cities in Flight novels could not be a clearer allegory of the Great Depression, complete with currency failure and the rise of totalitarian governments, but by the fourth and final volume in the series, the stakes have been raised, and the itinerant New Yorkers are called upon to save the universe itself. Another theme of particular interest to Blish was the question of what exactly makes us "human"—and are humans the only beings who can claim that nebulous entity, a soul? Blish wrote at length about men of God whose faith is challenged by the enormity and unknowability of the cosmos, of strange alien races who seem untouched by original sin ("A Case of Conscience," 1953), and of planets colonized by humans who have been modified to live in various alien environments (*Seedling Stars*, which includes the wonderful and moving "Surface Tension," 1952).

In an appreciation at the time of Blish's death, Darko Suvin wrote that "he always remained a scientist... a *doctor mirabilis*, a man to whom no knowledge, especially in its erudite branches, was uninteresting or foreign" (*Science Fiction Studies*). As "William Atheling," Blish was also an early and influential critic of SF, and he did much to encourage younger writers; he was a founder of both the Milford SF Writers Conference and the Science Fiction Writers of America. In the late 1960s he was given a standing order to write collections of stories based on scripts from the classic *Star Trek* series and, although it may seem an ironic fate for a writer whose simplest pulp adventures could turn on a dime to become involved in deep metaphysical considerations of the nature of good and evil, the revenue from the Star Trek books enabled him to live comfortably on his writing income. As well as the novelizations of the *Star Trek* scripts, Blish also wrote the first full-length, adult Star Trek spin-off, *Spock Must Die* (1970), thus opening up a whole new territory of fan fiction for readers and writers alike.

James Blish moved to England in 1968 to be closer to research libraries at Oxford University. A lifelong smoker, he died of lung cancer in Henley-on-Thames, in Oxfordshire, on July 30, 1975. On July 5, 2002, he was posthumously inducted into the Science Fiction and Fantasy Hall of Fame.

Awards

SF Hall of Fame (2002, posthumous)

Novels

A Case of Conscience (1953) **Hugo**

Short Fiction

"A Case of Conscience" (1953) **Retro Hugo 2004**
"Earthman, Come Home" (1953) **Retro Hugo 2004**

Works by the Author

Jack of Eagles (1952; aka *ESPer*)
The Duplicated Man (1953, with Robert A. W. Lowndes)
The Warriors of Day (1953; aka *Sword of Xota*)
The Seedling Stars (1956)
The Frozen Year (1957; aka *Fallen Star*)

VOR (1958, with Damon Knight)
Titan's Daughter (1961)
The Night Shapes (1962)
A Torrent of Faces (1967, with Norman L. Knight)
Welcome to Mars! (1967)
The Vanished Jet (1968)
Spock Must Die (1970)
. . . And All the Stars a Stage (1971)
Midsummer Century (1972)
The Quincunx of Time (1973)

After Such Knowledge

A Case of Conscience (1958)
Doctor Mirabilis (1964)
Black Easter: Or Faust Aleph-Null (1968)
The Day After Judgement (1971)

Cities in Flight

They Shall Have Stars (1956; aka *Year 2018!*)
A Life for the Stars (1962)
Earthman, Come Home (1955)
The Triumph of Time (1958; aka *A Clash of Cymbals*)

Heart Stars

The Star Dwellers (1961)
Mission to the Heart Stars (1965)

Other Notable Short Fiction

"Surface Tension" (1953). Later combined with "Seeding Program" (1956; aka "A Time to Survive") and other linked stories as the fix-up novel *The Seedling Stars*.
"There Shall Be No Darkness" (1950)
"Beep" (1954)
"How Beautiful With Banners" (1966)
"We All Die Naked" (1970)

Collections

Galactic Cluster (1959)
So Close to Home (1961)
Anywhen (1970)
Midsummer Century (1972)

Star Trek Readers I, II, III, IV (collection of script adaptations, 1976–1978)
The Best Science Fiction Stories of James Blish (1979)
The Devil's Day (1980)
A Work of Art and Other Stories (1993)
A Dusk of Idols (1996)
In This World, or Another (2003)
Cities in Flight (2004)
Works of Art (2008)

As Editor

Nebula Awards 5 (1970)
New Dreams This Morning (1966)

In Other Media

The Beast Must Die. British Lion Films, 1974. Directed by Paul Annett; starring Peter Cushing and Michael Gambon. Based on Blish's story "There Shall Be No Darkness."

Nonfiction Books

The Issue at Hand (1964, as "William Atheling")
More Issues at Hand (1970, as "William Atheling")
The Tale That Wags the God (1987) (edited by Cy Chauvin)

Articles and Essays

"Cathedrals in Space." In *Turning Points: Essays on the Art of Science Fiction,* ed. Damon Knight. New York: Harper & Row, 1977.

"The Development of a Science Fiction Writer." In *The Profession of Science Fiction: SF Writers on Their Craft and Ideas,* ed. Maxim Jakubowski and Edward James. New York: St. Martin's, 1992.

"On Science Fiction Criticism." In *SF: The Other Side of Realism*, ed. Thomas D. Clareson. Bowling Green, OH: Bowling Green University Popular Press, 1971.

"The Science in Science Fiction." In *The Tale That Wags the God*, ed. Cy Chauvin. Chicago: Advent, 1987 (orig. pub. 1971).

Bibliographies

Stephensen-Payne, Phil. *James Blish, Author Mirabilis: A Working Bibliography*. Leeds: Galactic Central, 1996.

For Further Information

Blish, Charles Benjamin. "James Blish." *Blish Genealogy.* August 2007. http://www.blish.org/gens/1380I.html. Not an official Web site, but a fascinating account of the Blish family by James Blish's son, who includes some personal reminiscences of his father.

Aldiss, Brian W. "James Blish and the Mathematics of Knowledge." In *This World and Nearer Ones,* 37–50. Kent, OH: Kent State University Press, 1981.

Blackman, S. James. "Cosmic Dust Bowl: James Blish and 'Cities in Flight'." *Space.com*, April 15, 2000. http://www.space.com/sciencefiction/books/cities_flight_000413.html

Devney, Bob. "A Case of Conscientiousness: James Blish and *The Tale That Wags the God.*" *Proper Boskonian* 38 (December 1996). http://users.rcn.com/devniad/otherw/PB38.html

Foyster, John. "William Atheling Jr.: A Critic of Science Fiction." In *The Tale That Wags the God,* 7–18. Chicago: Advent, 1987.

Ketterer, David. *Imprisoned in a Tesseract: The Life and Work of James Blish.* Kent, OH: Kent State University Press, 1987.

Stableford, Brian M. *A Clash of Symbols: The Triumph of James Blish.* San Bernardino, CA: Borgo, 1979

Suvin, Darko. "James Blish, 1921–1975." *Science Fiction Studies* 2 (1975): 294–95.

Ben Bova

Hard SF

Benchmark Title: *Mars* (1992)

b. 1932 (Philadelphia, Pennsylvania)

Photo credit: Beth Gwinn

My first published novel was written for teenagers, and there were rules laid down by the publisher: no sex, no smoking, no swearing. I blew up entire solar systems, I consigned billions of people to horrible death; they didn't seem to mind that at all. But no hanky-panky.

—MacDonald, "Men on Mars, Women on Venus,"
Bookpage (1999)

About the Author and the Author's Writing

Benjamin William Bova has been a professional writer all of his life. He was born and raised in Philadelphia; immediately following his graduation from Temple University—where he received a bachelor's degree in journalism in 1954—he worked as a technical editor for Project Vanguard, the United States Naval Research Laboratory (NRL) response to the Soviet Union's Sputnik program. During the 1960s he was employed as a science writer with Avco Everett Research Laboratory, a company at the forefront of aeronautics research and defense weapon development.

So it was a shift of emphasis, rather than career, in 1971 when Bova was appointed successor to John W. Campbell as editor of *Analog* SF magazine. His remit was to restore the magazine, which had become moribund and stagnant as Campbell became increasingly set in his editorial ways, to its place at the cutting edge of SF. The dangers that Bova had written about in his previous positions—being shot into space on top of a Vanguard missile, imagining Armageddon and its aftermath—was nothing compared to the response of some *Analog* readers to his editorial policy of broadening the magazine's horizons; as the *Encyclopedia of Science Fiction* (1999) describes it, even "such stories as 'The Gold at the Starbow's End' by Frederik Pohl and 'Hero' by Joe Haldeman, inoffensive though they might seem in the outside world, brought strong protests." For dragging *Analog* kicking and screaming out of the 1950s, Bova received the Hugo Award for Best Professional Editor six times. Later he became editorial director of *Omni Magazine*.

Meanwhile, Bova was also writing. His novels before 1971, starting with *The Star Conquerors* (1959), were all young adult fiction. Although all of his fiction tends to be straightforward adventure, in the 1970s he began to deal in more adult themes, in a more adult manner. For example, in the SF political thriller *The Multiple Man* (1976), a charismatic and radical U.S. president begins to behave in a way that suggests he has been replaced by a treacherous clone. In other novels, Bova deals with impending nuclear holocaust, first contact with more technologically advanced aliens, the first manned flight to Mars—all turning points for humanity which all, in their different ways, allow Bova to expand on his heart-felt belief that humankind's future is in the stars.

Like many writers of hard SF, Bova is a propagandist in the best possible sense. He has worked closely with groups dedicated to futuristic thought and research, in fact and fiction. He is the president emeritus of the National Space Society, a past president of Science-Fiction and Fantasy Writers of America, and a fellow of the American Association for the Advancement of Science (AAAS). He is a member of the Advisory Board of The Lifeboat Foundation, a nonprofit organization dedicated to science and research that would enable humanity to survive an extinction-level event. He has served as a technical advisor with filmmakers and television producers such as Woody Allen, George Lucas, and Gene Roddenberry. In 2005 Bova received the Lifetime Achievement award of the Arthur C. Clarke Foundation, "for fueling mankind's imagination regarding the wonders of outer space."

In the 1980s Ben Bova returned to school, earning an MA in communications from the State University of New York at Albany and a Ph.D. in education from California Coast University. He currently lives in Naples, Florida, with his wife Barbara, who is a literary agent. He writes a regular column for the local daily paper there, in which he holds forth on the topics dearest to his heart: the future, the environment, and the possibilities that science offers us all.

Awards

Edward E. Smith Memorial Award for Imaginative Fiction ("Skylark award") (1974)
Robert A. Heinlein Award (2008)

Novels

Titan (2006) **Campbell**

As Editor

Professional Editor, for *Analog Science Fiction and Fact* (1973, 1974, 1975, 1976, 1977, 1979) **Hugo**

Works by the Author

The Weathermakers (1967)
Out of the Sun (1968; rev. version 1984)
Escape! (1970)
THX 1138 (1971)
As on a Darkling Plain (1972)

When the Sky Burned (1973)
The Winds of Altair (1973; rev. version 1983)
Gremlins, Go Home! (1974, with Gordon R. Dickson)
The Starcrossed (1975)
The Multiple Man (1976)
City of Darkness (1976)
Colony (1978)
Test of Fire (1982)
Privateers (1985)
The Kinsman Saga (1987). A fix-up of two earlier novels, *Kinsman* (1979) and *Millennium* (1976).
The Peacekeepers (1988)
Cyberbooks (1989)
The Trikon Deception (1992, with Bill Pogue)
Triumph (1993)
Death Dream (1994)
Brothers (1995)
The Green Trap (2006)
The Immortality Factor (2009)

The Asteroid Wars

The Precipice (2001)
The Rock Rats (2002)
The Silent War (2004)
The Aftermath (2007)

Exiles Trilogy

Exiled from Earth (1971)
Flight of Exiles (1972)
End of Exile (1975)

The Grand Tour of the Universe

Mars (1992)
Empire Builders (1993)
Moonrise (1996)
Moonwar (1997)
Return to Mars (1999)
Venus (2000)
Jupiter (2000)
Saturn (2003)
Mercury (2005)

Powersat (2005)
Titan (2006)
Mars Life (2008)

Orion series

Orion (1984)
Vengeance of Orion (1988)
Orion in the Dying Time (1990)
Orion and the Conqueror (1994)
Orion among the Stars (1995)

Voyagers Trilogy

Voyagers (1981)
The Alien Within (1986)
Star Brothers (1990)

Watchmen Trilogy (YA)

The Star Conquerors (1959)
Star Watchman (1964)
The Dueling Machine (1969)

Notable Short Fiction

"Brillo" (1971, with Harlan Ellison)
"Floodtide" (1984)
"Inspiration" (1994)
"Acts of God" (1995)
"The Great Moon Hoax, or A Princess of Mars" (1996)

Collections

Forward in Time (1973)
Maxwell's Demons (1978)
Escape Plus (1984)
The Astral Mirror (1985)
Prometheans (1986)
Battle Station (1987)
Future Crime (1990)
Challenges (1993)
Twice Seven (1998)
Tales of the Grand Tour (2004)
The Sam Gunn Omnibus (2007)

As Editor

The Many Worlds of Science Fiction (1971)
Analog 9 (1973)
The Science Fiction Hall of Fame (1973)
Science Fiction Hall of Fame: The Novellas, 1, 2, and 3 (1975)
Analog Annual (1976)
The Best of Analog (1978)
Analog Yearbook (1978)
The Best of Omni Science Fiction, 1, 2, 3, and 4 (1980–1982, with Don Myrus)
The Best of the Nebulas (1989)
Future Quartet: Earth in the Year 2042: A Four-Part Invention (1994, with Frederik Pohl, Jerry Pournelle, and Charles Sheffield)
The Science Fiction Box: Eye for Eye, Run for the Stars, and Tales of the Grand Tour (2006, with Orson Scott Card and Harlan Ellison)
Nebula Awards Showcase 2008 (2008)

Three By . . . (Novellas)

Aliens (1977)
Exiles (1977)
Novella: 3 (1978)

In Other Media

The Starlost (1973). Short-lived SF TV series, devised and written by Harlan Ellison and starring (among others) Keir Dullea. Ben Bova was listed as science consultant for two episodes.

Nonfiction Books

The Milky Way Galaxy (1961)
The Fourth State of Matter (1974)
The Analog Science Fact Reader (1974)
Through Eyes of Wonder (1975)
In Quest of Quasars (1975)
Notes to a Science Fiction Writer (1975)
Viewpoint (1977)
Closeup: New Worlds (1977, with Trudy E. Bell)
The High Road (1981)
Vision of the Future: The Art of Robert McCall (1982, with Robert McCall)
Assured Survival: Putting the Star Wars Defense in Perspective (1984)
Star Peace (1986)
Welcome to Moonbase (1987)
The Craft of Writing Science Fiction That Sells (1994)

Space Travel: Science Fiction Writing Series (1997, with Anthony R. Lewis)

Time Travel: Science Fiction Writing Series (1997, with Anthony R. Lewis)

Immortality: How Science Is Extending Your Life Span—and Changing the World (2000)

Faint Echoes, Distant Stars: The Science and Politics of Finding Life Beyond Earth (2004)

Articles and Essays

Naples Daily News. http://www.naplesnews.com/. Column of local interest to Southwest Florida, but often with science and SF themes. For example: "Cloning's Potential Shows It's More Than Just a Funny Idea" (April 2004); "Human Race Straining the Ecosystem" (January 2007); "Science Fiction Can Teach Us Something If We Stop to Learn" (October 2004).

"O Brave New (Virtual) World." In *The World of 2044: Technological Development and the Future of Society,* ed. Charles Sheffield et al. St. Paul, MN: Paragon, 1994.

"The Role of Science Fiction." In *Science Fiction, Today and Tomorrow; A Discursive Symposium,* ed. Reginald Bretnor. New York: Harper & Row, 1974.

"Slowboat to the Stars!" *Analog Science Fiction and Fact* (February 2000).

For Further Information

Official Web site: http://www.benbova.net/

Auden, Sandy. "Scurrying Over the Rocks: An Interview with Ben Bova." *SF Site* (2005). http://www.sfsite.com/09b/sabb208.htm

James, Warren W. "Interviews." In *Mike Hodel's Hour 25: Science Fiction Radio for Southern California,* November 9, 2001, and July 18, 2005. http://www.hour25online.com/

Jenkins, Henry. "Ben Bova in Discussion at MIT" (edited version). *Media in Transition,* April 2, 2000. Massachusetts Institute of Technology. http://web.mit.edu/m-i-t/science_fiction/

Kilgore, DeWitt Douglas. "Ben Bova: Race, Nation and Renewal on the High Frontier." In *Astrofuturism: Science, Race, and Visions of Utopia in Space,* 186–221. Philadelphia: University of Pennsylvania Press, 2003.

Lilley, Ernest. "An Interview with Ben Bova." *SFRevu,* May 5, 2002. http://www.sfrevu.com/ISSUES/2002/0205/Feature%20-%20Ben%20Bova/interview.htm

MacDonald, Jay. "Men on Mars, Women on Venus." *BookPage,* June 1, 1999 (cached 5/30/09). http://www.bookpage.com/9906bp/ben_bova.html

Mullen, Leslie. "An Interview with Ben Bova." *Astrobiology Magazine Online,* April 21, 2004. http://www.astrobio.net/news/article933.html

Video Interviews. *Bookwrap Central.* n.d. http://www.bookwrapcentral.com/authors/benbova.htm

Leigh Brackett

Science Fantasy; Space Opera

Benchmark Title: *The Sword of Rhiannon* (1953)

b. 1915 (Los Angeles, California); d. 1978 (Lancaster, California)

> *The tale of adventure—of great courage and daring, of battle against the forces of darkness and the unknown—has been with the human race since it first learned to talk. . . . The so-called space opera is the folk-tale, the hero-tale, of our particular niche in history.*
> —The Best of Planet Stories No. 1 (1974)

About the Author and the Author's Writing

Like the names of the dishes on a particularly rich, particularly foreign menu, it is possible to dine out on Leigh Brackett's strange and wonderful titles alone; "Enchantress of Venus," "The Lake of the Gone Forever," "Lorelei of the Red Mist," and "Queen of the Martian Catacombs" suggest, before the reader even turns to the first page, the exotic wonders within. As a child Brackett was a great admirer of Edgar Rice Burroughs, and she is best known for deceptively simple adventures, in that style, set on the impossibly lush and exotic terrains of Mars and Venus. But whereas with Burroughs it is pretty much "what you see is what you get," with little in the way of narrative or character complications, Brackett's adventures conceal in their exoticism a keen sense of the individual who stands apart and humankind's tendency to shun what it does not understand. Brackett also had a unique talent for naturalistic, believable dialogue (however unlikely the situation in which it is being spoken), and for imagery that engages the reader's every sense in her exotic, wondrous worlds.

Leigh Douglass Brackett was born in Los Angeles, California, and was a professional writer from the age of twenty-four. Her first short story, "Martian Quest," was published in *Astounding Science Fiction* magazine in 1940, and thereafter her stories appeared regularly in magazines like *Astonishing Stories*, *Super Science Stories*, and *Thrilling Wonder Stories*. Most of Brackett's science fiction is unapologetic space opera or planetary romance, acted out against the background of the lush, fantastic Mars and Venus beloved of 1940s SF. It is a tribute to the way that she took this material and did something rare and different, and interesting, with it that this territory is now often described as the "Leigh Brackett Solar System." In 1949 she introduced her swashbuckling antihero Eric John Stark, who owed a huge (and acknowledged) debt to Burroughs's Tarzan and the Barsoom novels and to the Conan the Barbarian tales of Robert E. Howard. But Stark was no simple action hero, cast in the mold of John Carter, or Conan. Orphaned on Mercury, Stark is a perpetual outsider, a human raised by aliens, who owes allegiance to nothing but his own standards of friendship and honor. Beneath the simple veneer of her over-the-top adventures —Stark's encounter with the Venusian witch who steals men's souls in "Enchantress of Venus"; the clash of roguish archaeologist Matt Carse with the godlike Martian Rhiannon in *The Sword of Rhiannon*—Brackett plays with questions of loyalty and identity and with racial ambiguities that were well ahead of their time.

In 1946 Brackett married fellow SF writer Edmond Hamilton. Brackett and Hamilton earned their livings by writing, and as well as successful space operas and swashbucklers, Brackett wrote detective novels, and even an award-winning Western. She wrote, or co-wrote, the screenplays for acclaimed movies such as *The Big Sleep* (1946), *Rio Bravo* (1958), and *The Long Goodbye* (1973). In the 1970s she resumed the Stark series; tastes had changed, and readers demanded a degree of scientific plausibility, so Eric John Stark abandoned desert Mars and jungle Venus for the imaginary planet Skaith, which allowed Brackett to revisit the fantastic aspects of her Solar System worlds.

In 1978 Brackett was asked by George Lucas to submit a draft of a screenplay for the second movie in the *Star Wars* trilogy, *The Empire Strikes Back* (1980), based on his notes. The exact relationship between Brackett's draft script and the final version of the script is a source of some controversy. Many critics and fans have long believed that they could detect traces of Brackett's influence, both in the dialogue and in the space opera spirit of *Empire*; others (including some who have seen Brackett's script, which is available at the library of the Eastern New Mexico University in Portales, New Mexico) say that nothing of her work survived. However, her name appears, with Lawrence Kasdan, as screenwriter on the movie credits. Leigh Brackett died on March 24, 1978, in Lancaster, California. In 1980 she was posthumously given a Hugo Award for her work on *The Empire Strikes Back*. It is a further tribute to her long-term influence on SF that a new generation of SF writers have begun to colonize the Leigh Brackett Solar System for the twenty-first century. Writers as diverse as S. M. Stirling, in his Lords of Creation novels, and Kage Baker, in *The Empress of Mars* (2009), are bringing new life, and new readers, to the fantastic landscapes first described by Leigh Brackett.

Awards

Screenplay

The Empire Strikes Back (1981) **Hugo**

Works by the Author

Shadow Over Mars (1944; aka *The Nemesis from Terra*)

Sea-Kings of Mars (1949). Reissued in 1953 as *The Sword of Rhiannon*.

The Starmen (1952; aka *The Galactic Breed*). Reissued in 1976, in unabridged form, as *The Starmen of Llyrdis*.

The Big Jump (1955)

The Long Tomorrow (1955)

Alpha Centauri or Die! (1963). Fix-up of serialized novellas *The Ark of Mars* (1953), and *Teleportress of Alpha C.* (1954).

The Coming of the Terrans (1967)

The Secret of Sinharat and *People of the Talisman* (1964). Expanded versions of "Queen of the Martian Catacombs" (1949) and "Black Amazon of Mars" (1951). Republished in 1982 under one title as *Eric John Stark, Outlaw of Mars.*

Skaith Novels

The Ginger Star (1974)
The Hounds of Skaith (1974)
The Reavers of Skaith (1976)

Notable Mainstream and Other Genre Fiction

No Good from a Corpse (crime novel; 1944) (foreword by Ray Bradbury; "Epiphany (The Afterword)" by Michael Connolly). http://www.michaelconnelly.com/Other_Words/Epiphany/epiphany.html

Stranger at Home (crime novel, 1946). Bracket was ghost-writer for the actor George Sanders.

An Eye for an Eye (crime novel; 1957). Adapted for television as the CBS series *Markham*: 1959–1960)

The Tiger Among Us (crime novel; 1957; UK: *Fear No Evil*)

Follow the Free Wind (Western novel; 1963). Winner of the Spur Award from the Western Writers of America.

Silent Partner (crime novel; 1969)

Notable Short Fiction

"Martian Quest" (1940)
"The Jewel of Bas" (1944)
"The Veil of Astellar" (1944)
"Lorelei of the Red Mist" (1946, with Ray Bradbury)
"Enchantress of Venus" (1949)
"The Lake of the Gone Forever" (1949)
"Queen of the Martian Catacombs" (1949)
"Black Amazon of Mars" (1951)
"The Tweener" (1955)
"All the Colors of the Rainbow" (1957)
"The Other People" (1957; aka "The Queer Ones")

Collections

The Halfling and Other Stories (1973)
The Book of Skaith (1976)

The Best of Leigh Brackett (1977) (edited by Edmond Hamilton)
Martian Quest: The Early Brackett (2002)
Stark and the Star Kings (2005) (includes the previously unpublished title story, written with her husband, Edmond Hamilton)
Sea-Kings of Mars and Otherworldly Stories (2005)
Lorelei of the Red Mist: Planetary Romances (2008)

As Editor

The Best of Planet Stories No. 1 (1974)
The Best of Edmond Hamilton (1977)

In Other Media

The Vampire's Ghost. Republic Pictures, 1945. Directed by Lesley Selander; starring John Abbott.
The Big Sleep. Warner Bros. Pictures, 1946. Directed by Howard Hawks; starring Humphrey Bogart and Lauren Bacall.
Rio Bravo. Armada Productions, 1959; *El Dorado.* Paramount, 1966. Both directed by Howard Hawks; starring John Wayne.
The Long Goodbye. Lionsgate Films, 1973. Directed by Robert Altman; starring Elliott Gould and Nina Van Pallandt.
The Empire Strikes Back. Lucasfilm, 1980. Directed by Irvin Kershner; starring Mark Hamill, Harrison Ford, and Carrie Fisher. Draft screenplay, based on George Lucas's story notes.

Articles and Essays

"Barsoom and Myself." In *Edgar Rice Burroughs' Fantastic Worlds*, ed. James Van Hise. Yucca Valley, CA: James Van Hise, 1996.
"Introduction." In *The Best of Planet Stories No. 1*. New York: Ballantine Books, 1974.

For Further Information

Leigh Brackett, Queen of Space. Edited by Gary W. Thomas. http://www.gwthomas.org/brackett.htm

Carr, J. L. *Leigh Brackett: American Writer*. Polk City, IA: Chris Drumm, 1986.
Falk, Bertil. "Leigh Brackett: Much More Than the Queen of Space Opera!" *Bewildering Stories,* June 25, 2007. http://www.bewilderingstories.com/issue250/brackett1.html
Macklin, Tony, and Nick Pici, eds. Interview. In *Voices from the Set: The Film Heritage Interviews,* 219–37. Lanham, MD: Scarecrow, 2000. The audio version of this interview is available at http://tonymacklin.net/content.php?cID=242.

Moorcock, Michael. "Queen of the Martian Mysteries: An Appreciation of Leigh Brackett." *Projections: Science Fiction in Literature and Film,* ed. Lou Anders, 247–56. Austin, TX: Monkeybrain, 2004. http://www.fantasticmetropolis.com/i/brackett/

Sallis, James. "The Unclassifiable Leigh Brackett." *Boston Globe,* December 12, 2005. http://www.grasslimb.com/sallis/GlobeColumns/globe.09.brackett.html

Schweitzer, Darrell. "Edmond Hamilton and Leigh Brackett." In *Science Fiction Voices No. 5,* 35–41. San Bernardino, CA: Borgo, 1981.

Swires, Steve. "Leigh Brackett: Journeyman Plumber." In *Backstory 2: Interviews with Screenwriters of the 1940s and 1950s,* ed. Pat McGilligan, 15–26. Berkeley: University of California Press, 1991.

Valdron, Den. "Colonial Barsoon: Leigh Brackett. Part I: Spaceman's Burden. Part II: Appendices & Cover Gallery. *ERBzine* no. 1783 (n.d.). http://www.erbzine.com/mag17/1783.html

Ray Bradbury

Humor and Satire; Science Fantasy

Benchmark Titles: *The Martian Chronicles* (1950)

b. 1920 (Waukegan, Illinois)

There's a scene in "Moby Dick," where Ahab is going after the white whale, and Starbuck says to him, "Where's the profit in this?" And Ahab touches his heart and he says, "The profit is here, man, the profit is here."

—Testimony before the President's Commission on Implementation of U.S. Space Exploration Policy (2004)

Photo credit: Tom Victor. Reprinted by permission of Don Congdon Associates, Inc.

About the Author and the Author's Writing

With a career that spans *seven decades*, Ray Bradbury is probably the most likely candidate, of all the authors in this volume, for the title "National Treasure." Since his first short story, written in collaboration with Henry Hasse, appeared in *Super Science Stories* in 1941, Ray Bradbury has written more than 500 published works—short stories, novels such as *The Martian Chronicles* and *Fahrenheit 451*, plays, screenplays, television scripts, and verse. Hundreds of his short stories have been collected, anthologized, and published in magazines like *The Saturday Evening Post*, *The New Yorker*, *Amazing Stories*, and *Dime Detective*. From his early writing days, when he was a friend and collaborator of Golden Age SFers such as Forrest Ackerman, Leigh Brackett, and Henry Kuttner, to today, Bradbury has been one of the writers who has actively shaped that entity we point to when we say "SF."

Raymond Douglas Bradbury was born in Waukegan, Illinois. His mother emigrated to the United States from Sweden; his father was a power and telephone lineman, the son and grandson of newspaper publishers. The family spent some of his early years in Waukegan, and some in Tucson, Arizona; but this was the Great Depression, and when Bradbury was thirteen, the family followed his father to Los Angeles, where jobs were available. Bradbury's formative years belonged to Waukegan, however, and his semiautobiographical fantasy/horror novels *Dandelion Wine*, *Something Wicked This Way Comes*, and *Farewell Summer* draw on his childhood memories of the wonders and terrors of growing up in small-town USA.

As a child Bradbury was devoted to the works of L. Frank Baum, Jules Verne, H. G. Wells, and Edgar Rice Burroughs, four writers from whom he would have learned the importance of a sense of place, a strong moral center, and the strength of "ordinary" characters. His formal education ended when he graduated from Los Angeles High School in 1938, but he continued to read, take advantage of local libraries—and write. He received $15 for his first published story, in 1941, and by the end of 1942 Bradbury was a full-time, professional writer, described by *The Encyclopedia of Science Fiction* (1999) as, "poetic, evocative, consciously symbolic, with strong nostalgic elements and a leaning towards the macabre."

Bradbury's great contribution to SF was to recognize the possibilities of the "ordinary." Who else could have summed up the horrors of nuclear Armageddon in the last moments of a household computer and the appliances it doggedly keeps running for the family that is never going to come back? ("There Will Come Soft Rains," 1950). Bradbury is another of the SF greats who is resistant to having his work thoughtlessly labeled "scifi." In a 1999 interview in *Weekly Alibi*, he was emphatic: "*Martian Chronicles* is not science fiction, it's fantasy. It couldn't happen, you see?" (O'Leary).

In *The Martian Chronicles*, Bradbury transplants the formative experiences of small-town America to an imaginary Mars—a terrain even stranger than the Mars of pulp classics, such as those of Leigh Brackett (with whom Bradbury collaborated early in his career), because this is a Mars of the mind. As Bradbury says, it is not so much SF, as about our SF world, and how the myths and legends of a genre born in the twentieth century have shaped us and our perceptions. Bradbury's reluctance to be "boxed" with an SF label does not reflect a disrespect for the genre, however. In a 1999 *Book Magazine* interview, he said, "People are walking around the streets with phones to their heads talking to someone ten feet away.... We're surrounded by technology and the problems created by technology, and science fiction isn't important?" (Mesic).

More firmly in SF territory is Bradbury's great dystopian allegory *Fahrenheit 451*, in which anti-intellectualism has reached such a point that books are outlawed, and firemen are employed, not to put out fires, but as shock troops to burn the forbidden books. *Fahrenheit 451* has the dubious (and ironic) distinction of periodically being the target of attempts to remove it from school reading lists and public libraries.

Besides the "usual" array of awards for individual work and lifetime achievement, Bradbury's recent honors include, in 2007, a special citation from **The Pulitzer Board** "for his distinguished, prolific, and deeply influential career as an unmatched author of science fiction and fantasy"; in 2004, a **National Medal of Arts**, presented at the White House by President George W. Bush and Laura Bush; and in 2000, the **Distinguished Contribution to American Letters Award** from the National Book Foundation. But as is befitting such a unique talent, there are unique honors as well:

- a star with his name on it on the Hollywood Walk of Fame, at 6644 Hollywood Boulevard;

- an asteroid named in his honor—Bradbury 9766—and a crater on the moon called "Dandelion Crater," after his novel, *Dandelion Wine*; and

- honorary doctorates from Woodbury University, in California (2003), the National University of Ireland, Galway (2005), and Columbia College, Chicago (2009).

As well as a distinguished career in screenwriting, Bradbury was a consultant for the American Pavilion at the 1964 New York World's Fair and for the Spaceship Earth geosphere at Walt Disney World's Epcot Center.

Ray Bradbury and his wife Marguerite "Maggie" McClure were married from 1947 until her death in 2003. In spite of this loss and recent poor health, he continues to speak and write about the future—and the importance of the imagination.

Awards

World Fantasy Award Life Achievement (1977)
Science Fiction and Fantasy Writers of America, Grand Master (1989)
First Fandom Hall of Fame Award (1996)
SF Hall of Fame (1999)

Novels

The Martian Chronicles (1950) **Locus All-Time Collection, 1999**
Fahrenheit 451 (1953) **Prometheus Hall of Fame 1984, Retro Hugo 2004**

Collections

One More for the Road (2002) **National Book Award**

Works by the Author

The Martian Chronicles (1950)
The Illustrated Man (1951)
Fahrenheit 451 (1953)
Something Wicked This Way Comes (1962)
From the Dust Returned (2001)

Children and Young Adult

R Is for Rocket (1962)
S Is for Space (1966)
The Halloween Tree (1972)
Ahmed and the Oblivion Machine (1998)

Notable Mainstream and Other Genre Fiction

Dandelion Wine (1957)
Death Is a Lonely Business (1985)
A Graveyard for Lunatics (1990)
Green Shadows, White Whale (1992)
Let's All Kill Constance (2002)
Farewell Summer (2006)
Summer Morning, Summer Night (2008)

Other Notable Short Fiction

"R Is for Rocket" (1943)
"Mars is Heaven!" (1948)
"There Will Come Soft Rains" (1950)
"The Fog Horn" (1951; aka "The Beast from 20,000 Fathoms"). http://members.fortunecity.com/ymir1/beastfro9.html
"The Rocket Man" (1951)
"A Sound of Thunder" (1952)
"The Thing at the Top of the Stairs" (1988)

Collections

Dark Carnival (1947)
The Golden Apples of the Sun and Other Stories (1953)
A Medicine for Melancholy (1959; UK: *The Day It Rained Forever*)
The Small Assassin (1962)
The Machineries of Joy (1964)
The Autumn People (1965) and *Tomorrow Midnight* (1966) (EC Comics version of classic Bradbury stories, "illustrated in the good old comic book tradition"; adaptation by Albert B. Feldstein and various artists)
I Sing the Body Electric! (1969)
Long After Midnight (1976)
Beyond 1984: A Remembrance of Things Future (1979)
Long After Midnight and Other Stories (1981)
Dinosaur Tales (1983)
A Memory of Murder (1984)
The Toynbee Convector (1988)
Quicker Than the Eye (1996)
Driving Blind (1997)
Bradbury Stories: 100 of His Most Celebrated Tales (2003)
A Sound of Thunder and Other Stories (2004; prev. title *Classic Stories 1*)
Now and Forever: Somewhere a Band Is Playing & Leviathan '99 (2007)

As Editor

Timeless Stories for Today and Tomorrow (1952)
The Circus of Dr. Lao and Other Improbable Stories (1956)

In Other Media

The Beast from 20,000 Fathoms. Mutual Pictures of California, 1953. Directed by Eugène Lourié. Based on Bradbury's short story "The Fog Horn."
Budet Laskovyy Dozhd. Uzbekfilm Studio, 1984. Written and directed by Nazim Tulyakhodzayev. Intriguing Russian animated film, based on Bradbury's

classic 1950 short story "There Will Come Soft Rains." Winner of the Golden Dove Award at the Leipzig International Festival for Documentary and Animated Films in 1984.

Fahrenheit 451. Vineyard Film Ltd., 1966. Directed by François Truffaut; starring Oskar Werner and Julie Christie. An updated version of Bradbury's classic dystopian novel, with a screenplay by Frank Darabont, is planned for 2010.

The Halloween Tree. Hanna-Barbera Productions, 1993. Directed by Mario Piluso; starring Leonard Nimoy. Animated feature adaptation of Bradbury's 1973 children's novel, narrated by Bradbury.

Icarus Montgolfier Wright. Format Films, 1961. Produced by Jules Engel and Herbert Klynn. Bradbury is credited for the screenplay of this Oscar-nominated animated film based on his 1956 short story.

The Illustrated Man. Warner Brothers/Seven Arts, 1969. Directed by Jack Smight; starring Rod Steiger and Claire Bloom. Flawed, but interesting, film, hated by both Bradbury and Steiger.

It Came from Outer Space. Universal International Pictures, 1953. Directed by Jack Arnold; starring Richard Carlson and Barbara Rush.

King of Kings. Metro-Goldwyn-Mayer, 1961. Directed by Nicholas Ray; starring Jeffrey Hunter. Bradbury, uncredited, wrote the narration read by Orson Welles.

Moby Dick. Moulin Productions, 1956. Directed by John Huston; screenplay by Bradbury; starring Gregory Peck and Richard Basehart. *Green Shadows, White Whale* (1992) is a fictionalized account of Bradbury's experiences living in Ireland while he wrote the screenplay.

The Ray Bradbury Theater. Alliance Atlantis, 1985–1992. Starring, among others, Alan Bates, Drew Barrymore, Jeff Goldblum, Peter O'Toole, and William Shatner. Fifty-nine episodes, based on Bradbury stories and scripts.

Something Wicked This Way Comes. Bryna Productions, 1983. Directed by Jack Clayton; screenplay by Bradbury; starring Jason Robards and Jonathan Pryce.

Nonfiction

The Art of Playboy (1985)
Yestermorrow: Obvious Answers to Impossible Futures (1993)
Zen in the Art of Writing: Essays on Creativity (1994)
Bradbury Speaks: Too Soon from the Cave, Too Far from the Stars (2006)
Match to Flame: The Fictional Paths to Fahrenheit 451 (2007)

Articles and Essays

"Ray Bradbury: The Illustrated Spaceman" (edited testimony before the President's Commission on Implementation of U.S. Space Exploration Policy, April 15, 2004). *Astrobiology Magazine,* May 16, 2004. http://www.astrobio.net/news/article974.html

For Further Information

Official Web site: http://www.raybradbury.com

Aggelis, Steven I., ed. *Conversations with Ray Bradbury.* Jackson: University Press of Mississippi, 2004.

Bloom, Harold, ed. *Ray Bradbury.* Introduction by Damon Knight. New York: Chelsea House, 2000.

Eller, Jonathan R., and William F. Touponce. *Ray Bradbury: The Life of Fiction.* Kent, OH: Kent State University Press, 2004.

Mass, Wendy. *Ray Bradbury: Master of Science Fiction and Fantasy.* Berkeley Heights, NJ: Enslow, 2004.

McCarty, Michael. Interview. *Sci Fi Weekly,* March 26, 2007. http://reflectionsedge.com/index.php/2007/03/

Mesic, Penelope. "Cosmic Ray." *Book Magazine* (December 1998/January 1999). http://www.raybradbury.com/articles_book_mag.html

O'Leary, Devin D. "Grandfather Time." *Weekly Alibi,* September 27, 1999. Weekly Wire. http://weeklywire.com/ww/09-27-99/alibi_feat1.html

Reid, Robin Anne. *Ray Bradbury: A Critical Companion.* Westport, CT: Greenwood, 2000.

Swaim, Don. Audio Interviews. *Wired for Books* (1992 and 1993). WOUB/Ohio University. http://wiredforbooks.org/raybradbury/

Touponce, William F. *Naming the Unnameable: Ray Bradbury and the Fantastic after Freud.* Mercer Island, WA: Starmont, 1997.

Unangst, Kevin. *Ray Bradbury Online,* October 18, 2006. http://raybradburyonline.com/

Weist, Jerry, and Donn Albright. *Bradbury, an Illustrated Life: A Journey to Far Metaphor.* New York: William Morrow, 2002.

Weller, Sam. *The Bradbury Chronicles.* New York: William Morrow, 2005

Zebrowski, George. Interview. In *Synergy SF: New Science Fiction.* Waterville, ME: Five Star, 2004.

Marion Zimmer Bradley

Feminist SF; Science Fantasy; SF Romance

Benchmark Title: *The Heritage of Hastur* (1975)

b. 1930 (Albany, New York); d. 1999 (Berkeley, California)

Science fiction encourages us to explore the future—not the rosy future predicted to those who want to sell us technology, nor the bleak future predicted by professional Cassandras . . . but all *the futures, good and bad, that the human mind can envision.*

—Patti Peret, *The Faces of Science Fiction* (1984)

About the Author and the Author's Writing

Marion Eleanor Zimmer was born on a farm near Albany, New York, during the Great Depression. Her childhood dream was to be an opera singer, but because her family could not afford the training, she qualified as a teacher, married, and moved to Texas. Her first story as a professional was accepted by *Vortex Science Fiction* three years later.

Her earliest SF stories were typical "space opera," in the tradition of Leigh Brackett and C. L. Moore; even Darkover, which established her reputation, betrays their influence, "the lure of faraway places, faintly sinister desert towns, and flashing swords, frequently wielded by fighting women" (Schwartz 1996).

Bradley's first Darkover novels, *Planet Savers* and *Sword of Aldones*, were published in 1962. (The start of the saga is sometimes given as 1958 because *Planet Savers* made its first appearance that year, as a serial, in *Amazing Science Fiction Stories*.) Darkover is a lost Earth colony where psi powers have developed to an unusual degree, and the people there must challenge the hegemony of a galactic empire to preserve their way of life. The novels were an immediate success—*Sword of Aldones* was nominated for a Hugo in 1963; since then, it has grown in critical and popular esteem, for the depth of world building and its deft handling of a complicated mythology. The *Encyclopedia of Science Fiction* (1999) calls the Darkover saga "perhaps the most significant planetary-romance sequence in modern SF."

Bradley herself wrote twenty Darkover novels. (Subsequent volumes in the series, which bring the count to thirty-five, were coauthored with Mercedes Lackey or Adrienne Martine-Barnes, and since the death of MZB, the series has been continued by Deborah J. Ross.) From the very start, Bradley's female protagonists, such as the autonomous guild known as the Free Amazons or Renunciates, were strong, heroic types who were not held back by traditional gender roles, but by the late 1960s she came very close to ending the saga, complaining that "I was tired of writing the same novel over and over again. I was tired of reading the same novel over and over again" (Wolfson 1999).

In an interesting literary "symbiosis," Anne McCaffrey learned that Bradley was despairing of SF, and recommended that she try reading Ursula Le Guin's *Left Hand of Darkness*. Le Guin revived Bradley's interest in the possibilities that SF—and Darkover—had to offer, and convinced her that she did not have to write to the lowest common denominator of readership (Sparks and Holliday 1997). In *The World Wreckers* (1971) and the novels that followed it, Bradley showed the women of Darkover contending with the consequences and costs of freedom in whole new ways.

Bradley always insisted that, although the Darkover books can be arranged in a historical chronology, they are not a series, and they can be read in any order. In fact, in "A Darkover Retrospective," an afterword to a 1980 combined reissue of *The Planet Savers* and *The Sword of Aldones*, she admitted that the early Darkover novels were "fix-ups" of her youthful, unpublished work, and that she had never intended them as a coherent series. As time went on, and Bradley began to have higher aspirations for her writing, she recognized that this cobbled-together history was proving unsatisfactory. Bradley may not be the first SF author to "reboot" a popular series—fittingly, Leigh Brackett had done something of the kind with her Stark stories, "relocating" her popular hero to the fantasy planet of Skaith when post–New Wave readers would no longer swallow Venus and Mars as viable settings. But reboot is exactly what Bradley did: *The Heritage of Hastur* (1975) "revised" Darkover's history. Eventually Bradley's early novels were revised to conform with the new "official canon."

Marion Zimmer Bradley was a bundle of contradictions:

- She was considered a muse and a medium by pagan and Wiccan fans, who identify with her depiction of the psychic connectedness of all things. But she was in fact a devout Christian, a longtime communicant at St. Mark's Episcopal Church in Berkley, California. "I'm not a medium," she would say, "I'm a large."

- She was "one of the early manifestations of proto-feminist science fiction" (Jesser 1996), a woman writer who wrote about strong female characters, and who herself set milestones and broke glass ceilings, for other women writers, she was in fact deeply ambivalent about feminism.

- Although she was married twice and was the mother of three children, she was open about her bisexuality, and—again—broke with conventions in her work about same-sex love.

Bradley was—no contradiction here, just a statement of fact—a warm and supportive mentor to young writers. She founded *Marion Zimmer Bradley's Fantasy Magazine* as a resource for readers and writers, and acted as editor from 1988 until her death.

Although her books made her name, and brought her a large and devoted fan base, their financial success was modest. For many years she supported her family by writing *anything*: erotic romances, true confessions, mysteries, gothics, astrology articles, and daily horoscopes. Her first marriage ended in divorce in 1964. (Following her divorce, she earned her BA from Hardin-Simmons University in Abilene, Texas, in 1964, and went on to do graduate work at the University of California, Berkeley, in the late 1960s.) She remarried, but the marriage effectively ended in 1979 (possibly because she suspected that her husband was molesting a young boy). She was officially divorced in 1990, and her second husband died in prison in 1993. After suffering a series of strokes in the late 1980s, Marion Zimmer Bradley died in Berkeley, California, on September 25, 1999, following a massive heart attack. She was remembered in a funeral service that she had planned and written herself, featuring musical selections by Brahms and readings from *The Book of Common Prayer*. Her ashes were later scattered at Glastonbury Tor, in Somerset, England, the legendary location of Avalon and resting place of King Arthur and Guinevere.

Awards

World Fantasy Award Life Achievement (2000)

Novels

The Mists of Avalon (1983) **Locus**

Works by the Author

The Door through Space (1961)
Seven from the Stars (1962)
The Colors of Space (1963)

Darkover

Planet Savers (1962)
Sword of Aldones (1962)
The Bloody Sun (1964)
Star of Danger (1965)
Winds of Darkover (1970)
World Wreckers (1971)
Darkover Landfall (1972)
The Spell Sword (1974)
The Heritage of Hastur (1975)
Shattered Chain (1976)
Forbidden Tower (1977)
Stormqueen (1978)
Two to Conquer (1980)
Sharra's Exile (1981)
Hawkmistress (1982)
Thendara House (1983)
City of Sorcery (1984)
Heirs of Hammerfell (1989)

Subsequent Darkover novels were coauthored: *Rediscovery*, with Mercedes Lackey (1993); and with Adrienne Martine-Barnes, *Exile's Song* (1996), *The Shadow Matrix* (1997), and *Traitor's Sun* (1999). Since the death of MZB, the series has been continued by Deborah J. Ross.

Collections

The Dark Intruder and Other Stories (1964)
The Best of Marion Zimmer Bradley (1985)
Jamie and Other Stories (1988)

Darkover Omnibus Editions

Ages of Chaos (2002)
Forbidden Circle (2002)
Heritage and Exile (2002)
The Saga of the Renunciates (2002)
A World Divided (2003)
Darkover: First Contact (2004)
To Save a World (2004)

As Editor

Marion Zimmer Bradley's Fantasy Magazine (1988–2000)
The Best of Marion Zimmer Bradley's Fantasy Magazine (1994)
The Best of Marion Zimmer Bradley's Fantasy Magazine, Vol. II (1995, with Elisabeth Waters)
Greyhaven (1983, with Paul Edwin Zimmer)
Lythande (1986, with Vonda N. McIntyre)

Darkover

These are anthologies that may include stories by Bradley, but on the whole contain Darkover stories by various other authors.

The Keeper's Price (1980)
Sword of Chaos (1982)
Free Amazons of Darkover (1985)
The Other Side of the Mirror (1987)
Red Sun of Darkover (1987)
Four Moons of Darkover (1988)
Domains of Darkover (1990)
Renunciates of Darkover (1991)
Leroni of Darkover (1991)
Towers of Darkover (1993)
Snows of Darkover (1994)

In Other Media

The Mists of Avalon. Constantin Film Produktion, 2001. Directed by Uli Edel; starring Anjelica Huston, Julianna Margulies, and Joan Allen.

Nonfiction Books

The Necessity for Beauty: Robert W. Chambers & the Romantic Tradition (1974)

Articles and Essays

"Advice to New Writers." *Marion Zimmer Bradley Homepage.* 1996. http://mzbworks.home.att.net/

"A Darkover Retrospective." In The Planet Savers *and* The Sword of Aldones: *Two Novels of Darkover,* 303–59. New York: Ace, 1980.

"Experiment Perilous: The Art and Science of Anguish in Science Fiction." In *Experiment Perilous.* New York: Algol, 1976.

"Fandom: Its Value to the Professional." *Inside Outer Space: Science Fiction Professionals Look at Their Craft,* ed. Sharon Jarvis, 69–84. New York: Ungar, 1985.

"Feminine Equivalents of Greek Love in Modern Fiction." *International Journal of Greek Love* 1, no.1. (1965): 48–58.

"Of Men, Halflings, and Hero Worship." In *Tolkien and the Critics,* ed. Neil Isaacs and Rose A. Zimbardo. Notre Dame, IN: University of Notre Dame Press, 1968.

"One Woman's Experience in Science Fiction." In *Women of Vision,* ed. Denise DuPont, 84–97. New York: St. Martin's, 1988.

"Responsibilities and Temptations of Women Science Fiction Writers." In *Women Worldwalkers: New Dimensions of Science Fiction and Fantasy,* ed. Jane Branham Weedman, 25–42. Lubbock: Texas Tech, 1985.

Bibliographies

Benson, Gordon. *Marion Zimmer Bradley, Mistress of Magic: A Working Bibliography.* Leeds: Galactic Central, 1994.

For Further Information

Marion Zimmer Bradley Literary Works Trust: http://mzbworks.home.att.net/

Arbur, Rosemarie. *Marion Zimmer Bradley.* Mercer Island, WA: Starmont House, 1985.

Jesser, Nancy. "Marion Zimmer Bradley." In *Feminist Writers.* Detroit: St. James Press, 1996.

Shwartz, Susan M. "Marion Zimmer Bradley." In *St. James Guide to Science Fiction Writers,* ed. Jay Pedersen. Detroit: St. James, 1996.

———. "Marion Zimmer Bradley's Ethic of Freedom." In *The Feminine Eye: Science Fiction and the Women Who Write It,* ed. Tom Staicar, 73–88. New York: Ungar, 1982.

Sparks, Elisa Kay, and Katrina M Holliday. *Marion Zimmer Bradley on Writing SF and Fantasy.* Clemson University, February 14, 1997. http://hubcap.clemson.edu/~sparks/Mzb.html. This Web site is a particular useful resource to identify essays, reviews, and correspondence by and about MZB and Darkover that are no longer readily available anywhere else.

Wolfson, Jonquil. "Remembering the Queen of Darkover." *Space.com,* October 22, 1999. Imaginova Corp. http://www.space.com/sciencefiction/marion_zimmer_bradley_retro_991022.html

David Brin

Hard SF; Post-human SF

Benchmark Title: *Startide Rising* (1983)

b. 1959 (Glendale, California)

I'm known as a bit of an optimist, so it seems only natural that this novel projects a future where there's a little more wisdom than folly . . . maybe a bit more hope than despair.

In fact, it's about the most encouraging tomorrow I can imagine right now. What a sobering thought.

—Preface, *Earth* (1990)

Photo credit: Cheryl Brigham.
Courtesy of David Brin.

About the Author and the Author's Writing

Glen David Brin was born in Glendale, California. As a child he learned to use books, and particularly the SF of Robert Heinlein and Robert Sheckley, as a way to escape the "irrational and unreliable" adults in his life: "I dreamed about other places and times where things might be better . . . or where the challenges could at least be understood and taken on with a bit of courage and brains. Reading helped" (*Planetary Society*).

Brin has a BS in astronomy from CalTech, a master's in applied physics, and a PhD in space science from the University of California in San Diego. After earning his doctorate, he taught at San Diego State University and various San Diego community colleges. In other words, he is a professional who knows his stuff; a professional who, according to the *Encyclopedia of Science Fiction* (1999), "writes tales in which the physical constraints governing the knowable Universe are flouted with high-handed panache." This combination of knowledgeable scientist and skilled storyteller results in books like the Uplift series, which are "as compulsive reading as anything ever published in the genre."

The Uplift series depicts a huge galactic civilization in which man is a barely tolerated interloper in a hierarchy of races that, at one time or another, have had their intelligence and abilities "uplifted" to give them the ability to navigate space. In an allegiance with uplifted dolphins and chimpanzees, human spacefarers have to face off with various races that would exploit, destroy, or enslave them, while trying to solve the mystery of the Progenitors, the mythic, supposedly long-extinct race, who started the uplift cycle. The central personality clash of the novels—ambitious, energetic humans, not prone to stand on ceremony, versus the corrupt, feudal, and protocol-bound Patron races—reflects a central attitude that Brin returns to again and again, both in his fiction and in his critical nonfiction: the clash between Romanticism and the Enlightenment:

> The Romantic Movement has always distrusted democracy, production, industry, urban life, education, social mobility, craftsmanship, and co-operation—emphasizing instead the particular, the mysterious, the hierarchical and the feudal. . . . But I know where my loyalty lies. I'd have been a peasant or a burned heretic by now, if it weren't for Enlightenment civilization. (Means 2004)

His 1990 novel *Earth* is an ecological thriller, which marries his concern for future progress with his awareness of the fragility of the planet we call home. Another of his stand-alone novels, *The Postman*, a postapocalyptic fable of a drifter who rebuilds his shattered society, was made into a movie starring Kevin Costner. Of his experience with Hollywood, Brin says "their standard operating procedure is to hold you down, rip open your chest, tear out your still-beating heart, bounce it around the room . . . and then—if you're very , very lucky—they'll stuff it full of cash and sew it back in your chest" (Means 2004).

David Brin has been nominated for all the major SF awards a number of times. With Gregory Benford and Greg Bear, he was authorized by the estate of Isaac Asimov to complete the Second Foundation Trilogy; Brin's volume, *Foundation's Triumph*, carries Asimov's saga to its logical (and satisfying) conclusion. He is currently a full-time writer and lecturer and acts as a futurist consultant for various companies and agencies. He lives near San Diego with his family and, according to his official Web site, "a hundred very demanding trees."

Awards

Novels

Startide Rising (1983) **Hugo, Locus Poll, Nebula**
The Postman (1985) **Locus Poll, Campbell Memorial**
The Uplift War (1987) **Hugo, Locus Poll**

Short Fiction

"The Crystal Spheres" (1984) **Hugo**
"Thor Meets Captain America" (1986) **Locus Poll**

Collections

Otherness (1994) **Locus Poll**

Works by the Author

The Practice Effect (1984)
The Postman (1985)
Heart of the Comet (1986, with Gregory Benford)

Earth (1990)
Glory Season (1993)
Foundation's Triumph (1999; Second Foundation Trilogy)
Kil'n People (2002)
Sky Horizon: Colony High, Book One (2007; YA, illustrated by Scott Hampton)

Uplift Universe

Sundiver (1980)
Startide Rising (1983)
The Uplift War (1987)
Brightness Reef (1995)
Infinity's Shore (1996)
Heaven's Reach (1998)

Other Notable Short Fiction

"The Tides of Kithrup" (1981)
"The Crystal Spheres" (1984)
"The Giving Plague" (1989)
"Privacy" (1989)
"What Continues, What Fails . . ." (1991)
"Reality Check" (2000). http://www.concatenation.org/futures/reality_check_brin.pdf
"Stones of Significance" (2000)

Collections

River of Time (1986)
Otherness (1994)
Tomorrow Happens (2003)

As Editor

Project Solar Sail (1990, with Arthur C. Clarke)
King Kong Is Back!: An Unauthorized Look at One Humongous Ape (2005)
Star Wars on Trial: Science Fiction and Fantasy Writers Debate the Most Popular Science Fiction Films of All Time (2006)

In Other Media

Ecco the Dolphin: Defender of the Future (1992; Sega Genesis video game)
Forgiveness (2002; graphic novel set in the *Star Trek: The Next Generation* universe)
The Life Eaters (2003; graphic novel, art by Scott Hampton). Based on the 1986 short story "Thor Meets Captain America."

The Postman. Tig Productions, 1997. Directed by and starring Kevin Costner, from a screenplay by Eric Roth.

Nonfiction Books

Contacting Aliens: An Illustrated Guide to David Brin's Uplift Universe (2002, with Kevin Lenagh)

The Transparent Society: Will Technology Force Us to Choose Between Privacy and Freedom? (1998)—Won the Freedom of Speech Award of the American Library Association. The original December 1996 *Wired* article on which this book is based can be found at http://www.wired.com/wired/archive/4.12/fftransparent_pr.html

Extraterrestrial Civilization (1989, as Glen David Brin, with Thomas Kuiper)

Articles and Essays

"Gaia, Freedom, and Human Nature." In 1992 President's Program Presentations. LITA: Library and Information Technology Association, American Library Association, n.d. http://www.cni.org/pub/LITA/Think/Brin.html

"Our Favorite Cliché: A World Filled with Idiots . . . or, Why Fiction Routinely Depicts Society and Its Citizens as Fools." *Extrapolation* 41 (2000): 7–20.

"A Shaman's View." In *The Profession of Science Fiction: SF Writers on Their Craft and Ideas,* ed. Maxim Jakubowski and Edward James, 161–68. New York: St. Martin's, 1992.

"Singularities and Nightmares: Extremes of Optimism and Pessimism about the Human Future." *Lifeboat Foundation* (2006). http://lifeboat.com/ex/singularities.and.nightmares

"Tomorrow May Be Different." In *Exploring the Matrix: Visions of the Cyber Present,* ed. Karen Haber, 180–99. New York: St. Martin's, 2003.

For Further Information

Official Web site: http://www.davidbrin.com/

Interview. *Orbit,* July 19, 2002. http://www.sffworld.com/interview/13p0.html

Interview. *The Planetary Society,* April 30, 2002. http://mmp.planetary.org/artis/brind/brind70.htm

Means, Loren. "Interview with David Brin." *YLEM Journal* 24, no. 4 (2004): 11–14. http://www.ylem.org/Journal/2004Iss04vol24.pdf

Nicholls, Stan. "David Brin Won't Cop the Rap." In *Wordsmiths of Wonder: Fifty Interviews with Writers of the Fantastic,* 33–42. London: Orbit, 1993.

van Baardwijk, Jeroen. *Brin-L.* March 2005. http://www.brin-l.com/

Winter, Bill. "David Brin—Libertarian." *Advocates for Self-Government* (May 2007). http://www.theadvocates.org/celebrities/david-brin.html

John Brunner

Dystopias; Near Future; Space Opera

Benchmark Title: *Stand on Zanzibar* (1968)

b. 1930 (England: Oxfordshire);
d. 1995 (Scotland: Glasgow)

Photo credit: Mrs. Liyi Brunner

> *I wanted to make my living as a writer, I wanted to win a Hugo, have a nice home, be happily married, all the usual things. . . . I suddenly realized that I had achieved all of the ambitions that I was capable of visualizing when I was seventeen. . . . I suspect this happens to many people who reach that age which, in the wild state, would correspond to one becoming a tribal elder.*
> —Observation to Joe Haldeman,
> http://home.earthlink.net/~haldeman/biolong.html

About the Author and the Author's Writing

John Kilian Houston Brunner was born in Preston Crowmarsh, in Oxfordshire. He attended Cheltenham College, then served as an officer in the Royal Air Force from 1953 to 1955. He wrote his first novel, *Galactic Storm*, under a pen name at age seventeen, and from the late 1950s until ill-health forced him to slow down his writing pace in the 1980s, John Brunner published a novel a year in an ongoing struggle to make a living as a professional writer.

His early output is described in *The Encyclopedia of Science Fiction* (1999) as "literate space opera," although the pace of writing that he forced upon himself sometimes resulted in less-than literate carelessness. In his version of space opera, Brunner was fond of narratives in which humankind—either as a species or individuals—are pawns in the games of forces larger than themselves. His <u>Interstellar Empire</u> series, published in the 1970s, was about the predicament of humankind during the twilight of a galactic empire. In the <u>Zarathustra Refugee Planets</u>, 3,000 giant spaceships evacuate a planet threatened when its sun goes nova. After seven centuries the survivors have reverted to barbarism, and a corps of interstellar police are tasked with keeping their Zarathustra Refugee societies in protective isolation, to allow them to develop their cultures naturally.

In the late 1960s and early 1970s, Brunner wrote four dystopian novels, which took his favorite theme of the struggle against unbeatable odds and applied it to narratives closer to home. These four novels that have come to define his career—*Stand on*

Zanzibar (1968), *The Jagged Orbit* (1969), *The Sheep Look Up* (1972), and *The Shockwave Rider* (1975)—represent Brunner's most successful effort to combine style and substance with the tropes of SF. The novels are unconnected, but thematically similar, depicting all-too-plausible pictures of a future rendered unlivable by the Four Horsemen of our modern Apocalypse: pollution, overpopulation, a military industrial complex unchecked by the people it's supposed to serve, and a worldwide communications network that renders the planet's systems vulnerable to sabotage and infiltration. Some of the horrors that Brunner depicts had been done before, but each of his novels brought something fresh and believable to the old theme. In *The Jagged Orbit*, American society is disintegrating in the face of violence, drugs, and high-level corruption. In *The Shockwave Rider* (1975), Brunner anticipates the Internet, which had, of course, been done before—but Brunner is keenly aware of the wonderful World Wide Web's potential down sides: the blight of computer viruses and spam, the threat of information overload, and the vulnerability of personal information. In *The Shockwave Rider,* Brunner coined the term "worm" to describe software that could reproduce itself across a computer network, wreaking havoc. Upon its publication, some critics scoffed, but today Brunner's vision seems incredibly prescient.

Brunner made his only excursion into pure fantasy in five telling, short novels that make up the collection *The Traveller in Black* (1971). The "Traveller" in question is an enigmatic figure whose goal is to purge the universe of irrationality, drive back chaos, and force magic to give way to scientific law. Like the Traveller, Brunner was a passionate opponent of superstition, injustice, and anything that he saw as bogus science. He was a passionate supporter of left-wing causes such as the Campaign for Nuclear Disarmament—he wrote the song "The H-Bombs' Thunder," which later became the anthem of the CND—and was scathing in his criticism of pop science authors such as Erich von Daniken.

Although Brunner received major awards for *Stand on Zanzibar* and *The Jagged Orbit*, the resolutely skeptical views expressed in his novels may have hurt the marketing of his work in the United States and alienated that section of the SF audience looking for lighter, more optimistic fare. After the mid-1970s he returned to writing a sort of space opera, but with a noticeable lack of enthusiasm as his health began to decline. While attending the 1995 World Science Fiction Convention in Glasgow, Scotland, accompanied by his wife, Liyi, John Brunner died of a stroke. At the convention's awards ceremony, his friend Robert Silverberg recalled Brunner's SF achievements and suggested that, rather than a minute's silence, Brunner would have liked a last round of applause. The standing ovation continued for four minutes.

Awards

Novels

Stand on Zanzibar (1968) **BSF, Hugo**
The Jagged Orbit (1969) **BSF**

 ## Works by the Author

The 100th Millennium (1959; rev. as *Catch a Falling Star*, 1968)

Threshold of Eternity (1959)
The World Swappers (1959)
The Atlantic Abomination (1960)
Sanctuary in the Sky (1960)
The Rites of Ohe (1963)
To Conquer Chaos (1964)
The Whole Man (1964; UK: *Telepathist*)
The Day of the Star Cities (1965; rev. as *Age of Miracles*, 1973)
Stand on Zanzibar (1968)
The Jagged Orbit (1969)
The Sheep Look Up (1972)
The Shockwave Rider (1975)
A Maze of Stars (1991)

Interstellar Empire

Galactic Storm (1951, as Gill Hunt)
The Wanton of Argus (1953, as Kilian Houston Brunner) (later released as *The Space-Time Juggler*, 1963)
The Altar on Asconel (1965)

Zarathustra Refugee Planets

Secret Agent of Terra (1962)
Castaways' World (1963)
The Repairmen of Cyclops (1965)

Notable Short Fiction

"The Man from the Big Dark" (1958)
"Imprint of Chaos" (1960)
"The Totally Rich" (1963)
"The Last Lonely Man" (1964)
"Dread Empire" (1971)
"The Things That Are Gods" (1979)

Collections

Interstellar Empire (1976)
The Book of John Brunner (1976)
The Compleat Traveller in Black (1986)
The Best of John Brunner (1988) (introduction by Joe Haldeman)
Victims of the Nova (1989)

In Other Media

The Terrornauts. Amicus Productions, 1967. Screenplay by Brunner; based on a novel by Murray Leinster. Camp and delightfully silly effort which stars, among others, Charles Hawtrey of the British *Carry On* comedies.

Nonfiction Books

John Brunner Presents Kipling's Science Fiction (1992)
Tomorrow May Be Even Worse: An Alphabet of Science Fiction Cliches (1978)

Articles and Essays

"Science Fiction and the Larger Lunacy." In *Science Fiction at Large: A Collection of Essays, by Various Hands, about the Interface between Science Fiction and Reality,* ed. Peter Nicholls, 73–103. London: Gollancz, 1976.

Bibliographies

Sawyer, Andrew. "The John Brunner Archive." *SF Hub* (2004). University of Liverpool. http://www.sfhub.ac.uk/Brunner.htm

Stephensen-Payne, Phil, and Gordon R. Benson Jr. *John Brunner: Shockwave Writer, A Working Bibliography.* 3rd ed. Albuquerque: Galactic Central, 1989.

For Further Information

De Bolt, Joe. "The Development of John Brunner." In *Voices for the Future: Essays on Major Science Fiction Writers,* Vol. 2, ed. Thomas D. Clareson, 106–35. Bowling Green, OH: Bowling Green University Popular Press, 1979.

———. *The Happening Worlds of John Brunner: Critical Explorations in Science Fiction.* Port Washington, NY: Kennikat: 1975.

Langford, Dave. "Traveller in Black: John Brunner, 1934–1995." *The Skeptic* 9, no. 6 (1995). http://www.ansible.co.uk/writing/brunner.html

Robson, Alan. "John Brunner: An Appreciation." *Phlogiston Forty-Four* (1995). http://homepages.paradise.net.nz/triffid/trimmings/volume2/11_John_Kilian_Houston_Brunner.htm

Schweitzer, Darrell. "John Brunner Interview" (interview done in 1993). In *Speaking of the Fantastic,* ed. Darrell Schweitzer, 19–37. Holicong, PA: Wildside, 2002.

Walker, Paul. "John Brunner." In *Speaking of Science Fiction,* 315–24. Oradell, NJ: Luna, 1978.

Watson, Ian. "At the Wrong End of Time: An Appreciation of John Brunner (1934-1995)." In *Nebula Awards 31,* ed. Pamela Sargent, 116–24. New York: Harcourt, 1997.

Lois McMaster Bujold

Humor and Satire; SF Romance; Space Opera

Benchmark Title:
The Warrior's Apprentice (1986)

b. 1949 (Columbus, Ohio)

Everybody harbors some "cripplement," emotional if not physical. There is scarcely a more universal appeal to the reader. You can't judge anybody—you never know what backbreaking secret burdens they may be carrying.

"Highlights of Life," *Ohioana Authors* (2005)

Photo credit: Beth Gwinn

About the Author and the Author's Writing

Lois McMaster Bujold was born in Columbus, Ohio. Her father was a professor of welding engineering at The Ohio State University (the author of the definitive textbook *Nondestructive Testing Handbook*, which is known in the trade as "McMaster on Materials"), and a keen reader of SF; Bujold attributes her early interest in SF to her father's influence. She graduated from Upper Arlington High School, in Columbus, and attended The Ohio State University from 1968 to 1972; there, she tried several majors, including English and biology, but, as she told *SF Crowsnest* in a 2008 interview, "my heart was in the creative, not the critical end of things." Her real education at OSU may have come from her all-access pass to the two million books in the University Library, which she read voraciously, sometimes at a rate of five a week.

Bujold left OSU without receiving her degree, and during the early 1970s she worked as a pharmacy technician at OSU Medical Center. She married and had two children, and began to write. In an autobiographical essay on her Web site, she remembers that time: "I was unemployed with two small children (note oxymoron) on a very straitened budget in Marion [Ohio] at this point, but the hobby required no initial monetary investment. I wrote a novelette for practice."

However, Bujold underestimated the commitment and the emotional investment that writing would demand, and rapidly realized that, for her, it could never be merely a hobby—"only serious professional recognition would satisfy me." She sold her first story, "Barter," to the *Twilight Zone Magazine* in 1985; one year later, three novels she had submitted for consideration were bought by Jim Baen, of Baen books.

Bujold is best known for her hero, Miles Vorkosigan, a brilliant, charming young mercenary and spy, the scion of the noble house of Barrayar, a violent, class-bound society with very particular ideas about honor and the value of individuals. Miles is born with severe physical disabilities as a result of an attempt on the life of his aristocrat father, and from his very first appearance, in *The Warrior's Apprentice* (1986), he must deal with the backward attitudes toward disability and physical imperfection of his home planet. Throughout the course of his adventures, Miles grows as a character and is gradually transformed from a dashing scamp, leaping from one scrape to another, to an altogether more serious character who matures and (quite literally) confronts his dark side.

The Encyclopedia of Science Fiction (1999) describes Bujold's work as "both funny and humane.... [H]er novels and stories succeed on their own terms." Martha Bartter describes Bujold as a reluctant writer of military SF: Miles is a soldier, true, and many of the plots of Bujold's books deal with intergalactic intrigue and war, but she is too conscious of her characters as people (even the spear carriers and walk-ons) to kill them off without recognizing their basic humanity and making a note of what has been lost. In her short story "Aftermaths," a graves registration medtech remarks about an enemy corpse, "Nine months of pregnancy, childbirth ... Dozens of teachers. And all that military training , too. A lot of people went into making him.... That head held a universe, once."

Bujold alternates new episodes in the saga of Miles Vorkosigan and Barrayar with novels that are pure fantasy, such as the novels from the Chalion Universe, or the more recent The Sharing Knife series. Whenever she is asked in interviews—as she always is—if she can envisage ending the Barrayar novels, once and for all, she replies: "Properly, it should have ended at the end of *A Civil Campaign*—all comedies are supposed to end in weddings, Shakespeareanly, and the stories are ultimately comedies in the broadest sense, life-affirming" (Walton 2009). Fortunately for her devoted fans, Bujold keeps finding excuses—and stories—to make her return to Barrayar.

Since the start of her writing career in 1985, she has won four Hugo awards in the novel category, more than any other writer except Robert A. Heinlein. (She has also won a Hugo for her 1989 novella *The Mountains of Mourning*.) Her work has been translated into fifteen languages, including Hebrew, Bulgarian, and a short story in Chinese. After her marriage ended in the early 1990s, Lois McMaster Bujold moved with her children to Minneapolis, where she is an active part of the SF and writing scene.

Awards

Novels

Falling Free (1988) **Nebula**
The Vor Game (1990) **Hugo**
Barrayar (1991) **Hugo, Locus**
Mirror Dance (1994) **Hugo, Locus**
Paladin of Souls (2003) **Hugo, Nebula**

Short Fiction

"The Mountains of Mourning" (1989) **Hugo, Nebula**

Works by the Author

Ethan of Athos (1986)
Falling Free (1988)

Barrayar: Miles Vorkosigan

The Warrior's Apprentice (1986)
Brothers in Arms (1989)
The Vor Game (1990)
Mirror Dance (1994)
Cetaganda (1995)
Memory (1996)
Komarr (1998)
A Civil Campaign (1999)
Diplomatic Immunity (2002)

Barrayar: Cordelia Naismith

Shards of Honor (1986)
Barrayar (1991)

Other Notable Genre Fiction

The Spirit Ring (1993)

Chalion Universe

The Curse of Chalion (2001)
Paladin of Souls (2003)
The Hallowed Hunt (2005)

The Sharing Knife series

Beguilement (2006)
Legacy (2007)
Passage (2008)
Horizon (2009)

Other Notable Short Fiction

"Aftermaths" (1986)
"Labyrinth" (1989)
"Weatherman" (1990)
"Winterfair Gifts" (2004)

Collections
The Borders of Infinity (1989)
Dreamweaver's Dilemma: Short Stories and Essays (1995)

Barryar Compilations
Vorkosigan's Game (1990)
Young Miles (1997)
Cordelia's Honor (1999)
Miles, Mystery, and Mayhem (2001)
Miles Errant (2002)
Miles, Mutants and Microbes (2007)
Miles in Love (2008)

Articles and Essays
"The Future of Warfare." (Address to St Petersburg Con). Russian Fan Web site. 2000. http://bujold.lib.ru/b_wareng.htm

With Sylvia Kelso. "Letterspace: In the Chinks Between Published Fiction and Published Criticism," In *Women of Other Worlds,* ed. Helen Merrick and Tess Williams, 383–409. Nedlands, WA: University of Western Australia Press, 1999.

For Further Information
Official Web site: http://www.dendarii.com/

Aranaga, Carlos. "Interview." *SciFi Dimensions* (October 2006). http://www.scifidimensions.com/Oct06/loismcmasterbujold.htm

"Highlights of a Life." *Ohioana Authors,* December 6, 2005. WOSU Public Media. http://www.ohioana-authors.org/bujold/index.php

Kelso, Sylvia. "Lois McMaster Bujold: Feminism and 'The Gernsback Continuum' in Recent Women's SF." *Journal of the Fantastic in the Arts* 10, no. 1 (1998): 17–29.

Levy, Michael M. Interview. *Kaleidoscope: Exploring the Experience of Disability Through Literature and the Fine Arts* 34 (Winter–Spring 1997): 6–19.

Martini, Adrienne. Interview. *Bookslut* (May 2005). http://www.bookslut.com/features/2005_05_005637.php

Miller, Karen. "Fantastic Women: Lois McMaster Bujold." *SF Crowsnest,* January 1, 2008. http://www.sfcrowsnest.com

Thompson, Robert. "One Heckuva Turn: Lois McMaster Bujold Interviewed." *SF Crowsnest,* May 1, 2008. http://www.sfcrowsnest.com

Walton, Jo. Interview. *Tor.com,* April 20, 2009. http://www.tor.com/index.php?option=com_content&view=blog&id=23438

Anthony Burgess
[John Anthony Burgess Wilson]

Dystopias; Near Future

Benchmark Title: *A Clockwork Orange* (1962)

b. 1917 (England: Manchester); d. 1993 (England: London)

> *I typed a new title—A Clockwork Orange—and wondered what story might match it. I had always liked the Cockney expression and felt there might be a meaning in it deeper than a bizarre metaphor of, not necessarily sexual, queerness. Then a story began to stir.*
>
> —*You've Had Your Time* (1991)

About the Author and the Author's Writing

The English novelist "Anthony Burgess" was born John Burgess Wilson, in Harpurhey, a bleak northeastern suburb of Manchester, in the North of England. (The "Anthony" was added some years later, as a confirmation name; he began using his two middle names as a pen name in the mid-1950s.) He had an unhappy childhood, blighted by the death of his mother and older sister when he was a baby, during the influenza epidemic of 1918–1919. Throughout his life, Burgess believed that his father never forgave him for surviving when they had died, in spite of the fact that he seems to have been well looked after by both father and, eventually, stepmother. They at least saw to it that he was fortunate in his education; he was an exceptional student at the Catholic elementary schools he attended, sometimes to his personal cost, as he told his biographer, Roger Lewis, "I was either distractedly persecuted or ignored. I was one despised. . . . Ragged boys in gangs would pounce on the well-dressed like myself."

Eventually he earned a BA in English language and literature from the University of Manchester. From an early age, he also took considerable comfort in music (a single humane characteristic that he shared with Alex, the protagonist of his great dystopian novel, *A Clockwork Orange*); he taught himself to play the piano and violin and to read music. He was a talented composer and librettist, and his work was performed on Broadway, on BBC radio, and by the English National Opera. He was also a natural linguist, who picked up languages easily and spoke several fluently.

Burgess was an incredibly prolific writer of modern realist and historical fiction, as well as a critic, poet, and composer. Like many authors of his generation, he had no qualms about "slumming" in genre fiction, and several of his novels make use of the tropes of science fiction, especially scenarios of near-future dystopias. *The Wanting Seed* (1962) deals with a world suffering the effects of drastic overpopulation; *1985*

(1978) is partly dystopian novella, partly a critical work, discussing the importance and impact of George Orwell's *Nineteen Eighty-four*; *The End of the World News: An Entertainment* (1982) is a collection of linked novellas and, exactly as the title says, the final one is set in the future, shortly before the impact of a giant meteor with the earth.

But *A Clockwork Orange* is probably Burgess's best-known work, its well-deserved notoriety enhanced by the film version directed by Stanley Kubrick. Chosen by *Time Magazine* as one of the 100 best English-language novels from 1923 to 2005, *A Clockwork Orange* is set in a world at the mercy of youth gangs whose sport is "ultraviolence"—random, vicious attacks on anyone unlucky enough to cross their path. Burgess's central character is a fifteen-year-old gang leader named Alex, who speaks in a brutal slang that brilliantly renders the twisted nature of Alex's character and his environment.

A dystopian tour de force, *A Clockwork Orange* is an examination of free will and morality. Alex is captured and put through a brutal course of aversion conditioning. It stops the violence, but strips him of everything that made him human—particularly his love of music. As a SF novel, *A Clockwork Orange* is immensely important: the nadsat argot of Alex and his Droogs was a reminder of how SF can use language just as effectively as technological gimmicks. Burgess also stretched the boundaries of dystopia to include the "anti-utopia"—the state only wants to reform Alex, to make society safe from him. In *A Clockwork Orange*, Burgess asks, "At what cost?"

Throughout his career, Burgess was recognized as a renaissance man, a unique voice in twentieth-century arts and letters, and a critic of popular culture and society, who could be guaranteed to express blunt, and possibly unfashionable, opinions about any issue. Among the honors he received in his lifetime, he was created a Fellow of the Royal Society of Literature, a *Commandeur des Arts et des Lettres* of France's *Ordre National du Mérite*, and a *Commandeur de Merite Culturel* of the Principality of Monaco. He received honorary degrees from Birmingham and Manchester Universities in England and St Andrews in Scotland.

Anthony Burgess died in London on November 22, 1993, of lung cancer. He was working on his final novel on his deathbed. His ashes were interred in Monte Carlo.

Awards

Novels

A Clockwork Orange (1962) **Prometheus Hall of Fame 2008**

 Works by the Author

A Clockwork Orange (1962). A recording of Anthony Burgess reading from *A Clockwork Orange* is available online at http://town.hall.org/radio/HarperAudio/.

The Wanting Seed (1962)

1985 (1978)

The End of the World News: An Entertainment (1982)

Notable Mainstream Fiction

Nothing Like the Sun: A Story of Shakespeare's Love Life (1964)
Abba Abba (1977)
Earthly Powers (1980)
A Dead Man in Deptford (1993)

Enderby Quartet

Inside Mr. Enderby (1963, as Joseph Kell)
Enderby Outside (1968)
The Clockwork Testament, or Enderby's End (1974)
Enderby's Dark Lady, or No End of Enderby (1984)

The Long Day Wanes (Malayan Trilogy)

Time for a Tiger (1956)
The Enemy in the Blanket (1958)
Beds in the East (1959)

Collections

Homage to QWERT YUIOP: Essays (1986)
Future Imperfect (1994)
One Man's Chorus: The Uncollected Writings (1998)

In Other Media

A Clockwork Orange. Hawk Films, 1971. Directed and written by Stanley Kubrick; starring Malcolm McDowell and Patrick McGee.

Jesus of Nazareth. Radiotelevisione Italiana, 1977. Directed by Franco Zefferelli; starring (among many others) Robert Powell (as Christ), Lawrence Olivier, Peter Ustinov, James Earl Jones, and Anne Bancroft. A literate international television production.

A.D. Procter & Gamble Productions, 1985. Directed by Stuart Cooper; starring (among others) Anthony Andrews, Colleen Dewhurst, and Richard Kiley.

Cyrano de Bergerac. Channel 4 Television, 1985. Burgess's translation of the play by Edmund Rostand, performed by the Royal Shakespeare Company.

Nonfiction Books

The Novel Now: A Guide to Contemporary Fiction (1967)
Ninety-Nine Novels: The Best in English Since 1939: A Personal Choice (1984)
Little Wilson and Big God: The First Part of the Confession (1991)
You've Had Your Time: The Second Part of the Confessions (1991). "On *A Clockwork Orange*" (excerpt). http://www.visual-memory.co.uk/amk/doc/burgess.html
A Mouthful of Air: Language and Languages, Especially English (1992)

Articles and Essays

"Introduction." In *A Clockwork Orange.* London: Century Hutchinson, 1987. http://home.wlv.ac.uk/~fa1871/burgess.html

"Juice from a Clockwork Orange." In *Perspectives on Stanley Kubrick,* ed. Mario Falsetto, 187–90. New York: G. K. Hall, 1996.

For Further Information

The Anthony Burgess Center. January 2005. Universite d'Angers. http://bu.univ-angers.fr/EXTRANET/AnthonyBURGESS/. Burgess archive, donated by his widow, Liane; twice yearly publishes *The Anthony Burgess Newsletter.*

Aggeler, Geoffrey, ed. *Critical Essays on Anthony Burgess.* Boston: G. K. Hall, 1986.

Champion, Edward. "Books Blog: Burgess's Powers Are Still Strong." *The Guardian* (UK), February 5, 2008. http://www.guardian.co.uk/books/booksblog/2008/feb/05/burgessspowersarestillstro

Cullinan, John. Interview. *The Paris Review* (Spring 1973). http://www.theparisreview.com/viewinterview.php/prmMID/3994

Lewis, Roger. *Anthony Burgess.* London: St. Martin's, 2004.

Mathews, Richard. *The Clockwork Orange Universe of Anthony Burgess.* San Bernardino, CA: Borgo, 1978.

Stinson, John J. *Anthony Burgess Revisited.* Boston: Twayne, 1991.

Swaim, Don. Interview. *Wired for Books* (1985). Ohio University. http://wiredforbooks.org/anthonyburgess/

Edgar Rice Burroughs

Science Fantasy

Benchmark Title: *A Princess of Mars* (1912)

b. 1875 (Chicago, Illinois) d. 1950 (Encino, California)

> [A]nd I made up my mind that if people were paid for writing rot such as I read in some of those magazines, that I could write stories just as rotten.
> —"How I Wrote the Tarzan Books," *The World Magazine* (October 27, 1929)

About the Author and the Author's Writing

Edgar Rice Burroughs was born in Chicago, the son of a businessman. For the early part of his life, Burroughs drifted. He spent time on his brothers' ranch in Idaho, tried and failed to get into West Point, and enlisted with the U.S. 7th Cavalry in the Arizona Territory, but was discharged on medical grounds. He worked for his father, married, and went out West again, where he worked as a railway policeman in Salt Lake City, a door-to-door salesman, an accountant, the manager for the clerical department of Sears, Roebuck, and a peddler for a quack alcoholism cure. In 1911 Edgar Rice Burroughs was back in Chicago, working as a pencil sharpener wholesaler—and he had a lot of time on his hands. He began reading pulp fiction magazines and decided he had found his niche, as he told *The World Magazine,* in a 1929 interview: "As a matter of fact, although I had never written a story, I knew absolutely that I could write stories just as entertaining." His first story, "Under the Moons of Mars" (later retitled *A Princess of Mars*), was serialized in *All-Story* magazine in 1912 and he was paid $400 (roughly the equivalent of $7,600 today). Edgar Rice Burroughs was finished with pencil sharpeners.

Burroughs's Barsoom novels feature the heroic adventurer John Carter, who is transported by quasi-magical means to a fanciful Mars, where he meets and fights exotic warriors and woos the lovely red-skinned, egg-laying Princess. All of Burroughs's novels are as much fantasy as anything else, scientific plausibility not being high on their list of virtues. But SF writers as different as Leigh Brackett, Michael Moorcock, and Ray Bradbury have been inspired by Burroughs's exotic Mars and what *The Encyclopedia of Science Fiction* (1999) calls "storylines and venues as malleable as dreams, exotic and dangerous and unending." Inspired by the success of John Carter's adventures on Mars, Burroughs took up writing full time and had completed two more novels before *A Princess of Mars* had completed its run in *All-Story*. One of them was called *Tarzan of the Apes*. Edgar Rice Burroughs had officially passed from would-be purveyor of "rot" to cultural phenomenon.

Having found his niche, Burroughs devoted himself to the care and nurturing of its money-spinning potential, and in ways that would have made his businessman father proud. In the 1920s he set up his own company, Edgar Rice Burroughs, Inc., and cut out the middleman by printing his own books. He methodically exploited his series, especially Tarzan, through every possible medium—movies, syndicated comic strips, and merchandise—against the advice of the "experts," who predicted that it would dilute public interest in Burroughs's books, and the various media would end up competing against each other. They were wrong. Say "thank you" to Edgar Rice Burroughs for the *Star Trek* lunch box, the *Star Wars* action figures, and the *Battlestar Galactica* T-shirt.

In 1919 Burroughs purchased a large ranch north of Los Angeles, which he named "Tarzana." In 1928 the citizens of the community that grew up around his ranch voted to adopt that name when their town was incorporated. He was living in Hawaii when the Japanese Imperial forces attacked the U.S. Navy at Pearl Harbor in 1941; Burroughs immediately volunteered as a war correspondent. At sixty-six years of age, he was the oldest war correspondent to serve in the Pacific theater, flying from island to island, and even going out on bombing runs with the 7th Air Force. Edgar Rice Burroughs died of a heart attack on March 19, 1950, in Encino, California, having written almost seventy novels, including Westerns, historical romances, Tarzan and the Barsoom novels, and other science fantasy series such as the Venus stories, and Pellucidar, set in the hollow core of the Earth.

The Burroughs crater on Mars is named in his honor.

Awards

Science Fiction Hall of Fame (2003, Posthumous)
First Fandom Hall of Fame Award (2004)

Works by the Author

Barsoom

A Princess of Mars (1912)
The Gods of Mars (1914)
The Warlord of Mars (1918)
Thuvia, Maid of Mars (1920)
The Chessmen of Mars (1922)
The Master Mind of Mars (1928)
A Fighting Man of Mars (1931)
Swords of Mars (1936)
Synthetic Men of Mars (1940)
Llana of Gathol (1948)

Caspak
The Land That Time Forgot (1918)
The People That Time Forgot (1918)
Out of Time's Abyss (1918)
The Moon Maid (1926)

Pellucidar
At the Earth's Core (1914)
Pellucidar (1923)
Tanar of Pellucidar (1928)
Tarzan at the Earth's Core (1929)
Back to the Stone Age (1937)
Land of Terror (1944)
Savage Pellucidar (1941)

Venus
Pirates of Venus (1934)
Lost on Venus (1935)
Carson of Venus (1939)
Escape on Venus (1946)

Other Notable Genre Fiction
The Man-Eater (1915)
The Efficiency Expert (1921)
The Girl from Hollywood (1923)
The Cave Girl (1925)
The Bandit of Hell's Bend (1926)
The Mad King (1926)
The War Chief (1927)
The Outlaw of Torn (1927)
Jungle Girl (1932; aka *Land of the Hidden Men*)
Apache Devil (1933)
The Deputy Sheriff of Comanche County (1940)

Tarzan
Beginning with *Tarzan of the Apes* (1912)

Notable Short Fiction
"The Eternal Lover" (1914)
"The Lost Continent" (1916; aka "Beyond Thirty")

"The Resurrection of Jimber-Jaw" (1937)
"The Scientists Revolt" (1939)
"Beyond the Farthest Star" (1941)

Collections

Martian Tales of Edgar Rice Burroughs (1981)
Forgotten Tales of Love and Murder (2001)
Return to Mars (2004; aka *Three Martian Novels*)
John Carter's Chronicles of Mars (2007)
A Treasury of Edgar Rice Burroughs (2007)

In Other Media

In addition, of course, to the many, many movies based on Burroughs's Tarzan stories, there are the following:

The Land That Time Forgot. Amicus Productions, 1975. Directed by Kevin Connor; starring Doug McClure and John McEnery; screenplay by Michael Moorcock.

At the Earth's Core. American International Pictures, 1976. Directed by Kevin Connor; starring Doug McClure and Peter Cushing.

The People That Time Forgot. American International Pictures, 1977. Directed by Kevin Connor; starring Doug McClure and Patrick Wayne.

Articles and Essays

"How I Wrote the Tarzan Books." *The World Magazine* (*Washington Post* and *New York World* Sunday supplement), October 27, 1929. http://www.erbzine.com/mag0/0052.html

"Mr. Burroughs Describes His Publishing Methods." (Letter). *Writers' Digest* (1937). http://www.erbzine.com/mag0/0056.html

For Further Information

ERBzine. Ed. Bill and Sue-on Hillman. Edgar Rice Burroughs, Inc. http://www.erbzine.com/

The Burroughs Bulletin. Published quarterly for member of The Burroughs Bibliophiles since January 1990. http://www.erbzine.com/mag6/0650.html

Brady, Clark A. *The Burroughs Cyclopaedia.* Jefferson, NC: McFarland, 1996.

de Camp, L. Sprague. "Thoats, Tharks and Thews: A Literary Tour of John Carter's Mars Unearths the Inspirations for Edgar Rice Burroughs Red Planet Adventure." *Starlog* 10, no. 117 (1987): 18–25.

Famous Authors: Edgar Rice Burroughs. Kultur Video, 2008. The Famous Authors Series. Directed by Malcolm Hossick.

Fenton, Robert W. *Edgar Rice Burroughs and Tarzan: A Biography.* Jefferson, NC: McFarland, 2003.

Hanson, Alan. *The Wondrous Words of Edgar Rice Burroughs.* Spokane, WA: Waziri, 1998.

Pohl, Frederik. "Edgar Rice Burroughs and the Development of Science Fiction." *Burroughs Bulletin* 10 (1992): 8–14.

Taliaferro, John. *Tarzan Forever: The Life of Edgar Rice Burroughs, Creator of Tarzan.* New York: Simon & Schuster/Scribner, 1999.

Van Hise, James, ed. *Edgar Rice Burroughs' Fantastic Worlds.* Yucca Valley, CA: James Van Hise, 1996.

Octavia E. Butler

Myth and Legend; Utopias

Benchmark Title: *Patternmaster* (1976)

b. 1947 (Pasadena, California);
d. 2006 (Seattle, Washington)

I was attracted to science fiction because it was so wide open. I was able to do anything and there were no walls to hem you in and there was no human condition that you were stopped from examining.
—Balagun, Obituary and Interview, *New York City Independent Media Center* (2006)

Photo credit: Beth Gwinn

About the Author and the Author's Writing

Octavia Estelle Butler was born in Pasadena, California. Her father died when she was a baby, and she was raised by her grandmother and her mother, who worked as a cleaner to support the family. She was shy and socially isolated as a child (she was later diagnosed as dyslexic), and for entertainment she turned to SF—pulps, classics, and magazines—and to "terrible films" like *Devil Girl from Mars,* as she remembered in an essay with that same title, written for the MIT Media in Transition Project in 1998:

> As I was watching this film, I had a series of revelations. The first was that "Gee, I can write a better story than that." And then I thought, "Gee, anybody can write a better story than that." And my third thought was the clincher: "Somebody got paid for writing that awful story." So I was off and writing.

Butler attended Pasadena City College and received an associate degree there in 1968. She followed that up with classes at California State University, Los Angeles, and UCLA extension classes, but found that her creative writing instructors were dismissive of science fiction—"all that weird stuff," as they described it—and demanded stories based on her "real experience." The Octavia Butler who gave us *Earthseed* and *Kindred* could have been lost forever, had it not been for two writers' workshops she attended at this time: at the first, in 1969, sponsored by the Screenwriter's Guild, she met Harlan Ellison, who recognized a true, original talent. He encouraged her to attend a Clarion Science Fiction Writers' Workshop the following year, which gave Butler the encouragement she needed to embark upon *Patternmaster* (1976). Beginning with that novel, Butler found new ways to shape "all that weird stuff" into unique insights into the experience of being a black American woman; indeed, into the experience of being human.

Butler's novels and short stories are all, in their different ways, stories of "power: enslavement and freedom, control and corruption, survival and adjustment" (Salvaggio 1986). *Patternmaster*, and seven of Butler's eleven subsequent novels, are divided into the Patternist and the Xenogenesis series. (*Clay's Ark* is sometimes counted as a Patternist novel, but it is more like a bridge between the two series, with narrative references to both.) Both series tell wide-ranging, mythic stories of characters who are at the mercy of seemingly all-powerful alien beings; characters like Anyanwu in *Wild Seed* and Lillith in the Xenogenesis novel *Dawn* must devise strategies to accommodate the demands of creatures who hold the power of life and death over them, while holding on to their dignity and essential humanity. In *Kindred*, one of Butler's stand-alone novels, the central character, Dana, is at the mercy of a time-warping brainstorm, which whisks her back at arbitrary intervals to slave-owning, pre–Civil War Virginia. While *Kindred* is not SF, as Butler makes no attempt to rationally explain Dana's time traveling, the past that modern, independent, African American Dana encounters in antebellum Virginia is so alien, so horrible, that it might as well be the home planet of that Devil Girl that Butler watched as a child.

Butler's real coup is in the alien adversaries she provides for her beleaguered characters: Dana's white, slave-owning ancestor Rufus, the homicidal shape-shifter Doro of the Patternist series, the Oankali species of space-wanderers, who save Lillith from certain death on a nuclear wasted Earth—at a price. The twist in each novel is that Butler's protagonists need something from their nemeses: each set of characters are locked in a carefully balanced dance of survival, in which the death of one will exact a terrible price from the other.

In addition to the various SF awards she received for her work, in 1995 Butler was also the first science fiction writer to receive a MacArthur Fellowship, popularly known as the "genius grant." In 2000 she was presented with a lifetime achievement award from PEN, the worldwide association of writers. In later life she struggled with ill health and writers' block, but she remained a tireless campaigner for social, racial, and environmental issues and a generous, greatly loved mentor to young writers. Octavia E. Butler died on February 24, 2006, at age fifty-eight, of complications following a fall outside her Seattle, Washington, home. At the end of her life, Butler was still one of a few African American "big names" of SF—but thanks to her, that was changing. She had demonstrated to readers, and an upcoming generation of writers, that "all that weird stuff" can handle the important stories, the stories that they want to tell.

Awards

MacArthur Fellowship (1995)
PEN Lifetime Achievement (2000)

Novels

Parable of the Talents (1998) **Nebula**

Short Fiction

"Speech Sounds." (1984) **Hugo**
"Bloodchild" (1985) **Hugo, Locus Poll & Nebula**

 ## Works by the Author

Kindred (1979)
Clay's Ark (1984)
The Fledgling (2005)

Patternist

Patternmaster (1976)
Mind of My Mind (1977)
Survivor (1978)
Wild Seed (1980)

Xenogenesis

Dawn (1987)
Adulthood Rites (1988)
Imago (1989)

Earthseed

Parable of the Sower (1993)
Parable of the Talents (1998)

Other Notable Short Fiction

"The Evening and the Morning and the Night" (1987)
"Amnesty" (2003)
"The Book of Martha" (2004)

Collections

Xenogenesis (1989; aka *Lillith's Brood*)
Bloodchild and Other Stories (1995)
Seed to Harvest (2007)

Articles and Essays

"Aha! Moment! Eye Witness: Octavia Butler." *O, The Oprah Magazine* (May 2002). http://www.oprah.com/article/omagazine/aha/rys_omag_200205_aha
As O. E. Butler. "Birth of a Writer." *Essence,* 20 no. 1 (1989): 74+.
"Brave New Worlds: A Few Rules for Predicting the Future." *Essence* 31, no. 1 (2000): 164+.

"*Devil Girl from Mars*: Why I Write Science Fiction." MIT Media in Transition Project, February 19, 1998. http://web.mit.edu/m-i-t/articles/butler_talk_index.html

"The Monophobic Response." In *Dark Matter: A Century of Speculative Fiction from the African Diaspora,* ed. Sheree R. Thomas, 415–16. New York: Warner Books, 2000.

"A World without Racism." *NPR Weekend Edition: UN Racism Conference,* September 1, 2001. National Public Radio. http://www.npr.org/programs/specials/racism/010830.octaviabutler.html

For Further Information

Official Web site. January 2007. http://www.sfwa.org/members/butler/

Antczak, Janice. "Octavia Butler: New Designs for a Challenging Future." *African-American Voices in Young Adult Literature.* Ed. Karen Patricia Smith. Metuchen, NJ: Scarecrow, 1994. 311-336.

Ask the Experts: Octavia Butler (video interview). PBS.com. 2003. http://www.pbs.org/kcet/closertotruth/ask/butler.html

Balagun, Kazembe. Obituary and Interview. *New York City Independent Media Center,* February 27, 2006. http://nyc.indymedia.org/en/2006/01/63283.shtml

Barnes, Steven. "Octavia Butler, a Rememberance." *Internet Review of Science Fiction* (March 2006). http://www.irosf.com/q/zine/article/10262

Becker, Jennifer. "Biography & Bibliography." *Voices from the Gaps: Women Artists and Writers of Color,* August 21, 2004. Rev. and updated by Lauren Curtwright. University of Minnesota. http://voices.cla.umn.edu/vg/Bios/entries/butler_octavia_estelle.html

Champion, Edward. Podcast Interview. *The Bat Segundo Show,* December 1, 2005. Wordpress. http://www.edrants.com/segundo/the-bat-segundo-show-15/

Chau, Jen, and Carmen Van Kerckhove. Podcast Interview. *Addicted to Race,* February 6, 2006. New Demographic. http://www.addictedtorace.com/?p=29

Fowler, Karen Joy. "Remembering Octavia Butler." *Salon.com,* March 17, 2006. http://www.salon.com/books/feature/2006/03/17/butler/

Gonzalez, Juan, and Amy Goodman. "Science Fiction Writer Octavia Butler on Race, Global Warming and Religion." *Democracy Now!* November 11, 2005. http://www.democracynow.org/2005/11/11/science_fiction_writer_octavia_butler_on

Hairston, Andrea. "Octavia Butler—Praise Song to a Prophetic Artist." In *Daughters of Earth: Feminist Science Fiction in the Twentieth Century,* ed. Justine Larbalestier, 265–304. Middletown, CT: Wesleyan University Press, 2006.

"In Motion" Profile. *The Diamond Trail,* February 21, 2009. http://thediamondtrail.wordpress.com/

Moylan, Tom. "Octavia Butler's Parables." In *Scraps of the Untainted Sky: Science Fiction Utopia Dystopia,* 223–46. Boulder, CO: Westview, 2000.

Salvaggio, Ruth. "Octavia Butler." In *Starmont Reader's Guide 23*. Mercer Island, WA: Starmont, 1986.

Saunders, Joshunda. Interview. *In Motion Magazine*, March 14, 2004. NPC Productions. http://www.inmotionmagazine.com/ac04/obutler.html

Shaw, Heather. "Strange Bedfellows: Eugenics, Attraction, and Aversion in the Works of Octavia E. Butler." *Strange Horizons,* December 18, 2000. http://www.strangehorizons.com/2000/20001218/butler.shtml

Various press obituaries. *22 Over 7,* February 28, 2006. http://nmazca.com/3142857/archive/2006_02_01_archive.htm

Pat Cadigan

Cyberpunk; TechnoThriller

Benchmark Title: *Synners* (1991)

b. 1953 (Schenectady, New York)

Well, I wish I could erupt with some profoundly erudite and insightful pronouncement on literature in general and genre cross-pollination in particular, but the truth is, I write the kind of thing that I like to read, and afterwards, someone else tells me what it's called.
—Castellani, Interview in *The Well* (2001)

About the Author and the Author's Writing

Patricia Oren Kearney Cadigan was born in Schenectady, New York, and grew up in Massachusetts. She attended the University of Massachusetts, where she majored in theater, and the University of Kansas, where she studied with SF scholar James Gunn. After graduation she worked for a while as a writer and editor for Hallmark Cards. In the late 1970s and early 1980s, Cadigan edited the semiprofessional fan magazines *Shayol* and *Chacal*, where she earned repeated nominations and several awards for amateur publication and fanzine, and where she was able to publish her earliest short fiction.

Some critics may carp about her apocryphal title, "Queen of Cyberpunk"—a title that she herself treats with amused disdain (see quote above). It's true that the tough-minded vigor and icy black humor of her work place it squarely in the spirit of 1980s cyberpunk. But from her very earliest work, it seems her real interest has not been cyberpunk, *for its own sake,* as much as the "practical applications of cyberpunk." *Synners,* for example, has been described as "the best science fiction novel with a rock 'n' roll theme" (Leonard 1998). Her more recent novels, *Tea from an Empty Cup* and *Dervish Is Digital*, are detective stories in the *noir* style, in which the tension and the solution of the mystery itself hinge on the real-life implications of cyber-life. Some critics maintain that Cadigan is at her best in her short fiction; her stories have appeared in three personal anthologies, as well as collections such as *Alternate Kennedys* (1993), *Hackers* (1996), *The Web 2028* (1999), and *Letters from Home* (1991), which showcases otherwise uncollected stories by Cadigan, Karen Joy Fowler and Pat Murphy. Cadigan has also done a number of movie and TV tie-ins (*Twilight Zone, Jason X*), as well as "making of" books about the movies *Lost in Space* and *The Mummy*, which consider the ways that the "imaginings" of 1980s cyberpunk have become part of our lives today. "'The Mummy' is not a cyberpunk movie.... It's the way that it is made that is so cyberpunk—which I like even better. I get a big kick out of that" (Leonard 1998).

Cadigan moved to England in 1996 and for many years has been a visiting lecturer on creative writing and the SF genre at British universities. She currently lives in London, hanging out in techno clubs and indulging her passion for hard-edged rock. It seems fitting for the "been there, done that" tone of her fiction that she doesn't have a conventional Web site, but instead maintains an entertaining blog and posts amazing photographs of events and oddities of her life in London, such as "The World Naked Bike Ride on Charing Cross Road," on the photo-sharing Web site Flickr.

Awards

Novels

Synners (1991) **Arthur C. Clarke**
Fools (1992) **Arthur C. Clarke**

Short Fiction

"Angel" (1988) **Locus Poll**

Collections

Patterns (1989) **Locus Poll**

Works by the Author

Mindplayers (1987)
Synners (1991)
Fools (1992)
Tea from an Empty Cup (1998)
Dervish Is Digital (2001)
Datableed (1997)

Novelizations and Movie Tie-ins

Lost in Space—Promised Land (1999)
Cellular (2004)
Twilight Zone—Upgrade/Sensuous Cindy (2004)
Jason X (2005)
The Experiment (2005)

Young Adult

Avatar (1999—in omnibus volume *The Web 2028*)

Other Notable Short Fiction

"Death from Exposure" (1978)

"Second Comings—Reasonable Rates" (1981)
"The Sorceress in Spite of Herself" (1982)
"Pretty Boy Crossover" (1986)
"Two" (1988)
"The Power and the Passion" (1989)
"Fool to Believe" (1990)
"Dispatches from the Revolution" (1991)
"True Faces" (1992)
"No Prisoners" (1993)
"Paris in June" (1994)
"Among Strangers" (2007)

Collections

Patterns (1989)
Letters from Home (1991, with Karen Joy Fowler and Pat Murphy)
Dirty Work (1993)
Home by the Sea (1993)

As Editor

Chacal (1977, fanzine)
Shayol 1-7 (1977–1985, fanzine)
The Ultimate Cyberpunk (2004)

Nonfiction Books

The Making of Lost in Space (1998)
Resurrecting the Mummy: The Making of the Movie (1999)

Articles and Essays

"Introduction." In *Exploring the Matrix: Visions of the Cyber Present,* ed. Karen Haber, 10–15. New York: St. Martin's, 2003.
"Lateral Genius and the Persistence of *Neuromancer*." *Nova Express* 4, no. 4 (Winter/Spring 1998): 14+.
"Ten SF/Fantasy/Genre Films That Should Not Have Been Made." *The Magazine of Fantasy & Science Fiction* (July 1998): 127–29.
"Ten Years After." *Asimov's Science Fiction* (December 1993): 4–9.

For Further Information

Web sites: *Ceci N'est Pas Une Web site (Cadigan's Photos)*, http://www.flickr.com/photos/cadigan/ and *Ceci N'est Pas Une Blog* http://fastfwd.livejournal.com/

Castellani, Linda. "Pat Cadigan: Dervish Is Digital." *The Well,* August 10, 2001. Salon Media Group. http://www.well.com/conf/inkwell.vue/topics/120/Pat-Cadigan-Dervish-is-Digital-page01.html

Heuser, Sabine. "Pat Cadigan's Virtual Mindscapes." In *Virtual Geographies: Cyberpunk at the Intersection of the Postmodern and Science Fiction.* Amsterdam: Rodopi, 2003. 127–70.

Jenkins, Henry. "Exchange with Pat Cadigan: Queen of Cyberpunk." MIT, October 10, 1998 (edited version). In *Media in Transition.* Massachusetts Institute of Technology, November 3, 1998. http://web.mit.edu/m-i-t/science_fiction/

Jenssen, Stefanie. "Talking with Pat Cadigan." *InterContact'98* (1998). http://www.ii.uib.no/~bjornts/ICW/PR2/PR2_3.html

Kraus, Elisabeth. "Real Lives Complicate Matters in Schrodinger's World: Pat Cadigan's Alternative Cyberpunk Vision." In *Future Females, The Next Generation,* ed. Marleen S. Barr, 129–44. Lanham, MD: Rowman & Littlefield, 2000.

Leonard, Andrew. "The Return of the Queen of Cyberpunk." *Salon,* November 18, 1998. http://archive.salon.com/21st/books/1998/11/18books.html

Mathew, David. "Step Outside: An Interview with Pat Cadigan." *SF Site* (2000). http://www.sfsite.com/05b/pc224.htm

Schmidt, Jakob. Interview. *SF Site* (2006). http://www.sfsite.com/05b/pc224.htm

Seed, David. "Cyberpunk and Dystopia: Pat Cadigan's Networks." In *Dark Horizons: Science Fiction and the Dystopian Imagination,* ed. Rafaella Baccolini and Tom Moylan, 69–90. New York: Routledge, 2003.

Orson Scott Card

Myth and Legend; Science Fantasy; Sense of Wonder

Benchmark Title: *Ender's Game* (1985)

b. 1951 (Richland, Washington)

Photo credit: Beth Gwinn

The reader coming to my work will find that there is only rarely any science in my science fiction. I use the freedom of the genre to create the situations in which my stories take place, but I never try to predict of prescribe the future.
—Author Comments, *St. James Guide to Science Fiction Writers* (1996)

About the Author and the Author's Writing

There are two deep influences in the life and work of Orson Scott Card, which become immediately apparent in even the most superficial account of his career—his family and his faith. Card is a descendant of Charles Ora Card, a Mormon pioneer and son-in-law of Brigham Young, who fled the United States and founded the town of Cardston, in Alberta, Canada, as a refuge from religious persecution. The bare bones of this family history reveal themes that recur again and again in Card's fiction: courage, unwillingness to bend to pressure or persecution, and the knowledge that you must face the consequences of your choices.

Orson Scott Card was born in Richland, Washington, and grew up in Santa Clara, California, in Arizona, and in Utah. He has a BA in theater studies from Brigham Young University and an MA in English from the University of Utah. From 1971 to 1973 Card interrupted his college studies to spend two years as a volunteer Mormon missionary in Brazil, an experience that is reflected in several of his stories and novels. Upon his return from Brazil, while he was completing his undergraduate degree, he founded the Utah Valley Repertory Theatre Company, where he wrote and produced a number of plays on faith themes and Mormon history. He also worked as assistant editor at the Church's official magazine, *Ensign,* and it was in *Ensign* that Card's first short story, "Gert Fram" (under the pseudonym Byron Walley), was published in July 1977. In August 1977 "Ender's Game," Card's first SF story, was published in *Analog* magazine.

Ender's Game is an SF phenomenon. Its first incarnation, the 1977 novella, was nominated for a Hugo and short-listed for a Nebula award, and that became the basis of the 1985 novel of the same name. The novel *Ender's Game* (1985), and its sequel *Speaker for the Dead* (1986), remain the only two SF novels to earn their author both Hugo and Nebula awards two years in a row. Its popularity with young readers remains undimmed more than twenty years later. An interview with Tom Doherty of Tor books, reproduced on Card's Web site, quotes Doherty as saying that he has "given away 'hundreds of thousands of copies' . . . over the years, as a kind of science fiction gateway drug." But although the novella brought Card early recognition and in 1978 won him the John W. Campbell Award for Best New Writer, by the mid-1980s he was the victim of a slow economy's impact on publishing. He juggled various career possibilities: writing, working as editor for magazines and journals, and spending a year in a PhD program at the University of Notre Dame, with the objective of becoming an English teacher. As the young father of a growing family (he had also married in 1977), Card had to make his choices count, and although Ender established him with fans and critics, it was a contract for his Alvin Maker "trilogy" (now a six-volume series) that allowed him to set aside the "day job" and write full time.

Subsequently, Card has written mainstream fiction (*Woman of Destiny*, 1984), science fantasy (the alternative history Tales of Alvin Maker series), near-future post-apocalypse (*The Folk of the Fringe*, 1989), and far future human space colonization (the Homecoming series). Each of these has its narratives foundation in Card's faith, based on the history of the Latter Day Saints, its founder Joseph Smith, and its holy book, the Book of Mormon. The *Encyclopedia of Science Fiction* (1999) calls the Homecoming series "as close as humanly possible to the telling of an SF tale as Mormon parable."

Card is an outspoken critic, political writer, and speaker, whose views are guaranteed to raise somebody's blood pressure. He is a political and social conservative and a vocal supporter of former president George W. Bush's response to terrorism and conduct of the war in Iraq. His observations on homosexuality and adultery have upset many people who are unfamiliar with the teachings of the Church of the Latter Day Saints. He is robust in his contempt for modern literary criticism. However, he identifies himself as a Democrat: he is firmly pro-gun control/anti-National Rifle Association, highly critical of free-market capitalism, and forthright in his opinion that the Republican party in the South continues to tolerate racism. His "op-ed" writing appears in a weekly column published in the Greensboro *Rhinoceros Times* and is archived on his Web sites, named variously "War Watch," "World Watch," or "Civilization Watch," depending on the topic.

Orson Scott Card and his wife Kristine are the parents of five children, each named after an author he and his wife admire: Michael Geoffrey (Geoffrey Chaucer), Emily Janice (Emily Brontë and Emily Dickinson), Charles Benjamin (Charles Dickens), Zina Margaret (Margaret Mitchell), and Erin Louisa (Louisa May Alcott). Their son Charles was born with cerebral palsy and died shortly after his seventeenth birthday. He is buried with their daughter, Erin, who died as a newborn. Currently Card is Distinguished Professor at Southern Virginia University in Buena Vista, Virginia; he and his family live in Greensboro, North Carolina.

Awards

John W. Campbell Best New Author (1978)

Edward E. Smith Memorial Award for Imaginative Fiction ("Skylark award") (1992)

Novels

Ender's Game (1985) **Hugo, Nebula**

Speaker for the Dead (1986) **Hugo, Locus Poll, Nebula**

Short Fiction

"Eye for Eye" (1987) **Hugo**

"Dogwalker" (1989) **Locus Poll**

"Lost Boys" (1989) **Locus Poll**

Collections

Maps in a Mirror (2004) **Locus Poll**

Nonfiction

How to Write Science Fiction and Fantasy (2001) **Hugo**

Works by the Author

Songmaster (1979)

The Worthing Chronicle (1983). Revised edition of earlier novels *Hot Sleep* and *Capitol* (1978).

Wyrms (1987)

Treason (1988, rev. *A Planet Called Treason,* 1978)

The Abyss (1989) (novelization of James Cameron's film)

The Folk of the Fringe (1989)

Lovelock (1994, with Kathryn H. Kidd)

Empire (2006)

Ender Wiggins

Ender's Game (1985)

Speaker for the Dead (1986)

Xenocide (1991)

Children of the Mind (1996)

Ender's Shadow (1999)

Shadow of the Hegemon (2001)

Shadow Puppets (2002)

Shadow of the Giant (2005)

Homecoming

The Memory of Earth (1992)
The Call of Earth (1992)
The Ships of Earth (1994)
Earthfall (1995)
Earthborn (1995)

Mainstream and Other Genre Fiction

Hart's Hope (1983)
Saints (1983; aka *Woman of Destiny*)
Pastwatch: The Redemption of Christopher Columbus (1996)
Treasure Box (1996)
Stone Tables (1997)
Homebody (1998)
Enchantment (1999)
Magic Street (2005)
Invasive Procedures (2007, with Aaron Johnston)

The Tales of Alvin Maker

Seventh Son (1987)
Red Prophet (1988)
Prentice Alvin (1989)
Alvin Journeyman (1995)
Heartfire (1998)
The Crystal City (2003)

The Women of Genesis Series

Sarah (2000)
Rebekah (2001)
Rachel and Leah (2004)

Other Notable Short Fiction

"Ender's Game" (1977) (Available online at OSC's official Web site, http://www.hatrack.com/osc/stories/enders-game.shtml)
"Lifeloop" (1978)
"Songhouse" (1979)
"The Fringe" (1985)
"Hatrack River" (1986)
"Eye for Eye" (1987)
"Dowser" (1988)
"Dogwalker" (1989)
"Lost Boys" (1989)

Collections

Unaccompanied Sonata and Other Stories (1980)

Cardography (1987)

The Folk of the Fringe (1989)

The Changed Man (1992)

Maps in a Mirror: The Short Fiction of Orson Scott Card (2004). A cumulative anthology that contains all stories released in the *Maps in a Mirror* collections of the 1990s, such as *The Changed Man* (1992) and *Monkey Sonatas* (1993).

Keeper of Dreams (2008)

As Editor

Dragons of Light (1980)

Dragons of Darkness (1981)

Future on Fire (1991)

Black Mist and Other Japanese Futures (1997, with Keith Ferrell)

Future on Ice (1998)

Empire of Dreams & Miracles: The Phobos Science Fiction Anthology, Volume 1 (2002, with Keith Olexa)

Hitting the Skids in Pixeltown: The Phobos Science Fiction Anthology, Volume 2 (2003, with Keith Olexa and Christian O'Toole)

Masterpieces: The Best Science Fiction of the Twentieth Century (2004)

Orson Scott Card's InterGalactic Medicine Show (2008, executive editor, with Edmund R. Schubert, editor; http://www.intergalacticmedicineshow.com/)

In Other Media

The Secret of Monkey Island (1990) and *The Dig* (1995), LucasArts Entertainment. Computer game animations. Card is credited as "insults writer" for the sword-fighting scenes.

"Shelter" (*I Am Legend—Awakening, Story 3*). 100% Womon, 2008. Animated online featurette, developed by Jada Pinkett Smith, directed by Brooke Burgess from a screenplay by Card, shown on the official Web site as part of promotion for the movie *I Am Legend* (2007).

Nonfiction Books

Character and Viewpoint: Elements of Writing (1988)

How to Write Science Fiction and Fantasy (1990)

A Storyteller in Zion (1993)

Getting Lost*: Survival, Baggage, and Starting Over in J. J. Abrams'* Lost (2006)

Articles and Essays

"Fantasy and the Believing Reader." *Science Fiction Review* (Fall 1982). http://www.hatrack.com/osc/articles/fall82.shtml

"Morality in Videogames." *Forbes,* December 14, 2006. http://www.forbes.com/2006/12/10/games-orson-card-tech-cx_mn_games06_1212morality.html

"World Watch." *The Ornery American.* 2001–2009. http://www.ornery.org/essays/warwatch/index.html. Columns that originally appeared in *The Rhinoceros Times* (Greensboro, NC).

For Further Information

Official Web site: http://www.hatrack.com/

Allen, Moira. "Orson Scott Card: On Religion in Science Fiction and Fantasy." *Phantastes* (Spring 2000). http://www.writing-world.com/sf/card.shtml

Collings, Michael. *In the Image of God: Theme, Characterization, and Landscape in the Fiction of Orson Scott Card.* New York: Greenwood, 1990.

———. "Orson Scott Card." In *St. James Guide to Science Fiction Writers,* ed. Jay Pedersen. Detroit, MI: St. James, 1996. Includes extended Author Comments by OSC.

———. *Storyteller: The Official Orson Scott Card Bibliography and Guide.* Woodstock: Overlook Connection, 2001.

Gaudiosi, John. "Orson Scott Card Builds an Empire." *Wired,* October 11, 2006. http://www.wired.com/news/technology/0,72093-0.html?tw=rss.index

Interview. *Geeks On,* August 6, 2005. http://www.geekson.com/archives/archiveepisodes/2005/episode080605.htm

James, Warren W. Interview. *Mike Hodel's Hour 25,* January 12, 2001. http://www.hour25online.com/Hour25_Previous_Shows_2001-1.html#orson-scott-card_2001-01-12

Lilley, Ernest. "Interview with Orson Scott Card." *SFRevu,* October 2, 2002. http://www.sfrevu.com/ISSUES/2002/0210/Feature%20Interview%20-%20Orson%20Scott%20Card/Interview.htm

Orbit Interview. *SFFWorld,* February 1, 2002. http://www.sffworld.com/interview/18p0.html

Tyson, Edith S. *Orson Scott Card: Writer of the Terrible Choice.* Lanham, MD: Rowman & Littlefield/Scarecrow, 2003.

Willett, Edward. *Orson Scott Card: Architect of Alternate Worlds.* Berkeley Heights, NJ: Enslow, 2006.

Suzy McKee Charnas

Dystopias; Feminist SF

Benchmark Title: *Walk to the End of the World* (1974)

b. 1939 (New York City)

Africa equipped me, as a white American woman, to write about space and the future as inhabited by more kinds of people than just smart white guys doing imaginary techno speak at each other.
—Gordon, "Closed Systems Kill," *Science Fiction Studies* (1999)

Photo credit: Kyle Zimmerman.
Courtesy of Suzy McKee Charnas.

About the Author and the Author's Writing

Suzy McKee—the "Charnas" would come later—was born in New York City. Her parents were professional illustrators, and her first stories were written (and illustrated) in her father's sketch books. She attended progressive schools in Manhattan, and did her undergraduate degree at Barnard College. She already knew exactly what she wanted to do: write SF stories about parts of the world that most SF authors at that time ignored, like former African colonies and Caribbean islands. And to do that, she knew that she needed to be able to construct convincing societies and real worlds. She put together a major in economics and history because "I figured I would have to be able to give a reader a realistic sense of how my characters functioned in their world—what they did for a living, and where their attitudes and beliefs came from" (Gordon 1999). The young would-be writer also took geology to get some feel for landscape, and anthropology to improve her sense of the possibilities of cultural diversity.

After getting a master's degree in education from New York University, she joined the Peace Corps and taught English and history in Nigeria. On her return to New York in the late 1960s, she worked for a hospital mental health department, developing curriculum for its education program. She also married Steven Charnas. Eventually the couple moved to New Mexico, and Suzy McKee Charnas began her career as a freelance writer.

Her first novel, and the first volume in her four-part SF series <u>Holdfast</u>, was *Walk to the End of the World* (1974). "Holdfast" is a culture of free women who live a nomadic life beyond the reach of a postapocalyptic America, where women are enslaved and treated as breeding stock. In less skillful hands, this could have been a dull, "blame the guys" polemic. But "[r]ather than creating a straightforward, European-style patriarchy as a vehicle of male oppression or turning her feminine society into a lovey-dovey nurturefest, Charnas plays with social parameters, imagining the legacy of rage and fear" (Shulman 2000).

For example, in the male enclaves, any concept of "family" has been lost, along with any understanding between the sexes; men consider their sons natural enemies, and no man is supposed to know who his father is. Subsequent volumes in the Holdfast sequence describe the rebellion of the women and its bloody aftermath, a backlash in which the former oppressors are enslaved, and an ultimate resolution of the relations between genders and individuals is achieved. In Charnas's work, the characters you sympathize with, or learn to admire and trust, do not always do the right thing; the "bad guys" do not always behave as badly as you expect. Charnas is always aware, and always makes sure that the reader is aware, that the population of this nightmarish postapocalyptic United States are victims—all of them—of the terrible decisions that were made generations before they were born: "I love to take some hoary stereotype —jolly barbarism after the holocaust, breast-plated Amazons, blue-blooded vampires, the bold space-pilot fighting for independence—and turn it upside-down" (Author Comments, *St. James Guide*).

Apart from the Holdfast novels, Charnas has written horror (the Weyland Vampire stories); stand-alone fantasy; and the juvenile Sorcery Hall series, about the adventures of a trainee wizard dedicated to defending the world from the forces of evil. She lives with her husband in New Mexico.

Awards

Novels

Walk to the End of the World (1974) **Retro Tiptree 1996**
Motherlines (1978) **Retro Tiptree 1996**
The Conqueror's Child (1999) **Tiptree**

Short Fiction

"The Unicorn Tapestry" (1981) **Nebula**
"Boobs" (1989) **Hugo**

Works by the Author

Holdfast

Walk to the End of the World (1974)
Motherlines (1978)
The Furies (1994)
The Conqueror's Child (1999)

Other Genre Fiction

The Vampire Tapestry (1980)
Dorothea Dreams (1986)

The Kingdom of Kevin Malone (1993)
The Ruby Tear (1997)

Sorcery Hill

The Bronze King (1985)
The Silver Glove (1988)
The Golden Thread (1989)

Collections

Moonstone and Tiger-Eye (1992)
The Slave and the Free (1999)
Music of the Night (2001)
Stagestruck Vampires: And Other Phantasms (2006)

Other Notable Short Fiction

"Scorched Supper on New Niger" (1980)
"Listening to Brahms" (1986)
"Advocates" (1991, with Chelsea Quinn Yarbro)
"Beauty and the Opera or the Phantom Beast" (1996)

Nonfiction Books

My Father's Ghost: The Return of My Old Man, and Other Second Chances (2002)
Strange Seas (2002)

Articles and Essays

"No Such Thing as Tearing Down Just a Little: Post-Holocaust Themes in Feminist SF." *Janus* 6 (1980): 25–28.

"A Woman Appeared" In *Future Females: A Critical Anthology*, ed. Marleen Barr, 103–8. Bowling Green: Bowling Green State University Popular Press, 1981.

For Further Information

Official Web site: http://www.suzymckeecharnas.com/

Barr, Marleen. "Suzy McKee Charnas." In *St. James Guide to Science Fiction Writers,* ed. Jay Pedersen. Detroit, MI: St. James, 1996.

———. "Suzy McKee Charnas." In *Starmont Reader's Guide 23*. Mercer Island, WA: Starmont, 1986.

Clemente, Bill. "Of Women and Wonder: A Conversation with Suzy McKee Charnas." In *Women of Other Worlds,* ed. Helen Merrick and Tess Williams, 60–81. Nedlands: University of Western Australia Press, 1999.

Cranny-Francis, Anne. "Man Made Monsters: Suzy McKee Charnas' *Walk to the End of the World* as Dystopian Feminist Science Fiction." In *Science Fiction Roots and Branches,* ed. Rhys Garnett and R. J. Ellis, 183–206. Basingstoke: Macmillan, 1990.

Gordon, Joan. "Closed Systems Kill: An Interview with Suzy McKee Charnas." *Science Fiction Studies* 26 (1999): 447–68. http://www.depauw.edu/sfs/interviews/charnasinterview.htm

Grant, Gavin J. Interview. *Booksense,* November 11, 2002. American Booksellers Association. http://www.booksense.com/people/archive/c/charnassuzymckee.jsp

Shulman, Polly. "Matriarchy Blues." *Salon,* April 21, 2000. http://archive.salon.com/books/feature/2000/04/21/sf/index.html

Wilgus, Neal. "Walk to the End of the *Motherlines*." In *Seven by Seven: Interviews with American Science Fiction Writers of the West and Southwest,* 45–64. San Bernardino, CA: Borgo, 1996.

C. J. Cherryh

Space Opera; Science Fantasy

Benchmark Title: *Downbelow Station* (1981)

b. 1942 (St. Louis, Missouri)

Photo credit: Beth Gwinn

One thing you learn in archaeology is that there weren't any good old days—compared to now.... I'd rather live today than thirty years ago, or three hundred or three thousand. And I'd rather live in the future than now. I want to get into space. Maybe somebody will take my books where I can't go.
—Perret, *The Faces of Science Fiction* (1984)

About the Author and the Author's Writing

Carolyn Janice Cherry was born in St. Louis, Missouri and grew up in Lawdon, Oklahoma. Like many of the SF great, she started young, writing stories with "a fat-lead pencil on cheap tablets, illustrated, no less. I was young. I learned to type as soon as possible, and the stories consequently got longer. By the time I was sixteen, I had volumes" (*SFF World.com*). She was a member of Phi Beta Kappa at the University of Oklahoma and graduated with a BA in Latin in 1964, having specialized in archaeology, mythology, and the history of engineering. She received a master's degree in classics from Johns Hopkins University, in Maryland, where she was a Woodrow Wilson fellow. After graduate school she taught Latin, classics, and ancient history in the Oklahoma City public school system. "I wrote during the copious spare time a schoolteacher has ... with a sandwich for supper, the plate beside the typewriter and in front of the telly. My furniture lasted for much longer than it ought to: I only had to replace the typing chairs" (*SFF World.com*). During summer vacation she conducted student tours of the historical sites of England, France, Spain, and Italy, which gave her a chance to indulge her real passions: the history, religion, and culture of Rome and ancient Greece.

Meanwhile, Carolyn Janice Cherry was bombarding publishers with novels. No one had told her that the "usual" route to fame and fortune was to hawk your short stories around magazines for a penny a word, before having the temerity to progress to novels. She sent her work off to publishers, who not only refused them, but often lost the manuscripts. "Editors lost *Hunter of Worlds* three times. I always say that's the book that turned me into a real writer, because I kept having to improve it, and I learned on every pass" (*SFF World.com*).

Her breakthrough came in 1975, when Donald A. Wollheim of DAW Books purchased two manuscripts she had submitted, *Gate of Ivrel* and *Brothers of Earth*. The response was swift, and gratifying—on the strength of these two novels, in 1977 Cherry was awarded the John W. Campbell Award for Best New Writer. Don Wollheim had given her a three-book contract, with no due date and no specifications, so she quit teaching. "I figured since it amounted to more than a year's income as a teacher, I could take the risk" (Carmien 2004).

Carolyn Janice Cherry had become an award-winning, professional writer. She had also become "C. J. Cherryh." She reverted to her initials because her editors felt that her real name sounded like a romance writer, and because, in a genre that still had the reputation of being male-dominated, initials downplayed the fact that she was a woman. And "Cherryh"—pronounced "Cherry"—was chosen because it looked unique and stood out on bookshop shelves (which remains true to this day).

Since those breakthrough books, C.J. Cherryh has published more than sixty novels. She is widely admired for her versatility—she is as comfortable, and readable, in high fantasy as she is in hard SF, space opera, and science fantasy; but certain themes and motifs do recur. In a C. J. Cherryh novel, characters struggle to remain true to themselves in extremes: in the desperate circumstances of wartime (*Rimrunners*, *Downbelow Station*), in a society where wealth and power are based on identity-bending cloning (*Cyteen*), and among proud alien races that are forced to compromise their heritage, and make accommodations with enemies to survive (the Mri of *Kesrith*, part one of the Faded Sun sequence). Typically, an isolated human must deal with dangerous, difficult alien cultures, where the status quo has been shaken up by the advent of outsiders (whether the outsiders are the aliens, or the Earthmen who find themselves in the middle of a ruckus), and Cherryh uses all this to make clear the difficulty of real communication and affection crossing species. In *Hunter of Worlds*, the human character is a captive of a powerful, predatory alien race; the complicated interactions between human, dominant species and other client races in the novel makes the powerlessness and alienation of the human characters even more striking. Whatever genre Cherryh is working in, her stories depict alien worlds with great realism, they are "enriched with speculative ethnology, invented linguistics, and thoroughly imagined civilizations" (McAllister n.d.).

C. J. Cherryh lives near Spokane, Washington, with her partner, the science fiction/fantasy author and artist Jane Fancher. As well as three Hugos and a Locus Poll Award, in 2005 she was honored with two awards reserved for Sooners—the Oklahoma Book Award and the Arrell Gibson Lifetime Achievement Award, both administered by the Oklahoma Center for the Book. Her papers are housed at The Jack Williamson Science Fiction Library at Eastern New Mexico University. In March 2001 Asteroid 77185 was named in her honor, for—as California Institute of Technology's Jet Propulsion Laboratory puts it—"she has challenged us to be worthy of the stars by imagining how mankind might grow to live among them."

Awards

John W. Campbell Best New Author (1977)

Edward E. Smith Memorial Award for Imaginative Fiction ("Skylark award") (1988)

Novels

Downbelow Station (1981) **Hugo**
The Betrayal (1988) **Hugo**
Cyteen (1988) **Locus Poll**

Short Fiction

"Cassandra" (1979) **Hugo**

 # Works by the Author

Hestia (1979)
Wave Without a Shore (1981)

Alliance-Union Universe

Brothers of Earth (1976)
Hunter of Worlds (1977)
Serpent's Reach (1980)
Forty Thousand in Gehenna (1983)
Angel with the Sword (1985)
Cyteen (1988)
Regenesis (2009)

The Age of Exploration

Port Eternity (1982)
Voyager in Night (1984)
Cuckoo's Egg (1985)

Chanur

The Pride of Chanur (1981)
Chanur's Venture (1984)
The Kif Strike Back (1985)
Chanur's Homecoming (1986)
Chanur's Legacy (1992)

The Company Wars

Downbelow Station (1981)
Merchanter's Luck (1982)
Rimrunners (1989)
Heavy Time (1991)
Hellburner (1992)
Tripoint (1994)
Finity's End (1997)

The Faded Sun Trilogy
Kesrith (1978)
Shon'Jir (1978)
Kutath (1979)

The Morgaine Cycle
Gate of Ivrel (1976)
Well of Shiuan (1978)
Fires of Azeroth (1979)
Exile's Gate (1988)

Foreigner Universe
Foreigner (1994)
Invader (1995)
Inheritor (1996)
Precursor (1999)
Defender (2001)
Explorer (2003)
Destroyer (2005)
Pretender (2006)
Deliverer (2007)
Conspirator (2009)

Gene Wars
Hammerfall (2001)
Forge of Heaven (2004)

Nighthorse Universe
Rider at the Gate (1995)
Cloud's Rider (1996)

Other Genre Fiction
The Paladin (1988)
The Goblin Mirror (1992)
Faery in Shadow (1993)
Lois & Clark: A Superman Novel (1996)

Ealdwood
The Dreamstone (1983)
The Tree of Swords and Jewels (1983)

Heroes in Hell
Kings in Hell (1986)
Gates of Hell (1986)
Legions of Hell (1987)

The Russian Stories
Rusalka (1989)
Chernevog (1990)
Yvgenie (1991)

The Fortress Series
Fortress in the Eye of Time (1995)
Fortress of Eagles (1998)
Fortress of Owls (1999)
Fortress of Dragons (2000)
Fortress of Ice (2006)

Other Notable Short Fiction
"Homecoming" (1979)
"The Only Death in the City" (1981)
"The Scapegoat" (1985)

Collections
Sunfall (1981)
Visible Light (1986)
The Faded Sun Trilogy (1987)
Glass and Amber (1987). Includes essays such as "Perspectives in SF" (1987), "Romantic/Science Fiction: The Oldest Form of Literature" (1978), and "The Use of Archaeology in Worldbuilding" (1978).
Alternate Realities (2000)
The Chanur Saga (2000)
Devil to the Belt (2000)
The Morgaine Saga (2000)
At the Edge of Space (2003)
The Collected Short Fiction of C.J. Cherryh (2004)
The Deep Beyond (2005)
Chanur's Endgame (2007)
Alliance Space (2008)

As Editor

Merovingen Nights Anthologies
Festival Moon (1987)

Fever Season (1987)
Troubled Waters (1988)
Smugglers Gold (1988)
Divine Right (1989)
Flood Tide (1990)
Endgame (1991)

Nonfiction

"Goodbye Star Wars, Hello Alley-Oop." In *Inside Outer Space: Science Fiction Professionals Look at Their Craft,* ed. Sharon Jarvis, 17–26. New York: Ungar, 1985.

"Strong vs Weak Characters." *C. J. Cherryh World,* June 8, 2005 (orig. pub. 1995). http://www.cherryh.com/www/charac.htm

"Writerisms and Other Sins: A Writer's Shortcut to Stronger Writing." *C. J. Cherryh World,* June 8, 2005 (orig. pub. 1995). http://www.cherryh.com/www/advice.htm

For Further Information

Official Web site: http://www.cherryh.com/

Carmien, Edward, ed. *The Cherryh Odyssey.* Holicong, PA: Borgo, 2004.
———. "C. J. Cherryh Interview." *SFRevu* June 15, 2004. http://www.sfrevu.com/ISSUES/2004/0406/CJ%20Cherryh%20Interview/Review.htm
"Curiosity Killed This Cat." *Shejidan,* February 21, 2004. http://www.shejidan.com/main.html
Interview. *SFFWorld,* January 1, 2000. http://www.sffworld.com/interview/21p0.html
Jet Propulsion Laboratory, California Institute of Technology. "77185 Cherryh (2001 FE9)." *JPL Small-Body Database Browser.* July 14, 2004. http://ssd.jpl.nasa.gov/sbdb.cgi?sstr=77185
McAllister, Mick. "C. J. Cherryh, Science Fiction, and the Soft Sciences." *At Wanderer's Well,* April 7, 2007. http://www.dancingbadger.com/c_j_cherryh.htm
Raffel, Burton. "C.J. Cherryh's Fiction." *Literary Review* 44 (2001): 578+.

Ted Chiang

Myth and Legend; Slipstream

Benchmark Title: *Stories of Your Life, and Others* (2002)

b. 1967 (Port Jefferson, New York)

[M]agic is always esoteric, whereas science and technology are fundamentally egalitarian. Magic's something for the few, the select, the anointed, or someone who has a gift, but science is ultimately amenable to mass production, so we can all enjoy the benefits of science and technology.
—"Science, Language and Magic," *Locus* (2002)

Photo credit: Beth Gwinn

About the Author and the Author's Writing

Ted Chiang is one of a number of young writers whose work plays with the boundaries of SF, treating the fantastic as if it were hard science, and the hard sciences as if they were a form of magic. "Chiang's primary method is to change underlying natural laws or symbolic systems, creating worlds and situations that are fantastic to us but utterly rational to the characters that must live with them" (Smith 2002). Chiang's stories qualify as SF because they regularly deal in the ultimate in "what-ifs?": in "Tower of Babel" (1990), *what if* your work-a-day job was to be one of the crew on the most famous over-budget building project in history? In "Division by Zero" (1991), a mathematician suffers an identity crisis when she wonders *what if* a mathematical paradox undermines the professional and personal certainties on which she has built her life? *What if* ("Liking What You See: A Documentary") a cheap and readily available technology was available that meant that beauty became meaningless: no one is perceived as looking any better (or worse) than anyone else? And, in "Hell Is the Absence of God," in the ultimate *what if*, "God exists beyond a doubt. Angels behave like weather phenomena, the miracle of their appearances tracked, quantified, and reported on the nightly news" (Smith 2002). Chiang's single short novel, *The Merchant and the Alchemist's Gate*, is a time-travel story that tells a cautionary tale about the pointlessness of regret and second-guessing your own choices; a nesting box of stories, told in the traditional style of *One Thousand and One Nights*, which challenges the whole idea of *"what if"* in the narratives of the characters' lives.

Chaing is a minimalist writer, whose entire output to date totals a scant handful of short stories and novellas. As he said in an interview for *Interzone* magazine in 2002: "Because I don't get that many ideas for stories. If I had more ideas, I would write them, but unfortunately they only come at long intervals. I'm probably best described as an occasional writer." He consistently uses off-beat interpretations of historical themes, religious imagery, and philosophical ideas, to unsettling and thought-provoking effect. His critical acclaim is out of all proportion to his literary output: as well as several Nebula Awards for short fiction, he has won Nebula and Hugo Awards for "Hell Is the Absence of God" and *The Merchant and the Alchemist's Gate*. He turned down a Hugo nomination for his 2003 story, "Liking What You See: A Documentary," as the story was published before he could make what he saw as necessary revisions. His story "Seventy-Two Letters" has also received the Sidewise Award for Alternate History.

Ted Chiang was born in Port Jefferson, New York. He attended Brown University, graduating with a degree in computer sciences, and he has worked as a technical writer, writing software documentation. He credits the Clarion Writers' Workshop with giving him crucial encouragement at a time when he might have given up writing. "Clarion was the first time anyone told me they liked my work. Clarion also introduced me to the SF community. . . meeting my fellow students there was like discovering a family I'd never known I'd had" (Graff 2003).

Chiang lives near Bellevue, Washington, near Seattle. His 2008 short story "Exhalation," an evocative story of an all-metal world, its argon-breathing inhabitants, and a scientist who performs the ultimate self-examination, was the winner of the 2009 Hugo.

Awards

Campbell New Writer Award (1992)

Novels

The Merchant and the Alchemist's Gate (2007) **Hugo, Nebula**

Short Fiction

"Tower of Babylon" (1990) **Nebula**
"Story of Your Life" (1998) **Nebula, Sturgeon**
"Hell Is the Absence of God" (2001) **Hugo, Locus Poll, Nebula**
"Exhalation" (2008) **Hugo**

Collections

Stories of Your Life, and Others (2002) **Locus Poll**

Works by the Author

The Merchant and the Alchemist's Gate (2007)

Other Notable Short Fiction

"Division by Zero" (1991). http://www.fantasticmetropolis.com/i/division/
"Seventy-Two Letters" (2000)
"Understand" (2002). http://www.infinityplus.co.uk/stories/under.htm
"Liking What You See: A Documentary" (2002)

Collections

Stories of Your Life, and Others (2002)

Articles and Essays

"Science, Language and Magic." *Locus* (August 2002). http://www.scribd.com/doc/8681530/Ted-Chiang-Interview

For Further Information

Anders, Lou. Interview. *SFsite* (July 2002). http://www.sfsite.com/09b/tc136.htm

Graff, Rani. Interview. *Fantastic Metropolis,* December 13, 2003. http://www.fantasticmetropolis.com/i/chiang/

Grant, Gavin J. Interview *Booksense,* August 29, 2002. American Booksellers Association. http://www.booksense.com/people/archive/chiangted.jsp

Miéville, China. "Wonder Boy." *The Guardian* (London), April 24, 2004. http://www.guardian.co.uk/books/2004/apr/24/featuresreviews.guardianreview23

Robertson, Al. Interview. *Nebula Awards*, December 23, 2008. http://www.nebulaawards.com/index.php/interview/ted_chiang/

Smith, Jeremy. "The Absence of God: Ted Chiang Interviewed." *Interzone* 182 (September 2002): 23–26. http://www.infinityplus.co.uk/nonfiction/inttchiang.htm

Ted Chaing Page. *SFF Audio,* March 29, 2009. Includes link to *Starship Sofa* interview of May 2008, as well as links to various podcast versions of Chiang's fiction.

Arthur C. Clarke (Sir)

Hard SF; Sense of Wonder

Benchmark Title:
Childhood's End (1953)

b. 1917 (England: Minehead, Somerset);
d. 2008 (Sri Lanka: Colombo)

We stand now at the turning point between two eras. Behind us is a past to which we can never return. . . . The coming of the rocket brought to an end a million years of isolation . . . the childhood of our race was over and history as we know it began.
—*The Exploration of Space* (1951)

Photo credit: Rohan de Silva. Courtesy of the Estate of Sir Arthur C. Clarke.

About the Author and the Author's Writing

Sir Arthur C. Clarke was a writer of science fiction who was equally at home in the world of real-life scientific innovation and discovery. Throughout his long life, he dedicated himself to transforming the "stuff of science fiction"—radar early-warning systems, communication satellites, and space elevators—into realities. In a technical paper titled "Extra-terrestrial Relays" published in 1945, he first outlined the principles of global broadcasting by means of communication satellites in geostationary orbit. His wartime work on Ground Controlled Approach (GCA) radar was instrumental in the success of the Berlin Airlift of 1948–1949. Later, one of his short stories ("Dial F for Frankenstein," 1964) provided the inspiration for British computer scientist Tim Berners-Lee to invent the World Wide Web.

Arthur Charles Clarke was born in Minehead, in Somerset, England. His father died when he was fourteen, and his family was unable to afford university fees. After Clarke finished his studies at Huish's Grammar School, Taunton, he moved to London and took a job as a civil servant, in the British Exchequer and Audit Department. During World War II he served in the Royal Air Force as a radar specialist and instructor and worked on the early warning radar defense system that helped the RAF win the Battle of Britain. Following the war, Clarke entered King's College, London, and earned a BSc, with first-class honors, in physics and mathematics.

Clarke had first started writing SF while he was at school in Taunton; upon his arrival in London, he found like-minded souls as a member of the British Interplanetary Society—for many years his flat was its meeting place—and sold his first SF story in

1937. He continued to write short fiction throughout the war, and his first novels began to appear in 1951. *The Encyclopedia of Science Fiction* (1999) describes Clarke's early fiction as "optimistic propaganda for science." This all changed with his short story "The Sentinel" (1948), which became the basis of the classic movie *2001: A Space Odyssey*, written with director Stanley Kubrick. (Clarke and Kubrick shared an Oscar nomination for best screenplay.) While retaining the optimism and the love of pure science, "The Sentinel" marked a point when Clarke's fiction began to contemplate the possibilities that might await humankind in space. In novels such as *Childhood's End* and *Rendezvous with Rama*, science enables humans to take not only a physical journey to the stars, but also a transcendent journey of the spirit.

By 1952 Arthur C. Clarke was a professional writer: he was an assistant editor of the journal *Physics Abstracts* and had two novels and many short stories published. But he wanted to devote himself more wholeheartedly to his writing. Clarke took a personal leap of faith and moved to Sri Lanka (then known as Ceylon), where he could live cheaply and write full time, as well as indulge his interest in diving and underwater exploration. Sri Lanka eventually became his real *and* spiritual home, where he wrote, pioneered diving and underwater tourism, and played an active role as a public intellectual and a patron of art, science, and higher education. Clarke was also in great demand as a commentator on science and technology—for young people growing up in the 1970s and afterward, he was the popular face of science and "The Future." In 1969 Arthur C. Clarke sat side-by-side with Walter Cronkite on CBS television to cover the Apollo moon landings; from 1980 to 1994 he hosted three popular TV series—*Mysterious World*, *Strange Powers*, and *Mysterious Universe*—which were seen by tens of millions around the world.

Arthur C. Clarke was named Sri Lanka's first Resident Guest in 1975, but he remained a British citizen, and in 1998 he was knighted by HM Queen Elizabeth II for services to literature. In addition to the many SF awards for individual books and stories and his lifetime achievements, Sir Arthur also received many honorary doctorates, awards, and fellowships from literary, scientific, and academic bodies worldwide. He held senior positions with the H. G. Wells Society, the Institute for Cooperation in Space, and the National Space Society, as well as being a Distinguished Supporter of the British Humanist Association. He was chancellor of Sri Lanka's University of Moratuwa from 1979 to 2002, and in 2005 the Sri Lankan government presented him the country's highest civilian honor, *Sri Lankabhimanya* (The Pride of Sri Lanka), for his contributions to science and technology and his services to his adopted homeland.

Sir Arthur C. Clarke died on March 19, 2008, at his home near Colombo. At the time of his death he was, quite simply, the world's best known writer of science fiction, with a literary career spanning six decades, 100 books, and more than 1,000 short stories, including nonfiction on space travel, communication technologies, underwater exploration, and future studies. In addition to the knighthood, the honorary doctorates, the prizes, and the prestigious committees, there were other honors, too: quirkier honors, and perhaps even more fitting for the author who inspired other authors, the thinker and dreamer who inspired real-life discovery. In 1996 the International Astronomical Union named asteroid No. 4923 in his honor; in 2003 scientists at the University of Monash, Australia, named a newly discovered dinosaur species *Serendipaceratops arthurcclarkei*. Closer to home, there was his pioneering work on the use of geostationary satellites as telecommunications relays, which revolutionized worldwide communication. He never patented the idea and derived no financial benefit from his invention. But today, a geostationary orbit is known as a "Clarke" orbit.

Awards

SFWA Grand Master (1986)
Science Fiction Hall of Fame (1997)
Robert A. Heinlein Award (2004)

Novels

Rendezvous with Rama (1973) **BSF, Campbell Memorial, Hugo, Nebula, and Locus Poll**
The Fountains of Paradise (1979) **Nebula & Hugo**

Short Fiction

"The Star" (1955) **Hugo**
"The Nine Billion Names of God" (1953) **Retro Hugo 2004**
"A Meeting with Medusa" (1971) **Nebula**

Nonfiction

Astounding Days: A Science Fictional Autobiography (1989) **Hugo**

Screenplay

2001: A Space Odyssey (1968) **Hugo**
2010: Odyssey Two (1984) **Hugo**

Works by the Author

Prelude to Space (1951)
Sands of Mars (1951)
Islands in the Sky (1952)
Childhood's End (1953)
Earthlight (1955)
The City and the Stars (1956; orig. *Against the Fall of Night*, 1948)
The Deep Range (1957)
A Fall of Moondust (1961)
Dolphin Island (1963)
Glide Path (1963)
Rendezvous with Rama (1973)
Imperial Earth (1975)
The Fountains of Paradise (1979)
The Songs of Distant Earth (1986)

Beyond the Fall of Night (1990, with Gregory Benford)
The Ghost from the Grand Banks (1990)
The Hammer of God (1993)
Richter 10 (1996, with Mike McQuay)
The Trigger (1999, with Michael P. Kube-McDowell)
The Last Theorem (2008, with Frederik Pohl)

The 2001 series

2001: A Space Odyssey (1968)
2010: Odyssey Two (1982)
2061: Odyssey Three (1987)
3001: The Final Odyssey (1997)

With Gentry Lee

Cradle (1988)
Rama II (1989)
The Garden of Rama (1991)
Rama Revealed (1993)

With Stephen Baxter

The Light of Other Days (2000)
Time's Eye (2003)
Sunstorm (2005)
Firstborn (2007)

Other Notable Short Fiction

"Loophole" (1946)
"Rescue Party" (1946)
"The Sentinal" (1951)
"Sunjammer" (1964)
"The Hammer of God" (1992)
"The Wire Continuum" (1998, with Stephen Baxter)

Collections

Expedition to Earth (1953)
Reach for Tomorrow (1956)
Tales from the White Hart (1957)
The Other Side of the Sky (1958)
Tales of Ten Worlds (1962)
The Nine Billion Names of God (1967)
Of Time and Stars (1972)

The Wind from the Sun (1972)
The Best of Arthur C. Clarke (1973)
The Sentinel (1983)
Tales From Planet Earth (1990)
More Than One Universe (1991)
The Collected Stories of Arthur C. Clarke (2001)

In Other Media

Sir Arthur C. Clarke: 90th Birthday Reflections. TVAE Asia Pacific, December 2007. http://www.tveap.org/index.php?q=0712art_transcript_02.php

2001: A Space Odyssey. Metro-Goldwyn-Mayer, 1968. Directed by Stanley Kubrick; screenplay by Clarke; starring Keir Dullea, Gary Lockwood, and Leonard Rossiter.

2010: Odyssey Two. Metro-Goldwyn-Mayer, 1984. Directed by Peter Hyams; starring Roy Scheider, John Lithgow, and Helen Mirren.

Nonfiction Books

Interplanetary Flight (1950)
The Exploration of Space (1951)
The Exploration of the Moon (1954, with R. A. Smith)
The Coast of Coral (1956)
The Making of a Moon (1957)
The Challenge of the Spaceship (1959)
The Challenge of the Sea (1960)
Profiles of the Future (1962)
The Treasure of the Great Reef (1964)
Man and Space (1964)
Voices from the Sky—Previews of the Coming Space Age (1965)
The Coming of the Space Age (1967)
The Promise of Space (1968)
The Lost Worlds of 2001 (1972)
Report on Planet Three and Other Speculations (1972)
Voice Across the Sea (1974)
The View from Serendip (1977)
Ascent to Orbit: A Scientific Autobiography: The Technical Writings of Arthur C. Clarke (1984)
The Odyssey File (1984, with Peter Hyams)
1984: Spring, A Choice of Futures (1984)
Astounding Days: A Science Fictional Autobiography (1989)
How the World Was One: Beyond the Global Village (1992)
By Space Possessed: Essays on the Exploration of Space (1993)

The Snows of Olympus: A Garden on Mars (1994)

Greetings, Carbon-Based Bipeds! Collected Essays, 1934–1998 (2000)

Articles and Essays

"New Communications Technologies and the Developing World." *Analog Science Fiction/Science Fact,* March 29, 1982.

"Presidents, Experts, and Asteroids." *Science Magazine,* June 5, 1998. American Association for the Advancement of Science. http://www.sciencemag.org/cgi/content/full/280/5369/1532

"Son of Dr. Strangelove." In *Turning Points: Essays on the Art of Science Fiction,* ed. Damon Knight, 277–84. New York: Harper & Row, 1977.

For Further Information

Official Web site: http://www.arthurcclarke.net/

The Arthur C. Clarke Foundation, September 2006. http://www.clarkefoundation.org/

BBC Radio. Interviews. October 3, 1975, and January 4, 1987. BBC Four. BBC.co.uk. http://www.bbc.co.uk/bbcfour/audiointerviews/profilepages/clarkea1.shtml

Cherry, Matt. "God, Science, and Delusion: A Chat with Arthur C. Clarke." *Free Inquiry,* February 13, 2004. Secular Humanism. http://www.secularhumanism.org/index.php?section=library&page=clarke_19_2

Clareson, Thomas D. "The Cosmic Loneliness of Arthur C. Clarke." In *Voices for the Future: Essays on Major Science Fiction Writers, Vol. 1,* ed. Thomas D. Clareson. Bowling Green, OH: Bowling Green University Popular Press, 1976. 216–37.

Couper, Heather. *Sir Arthur C. Clarke: The Science and the Fiction*. BBC Radio 4, October 5, 2005. BBC.co.uk. http://www.bbc.co.uk/radio4/science/arthurcclarke.shtml

Harding, Luke. "The Space Odysseus." *The Guardian Online,* September 28, 2000. http://www.guardian.co.uk/books/2000/sep/28/sciencefictionfantasyandhorror.arthurcclarke

McAleer, Neil. *Arthur C. Clarke: The Authorized Biography*. Chicago: Contemporary, 1992.

Rabkin, Eric S. *Arthur C. Clarke*: *Starmont Reader's Guide 1.* West Linn, OR: Starmont, 1979.

Reid, Robin Anne. *Arthur C. Clarke: A Critical Companion*. Westport, CT: Greenwood, 1997.

Zebrowski, George. "Arthur C. Clarke." In *St. James Guide to Science Fiction Writers,* ed. Jay Pedersen. Detroit: St. James, 1996.

Samuel R. Delany

New Wave; Space Opera

Benchmark Title: *Babel-17* (1966)

b. 1942 (Harlem, New York)

> *Well, if one of us were to ask a New Yorker of a few centuries hence, 'How did you solve the problem of race hostility and gender oppression?' I'm pretty sure the answer will be much the same: 'We finally realized there weren't any such things as races or genders either."*
> —"Future Shock" (1999)

About the Author and the Author's Writing

In his 1988 memoir *The Motion of Light in Water*, Samuel R. Delany described himself, simply, as, "A black man. A gay man. A writer." Multitudes are contained in those eight words: Delany's work reflects the way science fiction has changed, presenting "a view of the world counter to the heroic individualism at the center of so much science fiction adventure" (Steiner 2004). His life story, and the story of his family, echoes the sea changes that have occurred, over the past 150 years, in American society itself.

Samuel Ray Delany Jr. was born in Harlem, New York. His mother was a librarian, his father the owner of the Levy & Delany Funeral Home, a successful Harlem business, a landmark that appears in stories by Langston Hughes and other writers of the Harlem Renaissance. Delany's grandfather, The Right Reverend Henry Beard Delany, vice principal of St. Augustine's College in Raleigh, North Carolina, was born in slavery in Georgia and ended his life as the Suffragan Bishop of the Archdiocese of North and South Carolina, the first African American elected an Episcopalian bishop. This summary of necessity skims over his maternal grandfather, chief red cap at Grand Central Terminal in New York, who was a friend of poet and novelist Paul Laurence Dunbar and polar explorer Matthew Hanson. It neglects to mention his paternal aunts, teachers who became published authors for the first time at the ages of 99 and 103. It regretfully sidelines the apocryphal family tale of the maternal great-grandmother who, as a child of eight and a slave, poisoned her cruel master to avoid another beating.

> But, along with another family lynching story from his father's family that he made use of in both his fiction (*Atlantis: Model 1924*) and his non-fiction ("The Semiology of Silence"), these were among the tales that came to Samuel Junior as part of his black heritage. (Steiner 2004)

Samuel Delany was a gifted child, attending The Dalton School, a prep school on Manhattan's Upper East Side, and the Bronx High School of Science. He was an excellent student in most subjects, but struggled with writing and spelling, due to what was later diagnosed as dyslexia. At summer camp one year he chose the nickname "Chip" for himself, and has been "Chip" to family, friends, and fans ever since. He attended City College in New York (now known as The City University of New York) for one year, but shortly after the death of his father in 1960, he left—at age eighteen—to write. He also married; his wife, the poet Marilyn Hacker, who was also eighteen, was working as an editorial assistant at Ace paperbacks, and she was in a position to bring her young husband's manuscript to the attention of an editor, saying she had found it in the slush pile. In December 1962, when he was just twenty, Ace Books published his first book, *The Jewels of Aptor*.

Delany has written extensively about his life and experiences in memoirs such as *The Motion of Light in Water*, in essays about New York life, in interviews such as the ones collected in *Silent Interviews*, and in his mainstream fiction. His science fiction is a potent blend of the conventions of space opera with well-turned phrases and provocative ideas, a lively combination of those conventions with "linguistic theory, female starship commanders, sexual triads, sword-wielding Orphic avatars, artist-criminals, pop culture, and the emotional complexities of sadomasochism" (Davis 2002). In her foreword to the 1996 revised edition of *Trouble on Triton*, the experimental novelist Kathy Acker described his fiction as "a conversation between you and Samuel Delany about the possibilities of being human."

His stories reflect a deep-seated belief that language affects our perception of reality: a recurrent motif is the poet or writer who undertakes a perilous quest or fantastic voyage. Another recurring feature is the role of "marginalized characters, people outside society's mainstream, such as slaves or those who have been biologically modified (through tattooing or piercing, for example)" (Boon and Gramlich 1981).

Stars in My Pocket Like Grains of Sand (1984), was Delany's last SF work (although "Future Shock" was an intriguing story-cum-essay on New York in the year 3000, written for the *Village Voice* on the eve of the millennium); since then he has written some pure fantasy, such as the Nevèrÿon series and *They Fly at Çiron* (1993). But on the whole, Delany has concentrated on his critical writing, and mainstream fiction, which is increasingly mined from his own personal experience: nonfiction such as *Times Square Red, Times Square Blue* (2001), and *1984* (2000); the semiautobiographical novel *Dark Reflections* (2007); and extreme erotica such as *Hogg* (1995). Over the years Delany has also held various academic positions. In January 2000 he joined the faculty in the English Department at the State University of New York at Buffalo, and since January 2001 he has been a professor of English and creative writing at Temple University in Philadelphia. He and his wife, Marilyn Hacker, were divorced in 1980; they are the parents of a daughter, Iva, born in 1972.

Samuel Delany is a black man, and a gay man, and as such he has brought fascinating —and difficult—new perceptions to the art of SF. As he said in "The Necessity of Tomorrows," a talk he gave at the Studio Museum of Harlem in November 1978, "We need images of tomorrow, and our people need them more than most." Fortunately for us, Samuel Delany is also a writer, and as readers, we are all his people. "[H]e freshens our eyes for what we had always accepted as familiar" (Dornemann and Lorberer 2000).

Awards

Science Fiction Research Association Pilgrim Award (1985)
Science Fiction Hall of Fame (2002)
Lambda Lifetime Award (1992) and Pioneer Award (2005)

Novels

Babel-17 (1966) **Nebula**
The Einstein Intersection (1967) **Nebula**

Short Fiction

"Aye, and Gomorrah" (1971) **Nebula**
"Time Considered as a Helix of Semi-Precious Stones" (1968) **Hugo, Nebula**

Nonfiction

The Motion of Light in Water: East Village Sex and Science Fiction Writing: 1960–65 (1988) **Hugo**

 ## Works by the Author

The Jewels of Aptor (1962)
Empire Star (1966)
Babel-17 (1966)
The Einstein Intersection (1967)
Nova (1968)
Dhalgren (1975)
Triton (1976; aka *Trouble on Triton*)
Empire (1978; with Howard Chaykin)
Stars in My Pocket Like Grains of Sand (1984)

The Fall of the Towers

Captives of the Flame (1963; aka *Out of the Dead City*)
The Towers of Toron (1964)
City of a Thousand Suns (1965)

Notable Mainstream and Other Genre Fiction

They Fly at Çiron (1993)
Equinox (1994; aka *Tides of Lust*)
The Mad Man (1994)
Hogg (1995)
Dark Reflections (2007)

The Nevèrÿon series

Tales of Nevèrÿon (1979)
Nevèrÿona (1983)
Flight from Nevèrÿon (1985)
The Bridge of Lost Desire (1987)

Other Notable Short Fiction

"The Ballad of Beta-2" (1965)
"Driftglass" (1967)
"The Star-Pit" (1967)
"We, in Some Strange Power's Employ, Move on a Rigorous Line" (1968; aka "Lines of Power")
"Aye, and Gomorrah" (1971)
"Time Considered as a Helix of Semi-Precious Stones" (1968)
"Prismatica" (1977)
"The Tale of Gorgik" (1979)
"The Tale of Rumor and Desire" (1987)

Collections

Driftglass: Ten Tales of Speculative Fiction (1971)
Distant Stars (1981)
The Complete Nebula Award-Winning Fiction (1983)
Driftglass/Starshards (1993)
Atlantis: Three Tales (1995)
Aye, and Gomorrah, and Other Stories (2003)
The Fall of the Towers (2004)

In Other Media

"The Star Pit." *The Mind's Eye Theater* (November 1967). WBAI-FM. With "Notes on 'The Star Pit," by Delany. http://www.pseudopodium.org/repress/TheStarPit/index.html

Nonfiction Books

The Jewel-Hinged Jaw: Notes on the Language of Science Fiction (1977)
Heavenly Breakfast: An Essay on The Winter of Love (1979)
Starboard Wine: More Notes on the Language of Science Fiction (1984)
The Motion of Light in Water: East Village Sex and Science Fiction Writing: 1960–65 (1988)
Silent Interviews: On Language, Race, Sex, Science Fiction, and Some Comics: A Collection of Written Interviews (1994)
Shorter Views: Queer Thoughts & the Politics of the Paraliterary (1999)

1984 (2000)

Times Square Red, Times Square Blue (2001)

About Writing: Seven Essays, Four Letters and Five Interviews (2006)

Articles and Essays

"Future Shock." *The Village Voice,* December 29, 1999. Village Voice Media Holdings. http://www.villagevoice.com/news/9952,delany,11385,1.html

"The Gestation of Genres: Literature, Fiction, Romance, Science Fiction, Fantasy." In *Intersections: Fantasy and Science Fiction,* ed. George E. Slusser and Eric S. Rabkin, 63–73. Carbondale: Southern Illinois University Press, 1987.

"The Necessity of Tomorrows." In *Starboard Wine: More Notes on the Language of Science Fiction,* 23–35. Pleasantville, NY: Dragon Press, 1984 (orig. pub. 1978).

"Orders of Chaos: The Science Fiction of Joanna Russ." In *Women Worldwalkers: New Dimensions of Science Fiction and Fantasy,* ed. Jane Branham Weedman, 95–124. Lubbock: Texas Tech University Press, 1985.

"Racism and Science Fiction." In *Dark Matter: A Century of Speculative Fiction from the African Diaspora,* ed. Sheree R. Thomas, 383–97. New York: Warner/Aspect, 2000.

"Science Fiction and 'Literature'—or, The Conscience of the King" and "Some Presumptuous Approaches to Science Fiction." In *Speculations on Speculation: Theories of Science Fiction,* ed. James Gunn and Matthew Candelaria, 95–118 and 289–300. Lanham, MD: Scarecrow, 2005.

For Further Information

Acker, Kathy. "Foreword: On Delany the Magician." In *Trouble on Triton: An Ambiguous Heterotopias,* rev. ed., by Samuel R. Delany. Middletown, CT: Wesleyan University Press, 1996.

Boon, Jo-Ellen Lipman, and Charles A. Gramlich. "Samuel R. Delany." In *Critical Survey of Short Fiction*, 2nd ed., ed. Frank N. Magill. Englewood Cliffs, NJ: Salem, 1981.

Davis, Ray. "Samuel Delany." In *Salon.com Reader's Guide to Contemporary Authors*. Bellona Times, 2002. http://www.pseudopodium.org/ht-20020401.html

Dornemann, Rudi, and Eric Lorberer. "A Silent Interview with Samuel R. Delany." *RainTaxi Review of Books* (November 2000). http://www.raintaxi.com/online/2000winter/delany.shtml

"Interview with Samuel Delany" (Audio). *The Paula Gordon Show*. Atlanta: WGUN, May 23, 2001. http://www.paulagordon.com/shows/delany/

Lunde, David. "Black Man/Gay Man/Writer . . . Prodigy: The Quest for Identity in Delany's Early Work." *The Review of Contemporary Fiction* 16, no. 3 (1996): 116–24.

Means, Loren. "Interview with Samuel R. Delany." *YLEM Journal* 24, no. 4 (2004): 8–11. http://www.ylem.org/Journal/2004Iss04vol24.pdf

Miller, Anthony. "Dangerous Visionary: Samuel R. Delany." *LA Weekly,* May 15, 2003. http://www.laweekly.com/2003-05-15/art-books/dangerous-visionary

Norvell, Forrest L., ed. *Starshards, a Samuel R. Delany Website.* December 2005. http://www.starshards.org/old-index.html

Philmus, Robert M. "On *Triton* and Other Matters: An Interview with Samuel R. Delany." *Science Fiction Studies* 17, no. 3 (November 1990). http://www.depauw.edu/sfs/interviews/delany52interview.htm

Rutledge, Gregory E. "Science Fiction and the Black Power/Arts Movement: The Transpositional Cosmology of Samuel R. Delany Jr." *Extrapolation* 41 (2000): 127–42.

Sallis, James, ed. *Ash of Stars: On the Writing of Samuel R. Delany.* Jackson: University Press of Mississippi, 1996.

Schuster, Jay, ed. *Samuel R. Delany Information.* The Physician's Computer Company, September 2001. http://www2.pcc.com/staff/jay/delany/

Slusser, George Edgar. *The Delany Intersection: Samuel R. Delany Considered as a Writer of Semi-Precious Words.* San Bernardino, CA: Borgo, 1977.

———. "Samuel R. Delany." In *St. James Guide to Science Fiction Writers,* ed. Jay Pedersen. Detroit, MI: St. James, 1996.

Special Samuel Delany Issue. *Review of Contemporary Fiction* 16 (Fall 1996).

Steiner, K. Leslie. "Samuel R. Delany." *Pseudopodium* (2004). http://www.pseudopodium.org/repress/KLeslieSteiner-SamuelRDelany.html

Tucker, Jeffrey Allen. *A Sense of Wonder: Samuel R. Delany, Race, Identity, and Difference.* Middletown, CT: Wesleyan University Press, 2004.

———. "Studying the Works of Samuel R. Delany." *Ohio University College of Arts and Sciences Forum* 15 (Spring 1998). http://wiredforbooks.org/scifi/delany.htm

Philip K. Dick

Humor and Satire; Near Future

Benchmark Title:
The Man in the High Castle (1962)

b. 1928 (Chicago, Illinois);
d. 1982 (Santa Ana, California)

I love SF. I love to read it; I love to write it. The SF writer sees not just possibilities but wild possibilities. It's not just "What if"—it's "My God; what if"—in frenzy and hysteria. The Martians are always coming.
—Introduction, *The Golden Man* (1980)

Photo credit: Anne Dick.
Courtesy of the Philip K. Dick Trust.

About the Author and the Author's Writing

When Philip K. Dick died of a stroke in 1982, at the age of fifty-three, his father took his ashes to Fort Morgan, Colorado, and buried them next to his twin sister Jane, who had died in 1929 as a six-week-old baby. Their headstone (which can be seen on his official Web site) is engraved on one side with Jane's name and the dates of her birth and death, and on the other with Dick's. He may not have known that this is where he would be laid to rest—by the time of his death he had been married five times and was the father of three children; he was a published author who had acquired a passionate and knowledgeable fan base. There was, you might say, a lot of water under the bridge. But whatever happened, whatever success he achieved, whatever difficulties he struggled with, there may have been a part of Dick that knew that Jane was there, waiting for him. All his life, he may have known exactly where he would one day be: next to his lost sister.

Philip Kindred Dick was born six weeks premature, in a freezing Chicago winter. Later, when he was old enough to take it all desperately to heart, but still too young to understand, his mother—from guilt, perhaps—told him all the terrible details: the two tiny babies, the young, inexperienced mother, the incompetent doctor. The infant Philip was saved, with hours to spare, when a visiting nurse had the babies rushed to the hospital for intravenous feeding; his sister died in the ambulance. Dick never forgot, and he never forgave his mother. Or perhaps he never forgave himself for surviving. "She fights for her life & I for hers, eternally. . . . My sister is everything to me. I am damned always to be separated from her/& with her, in an oscillation" (Introduction, *Four Novels of the 1960s*).

It is in that oscillation that Philip K. Dick found the narrative dynamic that powered some of his greatest SF works: the juxtaposition of what is real and what is not, and the shock when, like a character in one of his novels of "social satire and metaphysical uncertainty" (Bosky and Hlavaty 1996), we realize that we have not been told the whole story. In *Do Androids Dream of Electric Sheep* (1968), people have to take tests to prove that they "feel" deeply enough to be a real human, rather than android; people dial up emotions as if they were toasting their morning bagels and live their lives through 24/7 reality TV programs. According to *The Encyclopedia of Science Fiction* (199), if SF is the literature of "what if," then Dick's fears are "our own, spoken as we could not have spoken them."

Shortly after the death of his baby sister, the Dick family moved to San Francisco. His parents' marriage ended when he was five; except for two years in Washington, D.C., Dick lived in California for the rest of his life. He attended Berkeley High School. (One of his classmates was Ursula K. Le Guin, although they appear not to have encountered each other.) He registered at the University of California, Berkeley, but swiftly dropped out rather than participate in the then-mandatory ROTC. From 1948 to 1952 he worked in a record store. In 1952 Dick sold his first story, and from that point on, regardless of the financial insecurity it brought him, he was a professional writer.

Dick kept up a fearsome pace: seven of his stories appeared in one month in 1953. He had sixteen SF novels published between 1959 and 1964. He was desperate to be acknowledged as a mainstream author, but only one of his mainstream novels, *Confessions of a Crap Artist*, was published during his lifetime. He struggled with the poverty and uncertainty that many freelance writers know. On February 20, 1974, as he was recovering from the effects of surgery on an impacted wisdom tooth, he began to experience strange visions. "I experienced an invasion of my mind by a transcendentally rational mind, as if I had been insane all my life and suddenly I had become sane" (Platt 1980).

In spite of the fact that he was on heavy prescription medication when the symptoms began, and he had indulged in a certain amount of recreational drug-taking in the years prior to that, he was convinced that he had had a transcendent experience. Four semiautobiographical novels resulted from this experience, including *Valis* (1981), but the dark side was that, for the rest of his life, Dick suffered from paranoid delusions, imagining plots and break-ins by the FBI and the KGB. He wrote long, rambling letters to the FBI, 'informing' on other SF writers such as Stanislaw Lem and Thomas M. Disch. He died on March 2, 1982, the result of a combination of recurrent strokes accompanied by heart failure.

"Philip Dick does not lead his critics an easy life, since he does not so much play the part of a guide through his phantasmagoric worlds as give the impression of one lost in their labyrinth" (Lem 1986). Although he was not exactly neglected during his lifetime—he was, after all the recipient of a Hugo in 1963 for *The Man in the High Castle*, and in 1973 he placed twelfth in the *Locus Poll* for All-Time Favorite Author—it was after his untimely death that his reputation, as one might say, went platinum. Reams of academic paper have been devoted to careful consideration of his thirty-six novels and more than 100 short stories. While most academics and fans would probably agree that Dick has "written some of the best SF novels and some of the worst" (Bosky and Hlavaty 1996), they would probably disagree with his own, much harsher 1966 judgment in 1966: "I have written and sold 23 novels, and all are terrible except one. But I am not sure which one" ("Will the Atomic Bomb..."). And the writer who wanted to be taken seriously has, through the magic of science fiction, been given the ultimate accolade—he has entered the vocabulary. All very Dickian.

Awards

SF Hall of Fame (2005, posthumous)

Novels

The Man in the High Castle (1962) **Hugo**
Flow My Tears, the Policeman Said (1974) **Campbell Memorial**
A Scanner Darkly (1977) **BSF**

Works by the Author

Solar Lottery (1955; aka *World of Chance*)
The World Jones Made (1956)
The Man Who Japed (1956)
The Cosmic Puppets (1957; aka *A Glass of Darkness*)
Eye in the Sky (1957)
Time out of Joint (1959)
Dr. Futurity (1960)
Vulcan's Hammer (1960)
The Man in the High Castle (1962)
The Game-Players of Titan (1963)
Clans of the Alphane Moon (1964)
Martian Time-Slip (1964)
The Penultimate Truth (1964)
The Simulacra (1964)
The Three Stigmata of Palmer Eldritch (1964)
The Unteleported Man (1964; aka *Lies, Inc.*)
Dr. Bloodmoney: Or, How We Got Along After the Bomb (1965)
The Crack in Space (1966)
Now Wait for Last Year (1966)
Counter-Clock World (1967)
The Ganymede Takeover (1967, with Ray Nelson)
The Zap Gun (1967; aka *Operation Plowshare*)
Do Androids Dream of Electric Sheep? (1968)
Galactic Pot-Healer (1969)
Ubik (1969)
A Maze of Death (1970)
Our Friends from Frolix 8 (1970)

We Can Build You (1972)
Flow My Tears, the Policeman Said (1974)
Deus Irae (1976, with Roger Zelazny)
A Scanner Darkly (1977)
The Transmigration of Timothy Archer (1982)
Radio Free Albemuth (1985)

VALIS

Valis (1981)
The Divine Invasion (1981)

Notable Short Fiction

"Second Variety" (1953)
"The Minority Report" (1956)
"We Can Remember It for You Wholesale" (1966)
"Your Appointment Will Be Yesterday" (1966)
"Faith of Our Fathers" (1967)
"A Little Something for Us Tempunauts" (1974)

Collections

The Golden Man (1980)
The Collected Stories of Philip K. Dick
    Minority Report (1998)
    Second Variety (1998) (introduction by John Brunner)
    We Can Remember It For You Wholesale (1998)
    The Eye of the Sibyl and Other Classic Stories (2000)
    The Short Happy Life of the Brown Oxford (2002) (introduction by Roger Zelazny)
The Minority Report: 18 Classic Stories (2000)
The Philip K. Dick Reader (2001)
Selected Stories of Philip K. Dick (2002) (introduction by Jonathan Lethem)
Four Novels of the 1960s (2007) (edited by Jonathan Lethem)

In Other Media

Blade Runner. The Ladd Company, 1982. Directed by Ridley Scott; starring Harrison Ford and Rutger Hauer. Based loosely on *Do Androids Dream of Electric Sheep?* (1968), this is probably the greatest SF film ever made.

Total Recall. Carolco International N.V., 1990. Directed by Paul Verhoeven; starring Arnold Schwarzenegger and Sharon Stone. Based on the 1966 short story "We Can Remember It for You Wholesale."

Screamers. Allegro Films, 1995. Directed by Christian Duguay; screenplay by Dan O'Bannon; starring Peter Weller. Based on the 1953 short story "Second Variety."

Minority Report. DreamWorks SKG, 2002. Directed by Steven Spielberg; starring Tom Cruise and Samantha Morton. Based on the 1956 story of the same name.

Paycheck. DreamWorks SKG, 2003. Directed by John Woo; starring Ben Affleck and Uma Thurman. Based on the 1953 short story of the same name.

A Scanner Darkly. Warner Independent Pictures (WIP), 2006. Directed by Richard Linklater; starring Robert Downey Jr. and Keanu Reeves. Based on the 1977 novel.

Next. IEG Virtual Studios, 2007. Directed by Lee Tamahori; starring Nicholas Cage and Julianne Moore. Based on the 1954 short story "The Golden Man."

Productions are proposed or in progress for adaptations of the Dick stories "King of the Elves" (1953) and "The Adjustment Bureau" (1954), as well as the last novel published during his lifetime, *Radio Free Albemuth* (1985). In addition, work has started on *The Owl in Daylight*, a film based on Dick's own life, using story ideas left unpublished at the time of his death, which will star Paul Giamatti as Philip K. Dick.

Nonfiction Books

The Dark-Haired Girl (1988)

In Pursuit of VALIS (1991)

The Shifting Realities of Philip K. Dick: Selected Literary and Philosophical Writings (1995, ed. Lawrence Sutin). Includes "Will the Atomic Bomb Ever Be Perfected, and If So What Will Become of Robert Heinlein?" (1966) and other autobiographical and critical short pieces.

The Selected Letters of Philip K. Dick 1980–82 (1998)

What If Our World Is Their Heaven? The Final Conversations of Philip K. Dick (2001, ed. Gwen Lee and Doris Elaine Sauter)

Articles and Essays

"The Android and the Human." In *Science Fiction at Large: A Collection of Essays, By Various Hands, About the Interface between Science Fiction and Reality*, ed. Peter Nicholls, 199–224. London: Gollancz, 1976.

"Foreword to *The Preserving Machine*." (Unpublished) *Science Fiction Studies* 2, no.1 (1975): 22–24. http://www.depauw.edu/sfs/backissues/5/dick5art.htm

"Man, Android, and Machine" (Lecture delivered at London's Institute of Contemporary Art). In *Science Fiction at Large*, ed. Peter Nicholls. London: Gollancz, 1976.

Bibliographies

Butler, Andrew M., Salvatore Proietti, and Umberto Rossi, eds. *VALBS: Vast Active Living Bibliographic System, or Secondary Texts on PKD*. February 2004. http://web.tiscali.it/ausonia/

Willick, George C. "SF Bibliography." *Spacelight* (June 2006). http://www.gcwillick.com/Spacelight/dick.html

For Further Information

Official Web site: http://www.philipkdick.com/

Bosky, Bernadette Lynne, and Arthur D. Hlavaty. "Philip K. Dick." In *St. James Guide to Science Fiction Writers,* ed. Jay Pedersen. Detroit, MI: St. James, 1996.

Butler, Andrew M. *Philip K. Dick.* London: Trafalgar Square/Pocket Essentials UK, 2001.

Carrere, Emmanuel. *I Am Alive and You Are Dead: A Journey into the Mind of PKD.* Trans. Timothy Bent. New York: Henry Holt, 2004.

Corliss, Richard. "That Old Feeling: You Know Dick." *Time on Entertainment,* January 12, 2004. http://www.time.com/time/columnist/corliss/article/0,9565,575667-2,00.html

Dick, Anne R. *Search for Philip K. Dick, 1928–1982: A Memoir and Biography of the Science Fiction Writer.* Lewiston, NY: Edwin Mellen, 1995.

Enns, Anthony. "Media, Drugs, and Schizophrenia in the Works of Philip K. Dick." *Science Fiction Studies* 33 (2006): 68–88.

Jameson, Frederic. "Philip K. Dick." In *Archaeologies of the Future,* 345–83. New York: Verso, 2005.

Kaveney, Roz. "A Profile of Philip K. Dick." *Glamourous Rags,* January 23, 2006. http://glamourousrags.dymphna.net/philipkdick.html

Le Guin, Ursula K. "Science Fiction as Prophecy: Philip K. Dick." *The New Republic,* October 30, 1976. 34+.

Lem, Stanislaw. "Philip K. Dick: A Visionary amongst Charlatans." In *Microworlds,* 106–35. San Diego: Harvest/Harcourt Brace, 1986.

Mackey, Douglas A. *Philip K. Dick.* Boston: Twayne, 1988.

Mullen, R. D., et al., eds. *On Philip K. Dick: 40 Articles from Science-Fiction Studies.* Terre Haute, IN: SF-TH, 1992. Table of Contents: http://www.depauw.edu/sfs/PKD-book.htm. This collection contains a variety of interesting PKD essays and reviews from before 1992. Abstracts are available for all essays, and some of the texts are available in full online.

Palmer, Christopher, *Philip K. Dick: Exhilaration and Terror of the Postmodern.* Liverpool: Liverpool University Press, 2003.

Platt, Charles. Interview. In *Dream Makers: The Uncommon People Who Write Science Fiction.* New York: Berkley Publishing, 1980.

Sutin, Lawrence. *Divine Invasions: A Life of Philip K. Dick.* New York: Carroll & Graf, 2005 (orig. pub. 1989).

Thomas M. Disch

Apocalyptic SF; Near Future; New Wave

Benchmark Title:
Camp Concentration (1968)

b. 1940 (Des Moines, Iowa);
d. 2008 (New York)

It seemed to me to be perfectly natural to say, let's be honest, the real interest in this kind of story is to see some devastating cataclysm wipe mankind out. There's a grandeur in that idea that all the other people threw away and trivialized.

—Platt, "Thomas M. Disch," in *Dream Makers* (1980)

Photo credit: Beth Gwinn

About the Author and the Author's Writing

Thomas Michael Disch was born in Des Moines, Iowa, and grew up in Minneapolis. He was raised a Catholic; as a young man he attended a military academy run by the Christian Brothers, a religious order notorious in Ireland and the United States for their aggressive discipline. At eighteen he enlisted in the army, but before long he was committed to "psychiatric incarceration" and hustled out with a medical discharge. No explanation was given, but the likeliest guess is that his homosexuality, at a time when it was still classified as a mental illness, brought an end to his military career.

Disch moved to New York City. He attended, but did not graduate from, Cooper Union and New York University, and he had a number of "holding pattern" jobs: in offices and bookstores, on the nightshift for a newspaper, in a mortuary, with a life insurance company, and even as an extra in productions at the Metropolitan Opera. As soon as he sold his first story—"The Double Timer," in 1962—Disch lived on his income from his writing for the rest of his life. And he wrote almost anything: essays on literature and popular culture, book reviews, and books of criticism (for some years, he was theater critic for *The Nation* and the *New York Daily News*). As "Tom Disch" he was a well-respected poet. He wrote a number of children's books, including *The Brave Little Toaster: A Bedtime Story for Small Appliances* (1980), which was filmed by Disney. He taught at Wesleyan University, the University of Minnesota, and the Johns Hopkins Writing Seminars, and in the mid-1990s he was Artist-in-Residence at the College of William and Mary.

Thomas Disch never spared the feelings of the reader or the genre of science fiction. In a Disch novel, the alien invaders win, the price of understanding is death, and ordinary people treat each other no better than the aliens do. Much of his early short fiction was published first in *New Worlds*, the London-based magazine edited by Michael Moorcock, and his place is firmly among the writers of the New Wave, both British and American, who were steering SF away from "the Golden Age's blind faith in technology and science, towards a darker and more introspective focus on people and their problematic relationship to the technology they have created" (Miller 2008). His portrait of life in a desolate near-future New York, *334* (1972), is demanding but extremely moving. In *Camp Concentration* (1968), perhaps reminiscent of his experience with the army, political prisoners in a near-future United States are injected with a form of syphilis that is intended to make them geniuses—and which, within nine months, will make them dead. During the 1980s Disch moved away from SF. He was already writing a gothic romance, *Clara Reeve* (1975), under the name Leonie Hargrave; he had begun the "Supernatural Minnesota" sequence of metaphysical horror tales with the novel *The Businessman* (1984). His criticism—art, poetry, and theater—was assembled in two volumes, *The Castle of Indolence* (1995) and *The Castle of Perseverance* (2002). He also designed a computer game called *Amnesia* (1986).

Disch could be a difficult character. His reviews could be excoriating. (After a particularly acid review about a much-loved icon of SF, *The New York Times* dropped him as a reviewer.) In 1975, in an essay called "The Embarrassments of Science Fiction," Disch earned the eternal enmity of Robert A. Heinlein, and his entire fan base, by (as he himself put it) "outing *Starship Troopers* as a gay porn fantasy" (Miller 2008). When respected SF writer and critic Algis Budrys died in 2008—he and Disch had a long-standing feud—Disch reported the fact gleefully on his blog. He had a long-running, beyond the grave feud with Philip K. Dick, who wrote the FBI one of his conspiracy-theory letters about Disch (a distinction Disch shared with Stanislaw Lem), claiming that *Camp Concentration* contained illicit coded messages. (Interestingly, at the end of his life, Disch appears to have almost forgiven Dick: in his final novel, *The Word of God*, which appeared a few days before he died, Disch gave a fictionalized Dick the opportunity to go back in time and prevent the birth of one Thomas M. Disch.)

All this, and his extended self-exile from SF, had resulted in Disch feeling undervalued and excluded from the literary community that knew, and appreciated him, best. Then in 2005 his partner of over thirty years, Charles Naylor, died after a long and difficult illness; this left Disch severely depressed, suffering ill-health himself from the effects of sciatica and diabetes. Disch also faced difficult and expensive legal action to avoid being evicted from the apartment he had shared with Naylor. On July 4, 2008, depressed by grief and these personal problems, Thomas M. Disch took his own life.

His work strains at the boundaries of SF, and he made SF better for it.

Awards

Novels

On Wings of Song (1979) **Campbell Memorial**

Short Fiction
"The Brave Little Toaster" (1980) **BSF, Locus Poll**

Nonfiction
The Dreams Our Stuff Is Made Of (1998) **Hugo, Locus Poll**

Works by the Author
The Genocides (1965)
Mankind under the Leash (1966; aka *The Puppies of Terra*)
Echo Round His Bones (1967)
Camp Concentration (1968)
334 (1972)
On Wings of Song (1979)

Film Adaptations and Novelizations
The Prisoner (1969) (novel based on the cult 1960s TV series)
Alfred the Great (1969, as Victor Hastings)

Mainstream and Other Genre Fiction
The House That Fear Built (1966, as "Cassandra Knye," with John Sladek)
Black Alice (1968, as "Thom Demijohn," with John Sladek)
Clara Reeve (1975, as "Leonie Hargrave")
Neighboring Lives (1981, with Charles Naylor)
The Businessman: A Tale of Terror (1984)
The M.D.: A Horror Story (1991)
The Priest: A Gothic Romance (1994)
The Sub: A Study in Witchcraft (1999)
The Word of God (2008)

Other Notable Short Fiction
"Minnesota Gothic" (1964)
"102 H-Bombs" (1965)
"Come to Venus Melancholy" (1965)
"White Fang Goes Dingo" (1965)
"Casablanca" (1967)
"Fun with Your New Head" (1968). http://www.art.net/~hopkins/Don/text/head.html
"The Asian Shore" (1970)
"Et in Arcadia Ego" (1971)
"Angouleme" (1971)
"The Doomsday Machine" (1974)

"The Man Who Had No Idea" (1978)
"Understanding Human Behavior" (1981). http://www.strangehorizons.com/2001/20010730/human_behavior.shtml
"The Brave Little Toaster Goes to Mars" (1988)
"The Abduction of Bunny Steiner, or A Shameless Lie" (1992)
"The First Annual Performance Arts Festival at the Slaughter Rock Battlefield" (1998)

Collections

One Hundred and Two H-Bombs (1971)
Fun with Your New Head (1971; aka *Under Compulsion*)
White Fang Goes Dingo and Other Funny SF Stories (1971)
Getting into Death and Other Stories (1976)
The Early Science Fiction Stories of Thomas M. Disch (1977)
Fundamental Disch (1980) (introduction by Samuel R. Delany)
The Man Who Had No Idea (1982)
The Wall of America (2008)

Notable Poetry Collections

Yes, Let's: New and Selected Poems (1989)
Dark Verses & Light (1991)
About the Size of It (2007)
Winter Journey (forthcoming)

As Editor

The Ruins of Earth: An Anthology of Stories of the Immediate Future (1971)
Bad Moon Rising: An Anthology of Political Forebodings (1973)
The New Improved Sun: An Anthology of Utopian Fiction (1975)
New Constellations: An Anthology of Tomorrow's Mythologies (1976, with Charles Naylor)
Strangeness: A Collection of Curious Tales (1977, with Charles Naylor)

In Other Media

Amnesia. (1986). Text adventure computer game, written by Disch; created by Charles Kreitzberg's Cognetics Corporation.
The Brave Little Toaster (1987), *The Brave Little Toaster to the Rescue* (1997), and *The Brave Little Toaster Goes to Mars* (1998). Hyperion Pictures. Animated features with the voices of (among others), Deanna Oliver, DeForest Kelley, Jon Lovitz, Wayne Knight, Farrah Fawcett, Stephen Tobolowsky, and Alfre Woodard.
Can You Hear Me, Think Tank Two? Thought Crimes in Prose and Poetry (2001). Written and read by Disch; recorded and produced by David Garland.

Mecca|Mettle (2005). An audio anthology featuring works by Disch, BlöödHag, and Tim Kirk.

"Missing Hours." *Miami Vice.* (1987). An episode of the classic 1980s TV cop series, directed by Ate de Jong; starring Don Johnson, Philip Michael Thomas and Edward James Olmos.

Nonfiction Books

The Castle of Indolence: On Poetry, Poets, and Poetasters (1994)
The Dreams Our Stuff Is Made Of: How Science Fiction Conquered the World (1998)
The Castle of Perseverance: Job Opportunities in Contemporary Poetry (2002)
On SF (2005)

Articles and Essays

"The Embarrassments of Science Fiction." In *Science Fiction at Large: A Collection of Essays, By Various Hands, About the Interface between Science Fiction and Reality,* ed. Peter Nicholls, 139–56. London: Gollancz, 1976.

"Introduction." In *Solar Lottery,* by Philip K. Dick. Boston: Gregg, 1976.

"The Road to Heaven: Science Fiction and the Militarization of Space." *The Nation* 242 (May 10, 1986): 650–56.

Sermonettes. *Strange Horizons,* July 30, 2001. http://www.strangehorizons.com/2001/20010730/sermonettes.shtml

Bibliographies

Stephens, Christopher P. *A Checklist of Thomas M. Disch.* Hastings-on-Hudson, NY: Ultramarine 1992

For Further Information

Endzone. April 2006–July 2, 2008. Live journal. http://tomsdisch.livejournal.com/

Benford, Gregory. "The Stars My Consternation." *Reason* (August/September 1998). http://www.reason.com/news/show/30697.html

Clute, John. Obituary. *The Independent* (UK), July 10, 2008. http://www.independent.co.uk/news/obituaries/thomas-m-disch-poet-and-writer-of-death-haunted-science-fiction-who-won-plaudits-for-camp-concentration-863874.html.

Delany, Samuel R. *The American Shore: Meditations on a Tale of Science Fiction by Thomas M. Disch.* Elizabethtown, NY: Dragon Press, 1978.

Feeley, Gregory. "The Last Page of Thomas M. Disch." *SFRA Bulletin* (February –March 2009).

Hawtree, Christopher. Obituary. *Guardian Online,* July 9, 2008. http://books.guardian.co.uk/obituaries/story/0,,2289732,00.html

Heacox, Tom. "The Dish on Tom Disch." *Jump!* (Fall 1995). Posted at The College of William and Mary web site, February 29, 2004. http://web.wm.edu/so/jump/fall95/disch.html.

Henley, Jim. "The Child Knew Sin and the Snake Knew Love (Appreciation)." *Unqualified Offerings,* July 6, 2008. http://highclearing.com/index.php/archives/2008/07/06/8402

Horwich, David. Interview. *Strange Horizons,* July 30, 2001. http://www.strangehorizons.com/2001/20010730/interview.shtml

Miller, Sam J. "Who Killed Thomas M. Disch?" *Strange Horizons,* September 22, 2008. http://www.strangehorizons.com/2008/20080922/miller-a.shtml

Moorcock, Michael. "The Wall of America by Thomas M Disch." *The Telegraph* (UK), November 26, 2008. http://www.telegraph.co.uk/culture/books/bookreviews/3563693/The-Wall-of-America-by-Thomas-M-Disch.html

Platt, Charles. "Thomas M. Disch." In *Dream Makers: The Uncommon People Who Write Science Fiction.* New York: Berkley, 1980.

Sladek, John T. "Four Reasons for Reading Thomas M. Disch." *SF Commentary* 77 (2001): 3–10. http://www.ansible-editions.co.uk/authors/sladek-disch.htm

"Thomas M. Disch: It's All Methane to Me." *Locus* (June 2001). http://www.locusmag.com/2001/Issue06/Disch.html

Wymer, T. L. "Naturalism, Aestheticism and Beyond: Tradition and Innovation in the Work of Thomas M. Disch." In *Voices for the Future, Vol. 3,* ed. T. D. Clareson, 186–219. Bowling Green, OH: Bowling Green University Popular Press, 1984.

Cory Doctorow

Humor and Satire; Near Future; Techno-thriller

Benchmark Title: *Down and Out in the Magic Kingdom* (2003)

b. 1971 (Toronto, Ontario, Canada)

I was raised by technologists. . . . Socialists are by nature techno-utopians—Marx was a techno-utopian—and my dad was completely captivated by Disney, which is a techno-utopia . . . So I grew up in this science-fiction-y utopia, with these science-fiction-y utopians, and it left an indelible mark on my psyche.

—Macdonald, Interview in *Strange Horizons* (2003)

Photo credit: Beth Gwinn

About the Author and the Author's Writing

Cory Doctorow was born in Toronto, Ontario, Canada, the son of technologists, educators, Trotskyite activists, and from the stories he tells in various interviews, very entertaining people. On long car trips from Toronto to visit grandparents in Florida, Doctorow's dad would re-work classic tales of Conan the Barbarian into socialist parables, in which the original, politically unenlightened, muscle-bound grunt and sword-wielder Conan was transmogrified into a gender- and racially balanced threesome called Harry, Larry, and Mary. As Doctorow recalled years later for *Locus* magazine, "he would retell these half-remembered 'Conan' stories but they would all turn into the proletariat casting off their shackles, killing the king, and forming soviets!"

Hardly surprising, then, that Cory Doctorow has not only grown up to be passionately involved, from an early age, in advocacy and activism for nuclear disarmament, radical ecology, and the free movement of ideas, but has also developed into an anarchic bard of modern technology and alternative society, brightly cognizant of the liberating possibilities of the most unlikely bastions of the Establishment, such as Disneyland, and impishly dedicated to a personal subgenre of "found" stories, in which characters, settings, and narratives are liberated from the original intentions of their creators.

Doctorow was "noticed" as an up-and-coming talent in the late 1990s, for early short stories such as "Craphound" (1998), and "At Lightspeed, Slowing" (2000), and he was awarded the John W. Campbell Award for Best New Writer in 2000. His 2002 story "0wnz0red" was nominated for the 2004 Nebula. His breakthrough novel, *Down and Out in the Magic Kingdom* (2003), for which he won the Locus Award for Best First Novel, is set in a high concept future world dominated by the Bitchun Society, which has eliminated want and poverty and developed life extension technology so commonplace that death is merely a minor inconvenience. The only wealth is respect, and the world economy runs on karma credits, or "Whuffie points," since constant internal interfaces allow everyone to monitor exactly how successful they are at being liked. Everyone is free to do exactly as they please. And what pleases protagonist Jules is to move to Disney World, to devote himself to the preservation of that Nirvana of twentieth-century art and culture. But dark forces are at work . . . .

In *Someone Comes to Town, Someone Leaves Town* (2005), Doctorow moved into the territory of fantasy and magic, in a story about a mysterious stranger on the Toronto hacker scene, whose father is a mountain and whose mother is a washing machine: "[I]t's a kind of family revenge/wireless networking/urban fantasy novel," he told *Locus* magazine in 2005. But in *Little Brother* (2008), set in a near future beset with obsessive surveillance, Doctorow returns to SF and blurs the lines between current and potential technologies, in a story with echoes of Orwellian warnings and narrative links to post-9/11 security policies. In recent years, perhaps in a nod to memories of his father's politically enhanced "Conan plus Harry, Larry and Mary" stories, Doctorow began to write a number of short stories that use the titles of great SF stories as starting points for riffs on the classics of SF. Some "doctorow-ized" stories are "Anda's Game" (2004), "i, robot" (2005), "I, Row-Boat" (2006), and a new take on Vernor Vinge's "True Names," written with Benjamin Rosenbaum in 2008.

> [M]y next one might be a "Jeffty Is Five." Ellison's original "Jeffty" is an anti-technological story—Harlan's an antitechnological guy. He told us at Clarion that we should get offline and stop screwing around (the best advice I ever ignored). I'm just going to play with that for a while and see how it goes. Let a thousand "Nightfall's" bloom!

Doctorow also writes a vast amount of nonfiction, as coeditor of the online anthology *BoingBoing*, a "directory of wonderful things," and as columnist and writer of op-ed pieces in magazines such as *Wired*, *Popular Science,* and *MAKE*. For four years he lived in London, working as European Affairs Coordinator for the Electronic Frontier Foundation (EFF), a technology advocacy nonprofit, and helping to set up the Open Rights Group.

Doctorow attended an alternative SEED School in Toronto and took classes at four universities, although he went on to other interests without acquiring a degree. He is a frequent public speaker on copyright issues and a keen supporter of liberalized copyright laws. His work is usually issued under various versions of Creative Commons licenses, which allow readers to circulate electronic copies as long as they do not profit from doing that; his books are released in digital form, without charge, at the same time that the print versions are published.

In 2006 Cory Doctorow moved to Los Angeles to take up a position at The Public Diplomacy Center at the University of Southern California, where he teaches, researches, and writes about international copyright activism, technology, and the Net. He lives in Southern California with his partner, Alice Taylor; in February 2008 they became the parents of a daughter, Poesy.

Awards

Campbell New Writer Award (2000)

Novels

Down and Out in the Magic Kingdom. (2003) **Locus Poll**

Short Fiction

"I, Robot" (2005) **Locus Poll**
"When Sysadmins Ruled the Earth" (2006) **Locus Poll**
"After the Siege" (2007) **Locus Poll**

Works by the Author

Down and Out in the Magic Kingdom (2003)
Eastern Standard Tribe (2004)
Someone Comes to Town, Someone Leaves Town (2005)
Themepunks (2005, published online). http://dir.salon.com/story/tech/feature/2005/09/12/themepunks_1/index.html
Little Brother (2008)

Other Notable Short Fiction

"Craphound" (1998)
"At Lightspeed, Slowing" (2000)
"I Love Paree" (2000, with Michael Skeet)
"0wnz0red" (2002). http://dir.salon.com/story/tech/feature/2002/08/28/0wnz0red/index.html
"Jury Service" (2002, with Charles Stross)
"Flowers from Alice" (2002, with Charles Stross)
"Liberation Spectrum" (2003). http://dir.salon.com/story/tech/feature/2003/01/16/liberation_spectrum/index.html
"Nimby and the Dimension Hoppers" (2003) http://www.infinitematrix.net/stories/shorts/nimby.html
"Truncat" (2003). http://dir.salon.com/story/tech/feature/2003/08/26/truncat/index.html
"Visit the Sins" (2003). http://www.strangehorizons.com/2003/20030331/visit.shtml
"Appeals Court" (2004, with Charles Stross). http://www.infinitematrix.net/stories/shorts/appeals_court.html
"Human Readable" (2005)
"i, robot" (2005). http://www.infinitematrix.net/stories/shorts/i-robot.html
"I, Row-Boat" (2006)

"There's a Great Big Beautiful Tomorrow/Now Is the Best Time of Your Life" (2007)

"True Names" (2008, with Benjamin Rosenbaum)

Collections

A Place So Foreign and Eight More (2003)

Overclocked: Stories of the Future Present (2007)

As Editor

Tesseracts: Canadian Science Fiction; Tesseracts Eleven (2007, with Holly Phillips)

Nonfiction Books

The Complete Idiot's Guide to Publishing Science Fiction. (2000, with Karl Schroeder)

Essential Blogging: Selecting and Using Weblog Tools. (2002, with Shelley Powers et al.)

Content: Selected Essays on Technology, Creativity, Copyright, and the Future of the Future (2008)

Articles and Essays

"Ebooks: Neither E Nor Books." Talk initially given at the O'Reilly Emerging Technology Conference, February 12, 2004. http://craphound.com/ebooksneitherenorbooks.txt

"Thought Experiments: When the Singularity Is More Than a Literary Device (Interview with Ray Kurzweil)." *Asimov's Science Fiction* (May 2005). http://www.asimovs.com/_issue_0506/thoughtexperiments.shtml

"Trademarks." *Open P2P,* August 14, 2003. The O'Reilly Network. http://www.openp2p.com/pub/a/p2p/2003/08/14/trademarks.html

"Transparency Means Nothing Without Justice." *The Guardian,* April 29, 2009. http://www.guardian.co.uk/technology/2009/apr/29/cory-doctorow-police-transparency

"Wikipedia: A Genuine H2G2—Minus the Editors." In *The Anthology at the End of the Universe: Leading Science Fiction Authors on Douglas Adams'* The Hitchhiker's Guide to the Galaxy, ed. Glenn Yeffeth, 25–34. Dallas, TX: Benbella, 2005.

For Further Information

Official Web site: http://www.craphound.com/

Adams, John Joseph. "Interview: Information Wants to Be Free." *SciFi Weekly,* September 18, 2006.

"Everywhere, All at the Same Time: Interview." *Locus* (January 2005). http://www.locusmag.com/2005/Issues/01Doctorow.html

Harris, Bascha. "A Very Long Talk with Cory Doctorow." *Red Hat Magazine* (January and February 2006). http://www.redhat.com/magazine/016feb06/features/doctorow/interview.html

Koman, Richard. "An Interview with Cory Doctorow." *The O'Reilly Network,* March 4, 2005. http://www.oreillynet.com/pub/a/network/2005/03/04/corydoctorow.html

Lilley, Ernest. Interview. *SFRevu* (February 2003). http://www.sfrevu.com/

Macdonald, Katherine. Interview. *Strange Horizons,* March 31, 2003. http://www.strangehorizons.com/2003/20030331/doctorow.shtml

Harlan Ellison

Myth and Legend; New Wave

Benchmark Title: " 'Repent, Harlequin!' Said the Ticktockman" (1965)

b. 1934 (Cleveland, Ohio)

I am anti-entropy. My work is foursquare for chaos. I spend my life personally, and my work professionally, keeping that soup boiling. Gadfly is what they call you when you are no longer dangerous. . . . I much prefer troublemaker, malcontent, pain in the ass, desperado.
—"Introduction," *Shatterday* (1980)

Photo credit: Beth Gwinn

About the Author and the Author's Writing

What can you say about Harlan Ellison?

He is a writer. However, he is a writer who does not care for being pigeonholed or marginalized. He made this quite clear in 1992, in the first episode of *Sci-Fi Buzz*, a chat and discussion program he hosted for the Sci-Fi Channel, when he said: "Call me a science fiction writer and I will come to your house and nail your dog's head to the coffee table!" He is, at his best, an extremely fine writer, in whatever genre he works.

Harlan Ellison has a reputation for being abrasive and argumentative. A dust jacket from one of his own books describes him as "possibly the most contentious person on Earth." He has a reputation for embellishment and for elaborately plotted spoof biographies. So while it may not be true that he ran away from home at age thirteen to join the circus, and over the next half dozen years worked as a logger, a tuna fisherman, an actor, a floor walker in a department store, and a dynamite-truck driver, it probably is true that Harlan Jay Ellison was born in Cleveland and grew up in Painesville, Ohio, the only Jewish family in that small Midwest town:

> [Other kids] used to beat the [daylights] out of me. Regularly. It was this Jewish business. . . . I was the green monkey, the pariah. And I had no friends. Not just a few friends, or one good friend, or grudging acceptance by other misfits and outcasts. I was alone. (Salm 2005).

Upon the death of his father in 1949, the family returned to Cleveland. Ellison briefly attended Ohio State University, leaving midway through his sophomore year. According to his account, he hit a professor who said he had no talent. He claims to have sent that professor a copy of every story he published over the next forty-odd years. He moved to New York City in 1955 and began his writing career with vivid, violent accounts of city life, including *Rumble* (1958—aka *Web of the City*), an account of ten weeks he spent, incognito, with a youth gang in Red Hook, Brooklyn.

Ellison moved to California in the early 1960s. He worked on a number of popular TV series of the time, such as *Route 66, The Outer Limits, Star Trek,* and *The Flying Nun.* His TV work earned him equal amounts of praise—his teleplay for *Star Trek*, "The City on the Edge of Forever," is regularly cited by critics and fans as one of the best of all *Star Trek* episodes—and frustrations (scripts rewritten by producers and directors, ideas dumbed down). Ellison reserves the pen name "Cordwainer Bird" for productions that have tinkered with his script; it has been a source of lasting rancor to him that "The City on the Edge of Forever" was not filmed exactly as he wrote it. At around this time, he began publishing the short stories that made his name.

As of 1994 Ellison had published some 1,300 stories, essays, scripts, and reviews. In his own writing, Ellison is afraid of nothing—shocking subject matter, bold experimentation, dark themes. A story like "A Boy and His Dog," set in the aftermath of an apocalyptic war, is praised and damned equally as shocking, violent, misogynistic— and full of drama and telling insights into violence and survival. As in his life, his fiction reflects a mistrust of technology as a cure for all ills; the value of strong emotions of all sorts; the importance of myth, both personal and universal; and, most important of all, the absolute necessity of getting revenge against those who have done you wrong. Ellison has won vast numbers of every SF award available, including special WorldCon Convention awards for his lifetime achievement in SF, as well as for his groundbreaking anthologies *Dangerous Visions* (1968) and *Again, Dangerous Visions* (1972), which brought together stories by authors who, in Ellison's opinion, were reshaping the genre. He is widely acknowledged as a generous and tireless mentor to new SF talent.

Very few people are ambivalent about Harlan Ellison.
—Sullivan (1996)

Ellison has found other outlets for his fierce anger at prejudice and injustice of any kind. He took part in the 1965 march from Selma to Montgomery, Alabama, led by Martin Luther King Jr. He is a frequent guest on Bill Maher's *Politically Incorrect* and an outspoken advocate for gun control. He has been married five times. In 1994 he suffered a heart attack and was hospitalized for quadruple coronary artery bypass surgery. What can you say about Harlan Ellison? Perhaps Theodore Sturgeon said it best in his introduction to Ellison's 1967 short story collection *I Have No Mouth and I Must Scream*; according to Sturgeon, he is "a man on the move, and he is moving fast. He is, on these pages and everywhere else he goes, colorful, intrusive, ABRASIVE . . . and one hell of a writer."

Harlan Ellison lives in Los Angeles, California, with his wife, Susan.

Awards

Milford Award for lifetime achievement in SF publishing and editing (1986)
World Fantasy Award Life Achievement (1993)
Locus All-Time Poll: Short Fiction Writer (1999)

SFWA Damon Knight Memorial Grand Master (2006)
WorldCon Special Convention Awards (1968, 1972, 2006)

Short Fiction

"'Repent, Harlequin!' Said the Ticktockman" (1965) **Hugo, Nebula**
"I Have No Mouth, and I Must Scream" (1967) **Hugo**
"The Beast That Shouted Love at the Heart of the World" (1969) **Hugo**
"A Boy and his Dog" (1969) **Nebula**
"The Region Between" (1970) **Locus Poll**
"Basilisk" (1972) **Locus Poll**
"The Deathbird" (1973) **Hugo, Locus Poll**
"Adrift Just Off the Islets of Langerhans: Latitude 38° 54' N, Longitude 77° 00' 13' W" (1974) **Hugo, Locus Poll**
"Croatoan" (1975) **Locus Poll**
"Jeffty Is Five" (1977) Hugo, **Nebula, Locus Poll, Locus All-Time Poll 1999**
"Count the Clock That Tells the Time" (1978) **Locus Poll**
"Djinn, No Chaser" (1982) **Locus Poll**
"Paladin of the Lost Hour" (1985) **Hugo, Locus Poll**
"With Virgil Oddum at the East Pole" (1985) **Locus Poll**
"Eidolons" (1988) **Locus Poll**
"The Function of Dream Sleep" (1988) **Locus Poll**
"Mefisto in Onyx" (1994) **Locus Poll**

Nonfiction

Sleepless Nights in the Procrustean Bed: Essays (1984) **Locus Poll**

As Editor

Dangerous Visions (1966) **Locus All-Time Poll 1999, WorldCon Special Committee Award**
Again, Dangerous Visions (1972) **Locus Poll, WorldCon Special Committee Award**
Medea: Harlan's World (1985) **Locus Poll**

Collections

Deathbird Stories (1975) **BSF**
Angry Candy (1988) **Locus Poll**
Slippage (1997) **Locus Poll**

Dramatic Presentation

Star Trek: "The City on the Edge of Forever" (1967) **Hugo**
A Boy and His Dog (1975) **Hugo**

Works by the Author

The Man with Nine Lives (1960; aka *The Sound of a Scythe*)
Doomsman (1967)
The Starlost No. 1: Phoenix Without Ashes (1975, with Edward Bryant)

Mainstream and Other Genre Fiction

Web of the City (1958) (originally published as *Rumble*)
The Deadly Streets (1958)
Sex Gang (1959, as by Paul Merchant)
Children of the Streets (1961; orig. *The Juvies*)
Gentleman Junkie and Other Stories of the Hung-Up Generation (1961)
Spider Kiss (1961; orig. *Rockabilly*)

Other Notable Short Fiction

"Run for the Stars" (1957; rev. ed. 1991)
"Soldier" (1957)
"Pretty Maggie Moneyeyes" (1967)
"Shattered Like a Glass Goblin" (1968)
"Brillo" (1970, with Ben Bova)
"Runesmith" (1970, with Theodore Sturgeon)
"The Human Operators" (1971, with A. E. van Vogt)
"I'm Looking for Kadak" (1974)
"Shatterday" (1975)
"From A to Z, in the Chocolate Alphabet" (1976)
"The Man Who Was Heavily into Revenge" (1978)
"All the Lies That are My Life" (1980)
"Laugh Track" (1984)
"Paladin of the Lost Hour" (1985). http://harlanellison.com/iwrite/paladin.htm
"The Man Who Rowed Christopher Columbus Ashore" (1991)
"Susan" (1993). http://harlanellison.com/iwrite/susan.htm
"Chatting with Anubis" (1995)
"Incognita, Inc." (2001)
"Goodbye to All That" (2003)

Collections

A Touch of Infinity (1958)
Ellison Wonderland (1962; aka *Earthman, Go Home!*)
Paingod and Other Delusions (1965)
I Have No Mouth, and I Must Scream (1967)
From the Land of Fear (1967)

Love Ain't Nothing But Sex Misspelled (1968)

The Beast that Shouted Love at the Heart of the World (1969)

Over the Edge (1970)

Partners in Wonder (1971, collaborations with fourteen other writers)

Approaching Oblivion (1974)

Deathbird Stories (1975)

No Doors, No Windows (1975)

Strange Wine (1978)

Shatterday (1980)

Stalking the Nightmare (1982)

Angry Candy (1988)

Mind Fields (1994; stories inspired by the surrealist art of Jacek Yerka)

Slippage: Previously Uncollected, Precariously Poised Stories (1998)

Troublemakers: Stories by Harlan Ellison (2001)

The Essential Ellison: A 50 Year Retrospective (2005). A previous edition of this volume won the Bram Stoker Award for Superior Achievement in a Fiction Collection in 1987.

As Editor

Dangerous Visions (1967)

Again, Dangerous Visions (1972)

Medea: Harlan's World (1985)

In Other Media

"Soldier" (September 1964) and "Demon with a Glass Hand" (October 1964), *The Outer Limits*. The movie *The Terminator* had striking similarities to these Ellison *Outer Limits* scripts. Ellison eventually sued James Cameron, writer and director of *The Terminator*. The film's end credits now include the statement: "Acknowledgment to the works of Harlan Ellison."

"The City on the Edge of Forever." *Star Trek*. Episode 28, April 6, 1967. Starring William Shatner, Leonard Nimoy, and Joan Collins.

A Boy and His Dog. LQ/JAF, 1975. Directed by L. Q. Jones; starring Don Johnson and Tim McIntire.

The Starlost. 20th Century Fox Television, 1973–1974. Starring Keir Dullea. Ellison is credited as screenwriter for the sixteen episodes of this TV series.

Sci-Fi Buzz. The Sci-Fi Channel, 1992–1993.

Harlan Ellison's The City on the Edge of Forever: *The Original Teleplay That Became the Classic* Star Trek *Episode*. Stone Mountain, GA: White Wolf, 1996.

"The Human Operators" (1999), *The New Outer Limits*. Based on the short story written by Ellsion, in collaboration with A. E. Van Vogt; starring Malcolm McDowell.

Dreams with Sharp Teeth: A Film about Harlan Ellison. Creative Differences, 2007. Directed by Erik Nelson. http://www.creatvdiff.com/harlan_ellison.php

Harlan Ellison's Dream Corridor. Volume 1, 1996; Volume 2, 2007. Graphic art adaptations of some of Ellison's stories.

Nonfiction Books

Memos from Purgatory (1961)
The Glass Teat (1970)
The Other Glass Teat: Further Essays of Opinion on Television (1975)
The Book of Ellison (1978, ed. Andrew Porter)
Sleepless Nights in the Procrustean Bed: Essays. (1984, edited by Marty Clark)
An Edge in My Voice (1985)
Harlan Ellison's Watching (1989)
The Harlan Ellison Hornbook (1997)

Articles and Essays

"Goodbye to All That." In *Envisioning the Future: Science Fiction and the Next Millennium,* ed. Marleen S. Barr, 99–110. Middletown: Wesleyan University Press, 2003.

"Infamy: The New Fame." *Variety,* November 3, 2003.

"Introduction." In *The Nail and the Oracle: Volume XI: The Complete Stories of Theodore Sturgeon.* Berkeley, CA: North Atlantic, 2007.

Bibliographies

Fingerprints on the Sky: The Authorized Harlan Ellison Bibliography: The Fully Illustrated Reader's Guide. Hiram, GA: Overlook, 2007.

Islets of Langerhans: A Literary Topography. n.d. http://www.islets.net/index.html

For Further Information

Official Home page: http://harlanellison.com/home.htm

Blaschke, Jayme L. "A Conversation with Harlan Ellison." *Interzone* (June 2000). http://www.SFsite.com/07a/he107.htm

———. "Harlan Ellison." In *Voices of Vision,* 165–84. Lincoln: University of Nebraska Press, 2005. With substantial material that was cut from the interview as originally published.

De Los Santos, Oscar. "Clogging up the (In)human Works: Harlan Ellison's Apocalyptic Postmodern Visions." *Extrapolation* 40 (1999): 5–20.

Interview. *Locus* (July 2001). http://www.locusmag.com/2001/Issue07/Ellison.html

Lengel, Kerry. "Grand Master of Fabulism." *The Arizona Republic,* April 28, 2006. http://www.azcentral.com/ent/arts/articles/0428nebula28.html

Porter, Andrew, ed. *The Book of Ellison.* New York: Algol, 1978.

Salm, Arthur, "Harlan Ellison Is Fearless, and a Fearless Writer." *San Diego Union-Tribune,* March 20, 2005. http://www.signonsandiego.com/news/features/20050320-9999-1a20harlan.html

Slusser, George Edgar. *Harlan Ellison: Unrepentant Harlequin.* San Bernadino, CA: Borgo, 1977.

Strickland, Galen. Profile. *Templeton Gate.* n.d. http://templetongate.tripod.com/ellison.htm

Sturgeon, Theodore. "Introduction." In *I Have No Mouth and I Must Scream.* New York: Pyramid, 1967.

Sullivan, C. W., III, "Harlan Ellison." In *St. James Guide to Science Fiction Writers,* ed. Jay Pedersen. Detroit, MI: St. James, 1996.

Weil, Ellen, and Gary Wolfe, eds. *Harlan Ellison: The Edge of Forever.* Columbus: Ohio State University Press, 2002.

Philip José Farmer

Humor and Satire; Science Fantasy

Benchmark Title: *To Your Scattered Bodies Go* (1971)

b. 1918 (North Terre Haute, Indiana); d. 2009 (North Peoria, Illinois)

> *Any bad fiction, no matter the genre, is a wild exercise of the imagination which explodes in the night of our minds, makes garish pyrotechnics, then dies, leaving the night blacker than before. But good fiction is a steady light—even if sometimes a small one.*
> —"White Whales, Raintrees, Flying Saucers, . . ." (1954)

About the Author and the Author's Writing

The Encyclopedia of Science Fiction (1999) describes Phillip José Farmer as a "comparatively late starter," a distinction that resulted from a combination of family responsibilities and bad luck. Born in North Terre Haute, Indiana, he grew up in Peoria, Illinois, where his father was a civil engineer. Farmer's first attempt at getting a college degree, in journalism from the University of Missouri at Columbia, ended prematurely when he had to look for work to help his father pay off investment debts. The beginning of World War II, and starting his own family—he married in 1941—meant that it was 1949 before he completed his BA, at Bradley University in Peoria.

But during this time Farmer had been writing. He had been an avid reader of SF as a small boy, and in the late 1940s he had some success with hard-boiled detective stories. His novella *The Lovers* appeared in *Startling Stories* in 1952, and at first it appeared that Philip José Farmer had made it to the big time. *The Lovers* was an "explosive mixture" (*ESF* 1999) of lust and alien biology, single-handedly shattering the taboo on sex in SF, and fairly typical of Farmer's subsequent use of sexual themes. (However mild and unobjectionable—even touching—this story of an affair between a human and a shape-shifting insectoid alien might seem by today's standards, in the early 1950s *The Lovers* was hot stuff; when Farmer first submitted it to *Astounding*, the editor of that magazine and grand old man of SF, John W. Campbell, returned it, saying that the story had nauseated him.) On the strength of *The Lovers*, Farmer was presented with one of the first Hugo Awards, as most promising new talent of 1952. Critical praise was soon matched with financial success when, that same year, he won a $4,000 prize for his novel *I Owe for the Flesh*. He gave up the job he had held for over a decade with Keystone Steel & Wire Company in Peoria, called himself a full-time writer, and settled down to wait for the royalties to roll in.

And then it all went horribly wrong. The publishing company that had sponsored the writing prize went bankrupt without paying out his winnings; to add insult to injury, they lost his manuscript. Farmer lost his house and had to return to full-time work. But he continued to write. In 1957 his first novel was published. *The Green Odyssey* is picaresque novel about a shipwrecked spaceman on a strange and complicated barbarian planet, and it was one of the first of the planetary romance novels that became so popular in the 1960s and 1970s. He had learned caution, however, and over the next decade he juggled his fiction with various technical writing jobs—for General Electric, for Motorola's military electronics division, for McDonnell-Douglas—until he was laid off in 1969 and felt able to fall back on his earnings as a freelancer. Farmer won his second Hugo in 1968 for the novella *Riders of the Purple Wage*, a satire on a cradle-to-grave welfare state, written in an exuberant sexual and scatological style. In 1972 he won a third Hugo for a novel that revisited the premise of his lost prize-winning novel of 1952, *To Your Scattered Bodies Go,* the first volume of the imaginative and ambitious Riverworld series.

In Riverworld, real-life historical characters such as the explorer and adventurer Sir Richard Burton, author Samuel Clemens (Mark Twain), and even Nazi playboy Herman Goering are resurrected along the banks of a multi-million-mile-long river. Throughout the series, these mismatched and disconcertingly familiar figures explore the mysteries of Riverworld and the powers that have brought them back to life. Riverworld is an example of one of Farmer's favorite tricks—taking characters from elsewhere (history, pop-culture, and other people's novels), and tying them together into what *The Encyclopedia of Science Fiction* (1999) calls "one vast, playful mythology." Another example of this is Farmer's Wold Newton Family, a loosely connected series of stories that attempt to bring all of the superheroes and villains of nineteenth- and early twentieth-century adventure fiction together into one great *uber*-story, including alternative histories and unauthorized sequel adventures, for characters like Tarzan, Doc Savage, Phileas Fogg, and King Kong. His attempt to recruit Kurt Vonnegut's Kilgore Trout resulted in some serious unpleasantness between the two authors.

"Philip José Farmer is governed by an instinct for extremity. Of all SF writers of the first or second rank, he is perhaps the most threateningly impish, and the most anarchic" (*The Encyclopedia of Science Fiction* 1999). In 1970 Farmer returned with his wife and children to Peoria, where he had attended college, and over the next forty years, Peoria became the hub of what his loyal and highly motivated fan base called "all things Farmerian." He and his wife Bette had six grandchildren and four great-grandchildren. According to his official Web site, Farmer "passed away peacefully in his sleep," at the age of ninety-one, on February 25, 2009.

In an interview in *Science Fiction Review* in 1975, Farmer was asked about his thoughts about an afterlife, given his famous vision in the Riverworld series of what might await us in the hereafter. Farmer said, "I can't see any reason why such miserable, unhappy, vicious, stupid, conniving, greedy, narrow-minded, self-absorbed beings should have immortality." But he added, "When considering individuals, then I feel, yes, this person, that person, certainly deserves another chance." Life, he said, "is too short, too crowded, too hurried, too beset." Farmerphiles—the loyal fans of Philip José Farmer—would say that, for a while, thanks to him, life was made immeasurably better and more interesting.

Awards

Science Fiction and Fantasy Writers of America Grand Master (2001)
World Fantasy Award Life Achievement (2001)
First Fandom Hall of Fame Award (2003)

Novels

To Your Scattered Bodies Go (1971) **Hugo**

Short Fiction

Most Promising New Talent: "The Lovers" (1952) **Hugo**
"Riders of the Purple Wage" (1967) **Hugo**

Works by the Author

The Green Odyssey (1957)
Flesh (1960)
A Woman a Day, or The Day of Timestop (1960)
The Lovers (1961). An extended fix-up, combining the 1952 Hugo-winning novella and its sequel, *Moth and Rust* (1953).
Cache from Outer Space (1962)
Tongues of the Moon (1964)
Dare (1965)
Night of Light (1966)
Image of the Beast (1968)
Blown (1969)
Love Song (1970)
The Stone God Awakens (1970)
The Wind Whales of Ishmael (1971)
Venus on the Half-Shell (1975, as Kilgore Trout)
Jesus on Mars (1979)
Dark Is the Sun (1979)
Two Hawks from Earth (1979). A revised and expanded version of *The Gate of Time* (1966).
The Cache (1981)
The Unreasoning Mask (1981)
Stations of the Nightmare (1982)
Nothing Burns in Hell (1998)
Up from the Bottomless Pit (2005–2007; published in ten parts in *Farmerphile*)
The City Beyond Play (2007, with Danny Adams)

Dayworld
Dayworld (1984)
Dayworld Rebel (1987)
Dayworld Breakup (1990)

Riverworld
To Your Scattered Bodies Go (1971)
The Fabulous Riverboat (1971)
The Dark Design (1977)
The Magic Labyrinth (1980)
Gods of Riverworld (1983)
River of Eternity (1983). A rediscovered rewrite of the lost manuscript *I Owe for the Flesh*.

World of Tiers
The Maker of Universes (1965)
The Gates of Creation (1966)
A Private Cosmos (1968)
Behind the Walls of Terra (1970)
The Lavalite World (1977)
Red Orc's Rage (1991)
More Than Fire (1993)

Notable Mainstream and Other Genre Fiction
Fire and the Night (1962)
Inside Outside (1964)
Ironcastle (1976; translation/expansion of work by J.-H. Rosny)
Greatheart Silver (1982)
The Caterpillar's Question (1992, with Piers Anthony)
Naked Came the Farmer (1998; collaborative thriller with thirteen other authors)

Herald Childe Trilogy
The Image of the Beast (1968)
Blown: Or Sketches Among the Ruins of My Mind (1969)
Traitor to the Living (1973)

Wold Newton Family (Tarzan, Doc Savage, Sherlock Holmes and Other Characters)
A Feast Unknown (1969)
Lord of the Trees (1970)
Lord Tyger (1970)
The Mad Goblin (1970)

Tarzan Alive: A Definitive Biography of Lord Greystoke (1972)
Time's Last Gift (1972)
Doc Savage: His Apocalyptic Life (1973)
The Other Log of Phileas Fogg (1973)
The Adventures of the Peerless Peer (1974, as "John H. Watson")
Hadon of Ancient Opar (1974)
Flight to Opar (1976)
A Barnstormer in Oz (1982)
Escape From Loki (1991)
The Dark Heart of Time (1999)

Other Notable Short Fiction

"Mother" (1953)
"Father" (1955; the first of the Father Carmody stories)
"My Sister's Brother" (1960; aka "Open to Me, My Sister")
"Day of the Great Shout" (1965)
"Riverworld" (1966)
"The Sliced-Crosswise Only-on-Tuesday World" (1971)
"After King Kong Fell" (1973)
"Sketches Among the Ruins of My Mind" (1973)

Collections

The Alley God (1962)
The Celestial Blueprint: And Other Stories (1962)
Down in the Black Gang (1971)
The Book of Philip José Farmer (1973)
Mother Was a Lovely Beast: A Feral Man Anthology, Fiction and Fact about Humans Raised by Animals (1974)
Riverworld and Other Stories (1979)
Riverworld War: The Suppressed Fiction of Philip José Farmer (1980)
Father to the Stars (1981)
Stations of the Nightmare (1982)
The Purple Book (1982)
The Classic Philip José Farmer, 1952–1964 (1984)
The Classic Philip José Farmer, 1964–1973 (1984)
The Grand Adventure (1984)
Riders of the Purple Wage (1992)
Myths for the Modern Age: Philip José Farmer's Wold Newton Universe (2005)
The Best of Philip José Farmer (2006)
Pearls from Peoria (2006, edited by Paul Spiteri)
Strange Relations (2008)

Up from the Bottomless Pit and Other Stories (2007)
Venus on the Half-Shell and Others (2008)
The Other in the Mirror (2009)

In Other Media

Riverworld. Alliance Atlantis Communications, 2003. TV pilot, directed by Kari Skogland; starring Brad Johnson. Appears to bear little or no resemblance to the books whatsoever. According to the *Hollywood Reporter*, a new adaptation of *Riverworld*, starring Tahmoh Penikett, Laura Vandervoort, and Alan Cumming, is planned by RHI Entertainment as a TV mini-series.

Articles and Essays

"The Journey [as the Revelation of the Unknown]." In *The New Encyclopedia of Science Fiction*, ed. James Gunn. New York: Viking, 1988.

"White Whales, Raintrees, Flying Saucers, . . ." *Fantastic Universe* (July 1954).

"Why and How I Became Kilgore Trout." In *Venus on the Half-Shell*. Burton, MI: Subterranean Press, 2008.

Bibliographies

Nuninga, Zacharias L. A. "Philip José Farmer International Bibliography." November 27, 2006. http://www.philipjosefarmer.tk/

For Further Information

Official Web site: Edited by Michael Croteau and Craig Kimber. http://www.pjfarmer.com/

The Farmerphile: http://www.pjfarmer.com/farmerphile.htm

Adams, Danny. "A Brobdingnagian Education, Or, How Philip José Farmer Saved My Life in Four Easy Steps." *Some Fantastic* 4, no. 1(2005): 1–5. http://www.somefantastic.us/

Bibo, Terry. "A Conversation with Philip José Farmer." *Peoria Journal Star,* January 10, 1999. The 1999 Bibo interview is no longer available online, but it may be possible to contact the paper directly for a copy.

———. "Humble at Home, Farmer Enjoyed International Fame." *Peoria Journal Star,* February 25, 2009. http://www.pjstar.com/archive/x1749108393/Philip-Jose-Farmer-dead-at-91. Includes an archive of *PJF* photos.

Brizzi, Mary T., and Roger C. Sclobin. *Philip José Farmer: Starmont Reader's Guide 3*. Mercer Island, WA: Borgo, 1981.

Chapman, Edgar L. *The Magic Labyrinth of Philip José Farmer*. Milford Popular Writers of Today. San Bernardino, CA: Borgo, 1985.

Ellison, Harlan. "Philip José Farmer: Portrait of the Artist as the Great Wall of China." *Bulletin of the Science Fiction and Fantasy Writers of America* 35, no. 1 (2001): 32.

Jonas, Gerald. "Philip José Farmer, Daring Science Fiction Writer, Dies at 91." Obituary. *The New York Times,* February 26, 2009.

Kraft, David, and Mitch Scheele "SFR Interviews Philip José Farmer: The Inside Story of Kilgore Trout & Venus on the Half-Shell." *Science Fiction Review* 14 (August 1975).

Platt, Charles. "Philip José Farmer." *Dream Makers: The Uncommon People Who Write Science Fiction.* New York: Berkley, 1980.

Truesdale, Dave. "An Interview with Philip José Farmer (1918–2009)." *SF Site* (2009). http://www.SFsite.com/03a/pjf291.htm. The original interview appeared in *Tangent* No. 2, in 1975.

Vernon, William D. Interview. In *The Sound of Wonder: Interviews from "The Science Fiction Radio Show," Volume 2,* ed. Daryl Lane, David Carson and William Vernon. Phoenix, AZ: Oryx, 1985.

Wymer, Thomas L. "Philip José Farmer: The Trickster as Artist." In *Voices for the Future: Essays on Major Science Fiction Writers, Volume 2,* ed. Thomas D. Clareson, 34–55. Bowling Green, OH: University Popular Press, 1979.

Jack Finney

Science Fantasy; Time Travel

Benchmark Title: *Time and Again* (1970)

b. 1911 (Milwaukee, Wisconsin);
d. 1995 (Greenbrae, California)

Photo courtesy of the Literary Estate of Jack Finney. Reprinted with permission of Don Congdor Associates, Inc.

I don't like to and I could not reveal everything about myself.... So if now and then you think you can read between the lines, you may be right; or may not.

—*Time and Again* (1970)

About the Author and the Author's Writing

Jack Finney seems to have been an intensely private person. He appears to have given no formal interviews during his career. He didn't attend SF conventions (even when the party was in his honor). Well-meaning biographers are reduced to bulking out his life story with lines like, "[d]etails also have not survived about his first marriage, which most likely ended sometime in the late 1940s" (Seabrook 2006), as if he were a semilegendary character from the Dark Ages or a boy pharoah. But Jack Finney was neither of these things—he was a writer, a professional who learned the tricks of the trade in the advertising business. He was a writer who was not slavishly devoted to any particular genre; he wrote thrillers (*Five Against the House*, 1954, and *Assault on a Queen*, 1959) and comedies of manners (*Good Neighbor Sam*, 1963). He also wrote gentle fantasies of yearning for a lost past that becomes so strong, there is nothing for it but for his characters to snap back to that past, as if they are attached to it by bungee cords. He wrote a classic SF horror story, about fear of losing oneself to an evil force, that has been revisited by Hollywood again and again, as if someone there hopes they will someday live up to the original. And he wrote *Time and Again*.

What is known for sure about Jack Finney is that he was born in Milwaukee, Wisconsin, and christened "John." Three years later his father died, and little John was renamed Walter Braden Finney in his honor; but the name change did not take, and he was known as "Jack" all of his life. His mother returned with him to her parent's home, in Forest Park, Illinois, where she eventually remarried and gave young Jack a new family. Later in life he fondly remembered summer vacations spent with his mother, stepfather, and half-siblings, in a place called Galesburg, Illinois.

Following his graduation from Knox College in Galesburg, Finney had a career in advertising, in Chicago and for some years in New York City, working for companies with names like Dancer-Fitzgerald-Sample. It is possible to conjecture that Finney had mixed feelings about New York; many of his stories are about go-getting young professional guys, transplanted to the Big Apple for career purposes, who long for nothing more than the small town lives they left behind in the Midwest. On the other hand, *Time and Again* reads like a 400-odd-page love letter to New York, written by someone who has known it on its good days and its bad days, and loves it anyway.

Finney moved from advertising copy to fiction gradually. In 1946 he won a contest sponsored by *Ellery Queen's Mystery Magazine*, which resulted in his first published story. During the 1950s he churned out thrillers, which were in their turn churned into popular movies. His short stories appeared in all the best places, including *Cosmopolitan* and *Good Housekeeping*. During this period, as one popular periodical faded and dropped away (*Collier's*, *The Saturday Evening Post*), others would rise to take its place (*Playboy*), and Jack Finney stories would be there. Finney also wrote for the theater, and a good number of his stories were adapted for the TV drama series that were popular at the time, such as *Alcoa Premier*. Although the majority of Finney's other work can be described as mainstream thrillers and light fantasy, his status as a writer of SF is guaranteed by two novels—*Time and Again* (1970) and *Body Snatchers* (1954).

In *Body Snatchers,* alien invaders replicate the forms of ordinary people, dispose of the originals, and take their places on Main Street, USA. It is considered a classic Cold War allegory (although Finney always denied that it was anything more than a terrifying, paranoia thriller). It has been adapted for film four times, in 1956, 1978, 1993, and 2007. Unfortunately, Finney sold away all film rights for the novel for $7,500 in the 1950s. *Time and Again* is an "illustrated novel" in which the hero uses auto-hypnosis to transport himself back to 1880s New York City to solve a mystery. *The New York Times,* in Finney's obituary, described it as "beloved especially by New Yorkers for its rich, painstakingly researched descriptions of life in the city more than a century ago."

From the early 1950s, when Finney met and married his second wife, Marguerite, he lived in Marin County, California—in the same house for forty of those years. In 1987 he was given the World Fantasy Award for Life Achievement, which he received graciously and (it appears) in absentia. Jack Finney died in 1995 of pneumonia and emphysema, in Marin General Hospital in Greenbrae, California. Shortly before his death he delivered to his publisher his final novel, *From Time to Time,* the much-anticipated sequel to *Time and Again.*

Awards

World Fantasy Award Life Achievement (1987)

Grand Prix de l'Imaginaire (1994) (for the French translation of *Time and Again, Le Voyage de Simon Morley*)

Works by the Author

Invasion of the Body Snatchers. (1954)
Of Missing Persons (1955)
The Face in the Photo (1962; aka *Time Has No Boundaries*)
The Woodrow Wilson Dime (1968)
Time and Again (1970)
From Time to Time (1995)

Notable Mainstream and Other Genre Fiction

Five against the House (1954)
The House of Numbers (1957)
Assault on a Queen (1959)
Good Neighbor Sam (1963)
Marion's Wall (1973)
The Night People (1977)

Notable Short Fiction

"The Coin Collector" (1960)
"Of Missing Persons" (1955)
"I'm Scared" (1951)
"The Love Letter" (1959)
"Such Interesting Neighbors" (1951)
"Where the Cluetts Are" (1962)

Collections

The Third Level (1957; UK: *The Clock of Time*)
I Love Galesburg in the Springtime (1963)
About Time (1986)

In Other Media

"Time Is Just a Place." *Science Fiction Theater.* ZIV Television Programs, 1955.

5 Against the House. Columbia Pictures Corporation, 1955. Directed by Phil Karlson; starring Guy Madison, Kim Novak, and Brian Keith.

Invasion of the Body Snatchers. Walter Wanger Productions, 1956. Directed by Don Siegel; starring Kevin McCarthy and Dana Wynter.

The House of Numbers. Metro-Goldwyn-Mayer (MGM), 1957. Directed by Russell Rouse; starring Jack Palance.

Good Neighbor Sam. Columbia Pictures Corporation, 1964. Directed by David Swift; starring Jack Lemmon and Romy Schneider.

Assault on a Queen. Paramount Pictures, 1966. Directed by Jack Donohue; starring Frank Sinatra and Virna Lisi.

Invasion of the Body Snatchers. Solofilm, 1978. Remake, directed by Philip Kaufman; starring Donald Sutherland and Brooke Adams.

Maxie. Elsboy Entertainment, 1985. Directed by Paul Aaron; starring Glenn Close and Mandy Patinkin; based on *Marion's Wall.*

Body Snatchers. Warner Bros. Pictures, 1993. Yet another (less successful) remake of *Invasion of the Body Snatchers*, directed by Abel Ferrara; starring Gabrielle Anwar.

The Love Letter. Hallmark Entertainment, 1998. TV movie, directed by Dan Curtis; starring Campbell Scott and Jennifer Jason Leigh; based on the story of the same name.

The Invasion. Warner Bros. Pictures, 2007. And yet another lackluster remake of *Invasion of the Body Snatchers.* Directed by Oliver Hirschbiegel; starring Nicole Kidman and Daniel Craig.

Escape to Verna. 2008. Low-budget adaptation of Finney's short story *Of Missing Persons.* Directed by Joe Collesano and J. D. Marlow; screenplay by Elliot Rudmann. This short film is available online at the International Movie Database.

Nonfiction Books

Forgotten News: The Crime of the Century and Other Lost Stories (1983). True-crime story that inspired, and provided the research for, *Time and Again.*

For Further Information

Burns, Ric. "Why *Time and Again* Casts So Powerful a Spell." *New York Times,* January 28, 2001.

Kimmel, Daniel M. "Sleep No More: Why the Pod People Won't Go Away." *Internet Review of Science Fiction* (October 2005). http://www.iroSF.com/q/zine/article/10202

Seabrook, Jack. *Stealing Through Time: On the Writings of Jack Finney.* Jefferson, NC: McFarland, 2006.

Teich, Al, *Jack Finney: Time Traveler.* January 2004. http://www.alteich.com/tidbits/t010104.htm. A photo tour of New York City sites from Jack Finney's *Time and Again,* as they appeared in late 2003.

Willick, George C. "Biography, Obituaries and Bibliography." *Spacelight* (June 2006). http://www.gcwillick.com/Spacelight/finney.html

William Gibson

Cyberpunk; Near Future; TechnoThriller

Benchmark Title: *Necromancer* (1984)

b. 1948 (Conway, South Carolina)

> *It was a world of early television, a new Oldsmobile with crazy rocket-ship styling, toys with science fiction themes. . . . The trauma of my father's death aside, I'm convinced that it was this experience of feeling abruptly exiled, to what seemed like the past, that began my relationship with science fiction.*
>
> —"Since 1948" (2002)

About the Author and the Author's Writing

In his 2002 autobiographical essay, "Since 1948," William Gibson quotes Gene Wolfe, saying that "being an only child whose parents are dead is like being the sole survivor of drowned Atlantis." If alienation is the engine at the heart of cyberpunk, then one could argue that the catalyst that launched that engine began when "normal" childhood ended for William Gibson, with the death of his father when he was six years old. William Ford Gibson was born in Conway, South Carolina. His father was "something" (as he recalls it, in "Since 1948") in construction; the family moved around a lot, from one bright, "red brick Levittown-style" suburb to another, following his father's work on projects such as the Oak Ridge atomic facilities in Tennessee. His father was often away on business. "Then my father went off on one more business trip. He never came back. He choked on something in a restaurant, the Heimlich maneuver hadn't been discovered yet, and everything changed."

Following the death of his father, Gibson and his mother moved back to his parents' hometown in southwestern Virginia, where he spent the remainder of his childhood. He describes himself as "exactly the sort of introverted, hyper-bookish boy you'll find in the biographies of most American science fiction writers, obsessively filling shelves with paperbacks." His mother, who (not surprisingly) suffered from anxiety and depression, attempted to counter these mildly antisocial tendencies by sending him to a military-style boarding school in Arizona. And then, "my mother died with stunning suddenness. Dropped literally dead: the descent of an Other Shoe I'd been anticipating since age six" ("Since 1948") .

Gibson left high school without graduating. He took himself off to Canada to avoid the draft for the Vietnam War. (As he describes it, he "evaded" it so well that he was never even called up.) He lived in the "hippie" area of Toronto, vaguely considered becoming an artist, met his wife, Deborah Jean Thompson, spent some time with her in Europe, got married, and settled in her hometown of Vancouver. There he enrolled for a bachelor's degree in English at the University of British Columbia and began to write science fiction.

Gibson's short stories, such as "Burning Chrome" (1982) and "Johnny Mnemonic" (1981), and first novel, *Neuromancer*, were an immediate success—more than a success, they were a popular phenomenon. In the eyes of critics, pundits, and world readership at large, Gibson had done something amazing—something that, perhaps, corresponds to the impact that H. G. Wells had had a century before: He had shown them, in clear, shocking prose, the future that was awaiting them, just around the corner. Gibson did not exactly "invent" cyberpunk. The raw material was there, in Cordwainer Smith's Scanners and Habermen; in the jazzy, dislocated style of Alfred Bester and in James Tiptree Jr.'s wired-in style and ambivalence about future heroics; in Vernor Vinge's "True Names," which had appeared in 1981 and presented a prescient view of what a future of online shopping and 24/7 game-playing would really be like. In fact, Gibson did coin the term *cyberspace*, in "Burning Chrome," but more important than that, *Neuromancer* and Gibson's other work of the 1980s had a particular "tonality and attitude . . . a snappiness born of weary, hip cynicism" (Poole 2003); this, combined with the fact that Gibson's vision of the future seems to have become more real ever year since the novel was published, ensures that *Neuromancer* (and Gibson) will always be associated with the style and substance of that particular epiphany in SF. In addition, Gibson had the advantage (yes, advantage) of being relatively innocent about the science—he just understood the people. "I think I was really lucky, because I knew nothing about computing and consequently I could see the forest for the trees. . . . I just saw people. I sort of deduced functions from what these objects looked like" (Leonard 2003). *Neuromancer* swept the board of the major SF prizes that year—Hugo, Nebula, and Philip K. Dick—and since then it has sold more than 6.5 million copies worldwide.

Like all good "pioneers," Gibson has acquired a media persona that alternately fits and dissonates with the role he has been assigned as a "voice" of cyberpunk, cyberspace, and all things virtual. "Google me and you can learn that I do it all on a manual typewriter, something that hasn't been true since 1985, but which makes such an easy hook for a lazy journalist that I expect to be reading it for the rest of my life" ("Since 1948")

In the 1990s he was invited to script two episodes of *The X-Files* (cue spooky music); he has done edgy documentaries and multimedia projects, and has written the lyrics for a song recorded by Deborah Harry of Blondie. In his writing he continues to experiment with and push boundaries. *The Difference Engine* (1990), written with Bruce Sterling, was a "steampunk" alternative history, which imagined the impact on humanity and history if "difference engines" (steam-driven computers) had brought on the Information Revolution 100 years early. His 2003 novel *Pattern Recognition*, which was widely reviewed and praised outside the SF community, is about " 'the spontaneous perception of connections and meaningfulness in unrelated things.' In other words: Recognizing patterns that aren't actually there" (Leonard 2003). Many mainstream critics seemed to think that because it's set in August 2002, in a recognizable world still reeling from the impact of 9/11, and because it didn't involve cyborgs or alternate realities, *Pattern Recognition* isn't a science fiction novel. "But Gibson doesn't have to invent the future, any more, because it's already here. The world, as

Gibson notes repeatedly during our interview, is weird enough without needing to invent anything" (Leonard 2003).

Although he retains U.S. citizenship, William Gibson has spent most of his adult life in Canada. He lives in the Vancouver area.

Awards

SF Hall of Fame (2008)

Novels

Neuromancer (1984) **PKD, Hugo, Nebula**

Works by the Author

Other Notable Genre Fiction

The Difference Engine (1990, with Bruce Sterling)
Pattern Recognition (2003)
Spook Country (2007)

Bridge Trilogy

Virtual Light (1993)
Idoru (1996)
All Tomorrow's Parties (1999)

Neuromancer

Neuromancer (1984)
Count Zero (1986)
Mona Lisa Overdrive (1988)

Notable Short Fiction

"The Gernsback Continuum" (1981)
"Burning Chrome" (1982)
"Johnny Mnemonic" (1981)
"Red Star, Winter Orbit" (1983, with Bruce Sterling)
"Dogfight" (1985, with Michael Swanwick)
"The Winter Market" (1985)
"Rocket Radio" (1989). http://www.voidspace.org.uk/cyberpunk/gibson_rocketradio.shtml

Collections

Burning Chrome (1986)
Johnny Mnemonic: The Screenplay and the Story (1995)

In Other Media

Dream Jumbo: Working the Absolutes. With Robert Longo. Los Angeles, CA, October 1989. (text for performance art)

Agrippa (A Book of the Dead). With Dennis Ashbaugh. New York: Kevin Begar, 1992. http://www.antonraubenweiss.com/gibson/003otherworks.html. Autobiographical poem on limited edition encrypted diskette.

"Dog Star Girl." (song lyrics, with Chris Stein). *Debravation.* Deborah Harry. Sire/Reprise, 1993.

"Tomorrow Calling." Channel 4 Television Corporation, 1993. TV play directed by Tim Leandro; starring Colin Salmon and Toyah Wilcox; based on short story "The Gernsback Continuum."

Neuromancer. Audiobook. Read by William Gibson. Music by U2 and Black Rain. Los Angeles: Time Warner Audiobooks, 1994.

Johnny Mnemonic. TriStar Pictures, *1995.* Directed by Robert Longo; starring Keanu Reeves.

The X-Files: "Kill Switch" (February 1998, dir. Rob Bowman) and "First Person Shooter" (February 2000, dir. Chris Carter). 20th Century Fox Television. Co-written with Tom Maddox; starring Gillian Anderson and David Duchovny.

New Rose Hotel. Edward R. Pressman Film, 1998. Directed by Abel Ferrara; starring Christopher Walken and Willem Dafoe.

No Maps for These Territories. Documentary, 2003. Produced and directed by Mark Neale. http://www.nomaps.com/

Articles and Essays

"Disneyland with the Death Penalty." *Wired* (September/October 1993). http://www.wired.com/wired/archive/1.04/gibson.html

"God's Little Toys." *Wired* (July 2005). http://www.wired.com/wired/archive/13.07/gibson.html

"Modern Boys and Mobile Girls." *The Observer,* April 1, 2001. http://observer.guardian.co.uk/life/story/0,6903,466391,00.html

"My Own Private Tokyo." *Wired* (September 2001). http://www.wired.com/wired/archive/9.09/gibson.html

"The Road to Oceania." *The New York Times,* June 25, 2003. http://www.netcharles.com/orwell/articles/col-rtoceania.htm

"Since 1948." November 6, 2002. www.williamgibsonbooks.com/source/source.asp

"Time Machine Cuba (2004)." *Infinite Matrix,* January 23, 2006. http://www.infinitematrix.net/faq/essays/gibson.html

Bibliographies

Bibliography. *Centre for Language and Literature.* Athabasca University, May 17, 2007. http://www.athabascau.ca/writers/wgibson_biblio1.html

Page, S., ed. *William Gibson Bibliography/Mediagraphy*. October 2004. http://www.skierpage.com/gibson/biblio.htm

For Further Information

Official Web site: http://www.williamgibsonbooks.com

Barker, Clive. Interview. *Next Theatre,* December 13, 1997. Burning City. http://burningcity.com/CB_WG_P1.html

Cavallaro, Dani. *Cyberpunk and Cyberculture: Science Fiction and the Work of William Gibson.* London: Athlone, 2000.

Delany, Samuel R. "Zelazny/Varley/Gibson—and Quality." In *Shorter Views: Queer Thoughts & the Politics of the Paraliterary,* 271–91. Hanover, NH : University Press of New England/Wesleyan University Press, 1999.

Derra, Manuel, ed. "William Gibson Aleph." July 11, 2007. http://www.antonraubenweiss.com/gibson/

Gunn, Moira. Interview. *Tech Nation,* February 10, 2004. GigaVox Media Inc. http://www.itconversations.com/shows/detail389.html

Heuser, Sabine. "William Gibson's Construction of Cyberspace." In *Virtual Geographies,* ed. Mike Crang, 99–126. London: Routledge, 1999.

Kneale, James. "The Virtual Realities of Technology and Fiction: Reading William Gibson's Cyberspace." In *Virtual Geographies,* ed. Mike Crang, 205–21. London: Routledge, 1999.

Leonard, Andrew. "Nodal Point." *Salon.com,* February 13, 2003. http://dir.salon.com/story/tech/books/2003/02/13/gibson/index.html

———. "Riding Shotgun with William Gibson." *Salon.com,* February 7, 2001. http://archive.salon.com/tech/feature/2001/02/07/gibson_doc/index.html

Lim, Dennis. "Now Romancer." *Salon.com,* August 11, 2007. http://www.salon.com/books/int/2007/08/11/william_gibson/index.html

McMahon, Donna. "Redefining William Gibson." *SF Site* (January 2003). http://www.SFsite.com/06b/wg154.htm

Olsen, Lance. *William Gibson.* Starmont Reader's Guide 58. Mercer Island, WA: Starmont, 1992.

Parker, T. Virgil, ed. "William Gibson: Sci-Fi Icon Becomes Prophet of the Present." In *Sausage Factory: The College Crier's Infamous Interviews of the Freaks and the Famous,* 237–50. Portland, OR: Inkwater, 2009.

Poole, Steven. "Tomorrow's Man." *Guardian Online,* May 3, 2003. http://www.guardian.co.uk/books/2003/may/03/sciencefictionfantasyandhorror.williamgibson

Yoke, Carl B., and Carol Robinson, eds. *The Cultural Influences of William Gibson, the "Father" of Cyberpunk Science Fiction.* Lewiston, NY: Edwin Mellen Press, 2007.

Kathleen Ann Goonan

Apocalyptic SF; Post-human SF; Sense of Wonder

Benchmark Title: *Queen City Jazz* (1994)

b. 1952 (Cincinnati, Ohio)

Fiction's deep rhythms demand tales of human change. . . . To meld two major musical and literary ideas of the twentieth century, to portray human change in a technological, if musical, milieu, seems to me to be an interesting and almost inevitable enterprise.
—"Science Fiction and All That Jazz" (2000)

Photo credit: Joseph Mansy.
Courtesy of Kathleen Goonan.

About the Author and the Author's Writing

Kathleen Ann Goonan was born in Cincinnati and spent part of her childhood in Washington, DC. She attended Virginia Polytechnic Institute, earning a degree in English literature and philosophy and, after graduation, attended the Montessori Institute in Washington, D.C., acquiring her *Association Montessori Internationale* teaching certification. "My grand plan was to work three hours a day, nine months a year, and write the rest of the time. What actually transpired was that I taught year round, all day" (Sisson 2004).

After qualifying as a teacher, Goonan moved to Knoxville, Tennessee, where her husband was a family practice resident at the University of Tennessee, and there she opened a Montessori school, which prospered—she eventually had a hundred students and many employees working for her. But writing was never far from her mind, and shortly before her thirty-third birthday, when her school was running smoothly and she found she had some time, she started writing again.

> I wrote my trunk novel in a year. When my husband was offered a job in Hawaii, I decided to take the plunge, . . . mainly on the strength of personal rejection letters I was getting from Gardner Dozois, editor of *Asimov's*, and Ellen Datlow, fiction editor, at that time, of *OMNI*. (Sissons 2004)

By 1994, when *Queen City Jazz* appeared, Goonan had published about twenty stories.

In Goonan's <u>Nanotech Cycle</u>, there has been a catastrophic failure of all electronic communications on Earth, and nano- and biotechnologies ("bionan") have been developed to replace the lost technologies. They, in their turn, have produced deep changes in cities, in the environment, and indeed in humankind itself. The four novels are not a direct, lineal narrative, but instead provide snapshots, from the point of view of those who have the most to lose, of how this catastrophe came upon the planet, and the cultural and social changes that occur in the aftermath of this sudden apocalyse. The answer, in each novel, is linked to music, in the metaphors and in the structure used. "*Queen City Jazz* is improvisational in form, like jazz. . . . . *Mississippi Blues* is linear, like a river . . . *Crescent City Rhapsody* draws on the fact that Duke Ellington wrote several rhapsodies, [and] portrays a future history as a deliberate composition on the part of one powerful woman" (Kaveney n.d.).

Light Music, the final volume in the quartet, is about consciousness and storytelling and the human use of symbol to replicate our stories, saving them for consumption later. Goonan's 1996 novel, *The Bones of Time*, is set in near-future Hawaii and again deals with the perils of experimental biological nanotechnology. *In War Times* (2007) is set in an alternate universe in which the protagonist, an amateur saxophonist, is given the plans of a device that could change human nature, and with it time itself. The novel asks: Can technology be prevented from doing as much evil as good?

In a way, Goonan's entire life has served as source material. She credits her father with her love of music, particularly jazz. "My head is stuffed with Broadway tunes, popular music, folk music . . . [jazz] has been my music of choice for some time now. It is inexhaustible, complex, interesting, and beautiful, composed and played by musicians rather than technicians" (Prisco 2002). Her novels have made good use of the places she has known in the course of her various careers—Washington, D.C., rural Ohio, the area around Cincinnati, and Hawaii. Goonan says, modestly, that her science education was limited to mandatory classes, taken in high school without much enthusiasm:

> I enjoyed them when I had to take them, but they took away time from reading books. I think that the main thing that was missing from such classes was any sense of amazement. It was as if all science things had happened in the past, and that science was over. (Prisco 2002)

But, educator that she is, she has achieved a very high standard in science for her fiction, and her narratives reflect her keen interest in modern research on nanotechnology, biology, and chemistry.

In publicity material for *Queen City Jazz*, William Gibson described it as "[a]n unforgettable vision of America transfigured by a new and utterly apocalyptic technology." Goonan's work is sometimes bracketed with cyberpunk, but although Goonan, like the cyberpunks, is interested in exploring the virtual space that is the consciousness, and the impact that new technologies has on that, her emphasis is more on the transcendent than on the noir. "Transcendence, and the possibility of transcendence, is the aspect of being human—and of science fiction—that keeps me going" ("Extending Our Senses"). Kathleen Ann Goonan lives with her husband in Lakeland, Florida.

Awards

Novels

In War Times (2007) **Campbell Memorial**

Works by the Author

The Bones of Time (1996)
In War Times (2007)

Nanotech Cycle

Queen City Jazz (1994)
Mississippi Blues (1997)
Crescent City Rhapsody (2000)
Light Music (2002) (excerpt at http://www.infinitematrix.net/stories/excerpts/light_music1.html)

Notable Short Fiction

"Kamehameha's Bones" (1993)
"The String" (1995). http://www.goonan.com/string.html
"Sunflowers" (1995)
"Angels and You Dogs" (2003)
"Bride of Elvis" (1997)
"The Day the Dam Broke" (1995). http://www.goonan.com/dam.html

Articles and Essays

"The Biological Century and the Future of Science Fiction." Paper presented at The Library of Congress, December 13, 2001. http://www.goonan.com/loc.html
"Cities of the Future?" *Paradoxa* 2, no. 1 (1996): 30–35.
"Consciousness, Literature, and Science Fiction." *Iowa Review* (August, 2005). http://www.goonan.com/
"First Sale." In *Science Fiction and Fantasy Writer's Sourcebook,* ed. David H. Borcherding, 403–6. Cincinnati: Writer's Digest, 1996.
"More Than You'll Ever Know: Down the Rabbit Hole of *The Matrix.*" In *Exploring* The Matrix*: Visions of the Cyber Present,* ed. Karen Haber, 98–111. New York: St. Martin's, 2003.
"Science Fiction and All That Jazz." *Borders.com*, June 19, 2000. http://www.goonan.com/essay.html

For Further Information

Official Web site: http://www.goonan.com/

"Extending Our Senses." *Locus* (June 2001). http://www.locusmag.com/2001/Issue06/Goonan.html
Kaveney, Roz. "A World Altered by Nanotechnology (Interview)." *Amazon.co.uk.* n.d. http://www.amazon.co.uk/gp/feature.html?ie=UTF8&docId=18179

Prisco, Giulio. Interview. *Transhumanism.org,* May 12, 2002. World Transhumanist Association. http://www.transhumanism.org/index.php/th/more/291/

Sisson, Kate. Interview. *The Frankenstein Project.* February 2004. Georgia Tech. http://frankenstein.lcc.gatech.edu/GoonanInterview.html

Colin Greenland

Myth and Legend; Science Fantasy; Space Opera

Benchmark Title: *Take Back Plenty* (1990)

b. 1954 (England: Dover, Kent)

[G]enre fiction is a bloody brilliant toybox, and it's much more fun if you don't follow the manufacturers instructions.

—Bould & Butler, "Voices on the Boom," *Science Fiction Studies* (2003)

Photo credit: Duncan Mackay.
Courtesy of Colin Greenland.

About the Author and the Author's Writing

Colin Greenland began his career as a professional in SF in the early 1980s with a piece of critical nonfiction. Reworking the PhD thesis he had just undertaken at Pembroke College, Oxford, Greenland wrote *The Entropy Exhibition* (1983), which is still considered the foremost critical resource on Michael Moorcock, Brian Aldiss, J. G. Ballard, and the British New Wave; as Greenland describes it, "less a Wave than an explosion, starting at a definable centre and dissipating swiftly in all directions" (*The Entropy Exhibition*). His first three novels, a series of classic picaresque adventures, are sophisticated planetary romances. The settings are lush, complicated, and drawn in great detail; the characters are attractive and witty, and are as much in search of the meaning at the heart of their own lives as of the dark secrets that control their worlds. The decadent and decaying city of Thryn, in *Daybreak on a Different Mountain* (1984), has strong echoes of Mervyn Peake's Gormenghast, and in *The Hour of the Thin Ox* (1986) and *Other Voices* (1988), the warring empires of Bryland and Escaly have stylish, satisfying overtones of seventeenth-century England. All are on the brink of devastating changes, and the stories are firmly in the tradition of classic New Wave: exotic SF fantasies, with witty, angst-ridden heroes and heroines, deep symbolic undercurrents, and what *The Encyclopedia of Science Fiction* 1999) describes as an "entropy-laden plot and venue."In other words, they are serious, and although witty and enjoyable, are distinctly light on the old-fashioned SF hardware—and the fun.

In 1990 all that changed. *Take Back Plenty* is a jolly space romp; "[t]his is Greenland unbound" (Wilder 1996). In a wry, postmodernist take on the conventions of good-old fashioned pulp SF, Greenland brought new life to the old tropes: the decadent Mars of sparkling canals and murky bodegas; the all-knowing, all-powerful aliens with deep, dark secrets; and the feisty space trucker heroine with a hangover and a heart of gold. In *Plenty*, and the follow-ups in the trilogy, Greenland took the conventions out of the toybox, dusted them off, turned them on their heads, and rattled them around a bit—and in doing so, paid space opera the ultimate tribute of taking it seriously, on its own terms. Space opera had never gone away, of course, but Greenland's reinvention of the genre set off its own shock waves and reminded readers and critics alike that, in the right hands, there could be a lot more to it than meets the eye. "[T]he novel, and its unconventional heroine Tabitha Jute, is demonstrably a joy in itself as much as a prophecy of science fiction yet to come . . . the right time to read *Take Back Plenty* is always now" (Brialey 2007).

Colin Greenland was born in Dover, in the county of Kent, in England. He was a seasoned author at the age of five, with a genre-bending work (for family distribution only) about a fire engine that lays an egg. His first short story, "Miss Otis Regrets" (1982), won second prize in a Faber & Faber competition; *Take Back Plenty* was the winner of all three major British science fiction awards—the Eastercon, Arthur C. Clarke and British SF Association awards—a record that still stands. He describes his most recent novels, *Finding Helen* (2003) and *Losing David* (2005), as *slipstream*, "set here and now but the world is a little bit weird" (Hendrick 2006).

Greenland continues to write nonfiction and book reviews, to inspire future writers in the workshops he conducts, and to be active as an editor and as a member of the British Science Fiction Association. He is described by friend and colleague Neil Gaiman, in a profile in the online magazine *Infinity Plus*, as "looking a little like Gandalf's rock-and-rolling youngest brother would, if he were secretly a pirate." He lives in Cambridge with his partner, the fantasy writer Susanna Clarke.

Awards

Novels
Take Back Plenty (1990) **Arthur C. Clarke, BSF**

Works by the Author

Daybreak on a Different Mountain (1984)
The Hour of the Thin Ox (1986)
Other Voices (1988)
Harm's Way (1993)

The Tabitha Jute Trilogy
Take Back Plenty (1990)
Seasons of Plenty (1995)
Mother of Plenty (1998)

Other Genre Fiction
Spiritfeather (2000)
Finding Helen (2002)

Notable Short Fiction
"Miss Otis Regrets" (1982)
"A Passion for Lord Pierrot" (1990). http://www.infinityplus.co.uk/stories/pierrot.htm

"Nothing Special" (1991)

"Kings" (2005)

Collections

The Plenty Principle (1997)

As Editor

Interzone: The 1st Anthology (1985, with John Clute and David Pringle)

Storm Warnings: Science Fiction Confronts the Future (1987, with George E. Slusser and Eric S. Rabkin)

Nonfiction Books

The Entropy Exhibition: Michael Moorcock and the British "New Wave" in Science Fiction (1983)

The Freelance Writer's Handbook (1986, with Paul Kerton)

Michael Moorcock: Death is No Obstacle (1992) (introduction by Angela Carter)

Articles and Essays

"The 'Field' and the 'Wave': The History of *New Worlds*." In *Speculations on Speculation: Theories of Science Fiction,* ed. James Gunn and Matthew Candelaria, 247–57. Lanham, MD: Scarecrow, 2005.

"Images of *Nineteen Eighty-Four*: Fiction and Prediction." In *Storm Warnings: Science Fiction Confronts the Future,* ed. George E. Slusser, Colin Greenland, and Eric S. Rabkin, 124–34. Carbondale: Southern Illinois University Press, 1987.

"Unsettling the World (Article on M. John Harrison, with Nik Pratt)." In *Savoy Dreams,* ed. David Britton and Michael Butterworth. Manchester, UK: Savoy, 1984.

Writer's Talk: Michael Moorcock with Colin Greenland. VHS videocassette. Northbrooke, IL: The Roland Collection, 1989.

For Further Information

Bould, Mark, and Andrew M. Butler. "Voices on the Boom." *Science Fiction Studies* 30 (2003): 483–91.

Brialey, Claire. "*The Arthur C. Clarke Award: A Critical Anthology*: Review." *Strange Horizons*, February 5, 2007. http://www.strangehorizons.com/reviews/2007/02/the_arthur_c_cl.shtml

Hendrick, Dave. Interview. *Fractal Matter* (March 2006).

Nicholls, Stan. "Colin Greenland Brings Back Plenty." In *Wordsmiths of Wonder: Fifty Interviews with Writers of the Fantastic,* 71–79. London: Orbit, 1993.

Profile. *Infinity Plus* (July 6, 2007). http://www.infinityplus.co.uk/misc/cg.htm

Robson, Justina. "The Wild Ride (*Take Back Plenty*—Colin Greenland)." In *The Arthur C. Clarke Award: A Critical Anthology,* ed. Paul Kincaid and Andrew M. Butler. London: Serendip, 2006.

Wilder, Cherry. "Colin Greenland." In *St. James Guide to Science Fiction Writers*, ed. Jay Pedersen. Detroit, MI: St. James, 1996.

Joe Haldeman

Hard SF; Military SF

Benchmark Title: *The Forever War* (1975)

b. 1943 (Oklahoma City, Oklahoma)

Compared to "normal" writers, science fiction writers are a remarkably sane and friendly bunch.
—Perret, *The Faces of Science Fiction* (1984)

Photo credit: Beth Gwinn

About the Author and the Author's Writing

Joe (*not* Joseph) William Haldeman was born in Oklahoma City, Oklahoma, and as a child lived, among other places, in Puerto Rico, New Orleans, Bethesda, Maryland, and Anchorage, Alaska. He married in 1965 and two years later graduated from the University of Maryland with a degree in physics and astronomy. That same year he was drafted into the army.

In an honest, insightful, and extremely moving autobiographical sketch he wrote in the 1990s for Gale's *Contemporary Authors* series ("Interim Report: An Autobiographical Ramble"), Haldeman talks about that time: "Everybody's life takes sudden turns, and we all look back at major branches and wonder who we could have been if this or that had gone the other way. I very much didn't want to go to Vietnam."

Haldeman had taken his degree with the idea of becoming a scientist-astronaut —a NASA program which, he later learned, produced only one graduate who actually walked on the moon before the program became moribund in the 1970s. As he finished his degree (and watched his draft-exempt status slip away), Haldeman applied for a job with the Naval Observatory, for a place with the Peace Corps, and for conscientious objector status. "[B]ut the draft board wouldn't even start the process until you had a letter from your minister, and atheists don't have ministers. Stupidly, I let it go at that" ("Interim Report"). His draft notice arrived while the navy and the Peace Corps were deciding.

Haldeman served as a combat engineer, fighting in the Central Highlands of Vietnam. He was severely wounded in a massive explosion of booby-trapped enemy ordinance. "[O]ur topkick . . . asked the major in charge of the operation to move the GIs away so we could 'blow it in place,' . . . . Anybody who's read *Starship Troopers* knows that intelligent officers listen to their NCOs, but this major was a jerk."

For over thirty years, Haldeman believed that he was the only survivor of his squad of four engineers. (He later discovered that they had all survived but, like himself, were terribly wounded.) Haldeman received a Purple Heart, awarded by the army on May 23, 1969 ("Interim Report"). In his autobiographical profile, he speaks frankly about how he briefly used opium to cope with the pain of his wounds and even had a single, alarming experience with a heroin "cigarette." His wartime experiences were the basis for *War Year*, his first, non-SF novel.

On his return to civilian life, Haldeman did an MFA in creative writing at the University of Iowa Writer's Workshop, during which time he produced *The Forever War* (1974), "[t]he only master's thesis that won a Hugo and a Nebula" (Mead 2004). His body of work now includes over two dozen novels, numerous short stories, and scripts for both film and theater.

Hemingway is one of Haldeman's great literary influences (another is John Brunner, who became a friend). Like Hemingway, Haldeman writes in an economical style and lets dialogue and character do the work. The impact of his experiences in the Central Highlands, combined with his easy understanding of the possibilities and consequences of science, makes for intriguing narratives. In *The Forever War*, for example, soldiers in an interplanetary conflict are doomed to "jump" from one battleground planet to another, in a sort of one-way time travel that not only alienates them from the society they are supposed to be fighting to defend, but often fatally undermines their effectiveness as soldiers. (Because their enemy is also making similar leaps in time and space, they have no idea if they will be facing troops with spears or the weapons of a future they can hardly imagine.) In a conflict that is eventually exposed as a sham, all these "forever" soldiers have is their loyalty to each other, which is ruthlessly exploited by those they serve. As *The Encyclopedia of Science Fiction* (1999) puts it, "as a portrait of the *experience* of Vietnam, the book is remarkable . . . . In Joe Haldeman's novels, making sense of things is itself an act of heroism."

Forever Free (1998) is a straight sequel to *The Forever War*, but *Forever Peace* revisits the same themes, from the completely opposite "what-if" stance. The characters of *Forever War* are dragged through time, away from home and family; their military service strips it all away from them. But the central character of *Forever Peace* is a "virtual soldierboy": he gives up a week or so a month to operate a telepresence device that turns him into a virtually indestructible warrior robot, many light years away. This soldier—ironically, a university professor—is enabled to do terrible things, giving up nothing, and with no physical or emotional investment whatsoever. As metaphors for the cost of war to the human spirit, all three novels constitute a remarkable achievement.

Over his career, Haldeman has been nominated for a long list of all the major SF awards. *Forever Peace* (1997) is one of his most honored novels, earning a "trifecta" of Hugo, Nebula, and Campbell awards in 1998; it was the first SF fiction in twenty-two years to sweep all three prestigious prizes. Haldeman is also a respected and award-winning poet; in his spare time, he paints watercolors—figure studies and abstract works of evocative landscapes and still-life studies. He carries his paintbox with him on his travels. "[T]he preparation for both, is kind of talking apples and oranges, but there is a correspondence. . . . [S]ometimes there is no preparation at all; I just start and see where things go" (Haber 2001). He and his wife, Gay Haldeman, currently divide their time between Gainesville, Florida, and Cambridge, Massachusetts, where Joe Haldeman teaches science fiction and writing at MIT.

Awards

Edward E. Smith Memorial Award for Imaginative Fiction ("Skylark award") (1996)

Novels

The Forever War (1975) **Hugo, Nebula, Locus Poll**
Forever Peace (1997) **Campbell, Hugo, Nebula**
Camouflage (2004) **Nebula, Tiptree**

Short Fiction

"Tricentennial" (1977) **Hugo, Locus Poll**
"The Hemingway Hoax" (1990) **Hugo, Nebula**
"Graves" (1993) **Nebula**
"None So Blind" (1994) **Hugo, Locus Poll**

Collections

None So Blind (1994) **Hugo, Locus Poll**

Works by the Author

Attar's Revenge (1975, as "Robert Graham")
War of Nerves (1975, as "Robert Graham")
Mindbridge (1976)
All My Sins Remembered (1977)
Star Trek: Planet of Judgment (1977)
Star Trek: World Without End (1979)
Buying Time (1989; UK: *The Long Habit of Living*)
The Coming (2000)
Guardian (2002)
Camouflage (2004)
Old Twentieth (2005)
The Accidental Time Machine (2007)
Marsbound (2008)

Forever War

The Forever War (1975)
Forever Free (1998)
Forever Peace (1997)

The Worlds
Worlds (1981)
Worlds Enough and Time (1992)
Worlds Apart (1983)

Mainstream and Other Genre Fiction
War Year (1972)
Tool of the Trade (1987)
1968 (1995)
Saul's Death and Other Poems (1997)

Other Notable Short Fiction
"Hero" (1973)
"Anniversary Project" (1975)
"This Space for Rent" (1978)
"Blood Sisters" (1979)
"More Than the Sum of His Parts" (1985)
"Images" (1991)
"Feedback" (1993)
"None So Blind" (1994). http://home.earthlink.net/~haldeman/story1.html
"For White Hill" (1995)
"Faces" (2004)
"Angel of Light" (2005). http://www.cosmosmagazine.com/node/42
"The Mars Girl" (2006)

Collections
All My Sins Remembered (1977)
Infinite Dreams (1978)
There Is No Darkness (1983). A collection of linked short stories, written with his brother, Jack C. Haldeman.
Dealing in Futures (1985)
Vietnam and Other Alien Worlds. (1993). Includes short fiction, poetry, and essays such as "Not Being There," "Confessions of a Space Junkie," "War Stories," and "Photographs and Memories."
None So Blind (1996)
War Stories (2006). An omnibus edition, including Haldeman's two Vietnam novels, *War Year* and *1968*, as well as stories and essays about the Vietnam War.
A Separate War and Other Stories (2007)

As Editor

Cosmic Laughter (1974)
Study War No More (1977)
Nebula Award Stories 17 (1983)
Best Military Science Fiction of the 20th Century (2001)
Future Weapons of War (2007, with Martin H. Greenberg)

Tomorrow's Warfare series (with Charles G. Waugh and Martin H. Greenberg)

Body Armor: 2000 (1986)
Supertanks (1987)
Spacefighters (1988)

In Other Media

"I of Newton." *Twilight Zone*, 1985. Directed by Kenneth Gilbert; starring Sherman Hemsley and Ron Glass. According to Haldeman's autobiographical profile for *Contemporary Authors*, this story was originally written for his college creative writing class. In 1970, after his return from Vietnam, he sold it to *Fantastic* magazine for a penny a word, earning $15. Later it was adapted for *Twilight Zone*, for fifty times as much. "Not bad for a story banged out overnight to meet a class deadline."

Articles and Essays

"Interim Report: An Autobiographical Ramble." *Contemporary Authors Autobiography Series*, Volume 25, 1996. http://home.earthlink.net/~haldeman/biolong.html
"The Matrix as Sci-Fi." In *Exploring* The Matrix*: Visions of the Cyber Present,* ed. Karen Haber, 168–79.. New York: St. Martin's, 2003.
"Point of View." In *Paragons: Twelve Master Science Fiction Writers Ply Their Craft,* ed. Robin Wilson, 273–79. New York: St. Martin's, 1996.

For Further Information

Official Web site*:* http://home.earthlink.net/~haldeman/

Blackmore, Tim. "Warring Stories: Fighting for Truth in the Science Fiction of Joe Haldeman." *Extrapolation* 34 (1993): 131–46.
de Beer, David. Interview. *Nebula Awards,* July 23, 2008. http://www.nebulaawards.com/index.php/interview/joe/
DeForest, Roger. "The Bulk of Haldeman's Brane." *Hard SF.com,* July 4, 2006. http://www.hardsciencefiction.rogerdeforest.com/?mode=8&id=3
Gordon, Joan. *Joe Haldeman.* Mercer Island: Starmont House, 1980.

———. "Joe Haldeman: Cyberpunk Before Cyberpunk Was Cool?" In *The Celebration of the Fantastic,* ed. Donald E. Morse, 251–57. Westport: Greenwood, 1992.

Haber, Karen. "Joe Haldeman: Art for Art's Sake." *Locus* (October 2001). http://www.locusmag.com/2001/Issue10/Haldeman.html

Jason, Philip K. "Joe Haldeman and the Wounds of War." In *Acts and Shadows: The Vietnam War in American Literary Culture.* Lanham, MD: Rowman & Littlefield, 2000.

McShane, Shamrock. "Joe Haldeman's Cosmological Adventure." *The New Moon Rising,* January 18, 2007. http://www.thenewmoonrising.com/archives/haldeman.htm

Mead, Donald. "Interview." *Strange Horizons,* February 23, 2004. http://www.strangehorizons.com/2004/20040223/haldeman.shtml

Podcast Interviews. *The Future and You.* 2006. http://www.thefutureandyou.libsyn.com/?search_string=haldeman&Submit=Search&search=1

Rand, Ken. "Joe Haldeman." *Internet Review of Science Fiction* (June 2004). http://www.irosf.com/q/zine/article/10061

Harry Harrison

Graphic Novels; Humor and Satire; Space Opera

Benchmark Title:
The Stainless Steel Rat (1961)

b. 1925 (Stamford, Connecticut)

Photo credit: Paul Tomlinson. Courtesy of Paul Tomlinson and Harry Harrison.

I have found that an action story with two or three levels of intellectual content below the surface enables me to say just what I want to say. I have also found that humor—and black humor—can carry ideas that can be expressed in no other way.

—www.harryharrison.com/

About the Author and the Author's Writing

Henry Maxwell Dempsey was born in Stamford, Connecticut. His father, who was a printer, changed the family's surname to Harrison shortly after the birth of his son. His mother was a schoolteacher, a Latvian immigrant who came to the United States when she was about fifteen years old. When Harrison was a baby, the family relocated to the New York borough of Brooklyn, and then to Queens, but the pressures of Depression life kept them unsettled. In a 1984 interview with biographer Paul Tomlinson, he recalled, "We'd do midnight flits: rent a new apartment, get a month's concession, pay for one month, stay for the two months, then for a third and owe the rent."

The frequent moves caused Harrison to do poorly in school and find it difficult to make friends, and he took refuge in SF and the Queens Public Library. When Harrison graduated from Forest Hills High School in 1943—in the midst of World War II—expecting to be drafted at any moment, he decided that, as he "didn't really want to drown, . . .[and] didn't want to be shot," he would join the Army Air Corps. He spent four years in the Army Air Corps as an armorer and gunnery instructor and reached the rank of sergeant. It wasn't the happiest of times, but like any good writer (even if he didn't realize it at that point), Harrison was storing up material: "Did I enjoy my stint in the army? No. If you read *Bill, the Galactic Hero* you'll see how I feel about the army" (Tomlinson 1984, 1999).

When the war ended, Harrison took advantage of the GI Bills of Rights and attended art classes, first at Hunter College in New York City, where he was a student of noted painter John Blomshield, and then at the Cartoonists and Illustrators School, where one of his instructors was Burne Hogarth—"the fellow who drew Tarzan." Harrison set up his own "comic book factory," where he did comics, advertising, and magazine illustrations. His status as professional illustrator for SF magazines brought him into contact with greats like Isaac Asimov, Damon Knight, and Theodore Sturgeon, and when Harrison wrote a SF story while he was recovering from the flu, it was Damon Knight who bought it, for the February 1951 issue of his magazine *Worlds Beyond*. Although Harrison's move from illustration to writing was gradual (and the two threads of his career overlapped for some years), it was hurried along when the Comics Code was introduced by Congress in 1955 and, amid sensationalist claims that they were corrupting the nation's youth, the golden age of the pulps came to an end.

In the irreverent humor of his Stainless Steel Rat novels and of Bill the Galactic Hero (a non-too-gentle spoof of writers like Heinlein and his gung-ho SF like *Starship Troopers*), Harrison's naturally iconoclastic style and attitude began to assert itself.

> In the classic opening to The Stainless Steel Rat, Slippery Jim DiGriz causes a safe to fall on the policeman who is trying to arrest him. While this could seem impossibly cruel and violent, the voice of the policeman is heard from beneath the safe, adding destruction of a police robot to the charges. (Barzier 1996)

There you have classic Harrison: shocking, if cartoonish violence, a quick punch line, and the equally fast restoration of the reader's sense of his hero as a basically good man.

Harrison also wrote other series, such as the West of Eden trilogy, and stand-alone SF such as *Captive Universe* (1969) and *Make Room! Make Room!* This 1966 novel was the basis for the 1973 Charlton Heston film *Soylent Green*, which won a Nebula Award for Dramatic Presentation, although Harrison's plot was greatly "Hollywood-ized." But Harrison could not say that he didn't see it coming: *The Technicolor Time Machine* (1968) is a movie industry satire, "making it clear that Hollywood will trivialize anything in the interest of making money" (Barzier 1996). For Bill the Galactic Hero, he has worked with Robert Sheckley and Jack C. Haldeman, as well as collaborating with Gordon R. Dickson and Leon Stover. Harrison also has a long list of collaborations as editor with Brian W. Aldiss.

In 1954 Harry Harrison married Joan Merkler, a dress designer and ballet dancer. From the late 1950s, their married life reads like a summary of the *World Almanac*, with extended and adventurous stays in London, Capri (chosen to escape a London winter), Copenhagen (chosen because Harrison learned from a fan that most Danes speak English), and Mexico. Why Mexico? "Because it is connected to America by road and you can drive there. . . . It was very cheap [in Mexico] in those days" (Tomlinson 1984, 1999).

The arrival of a son, Todd, and a daughter, Moira, did not curb the Harrison wanderlust. In the 1970s the family settled in Ireland, which is where Harry Harrison continues to make his home today.

Awards

Science Fiction Hall of Fame (2004)
SFWA Damon Knight Memorial Grand Master (2009)

Dramatic Presentation
Soylent Green (1973)

As Editor
Astounding: The John W. Campbell Memorial Anthology (1974) **Locus Poll**

Works by the Author

Planet of the Damned (1962; aka *A Sense of Obligation*)
Plague from Space (1965)
Make Room! Make Room! (1966)
The Technicolor Time Machine (1968)
Captive Universe (1969)
In Our Hands the Stars (1970; aka *The Daleth Effect*)
Spaceship Medic (1970)
Tunnel Through the Deeps (1972; aka *A Transatlantic Tunnel, Hurrah!*)
Star Smashers of the Galaxy Rangers (1974)
Skyfall (1976)
Lifeboat (1977; aka *Lifeship,* with Gordon R. Dickson)
Planet Story (1979)
Invasion: Earth (1982)
The Jupiter Plague (1982)
A Rebel in Time (1983)
The Turing Option (1992, with Marvin Minsky)

The Adventures of Bill, the Galactic Hero

Bill, the Galactic Hero (1965)
Bill, the Galactic Hero on the Planet of Robot Slaves (1989)
Bill, the Galactic Hero on the Planet of Bottled Brains (1990, with Robert Sheckley)
Bill, the Galactic Hero on the Planet of Tasteless Pleasure (1991, with David Bischoff)
Bill, the Galactic Hero on the Planet of Zombie Vampires (1991, with Jack C. Haldeman II)
Bill, the Galactic Hero on the Planet of Ten Thousand Bars (1991, with David Bischoff)
Bill, the Galactic Hero: the Final Incoherent Adventure (1991, with David Harris)

Deathworld Trilogy

Deathworld (1960)
Deathworld Two (1964)
Deathworld Three (1968)

Eden

West of Eden (1984)
Winter in Eden (1986)
Return to Eden (1988)

The Stainless Steel Rat

The Stainless Steel Rat (1961)
The Stainless Steel Rat's Revenge (1970)
The Stainless Steel Rat Saves the World (1972)
The Stainless Steel Rat Wants You! (1978)
The Stainless Steel Rat for President (1982)
You Can Be the Stainless Steel Rat (1985)
The Stainless Steel Rat Goes to Hell (1996)
The Stainless Steel Rat Joins the Circus (1999)

To the Stars

Homeworld (1980)
Starworld (1981)
Wheelworld (1981)

Other Genre Fiction

Vendetta for the Saint (1964)
Stonehenge (1972, with Leon Stover)
Stonehenge: Where Atlantis Died (1983, with Leon Stover)

Notable Short Fiction

"Rock Diver" (1951)
"The Stainless Steel Rat" (1957)
"American Dead" (1970)
"By the Falls" (1970)
"The Mothballed Spaceship" (1973)
"The Golden Years of the Stainless Steel Rat" (1993)
"Bill, the Galactic Hero's Happy Holiday" (1995)

Collections

War with the Robots (1962)
Two Tales and Eight Tomorrows (1968)
One Step from Earth (1970)
Prime Number (1970)
The Men from P.I.G. & R.O.B.O.T. (1974)
To the Stars (1987)

The Best of Harry Harrison (1991)

Stainless Steel Visions (1993)

Galactic Dreams (1994)

The Adventures of the Stainless Steel Rat (1996)

A Stainless Steel Trio (2003)

50 in 50: Fifty Stories for Fifty Years! (2002). Fifty stories, marking Harrison's fiftieth anniversary as a published SF writer. Contains personal favorites, as well as some stories that have never been collected before. Introduction by Harrison.

As Editor

Farewell Fantastic Venus (1968, with Brian W. Aldiss)

Nebula Award Stories 2 (1967, with Brian W. Aldiss)

Nova series (1970–1974)

Best SF series (1967–1976, with Brian W. Aldiss)

SF: Authors' Choice series (1968–1974)

Hell's Cartographers (1975, with Brian Aldiss). Collection of SF essays, including "The Beginning of the Affair" by Harrison himself, which is available online at http://www.harryharrison.com/.

Decade series (with Brian W. Aldiss)

Decade the 1940s (1975)

Decade the 1950s (1976)

Decade the 1960s (1977)

In Other Media

Soylent Green. Metro-Goldwyn-Mayer (MGM), 1973. Directed by Richard Fleischer; starring Charlton Heston and Edward G. Robinson. Extremely loose adaptation of Harrison's 1966 novel *Make Room! Make Room!*

Nonfiction Books

Great Balls of Fire! A History of Sex in Science Fiction (1977)

Spacecraft in Fact and Fiction (1979, with Malcolm Edwards)

Articles and Essays

"A Cannibalized Novel Becomes *Soylent Green.*" In *Omni's Screen Flights—Screen Fantasies: The Future According to SF Cinema,* ed. Danny Peary. New York: Doubleday, 1984. http://www.iol.ie/~carrollm/hh/soycann.htm

"Introducing the Future: the Dawn of Science-Fiction Criticism." In *Histories of the Future: Studies in Fact, Fantasy and Science Fiction,* eds. Alan Sandison and Robert Dingley, 1–7. Basingstoke, UK: Palgrave, 2000.

"Worlds Beside Worlds." In *Science Fiction at Large: A Collection of Essays, By Various Hands, About the Interface between Science Fiction and Reality*, ed. Peter Nicholls, 105–14. London: Gollancz, 1976. http://www.iol.ie/~carrollm/hh/n13-tt-worlds.htm

Bibliographies

Tomlinson, Paul. *Harry Harrison: An Annotated Bibliography*. Holicong, PA: Wildside/Cosmos, 2002. http://www.iol.ie/~carrollm/hh/map-bib.htm

For Further Information

Official Web site: Edited by Paul Tomlinson. http://www.harryharrison.com/
Harry Harrison Official News Blog: http://harryharrison.wordpress.com/

Barzier, Paul. "Harry Harrison." In *St. James Guide to Science Fiction Writers*, ed. Jay Pedersen. Detroit, MI: St. James, 1996.

Molson, F. J. "Harry Harrison." *Extrapolation* 32 (1991): 95–99.

"Science Fiction Should be Humane: A Talk with Harry Harrison." *Soviet Literature* 12 (1987):178–80.

Shreeve, John. "A Stainless Steel Rap: Harry Harrison Interviewed." *Interzone* 72 (June 1993): 23–26.

Stover, Leon. *Harry Harrison*. Boston: Twayne, 1990.

Tomlinson, Paul. *A Brief Biography*. 1984, 1999. http://www.harryharrison.com/

M. John Harrison

New Wave; Science Fantasy

Benchmark Title: *In Viriconium* (1982)

b. 1945 (England: Rugby, Warwickshire)

I am often thought of as a pessimistic writer. I believe this is an over-simplification and prefer to think of myself as a compassionate but realistic one.
—Author Comments, *St. James Guide to Science Fiction Writers* (1996)

About the Author and the Author's Writing

Up until the turn of the twenty-first century, M. John Harrison was regularly described by interviewers and profilers as a "brooding hermit," "the most underrated writer of his day," dark, bleak, and remote. "He frequently uses entropy as a metaphor for the meaningless struggle of everyday existence" (Hughes 2001). For the Author Comments in the fourth edition of the *St. James Guide to Science Fiction Writers* in 1996, Harrison wrote, of his own work, that his fiction is "concerned with the inability of people to feel ordinary emotions, or to communicate them successfully to one another."

His first novel, *The Committed Men* (1971), is a bleak (that word again!) story of postapocalyptic Britain, peopled with a grotesque band of characters—a dwarf, a cripple, and a girl who has just given birth to a mutant baby—who are on a quest through the a ravaged countryside to save the baby by delivering it to the new race of mutants that has carved its own territory in the south. His best known (but probably weakest) novel, *The Centauri Device* (1974), of which the author is extremely dismissive (see his comments in the 2002 *SF Site* interview), is a "deliberate and systematic overturning of the form's conventions" (Langan 2006): the "hero," John Truck, is not a hero. He gets through most of the novel as a passive loser and, to avoid serious spoilers, let's just say that it does not end well. Harrison's Viriconium series—which includes *The Pastel City* (1971), *In Viriconium* (1982), and numerous shorter works—is distinctly *downbeat* sword and sorcery. The novels use entropy, a civilization in decline, mysterious plagues, the psychology of sensory deprivation, and even what in other hands could be a ridiculous tale of invading sentient insects, as dark metaphors of the human condition. According to Rhys Hughes, in a profile originally published in *The Zone* magazine in 1996, Harrison is "at his best when depicting individuals struggling to preserve their identities in the face of abstract uncertainties."

But although he may be a little bleak, and quick to destroy whole galaxies on a whim, Harrison is also wonderful. As critic and writer Gabriel Chouinard says in his introduction to his 2002 *SF Site* interview, "[h]is prose sparkles, his ideas burn incessantly, and his characters sear their wily ways into the consciousness of all who read them."

It's hardly surprising that M. John Harrison was often referred to as SF's best-kept secret. But in recent years, to the delight of anyone who was in on the secret, M. John Harrison has emerged (after only forty-odd years) as a hot "new" property. This may have had as much to do with personal choices about his writing style as with a possible "smartening up" of his potential audience: as he tells it in the *SF Site* interview, one evening he was taken out for a drink by his agent and Iain M. Banks, "who I'm told is a bit of a novelist when he isn't driving fast cars . . . . At about two in the morning, Iain fixed me with a watery but evil eye and said, 'You know your trouble, Mike? You don't have enough fun.' I went away and thought about that; then I sat down at the iMac and had some fun."

Harrison is, as Chouinard puts it, "a cross-genre guerrilla." One of his finest novels is the semiautobiographical, and almost-mainstream, *Climbers* (1989)—he is a keen rock climber, and the book was "at its most autobiographical when you thought it was least, and vice versa." *Climbers* won the Boardman Tasker Prize for Mountain Literature, the first work of fiction to do so. *Viriconium,* and his most recent novels, *Light* (2002) and *Nova Swing* (2006), teeter on a sharp line between SF and fantasy but, as says, "My urge is less to transgress genre boundaries than *insult them*, in the medical sense" (Chouinard 2002).

Michael John Harrison was born in Rugby, in Warwickshire, England. In the early 1960s he trained to become a teacher; he sold his first story in 1966, to *New Worlds*, the New Wave SF magazine that was shaking up the genre under the general editorship of Michael Moorcock. From 1968 to 1975 Harrison worked as literary editor of *New Worlds*, and like others, started writing stories for Moorcock's Jerry Cornelius Multiverse. "His Cornelius stories have often been judged to be the best of the bunch—his treatment of the anarchic demagogue was both rigorous and careful . . . , showing a flair for characterisation, dynamic and description" (Hughes 2001).

Harrison is a regular fiction reviewer for the *Times Literary Supplement* and for the London newspapers *The Guardian* and *The Daily Telegraph*. Under the name Gabriel King he has written a number of more traditional fantasy novels, with Jane Johnson. M. John Harrison currently lives near the River Thames, in West London, with his girlfriend, Cath Phillips.

For forty years M. John Harrison has been at the cutting edge of every important development in SF: New Wave, the revival of the intelligent space opera, the transmigration of SF sensibilities to mainstream themes, and, most recently, the melding of the tropes of fantasy and SF into a seamless whole, which some call "the Weird." His last word about his writing, from the *SF Site* interview? "If it isn't two words away from falling over, it's not worth doing."

Awards

Novels

Light (2002) **Tiptree**
Nova Swing (2006) **ACC, PKD**

Works by the Author

The Committed Men (1971)
The Centauri Device (1974)
Signs of Life (1997)
Light (2002)
Nova Swing (2006)

The Viriconium sequence

The Pastel City (1971)
A Storm of Wings (1980)
In Viriconium (1982; aka *The Floating Gods*)

Notable Mainstream and Other Genre Fiction

Climbers (1989)
The Luck in the Head (1991; graphic novel, with Ian Miller)
The Course of the Heart (1992)

As Gabriel King (with Jane Johnson)

The Wild Road (1997)
The Golden Cat (1998)
The Knot Garden (2001)
Nonesuch (2002)

Notable Short Fiction

"Lamia Mutable" (1967)
"Running Down" (1975)
"Egnaro" (1981)
"A Young Man's Journey to Viriconium" (1985)
"Isobel Avens Returns to Stepney in the Spring" (1994). http://www.infinityplus.co.uk/stories/isobel.htm
"The East" (1996). http://www.mjohnharrison.com/archive/east.htm
"Suicide Coast" (1999)
"The Neon Heart Murders" (2000)
"I Did It" (2003). http://www.mjohnharrison.com/archive/ididit.htm
"Tourism" (2004). http://www.amazon.com/exec/obidos/tg/feature/-/536970/002-2458924-6179268

Stories in the Jerry Cornelius Universe

"The Ash Circus" (1969)
"The Nash Circuit" (1969)
"The Flesh Circle" (1971)

Collections

The Machine in Shaft Ten & Other Stories (1975)
The Ice Monkey & Other Stories (1983)
Viriconium Nights (1984)
Travel Arrangements (2000)
Things That Never Happen (2002) (introduction by China Miéville)
Viriconium (2005) (introduction by Neil Gaiman). An omnibus version that includes almost all the Viriconium stories.

Nonfiction Books

Fawcett on Rock (1987). Autobiography of rock climber Ron Fawcett, ghostwritten by Harrison.
Parietal Games: Critical Writings by and on M. John Harrison. (2005, ed. Mark Bould and Michelle Reid)

Articles and Essays

"Clone Alone." *The Guardian,* February 26, 2005. http://www.guardian.co.uk/books/2005/feb/26/bookerprize2005.bookerprize
"Introduction." In *The Chrysalids,* by John Wyndham. New York: Penguin, 2000.
"A Literature of Comfort." In *New Worlds Quarterly,* ed. Michael Moorcock, 182–90. New York: Berkley, 1971.
"The Profession of Fiction." In *The Profession of Science Fiction: SF Writers on Their Craft and Ideas,* ed. Maxim Jakubowski and Edward James, 140–53. New York: St. Martin's, 1992.
"What It Might Be Like to Live in Viriconium." *Fantastic Metropolis,* October 15, 2001. http://www.fantasticmetropolis.com/i/viriconium/
"How I Write." *Time Out Magazine* (December 2006). http://www.mjohnharrison.com/archive/tointerview.htm

For Further Information

Official Web site: http://www.mjohnharrison.com/

The M. John Harrison Blog: http://ambientehotel.wordpress.com/
Bould, Mark, and Michelle Reid, eds. *Parietal Games: Critical Writings by and on M. John Harrison.* Liverpool: Science Fiction Foundation, 2005.
Chouinard, Gabriel. "A Conversation with M. John Harrison." *SF Site* (September 2002). http://www.SFsite.com/12b/mjh142.htm
Clute, John. "M. John Harrison." In *Look at the Evidence: Essays and Reviews,* 430–35. Liverpool: Liverpool University Press, 1995.
Hudson, Patrick. "Disillusioned By the Actual." *The Zone Online* (November 2002). Pigasus Press. http://www.zone-SF.com/mjharrison.html

Hughes, Rhys. "Climbing to Viriconium: The Work of M. John Harrison." *Fantastic Metropolis,* October 15, 2001. http://www.fantasticmetropolis.com/i/harrison/

Langan, John. "Significant Stories, Stylishly Told." *Science Fiction Studies* 33 (2006): 348–52.

Mathew, David. Interview. *Infinity Plus* (November 2002). http://www.infinityplus.co.uk/nonfiction/intmjh.htm

Miéville, China. "The Limits of Vision(aries): Or M. John Harrison Returns to London and It Is Spring." *Vector* 226 (2002): 10–13.

Morgan, Cheryl. Interview. *Strange Horizons,* June 9, 2003. http://www.strangehorizons.com/2003/20030609/harrison.shtml

"No Escape." *Locus* (December 2003). http://www.locusmag.com/2003/Issue12/Harrison.html

Nussbaum, Abigail. "Is There Someone at the End of This Rope? A Long Day's Struggle with M. John Harrison." *Asking the Wrong Questions,* September 17, 2005. http://wrongquestions.blogspot.com/2005/09/is-there-someone-at-end-of-this-rope.html

Robert Heinlein

Hard SF

Benchmark Title: *Stranger in a Strange Land* (1961)

b. 1907 (Butler, Missouri); d. 1988 (Carmel, California)

A human being should be able to change a diaper, plan an invasion, butcher a hog, conn a ship, design a building, write a sonnet, balance accounts, build a wall, set a bone, comfort the dying, take orders, give orders, cooperate, act alone, solve equations, analyze a new problem, pitch manure, program a computer, cook a tasty meal, fight efficiently, die gallantly.
—Time Enough for Love (1973)

About the Author and the Author's Writing

Robert Anson Heinlein was born in Butler, Missouri, and grew up in Kansas City. He graduated from the U.S. Naval Academy at Annapolis in 1929 and achieved the rank of lieutenant, serving in radio communications on the newly commissioned aircraft carrier USS *Lexington*, and later on the destroyer USS *Roper*. However, by 1934 Heinlein had developed pulmonary tuberculosis and had to retire from the service on medical grounds. Following his discharge, while he was recuperating Heinlein attended graduate classes in mathematics and physics at the University of California at Los Angeles (UCLA) and became involved in local politics. He worked on a newspaper that supported socialist firebrand Upton Sinclair's "End Poverty in California" movement and later worked for Sinclair's unsuccessful gubernatorial campaign; in 1938 Heinlein himself ran for the California State Assembly as a Sinclair Democrat. (His friend and fellow writer L. Sprague de Camp noted affectionately in the *Requiem* he wrote on Heinlein's death, "His political orientation then was quite different from the emphatic conservatism that he later embraced.") Heinlein lost his bid for public office, and for a while he tried to support himself by selling real estate, with a brief foray into silver mining. When neither of those options worked out very well, he turned to writing science fiction.

Robert Heinlein is one of the true classics; his prolific output shaped the twentieth century's perception of space and the universe, not only the fiction, but the fact as well. Heinlein's career closely shadowed, or even anticipated, the trends that were shaping mass-marketing publishing in the twentieth century. There was his intense activity on the SF pulp magazine story factories in the later 1930s and 1940s and the postwar "coming-of-age" novels depicting keen young inventors, starmen, and astronauts of the late 1940s and 1950s. There was the more didactic tone of his later work: Heinlein scholar George Slusser, in his argument for Heinlein as a great American novelist and technical innovator, calls his late novels, beginning with *Stranger in a Strange Land*

(1961), "meta-fiction," in which the author speaks through the novel as one of the characters. And Slusser (1996) adds: "Loony Tunes did not wait for Roland Barthes to create "mise en ablime" narrative, so Heinlein, in a work like *Number of the Beast*, invented out of the stuff of his own created world (and the SF genre itself) a fascinating piece of self-reflexivity."

Heinlein's scrupulous attention to technical detail, as well as his efforts to maintain plausibility in both plot and character, "raised the bar" for the whole genre of SF, but also created an environment in which readers—ordinary readers, not just fans—*believed* that interplanetary travel could and would happen, that it was just a matter of time. Heinlein may be the classic that he is because, in fact and fiction, he was a "man of the future"—a forward thinker who as a naval officer worked at the cutting edge of communication technology for the U.S. Navy, and as a civilian, years later, designed a "modern" home with his wife Virginia, incorporating labor- and energy-saving features that are standard or commonplace today, but in the 1950s really did seem like science fiction. That sort of forward thinking translated itself easily into Heinlein's fiction. It wasn't exactly that Heinlein saw inventions like cell phones, microwave ovens, and guided missiles in his "crystal ball"; it was more that Heinlein could see that things like that would have to be invented to enable the future that his characters inhabited. Consequently, Robert Heinlein's future felt used, comfortable, and *right*. He even identified the vocabulary that we would all need in this future of his; words and phrases from his writing have slipped effortlessly the language, because they pin down very specific aspects of our modern world: to "grok" (meaning to understand or deeply appreciate), "TANSTAAFL" (that is, "There ain't no such thing as a free lunch") and "waldo" (for a robotic device or prosthetic limb, named after a character in a 1942 Heinlein story who builds a technology empire by using such a device).

Heinlein is one of a handful of SF authors who, in their own lifetimes, came to be seen and respected as "emissaries" of the future they wrote about. On July 20, 1969, he joined Walter Cronkite and Arthur C. Clarke to provide television commentary as Neil Armstrong set foot on the surface of the moon.

As a writer, Heinlein is almost impossible to pin down—the young naval officer and child of solid, conventional Midwestern morals and values coexists comfortably with the author who wrote about unconventional values and sexual relationships. The radical and the conservative coexist comfortably, and just when you think you have his number, he surprises you. Heinlein can simultaneously be perceived as patron saint of militarism (*Starship Troopers*) and free love (*Stranger in a Strange Land*). In answer to the question, "Is Heinlein right-wing?" Spider Robinson replies that he might be—if you stretch the definition to include

> a man who bitterly opposes military conscription, supports consensual sexual freedom . . . , champions massive expenditures for scientific research, suggests radical experiments in government; and has written with apparent approval of anarchists, communists, socialists, technocrats, limited-franchise-republicans, emperors and empresses, capitalists, dictators, thieves, whores, charlatans and even career civil servants. (Robinson 1980, 2001)

Given the breadth of his writing and the scope of his interests, it is incredible to note that Heinlein suffered from varying degrees of ill health for most of his adult life. In July 1979 he was invited to Washington, D.C., to testify before a joint session of the

House Committee on Aging and the House Committee on Science and Technology, on the applications of space technology to the elderly and the handicapped. Robert Heinlein died of cardiovascular disease and emphysema in Carmel, California, on May 8, 1988. In 1994 a crater on Mars was named after him.

Awards

Locus All-Time Polls—All-time Author (1973 and 1977)
SFWA Grand Master (1977)
Science Fiction Hall of Fame (1998, posthumous)

Novels

The Future History series: **All-Time Series, Hugo** (1966)
Red Planet (1949) **Prometheus Hall of Fame 1996**
The Farmer in the Sky (1951) **Retro Hugo 2001**
Double Star (1956) **Hugo**
Methuselah's Children (1958) **Prometheus Hall of Fame 1997**
Starship Troopers (1959) **Hugo**
Stranger in a Strange Land (1961) **Hugo, Prometheus**
The Moon Is a Harsh Mistress (1966) **Hugo, Nebula, Prometheus**
Time Enough for Love (1973) **Prometheus**
Job: A Comedy of Justice (1984) **Locus Poll**

Short Fiction

"Requiem" (1940) **Prometheus Hall of Fame 2003**
"The Man Who Sold the Moon" (1951) **Retro Hugo 2001**

Nonfiction

Grumbles from the Grave (1989) **Locus Poll**

Dramatic Presentation

Destination Moon (1947)

Works by the Author

Beyond This Horizon (1942)
Rocket Ship Galileo (1947)
Space Cadet (1948)
Red Planet (1949)
Sixth Column (1949)
The Farmer in the Sky (1951)
The Puppet Masters (1951)

Between Planets (1951)
The Rolling Stones (1952)
Starman Jones (1953)
The Star Beast (1954)
Tunnel in the Sky (1955)
Double Star (1956)
Time for the Stars (1956)
The Door into Summer (1957)
Citizen of the Galaxy (1957)
Have Space Suit—Will Travel (1958)
Starship Troopers (1959)
Stranger in a Strange Land (1961)
Podkayne of Mars (1963)
Glory Road (1963)
Farnham's Freehold (1964)
The Moon Is a Harsh Mistress (1966)
Waldo and Magic, Inc. (1966)
I Will Fear No Evil (1970)
The Notebooks of Lazarus Long (1978)
Job: A Comedy of Justice (1984)
Variable Star (2006, completed by Spider Robinson)

The "Future History" series

Methuselah's Children (1958)
Orphans of the Sky (1963)
Time Enough for Love (1973)
The Number of the Beast (1980)
Friday (1982)
The Cat Who Walks Through Walls (1985)
To Sail Beyond the Sunset (1987)

Other Notable Short Fiction

"Life-Line" (1939)
"The Roads Must Roll" (1940)
"By His Bootstraps" (1941)
"—And He Built a Crooked House" (1941)
"The Green Hills of Earth" (1947)
"The Man Who Sold the Moon" (1951)
"The Year of the Jackpot" (1952)
"All You Zombies—" (1959)

Collections

To read all of Heinlein's short fiction, you would need the following:
The Past Through Tomorrow (1967)
Expanded Universe (1980)
The Fantasies of Robert A. Heinlein (2002)
Off the Main Sequence (2005)

In Other Media

Destination Moon. George Pal Productions, 1950. Directed by Irving Pichel; screenplay by Heinlein, based on the 1947 novel *Rocket Ship Galileo.*

Project Moon Base. Galaxy Pictures Inc., 1953. Pilot for abandoned TV series; directed by Richard Talmadge.

The Puppet Masters. Hollywood Pictures, 1994. Directed by Stuart Orme; starring Donald Sutherland.

Starship Troopers. Tristar Pictures, 1997. Directed by Paul Verhoeven; starring Casper Van Dien and Neil Patrick Harris.

Nonfiction Books

Grumbles from the Grave (1989)
Take Back Your Government: A Practical Handbook for the Private Citizen Who Wants Democracy to Work (1992)
Tramp Royale (1996). An account of his travels with his wife, Virginia.

Articles and Essays

"On the Writing of Speculative Fiction." In *Writing Science Fiction & Fantasy,* ed. The Staff of *Analog & Isaac Asimov's Science Fiction Magazine,* 5–12. New York: St. Martin's Griffin, 1993.

"Science Fiction: Its Nature, Faults and Virtues." In *Turning Points: Essays on the Art of Science Fiction,* ed. Damon Knight, 3–28. New York: Harper & Row, 1977.

Bibliographies

Ormes, Marie Guthrie. "Surprises in the Heinlein Bibliography." In *Imaginative Futures,* ed. Milton T. Wolf and Daryl F. Mallett, 95–114. San Bernardino, CA: Borgo, 1995.

Stephenson-Payne, Phil. *Robert Heinlein, Stormtrooping Guru: A Working Bibliography.* Albuquerque, NM: Galactic Central, 1993.

For Further Information

The Heinlein Society: http://www.heinleinsociety.org/

Site RAH: The Home Page for Science Fiction's Grand Master. Ed. James Gifford. Nitrosyncretic Press. 2005. http://www.nitrosyncretic.com/rah/

Angelo, Darlos, ed. *Robert A. Heinlein: The Dean of Science Fiction Writers*. April 21, 2002. http://www.wegrokit.com/index.htm

Doherty, Brian. "Robert Heinlein at 100: How the Science Fiction Master Created the Template for Our Looser, Hipper, More Pluralist World." *Reason* (August/September 2007). http://reason.com/archives

Franklin, H. Bruce. *Robert A. Heinlein: America as Science Fiction*. New York: Oxford University Press, 1980.

Gifford, James. *Robert A. Heinlein: A Reader's Companion*. Sacramento, CA: Nitrosyncretic, 2000.

Pace, Eric. Obituary. *The New York Times,* May 10, 1988.

Platt, Charles. "Heinlein Speaks?" In *Loose Canon,* 100–111. Holicong, PA: Cosmos/Wildside, 2001.

Robinson, Spider. "Rah, Rah, R. A.H.!" *Destinies* (Summer 1980). (Reprinted in *Time Travelers Strictly Cash.* New York: Tor, 2001). http://www.heinleinsociety.org/rah/works/articles/rahrahrah.html

Slusser, George Edward. *Robert A. Heinlein: Stranger in His Own Land*. San Bernardino, CA : Borgo, 1977.

———. "Robert A. Heinlein." In *St. James Guide to Science Fiction Writers,* ed. Jay Pedersen. Detroit, MI: St. James, 1996.

Stimson, Thomas E., Jr. "A House to Make Life Easy." *Popular Mechanics* (June 1952). http://www.nitrosyncretic.com/rah/pm652-art-hi.html. Fascinating article on, and photographs of, Robert and Virginia Heinlein showing off the "futuristic" house they designed.

Stover, Leon. *Robert Heinlein*. Boston: Twayne, 1987.

Vonnegut, Kurt. "Heinlein Gets the Last Word." *New York Times Book Review*, December 9, 1990, 13.

Frank Herbert

Post-human SF; Space Opera

Benchmark Title; *Dune* (1965)

b. 1920 (Tacoma, Washington); d.1986 (Madison, Wisconsin)

Like the best muckraking yellow journalists of the news media, I ask questions that other people aren't asking, and do a lot of investigating into the world around me. So even though I try to write entertaining, future-oriented stories, my books always contain messages that—I believe—are relevant to our situation today.
—Stone, "The Plowboy Interview," *Mother Earth News* (1981)

About the Author and the Author's Writing

Frank Patrick Herbert was born in Tacoma, Washington, and grew up on the family's small farm in Kitsap County. As he described it in an interview with *Mother Earth News* in 1981, "[t]here were pigs to feed, and I had corn and such to hoe. I once even reared and canned 500 chickens as a 4-H project. We raised all our own food."

He grew up surrounded by a large extended family—ten maternal aunts and six paternal uncles. Times were hard, but the responsibility, self-sufficiency, and support of a close community shaped Herbert's attitudes and his fiction. And from a very young age, much to the amusement of his family, Herbert was sure that he wanted to be a writer. In 1939 he moved to California, lied about his age, and got himself a job as reporter for the *Glendale Star*. "Country pragmatism doubtless contributed as well to his choice of journalism as the compromise career for a fledgling storyteller. 'You do things which are necessary,' he says" (O'Reilly 1981).

For most of his working life, Herbert was a professional journalist writing for dailies such as the *Seattle Star*, *The Oregon Statesman*, and *The San Francisco Examiner*. During World War II he served in the Seabees, as a photographer. He attended the University of Washington for a while, where he met his future wife, Beverly, but did not graduate: "I wasn't interested in a degree. I was always interested in writing. I looked on schools, especially the higher levels, as a kind of cafeteria line" (O'Reilly 1981).

During the 1950s and early 1960s, Herbert had more than twenty short stories accepted in various magazines. The first to be published under his own name—"The Survival of the Cunning," published by *Esquire* in 1945—is a war story set in the Arctic, in which an Eskimo guide uses his superior understanding of his harsh environment to save a navy scout. His first novel, *The Dragon in the Sea* (1955, also know as *Under Pressure*), is a submarine thriller set in an ongoing future war caused by a worldwide oil shortage. Both of these early works deal with themes that Herbert would one day weave into a more substantial narrative: life in extreme environments, respect for nature, and the consequences of carelessness with limited resources. But more substantial success eluded him, and for some years Beverly was the family breadwinner, while he was a "house-husband" and child-carer to their two sons; meanwhile, he was doing journalism pieces and working on a particular project that had caught his imagination.

In 1957 Herbert had done extensive research on a government project in the town of Florence, Oregon, that aimed to control sand dunes by ecological rather than mechanical means. Herbert became fascinated by the variety of life that survived on the shifting slopes of the dunes, and the lengths that plant and animal life went to in order to make the most of the scant resources. "[I]t was, for a science-fiction writer anyway, an easy step from that to think: What if I had an entire planet that was desert?" (McNelly 1987).

Dune is a gothic political thriller set on Arrakis, a desert planet that is the only natural source of the spice *mélange*, an all-important hallucinogen that not only makes interstellar travel possible, but (it gradually emerges) also prolongs life and provides a gateway to a higher consciousness. With *Dune*, Herbert introduced a science fiction in which technology comes second to character, philosophy, and world-building. Herbert's message "is an interest in ecology and a respect for rural values, a fear of man's tampering with nature coupled with the realization that he must tamper with himself if he is to advance" (Macdonald 1996).

Although *Dune* immediately made Herbert's name, it was not an instant money-maker, and for some years he continued to write for newspapers. But like the spice *mélange*, *Dune* gradually took over and transformed his life: from 1970 to 1972, he was a lecturer at the University of Washington. He was invited to write and speak on ecological issues. He went to Vietnam and Pakistan as a social and ecological consultant in 1972 and then produced a documentary based on his experiences, called *The Tillers*. *Dune* enabled him to "practice what he preached," and by the time he was interviewed by *Mother Earth News* in 1981, his home was a model of a sustainable lifestyle: "I'm slowly but surely thermopaning all the house's windows.... I intend to add a solar collector over our swimming pool building to heat its water . . . and—for a time—I even raised chickens to provide manure for my methane experiments."

Dune is the single work that will always be associated with Frank Herbert's name. He wrote many other stories, which are well worth reading, such as *Destination: Void* (1966), *Whipping Star* (1970), and *The White Plague* (1982). And, of course, there are additional chapters of the Dune saga, which stir mixed feelings in readers—depending on who you ask, they are either a triumphant development of the themes of the first volume, with a "life and interest beyond mere plot"(Macdonald 1996) or an overinflated extension: "none has anything like the power of the first book" (Andrews and Rennison 2006). But *Dune* is regularly voted the "greatest" SF novel of all time.

Frank Herbert was planning and working with his son Brian Herbert on a seventh novel in the Dune saga when he died on February 11, 1986, in Madison, Wisconsin, the result of a pulmonary embolism brought on by surgery to treat pancreatic cancer. Since 1999 Brian Herbert and Kevin J. Anderson have produced a number of prequel novels, as well as two—*Hunters of Dune* (2006) and *Sandworms of Dune* (2007)—that complete the original Dune series, based on notes Frank Herbert left behind.

Awards

Science Fiction Hall of Fame (2006, posthumous)

Novels

Dune (1965) **Hugo, Nebula**
All-Time Best Novel: (1975, 1987, 1998) **Locus Poll**

Works by the Author

Under Pressure (1955; aka *The Dragon in the Sea*)
The Eyes of Heisenberg (1966)
The Green Brain (1966)
The Santaroga Barrier (1968)
The Heaven Makers (1968)
The Godmakers (1972)
Soul Catcher (1972)
Hellstrom's Hive (1973)
Direct Descent (1980)
The White Plague (1982)
Man of Two Worlds (1986, with Brian Herbert)

ConSentiency Universe

Whipping Star (1970)
The Dosadi Experiment (1977)

Dune

Dune (1965)
Dune Messiah (1969)
Children of Dune (1976)
God Emperor of Dune (1981)
Heretics of Dune (1984)
Chapterhouse: Dune (1985)

WorShip novels

Destination: Void (1966, rev. 1978)
The Jesus Incident (1979, with Bill Ransom)
The Lazarus Effect (1983, with Bill Ransom)
The Ascension Factor (1988, with Bill Ransom)

Collections

The Worlds of Frank Herbert (1970)

The Book of Frank Herbert (1973)

The Priests of Psi (1980)

Eye (1985, illustrated by Jim Burns)

Songs of Muad'Dib: Poems and Songs from Frank Herbert's "Dune" Series and His Other Writings (1992)

The Road to Dune (2005, with Brian Herbert and Kevin J. Anderson)

As Editor

New World or No World (1970)

Nebula Winners 15 (1981)

In Other Media

Dune. HarperAudio! May 24, 1994. Internet Town Hall. http://town.hall.org/radio/HarperAudio/052494_harp_ITH.html. Frank Herbert reading excerpts.

Dune. Universal Pictures, 1984. Directed by David Lynch; starring Kyle McLachlan, Francesca Annis, Patrick Stewart, Max von Sydow, and Sting.

Dune. Evision, 2000. TV mini-series directed by John Harrison; starring Alec Newman and William Hurt.

Children of Dune. Blixa Film Produktion GmbH & Co. KG, 2003. TV mini-series, sequel, directed Greg Yaitanes; starring Alec Newman.

Nonfiction Books

Threshold: The Blue Angels Experience (1973)

Without Me, You're Nothing: The Essential Guide to Home Computers (1981, with Max Barnard)

Articles and Essays

"The ConSentiency and How It Got That Way." *Galaxy* (May 1977).

"Dune Genesis." *Omni Magazine* (July 1980).

"Introduction." In *Saving Worlds,* by Roger Elwood and Virginia Kidd. New York: Doubleday, 1973. (Reissued as *The Wounded Planet*)

"Listening to the Left Hand." *Harper's Magazine* (1973). http://www.aeriagloris.com/Resources/FrankHerbertEssay/index.html

"Men on Other Planets." In *The Craft of Science Fiction,* ed. Reginald Bretnor. New York: Harper and Row, 1976.

"Science Fiction and a World in Crisis." In *Science Fiction, Today and Tomorrow; A Discursive Symposium,* ed. Reginald Bretnor, 69–97. New York: Harper & Row, 1974.

Bibliographies

Kahl, Kris. Bibliography. *Cave of Birds.* May 2007. http://www.caveofbirds.com/bib.html

For Further Information

Official Web site: http://www.dunenovels.com/

Andrews, Stephen E., and Nick Rennison. "Frank Herbert." In *100 Must-Read Science Fiction Novels*. London: A. & C. Black, 2006.

Herbert, Brian. *The Dreamer of Dune: A Biography of Frank Herbert*. New York: Tor, 2003.

"An Interview with Brian Herbert." *Space.com,* July 31, 1999. http://www.space.com/sciencefiction/herbert.html

Jonas, Gerald. "The Sandworm Sage." *The New York Times,* May 17, 1981.

Macdonald, Gina. "Frank Herbert." In *St. James Guide to Science Fiction Writers,* ed. Jay Pedersen. Detroit, MI: St. James, 1996.

McNelly, Willis E., ed. *The Dune Encyclopedia*. New York: Berkley Trade, 1987.

———. Transcript of an interview recorded with Frank Herbert on February 2, 1969 in Sexek (Turkey). Plan B. July 2005. http://www.sinanvural.com/seksek/inien/tvd/tvd2.htm

Merritt, Byron. "Frank Herbert Lives." *The Zone Online* (November 2005). Pigasus Press. http://www.zone-SF.com/frankherbert.html

Miller, D. M. *Frank Herbert*. Starmont Reader's Guide, 5. Mercer Island, WA: Starmont, 1981.

O'Reilly, Timothy. *Frank Herbert*. New York: Frederick Ungar, 1981. http://tim.oreilly.com/herbert/

Platt, Charles. "Frank Herbert." In *Dream Makers: The Uncommon People Who Write Science Fiction,* 183–92. New York: Berkley, 1980.

Stone, Pat. "The Plowboy Interview: Frank Herbert." *Mother Earth News* (May/June 1981). http://www.motherearthnews.com/Nature-Community/1981-05-01/Interview-With-A-Science-Fiction-Author.aspx

Touponce, William F. *Frank Herbert*. Boston: Twayne, 1988.

Turner, Paul. "Vertex Interviews Frank Herbert." *Vertex* (October 1973). http://members.lycos.co.uk/Fenrir/ctdinterviews.htm

Russell Hoban

Apocalyptic SF; Myth & Legend

Benchmark Title: *Riddley Walker* (1981)

b. 1925 (Lansdale, Pennsylvania)

I myself would say I'm dedicated to strangeness. I find myself wondering what it is that looks out through my eyeholes, and I really don't know. And it's this strangeness that I'm always pursuing in my writing and it's this sorrow in each of us that I'm trying to get to and depict as accurately as I can.
—Martin, "Russell Hoban," *The Independent* (2006)

Photo credit: Permission of David Higham Associates.

About the Author and the Author's Writing

On my naming day when I come 12 I gone front spear and kilt a wild boar he parbly ben the las wyld pig on the Bundel Downs any how there hadn't ben non for a long time befor him nor I ain't looking to see none agen. (*Riddley Walker*, 1981)

Prior to 1973, Russell Hoban was an author of children's fiction. Grateful parents, when confronted with the sticky question of something to read to their darlings at bedtime, would bless the man who gave us Frances, the badger child whose simple, familiar adventures *some* parents can still quote, from memory, twenty-odd years after the event. Hoban was already the author of about fifty books for children, some illustrated with charming, witty pencil drawings by his wife Lillian, when in the early 1970s he began to write adult fiction—stories darker, stranger, and altogether different, that nonetheless blended strangeness, allegory, and wordplay with the same humor that made the Frances books such a pleasure for both parent and child. What happened next, as Earl Rovit described in a 1997 survey of Hoban's work in *Hollins Critic*, was "the kind of stunning miracle which devoted readers have learned to recognize and accept with gratitude . . . *Riddley Walker* arrived, whole-hewn, unpredictable, inimitable."

Riddley Walker is set about 2,000 years in the future, long after the now-apocryphal splitting of "the little shining man, the Addom" and the explosion of the "1 Big 1," which had blasted England back to hard-scrabble primitivism. In *Riddley Walker*, the Iron Age meets Heironymous Bosch, in a world that is suspicious of "clevverness," a world in which the powers-that-be communicate to the huddled masses though Punch and Judy shows that recycle misremembered lessons of the past. It is a world in which the language spoken is a version of English that is, like the landscape, rusted and eroded, and "just woar down a littl." Riddley himself—"courageous, endearing, wonderfully articulate, and shrewd beyond his years" (Rovit 1997)—is a twelve-year-old boy who is thrust into the machinations of adulthood by the death of his father and various mysterious indications that he has been chosen for some important role in his hard little world. "*Riddley Walker* is not SF at its most edifying and highbrow, but at its most linguistically and imaginatively exuberant; it is a thought-experiment with a heart and a sensibility as well as a mind" (McGuirk 1999).

Russell Conwell Hoban was born just outside of Philadelphia, Pennsylvania, the son of Jewish Ukrainian immigrants who named their son after Russell Conwell, the charismatic preacher and inspirational speaker who founded Philadelphia's Temple University. Hoban briefly attended Temple, until he left to enlist in the army during World War II. During his military service, he met and married his first wife, the illustrator Lillian Hoban. For many years he worked as a magazine illustrator and advertising copywriter, as well as a prolific writer of books for young children. In 1969 he took his family to London, intending to stay only a short time. But in England the Hobans' marriage ended, and although the rest of the family returned to the United States, he remained in London and has lived there ever since.

Russell Hoban is the author of over a dozen adult novels. His two most obviously SF works are *Riddley Walker* and *Fremder* (1996), the mysterious story of the sole survivor of the disappearance of a deep-space freighter; but everything he writes plays with the conventions of various genres—SF, fantasy, mythology, historical fiction, as well as mainstream. His fantasy often has SF embellishments—in a near-future where lions have become extinct, the love between a father and son restores them to the world (*The Lion of Boaz-Jachin and Jachin-Boaz,* 1973); in *Pilgermann* (1983), time travel enhances a retelling of the legend of the Wandering Jew. His mainstream fiction, such as *Turtle Diaries* (1975), and his most recent work, *My Tango with Barbara Strozzi* (2007), sparkles with magical touches. Although he has never been a best seller, he has achieved cult status: in an annual worldwide tribute called the "Slickman A4 Quotation Event," fans celebrate his birthday by leaving quotations from his works, typed neatly on yellow paper, in unlikely places, to be found by the uninitiated. In 2005 fans organized an international convention—a *Some-Poasyum*, as young Riddley Walker would call it—to celebrate his eightieth birthday. Russell Hoban lives in London with his wife, Gundula Ahl; they have three children, one of whom is the composer Wieland Hoban, to whom *Riddley Walker* is dedicated. "What ben makes tracks for what wil be. Words in the air pirnt foot steps on the groun for us to put our feet in to."

Awards

Novels

Riddley Walker (1980) **Campbell Memorial**

Works by the Author

Riddley Walker (1980)
Fremder (1996)

Notable Mainstrean and Other Genre Fiction

The Lion of Boaz-Jachin and Jachin-Boaz (1973)
Turtle Diary (1975)
Pilgermann (1983)
Turtle Diary (1986)
The Medusa Frequency (1987)
Mr. Rinyo-Clacton's Offer (1998)
Amaryllis Night and Day (2001)
Her Name Was Lola (2003)
My Tango with Barbara Strozzi (2007)

Children's Books

The Mouse and His Child (1968)
Emmet Otter's Jug-Band Christmas (1971, illustrated by Lillian Hoban)
Egg Thoughts and Other Frances Songs (1972)
The Marzipan Pig (1986)

Frances the Badger series

Bedtime for Frances, Bread and Jam for Frances, etc. (1960–1970, all illustrated by Lillian Hoban)

Collections

A Russell Hoban Omnibus (1999)

In Other Media

Emmet Otter's Jug-Band Christmas. Canadian Broadcasting Corporation (CBC) and Jim Henson Associates, 1977. A Muppets production of the Hobans' story. Directed by Jim Henson; starring Frank Oz and Jerry Nelson.

The Mouse and His Child. Walt DeFaria Productions, 1977. Directed by Charles Swenson and Fred Wolf; starring Peter Ustinov and Cloris Leachman.

Turtle Diary. British Lion Film Corporation, 1985. Adapted by Sir Harold Pinter; directed by John Irvin; starring Glenda Jackson and Ben Kingsley.

The Marzipan Pig. Michael Sporn Animation, 1990. Directed by Michael Sporn; starring Tim Curry.

Nonfiction Books

"Writers' Rooms: Russell Hoban." *The Guardian*, March 22, 2009. http://books.guardian.co.uk/graphic/0,,2208617,00.html

For Further Information

Official Web site: http://www.ocelotfactory.com/hoban/index.html

The Russell Hoban Some-Poasyum: February 11–13, 2005. http://www.hoban2005.co.uk/. A celebration of the work and eightieth birthday of "the most original novelist we have" (*The Times*).

"All My Soups: Interview." *BookGroup.info,* February 4, 2003. http://www.bookgroup.info/041205/interview.php?id=9

Kohlhaas, Alidë. "Novels from the Pen of a Mature Writer." *Lancette Arts Journal* (December 2005).

Martin, Tim. "Russell Hoban: Odd, and Getting Odder." *The Independent* (London), January 22, 2006. http://arts.independent.co.uk/books/features/article340500.ece

McCalmont, Katie. "Interview: Russell Hoban." *untitledbooks.com,* November 6, 2008. http://www.untitledbooks.com/features/interviews/russell-hoban/

McGuirk, Carol. "*Riddley Walker*: Expanded Edition." *Science Fiction Studies* 26 (1999). http://www.depauw.edu/SFs/birs/bir77.htm#hoban

Rovit, Earl. "The Fiction of Russell Hoban." *Hollins Critic* 34, no. 5 (December 1997): 1–12.

Swaim, Don. Interview. *Wired for Books* (1987). http://wiredforbooks.org/russellhoban/

Wilkie, Christine. *Through the Narrow Gate: The Mythological Consciousness of Russell Hoban.* Rutherford, NJ: Farleigh Dickinson University Press, 1989.

Nalo Hopkinson

Myth and Legend; Near Future; Science Fantasy

Benchmark Title:
Brown Girl in the Ring (1998)

b. 1960 (West Indies: Jamaica)

Do you think of yourself as a Canadian writer or a Caribbean writer? A: Both. Q:. Do you think of yourself as a queer writer or just as a writer? A: Both. Q: Do you think of yourself as a woman writer, or— A: Both. All of the above, and more.

—FAQ, nalohopkinson.com

Photo credit: D. C. Findlay © 2007.
Courtesy of Nalo Hopkinson.

About the Author and the Author's Writing

Nalo Hopkinson is the Persephone of SF, visiting the underworld of Caribbean *obeah*, with its duppies and jumbies (Jamaican ghosts and dark spirits), soucouyants (a sort of succubus, or vampire), *voudoun* ladies, and other powerful spirits, and bringing them back, for the benefit of her readers, to meet an unpredictable future. Since 1998, when Hopkinson's *Brown Girl in the Ring* won the Warner Aspect First Novel contest, she has been demonstrating that SF does not have to be just "adventure stories in which white people use technology to overpower alien cultures. Small wonder that black writers haven't been drawn to it in large numbers—we've been on the receiving end of colonization, and for us it's not an entertaining adventure story" (Rutledge 1999).

Nalo Hopkinson was born in Kingston, Jamaica; she grew up there and in Trinidad and Guyana. For a while her family lived in the United States, in Connecticut. Her father, the late Abdur Rahman Slade Hopkinson, was a Guyanese actor, poet, and playwright and a member of Derek Walcott's Trinidad Theatre Workshop. When Hopkinson was seventeen her family moved to Toronto, to enable her father to get the treatment he needed for chronic kidney failure. She has lived in Canada ever since. Her education was disrupted by all the moving around; as she told Gregory E. Rutledge in an interview for *African American Review*, "Four high schools in four different countries.... Was good at biology, literature, and languages; indifferent at geography, history, civics, and art; horrible at math, physics, and chemistry. Now I have to study it all in order to write what I do, and it's much more fun this way."

She graduated with honors in Russian and French from York University and considered a career as a chiropractor or in recreation management. ("I guess you don't want to know about the aerobics instructor training courses" [Rutledge 1999].) In 1995 she attended the Clarion Science Fiction and Fantasy Writers' Workshop, where she met Samuel Delany, one of her long-time literary role models, and also earned an MA degree in writing popular fiction at Seton Hill University, where she studied with science fiction writer James Morrow.

To say that her fiction draws upon Caribbean history and language, and its traditions of oral and written storytelling, is like saying Ernest Hemingway writes fishing stories. Her fictions glow with the possibilities of a fruitful cross-pollination of science and magic, social extrapolation and tradition. *Brown Girl* is set in late twenty-first-century, inner-city Toronto, a "donut city" in which everyone who has the resources has fled to the 'burbs, and the center has collapsed in on the poor and the predatory. She creates a vivid world of urban decay and startling, dangerous magic, where the human heart is both a metaphor and the key to her characters' dilemmas. In this bleak setting, a young woman, Ti-Jeanne, unwed mother and nascent mystic and healer like her own mother, Mami Gros-Jeanne, struggles to survive. The story is told in a dizzying mixture of Caribbean *patois* and a stripped down street slang as rough as the dying Toronto that surrounds them.

> "But doux-doux," Prince of Cemetery said, "Your granddaughter head full of spirits already; she ain't tell you? All kind of duppy and thing. When she close she eyes, she does see death. She belong to me. She is my daughter. You should 'fraid of she." (*Brown Girl in the Ring*)

In her most recent novel, *The New Moon's Arms* (2007), her central character, Chastity, is a fifty-year-old woman whose two big life transitions—the death of her beloved father and the beginning of menopause—signal the return of a special gift for finding lost things. Like an old toy truck, or her hairbrush. Or a four-year-old boy, who is the key to a mystery at the heart of Chastity's life. As Hopkinson told David Soyka in a 2001 interview for *SciFi Weekly*, "I try to write from my center. In order to do that in a literary milieu that presumes ground zero to be white middle-class experience, I have to shift the reader's vision over to the margins."

In addition to repeated nominations for a Nebula (2008), the Philip K. Dick Award (1998, 2001), and the Tiptree Prize, for fiction that "explores and expands the roles of women and men" (1998, 2000), Hopkinson has repeatedly been honored by Canadian arts organizations. She received the Ontario Arts Council Foundation Award for Emerging Writers and two Aurora Awards (2006 for *Tesseracts 9*, an anthology of Canadian science fiction and fantasy that she edited with Geoff Ryman; and 2008, for *The New Moon's Arms*). She has also won the Sunburst Award for Canadian Literature of the Fantastic twice, the first author to do so.

Since the publication of *Brown Girl in the Ring,* Hopkinson has been writing and teaching writing at various programs around the world. She has been a writer-in-residence at Clarion several times, and she is one of the founding members of the Carl Brandon Society, a group "dedicated to addressing the representation of people of color in the fantastical genres." She is working on a new novel, *Taint*; CBC Radio recently made a recording of her reading one of her short stories to an original musical composition by William Sperandei, a jazz trumpeter.

Nalo Hopkinson continues to push the boundaries of what SF and fantasy can do.

Awards

Campbell New Writer Award (1999)

Novels

Brown Girl in the Ring (1998) **Locus Poll**

Works by the Author

Brown Girl in the Ring (1998)
Midnight Robber (2000)
The Salt Roads (2003)
The New Moon's Arms (2007)

Other Notable Short Fiction

"Slow Cold Chick" (1998)
"The Glass Bottle Trick" (2000)
"Greedy Choke Puppy" (2000)
"Something to Hitch Meat To" (2001)
"The Smile on the Face" (2004)
"Soul Case" (2007)

Collections

Skin Folk (2001)

As Editor

Whispers from the Cotton Tree Root: Caribbean Fabulist Fiction (2000)
Mojo: Conjure Stories (2003)
So Long Been Dreaming (2004)
Tesseracts Nine (2005, with Geoff Ryman)

Articles and Essays

"Delany's Mad Man: The Dark Side of Human Desire." *WORD: Toronto's Black Culture Magazine* (October 27, 1994): 10.

"Dropping Science: Black Science Fiction in the 90's," *Possibilities* 1, no. 4 (1995): 16–19.

"Looking for Clues (WisCon GOH Speech 2002)." *Extrapolation* 44, no. 1 (2003): 112–17.

"Où Suis-Je? Or, Where Am I?" *Indie Bound*. American Booksellers Association, n.d. http://www.indiebound.org/author-interviews/hopkinsonnalo2

Bibliographies

Rutledge, Gregory E. "Nalo Hopkinson: Bibliography and Appreciation." *University of Nebraska-Lincoln DigitalCommons*, May 30, 2002. http://

digitalcommons.unl.edu/cgi/viewcontent.cgi?article=1024&context=englishfacpubs

For Further Information

Official Web site and blog: http://www.nalohopkinson.com/

Aylott, Chris. "Filling the Sky with Islands: An Interview with Nalo Hopkinson." *Space.com*, January 11, 2000. http://www.space.com/sciencefiction/books/hopkinson_intv_000110.html

Batty, Nancy. "Caught by a . . . Genre" (Interview). *Ariel* 33, no. 1 (2002): 175–201.

Brown, Charles N. "Nalo Hopkinson: Multiplicity." *Locus* (June 2007). http://www.locusmag.com/2007/Issue06_Hopkinson.html

Burwell, Jennifer, and Nancy Johnson, "A Dialogue on SF and Utopian Fiction, between Nalo Hopkinson and Élisabeth Vonarburg." *Foundation* 81 (Spring 2001): 40–47.

"A Conversation with Nalo Hopkinson." *SF Site* (2000). http://www.SFsite.com/03b/nh77.htm

Glave, Dianne D. "An Interview with Nalo Hopkinson." *Callaloo* 26, no.1 (2003): 146–59.

Grant, Gavin J. Interview. *Indie Bound*. American Booksellers Association, n.d. http://www.indiebound.org/author-interviews/hopkinsonnalo

Haugan, Robyn, and Kelly Hanson. Biography and Bibliography. *VG.com*, December 16, 2004. University of Minnesota. http://voices.cla.umn.edu/vg/Bios/entries/hopkinson_nalo.html

Interview. *SFFworld.com*, March 13, 2000. http://www.SFfworld.com/interview/76p0.html

Nelson, Alonda, ed. "Making the Impossible Possible: An Interview with Nalo Hopkinson." In *Afrofuturism: A Special Issue of Social Text*. Durham, NC: Duke University Press, 2002.

Rambo, Cat. Interview. *Nebula Awards*, February 1, 2009. http://www.nebulaawards.com/index.php/interview/nalo_hopkinson/

Rutledge, Gregory E. "Speaking in Tongues: An Interview with Science Fiction Writer Nalo Hopkinson." *African American Review* 33, no. 4 (1999): 589–601.

Schellenberg, James, and David M. Switzer. Interview. *Challenging Destiny,* April 10, 2001. http://www.challengingdestiny.com/interviews/hopkinson.htm

Soyka, David. "Nalo Hopkinson Uses SF to Probe the Inner and Outer Worlds of Alienation." *Sci Fi Weekly,* October 1, 2001. (Since this excellent interview was accessed in May 2009, the SciFi channel, now SyFy, appears to have removed all SciFi Weekly Archives.)

Watson-Aifah, Jené. "A Conversation with Nalo Hopkinson." *Callaloo* 26, no.1 (2003): 160–69.

Aldous Huxley

Dystopias; Humor and Satire; Utopias

Benchmark Title: *Brave New World* (1932)

b. 1894 (England: Godalming, Surrey); d. 1963 (Los Angeles, California)

> *Within the next generation I believe that the world's leaders will discover that infant conditioning and narco-hypnosis are more efficient, as instruments of government, than clubs and prisons, and that the lust for power can be just as completely satisfied by suggesting people into loving their servitude as by flogging them and kicking them into obedience.*
> —Letter to Eric Blair (George Orwell), 1949,
> in *Letters of Aldous Huxley* (1969, ed. Grover Smith)

About the Author and the Author's Writing

If George Orwell's *Nineteen Eighty-Four* is the great totalitarian dystopian novel of the mid-twentieth century, *Brave New World,* by Aldous Huxley, provides its mirror image—Utopia *as* dystopia, a darkly ironic picture of a future "perfect society" in which an infantile hedonism is the norm, and humankind has been drugged and genetically manipulated into mindless compliance. Huxley was a social satirist, who used irony and caricature in his mainstream novels like *Crome Yellow* (1921) and *Antic Hay* (1923) to capture the essence of the world that emerged from the horror of the trenches of World War I. His novels were notorious for their matter-of-fact attitude to sex, free-thinking, and all-around iconoclasm, stances intended to express the disruption of life and society that he had witnessed in British society after the war.

Aldous Leonard Huxley was born in Godalming, Surrey, in England. His family pedigree was uniquely blended to produce an evangelical freethinker and challenger of the status quo. Huxley was the grandson of T. H. Huxley, a prominent nineteenth-century English naturalist, advocate of the superiority of the scientific method, and originator of the term "agnostic." (T H. Huxley was also the much-admired professor who inspired young H. G. Wells with ideas about evolution and society.) On his mother's side, Aldous Huxley was an Arnold: Julia Arnold Huxley was the niece of the great Victorian poet and critic Matthew Arnold and the novelist Mrs. Humphrey Ward, as well as being the granddaughter of Dr. Thomas Arnold, the inspirational educator and original embodiment of "muscular Christianity," who featured as a character in the novel *Tom Brown's Schooldays*. Huxley's first school was his father's well-equipped botanical laboratory, and his first tutor was his mother; after her death, in 1908, he attended Eton College, and he graduated from Balliol College, Oxford, in 1916 with first-class honors.

An illness he suffered as a teenager left Huxley blind for several years and with very poor eyesight for the remainder of his life. His disability spared him military service in World War I; he spent some time during the war years on the estate of the radical society hostess Lady Ottoline Morrell, where he met and befriended many of the great writers and artists of the day, such as D. H. Lawrence, Bertrand Russell, and Lytton Strachey. There he also met and married his first wife, Maria Nys. Huxley also taught French at Eton for a year. Eric Blair (George Orwell) was one of his pupils, and although he was remembered as a hopeless teacher, he also impressed Blair with his way with words.

In 1937 Huxley moved to California with his wife and son; he lived in the United States for the rest of his life. He supplemented his writing income with screenwriting, and his name appeared in the credits of a number of movies, such as *Pride and Prejudice* (1940) and *Jane Eyre* (1944); however, his unhurried working pace and unconventional narrative style soon put an end to his Hollywood career. (Walt Disney supposedly said that he only understood every third word of Huxley's rejected script for *Alice in Wonderland*.) As time passed, his writing became more mystical, reflecting his interest in the effects of psychedelic drugs. In his 1954 memoir *The Doors of Perception*, Huxley argued that two substances he had been experimenting with, lysergic acid (soon to become better know as LSD) and mescaline, should be widely used for the visionary experience they offered. This book became a cult text in the psychedelic 1960s—the title inspired the name of the rock band The Doors, and Huxley's impassioned advocacy of the use of mind-bending drugs won him a place of honor on the cover of The Beatles' 1967 album *Sgt. Pepper's Lonely Hearts Club Band*.

Huxley's four novels with SF themes cover quite a range of SF tropes. *After Many a Summer* (1939) is a dark consideration of the cost of eternal life; *Ape and Essence* (1948) is a postapocalyptic fantasy. But it is for *Brave New World* that he will undoubtedly be remembered, with its frightening vision of how relaxed social trends and scientific "progress" (test tube babies, chemical and genetic engineering, Pavlovian conditioning) could, by the twenty-sixth century, result in a nearly irresistible form of dictatorship. In his final years he wrote the Utopian novel *Island* (1962), an altogether more positive and gentler look at what the future might hold. As he put it in an essay he wrote as a foreword to the twentieth anniversary edition of *Brave New World*, *Island* offers "a third alternative. Between the Utopian and primitive horns of his dilemma would lie the possibility of sanity. . . . Science and technology would be used as though, like the Sabbath, they had been made for man, not . . . as though man were to be adapted and enslaved to them."

When Huxley's first wife, Maria, was dying of breast cancer in 1955, Huxley used hypnotic techniques in her final hours to talk her through the memory of ecstatic experiences she had had earlier in life. His own health deteriorated after 1960, and when he himself was dying, he asked his second wife, the writer Laura Archera, to inject him with LSD. He died on November 22, 1963, as the world was reeling from the assassination of President John F. Kennedy. Huxley's ashes were interred in the family grave in the cemetery in Compton, a village near, Guildford, Surrey.

Works by the Author

Brave New World (1932)
After Many a Summer (1939)
Ape and Essence (1948)
Island (1962)

Notable Mainstream Fiction

Crome Yellow (1921)
Antic Hay (1923)
Point Counter Point (1928)
Eyeless in Gaza (1936)
The Genius and the Goddess (1955)

Collections

On the Margin (1923)
The Art of Seeing (1942)
The Perennial Philosophy (1945)
The Doors of Perception (1954). http://www.mescaline.org/huxley.htm
Heaven and Hell (1956)
Brave New World Revisited (1958)
Literature and Science (1963)
The Collected Short Stories of Aldous Huxley (1992)
Huxley and God: Essays (2003)

In Other Media

A Woman's Vengeance. Universal International Pictures (UI), 1948. Directed by Zoltan Korda; starring Charles Boyer and Ann Blyth. The first of at least nine adaptations of Huxley's noir short story, "The Giaconda Smile."

"Ape and Essence." British Broadcasting Corporation (BBC), 1966. A TV play in *The Wednesday Play* series; directed by David Benedictus; starring Alec McCowen.

The Devils. Russo Productions, 1971. Wild adaptation of *The Devils of Loudun*, Huxley's nonfiction account of accusations of witchcraft in seventeenth-century France; directed by Ken Russell; starring Oliver Reed and Vanessa Redgrave.

Brave New World. Dan Wigutow Productions, 1998. Directed by Leslie Libman and Larry Williams; starring Peter Gallagher and Leonard Nimoy. Not a great adaptation, but better than the 1980 mini-series.

Aldous Huxley: The Gravity of Light. Cinéma Esperança International Inc., 2005. Documentary, directed by Oliver Hockenhull.

Nonfiction Books

Jesting Pilate (1926)
Grey Eminence (1941)
The Devils of Loudun (1953)
Letters of Aldous Huxley (1969, ed. Grover Smith)
Selected Letters (2007)

Articles and Essays

"Chemical Persuasion." In *Turning Points: Essays on the Art of Science Fiction,* ed. Damon Knight, 231–37. New York: Harper & Row, 1977.

"Culture and the Individual." *Playboy* (1963). http://www.psychedelic-library. org/ huxcultr.htm

"Foreword." In *Brave New World*. London: Penguin Modern Classics, 1950.

"On Self-Transcendence," epilogue to *The Devils of Loudun.* (1953). http://www.psychedelic-library.org/loudun.htm

"The Ultimate Revolution." Berkeley Language Center—Speech Archive (SA 0269).University of California, Berkeley, March 20, 1962. http://sunsite.berkeley.edu/Speech/VideoTest/audiofiles.html#huxley

Bibliographies

"Aldous Huxley: Bibliography." *Erowid Character Vaults* (July 2007). Erowid.org. http://www.erowid.org/culture/characters/huxley_aldous/huxley_aldous.shtml

For Further Information

Aldiss, Brian. "Between Privy and Universe: Aldous Huxley (1894–1963)." In *The Detached Retina: Aspects of SF and Fantasy,* 31–36. Syracuse, NY: Syracuse University Press, 1995.

The Aldous Huxley Society. The Centre for Aldous Huxley Studies, Department of English, Westfälische Wilhelms-Universität Münster. March 19, 2009. http://www.anglistik.uni-muenster.de/Huxley/ahs.html. The Centre also publishes *The Aldous Huxley Annual*: *A Journal of Twentieth-Century Thought and Beyond*, in association with the University of Kentucky.

Barfoot, C. C., ed. *Aldous Huxley: Between East and West*. Amsterdam: Rodopi, 2001.

Bedford, Sybille. *Aldous Huxley: A Biography*. Chicago: Ivan R. Dee, 2002. Readable 1974 biography, based on the author's forty-year friendship with Huxley.

Desmond, Adrian. *Huxley: From Devil's Disciple to Evolution's High Priest*. London: Penguin, 1997.

Dunaway, David K. *Aldous Huxley Recollected: An Oral History*. New York: Carroll & Graf, 1995.

Fraser, Raymond, and George Wickes. Interview. *The Paris Review* (Spring 1960). http://www.theparisreview.com/viewinterview.php/prmMID/4698

Huxley, Laura Archera. *This Timeless Moment: A Personal View of Aldous Huxley*. Berkeley, CA: Celestial Arts, 2000 (orig. pub. 1968).

Murray, Nicholas. *Aldous Huxley: A Biography*. New York: St. Martin's, 2003.

Somaweb: The Intellectual, Satirical, Spiritual, Hypnotic, and Philosophical World of Aldous Huxley. April 25, 2009. http://somaweb.org/

Texas Archival Resources Online. *Aldous Huxley Papers, 1916–1963*. University of Houston, 1995. http://www.lib.utexas.edu/taro/uhsc/00008/hsc-00008.html

Gwyneth Jones

Myth and Legend; Near Future

Benchmark Title: *Divine Endurance* (1984)

b. 1952 (England: Manchester)

I've always liked Hans Andersen's stories, because of their cruelty. I like the way his magic makes things marvellous without making them any easier.
—"Deconstructing *Divine Endurance*" (1998)

Photo credit: Trisha Turchas, Archer Photography. Courtesy of Gwyneth Jones.

About the Author and the Author's Writing

In an interview in *Cold Print* in 2002, Gwyneth Jones referred to science fiction as "fairytales with technology in them." Although this is a definition that might drive some readers of SF mad, it is a very apt five-word summary of the impressive work of an author who writes fantasy with a cold, hard spine of science; near-future SF with a thoughtful leavening of Arthurian romance and rock 'n' roll; young adult fiction that is compelling and frightening enough for the most demanding adult; and an alien invasion saga that re-creates, with hermaphrodite aliens, the sorry history of Western Europe's imperialistic adventures in Africa. "It seems," as she told *SF Site* online magazine in a 2004 interview, "that, originally, a fairy was a story about fated events, about someone's destiny working out, in noteworthy ways." If so, then Gwyneth Jones is fulfilling her "fairy" by telling well-written, provocative stories that are an interesting combination of SF and high fantasy—sometimes in the same novel.

Gwyneth Ann Jones was born in Manchester, England, and graduated from the University of Sussex with a degree in European history of ideas. In addition to the SF and fantasy novels she has written under her own name, she has been writing fantasy, horror, and ghost stories for young readers since 1980 under the name Ann Halam. Her first published SF for adults, *Divine Endurance*, was written at a time when Jones was, more or less by choice, living in Singapore as a stay-at-home wife:

> I was surrounded by people who didn't see my situation as the dutiful little pleasure-machine as a free, temporary choice. As far as they were concerned it was my natural role, I was designed that way. This was a shock. I'm sure that's part of where Cho came from. ("Deconstructing *Divine Endurance*" 1998)

In *Divine Endurance*, the "orphaned" princess, Chosen Among the Beautiful (Cho, for short), has grown up in mysterious isolation, looked after (or is it imprisoned?) by machines, with only the imperious, all-knowing cat Divine Endurance as a companion. Dramatic events force child and cat—who are not exactly what they seem—on a quest that takes them through a far-future Southeast Asia peopled with princes, clans, gangsters, and revolutionaries. In fact, if there is a common thread running through the disparate styles of Gwyneth Jones, it is that things are never precisely what they seem. The novels that comprise The Aleutian Trilogy may appear, on the surface, to be a good old-fashioned alien invasion saga, complete with gender-bending aliens—the "Aleutians"—who are humanlike enough to be provocative, but alien enough to pose a real challenge to the humans who must survive their reign on Earth. But as the series progresses, it becomes obvious that no one is who or what he appears. In her work, Jones consistently shows that SF does not have to depend on "raygun death and heroic derring-do; rather, it heads off into disturbing territories" (Mitchell 1997).

Jones has recently claimed to have forsworn SF for fantasy, at least for the time being. *Bold as Love*, the first volume in her extended "fantasy" cycle, combines elements of science fiction, fantasy, and horror in a near-future Britain in which ecological and social disasters have lead to the ascendance of a Green counterculture government of rock musicians. In fact, when the first volume appeared, some reviewers complained that she had gone beyond the fantastic. Celebrities and rock stars leading a country? Who ever heard of such thing? But, as David Soyka admits in his *SF Site* interview, Jones was merely ahead of the curve: "Now that the Terminator is governor of California, I feel as if I owe you an apology."

Gwyneth Jones is also a respected critic, whose essays and reviews have appeared in a wide range of periodicals, as well as online. In addition to SF awards, she has received two World Fantasy Awards and the Children of the Night Award from the Dracula Society, She was a co-winner of the very first Tiptree award, the annual literary prize for "science fiction or fantasy that explores and expands the roles of women and men," awarded for *White Queen* (the first volume of The Aleutian Trilogy). She lives with her husband and son in Brighton, England. "Whether or not the technology is plausible, or the political-sociological-philosophical ideas are interesting, you have the story to fall back on . . . and maybe the story is what lasts" ("Building Sandcastles" 2002).

Awards

Novels

White Queen (1991) **Tiptree**
Bold as Love (2001) **ACC**
Life (2004) **PKD**

Short Fiction

"La Cenerentola" (1998) **BSF**

Works by the Author

Divine Endurance (1984)
Escape Plans (1986)

Kairos (1988)
The Hidden Ones (1988)
Spirit: or The Princess of Bois Dormant (2008)

The Aleutian Trilogy

White Queen (1991)
North Wind (1994)
Phoenix Café (1997)

Bold as Love Cycle

Bold as Love (2001)
Castles Made of Sand (2002)
Midnight Lamp (2003)
Band of Gypsies (2005)
Rainbow Bridge (2006)
Life (2004)

Other Notable Genre Fiction

Water in the Air (1977)
The Influence of Ironwood (1978)
The Exchange (1979)

As Ann Halam

Ally, Ally, Aster (1981)
The Alder Tree (1982)
King's Death's Garden (1986)
Dinosaur Junction (1992)
The Haunting of Jessica Raven (1994)
The Fear Man (1995)
Don't Open Your Eyes (2000)
Taylor Five: The Story of a Clone Girl (2001)
Dr. Franklin's Island (2002)
Siberia (2005)

Zanne series

The Daymaker (1987)
Transformations (1988)
The Skybreaker (1990)

Notable Short Fiction

"Bold as Love" (1992) http://www.infinityplus.co.uk/stories/boldlove.htm
"The Grass Princess" (1995)

"Red Sonja and Lessingham in Dreamland" (1996)
"Balinese Dancer" (1997)
"The Tomb Wife" (2007)

Collections

Identifying the Object (1993)
Seven Tales and a Fable (1995)
Grazing the Long Acre (2009)
The Buonarotti Quartet (2009)

In Other Media

Telebugs. Telemagination, 1986. Children's animated adventure, featuring cute robots; broadcast on British ITV. Episodes were directed by Elphin Lloyd-Jones and John M. Mills, featuring the voice of Ron Moody as the various characters.

Nonfiction Books

Deconstructing the Starships: Science, Fiction and Reality (1998)
Imagination/Space (2009)

Articles and Essays

"Deconstructing *Divine Endurance*—Chosen Among The Beautiful: Encountering the Object of Desire." Guest of Honour speech, "Intercontact," Oslo, July 1998. http:// homepage.ntlworld.com/gwynethann/OSLO.htm

"Flight into Fancy." *Insanity: WisCon 29*, May 27–30, 2005. http://www.wiscon.info/downloads/jones.pdf

"The Icons of Science Fiction." In *The Cambridge Companion to Science Fiction*, ed. Edward James and Farah Mendelsohn, 163–73. Cambridge: Cambridge University Press, 2003.

"Kairos: The Enchanted Loom." In *Edging into the Future: Science Fiction and Contemporary Cultural Transformation,* ed. Veronica Hollinger and Joan Gordon, 174–89. Philadelphia: University of Pennsylvania Press, 2002.

"Metempsychosis of the Machine: Science Fiction in the Halls of Karma." *Science Fiction Studies* 24 (1997): 1–10.

"The Neuroscience of Cyberspace: New Metaphors for the Self and Its Boundaries." In *The Governance of Cyberspace: Politics, Technology and Global Restructuring,* ed. Brian D. Loader, 46–63. London: Routledge, 1997.

"Riddles in the Dark." In *The Profession of Science Fiction: SF Writers on Their Craft and Ideas,* ed. Maxim Jakubowski and Edward James, 169–81. New York: St. Martin's, 1992.

"Secret Characters: The Interaction of Narrative and Technology." Keynote Speech at Computers and Writing Conference 2001, Ball State University, May 19, 2001. http://english.ttu.edu/Kairos/6.2/coverweb/jones.htm

"Two Thousand Words." *Infinity Plus*, August 14, 2006. http://www.infinityplus.co.uk/nonfiction/twothou.htm

"The Universe of Things." In *Women of Other Worlds*, ed. Helen Merrick and Tess Williams, 329–41. Nedlands, WA: University of Western Australia Press, 1999.

Bibliographies

Bould, Mark. "Gwyneth Jones: An Introduction." *Femspec* 5, no. 1 (2004): 190–96.

For Further Information

Official Web site: http://homepage.ntlworld.com/gwynethann/

Auden, Sandy. "Winning with a Bold Streak: An Interview with Gwyneth Jones." *SF Site* (2005). http://www.SFsite.com/10b/sagj210.htm

"Building Sandcastles: Gwyneth Jones Interviewed." *Cold Print,* March 10, 2002. http://www.cold-print.freeserve.co.uk/gjones.htm

Butler, Andrew. "Going Up Hill: An Interview with Gwyneth Jones." *Femspec* 5, no. 1 (2004): 216–33.

Emsley, Iain. Interview. *Infinity Plus* (2003). http://www.infinityplus.co.uk/nonfiction/intgj.htm

Mitchell, Chris. "Gwyneth Jones: Phoenix Cafe: Phoenix Rising." *Spike Magazine* (February 1997). http://www.spikemagazine.com/029jones.php

Sawyer, Andy. "Gwyneth Jones: Anxieties of Science Fiction." In *A Companion to Science Fiction,* ed. David Seed, 420–30. Malden: Blackwell, 2005.

Soyka, David. "Playing the Power Chords of SF: A Conversation with Gwyneth Jones." *SF Site* (January 2004). http://www.SFsite.com/02a/gj169.htm

VanderMeer, Jeff. "Gwyneth Jones Walks the Plank: Interview." *VanderWorld,* July 16, 2006. http://vanderworld.blogspot.com/2006/07/gwyneth-jones-walks-plank.html

James Patrick Kelly

Near Future; Slipstream

Benchmark Title: "Mr. Boy" (1990); "Think Like a Dinosaur" (1995)

b. 1951 (Long Island, New York)

I have quite resigned myself at this point in my career to accepting that my obit will start with something like "This was the guy who wrote 'Think Like a Dinosaur',"although I would argue that it's neither the best of all my work—although damn close—nor my personal favorite.
—McManus, Interview in *Strange Horizons* (2006)

Photo credit: Courtesy of Beth Gwinn

About the Author and the Author's Writing

This is the guy who wrote "Mr. Boy" (1990), the sharp and imaginative story of a near-future Peter Pan who, thanks to a genetic process called "twanking," is perpetually frozen at twelve years old. (Peter Pan's mother has "twanked" herself into three-quarter-size replica of the Statue of Liberty, and his best friends are an AI with attitude and a little yellow dinosaur.) This is the guy whose Hugo award-winning 1999 story "10^{16} to 1" is about a twelve-year-old who is convinced by a time traveler that he must prevent the third world war from being the war that really does end all wars. This is the guy who *Booklist*, in a 1997 review, described as writing "thoughtful, beautifully written stories, just a few degrees north of realism."

This is the guy who has admitted the influence of Ursula K. Le Guin on his early writing saying that his first SF novel *The Planet of Whispers* was "an Ursula Le Guin novel with the serial numbers filed off" (Gevers 2006). This is the guy who works regularly with John Kessel, producing the canny psychological fantasy *Freedom Beach,* as well as a number of thoughtful and well-regarded anthologies reflecting current SF trends. This is the guy whose funny, thoughtful, clever, moving and challenging stories are as likely to be about time-traveling revolutionary fighting utopians, trapped in the far-future ("Undone," 2001), as it is to be his take on a near-future "world without men" story ("Men Are Trouble," 2004), about a hard-boiled PI who must solve the murder of a newlywed and then go home to her own wife.

And, yes, this is the guy who wrote "Think Like a Dinosaur," the story in which the assumptions of classic 1950s hard SF are put to an altogether bleaker, more interesting test. In "Dinosaur," reptilian aliens offer humankind wonderful alien tech that, in effect, "faxes" people to far-off planets—at a price. "Dinosaur" is a clever, thought-provoking spin on the classic 1950s short story "The Cold Equations," and like many of the stories of James Patrick Kelly, it demonstrates that if there is any thread running through his finely crafted stories, it is that what we yearn for comes at a price: "My ideal reader would have to be someone with extremely eclectic tastes. I'm hoping that, like me, she hasn't quite made up her mind about what's important in life, but has formed some educated opinions" (McManus 2006).

James Patrick Kelly was born 1951 in Mineola, on Long Island, New York.

> I got sick when I was 11 while visiting my Grandma Kelly in St. Louis, and to keep me busy she showed me my uncle's old SF collection. But actually I was well prepared as a kid for my lifelong infatuation with the fantastic, having obsessively read the Oz series and, have mercy on me, the Tom Swift Jr. series. (Gevers 2006)

He is a graduate of the University of Notre Dame and a two-time alumnus of the Clarion science fiction workshop. In the 1980s Kelly and Kessel, along with writers such as Connie Willis, were labeled as "humanists" as a challenge to the cyberpunks. But the inclusion of Kelly's story "Solstice" (1985) in Bruce Sterling's definitive 1988 cyberpunk anthology *Mirrorshades* only served to demonstrate that, from a very early point in his career, he has been impossible to pigeonhole.

For the past twenty-five years, Kelly has had a story appear in the June issue of *Asimov's Science Fiction*—a record which was commemorated in June 2009 by "a kind of JPK tribute issue" (jimkelly.net). He also has a regular nonfiction column in *Asimov's* called "On the Net" and posts two weekly podcasts, *Free Reads* and *James Patrick Kelly's StoryPod*. Kelly has become a great believer in the viral marketing potential of podcasting since his novella *Burn* won the 2006 Nebula Award after he made it available on his Web site as a free podcast. "There were upwards of twenty thousand downloads that I know about . . . . So podcasting has been very good to me" (Tan 2009). Kelly lives in New Hampshire and teaches in the Stonecoast Creative Writing MFA program at the University of Southern Maine. The governor of New Hampshire appointed him to the State Council on the Arts, and he served as chair from 2003 to 2006. He is the vice chair of the Clarion Foundation, which oversees the Clarion Science Fiction Workshop. He has also served on the board of directors of the New England Foundation for the Arts.

As he tells it, in an interview to celebrate the nomination of his short story "Don't Stop" for a 2009 Nebula Award, "[i]t took me a long time to become James Patrick Kelly" (Tan 2009). Fortunately for his fans, "becoming" a lifelong James Patrick Kelly fan is usually only a matter of reading one—any one—of his thoughtful, well-crafted stories.

Awards

Short Fiction

"Think Like a Dinosaur" (1995) **Hugo**
"Itsy Bitsy Spider" (1997) **Locus Poll**
"10^{16} to 1" (1999) **Hugo**
"Burn" (2006) **Nebula**

Works by the Author

Planet of Whispers (1984)
Freedom Beach (1985, with John Kessel)
Look into the Sun (1989). http://freereads.blogspot.com/
Wildlife (1994)

Other Notable Short Fiction

"Dea Ex Machina" (1975)
"Saint Theresa of the Aliens" (1984)
"Solstice" (1985)
"The Prisoner of Chillon" (1986)
"Rat" (1986)
"Glass Cloud" (1987)
"Heroics" (1987)
"Mr. Boy" (1990)
"The Propagation of Light in a Vacuum" (1990)
"Monsters" (1992). http://www.infinityplus.co.uk/stories/monsters.htm
"Think Like a Dinosaur" (1995)
"Why the Bridge Stopped Singing" (1996). http://www.fantasticmetropolis.com/i/bridge/
"Ninety Percent of Everything" (1999, with Jonathan Lethem and John Kessel)
"Feel the Zaz" (2001)
"Undone" (2001)
"barry westphall crashes the singularity" (2002). http://www.infinitematrix.net/stories/shortshorts/riohondo/kelly-rh9.html
"Bernardo's House" (2003)
"Burn" (2005). http://www.infinitematrix.net/downloads/burn/Burn.pdf
"Men Are Trouble" (2004)
"The Wreck of the *Godspeed*" (2004)
"Don't Stop" (2007)
"Surprise Party" (2008)

Collections

Heroines (1990)
Think Like a Dinosaur and Other Stories (1997)
Strange But Not a Stranger (2002)
The Wreck of the Godspeed and Other Stories (2008)

As Editor

Feeling Very Strange: The Slipstream Anthology (2006)
Rewired: The New Cyberpunk Anthology (2007, with John Kessel)

In Other Media

"Think Like a Dinosaur." *The Outer Limits*, 2001. Directed Jorge Montesi; starring Enrico Colantoni.

"The Pyramid of Amirah." *Audio Fun.* Mind Mined Productions, 2004. http://www.mindmined.com/audiofun/jamespatrickkelly/the_pyramid_of_amirah.html

Articles and Essays

"Making Monsters." In *Paragons,* ed. Robin Wilson. New York: St. Martin's, 1997.

"Meditation on the Singular Matrix." In *Exploring the Matrix: Visions of the Cyber Present,* ed. Karen Haber, 222–34. New York: St. Martin's, 2003.

"Murder Your Darlings." *Writer's Digest* (July 1995). http://www.sfwa.org/2009/06/murder-your-darlings/

"On the Net." In *Asimov's Science Fiction* (June 1998–December 2005).

"Slipstream." In *Speculations on Speculation: Theories of Science Fiction,* ed. James Gunn and Matthew Candelaria. Lanham, MD: Scarecrow, 2005.

"Writer's Workshops." *The Bulletin of the Science Fiction Writers of America* (Spring 1988). http://www.sfwa.org/2009/06/writers-workshops/

"You and Your Characters." In *Writing Science Fiction and Fantasy,* ed. Gardner Dozois et al. New York, St. Martin's Press, 1991. http://www.sfwa.org/2005/01/you-and-your-characters/

For Further Information

Official Web site: http://www.jimkelly.net/

Adams, John Joseph. "A Genre That . . . Well . . . Isn't." *Sci Fi Weekly,* June 12, 2006.

D'Ammassa, Don. "James Patrick Kelly." In *St. James Guide to Science Fiction Writers,* ed. Jay Pedersen. Detroit, MI: St. James, 1996.

Gevers, Nick. "New-fashioned Romantic James Patrick Kelly Smokes, But Never Inhales." *SciFi.com,* January 30, 2006.

Introduction to "Think Like a Dinosaur." In *The Hard SF Renaissance,* ed. David G. Hartwell and Kathryn Cramer. New York: Macmillan, 2003.

"James Patrick Kelly: Writing on the Edge." *Locus* (November 2002). http://www.locusmag.com/2002/Issue11/Kelly.html

McManus, Victoria. Interview. *Strange Horizons*, May 15, 2006. http://www.strangehorizons.com/2006/20060515/kelly-int-a.shtml

Slusher, Dave. "Voices in Your Head. (Audio Interview)" *IT Conversations*, October 11, 2004. GigaVox Media. http://www.itconversations.com/shows/detail219.html

Snider, John C. Interview. *SciFiDimensions* (September 2002). http://www.scifidimensions. com/Sep02/jamespatrickkelly.htm

———. "Strange But Not a Stranger." *SciFiDimensions* (September 2002). http://www.scifidimensions.com/Sep02/stranger.htm

Tan, Charles. Interview. *Nebula Awards*, June 10, 2009. http://www.nebulaawards.com/index.php/interview/james_patrick_kelly_2009/

Ursula K. Le Guin

Feminist SF; New Wave; Utopias

Benchmark Title: *The Left Hand of Darkness* (1969)

b. 1929 (Berkeley, California)

> *I stare and see something, maybe a person in a landscape, and have to find out what it is.*
> —Jaggi, "The Masgician," *The Guardian* (2005)

About the Author and the Author's Writing

It is difficult to image a reader who has not been touched by the work of Ursula K. Le Guin at some time or other in his or her reading life. Over nearly forty years as a published writer, she has produced more than twenty novels, numerous children's books, and more than a hundred short stories. She is a notable essayist, translator, and poet; she has developed screenplays of her own work. Titles by her regularly appear on "best of" and "most influential" lists—fantasy such as the Earthsea chronicles and the *Orsinian Tales*; science fiction such as *The Dispossessed* (1974), *The Left Hand of Darkness* (1969), and *Always Coming Home* (1985). Most of her major titles have remained continuously in print, some for over forty years. The appeal of her writing lies in the fact that it is grounded by its intensely human approach to the most fantastic subject matter; as Le Guin said in a 2001 interview with *Salon Magazine* online, "These are human stories. I'm using the other worlds and the other races as metaphors. All I know how to write about are people and animals—and trees. Still, nothing that is alien" (Justice 2001).

Born Ursula Kroeber in Berkeley, California, she grew up in a house filled with books, stories, and intellectual curiosity, the daughter of academics. Her father was the anthropologist Alfred Kroeber, her mother the writer Theodora Kroeber, author of *Ishi in Two Worlds*, a groundbreaking anthropological work that told the story of Ishi, the last survivor of the Yahi Indian tribe: "We had a house full of folktales; I liked the Norse better than the Greek" (Jaggi 2005).

She fell in love with SF at an early age and was writing it—and receiving her first rejection slips—at age eleven. A BA from Radcliffe College was followed by an MA from Columbia University in the literature and languages of the Middle Ages and Renaissance, then a Fulbright Scholarship and plans for further study in France. But while she was traveling to Europe on the *Queen Mary*, "in steerage," as she puts it, she met Charles Le Guin, fellow student historian; a few months later the young couple married in Paris. They lived in Macon, Georgia, for a while, where Le Guin taught

French at Mercer University, but she found that "[g]oing to a totally segregated society was quite a shock. I pulled him west" (Jaggi 2005).

Charles Le Guin took up a post at Portland State University in 1958; the couple, with their three children, settled in Oregon. Like most mothers with a young family, Le Guin had to work in and around her family's schedule; that, and the discomfort of publishers who found her work impossible to pigeonhole, meant that her first novel wasn't published until she was thirty-seven years old. Beginning in 1966, with *Planet of Exile* and *Rocannon's World*, Le Guin established the Hainish sequence, a cycle of stories about planets—including Earth—long ago "seeded" with humanoid life by mysterious, superior beings.

Her first three novels, all episodes of the Hainish Cycle, were entertaining and interesting, and demonstrated that she was "not interested in space conquest or wiring, but using the form as a wonderful box of fixed metaphors you can play with endlessly" (Jaggi 2005). But it was her fourth novel, *The Left Hand of Darkness* (1969), that really showed the world what Le Guin could do. Set on the snowbound world of Gethen (or, as it's known to Genly Ai, the Hainish diplomat who is enduring an uncomfortable assignment there, "Winter") , it is one of the outermost seedings of the Hainish Expansion and has been cut off from the human community for 500 millennia. The Hainish, for reason known only to themselves, genetically manipulated Gethenians to be androgynous; they can become male or female in the course of their sexual cycle—resulting in the immortal line, "the King was pregnant." The cold is not the only source of Genly Ai's discomfort. Because the Gethenians are otherwise so like us, Genly (and, through him, the reader), is forced to confront "the nature of sex and sexism in our world, and of cultural chauvinism generally" (*The Encyclopedia of Science Fiction* 1999).

Some readers and critics carp that Le Guin's tales are little more than vehicles for her views—utopian ideals in *The Dispossessed* and *The Lathe of Heaven* (1971), Taoism in *The Telling* (2000), the environment in *Always Coming Home*, and gender roles in *The Left Hand of Darkness* (and almost anything else she writes). But this entirely misses the point of what Le Guin does so well. The Taoism that pervades Le Guin's work only serves to emphasize balance and the fact that the world—any world—is far more complicated than our limited intellects could imagine. Her work has a tradition of challenging assumptions, even her own. "Sometimes one's very angry and preaches, but I know that to clinch a point is to close it. To leave the reader free to decide what your work means, that's the real art; it makes the work inexhaustible" (Jaggi 2005)

Ursula K. Le Guin is a recipient of the National Book Award, five Hugos, five Nebulas, the Kafka Award, a Pushcart Prize, and several lifetime achievement awards, among dozens of other honors. Over the years she has taught, held workshops, and done readings at universities and writers' forums, from Seattle, Washington, to Melbourne, Australia; according to her official Web site, she leads "an intensely private life, with sporadic forays into political activism and steady participation in the literary community of her city." At the age of seventy-four she is still writing, but she has decided to give herself permission to limit her public appearances to her home area of Portland, Oregon. As she puts it on her Web site, "Please don't ask me to come give a speech, unless you are the King of Sweden."

Awards

Science Fiction Research Association Pilgrim Award (1989)
World Fantasy Award Life Achievement (1995)
Science Fiction Hall of Fame (2001)
SFWA Damon Knight Memorial Grand Master (2003)

Novels

The Left Hand of Darkness (1969) **Hugo, Nebula, Tiptree Retro 1996**
The Lathe of Heaven (1971) **Locus Poll**
The Dispossessed (1974) **Hugo, Nebula, Locus Poll, Prometheus Hall of Fame 1993**
The Telling (2000) **Locus Poll**

Short Fiction

"The Word for World Is Forest" (1972) **Hugo**
"The Ones Who Walk Away from Omelas" (1974) **Hugo**
"The Day Before the Revolution" (1975) **Locus Poll, Nebula**
"The New Atlantis" (1975) **Locus Poll**
"Sur" (1983) **Locus Poll**
"Buffalo Gals, Won't You Come Out Tonight" (1987) **Hugo**
"Forgiveness Day" (1994) **Locus Poll, Sturgeon**
"The Matter of Seggri" (1994) **Tiptree**
"Solitude" (1994) **Nebula**
"Mountain Ways" (1996) **Locus Poll, Tiptree**
"The Birthday of the World" (2000) **Locus Poll**
"The Bones of the Earth" (2001) **Locus Poll**
"The Finder" (2001) **Locus Poll**
"The Wild Girls" (2002) **Locus Poll**

Collections

The Wind's Twelve Quarters (1975) **Locus Poll**
The Compass Rose (1982) **Locus Poll**
Four Ways to Forgiveness (1995) **Locus Poll**
Changing Planes (2003) **Locus Poll**

Nonfiction

The Wave in the Mind (2004) **Locus Poll**

Works by the Author

The Lathe of Heaven (1971)
Eye of the Heron (1978)
Always Coming Home (1985)

The Hainish sequence

Planet of Exile (1966)
Rocannon's World (1966)
City of Illusions (1967)
The Left Hand of Darkness (1969)
The Dispossessed: An Ambiguous Utopia (1974)
The Telling (2000)

Other Notable Genre Fiction

Orsinian Tales (1976)
Malafrena (1979)
The Beginning Place (1980; aka *Threshold*)
Lavinia (2008)

Earthsea

Includes *A Wizard of Earthsea* (1968) and the Nebula award-winning *Tehanu: The Last Book of Earthsea* (1990)

Other Notable Short Fiction

"Nine Lives" (1969)
"Winter's King" (1969)
"Vaster Than Empires and More Slow" (1970)
"The Pathways of Desire" (1979)
"She Unnames Them" (1985)
"The Shobies' Story" (1990)
"Another Story or A Fisherman of the Inland Sea" (1994)
"Coming of Age in Karhide" (1995)
"A Man of the People" (1995)
"A Woman's Liberation" (1995)
"Dragonfly" (1998)
"Old Music and the Slave Women" (1999)
"The Bones of the Earth" (2001)
"The Seasons of the Ansarac" (2002). http://www.infinitematrix.net/stories/shorts/seasons_of_ansarac.html
"Paradises Lost" (2002)

Collections

The Wind's Twelve Quarters (1975)
The Compass Rose (1982)
Buffalo Gals, and Other Animal Presences (1987)
Searoad (1991)
A Fisherman of the Inland Sea (1994)
Four Ways to Forgiveness (1995)
Unlocking the Air and Other Stories (1996)
The Birthday of the World (2002)
Changing Planes (2003)
Science Fiction Stories (2003)

As Editor

Nebula Award Stories 11 (1976)
Edges (1980, with Virginia Kidd)
Interfaces (1980, with Virginia Kidd)
The Norton Book of Science Fiction: North American SF, 1960–1990 (1993, with Brian Attebery)

In Other Media

The Lathe of Heaven. Taurus Film, 1980. Directed by Fred Barzyk and David R. Loxton; starring Bruce Davison. A much inferior adaptation was made by A&E Television Network in 2002.
Earthsea. Hallmark Productions, 2004. Directed by Robert Lieberman. "Reimagined" version that is so bad, it provoked Mrs. Le Guin to post a denunciation of it on IMDb.

Nonfiction Books

The Language of the Night: Essays on Fantasy and Science Fiction (1980)
Dancing at the Edge of the World: Thoughts on Words, Women, Places (1989)
Steering the Craft: Exercises and Discussions on Story Writing for the Lone Navigator or the Mutinous Crew (1998)
The Wave in the Mind: Talks and Essays on the Writer, the Reader, and the Imagination (2004)

Articles and Essays

"Science Fiction and Mrs. Brown." In *Speculations on Speculation: Theories of Science Fiction,* ed. James Gunn and Matthew Candelaria, 119–40. Lanham: Scarecrow, 2005.
"A Whitewashed *Earthsea*: How the SciFi Channel Wrecked My Books." *Slate,* December 16, 2004 http://www.slate.com/id/2111107/

Bibliographies

"Ursula K. Le Guin: Short Bibliography 2006." Official Web site. October 27, 2006. http://www.ursulakleguin.com/Biblio-Short.pdf

"Ursula K. Le Guin: Partial List of Secondary Sources." Official Web site. September 7, 2007. http://www.ursulakleguin.com/SecondarySources.html

For Further Information

Official Web site: Edited by Vonda N. McIntyre. 2006. Science Fiction and Fantasy Writers of America. http://www.ursulakleguin.com/

Awl, Dave. *The Ekumen: An Ursula K. Le Guin Reference Page.* The Ocelot Factory, 2002. http://www.ocelotfactory.com/leguin/

Bernardo, Susan M., and Graham J. Murphy. *Ursula K. Le Guin: A Critical Companion.* Westport, CT: Greenwood, 2006.

Delany, Samuel R. "To Read *The Dispossessed.*" In *The Jewel-Hinged Jaw,* 239–308. New York: Dragon, 1977.

Gevers, Nick. "Driven by a Different Chauffeur: An Interview with Ursula K. Le Guin." *SF Site* (November/December 2001). http://www.SFsite.com/03a/ul123.htm

Herbert, Rosemary. "Ursula K. Le Guin." In *St. James Guide to Science Fiction Writers,* ed. Jay Pedersen. Detroit, MI: St. James, 1996.

Jaggi, Maya. "The Magician." *The Guardian*, December 17, 2005. Guardian Unlimited. http://www.guardian.co.uk/books/2005/dec/17/booksforchildrenandteenagers.shopping

James, Warren W. Interview. *Mike Hodel's Hour 25: Science Fiction Radio for Southern California,* September 29, 2000 and August 17, 2003. http://www.hour25online.com/Hour25_Audio_Index.html

Justice, Faith L. "Ursula K. Le Guin." *Salon,* January 23, 2001. http://archive.salon.com/people/bc/2001/01/23/le_guin/

McIntyre, Vonda, N. "Ursula K. Le Guin: Mutinous Navigator." *Nebula Grand Master Awards* (April 2003). Science Fiction and Fantasy Writers of America, Inc. http://www.sfwa.org/awards/2003/ukl-gm.html

Philips, Julie, ed. "Dear Starbear: Letters between Ursula K. Le Guin and James Tiptree Jr." *Fantasy & Science Fiction* 111, no. 3 (2006): 77–115.

Reid, Suzanne Elizabeth. *Presenting Ursula K. Le Guin.* New York: Twayne, 1997.

Stanislaw Lem

Hard SF; Humor and Satire; Myth and Legend

Benchmark Title: *Solaris* (1961)

b. 1921 (Poland: Lvov);
d. 2006 (Poland: Krakow)

Good books tell the truth, even when they're about things that never have been and never will be. They're truthful in a different way. When they talk about outer space, they make you feel the silence, so unlike the Earthly kind.
—*More Tales of Pirx the Pilot* (1982)

Photo credit: By permission of Stanislaw Lem's archive.

About the Author and the Author's Writing

Stanisław Lem was born in Lvov, in eastern Poland, shortly after that country regained its independence from Russia after World War I. His father was a physician, and Lem had just begun his own medical studies when World War II began in 1939; Poland was first invaded and occupied by the Soviet Union and then, twenty months later, in June 1941, by Nazi Germany. Lem, who had Jewish ancestry although he had been raised as a Catholic, used false papers to survive the war and avoid the concentration camps that were the fate of so many other Poles; he worked as an automobile mechanic and learned to sabotage German military vehicles. His work gave him access to a Luftwaffe depot and enabled him to steal weapons and other equipment for the Polish Resistance. The great personal risk that this involved is almost unimaginable.

When the war ended Lvov became part of the Soviet Union and the Lem family was forced to relocate to Kraków, in southwest Poland. Lem resumed his medical studies, and while a student he began to write—poems and stories, and pulp thrillers. He was unable to qualify as a doctor because he refused to subscribe to the crackpot pseudo-science then being forced on schools by Stalin and the Polish Communist Party; he failed his exams. Instead, he became a junior research assistant and began to write in earnest.

At first Lem's work conformed to the officially sanctioned "Soviet realist" and optimistic Communist utopian style of SF. He had very little choice; in art, as well as in life, every word was weighed by busy censors who pored over texts looking for internationalist sympathies or any suggestion that the author felt that all was not for the best in this best of all possible Marxist-Leninist worlds. Lem later dismissed his early SF, such as *The Man from Mars* (*Człowiek z Marsa*, 1946), *The Magellanic Cloud* (*Obłok*

Magellana, 1955), and juvenile SF *The Astronauts* (*Astronauci*, 1951), which were, by his standards, "SF lite," so hamstrung by the Soviet conventions forced upon them that Lem often said that they should be forgotten. But Lem came into his own after 1956, when the death of Josef Stalin resulted in the lifting of some restrictions on freedom of speech. Between 1956 and 1968 Lem wrote, and saw published, seventeen books.

Of these, *Solaris* (1961) is undoubtedly the most famous novel available in English. It's a deceptively simple story: A strange ocean planet, possibly sentient, begins to have weird effects on the scientists studying it, conjuring up manifestations of lost loved ones and incidents from their past that they would rather forget. The researchers study the mysterious planet Solaris: they measure it and "collect reams of frustrating and contradictory data, write volumes of theories" (Macdonald 1996), only to find that it contradicts all of their laws, and instead holds up a mirror to their souls. It's hardly surprising that *Solaris* has captured the imagination of filmmakers, resulting in two adaptations, one Russian, directed by Andrei Tarkovsky, the other American, starring George Clooney.

The work of Stanislaw Lem explores philosophical themes: speculation on technology, the nature of intelligence, the futility of attempts to comprehend the truly alien, and despair about human limitations and humankind's place in the universe. Lem also wrote nonfiction; his two most famous philosophical texts are *Dialogi* (*Dialogues*) and *Summa Technologiae* (1964), in which Lem discusses philosophical implications of technologies that were completely in the realm of science fiction at the time he was writing but are part of our everyday reality today—for example, virtual reality and nanotechnology. As he told Istvan Csicsery-Ronay when he was interviewed for *Science Fiction Studies* in 1986, "I am interested primarily in the line of junction, the border between science and philosophy, and also in the fact that a certain species of 'brained animals' on Earth, I mean Man, has made science one of its main preoccupations."

A catalog like this sounds rather grim, but some of Lem's best work is hilariously funny and wonderfully absurd. Comparisons have been made to Franz Kafka, Kurt Vonnegut, and even Douglas Adams. *The Cyberiad* (1967) is a series of humorous short stories from a mechanical universe ruled by robots, "satiric parodies of human avarice, cruelty and stupidity" (Macdonald 1996). *Tales of Pirx the Pilot* and the "memoirs" of Ijon Tichy the Star Traveller take ordinary men and use their absurd and outlandish adventures in space to illustrate the thin line between the inherent goodness of particular individuals and Lem's deep pessimism about humanity as a whole.

And is this really surprising? Polish writers who came to maturity after World War II are often referred to in Poland as "*Kolumbowie*," or "Columbuses," because they had to explore new political and social territory. Stanislaw Lem's writing, like that of his compatriots of his generation, was deeply marked by the terrible suffering of Poland and the Polish people during the twentieth century—when Lem writes about guilt, civilization, and responsibility in his SF, the context may be futuristic, but the questions are clearly rooted in the terrible events of our recent past and in the here and now.

In the early 1980s Stanislaw Lem took advantage of relaxed travel restrictions in Poland to move to Vienna. There he enjoyed the new freedom and the physical comforts of life in the West, but he found the commercialism and foreignness disturbing and distracting. In 1988 he returned to Krakow and spent his final years in the company of fellow Polish writers, surrounded by family; he died in Krakow on March 27,

2006, at the age of eighty-four. He left behind him books translated into forty languages, sales of more than twenty-five million copies internationally, and more than twenty titles in print in the United States alone.

Awards

Lem's work has, to date, won only two SF prizes—the Israeli *Geffen* (2003, for *Solaris*) and the Japanese *Seiun* (1977, for his Pirx the Pilot story "Rozprawa") . He has, however, won a number of literary prizes in Poland and received honorary doctorates from Wrocław Polytechnic and the Universities of Opole, Lwów, Jagiellonian, and Bielefeld. He was awarded the Grand Prix de Littérature Policière in 1979 for his novel *Katar*. In 1997 he was made an honorary citizen of Kraków.

Works by the Author

Eden (1959)
The Investigation (1959)
Memoirs Found in a Bathtub (1961)
Return from the Stars (1961)
Solaris (1961)
The Invincible, (1964)
His Master's Voice (1968)
The Futurological Congress: From the Memoirs of Ijon Tichy (1971)
The Chain of Chance (1975)
Fiasco (1986)
Peace on Earth (1986)

Collections

The Cyberiad: Fables for the Cybernetic Age (1974)
Mortal Engines (1977)
Tales of Pirx the Pilot (1979)
The Cosmic Carnival of Stanislaw Lem (1981)
Memoirs of a Space Traveler: Further Reminiscences of Ijon Tichy (1982)
More Tales of Pirx the Pilot (1982)

In Other Media

Solaris. Mosfilm, 1972. Directed by Andrei Tarkovsky.
Solaris. Twentieth Century-Fox Film Corporation, 2002. Directed by Steven Soderbergh; starring George Clooney and Natascha McElhone.

Nonfiction Books

Highcastle: A Remembrance (1975)

Microworlds: Writings on Science Fiction and Fantasy (2006)
A Stanislaw Lem Reader (Rethinking Theory) (1997, edited by Peter Swirski)
Summa Technologiae (1984, translated by Frank Prengel)

Bibliographies

Graefrath, Bernd. "Taking Science Fiction Seriously: A Bibliographic Introduction to Stanislaw Lem's Philosophy of Technology." *Research in Philosophy and Technology* 15 (1995): 271–85.

For Further Information

Solaris: The Official Stanislaw Lem Site: http://english.lem.pl/

Csicsery-Ronay, Istvan, Jr. Obituary. *Science Fiction Studies* 33 (2006): 564–66.
———. "Twenty-two Answers and Two Postscripts: An Interview with Stanislaw Lem." *Science Fiction Studies* 13 (1986): 242–60. http://www.depauw.edu/SFs/interviews/lem40interview.htm
Davis, J. Madison. *Stanisław Lem*. Mercer Island, WA: Starmont, 1990.
Federman, Raymond. Interview. *Science Fiction Studies* (March 1983). http://www.depauw.edu/SFs/interviews/federman29.htm
"Life After Lem." *The Polish Science Voice,* April 5, 2006. http://www.warsawvoice.pl/view/11034
Macdonald, Gina. "Stanislaw Lem." In *St. James Guide to Science Fiction Writers,* ed. Jay Pedersen. Detroit, MI: St. James, 1996.
Powers, Nathan M. "Stanislaw Lem." *The Scriptorum,* October 1, 1999. http://www.themodernword.com/scriptorium/lem.html
Saunders, Alan. "To Solaris and Beyond." *The Philosopher Zone,* April 29, 2006. Australian Broadcasting Corporation. http://www.abc.net.au/rn/philosopherszone/stories/2006/1622605.htm
Swirski, Peter. ed. *The Art and Science of Stanislaw Lem.* Montreal: McGill-Queen's University Press, 2006.
Ziegfeld, Richard E. *Stanislaw Lem*. New York: Ungar, 1985.

Madeleine L'Engle

Science Fantasy; Sense of Wonder

Benchmark Title: *A Wrinkle in Time* (1962)

b. 1918 (New York); d. 2007 (Goshen, Connecticut)

In art . . . we are helped to remember some of the glorious things that we have forgotten and some of the terrible things we are asked to endure.
—*Walking on Water* (2001)

About the Author and the Author's Writing

Madeleine L'Engle Camp was born in New York City; her father, Charles Wadsworth Camp, was a journalist and her mother a pianist. L'Engle was a shy, bookish child; the only child of older parents, she wrote stories and kept a journal from a very early age. But her childhood was blighted by the poor health of her father and the insensitivity of the adults around her. The teachers at the posh schools she attended seemed content to brand her shyness and childish clumsiness as stupidity; her parents overcompensated by changing her schools frequently, hiring one governess after another, and quarreling. (It should be noted that revisionist biographers have suggested that Mr. Camp's health problems stemmed, not from encounters with mustard gas suffered during the Great War, as the family claimed, but alcoholism.) A series of boarding schools, and frequent moves to find a climate that might suit her father's health, alienated her from both family and potential friends of her own age. When her father died in Florida in 1935, L'Engle was away at her boarding school, in Charleston, South Carolina; she did not make it back in time to say her farewells.

L'Engle graduated from Smith College in Massachusetts in 1941. During the following decade she moved back to New York, had two novels published, and became an off-Broadway actress. She met her husband, Hugh Franklin, also an actor, while they were performing in a production of *The Cherry Orchard*. For a while the young couple, with their growing family, lived in a 200-year-old farmhouse in rural Connecticut and ran a general store. In the late 1950s the Franklins moved back to New York City so her husband could resume his acting career. (He became well known as Dr. Charles Tyler in the soap opera *All My Children*.) During a family camping trip that preceded the move, L'Engle had the idea for her most famous novel, *A Wrinkle in Time*. Twenty-six publishers rejected the story before Farrar, Straus & Giroux finally published it in 1962. Winner of the Newbery Medal in 1963, the Lewis Carroll Shelf Award in 1965, and a runner-up for the Hans Christian Andersen Award in 1964, it is one of the best-selling children's books of all time and, like many of her books, equally popular with adults and children. In 1998 L'Engle received the Margaret Edwards

Award of the American Library Association, a lifetime achievement award for writing young adult literature.

A Wrinkle in Time is the first in a quartet of novels called the Time Fantasy series, in which the author uses popular tropes of science fiction and fantasy, such as a quest to a distant planet, time travel, and a battle against interplanetary evil to tell a story of love and family. Given the unhappiness of her childhood and the traumatic loss of her father, L'Engle's science fantasy offers hope to the young reader—that the young protagonists can triumph against evil, can save their kidnapped father—that life can go on. "Whatever the literary genre, L'Engle upholds that a writer's responsibility is to radiate hope, to bring healing, to say yes to life. Her works wrestle with the unanswerable questions of life and death, God and darkness" (St. Yves 1995).

During the 1960s L'Engle became active at the Cathedral of St. John the Divine, in New York, first as a volunteer librarian and eventually in a long-standing position as writer in residence. During that time she wrote dozens of books for children and adults. She was created a Dame of the Order of St. John by H.M. Queen Elizabeth II in 1977. Well into the 1990s L'Engle was lecturing, traveling, and corresponding with fans all over the world, in spite of the deaths of her husband, in 1986, and her son Bion, in 1999; even osteoporosis and the effects of a cerebral hemorrhage suffered in 2002 did not cramp her style, or stop her from working on a book about aging; describing it in an interview with *Newsweek* in 2006, she said "enjoy it, you might as well. And it's not all bad. I can say what I want, and I don't get punished for it."

Madeleine L'Engle passed away on September 6, 2007, at age eighty-eight, near her home in Goshen, Connecticut.

Awards

World Fantasy Life Achievement (1997)

Novels

A Wrinkle in Time (1962) **Newbery Award**
A Ring of Endless Light (1980) **Newbery**

Works by the Author

The Time Quartet

A Wrinkle in Time (1962)
A Wind in the Door (1973)
A Swiftly Tilting Planet (1978)
Many Waters (1986)

O'Keefe Family Trilogy

The Arm of the Starfish (1965)
The Young Unicorns (1968)
An Acceptable Time (1989)

Other Notable Genre Fiction

Camilla Dickinson (1951; aka *Camilla*)
A Severed Wasp (1982)
A Live Coal in the Sea (1996)

Austin Family Stories

Meet the Austins (1960)
The Moon by Night (1963)
The Young Unicorns (1968)
A Ring of Endless Light (1980)
Troubling a Star (1994)

Notable Short Fiction

Austin Family Christmas Stories

"The Anti-Muffins" (1980)
"The Twenty-four Days Before Christmas" (1984)
"A Full House: An Austin Family Christmas" (1999)

Collections

The Sphinx at Dawn: Two Stories (1989)
The Ordering of Love: The New and Collected Poems of Madeleine L'Engle (2005)

In Other Media

*Madeleine L'Engle: Star*Gazer*. Ishtar Films, 1989. Directed by Martha Wheelock.
A Ring of Endless Light. Disney Channel, 2002. Directed by Greg Beeman; starring James Whitmore and Mischa Barton.
A Wrinkle in Time. BLT Productions, 2003. Directed by John Kent Harrison; starring Kate Nelligan and Alfre Woodard.

Nonfiction Books

Dare to Be Creative! A Lecture Presented at the Library of Congress (1984)
Trailing Clouds of Glory: Spiritual Values in Children's Literature (1985, with Avery Brooke)
The Rock That Is Higher: Story as Truth (1993)
Walking on Water: Reflections on Faith and Art (2001). Includes the essay "Aslan's Kin: Interfaith Fantasy and Science Fiction," which is available online at http://greenbelt.com/news/aslan/lengle.htm.
Madeleine L'Engle Herself: Reflections on a Writing Life (2001, edited by Carole Chase)

The Crosswicks Journals
A Circle of Quiet (1972)
The Summer of the Great-grandmother (1974)
The Irrational Season (1977)
Two-Part Invention: The Story of a Marriage (1988)

Articles and Essays

Acceptance Speech for The Margaret Edwards Award, June 27 1998. http://gos.sbc.edu/l/lengle.html

"The Expanding Universe" (Newbery Award Acceptance Speech), August 1963. http://www.madeleinelengle.com/reference/newberyspeech.htm

"Foreword." In *Companion to Narnia,* by Paul F. Ford. San Francisco: Harper, 1994.

"Tell Me a Story." In *The Quiet Center: Women Reflecting on Life's Passages,* ed. Katherine Ball Ross, 163–68. New York: Hearst, 1997.

Bibliographies

Blocher, Karen Funk, ed. *The Tesseract: A Madeleine L'Engle Bibliography in 5 Dimensions.* May 2005. http://lengleweb.mavarin.com/murry.html

Buswell Library: Wheaton College Archives & Special Collections. *The Madeleine L'Engle Collection.* Wheaton College, January 2006. http://www.wheaton.edu/learnres/ARCSC/collects/sc03/bio.htm

For Further Information

Official Web site: http://www.madeleinelengle.com/

Chase, Carole F. *Suncatcher: A Study of Madeleine L'Engle and Her Writing.* 2nd ed. Philadelphia, PA: InniSFree, 1998.

Gonzales, Doreen. *Madeleine L'Engle: Author of* A Wrinkle in Time. New York: Dillon, 1991.

Hein, Rolland. *Christian Mythmakers: C. S. Lewis, Madeleine L'Engle, J. R. R. Tolkien, George MacDonald, G. K. Chesterton and Others.* Chicago: Cornerstone, 1998.

Hettinga, Donald. *Presenting Madeleine L'Engle.* New York: Twayne, 1993.

Podell, Tim. "Good Conversation!: A Talk with Madeleine L'Engle." (videorecording) Scarborough, NY: Tim Podell Productions, 1993.

Shaw, Luci, ed. *The Swiftly Tilting Worlds of Madeleine L'Engle.* Wheaton, IL: Harold Shaw, 1998.

St. Yves, Suzanne. "Into the Depths of the Human Heart: Madeleine L'Engle's Search for God." *Sojourner's* (March–April 1995). http://www.sojo.net/index.cfm?action=magazine.article&issue=soj9503&article=950331

Webb, Heather. "A Conversation with Madeleine L'Engle." *Mars Hill Review* 4 (1996): 51–65. http://www.leaderu.com/marshill/mhr04/lengle1.html

Zarin, Cynthia. "The Storyteller." *The New Yorker,* April 12, 2004.

Jonathan Lethem

Slipstream

Benchmark Title:
Gun, with Occasional Music (1994)

b. 1964 (Brooklyn, New York)

It's probably obvious already that I'm engaged with genres but not bound by them. Technology in my work is iconographic and metaphoric. I wouldn't know an extrapolation if it came in bearing flowers. I write about myself and my friends.

—Author Comment, *St. James Guide to Science Fiction Writers* (1996)

Photo credit: Peter Bellamy.
Permission of Jonathan Lethem.

About the Author and the Author's Writing

A recent profile of Jonathan Lethem in a major English newspaper was entitled "The Borrower," and it is as a borrower—a writer who makes free with the storylines of many genres and the conventions of other times and other artists, and makes them uniquely *now* and uniquely *his own*—that he has made his mark on both SF and mainstream fiction. Lethem burst on the writing scene in 1994 (after, of course, many years of working on his craft, steadfastly and relatively unnoticed) with his SF/noir detective novel, *Gun, with Occasional Music. Gun* is set in a near-future Los Angeles (where else?) in which gene therapy has allowed the "evolution" of animals into a sentient underclass. "Raymond Chandler, Dashiell Hammett and Ross McDonald . . . bequeath as much to the gritty tone . . . as Philip K. Dick, Stanislaw Lem and Cordwainer Smith contribute to its crowded furniture" (Kelleghan 1996). In the best tradition of Chandler and Hammett, Lethem's PI, Conrad Metcalfe, finds that however mean the streets he must walk down, honor requires him to untangle the complicated web of deceit spun around his clients, whatever the cost.

Gun, with Occasional Music was followed by *Amnesia Moon* (1995), a fix-up of unpublished short stories, and Lethem's riff on an absurd, over-the-top dystopia that was the specialty of Phillip K. Dick: "I was trying to write out an obsession with dystopias, with collapsed or oppressed realities" ("Breeding Hybrids in the Genre Garden" 1997). In *Amnesia Moon,* the United States has been beset by a mysterious apocalypse that strips memories and splits up the landscape into a patchwork of alternate societies with different pasts and rules: very Dickian, indeed. In his 2005 autobiographical essay "The Disappointment Artist," Lethem describes Dick's role in his life being "as formative an influence as marijuana or punk rock . . . bending it irreversibly along a course I still travel." In *Girl in Landscape* (1998), a motherless girl must grow up fast amid the xenophobia and strange goings-on of a frontier colony on the Planet of the Archbuilders. Here, Lethem brings an SF spin to the great John Ford film *The Searchers:* "In some ways, it's a book that takes the point of view of the Natalie Wood character . . . and gives her her own book" ("Breeding Hybrids in the Genre Garden" 1997). Even in Lethem's mainstream novels, such as *Motherless Brooklyn* (1999) and *Fortress of Solitude* (2005), reality is filtered through the lens of pop culture references, which, of course, include SF.

Jonathan Allen Lethem was born and raised in Brooklyn, New York, growing up in the "pregentrified" neighborhood of Boerum Hill, an experience he describes in interviews as "thrilling." His parents were artists and activists; his mother died of a brain tumor when he was thirteen years old, an event that has had a tremendous effect on him as a writer and that often resonates in his work. "My books all have this giant, howling missing [center]—language has disappeared, or someone has vanished, or memory has gone" (McGlone 2007).

His original ambition was to follow his father and become a visual artist, but he describes his style while at The High School of Music & Art in Manhattan as "glib, show-offy, usually cartoonish" (Interview in *Postroad* 2002); he spent most of his time writing and illustrating his own 'zine and writing a novel (unpublished), about which he has said he "learned to type, at least" (Kelleghan 1998). Lethem went to Bennington College in Vermont, briefly and sporadically, and then hitchhiked cross-country to San Francisco, living in the Bay Area for a decade, working in bookstores and writing. His first novel, *Gun, with Occasional Music* (1994), was a finalist for the Nebula, and placed first in the Best First Novel category of the 1995 *Locus Magazine* reader's poll.

In 1996 Lethem moved back to Brooklyn with his family, to Boerum Hill, the neighborhood where he grew up. Both *Motherless Brooklyn* and *Fortress of Solitude* are set in this familiar territory. *Fortress of Solitude* won the National Book Critic's Circle Award, The Macallan Gold Dagger for crime fiction, and the Salon Book Award. Lethem is a tireless essayist and a past editor of the magazines *Paradoxa* and *Fence*. In 2005 he was awarded a MacArthur Fellowship, often referred to as the "genius grant." Also in 2005 he announced that he would write a series for Marvel Comics resurrecting the character "Omega the Unknown."

Lethem has a three-inch tattoo on his upper left arm of a spray can shooting red-pink paint. The can is labeled "UBIK," the title of a Philip K. Dick novel, which, as Lethem explained to an interviewer for *The San Francisco Chronicle*, is "a spray that reverses entropy," an appropriate image for a writer who has done so much to impose the order of fiction on the chaos of modern popular culture.

Awards

Novels

Gun with Occasional Music (1994) **Locus Poll**

 Works by the Author

Gun with Occasional Music (1994)
Amnesia Moon (1995)
As She Climbed Across the Table (1997)
Girl in Landscape (1998)

Notable Mainstream Fiction

Motherless Brooklyn (1999)
The Fortress of Solitude (2003)
You Don't Love Me Yet (2007)
Chronic City (2009)

Notable Short Fiction

"The Happy Man" (1991)

"Vanilla Dunk" (1992)

"The Insipid Profession of Jonathan Horneboom" (1995)

"Receding Horizon" (1995)

"Ninety Percent of Everything" (2000, with James Patrick Kelly and John Kessel)

"This Shape We're In" (2000)

"The Glasses" (audio file) (2004). http://dir.salon.com/story/books/feature/2004/11/01/lethem/index.html

"Super Goat Man" (2004). http://www.newyorker.com/fiction/content/articles/040405fi_fiction?040405fi_fiction

"Phil in the Marketplace" (2006). http://www.vqronline.org/articles/2006/fiction/lethem-phil-marketplace/

Collections

The Wall of the Sky, the Wall of the Eye (1996)
Kafka Americana (1999, with Carter Scholz)
Men and Cartoons (2004)
How We Got Insipid (2006)

Nonfiction Books

The Disappointment Artist (2005)
Believeniks!: 2005: The Year We Wrote a Book About the Mets (2006, with Christopher Sorrentino, as "Ivan Felt and Harris Conklin")

Articles and Essays

"Defending the Searchers." *Tin House* (2001)

"The Ecstasy of Influence: A Plagiarism." *Harpers* (February 2007). http://www.harpers.org/archive/2007/02/0081387

"First Sales." In *Science Fiction and Fantasy Writer's Sourcebook*, ed. David H. Borcherding, 406–9. Cincinnati, OH: Writer's Digest, 1996.

"Hitchhiking in Nevada Is Illegal." *Rolling Stone,* July 6, 2000. http://www.verysilly.org/lethem/hitching.html

"L Alone at the Movies." *The New Yorker,* June 17, 2002. http://www.newyorker.com/talk/content/articles/020617ta_talk_lethem?020617ta_talk_lethem

"The Many Dimensions of Rod Serling." *Gadfly* (September–October 1999). http://www.gadflyonline.com/archive/SepOct99/archive-serling.html

"My Marvel Years." *London Review of Books* 26, no. 8 (April 15, 2004). http://www.lrb.co.uk/v26/n08/leth01_.html

"Nine Failures of the Imagination" *New York Times,* September 23, 2001.

"The Squandered Promise of Science Fiction." *Village Voice* (June 1998). http://www.verysilly.org/lethem/lethems_vision.html

"Top Five Depressed Superheroes." *Shout Magazine* (December 2002).

"You Don't Know Dick." *Bookforum Summer 2002.* http://www.verysilly.org/lethem/lethemBF.html

Bibliographies

Lethem in Landscape. October 26, 2004. http://www.verysilly.org/lethem/

For Further Information

Official Web site: http://www.jonathanlethem.com/

Benson, Heidi. "Jonathan Lethem Finds Urban Utopias Lost in New Novel." *The San Francisco Chronicle,* October 6, 2003. http://www.SFgate.com/c/a/2003/10/06/DD14158.DTL

"Breeding Hybrids in the Genre Garden." *Locus* (October 1997). http://www.locusmag.com/1997/Issues/10/Lethem.html

Edemariam, Aida. "The Borrower." *The Guardian Online,* June 2, 2007. http://www.guardian.co.uk/books/2007/jun/02/featuresreviews.guardianreview8

Flannagan, Sean, and Andrew Krucoff. Interview. *92Y Blog,* November 14, 2005. http://blog.92y.org/index.php/item/jonathan_lethem_interview/

Houle. Zachary. "A Conversation with Jonathan Lethem." *SF Site* (November 2000). http://www.SFsite.com/11b/jl93.htm

Interview. *Amazon.com.* 1999. http://www.amazon.com/gp/feature.html?ie=UTF8&docId=12096

Interview. *Postroad* 5 (Fall–Winter 2002). http://www.postroadmag.com/Issue_5/Etcetera5/Lethem.htm

Interviews to 2004. *Lethem in Landscape.* October 26, 2004. http://www.verysilly.org/lethem/interviews.html

Kelleghan, Fiona. "Jonathan Lethem." In *St. James Guide to Science Fiction Writers,* ed. Jay Pedersen. Detroit, MI: St. James, 1996.

———. "Private Hells and Radical Doubts: An Interview with Jonathan Lethem." *Science Fiction Studies* 25 (1998). http://www.depauw.edu/SFs/interviews/letheminterview.htm

McGlone, Jackie. "Brooklyn Dodger." *The Scotsman* (UK), May 26, 2007.

Stein, Lorin. Interview. *The Paris Review* (Summer 2003).

Zeitchik, Steven. "Jonathan Lethem: A Booklyn of the Soul." *Publishers Weekly* 19 (September 2003): 37–38.

Ken MacLeod

Space Opera

Benchmark Title: *The Star Fraction* (1995)

b. 1954 (Outer Hebrides, Scotland)

Hey, this is Europe. . . . The bones of our ancestors, and the stones of their works, are everywhere. Our liberties were won in wars and revolutions so terrible that we do not fear our governors: they fear us. Our children giggle and eat ice-cream in the palaces of past rulers. We snap our fingers at kings.
—USENET posting, rec.sf.arts.fandom (September 2000)

Photo credit: Ian Whates.
Courtesy of Ken MacLeod.

About the Author and the Author's Writing

Kenneth Macrae MacLeod was born in Stornoway on the island of Lewis, in the Outer Hebrides of Scotland, and grew up in Greenock, on the south bank of the River Clyde. After graduating from Glasgow University with a degree in zoology, he pursued a career as a computer programmer. He put his writing ambitions on hold until, having completed his master's thesis in biomechanics, he challenged himself to write. His first novel, *The Star Faction*, was an immediate success, runner up for the Arthur C. Clarke Award and winner of the Prometheus Award for best libertarian novel. In the Fall Revolution sequence and the Engines of Light trilogy, MacLeod combines space opera spirit with the substance of political ideas; his fiction shows "how mindless adherence to a creed, even a beneficent one, creates a nation of unimaginative sheep" (*Emerald City* 2000).

Cosmonaut Keep (2000), the first volume of the Engines of Light trilogy, juggles two strands. The first is a near-future account of a young Scottish computer programmer, living in a world in which the cold war between an American dominated by the right, and a European Union dominated by Russia, is heating up; he finds himself in possession of the secret of interstellar flight. The second is the far-future vision of the young programmer's distant descendant, who shares his world with intelligent dinosaurs and star-ship piloting squid. *The Night Sessions* (2008) is a futuristic thriller, set in 2037, in the aftermath of the "Faith Wars"—a disastrous conflict also known as the Oil Wars. Western society has rejected religion, and its nations have become secular states. Robots have gained self-awareness and are now part of society. MacLeod has previously stated that the one common thread in his books is that they are about the clash between human beings and post-human artificial intelligence. He confesses to having once been skeptical about AI, and the Singularity: "'Computers can't argue,' [they] said. Of course, in those days computers were built by IBM and filled a room. These days you get more computing power on your phone, and they do argue. I'm not as sceptical as I once was about AI, but no less suspicious" (Wilson n.d.).

Ken MacLeod's worlds may be far futures, flirting with singularities and post-human cyborg resurrection; or they may be more immediate, alternative tomorrows, taking the problems we have now to the next logical (and terrifying) level. But as he told *Locus* magazine in 2006, "If I have any political motivation in my writing, it is to make people think." His heroes are usually anarchists/libertarians, with a skeptical attitude toward authority in general, and government in particular. MacLeod can best be described as a techno-utopian socialist, resolutely pro-technology, whose anarcho-primitivist characters are often (but not always) villains. "One of the very first socialist pamphlets I ever read, from *Socialist Worker* way back in 1970 or so, said that with atomic power and automation we could build a world of 'peace, leisure and abundance beyond the wildest dreams of the utopians.' I'd still hold out for that" ("Interview" 2005).

In case all this sounds too dry and political, it's worth mentioning that Ken MacLeod is very funny, well known for the jokes and puns that he manages to construct from the head-on clash of futuristic drama, socialist ideology, and computer programming. In 1997 he was able to put aside computer programming and become a full-time writer. He lives in West Lothian, Scotland, and continues to explore the future possibilities of evolution, revolution, and technological upheaval.

Awards

Novels

The Star Fraction (1995) **Prometheus**

The Stone Canal (1996) **Prometheus**

The Sky Road (1999) **BSF**

Learning the World: A Novel of First Contact (2005) **Prometheus**

Short Fiction

"Lighting Out" **BSF**

Works by the Author

Newton's Wake: A Space Opera (2004)

Learning the World: A Novel of First Contact (2005)

The Highway Men (2006)

The Execution Channel (2007)

The Night Sessions (2008)

The Restoration Game (2009)

Fall Revolution series

The Star Fraction (1995)
The Stone Canal (1996)
The Cassini Division (1998)
The Sky Road (1999)

Engines of Light Trilogy

Cosmonaut Keep (2000)
Dark Light (2001)
Engine City (2002)

Notable Short Fiction

"The Downloadable Boy" (1999; excerpt from *The Cassini Division*). http://www.salon.com/books/feature/1999/07/27/macleod_excerpt/
"Cydonia (THE WEB)" (1998)
"The Human Front" (2002)
"The Highway Men" (2006)
"Jesus Christ, Reanimator" (2007)
"Who's Afraid of Wolf 359?" (2007)

Collections

Giant Lizards from Another Star (2006)

Articles and Essays

"History in SF: What (Hasn't Yet) Happened in History." In *Histories of the Future: Studies in Fact, Fantasy and Science Fiction,* ed. Alan Sandison and Robert Dingley, 8–14. Basingstoke, UK: Palgrave, 2000.
"Libertarianism, the Looney Left and the Secrets of the Illuminati." *Matrix* (September/October 1997). http://www.libertarian.co.uk/lapubs/persp/persp010.pdf
"Politics and Science Fiction." In *The Cambridge Companion to Science Fiction,* ed. Edward James and Farah Mendlesohn, 230–40. Cambridge: Cambridge University Press, 2003.
"Science Fiction after the Future Went Away." *Revolution* 5 (1998). http://www.infinityplus.co.uk/nonfiction/kensf.htm
SF Crowsnest. Regular Features Column. http://www.sfcrowsnest.com/: For example: "2001 and All That (or, Life Before and After the End of History)," June 2003; "Does Science Fiction Have to Be About the Present?" November 2003; "Where I Get My Other Ideas From. (NESFA Guest of Honor Speech)," April 2006.

For Further Information

Author's Blog: *The Early Days of a Better Nation.* http://kenmacleod.blogspot.com/

Butler, Andrew M., and Farah Mendlesohn. *The True Knowledge of Ken MacLeod.* Cambridge: Science Fiction Foundation, 2003.

Emerald City: Fantasy and Science Fiction. "Ken MacLeod Issue" (May 2000). http://www.emcit.com/emcitS01.shtml

"Interview: Ken MacLeod: Politics & SF." *Locus* (September 2006). http://www.locusmag.com/2006/Issues/09MacLeod.html

"Interview: Science Fiction Can Help Us Learn to Change the World." *Socialist Worker.* November 12, 2005. http://www.socialistworker.co.uk/article.php?article_id=7729

Leonard, Andrew. "An Engine of Anarchy." *Salon,* July 27, 1999. http://www.salon.com/books/feature/1999/07/27/macleod_interview/

Lilley, Ernest. "Interview with Ken Macleod." *SFRevu* (March 2006). http://sfrevu.com/Review-id.php?id=3776

Walker, Jesse. "Anarchies, States and Utopias: The Science Fiction of Ken MacLeod." *Reason* (November 2000). http://www.reason.com/news/show/27843.html

Wilson, Andrew J. "Tomorrow Lies in Ambush: A Conversation with Ken MacLeod." *One Magazine,* n.d. http://www.iamone.co.uk/index.php?option=com_content&view=article&id=102&Itemid=0

Anne McCaffrey

Science Fantasy; SF Romance

Benchmark Title: *Dragonflight* (1969)

b. 1926 (Cambridge Massachusetts)

Photo credit: Beth Gwinn

Why dragons? To which I generally retort, Why not? They've had a bad press for years. And I was turning them on their tails and making them useful.
—Jamneck, "An Interview with Anne McCaffrey," *Writing World* (2004)

About the Author and the Author's Writing

First of all, a clarification is in order: the Pern stories, and indeed almost all stories by Anne McCaffrey are science fiction, even if they are what the *Encyclopedia of Science Fiction* (1999) calls "tinged with the tone and instruments of Fantasy." To quote the lady herself, "People have freaked out when I tell them that my dragons are scientifically based.... What else can you call a genetically engineered life form? But I must say I get a kick out of cutting them short when they call me a 'fantasy' writer" (Jamneck 2004).

The Dragonrider stories are set on an Earth colony which, due to the hardscrabble nature of its world, has reverted to a medieval stage of society and technology. But it has also produced dragons with psionic abilities, which are the only things that stand between the colonists and "thread," a spore that periodically rains down on Pern, consuming crops, animals, and any humans in its path. The dragons are paired for life with elite "dragonriders," who bond with their mounts at birth and communicate with them telepathically. Later books in the series have backtracked, to deal with the colonization of Pern and the bio-engineering that resulted in the dragons, and as the series has progressed, some of the SF conventions and themes have become more obvious, as the colonists rediscover their links to their Mother Planet and gradually develop much higher levels of technology.

Anne Inez McCaffrey was born in Cambridge, Massachusetts, "on April 1st, 1926, ... at 1:30 p.m., in the hour of the Sheep, year of the Fire Tiger, sun sign Aries with Taurus rising and Leo mid-heaven (which seems to suggest an early interest in the stars)" (official Web site). Her father was a retired colonel in the U.S. Army, and her mother was an estate agent. She attended schools in Virginia and New Jersey and received a BA from Radcliffe, majoring in Slavonic languages. After graduation she became a character actress, studied voice for nine years, and became involved in the stage direction of opera and operetta. In 1950 she married and subsequently had three children.

McCaffrey's first story was published in 1953; she had some steady success with the short form during the 1950s and early 1960s, but her first novel had to wait until her children were settled in school. *Restoree*, published in 1966, was written as a pastiche of what McCaffrey saw as the "absurd and unrealistic" portrayal of women in SF novels at that time. "No one had told me that women were not supposed to write [SF] and that few read it. After seven years of voracious reading in the field, I had it up to the eyeteeth with vapid women. I rebelled" ("Hitch Your Dragon to a Star . . ." 1974). *Restoree* is not great fiction, but it is a terrific romp, and like the Dragonriders series and *The Ship Who Sang* (1969)—which McCaffrey claims is her favorite of *all* her books—it reflects some of her favorite thematic elements: strong female characters, teamwork, birth, rebirth, and reinvention, "the buoyant persistence of human personality despite physical differences" (Brizzi 1996), all leavened with generous helpings of romance. In *The Ship Who Sang* (1969), based on a beautifully crafted 1961 short story, and the first book in The Brain & Brawn Ships series, infants who are physically handicapped but otherwise extremely intelligent are transformed into the cyborg brains of powerful spacecraft, piloted by ordinary human pilots.

McCaffrey was the first woman to win both the Hugo and Nebula Awards, in 1968 and 1969, for short stories, which were eventually incorporated into her second novel, *Dragonflight*. In 2005 McCaffrey was named the Damon Knight Grand Master by the SFWA, and in 2006 she was inducted into the Science Fiction Hall of Fame. She is nothing less than an icon of SF, the wellspring of a literary industry that has been the delight of legions of fans. The Pern saga will, in future, be written by her son Todd, who has been gradually picking up the torch of the family franchise: "[H]e grew up with the dragons, he knows the canon, and he helped me work through a couple of things. So he and my daughter Gigi (Georgeanne) have the right to continue the dragon series" ("Heirs to Pern" 2004). In her many other series, such as Doona, the Crystal Singers, the Dinosaur Planet, and Acorna, McCaffrey has worked with some of the best writers of science fantasy on the current scene, such as Jody Lynn Nye and Elizabeth Moon, Margaret Ball, and Elizabeth Ann Scarborough.

When her marriage ended in 1970, McCaffrey and her children moved to Ireland, where she had a successful second—or third—career running a livery stable, raising horses, and showing them in horse trials and show-jumping competitions. Until arthritis made it impossible, she also rode for pleasure; arthritis also put a stop to her regular attendance at SF cons all over the world. Anne McCaffrey currently lives in County Wicklow in Ireland, in "Dragonhold-Underhill," the home she designed herself for the rolling Wicklow countryside.

Awards

Edward E. Smith Memorial Award for Imaginative Fiction ("Skylark award") (1976)
SFWA Damon Knight Memorial Grand Master (2005)
Science Fiction Hall of Fame (2006)
Robert A. Heinlein Award (2007)

Short Fiction
"Dragonrider" (1967) **Nebula**
"Weyr Search" (1967) **Hugo**

Works by the Author

Restoree (1967)
The Coelura (1987)
Nimisha's Ship (1999)

The Brain & Brawn Ships
The Ship Who Sang (1969). Subsequent volumes in the series are collaborations with Margaret Ball, Mercedes Lackey, S. M. Stirling, and Jody Lynn Nye.

The Catteni
Freedom's Landing (1995)
Freedom's Choice (1997)
Freedom's Challenge (1998)
Freedom's Ransom (2002)

The Crystal Singers
Crystal Singer (1982)
Killashandra (1985)
Crystal Line (1992)

The Dinosaur Planet
Dinosaur Planet (1984)
Dinosaur Planet Survivors (1984)

Subsequent volumes—referred to as the Planet Pirates series—are collaborations with Jody Lynn Nye and Elizabeth Moon.

The Doona series
Decision at Doona (1969)
Crisis on Doona (1992, with Jody Lynn Nye)
Treaty at Doona (1994)

The Dragonriders of Pern
Dragonflight (1969)
Dragonquest (1971)
Dragonsong (1976)
Dragonsinger (1977)

The White Dragon (1978)
Dragondrums (1979)
Moreta: Dragonlady of Pern (1983)
Nerilka's Story (1986)
Dragonsdawn (1988)
All the Weyrs of Pern (1991)
The Dolphins of Pern (1994)
Dragonseye (1996; aka *Red Star Rising: Second Chronicles of Pern*)
The Masterharper of Pern (1998)
The Skies of Pern (2001)
Dragon's Kin (2003, with Todd McCaffrey).

Subsequent Pern novels, up to and including *Dragon Harper* (2007), were written in collaboration with her son, Todd McCaffrey. *Dragonheart* (2008) is credited to Todd McCaffrey alone.

The Talent series

To Ride Pegasus (1973)
Pegasus in Flight (1990)
Pegasus in Space (2000)
The Rowan (1990)
Damia (1991)
Damia's Children (1993)
Lyon's Pride (1994)
The Tower and the Hive (1999)

Other Notable Genre Fiction

Ring of Fear (1971)
The Mark of Merlin (1971)
The Kilternan Legacy (1975)
Stitch in Snow (1984)
The Year of the Lucy (1986)
The Lady (1987; aka *The Carradyne Touch*)

Acorna series

With Margaret Ball

Acorna the Unicorn Girl (1997)
Acorna's Quest (1998)

With Elizabeth Ann Scarborough

Acorna's People (1999)
Acorna's World (2000)
Acorna's Search (2001)
Acorna's Rebels (2003)
Acorna's Triumph (2004)

Petaybee series, with Elizabeth Ann Scarborough

Powers That Be (1993)
Power Lines (1994)
Power Play (1995)
Changelings (2005)
Maelstrom (2006)
Deluge (2008)

Juvenile Fantasy

An Exchange of Gifts (1995)
No One Noticed the Cat (1996)
If Wishes Were Horses (1998)
Black Horses for the King (1998)

Notable Short Fiction

"The Ship Who Sang." (1961)
"Dramatic Mission" (1969)
"Rescue Run" (1991)
"Beyond Between" (2003)

Collections

Get Off the Unicorn (1977)
Dragonriders of Pern (1988)
The Renegades of Pern (1989)
The Chronicles of Pern: First Fall (1994)
The Girl Who Heard Dragons (1994)
A Gift of Dragons (2002)

As Editor

Alchemy & Academe (1970)
Cooking Out of This World (1973)
Space Opera (1996, with Elizabeth Ann Scarborough)
Serve It Forth—Cooking with Anne McCaffrey (1996, with John Gregory Betancourt)

Nonfiction Books

People of Pern (1988, with Robin Wood)
The Dragonlover's Guide to Pern (1989, with Jody Lynn Nye)

Articles and Essays

"Hitch Your Dragon to a Star: Romance and Glamour in Science Fiction." In *Science Fiction, Today and Tomorrow,* ed. Reginald Bretnor, 278–92. New York: Harper & Row, 1974.

For Further Information

Official Web site: *The Worlds of Anne McCaffery.* http://www.annemccaffrey.net/index.php

Brizzi, Mary T. *Anne McCaffrey.* Starmont Reader's Guide, 30. San Bernardino, CA: Borgo, 1986.

———. "Anne McCaffrey." In *St. James Guide to Science Fiction Writers,* ed. Jay Pedersen. Detroit, MI: St. James, 1996.

Dohmen, Teri. "Anne McCaffrey: Year of the Dragons." *Crescent Blues* (February 1999). http://www.crescentblues.com/2_1issue/mccaffrey.shtml

"Heirs to Pern." *Locus* (November 2004). http://www.locusmag.com/2004/Issues/11McCaffrey.html

Jamneck, Lynne. "An Interview with Anne McCaffrey." *Writing World* (2004). http://www.writing-world.com/sf/mccaffrey.shtml

McCaffrey, Todd. *Dragonholder: The Life and Dreams (So Far) of Anne McCaffrey.* New York: Ballantine/Del Rey, 1999.

Miller, Cheryl B., ed. *The Many Works of Anne McCaffrey.* October 16, 2006. http://mccaffrey.srellim.org/

Roberts, Robin. *Anne McCaffrey: A Critical Companion.* Westport, CT: Greenwood, 1996.

Swaim, Don. Audio Interview. *Wired for Books* March 22, 1988). http://wiredforbooks.org/annemccaffrey/

Trachtenberg, Martha P. *Anne McCaffrey: Science Fiction Storyteller.* Berkeley Heights, NY: Enslow, 2001.

Maureen F. McHugh

Near Future

Benchmark Title:
China Mountain Zhang (1992)

b. 1959 (Loveland, Ohio)

Photo credit: Beth Gwinn

My characters have faulty memories, but that's not because they are postmodern, that's because they are something much older than that, unreliable narrators. My characters are sometimes forgetful, always biased, but always in an attempt to mimic human failings, to let you pretend, dear reader, that they are real.
—"Why I Am Not Post-Modern" (2001)

About the Author and the Author's Writing

A common thread running through the novels and stories of Maureen F. McHugh is the struggle of characters who lack *guanxi*, or significance. In the near future of *China Mountain Zhang*, the novel with which McHugh "virtually erupted into the science fiction scene" (Bogstad 1996) in 1992, almost any difference from the "norm" is fatal to that all-important *guanxi*: discrimination is endemic, indeed institutionalized. The central character, the eponymous China Mountain Zhang, is a young American of Chinese descent, in a world in which China is the new dominant economic and political empire. But he is gay (strike one, in an intensely gender-sensitive culture), and he is "only" half-Chinese, although he has been genetically altered to play down the Hispanic elements of his appearance. McHugh tells the story as first-person episodes, through the eyes of Zhang and his friends and acquaintances, characters who, because of their sexuality, race, appearance, or birth, have even less *guanxi*, or as one puts it, "no connection, no string. Everybody just wants to get rid of us. We're human trash, disposable." They are characters who, like China Mountain Zhang, must negotiate the minefield that is their world.

McHugh has a talent for constructing settings and societies that are convincing, fascinating, and even attractive, in spite of the demands they make on her characters: in *China Mountain Zhang*, China and Chinese culture are in the ascendant. Food is harvested from the South Pole, and humankind has begun to colonize Mars. People live beneath the oceans, harvesting its wealth of resources. The action of her second novel, *Half the Day Is Night* (1994), takes place in one of these underwater cities, a common SF setting, but McHugh makes it come to life in its discomfort and darkness and strips it of any pretense at sparkling hi-tech glamour; instead, through her character's eyes, she reveals it as "like a second rate airport, full of soldiers and pre-form furniture in bright grimy orange and aqua. A third world country underwater. He had not realized that it would be so dark."

Her most recent book, *Nekroplis* (2002), is set in a near-future Morocco where the underclass live in old mausoleums, on the fringes of the city, while the affluent maintain their lifestyles with high-tech slaves, either genetically engineered from animals or, like the central character Hariba, "jessed"—physically bonded to her "employer" —by chemical alteration.

Maureen F. McHugh was born and grew up in Loveland, Ohio, near Cincinnati. She received a BA from Ohio University in 1981 and got a master's degree in English literature at New York University. After several years as a part-time college instructor and temping in technical writing and miscellaneous clerical jobs, she spent a year teaching in Shijiazhuang, China, an experience that provided rich material for *China Mountain Zhang* and a number of her finely crafted short stories. Her life has not been all plain sailing: in interviews, she has spoken of her struggle with depression, the effect of alcoholism on her family, and her mother's gradual decline into dementia. However, as she says in an essay on her official Web site, "I have my doubts about talking about it. It seems utterly American and foolish to share intimate details about my life with people but I keep thinking that if it was insulin I was taking instead of anti-depressant medication I wouldn't think so much about it" ("The Self-World of Depression" 1997).

After the success of *China Mountain Zhang* and her subsequent novels in the 1990s, McHugh has most recently been receiving critical praise for her short fiction. In December 2005 her extraordinary collection of speculative and slipstream stories, *Mothers and Other Monsters*, was shortlisted as a finalist for the prestigious Story Prize—and received the ultimate compliment from shocked mainstream reviewers, who said, "*It can't be science fiction, it's too good.*" In recent years she has been working as a scriptwriter for companies that produce alternative reality games, such as *Year Zero* and *I Love Bees*. In early 2009 she became a cofounder of No Mimes Media, an alternate reality game company.

Maureen F. McHugh lives in Austin, Texas, with her husband, Bob Yeager. She has described her relationship to their son Adam with great wit and sensitivity in essays such as "The Evil Stepmother": "We joke about me being the evil stepmother. In fact, the joke is that I am the Nazi Evil Stepmother From Hell. It dispels tension to say it out loud." In November 2004 McHugh was diagnosed with Hodgkin's lymphoma. Her blog *No Feeling of Falling* has been an ongoing account of her treatment and recovery; fortunately, according to a note on her official Web site in October 2006, "[t]hat's so much old news. I'm healthy and fine now."

Awards

Novels

China Mountain Zhang (1992) **Locus Poll, Tiptree**

Short Fiction

"The Lincoln Train" (1995) **Hugo, Locus Poll**

Works by the Author

China Mountain Zhang (1992)
Half the Day Is Night (1994)
Mission Child (1998)
Nekropolis (2002)

Other Notable Short Fiction

"Protection" (1992)
"Render Unto Caesar" (1992)
"Nekropolis" (1994)
"Virtual Love" (1994)
"The Cost to Be Wise" (1996)
"Strings" (1996)
"Interview: On Any Given Day" (2001)
"Makeover" (2002). http://www.infinitematrix.net/stories/shortshorts/riohondo/mchugh-rh10.html
"Presence" (2002)
"Alternate History" (2003)
"Ancestor Money" (2003)
"Eight-Legged Story" (2005). http://www.lcrw.net/trampoline/stories/mchugheight.htm

Collections

Mothers and Other Monsters (2005)

In Other Media

Alternate Reality Games: Viral Marketing

Year Zero. 42 Entertainment, 2007. Writer. Marketing for the Nine Inch Nails concept album of the same name.
I Love Bees. 42 Entertainment, 2004. Writer and Managing Editor. Marketing for video game *Halo 2*.
Last Call Poker. 42 Entertainment, 2005. Writer and Managing Editor. Marketing for the Neversoft video game *Gun*.

Articles and Essays

"The Anti-SF Novel." Talk given to the Philadelphia SF Society, September 12, 1997. http://my.en.com/~mcq/antisf.html
"Creating and Using Near Future Settings." In *Science Fiction and Fantasy Writer's Sourcebook,* ed. David H. Borcherding, 18–25. Cincinnati, OH: Writer's Digest, 1996.
"The Evil Stepmother." *Maureen F. McHugh Official Website*. December 12, 2000. http://my.en.com/~mcq/stepmother.html

"The Self-World of Depression." *Maureen F. McHugh Official Website.* October 12, 1997. http://my.en.com/~mcq/umwelt.html

"Why I Am Not Post-Modern." *Book Sense,* September 28, 2001. http://www.booksense.com/people/archive/mchughmaureen.jsp

For Further Information

Official Web site: http://my.en.com/~mcq/

Author Blog: "No Feeling of Falling." http://maureenmcq.blogspot.com/

Bogstad, Janice M. "Maureen McHugh." In *St. James Guide to Science Fiction Writers,* ed. Jay Pedersen. Detroit, MI: St. James, 1996.

Bond, Gwenda. Interview. In *Reading Guide.* Small Beer Press. 2005. http://www.lcrw.net/mchugh/mchugh-interview.htm

Hogan, Ron. "Author, Author: Maureen McHugh and Sarah Willis." *Beatrice.com,* October 26, 2005. http://www.beatrice.com/archives/001809.html

Lindow, Sandra, and Michael Levy. Interview. *SFRA Review* (September–December 2001): 2–18. http://www.sfra.org/sfra-review/254-255.pdf

"Maureen F. McHugh: Filling the Void." *Locus* (February 2008). http://www.locusmag.com/2008/Issue02_McHugh.html

Stansberry, Pat. Interview. *Strange Horizons,* September 9, 2002. http://www.strangehorizons.com/2002/20020909/mchugh.shtml

Zhou, Yupei. "Beyond Ethnicity and Gender: *China Mountain Zhang*'s Transcendent Techniques." *Extrapolation* 42 (2001): 374–83.

Vonda N. McIntyre

Apocalyptic SF; Feminist SF; Myth and Legend

Benchmark Title: *Dreamsnake* (1978)

b. 1948 (Louisville, Kentucky)

Photo credit: Alice Lengers.
Permission of Vonda N. McIntyre.

[T]he customs officer asked if I had anything else to declare. "I have this award," I said . . . And I opened up my ratty shopping bag and revealed my Hugo . . . . He read the plaque, said, "That's all right. Awards aren't dutiable. I've read your books. Please go right on through, and welcome home."
He made my day.
—Stevenson, Interview in *Book View Cafe News* (2009)

About the Author and the Author's Writing

Vonda N. McIntyre, like many other SF fans of her generation, remembers exactly what she was doing on the evening of September 8, 1966, one week before she set off for college. But while most "Trekkers" of a certain age might remember where they were and how they reacted when they saw the first adventure of Captain Kirk and Mr. Spock that night, Vonda McIntyre has more reason to recall the moment than most of us. "I started writing a screenplay for *Star Trek* during the first commercial break. . . . I watched that show and thought, 'I've never seen anything like this in my life. It's wonderful. I want to write for it'" ("To Hollywood and Beyond" 1998). McIntyre completed that screenplay, and it made it as far as Gene Roddenberry's production offices, when the series was canceled. She was "heartbroken"; little did she know that this setback, sad as it was, was a relatively minor speed bump in a career in which she would have the opportunity to create original SF every bit as dramatic and memorable as the adventures of the Starship *Enterprise*—and she would eventually have opportunities, as a professional SF writer, to shape the direction of the program that had impressed her so much.

Vonda Neel McIntyre was born in Louisville, Kentucky. Her family moved to the Seattle area when she was twelve, and she became involved with SF fandom as a freshman at the University of Washington. In a 2005 interview with SF fanzine *Trufen*, she recalled that it was a revelation to her: "[Not] so much love at first sight as home at first sight. As a girl science geek in a suburban high school, I had always felt seriously out of place" (O'Brien 2005). McIntyre graduated with a BS, with honors, and attended Clarion Science Fiction writers' workshop in 1970. After one year of graduate work in genetics, she fled "to live four miles down a logging road in Oregon, where she finished her first novel" (official Web site), more than convinced that "as a research scientist, I make a pretty good science fiction writer."

That first novel was *The Exile Waiting* (1975), in which the rulers of the last city on Earth exile two malcontents, a young empath and an off-world poet, to the deep underground. They find a world of crystalline caverns, strange, isolated people, and simmering rebellion. In 1973 McIntyre's novelette "Of Mist, and Grass, and Sand" had appeared in *Analog*, immediately drawing praise and high honors. The story, which later served as the opening chapter of the 1978 novel *Dreamsnake*, takes place on an Earth that uses genetic technology, as mechanical technology is no longer sustainable. Her protagonist, a traveling healer, is on a quest to find a rare alien "dreamsnake" and sees the best and the worst on her journey. "Believe it or not, a lot about the book was relatively controversial when it came out. Not too many SF novels had a woman protagonist. Child abuse was not much discussed in SF. The sexuality was edgy for the time" (Stevenson 2009). *Dreamsnake* swept the board of SF prizes for its year. McIntyre's most recent novel, *The Moon and the Sun* (1997), is an alternate history of King Louis XIV of France, the "Sun King," and his court's encounter with a living, breathing, and *sentient* sea monster.

McIntyre's works invariably reveal her skill in depicting strong female characters and her ability to develop an idea. "A hallmark of Vonda McIntyre's writing is her theme of physical transformation, either through genetic engineering or mechanical means" (Carter 1996). She has written the novelizations of three *Star Trek* films, and came up with a name for the character of Mr. Sulu—"Hikaru"—as well as writing a number of original Star Trek novels, beginning with *The Entropy Effect* in 1981. In a wonderful illustration of the principle that no good idea should ever be wasted, *The Entropy Effect* was based on that screenplay McIntyre had begun during the commercial break on September 8, 1966. "A few critics have claimed that I both derailed my writing career and damaged my ethics, morals, and precious bodily fluids by writing Star Trek novels but I have to disagree" ("Writing Star Trek Novels" 2009). True *Star Trek* fans would also disagree, as it is widely agreed that McIntyre's tie-in fiction is recognized as among the very best of the spin-offs of the Star Trek series, keeping the bar high for anyone who wishes to add his or her own narrative diversity to the long-running series.

McIntyre is a generous supporter of writers and SF fandom. Her Web site features a number of articles about the craft of writing, as well as resources for writers at all stages of their careers. She has taught at Clarion many times. In 1994, based on a screenplay she had done for *Dreamsnake*, the Chesterfield Film Company offered her a fellowship, sponsored by Universal Studios and Amblin Entertainment. She spent the year in Los Angeles working on a screenplay of her young adult novel *Barbary*, and an idea that became her Nebula award-winning novel *The Moon and the Sun*. In 2000 she was Evans Chair at The Evergreen State College at Olympia, Washington.

Vonda N. McIntyre is a "card-carrying member" of the American Civil Liberties Union. She has exhibited horses and has earned *shodan* (first degree black belt) in the martial art Aikido. She lives in the Seattle area.

Awards

Novels

Dreamsnake (1978) **Hugo, Locus Poll, Nebula**
The Moon and the Sun (1997) **Nebula**

Short Fiction

"Of Mist, Grass, and Sand" (1973) **Nebula**

 ## Works by the Author

The Exile Waiting (1975)
Dreamsnake (1978)
Superluminal (1983)
The Bride (1985)
Barbary (1986)
The Moon and the Sun (1997)

Star Wars

The Crystal Star (1994)

Star Trek

The Entropy Effect (1981)
Star Trek: The Wrath of Khan (1982)
Star Trek III: The Search for Spock (1984)
Star Trek IV: The Voyage Home (1986)
Enterprise: The First Adventure (1986)

Starfarers Quartet

Starfarers (1989)
Transition (1991)
Metaphase (1992)
Nautilus (1994)

Other Notable Short Fiction

"Wings" (1973)
"The Mountains of Sunset, the Mountains of Dawn" (1974)
"Aztechs" (1977)
"Fireflood" (1979)
"Transit" (1983)
"Steelcollar Worker" (1992)

"The Adventure of the Field Theorems" (1995)

"Little Faces (2005)

"The Natural History & Extinction of the People of the Sea" (2008). http://www.bo_Hlt229613402oBM_86_kview_Hlt231554915cBM_87_afe.com/index.php/Ursula-K.-Le-Guin/Short-Stories/A-Book-View-Caf%C3%A9-Bonus. The faux-encyclopedia article that inspired *The Moon and the Sun.* Illustrated by Ursula K. Le Guin.

Collections

Fireflood and Other Stories (1979)

Duty, Honor, Redemption (2004)

As Editor

Aurora: Beyond Equality (1976, with Susan Anderson)

Nebula Awards Showcase 2004 (2004)

Articles and Essays

"Mr. Spock's Dad." *Book View Café,* February 22, 2009. http://blog.bookviewcafe.com/2009/02/22/mr-spocks-dad/

"Pitfalls of Writing Science Fiction & Fantasy: General Useful Information & Other Opinionated Comments." *Sff.net,* September 8, 2003. http://www.sff.net/people/Vonda/Pitfalls.html

"Writing Star Trek Novels, or, Why Don't You Get a Morally Acceptable Job?" *Bookview Café*, February 15, 2009. http://blog.bookviewcafe.com/2009/02/15/writing-star-trek-novels/

Bibliographies

Annotated Bibliography: http://www.oz.net/~vonda/vnm_bib.htm

For Further Information

Official Web site: http://www.vondanmcintyre.com/

Author's Blog: *Book View Café.* http://blog.bookviewcafe.com/

Carter, Gay. E. "Vonda McIntyre." In *St. James Guide to Science Fiction Writers,* ed. Jay Pedersen. Detroit, MI: St. James, 1996.

Kilgore, De Witt Douglas. "Changing Regimes: Vonda N. McIntyre's Parodic Astrofuturism." *Science Fiction Studies* 27, no. 2 (July 2000): 256–77. http://www.depauw.edu/sfs/backissues/81/kilgore81art.htm

Kolm, Peggy. "Vonda McIntyre and 'Of Mist and Grass and Sand'." *Biology in Science Fiction,* March 23, 2007. http://sciencefictionbiology.blogspot.com/2007/03/vonda-mcintyre-and-of-mist-and-grass.html

O'Brien, Ulrika. "The Fannish Inquisition: Vonda McIntyre." *Trufen.net,* April 13, 2005.

Stevenson, Jennifer. Interview. *Book View Cafe News,* 1, no. 4 (April 2009). http://www.bookviewcafe.com/index.php/Newsletter-April-2009

"To Hollywood and Beyond." *Locus* (February 1998). http://www.locusmag.com/1998/Issues/02/McIntyre.html

Van Natta, Carol, and Ann Harbour. *Vonda N. McIntyre.* 1997. http://www.oz.net/~vonda/

Wood, Diane S. "Breaking the Code: Vonda N. McIntyre's *Dreamsnake.*" *Extrapolation* 31 (1991): 63+.

Frank Miller

Graphic Novels

Benchmark Title: *Batman: The Dark Knight Returns* (1986)

b. 1957 (Olney, Maryland)

> *It's one craft. My pictures are incomplete with words. My words make no sense without pictures. Mostly, I do the whole job myself. Sometimes I share the job with other talents. But it's one, single craft, not a shotgun wedding between two.*
> —Sakaridis, "Frank Miller," *Comicdom* (2006)

About the Author and the Author's Writing

In the course of his career, Frank Miller's words and pictures have been responsible for "rebooting" the narratives of some of the leading archetypes of twentieth-century popular culture—Batman, Spiderman, Wolverine of the X-Men, Superman, and Daredevil—bringing a darker and more mature mythology to uniquely American characters and a unique American story form. He was born in Olney, Maryland, the fifth of seven children. His mother was a nurse, and his father was a carpenter and electrician. The family moved to Montpelier, Vermont, where he spent most of his childhood, reading comic books and thrillers and watching movies. Miller was thirteen when he discovered Will Eisner, comic book writer and artist, whose dark, substantial work of the 1940s prefigured the graphic novel revolution of the 1970s. Later in life Miller had the opportunity to work with Eisner and call him a friend, and he engaged in friendly arguments with his boyhood idol about the "importance" of what they were doing: "'He and I had so many arguments about that,' says Miller, laughing. 'He would deny the obvious cinematic influence on him. . . . And he sought for comics to be next to prose, where I always thought of comics as being another scrappy form, messing in popular culture'" (Applebaum 2008). Eventually Miller was able to bring Eisner's classic 1940 comic book character The Spirit to film, in a deeply personal tribute to a man who shaped his ideas of what graphic art could achieve.

Miller's first work in comic books was in Gold Key's *Twilight Zone* in 1978, and he worked with DC Comics and Marvel on titles such as *John Carter, Warlord of Mars* and *Weird War Tales*. Miller was with Marvel, filling in on Spiderman in the late 1970s, when he casually asked if he could take over the storyline of Daredevil—the "hero without fear"—a minor character in the Spiderman universe. His debut on that title, although tame by the standards of the style he developed later, was pure film noir, and it gave the whole genre a new dynamism and drama. As well as the well-known hallmarks of his visual style—the dark, blocky drawings, the movement expressed by breaking up and repeating bits of images—Miller made important narrative changes;

for example, he brought a new realism to the Daredevil's antagonists, moving away from the costumed villains that the comics had churned over for so long, and introducing, in Kingpin, a close-to real-life representative of organized crime. And Miller did not shy away from the darkest possibilities, such as when longstanding love interest and very popular crime-fighter in her own right, Elektra, was killed off. Miller seemed to take delight in a fan's mournful resistance to the idea that, even in comics, dead *can* mean Dead. "Did I mention that Elektra is dead? . . . But Elektra is still dead. . . . Have I mentioned that Elektra is dead?" (Sakaridis 2006). Eventually he would revive her, but only on his own terms.

With Daredevil one of Marvel's best-selling characters, Miller was given the sensitive task of bringing new life to one of Marvel's most treasured assets. *The Dark Knight Returns* is not the Batman of the naïve, adolescent comics, or the cartoon Batman of the 1960s TV series. This older, darker Batman is vigilante and conflicted antihero; Miller's more complicated and interesting take on the story brought the Caped Crusader to a whole new audience. But it also changed the entire comic industry. *The Dark Knight Returns* became one of the biggest selling trade paperbacks of the 1980s and remained in print for over twenty years. The idea of "comics" as ephemera—in fact, the idea of labeling graphic novels as "comics" at all—was gone and, like Elektra, Frank Miller had killed it stone dead. In the future no one could deny that a graphic story could carry a serious theme and hold on to the public imagination, as well as any traditional text or cinematic narrative.

Much of Miller's best-known work could not exactly be labeled SF—*Sin City*, for example, is pure noir, a moody, violent crime drama set in a fictional version of Las Vegas, where an unlikely cast of antiheroes must fend for themselves against a greedy and corrupt Establishment. Miller is clearly interested in the visual and narrative possibilities of history and legend—such as in *300*, Miller's gorgeously visual and dramatic take on the battle of Thermopylae, where the Spartan army made a suicidal stand against a vastly superior force of Persian invaders, and in *Ronin*, in which Miller brings a modern American, postapocalyptic take to a tale of samurais in feudal Japan. But even Miller's non-SF superhero work demonstrates a sense of the world being not quite what it seems, and characters as different as King Leonidas of the Spartans and Hartigan of "Basin City" force the reader to focus on "what makes a hero and what doesn't" (Brownstein 2000).

Before he began his *IGN* interview with Miller, Todd Gilchrist observed that "his consistency as a creator of fantastic new worlds has elevated him beyond the pages of mere funny books." Frank Miller might disagree—as in his friendly arguments with his hero, Will Eisner; he refuses to be lured into overanalysis of what he does and how he does it. For Frank Miller, it all seems deceptively easy. "I don't strain for Importance: I play, bringing every ounce I've got to the game" (Sakaridis 2006).

Awards

Will Eisner Comic Industry Awards

Best Writer/Artist (1991)
Best Writer/Artist: *Sin City* (1993)
Best Writer/Artist: *300* (1996)
Bob Clampett Humanitarian (1998)

Kirby Awards

Best Single Issue (1986, 1987)
Best Graphic Album (1987)
Best Writer/Artist (1986)
Best Art Team (1987)

Harvey Awards

Best Series (1996, 1999)
Best Graphic Album of Original Work (1998)
Best Domestic Reprint Project (1997)

Works by the Author

Batman (1985–)

Batman: The Dark Knight Returns (1986, with Klaus Janson and Lynn Varley)
Batman: Year One (1988, with Richmond Lewis and David Mazzucchelli)
Spawn: Batman (1994, with Todd McFarlane)
Batman: The Dark Knight Strikes Again (2004)
Holy Terror, Batman! (in production)

Daredevil and Elektra (1979–1983, 1986–)

Elektra Lives Again (1990)
Daredevil: The Man without Fear (1993)
Daredevil Visionaries—Frank Miller, Vols. 1, 2, 3 (2001, 2002)
Elektra by Frank Miller Omnibus (2008, with Bill Sienkiewicz)

Hardboiled (1990)

Hardboiled (2000, with Geof Darrow)

Martha Washington (1992–1997)

Martha Washington Dies (2007)
The Life and Times of Martha Washington in the Twenty-First Century (2009, with Dave Gibbons)

Robocop (1990/1993)

Frank Miller's Robocop (2007, with Juan Jose Ryp)

Ronin (1983–1984)

Absolute Ronin (2008, with Lynn Varley)

Spider-Man (1979)
The Complete Frank Miller Spider-Man (2002)

Wolverine: X-Men (1982)
Wolverine (2009, with Chris Claremont)

Other Notable Work
300 (1999, with Lyn Varley)

Sin City (1990s)
Complete Sin City Library (2005). Includes individual titles such as *Family Values* (1997) and *Booze, Broads, & Bullets* (1998).

Cover Art
Space and Time (January 1975)
Mefisto in Onyx (1993) By Harlan Ellison
Gravity's Rainbow (2006) By Thomas Pyncheon

In Other Media
RoboCop 2. Orion Pictures Corporation, 1990. Directed by Irvin Kershner; screenplay by Frank Miller; starring Peter Weller.

RoboCop 3. Orion Pictures Corporation, 1993. Directed by Fred Dekker; screenplay by Frank Miller. This is supposedly a dreadful movie, but has minor Miller interest because of two characters: a cyborg samurai is a nod to *Ronin*, in which a masterless samurai's spirit is reanimated with futuristic biotechnology. And Bertha Washington, a freedom fighter in the film, is a reference to the freedom fighter with a similar name in Miller's *Give Me Liberty*.

Elektra. Twentieth Century-Fox Film Corporation, 2005. Directed by Rob Bowman; starring Jennifer Garner and Goran Visnjic.

Sin City. Dimension Films, 2005. Directed by Frank Miller and Robert Rodriguez; starring Mickey Rourke, Bruce Willis, Benicio Del Toro, Clive Owen, and Jessica Alba.

300. Warner Bros. Pictures, 2006. Directed by Zack Snyder; starring Gerard Butler and Lena Headey.

The Spirit. Lionsgate, 2008. Directed by Frank Miller; starring Gabriel Macht and Eva Mendes.

Acting or Appearing as Himself
Sin City, Daredevil, RoboCop, Jugular Wine: A Vampire Odyssey

Nonfiction Books
The Art of Sin City (2002).

Articles and Essays

With Gordon Linzner. "Midnight Swordsman." *Space & Time* (May 1973).

"Introduction." In *Mefisto in Onyx,* by Harlan Ellison. Shingletown, CA: Mark V. Ziesing, 1994.

"The Mark of Batman: An Introduction." In *Batman: The Dark Knight Returns.* New York: DC Comics, 1986. 6-8.

Official Web site, *The Spirit,* February–November 2008: http://www.mycityscreams.com/index2.html?swf=blog

For Further Information

Official Web site: *The Complete Works of Frank Miller.* http://www.moebiusgraphics.com/

Applebaum, Stephen. "It's No Sin: Frank Miller Interview." *The Scotsman* (UK), December 22, 2008. http://thescotsman.scotsman.com/features/Frank-Miller-interview-It39s-no.4812742.jp

Brownstein, Charles. "Returning to the Dark Knight: Frank Miller Interview." *Comic Book Resources,* April 21, 2000. http://www.comicbookresources.com/?page=article&id=192

The Comics Journal Library: Frank Miller. Fantagraphics Books, 2003.

"Frank Miller." In *Authors & Artists for Young Adults, Volume 45,* 127–32. Farmington Hills, MI: Gale Group, 2002.

"Frank Miller Time." Video profile. *A Comicbook Orange,* August 1, 2007 http://www.youtube.com/watch?v=NCO6y2ML7kw

George, Milo, ed. *Frank Miller: The Interviews, 1981–2003.* Seattle, WA: Fantagraphics, 2003.

Gross, Edward. "The CFQ Interview: Original Sinners, Frank Miller and Robert Rodriguez." *Cinefantastique* 37, no. 2 (April/May 2005): 24–31.

Gilchrist, Tod. Interview. *IGN.com,* August 19, 2005. http://dvd.ign.com/articles/643/643778p1.html

Interview. *G4TV.com,* March 31, 2005. http://g4tv.com/gamemakers/features/51443/Icons-Interview-Frank-Miller.html

Jensen, G.O. *The Frank Miller Library.* July 2005. http://fmi.gojensen.no/

Lovece, Frank. "Spirit Guide: Frank Miller Adapts Will Eisner's Cult Comic." *Film Journal International,* December 22, 2008. http://www.filmjournal.com/filmjournal/content_display/esearch/e3i8a7ba6d185c56a44dde220cb5168caff

Pizzino, Christopher. "Art That Goes Boom: Genre and Aesthetics in Frank Miller's *Sin City.*" *English Language Notes* 46, no. 2. (Fall/Winter2008): 115–28.

Sakaridis, Dimitris. "Frank Miller: I Stole From the Best!" *Comicdom,* January 22, 2006. http://archive.comicdom.gr/interviews.php?id=17&lang=en

Sharrett, Christopher. "Batman and the Twilight of the Idols: An Interview with Frank Miller." In *The Many Lives of the Batman*, ed. Roberta E. Pearson and William Uricchio, 33–46. London: BFI, 1991.

Walter M. Miller

Apocalyptic SF

Benchmark Title: *A Canticle for Leibowitz* (1959)

b. 1922 (New Smyrna Beach, Florida); d. 1996 (Daytona Beach, Florida)

> *You ask me where I have been for twenty-five years.*
> *I will tell you.*
> *I live here in the swamp.*
> *I live here to save my hide.*
>
> —"Alibi," in *Beyond Armageddon* (1985)

About the Author and the Author's Writing

A Canticle for Leibowitz (1959) is a wonder among one-hit wonders. Written by Walter M. Miller, it was the single novel published during a lifetime blighted by severe depression—probably what would today be called post-traumatic stress disorder— and guilt about his role as a young airman in World War II, particularly his part in the destruction of Monte Casino, an Italian monastery found by St. Benedict in the twelfth century. *Canticle* is a work that is very much *of* its time, a novel of "nuclear anxiety," written in that time of supreme nuclear anxiety, the 1950s. But it is also a novel that transcends its time, with its weird, proto-Catholic spirituality; its stunning imagery; and its clear, memorable prose. It is that very rare thing, an SF novel written by one who saw himself as an SF writer, that is read and appreciated by people who "don't read science fiction."

Walter Michael Miller Jr. was born in New Smyrna Beach, Florida. He attended the University of Tennessee until he enlisted in the Army Air Corps in 1942, shortly after Pearl Harbor. He served as a radioman and tail gunner in B-52 bombers, flying fifty-three bombing missions over Italy and the Balkans, among them the raids that helped to destroy Monte Casino. The question that hangs over the bombing of the monastery is not just the destruction of a thousand-year-old site of worship, but the fact that subsequent investigations revealed that the German army was not using the monastery as a command post; the only casualties were monks and refugees from the nearby village, women and children and old men, who had taken shelter in what they assumed would be an off-limits sanctuary. Pictures of the aftermath of the B-52 raids show a scene of utter devastation: "the ruins all about him here were very old . . . gradually eroded into these anomalous heaps by generations of monks and occasional strangers . . . . The human erosion had all but obliterated the resemblance to buildings" (*Canticle*, Chapter 1).

Following the war, Miller resumed his education at the University of Texas at Austin; he studied engineering, but did not complete his degree. He married, had four children, returned to live in Florida at Daytona Beach, and converted to Roman Catholicism. He may have worked for a railroad company, as he eventually retired on a railroad pension and Social Security following a car accident. While he was hospitalized following the accident, he began writing, and between 1951 and 1957 he had between thirty and forty short stories published. His story "The Darfsteller," about an elderly actor who hatches a desperate plan to get back on the stage, won a Hugo in 1955. *A Canticle for Leibowitz* (1959) was a "fix-up," assembled from three novellas that had been published in *The Magazine of Fantasy and Science Fiction* in 1955, 1956, and 1957. It won the 1961 Hugo Award for Best Novel. "A commercial writer who boasted a million words by 1955, including scripts for television's *Captain Video*, he came to write progressively more complex, sophisticated, problematic stories until, having more or less perfected his art, he stopped writing at the pinnacle of his success, at the age of 36" (Samuelson 1978).

Miller never published another new novel or story in his lifetime, although several compilations of his 1950s stories appeared in the 1960s and 1970s. He told Terry Bisson, with whom he engaged in a long-distance collaboration on the eagerly awaited sequel to *Canticle*, that he found that writing was like "trying to spit through a screen." As time went on, he became more and more of a recluse. Bisson adds, "When [Lucius Shepard] was living in south Florida, [he] received a fan letter (an unheard of thing!) from Walt Miller, who lived only a few miles away. It praised his writing at some length. Then, at the bottom, it said: *PS: This does not mean I want to meet you!*"

Five months after the death of his wife in 1996, Walter M. Miller shot himself. He had written most—about 600 pages—of *Saint Leibowitz and the Wild Horse Woman*, the sequel to *A Canticle for Leibowitz*. It was finished by Terry Bisson and published in 1997. "It may be that his novel obsessed him, draining off his writing energy; it may be that it set him a standard he felt unable to maintain; perhaps it expressed so well the themes which concerned him that its completion left him nothing to say" (Samuelson 1978).

Awards

Novels

A Canticle for Leibowitz (1959)

Short Fiction

"The Darfsteller" (1955)

Works by the Author

A Canticle for Leibowitz (1959)
Saint Leibowitz and the Wild Horse Woman (1997, completed by Terry Bisson)

Other Notable Short Fiction

"The Big Hunger (1952)
"Conditionally Human" (1952)
"Crucifixus Etiam" (1953)
"I, Dreamer" (1953)

Collections

Conditionally Human (1962)
The View from the Stars (1964)
The Best of Walter M. Miller, Jr. (1980; reissued as *Dark Benediction*, 2007)
The Science Fiction Stories of Walter M. Miller, Jr. (1978, edited by D. N. Samuelson)
Conditionally Human and Other Stories (1982)
The Darfsteller and Other Stories (1982)

As Editor

Beyond Armageddon (1985, with Martin H. Greenberg)

In Other Media

A Canticle for Leibowitz, Soundtrack. Nishi, 2005. Compiled and performed by John Kannenberg. http://www.notype.com/nishi/releases/87/index.html

Articles and Essays

"Forewarning (An Introduction)." In *Beyond Armageddon,* ed. Walter Miller and Martin H. Greenberg. Lincoln: University of Nebraska Press, 2006 (orig. pub. 1985).

Bibliographies

Roberson, William H., and Robert L. Battenfeld. *Walter M. Miller, Jr.: A Bio-Bibliography*. Westport, CT: Greenwood, 1992.
Bibliography. Edited by Susan Stepney. University of York, Department of Computer Science, July 1, 2007. Unofficial Pages. http://www-users.cs.york.ac.uk/susan/sf/books/m/wltrmmll.htm

For Further Information

Aldiss, Brian. "All Doomed Again." *New Statesman,* September 26, 1997, 65+.
Bisson, Terry. "A Canticle for Miller: or, How I Met Leibowitz and the Wild Horse Woman, But Not Walter M. Miller, Jr." *Locus* (December 1997). http://www.sff.net/people/tbisson/miller.html
Garvey, John. "*A Canticle for Leibowitz*: A Eulogy for Walt Miller." *Commonweal*, April 5, 1996.
Samuelson, D. N. "Introduction." In *The Science Fiction Stories of Walter M. Miller, Jr.*, vii–xxv. Boston, MA: Gregg, 1978.
———. "The Lost Canticles of Walter M. Miller, Jr." *Science Fiction Studies* 3 (1976): 3–26. http://www.depauw.edu/sfs/backissues/8/samuelson8art.htm
Secrest, Rose. *Glorificemus: A Study of the Fiction of Walter M. Miller, Jr.* Lanham, MD: University Press of America, 2002.
Roberson, William H., and Robert L. Battenfeld. *Walter M. Miller, Jr.: A Bio-Bibliography*. Westport, CT: Greenwood, 1992.

Elizabeth Moon

Military SF; Space Opera

Benchmark Title: Hunting Party (1993)

b. 1945 (McAllen, Texas)

The first book was an enormous thrill, and the award is a thrill, and it's still a thrill to have a book come out, but the real thing that keeps me going is when the writing is alive and making the story a reality that other people can play in. It's creation. Creation is the whole thing.

—Dow, "Making Contact," *Rice* (2006)

Photo credit: Beth Gwinn

About the Author and the Author's Writing

Like many of the most popular and successful writers of SF, the details of Elizabeth Moon's personal life and upbringing have had a major impact on her writing, in ways that might not be immediately obvious or expected for one who is best known for tales of futuristic empires and interplanetary warfare. The only child of a single mother, Moon saw firsthand as she was growing up how a capable woman can manage the challenges that life throws at her. In an interview at *SF Site*, Moon recalled, "She did carpentry. We painted the house together. We built things together. When I was quite young, she was working in a hardware store, so I grew up knowing about hardware." Moon's mother went on from the hardware store to become a graduate student in engineering and an aeronautical engineer, another way in which she convinced her observant daughter that "more things should be open to women," and possibly provided a role model for characters in the popular Vatta's War series.

For ideas about the adventures of central character Kylara Vatta, Moon actually did not need to look farther than her own term of service in the U.S. Marine Corps from 1968 to 1971, which would have given her a firm grounding in the life of a resourceful young woman who has trained for military service at the Spaceforce Academy. In the first volume of the series, cadet Ky has been forced by intrigue and poor leadership to resign in disgrace and instead captain an old trading ship for her family's interstellar trading company. Her military training is put to good use, however, as in the course of the series she faces mercenaries, mutineers, assassins, pirates, and official treachery, first as a ship captain in tricky situations and later as the representative of a family under attack.

Moon was born Susan Elizabeth Norris, on March 7, 1945, and grew up in McAllen, Texas. Like many SF writers, she started young, writing stories and poems as a small child; her first "book" was an illustrated biography of the family dog. She acquired a BA in history from Rice University in the late 1960s, and another in biology from the University of Texas at Austin in 1975. She also did graduate work in biology at the University of Texas, San Antonio. In 1969 she married Richard Moon, a Rice classmate and army officer; in the late 1970s they moved to the small central Texas town where they live today, with their son Michael, whom they adopted as an infant in 1983.

Moon's first fiction sale—in 1985, "at age forty," as she is proud to point out—was to Marion Zimmer Bradley's *Sword & Sorceress III*, and her first SF was a story called "ABCs in Zero G," published in *Analog* that same year. Her first novel, *Sheepfarmer's Daughter*, was also the first in the Deed of Paksennarion fantasy trilogy, which *SF Site* described as "a starkly realistic fantasy world." *Sheepfarmer's Daughter* won the Compton Crook Award in 1989.

In addition to the Vatta's War series and her fantasy work, Moon has written a number of novels in the *Familias Regnant* universe, a stylish and imaginative space opera of the far future; and she has written stand-alone titles such as the critically acclaimed *Remnant Population* (1996) and *The Speed of Dark* (2002). *Remnant Population* is much admired because it breaks down one important barrier in the annals of SF characters: protagonist Ofelia Falfurrias is not a babe in a lab coat, or titanium breastplate. "[S]he's a poor old person. A working-class person, which makes her very different. Other people, including me, have written books with main characters who were old and rich. Or old and brilliant. Old sages, old wizards, old rich people. Ofelia isn't any of those, so she is different" (*SF Site*).

The Speed of Dark, a novel about identity and self-worth and the true meaning of diversity, is another example of Moon's sensitive and thoughtful use of her own life story: the central character is an intelligent and personable young man who is autistic. Moon's research for the character of Lou Arrendale was intensely personal; her son Michael is autistic:

> Since there was no early intervention available when he was little, and inadequate special education in local schools later, I did all his therapy and also homeschooled him for over a decade.... The character Lou is not much like our son—he's higher-functioning and less exuberant—but there are spectrum-wide similarities. (Weller 2007)

The Speed of Dark, "compelling and deeply personal" (Snider 2003) deals with Lou's dilemma when he is pressured into undergoing an experimental procedure that will "cure" him of his autism, and the true cost of such a cure.

In addition to the demands of life as a writer and mother, Elizabeth Moon finds time for an impressive array of activities in her local community. Her official Web site lists service as an EMS volunteer, member of the city council, Chamber of Commerce president, and library board member. She has been a singer in various church and community choirs and taught Sunday school, worked with church youth groups, and served in the vestry. This is not surprising for one who was willing to give up three years of her life to serve with one of our nation's toughest, and most honored, services. Her other, nonwriting interests include riding horses and fencing (Renaissance style: rapier, dagger, etc.) and "space exploration, ... restoration ecology, wildlife management, classical music, just about anything but housework" (official Web site).

Awards

Robert A. Heinlein Award (2007)

Novels

The Speed of Dark (2002) **Nebula**

 Works by the Author

Remnant Population (1996)
The Speed of Dark (2002)

Familias Regnant

Hunting Party (1993)
Sporting Chance (1994)
Winning Colors (1995)
Once a Hero (1997)
Rules of Engagement (1998)
Change of Command (1999)
Against the Odds (2000)

The Planet Pirates

Sassinak (1990, with Anne McCaffrey)
The Death of Sleep (1990, with Anne McCaffrey and Jody Lynn Nye)
Generation Warriors (1991, with Anne McCaffrey)

These novels are part of a sequence that began with two books by Anne McCaffrey, *Dinosaur Planet* and *Dinosaur Planet Survivors*.

Vatta's War

Trading in Danger (2003)
Marque and Reprisal (2004; aka *Moving Target*)
Engaging The Enemy (2006)
Command Decision (2007)
Victory Conditions (2008)

Other Notable Genre Fiction

The Legacy of Gird Novels

Surrender None (1990)
Liar's Oath (1992)

Paksenarrion

Sheepfarmer's Daughter (1988)
Divided Allegiance (1988)
Oath of Gold (1989)

Collections

Lunar Activity (1990)
Phases (1997)
Moon Flights (2007)

Articles and Essays

"Autism: Past, Present, Future, Speculative." Elizabeth Moon.com. 2003 http://www.elizabethmoon.com/autism-general.htm

"Real Weather, Small Towns, and Science Fiction" (Introduction to *Lunar Activity,* 1990)

For Further Information

Official Web site: http://www.elizabethmoon.com

Blaschke, Jayme L. "A Conversation with Elizabeth Moon, Part 1 and Part 2." *SF Site* (November 1999). http://www.sfsite.com/02a/em74.htm

———. "Elizabeth Moon." In *Voices of Vision*, 85–98. Lincoln: University of Nebraska Press, 2005. With substantial material that was cut from the interview as originally published.

Branovacki, Maya. Interview. *Wotmania.com,* August 18, 2006.

Dow, Christopher. "Making Contact: Elizabeth Moon's Path to the Stars." *Rice: The Magazine of Rice University* (September 2006). http://www.rice.edu/sallyport/2006/summer/features/moon.html

"Elizabeth Moon: Explorations. *Locus* (March 2004). http://www.locusmag.com/2004/Issues/03Moon.html

Interview. *Fast Forward: Contemporary Science Fiction* (March 2008). http://fast-forward.tv/blog/?p=52

Snider, John C. Interview. *SciFi Dimensions* (2003). http://www.scifidimensions.com/Feb03/elizabethmoon.htm

Weller, Kurt. Interview. *Plaza of the Mind* (March 2007). http://plazaofthemind.blogspot.com/2007/03/plaza-of-mind-interview-with-author.html

Michael Moorcock

New Wave; Science Fantasy; Time Travel

Benchmark Title:
The Final Program (1968)

b. 1939 (England: London)

The past is a script we are constantly rewriting. Experience changes over the years to suit whatever story we believe we are telling.
—Introduction, *Elric: The Stealer of Souls* (2008)

Photo credit: Beth Gwinn

About the Author and the Author's Writing

Michael Moorcock's prodigious output includes rock songs, comics, screenplays, essays, and more than 100 novels and novellas. In the 1960s, as editor of *New Worlds* magazine and the anthology *New Worlds Quarterly*, he was a moving force behind the 1960s New Wave, which reshaped the expectations of the SF genre. In his own writing, Moorcock was an early practitioner of "genre-bending" fiction—he did not just break through the dividing lines between SF, fantasy, and realistic fiction, but ground the lines in the dust under his heel and moved on.

Moorcock was born in December 1939, in Mitcham, Surrey, a district of South London, at the beginning of World War II. As Moorcock wrote in an autobiographical profile for Hachette Books in 2001, "[f]rom the Day I was born someone was trying to kill me.... I grew up in a city with thousands of tons of bombs and rockets falling on it." He spent his early years in Norbury, London, which was not safer, but slightly leafier; there, his mother worked as accountant for a lumberyard. His father, an otherwise "very sober engineer" (*Moorcock's Miscellany*: Norbury), introduced his son to fantasy and SF through his collection of Edgar Rice Burroughs. Growing up as the child of a Jewish mother, surrounded by a family circle that was predominantly Jewish (although his own immediate family was not religious), it is likely that young Moorcock was well aware that Hitler's threat to his personal safety didn't end with the bombs that were raining down on his home city.

Moorcock's parents' marriage ended with, as he has put it, "the end of European hostilities" ("Introduction," in *Elric* 2008), a development that he described as a "blessing"; he completed his education at Pitman's College, probably in preparation for a life as a clerk or administrator. At fifteen he was a messenger for a shipping company; at sixteen he became editor of the comic book *Tarzan Adventures*, for which he had already been writing for a year or so. He worked as editor for pulp magazines such as *Sexton Blake Library*, *Thriller Picture Library*, and various comics, as well as the policy discussion magazine of the Liberal Party.

Then he became editor of *New Worlds*. According to Colin Greenland in *The Entropy Exhibition*, his history of Moorcock and the New Wave, "Moorcock and the writers he gathered around him were conscious, even self-conscious, about science fiction, its symbolism, its immediacy, its responsibilities, and above all its possibilities."

The possibilities of Moorcock's fiction center on the Multiverse, a kaleidoscope of alternate realities, where characters like Jerry Cornelius—a kind of hip secret agent of ambiguous sexuality—range from the near present to the far future, averting (or inciting) catastrophe. Cornelius and the other denizens of the Multiverse provide a ringing challenge to the jaded archetypes of sword and sorcery fantasy and complacent "swinging sixties" futurism. And Cornelius is a manifestation of another standard Moorcock fixture, the Eternal Champion: a figure who exists outside time and space and outside the normal laws of humanity; he reappears, again and again, in various guises, throughout Moorcock's narrative history (in *Dancers at the End of Time,* there is a character who *could* be Jerry Cornelius, but isn't). From an early stage in the story's development, Moorcock opened up the narrative of Jerry Cornelius and the narrative stage of the Multiverse to other writers, more or less inventing the "shared universe" style of storytelling.

During the 1960s he was a singer and songwriter and member of various rock bands, including Hawkwind and Deep Fix. Since the later 1970s Moorcock has broken out of the confines of SF. *Gloriana; or, The Unfulfill'd Queen* (1978) is alternative history, or perhaps a Spenserian fantasy: dark, ironic, and enigmatic. His 1988 novel *Mother London*—generally considered to be his finest work—is neither SF nor fantasy, but contains enough SF touches, like telepathy and occasional manifestations of psi powers, to show that the bond is still there. Moorcock is a good friend of graphic novelist Alan Moore, and together they have worked on various projects that connect their most famous works in a new medium.

Michael Moorcock holds multiple British Fantasy Awards, the *Guardian* Fiction Award (for *The Condition of Muzak*, 1977), and the World Fantasy Award; he was a finalist for the Whitbread Prize for *Mother London*. In 2004 he was awarded the *Prix Utopiales* Grandmaster Lifetime Achievement Award. He won a Nebula for his novella *Behold the Man*, an alternative interpretation of the life of Christ, the protagonist of which is a young Jewish boy from a broken home, bullied for not fitting in, struggling to understand the interwoven mix of illusion and truth of human beliefs and religion.

In the early 1990s, following problems with Her Majesty's Inland Revenue (the UK equivalent of the IRS), Michael Moorcock moved to Lost Pines, Texas, where he lives with his wife, Linda. Of all the writers and editors of SF, Moorcock can lay the most serious claim to having shaped SF, as it is told, at the beginning of the twenty-first century.

Awards

World Fantasy Award Life Achievement (2000)
Science Fiction Hall of Fame (2002)
Prix Utopia (2004)
SFWA Damon Knight Memorial Grand Master (2008)

Short Fiction

"Behold the Man" (1966) **Nebula**

Works by the Author

The Fireclown (1965; aka *The Winds of Limbo*)
The Sundered Worlds (1965; aka *The Blood Red Game*)
The Twilight Man (1966; aka *The Shores of Death*)
The Wrecks of Time (1967; aka *The Rituals of Infinity*)
The Black Corridor (1969, with Hilary Bailey)
The Ice Schooner (1969)
Behold the Man (1969)
Breakfast in the Ruins (1972). http://www.revolutionsf.com/fiction/breakfast/1990/02.html

The Dancers at the End of Time

An Alien Heat (1972)
The Hollow Lands (1974)
The End of All Songs (1976)
The Transformation of Miss Mavis Ming (1977)

Jerry Cornelius

The Final Program (1968)
A Cure for Cancer (1971)
The English Assassin (1972)
The Adventures of Una Persson and Catherine Cornelius in the Twentieth Century (1976)
The Condition of Muzak (1977)
The Great Rock 'n' Roll Swindle (1980)
The Entropy Tango (1981)
The Alchemist's Question (1984)

Nomad of the Time Streams (Oswald Bastable)

The Warlord of the Air (1971)
The Land Leviathan (1974)
The Steel Tsar (1981)

Warrior of Mars

Warriors of Mars (1965)
Blades of Mars (1965)
Barbarians of Mars (1965)

Mainstream and Other Notable Genre Fiction

Gloriana (1978)
Mother London (1988)
King of the City (2000)
Silverheart (2000, with Storm Constantine)

Between the Wars

Byzantium Endures (1981)
The Laughter of Carthage (1984)
Jerusalem Commands (1992)
The Vengeance of Rome (2006)

The Elric sequence

Elric: The Stealer of Souls (1963; rev. and illus. ed. 2008)
Stormbringer (1965, revised 1977)
Elric of Melniboné (1972)
The Sailor on the Seas of Fate (1976)
The Vanishing Tower (1977; aka *The Sleeping Sorceress*)
The Bane of the Black Sword (1977)
The Fortress of the Pearl (1989)
The Revenge of the Rose (1991)
Elric in the Dream Realms (2009)

The Second Ether sequence

Blood: A Southern Fantasy (1994)
Fabulous Harbours (1995)
The War Amongst the Angels (1996)

Ulrich and Oona von Bek

The War Hound and the World's Pain (1981)
The Brothel in Rosenstrasse (1982)
The City in the Autumn Stars (1986)
The Dreamthief's Daughter (2001)
The Skrayling Tree (2003)
The White Wolf's Son (2005)

Other Notable Short Fiction

"The Peking Junction" (1969)
"Pale Roses" (1974)
"Ancient Shadows" (1975)
"Crossing Into Cambodia" (1979)
"Elric at the End of Time" (1981)

"The Cairene Purse" (1990)
"London Bone" (1997)
"The Spencer Inheritance" (1997). http://www.theedge.abelgratis.co.uk/spencer.htm
"Cheering for the Rockets" (1998). http://www.fantasticmetropolis.com/i/rockets/full/
"Through the Shaving Mirror . . . or, How We Abolished the Future" (2001). http://www.fantasticmetropolis.com/i/mirror/
"A Slow Saturday Night at the Surrealist Sporting Club" (2001)
"An Evening at Home" (2002). http://www.fantasticmetropolis.com/i/evening/
"Firing the Cathedral" (2002)
"The Visible Men" (2006)

Collections

The Deep Fix (1966, as James Colvin)
The Time Dweller (1969)
Moorcock's Book of Martyrs (1976; aka *Dying for Tomorrow*)
Sojan (1977)
Jerry Cornell's Comic Capers (1980)
My Experiences in the Third World War (1980)
Elric at the End of Time (1984)
The Opium General (1984)
Casablanca (1989)
Lunching with the Antichrist (1995)
Tales from the Texas Woods (1997)
The Cornelius Quartet (2001; rev. version of *The Cornelius Chronicles*)
London Bone (2001)
The Lives and Times of Jerry Cornelius: Stories of the Comic Apocalypse (2003)
The Metatemporal Detective (2007)
The Best of Michael Moorcock (2009)

The Tale of the Eternal Champion

The Eternal Champion (1996)
Von Bek (1995)
Hawkmoon (1995)
A Nomad of the Time Streams (1995)
Elric: Song of the Black Sword (1995)
The Roads Between the Worlds (1996)
Corum: The Coming of Chaos (1997)
Sailing to Utopia (1997)
Kane of Old Mars (1998)
The Dancers at the End of Time (1996)
Elric: The Stealer of Souls (1998)

Corum: The Prince With the Silver Hand (1999)
Legends from the End of Time (1999)
Earl Aubec and Other Stories (1999)
Count Brass (2000)

As Editor

New Worlds. (May 1964–March 1971)
Best S.F. Stories from New Worlds (1967–1974)
New Worlds Quarterly (1971–1973)
SF Reprise (1966)
The Best of New Worlds (1965)
The Traps of Time (1968)
The Inner Landscape (1969)
The Nature of the Catastrophe (1971, with Langdon Jones)
Before Armageddon (1975)
England Invaded (1977)
New Worlds: An Anthology (1983)
New Worlds (2004)

In Other Media

The Final Programme. Anglo-EMI, 1973. Directed by Robert Fuest; starring Jon Finch as Jerry Cornelius. Also released as *The Last Days of Man on Earth*.

The Land That Time Forgot. Amicus Productions, 1975. Directed by Kevin Connor; screenplay by Moorcock; starring Doug McClure and John McEnery.

Hawkwind: The Chronicle of the Black Sword. Alpha Video Distributors, 1985. Based on the "Elric" stories by Michael Moorcock; stage production as performed by Hawkwind at London's Hammersmith Odeon, 1985. Moorcock performs as Narrator.

Writer's Talk: Michael Moorcock with Colin Greenland. VHS Videocassette. Northbrooke, IL: The Roland Collection, 1989.

Michael Moorcock's Multiverse. Vertigo/DC Comics, 1999. An attempt to express the totality of the Multiverse in graphic novel form.

Nonfiction Books

The Retreat from Liberty: The Erosion of Democracy in Today's Britain (1983)
Letters from Hollywood (1986)
Wizardry and Wild Romance: A Study of Epic Fantasy (1987)
Fantasy: The 100 Best Books (1988, with James Cawthorn)

Articles and Essays

"Introduction." In *Elric: The Stealer of Souls*. Illustrated by John Picacio. New York: Random House, 2008 (orig. pub. 1963).

"Michael Moorcock Speaks." In *Author! Author!* Hachette Book Group, March 2001. http://www.hachettebookgroup.com/

"A New Literature for the Space Age." *New Worlds* 142 (May–June 1964): 2–3.

"Putting a Tag on It (1961)." In *Elric: The Stealer of Souls* (1963). Illustrated by John Picacio. New York: Random House, 2008.

"Queen of the Martian Mysteries: An Appreciation of Leigh Brackett." *Fantastic Metropolis,* June 13, 2002. http://www.fantasticmetropolis.com/i/brackett/

"Starship Stormtroopers." In *The Opium General.* London: Harrap, 1984. http://flag.blackened.net/liberty/moorcock.html. An essay that originally appeared in the Cienfuegos Press *Anarchist Review* in 1978.

"Triumph of the City." *Booksense,* October 19, 2001. http://www.indiebound.org/author-interviews/moorcockm

Bibliographies

Davey, Ian. "Complete Bibliography." In *Michael Moorcock: Cartographer of the Multiverse*. June 2005. Sweet Despise. http://www.eclipse.co.uk/sweetdespise/moorcock/bib/

For Further Information

Moorcock's Miscellany. 2009. http://www.multiverse.org/

Online interviews, articles, etc.: http://www.multiverse.org/fora/showthread.php?t=3701

"Your Norbury" thread, containing personal reminiscences: http://www.multiverse.org/fora/showthread.php?t=1824

Auden, Sandy. "Chaotic Lives: An Interview with Michael Moorcock." *SF Site* (2005). http://www.sfsite.com/05b/samm200.htm

BBC3 Radio. Audio Interview. *Nightwaves,* January 16, 2006. http://www.multiverse.org/imagehive/v/mediahive/mp3z/nightwaves/

Coombes, Mike. "An Interview with Michael Moorcock." *Internet Review of Science Fiction* (February 2005). http://www.irosf.com/q/zine/article/10115

Davey, Ian. *Cartographer of the Multiverse*. Sweet Despise, June 2005. http://www.eclipse.co.uk/sweetdespise/moorcock/

———. Interview. Author Information Page, Hachette Book Group, n.d. http://www.hachettebookgroup.com/Michael_Moorcock_(1015067)_Author Interview(1).aspx

"*The Edge's* Michael Moorcock Pages. *The Edge"* (May 2004). http://www.theedge.abelgratis.co.uk/michaelmoorcockindex.htm

Gardiner, Jeff. *The Age of Chaos: The Multiverse of Michael Moorcock*. The British Fantasy Society, 2002.

Greenland, Colin. *The Entropy Exhibition: Michael Moorcock and the British "New Wave" in Science Fiction*. London: Routledge, 1983.

———. *Michael Moorcock: Death Is No Obstacle*. Manchester, UK: Savoy, 1992.

Hudson, Patrick. "Fifty Percent Fiction: Michael Moorcock Interviewed." *The Zone* (November 2005). http://www.zone-sf.com/mmoorcock.html

Interview. *Quantum Muse* (October 2001). http://www.quantummuse.com/michael_moorcock_interview.html

Kenny, John. "Another Sunny Day in Texas: John Kenny Talks to Michael Moorcock." *Albedo One,* October 13, 2006. http://www.albedo1.com/html/michael_moorcock.html

Means, Loren. "Interview with Michael Moorcock." *YLEM Journal* 25, nos. 10/12 (2005): 9–14. http://www.ylem.org/Journal/2005Iss10&12vol25.pdf

"Michael Moorcock: Movements & Myths." *Locus* (March 2003). http://www.locusmag.com/2003/Issue03/Moorcock.html

Mondschein, Ken "Michael Moorcock on Politics, Punk, Tolkien, and Everything Else." *Corporate Mofo*, January 1, 2002. http://corporatemofo.com/

Neves, José Carlos. "Entrevistas (Interviews): Acclaimed British Writer Michael Moorcock." October 15, 2003. http://www.alanmooresenhordocaos.hpg.ig.com.br/entrevistas33.htm

Robson, Alan. "The Lesser Spotted Science Fiction Writer, Part 6: Michael Moorcock." In *Trimmings from the Triffid's Beard*. Wellington, New Zealand: Burning Tiger Press, 1999. Originally published in *Phlogiston Forty* (1994). http://homepages.paradise.net.nz/triffid/trimmings/volume2/06_The_Lesser_Spotted_Michael_Moorcock.htm

"Strange Connections—An Interview with Michael Moorcock." *3am Magazine* (2002). http://www.3ammagazine.com/litarchives/2002_jun/interview_michael_moorcock.html

Alan Moore

Graphic Novels

Benchmark Title: *Watchmen* (1987)

b. 1953 (England: Northampton)

It's all down to functionality eventually. If you're functional it doesn't matter if you're mad.
—Rose, "Moore's Murderer," *The Guardian* (2002)

About the Author and the Author's Writing

Alan Moore was born in Northampton, England, a market town in the East Midlands, about fifty miles southeast of Birmingham. His father worked for a local brewery; his mother was a printer, and the family lived in a typically working-class area of the town. Moore was fascinated by storytelling at an early age. "I had joined the library by the age of five and I naturally gravitated towards mythology, fairy stories, Arthurian romances and the legends of the Greeks and Romans" (Rigby 2008). He also read comics; as he put it, "[i]f you were working-class, you had comics. It was like rickets" (Robinson 2001).

Passing the secondary school entrance exam, the "Eleven Plus" gave Moore a place at the academically focused Northampton Grammar School (instead of being channeled into a technical high school, which would have put him on a fast track to a blue-collar job). However, in 1970, at the age of seventeen, he was expelled from Northampton Grammar for dealing LSD. He later described himself as "one of the world's most inept LSD dealers. . . . If you're sampling your own product . . . you may believe . . . you are completely immune to any form of retaliation and prosecution, which is not the case" (Rigby 2008). Following his expulsion, with no qualifications Moore went through a series of dead-end jobs, working for the gas board and cleaning toilets in a Northampton hotel. Meanwhile, however, he was producing comic strips for underground magazines; short strips for *Doctor Who Magazine*, *Star Wars Weekly*, and *Judge Dredd;* and for the *Northamptonshire Post*, a cartoon called "Maxwell the Magic Cat," which he described as an "antidote to Garfield" (Rigby 2008), for which he was paid £10 a week.

In1983 Moore was hired by DC Comics; initially, he was charged with the missions of revitalizing DC's Swamp Thing character. Eventually he worked on *Hellblazer*, for which he created the character John Constantine. He was rapidly recognized as one of the new generation of graphic storytelling writers and artists who were breathing new life into the genre. As ComicCon put it in a profile for his guest appearance, "he cut an elegant and erudite swath through American comics; . . . and gave a mighty heave-ho push to the creative envelope (not only farther than anyone else had, but farther than anyone else could imagine!).”

Moore's 1987 graphic novel *Watchmen*, with artist Dave Gibbons, featured multilayered storytelling that redefined what a comic could do. In *Art of the Comic Book: An Aesthetic History*, Robert Harvey wrote that with *Watchmen*, Moore and Gibbons "had demonstrated as never before the capacity of the [comic book] medium to tell a sophisticated story that could be engineered only in comics." *Watchmen* was the only graphic novel to appear on *Time*'s 2005 "All-TIME 100 Greatest Novels" list. Disagreements about the ownership of *Watchmen* led Alan Moore to sever ties with DC Comics, but success has enabled him to do as he pleases and follow his own artistic instincts, "pursuing creative projects that had little to do with fantasy-horror and science fiction and adult men with capes" (Babcock 2003).

Moore is an intensely private person. "Recoiling in horror from the celebrity status being foisted on him" (Babcock 2003), he strictly limited his personal appearances and has resolutely refused to become involved in the hoopla surrounding the filming of three of his works—*Watchmen* (Warner Bros., 2009), *The League of Extraordinary Gentlemen* (Angry Films, 2003), and *V for Vendetta* (Silver Pictures, 2006). (There have been others that he has not even bothered to be rude about.) "I haven't seen the *From Hell* movie yet. I might see it when it comes out on video.... I've tried to keep an emotional distance" (Rose 2002). He was less generous—and restrained—on the subject of *Watchmen*, especially when director Zack Snyder expressed a good-natured hope that one day Moore might sit down and watch the DVD in his home in *London*. Moore, of course, lives in Northampton (sixty-seven miles, as the crow flies, from London), in an unassuming house very similar to the one where he grew up; he was not amused. Zack Snyder should not expect to hear a Moore DVD player, in London or anywhere, warming up any time soon.

In 2007 Moore married Melinda Gebbie, his second wife, with whom he has worked on several comics. He is a vegetarian, an anarchist, a practicing magician, and an occultist, and claims to worship a Roman snake deity named Glycon, which, he cheerfully acknowledges, was "exposed as a glove-puppet in the second century" (Rose 2002). And he lives in Northampton.

Awards

Novels

Watchmen (1987) **Hugo, Locus Poll**

V for Vendetta (1989) **Prometheus Hall of Fame 2006**

Works by the Author

Marvelman (1982–1984, 1985–1989, with Garry Leach, Alan Davis, John Totleben, and others; later retitled *Miracleman* for legal reasons)

V for Vendetta (1982–1985 and 1988–1989, with David Lloyd; collection published 1995)

The Bojeffries Saga (1983–1984, 1986, with Steve Parkhouse; collection published 1992)

Swamp Thing (1983–1987, with Stephen R. Bissette, Rick Veitch, and others)
Watchmen (1986–1987, with Dave Gibbons; collection published 1987)
From Hell (1989–1992, with Eddie Campbell; collection published 1999). A retelling of the Jack the Ripper story, inspired by Douglas Adams's Holistic Detective novels.
WildC.A.T.S (1995–1998, with Travis Charest and others; collection published 2007)
Promethea (1999–2005, with J. H. Williams III and others)
The League of Extraordinary Gentlemen (1999–2003, with Kevin O'Neill; collection published as *Black Dossier*, 2007)
Tomorrow Stories (1999–2006, with various artists; collection published in 2006)

Other Notable Short Fiction

"A Hypothetical Lizard" (1987)

Collections

Alan Moore's Shocking Futures (1986)
Alan Moore's Twisted Times (1987)
DC Universe: The Stories of Alan Moore (2003)
The Complete Alan Moore (2006)
Alan Moore: Wild Worlds (2007)
The Extraordinary Works of Alan Moore: Indispensable Edition (2008)

In Other Media

Ragnarok. Nutland Video Ltd., 1982. A little-known British sci-fi adventure, lightly animated; essentially an on-screen comic, with story/script by Moore. Character designed by Bryan Talbot.
The Return of Swamp Thing. Millimeter Films, 1989. Directed by Jim Wynorski; inspired by Moore's series. Featuring the voices of Louis Jordan and Heather Locklear.
From Hell. Twentieth Century-Fox Film Corporation, 2001. Directed by Albert Hughes and Allen Hughes; starring Johnny Depp and Heather Graham.
The League of Extraordinary Gentlemen. Angry Films, 2003. Directed by Stephen Norrington; starring Sean Connery.
The Mindscape of Alan Moore. Shadowsnake Films, 2003. Directed by DeZ Vylenz. Feature documentary on Moore.
Constantine. Warner Bros. Pictures, 2005. Directed by Francis Lawrence; starring Keanu Reeves and Rachel Weisz. Based on the character John Constantine, who was created by Moore with others for the series Swamp Thing.
V for Vendetta. Silver Pictures, 2006. Adaptation written by the Wachowski Brothers; directed by James McTeigue; starring Natalie Portman and Hugo Weaving. Moore had his name removed from the film, which is credited as "Based on the graphic novel illustrated by David Lloyd."

Watchmen. Warner Bros. Pictures, 2009. Directed by Zack Snyder; starring Billy Crudup and Jackie Earle Haley. Moore had his name removed from the film.

Nonfiction Books

Alan Moore's Writing for Comics (2003). Essays published previously in *Fantasy Advertiser* and *Comics Journal*; illustrations by Jacen Burrows.

Bibliographies

Karpas, Michael. "Alan Moore: General Bibliography." *EnjolrasWorld.com*, May 9, 2009. http://www.enjolrasworld.com/HTML%20Bibliographies/Alan%20Moore%20Bibliography.htm

Alan Moore Interview Index: http://www.alanmooreinterview.co.uk/

For Further Information

"Alan Moore." *Comicon.com* (February 2009). http://www.comicon.com/moore/

Babcock, Jay. "Magic Is Afoot: A Conversation with Alan Moore about the Arts and the Occult." *Arthur* (May 2003). http://www.arthurmag.com/2007/05/10/1815/

Baker, Bill. *Alan Moore Spells It Out*. Bel Air, CA: Airwave Publishing, 2005.

———. *Alan Moore's Exit Interview*. Bel Air, CA: Airwave Publishing: 2007.

Bernard, Mark, and James Bucky Carter. "Alan Moore and the Graphic Novel: Confronting the Fourth Dimension." *ImageTexT: Interdisciplinary Comics Studies* 1, no. 2 (2004). University of Florida. http://www.english.ufl.edu/imagetext/archives/v1_2/carter/

Camper, Stephen. *Alan Moore Fan Site*. January 2009. http://www.alanmoorefansite.com/

Carney, Sean. "The Tides of History: Alan Moore's Historiographic Vision." ImageTexT: Interdisciplinary Comics Studies 2, no.2 (2006). University of Florida. http://www.english.ufl.edu/imagetext/archives/v2_2/carney/

Clarke, Susanna. "Alan Moore: The Wonderful Wizard of . . . Northampton." *The Telegraph* (UK), October 9, 2007. http://www.telegraph.co.uk/culture/3668393/Alan-Moore-the-wonderful-wizard-of...-Northampton.html

Davis, Lauren. "Alan Moore Explains Why He Is the Comic Book Messiah." *io9.com,* September 7, 2008. http://io9.com/5046375/alan-moore-explains-why-he-is-the-comic-book-messiah

Gaiman, Neil. "Moore About Comics." *Knave* (March 1986). Vintage interview posted in full on Gaiman's blog, February 25, 2009. http://journal.neilgaiman.com/2009/02/from-before-he-was-wizard.html

Khoury, George. *The Extraordinary Works of Alan Moore*. Raleigh, NC: TwoMorrows Publishing, 2003.

Millidge, Gary Spencer, and Smoky Man. *Alan Moore: Portrait of an Extraordinary Gentleman*. Leigh-on-Sea, Essex, UK: Abiogenesis, 2003.

Neves, José Carlos. *Alan Moore: Senhor do Caos/ Lord of Chaos*. April 12, 2004. http://www.alanmooresenhordocaos.hpg.ig.com.br/introducao.htm

Parker, James. "The Sorcery of Alan Moore: How Pop Culture Fell under a Comic-Book Writer's Strange Spell." *The Atlantic* (May 2009). http://www.theatlantic.com/doc/200905/alan-moore-watchmen

Parkin, Lance. *Alan Moore: The Pocket Essentials.* London: Trafalgar Square Publishing, 2002.

Peters, Jefferson M. "Alan Moore." In *British Fantasy and Science-Fiction Writers since 1960*, ed. Darren Harris-Fain, 312–20. Farmington Hills, MI: Thomson/Gale, 2002.

Rigby, Nic. "Comic Legend Keeps True to Roots." *Inside Out,* March 21, 2008. BBC Northamptonshire.

Robinson, Tasha. Interview. *The Onion A.V. Club,* October 24, 2001. http://www.avclub.com/articles/alan-moore,13740/

Rose, Steve. "Moore's Murderer." *The Guardian* (UK), February 2, 2002.

Stone, Brad. Interview. *CBR News,* October 22, 2001. Comic Book Resources. http://www.comicbookresources.com/?page=article&id=511

Thorpe, Vanessa. Profile. *The Guardian* (UK), March 1, 2009. http://www.guardian.co.uk/books/2009/mar/01/alan-moore-profile-watchmen

Larry Niven

Hard SF; Space Opera

Benchmark Title: *Ringworld* (1970)

b. 1939 (Los Angeles, California)

I knew what I wanted when I started writing. I've daydreamed all my life, and told stories too: stories out of magazines and anthologies, aloud, to other children. One day my daydreams began shaping themselves into stories. . . . I longed to touch the minds of strangers and show them wonders.

—*Playgrounds of the Mind* (1991)

Photo credit: Marilyn Niven.
Permission of Larry Niven.

About the Author and the Author's Writing

Laurence van Cott Niven was born in Los Angeles, California, and grew up in Beverly Hills. He attended the California Institute of Technology in Pasadena from 1956 to 1958. "Flunked out after discovering a book store jammed with used science fiction magazines" (Wolfman 2003). He continued his education at Washburn University in Topeka, Kansas, obtaining a BA in mathematics in 1962 and followed that briefly with graduate work at the University of California, Los Angeles. He sold his first story, "The Coldest Place," for $25 in 1964, and gave up his studies altogether once he proved to himself that his writing could pay. He has earned his living as a writer ever since. "Honest employment: gas station attendant, summer 1960" (Wolfman 2003).

With the encouragement of friend and publisher Frederik Pohl, Niven quickly established himself in the forefront of a hard SF renaissance. From an early stage in his career he displayed the uncanny ability to dramatize the big ideas of physics, biology, astronomy, and mathematics, and make them exciting and appealing to a wide readership. With the wide-ranging and complicated web of stories that make up his Tales of Known Space, Niven was soon identified as a worthy successor to Heinlein and Clarke, an author whose sense of wonder, and pure joy in the possibilities of technology and discovery, brought new readers—and new writers—to the cause. He was a major influence on hard SF writers of the 1980s and 1990s; according to *The Encyclopedia of Science Fiction* (1999), many SF writers "owe much to the scope of [his] inventiveness, the sense he conveys of technological ingenuity as being ultimately beneficial, and his cognitive exuberance."

Because of his scientific background and his openness to new scientific concepts wherever they may be found, there are few phenomena of the universe that have not been given the Niven narrative treatment. With his character Beowulf Shaeffer, "out-of-work space pilot and born tourist" (*Larryniven.org*), Niven takes his readers on a tour of the "odd pockets of the universe": dark matter, neutron stars, the rings of Saturn, antimatter planets, and the core of the galaxy. Two Hugo Award–winning stories, "The Hole Man" (1974) and "The Borderland of Sol" (1975), resulted from an interview that Niven and his "new friend" Jerry Pournelle conducted in the early 1970s with physicist Steven Hawking. And what is almost certainly Niven's most famous contribution to the hardware available to SF's box of tricks resulted from his efforts to imagine a more efficient version of a "Dyson Sphere," the theoretical construct that offers an almost limitless habitat by enclosing a star in a giant ping-pong ball. Other writers might have shrugged and left it at that, but he "looked at [it] and started redesigning" (McCarty 2004).

Niven's clever refinement—he removes all the extraneous parts of the structure, leaving a spinning band, landscaped on the sun-facing side, with the atmosphere and inhabitants kept in place through centrifugal force—is the setting for *Ringworld* (1970). If this idea's genesis is a perfect example of how Niven turns real science into entertaining and memorable story ideas, it could also be an illustration of a recurring criticism of his work—that plot and character are sacrificed for the real star of the show—the science, and Niven's fantastically vivid environments. But he counters this criticism passionately; in a 2004 interview in *SF Weekly*, he said, "I've always done my best for development of characters, . . . The environment might come first, or a question might come first, or a puzzle might come first—all of those will shape the characters."

Niven has also written comic material, such as *The Draco Tavern*, and science fantasy, such as *The Magic Goes Away (1977)*, but even his humor has a solid core of scientific fact, and his magic "might be termed 'hard' fantasy, in which the magic is as strictly regulated as the science in an *Analog* story" (Laskowski 1996). He is a successful collaborator, working with authors such as Jerry Pournelle and Stephen Barnes, and generous with his ideas: one of Niven's Known Space scenarios, the war with the vicious and cunning catlike race the Kzinti, has been opened up to other writers in the shared-world anthology series The Man-Kzin Wars. Niven has also written for the DC Comics character Green Lantern, working into his narratives hard SF concepts such as entropy and the red-shift effect, bringing an unusual scientific rigor to that genre. Niven also wrote the Green Lantern "Bible."

Larry Niven is an intensely political writer. A bumper sticker on his car proudly proclaims him as "Tactless" (Wolfman 2003). He is a passionate advocate for space exploration and is a founder member of SIGMA, a "science fiction think tank" led by Jerry Pournelle, which has advised various government departments, including the Department of Homeland Security, on future trends affecting national policy and security. He and his wife Marilyn Joyce Wisowaty—who is known in SF circles as "Fuzzy Pink"—were introduced by Frederik Pohl, and have been married since 1969. They live in the suburbs of Los Angeles, and together they are active participants in SF conventions and fan life.

Awards

Edward E. Smith Memorial Award for Imaginative Fiction ("Skylark award") (1973)
Robert A. Heinlein Award (2005)

Novels

Ringworld (1970) **Hugo, Locus Poll, Nebula**
The Integral Trees (1983) **Locus Poll**
Fallen Angels (1991, with Jerry Pournelle and Michael F. Flynn) **Prometheus**

Series

<u>Convergent Series</u> **Locus Poll**

Short Fiction

"Neutron Star" (1966) **Hugo**
"Inconstant Moon" (1971) **Hugo**
"The Hole Man" (1974) **Hugo**
"The Borderland of Sol" (1975) **Hugo**
"The Missing Mass" (2000) **Locus Poll**

Works by the Author

The Flying Sorcerers (1971, with David Gerrold)
Protector (1973)
Berserker Base: A Collaborative Novel (1984) (written with, among others, Poul Anderson, Fred Saberhagen, Connie Willis, and Roger Zelazny)
Destiny's Road (1997)
Rainbow Mars (1999)
Building Harlequin's Moon (2005, with Brenda Cooper)

Ringworld

Ringworld (1970)
The Ringworld Engineers (1979)
The Ringworld Throne (1996)
Ringworld's Children (2004)

Smoke Ring

A World Out of Time (1976)
The Integral Trees (1983)
The Smoke Ring (1987)

With Jerry Pournelle

Inferno (1976)
Lucifer's Hammer (1977)
Oath of Fealty (1982)
Footfall (1985)
Fallen Angels (1991, also with Michael F. Flynn)
Escape from Hell (2009)

The Moties
The Mote in God's Eye (1974)
The Gripping Hand (1993, aka *The Moat Around Murcheson's Eye*)

With Stephen Barnes

The Descent of Anasi (1981)
Achilles' Choice (1991)
Saturn's Race (2001)

Dream Park Trilogy
Dream Park (1981)
The Barsoom Project (1989)
The California Voodoo Game (1992; aka *The Voodoo Game*)

With Stephen Barnes and Jerry Pourelle

The Legacy of Heorot, 1987)
The Dragons of Heorot (1995; aka *Beowulf's Children*)

Other Notable Genre Fiction

The Magic Goes Away (1978)
The Magic May Return (1981)
More Magic (1984)
The Time of the Warlock (1984)

The Golden Road, with Jerry Pournelle
The Burning City (2000)
The Burning Tower (2005)

Other Notable Short Fiction

"Becalmed in Hell" (1965)
"Wrong-Way Street" (1965)
"A Relic of Empire" (1966)
"Flatlander" (1967)
"The Jigsaw Man" (1967)
"All the Myriad Ways" (1968)

"Not Long Before the End" (1969)
"The Fourth Profession" (1971)
"What Good Is a Glass Dagger?" (1972)
"The Defenseless Dead" (1973)
"Flare Time" (1978)
"The Locusts" (1979, with Steve Barnes)
"Spirals" (1979, with Jerry Pournelle)
"The Patchwork Girl" (1980)
"The Return of William Proxmire" (1989)
"Fly-by-Night" (2000)
"Free Floaters" (2002, with Brenda Cooper)

Collections

Neutron Star (1968)
The Shape of Space (1969)
All the Myriad Ways (1971)
The Flight of the Horse (1973)
Inconstant Moon (1973)
A Hole in Space (1974)
Tales of Known Space: The Universe of Larry Niven (1975)
The Children of the State (1976)
A World Out of Time (1976)
Convergent Series (1979)
Niven's Laws (1984)
Limits (1985)
Bridging the Galaxies (1993)
Crashlander (1994)
Flatlander: The Collected Tales of Gil "the Arm" Hamilton (1995)
Larry Niven Short Stories, Volumes 1–3 (2003)
The Draco Tavern (2006)
Man-Kzin Wars, Volumes 1–12 (1988–2009)

In Other Media

Unknown Worlds of Science Fiction (1975). Marvel Comics' black-and-white anthology magazine, featuring Niven stories "Not Long before the End" (adapted by Doug Moench and Vicente Alcazar) and "All the Myriad Ways" (adapted by Howard Chaykin).
The Magic Goes Away (1986). Graphic novel illustrated by Jan Duursema, for DC Comics.
Death by Ecstasy: Illustrated Adaptation of the Larry Niven Novella (1991)
Green Lantern: Ganthet's Tale (1992, with John Byrne)

"Inconstant Moon." *The Outer Limits* (1996). Directed by Joseph L. Scanlan; starring Michael Gross and Joanna Gleason.

Nonfiction Books

N-Space (1990)
Playgrounds of the Mind (1991)
Scatterbrain (2003)

These three collections include essays such as "Where Do I Get My Crazy Ideas?" and "Epilog: What I Tell Librarians," as well as selections of novel excerpts and short fiction.

Articles and Essays

"Man of Steel, Woman of Kleenex." In *The Man from Krypton : A Closer Look at Superman,* ed. Glenn Yeffeth, 51–58. Dallas, TX: BenBella, 2005. http://www.rawbw.com/~svw/superman.html

Bibliographies

Guptill, Paul, and Chris Drumm. *The Many Worlds of Larry Niven.* Polk City, IA: Drumm, 1989.

Lambert, David, and Carol Phillips. "Larry Niven's Bibliography." *Known Space* (2007). http://www.larryniven.org/biblio/

For Further Information

Officially recognized fan Web site: *Known Space: The Future Worlds of Larry Niven.* Edited by Ted Scribner et al. April 15, 2009. http://www.larryniven.org/

Farrell, Shaun. Interview. *Shaun's Quadrant* (August 2006). Far Sector. http://www.farsector.com/quadrant/interview-larryniven.htm

Hughes, Aaron. "Larry Niven Interview." *Fantastic Reviews* (August 2004). http://www.geocities.com/fantasticreviews/niven_interview.htm

James, Warren W. Interview. *Mike Hodel's Hour 25,* February 21, 2005. http://www.hour25online.com/Hour25_Previous_Shows_2005-02.html#larry-niven_2005-02-21

Jameson, Frederic. "Science Fiction as Politics: Larry Niven." *New Republic,* October 30, 1976, 34–38.

Laskowski, William Jr. "Larry Niven." In *St. James Guide to Science Fiction Writers,* ed. Jay Pedersen. Detroit, MI: St. James, 1996.

Lilley, Ernest. Interview. *SFRevu* (August 2003). http://www.sfrevu.com/ISSUES/2003/0308/Larry%20Niven%20Interview/Review.htm

McCarty, Michael. "To Our Ringworld's Children's Children: Larry Niven." In *Modern Mythmaker.* Jefferson, NC: McFarland, 2008.

Wolfman, Marv. "Speaking with . . . Larry Niven." SBC, 2003. http://www.silverbulletcomicbooks.com/wolfman/103572529241628.htm

George Orwell [Eric Arthur Blair]

Dystopias

Benchmark Title: *Nineteen Eighty-Four* (1949)

b. 1903 (India: Bengal); d. 1950 (England: London)

Every novelist has a "message," whether he admits to it or not, and the minutest details of his work are influenced by it. All art is propaganda.
—"Charles Dickens" (1940)

About the Author and the Author's Writing

Eric Arthur Blair compressed the experiences of several busy lifetimes into the few years that were allotted to him. His early experiences equipped him with a keen socialist political conscience; fragile health; and plentiful material for his extensive writing. He was born on June 25, 1903 in Motihari, Bengal Presidency, British India, where his father worked in the Opium Department of the Indian Civil Service. When he was a baby, his mother returned to England with Eric and his elder sister Marjorie; they settled at Henley-on-Thames, a genteel Home Counties town. Apart from a brief visit in 1908 (after which his sister Avril was born), Blair did not see his father again until 1912. His family was not wealthy enough to afford the fees for a top-flight public school, but family connections made it possible for the boy to attend St Cyprian's School, in Eastbourne, Sussex, on a scholarship. The memoir "Such, Such Were the Joys" (1952) was an account of his unhappy time at that school. At St. Cyprian's Blair earned scholarships that enabled him to complete his secondary education at Wellington College and then go on to Eton, where he was a King's Scholar from 1917 to 1921. (An irony of this is that one of the young Masters, an incompetent and hopeless teacher who couldn't keep discipline, was the novelist Aldous Huxley, who went on to write *Brave New World*, a novel that is often bracketed with Orwell's great work.)

University was impossible without another scholarship, so Blair decided to become an officer in the Indian Imperial Police. He served in Burma, in the Irrawaddy Delta region, from the beginning of 1924, but three years later he contracted Dengue fever and returned to England, effectively ending his service. Blair had decided to become a writer. His experiences in Burma yielded the novel *Burmese Days* (1934) and the essays "A Hanging" (1931) and "Shooting an Elephant" (1936).

Young Eric Blair greatly admired Jack London, and he began his writing career as he believed London would have done, making exploratory expeditions to the poorer parts of London, spending his nights in common lodging houses, and eventually going about the country dressed like a tramp. This experience became his first book, *Down* and *Out in Paris and London* (1933), for which he chose the pen name "George Orwell" because, as he told a friend, it was a good round English name. While he was looking for a publisher for *Down and Out*, he lived with his parents in Southwold; he taught for a while and schemed to get arrested so he could spend Christmas in prison ("George Orwell: A Life in Quotes" 2009) so he could write about it. He wrote about his scheme; the resulting essay, "Clink" (1932), and others were published by magazines like *Adelphi*. He caught pneumonia and almost died. He also worked in a secondhand bookstore in London, where he met and married Eileen O'Shaughnessy. In 1936 Eric Blair went to Spain to join the Nationalists in the fight against Fascism (joined by Eileen, who volunteered in the offices of the Independent Labour Party in Barcelona and kept him supplied with English tea, chocolate, and cigars). While at the front in Aragon, Blair was shot in the neck by a sniper and almost died. But what he saw in Spain convinced him that Fascism and Stalinist Communism presented almost equal threats of a bleak, totalitarian future, and he devoted the remainder of his life and his writing to seeing that that did not happen.

During and immediately after World War II, George Orwell worked as a journalist and war correspondent, writing book reviews and columns on popular culture and politics, which continue to be read and respected today. He did propaganda broadcasts to India for the BBC and covering the liberation of France and occupation of Germany for *The Observer*. In 1944 his anti-Stalinist allegory *Animal Farm* was published, to critical and popular acclaim. However, Eric Blair's personal life was in turmoil. In 1945 Eileen died during routine surgery, leaving him with the baby son whom they had adopted only a few months before. His health was very poor; he had contracted tuberculosis, probably during his "down and out" period, and he was in and out of hospitals for the last three years of his life. But Eric Blair had made up his mind that he wanted to "push the world in a certain direction, to alter other peoples' ideas of the kind of society that they should strive after" ("Why I Write" 1946). And in spite of his illness, in spite of his grief and the complications of his life, before Eric Arthur Blair died in London on January 21, 1950, as George Orwell he managed to write *Nineteen Eighty-Four*, "a cautionary tale on a heroic scale" (Cowper 1996), about a little man in a totalitarian world. He gave the world Big Brother, Newspeak, doublethink, Room 101, Thought Police, and another word—"Orwellian"—for a nightmare future that was "a boot stamping on a human face—forever."

Awards

Novels

Animal Farm (1945) **Retro Hugo 1996**
Nineteen Eighty-Four (1949) **Prometheus Hall of Fame 1984**

Works by the Author

Animal Farm (1945)
Nineteen Eighty-Four (1949)

Notable Mainstream Fiction

Burmese Days (1934)
A Clergyman's Daughter (1935)
Keep the Aspidistra Flying (1936)
Coming Up for Air (1939)

Collections

Inside the Whale and Other Essays (1940)

Critical Essays (1946)

The Complete Works of George Orwell (1997, edited by Peter Davison). Twenty-volume series.

The Collected Essays, Journalism and Letters of George Orwell (2000, edited by Sonia Orwell, and Ian Angus). Four volumes:
  An Age Like This, 1920–1940
  My Country Right or Left, 1940–1943
  As I Please, 1943–1945
  In Front of Your Nose, 1945–1950

Essays. Everyman's Library Classics (2002, edited by John Carey)

All Art Is Propaganda: Critical Essays (2008, edited by George Packer)

Facing Unpleasant Facts: Narrative Essays (2008, edited by George Packer)

In Other Media

George Orwell's 1984. NBC Radio, August 27, 1949. Starring David Niven as Winston Smith. http://greylodge.org/gpc/?p=78

1984. BBC Sunday Night Theatre, 1954. Directed by Rudolph Cartier; starring Peter Cushing and Andre Morell. British Broadcasting Corporation.

Animal Farm. Halas and Batchelor Cartoon Films, 1954. Directed by Joy Batchelor and John Halas; featuring the voice of Maurice Denham.

Nineteen Eighty-Four. Umbrella Rosenblum Films. 1984. Directed by Michael Radford; performed by John Hurt and Richard Burton.

Keep the Aspidistra Flying. BBC Films, 1997. Directed by Robert Bierman; starring Richard E. Grant and Helena Bonham Carter.

Animal Farm. Animal Farm Productions Ltd., 1999. Directed by John Stephenson; featuring the voices of, among many others, Patrick Stewart and Peter Ustinov.

Nonfiction Books

Down and Out in Paris and London (1933)
The Road to Wigan Pier (1937)
Homage to Catalonia (1938)

Articles and Essays

"A Hanging" (1931)

"Shooting an Elephant" (1936)

"Charles Dickens" (1940)

"My Country Right or Left" (1940)

"The Lion and the Unicorn: Socialism and the English Genius" (1941)

"England Your England" (1941)

Unpublished preface to *Animal Farm* (1945). http://home.iprimus.com.au/korob/Orwell.html

"Politics and the English Language" (1946)

"Why I Write" (1946)

"Such, Such Were the Joys" (1952, published posthumously)

George Orwell's Library. Ed. O. Dag. Orwell Project, December 2004. http://orwell.ru/home.html. A comprehensive online selection of Orwell's fiction and nonfiction, including "Good Bad Books" (1945), "In Defense of the Novel" (1936), "Politics and the English Language" (1946), "Wells, Hitler and the World State" (1941), and "Why I Write" (1946).

Bibliographies

Charles' George Orwell Links. March 2007. http://www.netcharles.com/orwell/

Fenwick, Gillian. *George Orwell: A Bibliography.* New Castle, DE: Oak Knoll, 1998.

Pridmore, Donna J. Selective Secondary Bibliography. *Literary History*, May 10, 2005. http://www.literaryhistory.com/20thC/Orwell.htm

For Further Information

Bhattacharyya, Debashis. "All's Not Well with Orwell." *The Telegraph* (Calcutta, India), November 14. 2004. A report from the province of Bihar, in India, the birthplace of George Orwell, about attempts to put the run-down town on the literary map. http://www.netcharles.com/orwell/misc.htm

Bowker, Gordon. *George Orwell.* London: Little Brown, 2003.

Brunsdale, Mitzi M. *Student Companion to George Orwell.* Westport, CT: Greenwood, 2000.

Buitenhuis, Peter, and Ira B. Nadel, eds. *George Orwell: A Reassessment.* New York: St. Martin's, 1988.

Cowper, Richard. "George Orwell." In *St. James Guide to Science Fiction Writers*, ed. Jay Pedersen. Detroit, MI: St. James, 1996.

Davison, Peter. *George Orwell: A Literary Life.* New York: St. Martin's, 1996.

Ershler, Norman, ed. *Orwell Reader.* n.d. http://www.theorwellreader.com/orwell.shtml

"George Orwell: A Life in Quotes." *The Telegraph* (UK), May 29, 2009. http://www.telegraph.co.uk/culture/books/5386818/George-Orwell-a-life-in-quotes.html

"George Orwell: From *Animal Farm* to Zog, an A-Z of Orwell." *The Telegraph* (UK), May 26, 2009. http://www.telegraph.co.uk/culture/books/5386673/George-Orwell-from-Animal-Farm-to-Zog-an-A-Z-of-Orwell.html

Hammond, J. R. *A George Orwell Chronology.* New York: Palgrave, 2000.

Hitchens, Christopher. *Why Orwell Matters.* New York: Basic, 2002.

Hurst, L. J. "George Orwell in the World of Science Fiction." *L.J. Hurst Homepages,* December 1998. http://dialspace.dial.pipex.com/l.j.hurst/orwellsf.htm

Ingle, Stephen. *George Orwell: A Political Life.* Manchester, UK: Manchester University Press, 1993.

James, Clive. "The Truthteller: George Orwell." *The New Yorker,* January 18, 1999.

Lazaro, Alberto, ed. *The Road to George Orwell: His Achievement and Legacy.* New York: Peter Lang, 2001.

Lucas, Scott. *George Orwell and the Betrayal of Dissent.* London: Verso, 2003.

Menand, Louis. "Honest, Decent, Wrong: The Invention of George Orwell." *The New Yorker,* January 27, 2003.

Meyers, Jeffrey. *Orwell: Wintry Conscience of a Generation.* New York: Norton, 2000.

Newsinger, John. *Orwell's Politics.* London: Macmillan, 1999.

O. Dag's Orwell Project. December 2004. http://orwell.ru/home.html

Paxman, Jeremy. "The Genius of George Orwell." *The Telegraph* (UK), June 5, 2009. http://www.telegraph.co.uk/culture/books/5453633/The-genius-of-George-Orwell.html

Rodden, John. *Scenes from an Afterlife: The Legacy of George Orwell.* Wilmington, DE: Intercollegiate Studies Institute, 2003.

Shelden, Michael. *Orwell: The Authorized Biography.* London: Heinemann, 1991.

University College London. *The George Orwell Archive.* October 16, 2008. http://www.ucl.ac.uk/Library/special-coll/orwell.shtml

Marge Piercy

Feminist SF; Myth and Legend; Time Travel; Utopias

Benchmark Title:
Woman on the Edge of Time (1976)

b. 1936 (Detroit, Michigan)

There were no role models for women like me.
—*Sleeping with Cats* (2002)

Photo credit: Ira Wood.
Permission of Ira Wood and Marge Piercy.

About the Author and the Author's Writing

Marge Piercy was born in Detroit, Michigan. The story of Piercy's family could be described as the American experience in miniature: her father and mother were forced by the Great Depression to leave the coalfields and industrial cities of Pennsylvania to find work; her maternal grandfather was a union organizer who was murdered while organizing bakery workers. Her maternal grandmother was born in a Lithuanian *shtetl*, the daughter of a rabbi. As a child, Piercy was particularly close to her grandmother, who gave her the Hebrew name Marah. "Grandmother Hannah was a great storyteller. She and my mother told many of the same stories, but always the stories came out differently" (McManus 2005).

Although Piercy's father was not Jewish (he was raised a Presbyterian but observed no religion), her grandmother and mother raised her in the tradition of Judaism, and she remains observant to this day.

Like so many young people of her generation and her class, Piercy was the first in her family to attend college. She was the beneficiary of a number of scholarships endowed by the playwright Avery Hopwood, a now-forgotten writer of sex farces, who left his fortune to the University of Michigan to be used to encourage good and original student writing. These scholarships meant that during her senior year Piercy didn't have to work to support herself, and they paid for a trip to France after her graduation. Later she received a fellowship to pursue an MA at Northwestern University.

Following a short-lived marriage to a French physicist, who expected her to play the role of a conventional wife and put her writing ambitions aside for him, Piercy lived in Chicago and did menial jobs to support herself while she worked toward becoming the writer she wanted to be. "[S]he knew . . . she wanted to write about women she could recognize, working class people who were not as simple as they were supposed to be" (McManus 2005).

Meanwhile, Piercy was active in the civil rights movement, an early protestor against the war in Vietnam, and closely involved with the Students for a Democratic Society. She married again, an "open" marriage that "wasn't conventional and in many ways wasn't a marriage at all." She and her husband shared their activism and moved from East Coast to West, from San Francisco to Boston and New York. They finally settled in Cape Cod in 1971, partly because of Piercy's health and also to escape the internal quarrels that were tearing apart the anti-Vietnam War movement. Her second marriage foundered as the couple reacted differently to the relative quiet and isolation of Cape Cod life. As Piercy's second marriage dwindled away and finally ended, she found herself growing closer to Ira Wood, a novelist and playwright with whom she had collaborated on a play called *The Last White Class*, and who shared many of her writing ambitions and social concerns. They were married in 1982. "In the past, when she did not have support at home, she has felt as if she were fighting on all fronts at once with no base. One gift Wood has given her is that warm place of support" (McManus 2005.)

Piercy is as well-known and respected as a poet as she is for her fiction, both mainstream and SF; she has also published a wide range of memoirs, essays, reviews, and social commentary. Her 1996 *City of Darkness, City of Light* is set during the French Revolution. Novels such as *Summer People* and *The Longings of Women* are set in the modern day. All of her books share a focus on women's lives; all of her work also has in common a focus on feminist and social concerns. *Woman on the Edge of Time* (1976) uses time travel to depict a future United States in which men and women are truly equal, while at the same time it raises issues of social justice, feminism, and the treatment of the mentally ill. *He, She and It* (1991, published outside the United States as *Body of Glass*), winner of the Arthur C. Clarke Award, is set in a near future in which small matriarchal enclaves hold out against a world ruined by corporate greed. The lore and language of Jewish tradition suffuses Piercy's work, and particularly in *He, She and It* she incorporates the legend of the Golem, a man of clay animated by the chief rabbi of the medieval Prague ghetto to protect his congregation. All of her work—poetry, nonfiction, realistic fiction, and SF—demonstrates her commitment to a dream of social change, a concept that might best be expressed in the Hebrew phrase *tikkun olam*, or the "repair of the world."

Today Marge Piercy lives on Cape Cod in a house on a freshwater marsh, surrounded by mixed oak and pine woods, with her husband, Ira Wood. They have written a novel together, *Storm Tide* (1998), and in 1997 they founded the Leapfrog Press, a small literary publishing company. She writes and lectures, and she is active in groups and organizations devoted to the renewal of Jewish *Shabbat* worship and communal prayer; she often teaches at the Jewish renewal retreat center, *Elat Chayyim*.

Awards

Novels

He, She And It (1991; aka *Body of Glass*) **ACC**

Works by the Author

Other Notable Genre Fiction

Dance the Eagle to Sleep (1970)
Woman on the Edge of Time (1976)
He, She And It (1991; aka *Body of Glass*)

Notable Mainstream Fiction

Small Changes (1973)
Vida (1980)
Gone to Soldiers (1988)
City of Darkness, City of Light (1996)
Storm Tide (1998, with Ira Wood)
Three Women (1999)
Sex Wars (2005)

Collections

Poetry

The Moon Is Always Female (1980)
My Mother's Body (1985)
Early Grrrl: The Early Poems of Marge Piercy (1999)
The Art of Blessing the Day: Poems with a Jewish Theme (2000)
The Crooked Inheritance: Poems (2009)

In Other Media

Louder: We Can't Hear You (Yet!): The Political Poems of Marge Piercy (2004) (audiobook)

Nonfiction Books

Sleeping with Cats: A Memoir (2002)
So You Want to Write: How to Master the Craft of Writing Fiction and Memoir (2nd ed. 2005, with Ira Wood)
Pesach for the Rest of Us: Making the Passover Seder Your Own (2007)

Articles and Essays

"Active in Time and History." In *Paths of Resistance: The Art and Craft of the Political Novel,* ed. William Zinsser, 89–123. Boston: Houghton Mifflin, 1989.

"Foreword." In *Lost In Space: Probing Feminist Science Fiction and Beyond,* ed. Marleen Barr. Chapel Hill: University of North Carolina Press, 1993.

"In Your Name." *Monthly Review* (September 2004). http://www.monthlyreview.org/0904piercy.htm

"Joanna Russ." In *Contemporary Novelists,* 730. 4th ed. London: St. James, 1986.

"Life of Prose and Poetry: An Inspiring Combination" (Writers on Writing). *The New York Times,* December 20, 1999. http://www.margepiercy.com/essays/NYTLife.htm

"Love and Sex in the Year 3000." In *Envisioning the Future: Science Fiction and the Next Millennium,* ed. Marleen S. Barr, 131–45. Middletown: Wesleyan University Press, 2003.

"Traveling Into Darkness (Introduction)." In *The Last Man,* by Mary Shelley. New York: Bantam Books, 1994

Bibliographies

Doherty, Patricia. *Marge Piercy: An Annotated Bibliography.* Westport, CT: Greenwood, 1997.

For Further Information

Official Web site: http://www.margepiercy.com/

Booker, M. Keith. "Woman on the Edge of a Genre: The Feminist Dystopias of Marge Piercy." *Science Fiction Studies* 21 (1994): 337–50. http://www.depauw.edu/sfs/backissues/64/booker.htm

Friedmann, Peggy, and Ruthann Robson. Interview. *Kalliope.* In *Parti-Colored Blocks for a Quilt, Essays.* University of Michigan Press, 1982. http://www.margepiercy.com/interviews/kalliope.htm

Keulen, Margarete. *Radical Imagination: Feminist Conceptions of the Future in Ursula Le Guin, Marge Piercy, and Sally Miller Gearhart.* New York: Peter Lang, 1991.

McManus, Terry. Official Biography. 2005. http://www.margepiercy.com/

Moylan, Tom. "Marge Piercy's Tale of Hope." In *Scraps of the Untainted Sky: Science Fiction Utopia Dystopia,* 247–72. Boulder, CO: Westview, 2000.

Rheannon, Francesca. Interview. *Writers Voice,* March 2, 2007. Valley Free Radio. http:// www.writersvoice.net/2007/03/marge-piercy-sex-wars/

Shands, Kerstin W. *The Repair of the World: The Novels of Marge Piercy.* Westport, CT: Greenwood, 1994.

Swaim, Don. Interview. *Wired for Books* (March 12, 1984). WOUB Ohio University. http://wiredforbooks.org/margepiercy/

Weinbaum, Batya. "Interview with Marge Piercy." *Femspec* 3, no. 2 (2001): 101–3.

Frederik Pohl

Humor and Satire; Space Opera

Benchmark Title: *Gateway* (1977)

b. 1919 (Brooklyn, New York)

> *SF looks toward an imaginary future, while fantasy, by and large, looks toward an imaginary past. Both can be entertaining. Both can possibly be, perhaps sometimes actually are, even inspiring. But as we can't change the past, and can't avoid changing the future, only one of them can be* real.
> —"Pohlemic: Mail Call" (1992)

About the Author and the Author's Work

Frederik George Pohl Jr. was born in Brooklyn, New York. His father took work wherever he could find it, so young Pohl's early years were spent roaming from Texas, to California, to Central America, where his father worked on the locks of the Panama Canal. When he was about seven the family returned to New York, and he eventually attended the prestigious Brooklyn Tech High School. He was already a passionate reader of SF when he arrived there, and while there he formed a lifelong friendship with fellow student Isaac Asimov, whose parents owned a candy store in the neighborhood. With an influence like this, it is hardly surprising that Pohl was writing and editing SF fanzines in his early teens. "The first SF movie I ever saw was called *Just Imagine*. It was released in 1930. It was about the incredible far future of 1980. In it, New York was all skyscrapers and people lived on pills" (McCarty 2001).

The Great Depression forced Pohl to drop out of school at age fourteen to find work, and the desperate circumstance of the 1930s influenced him to such an extent that, at seventeen, he joined the Young Communist League, to express his support of trade unions and his opposition to racial prejudice and the policies of fascist leaders such as Hitler and Mussolini. However, the young Pohl was not an entirely comfortable fit with the Communist Party, as they believed that SF was a corrupting influence on the young and writing SF was an unsuitable occupation for a good young Communist. Following the pact Stalin made with Hitler in 1939, Pohl decided the Communist Party had changed and he could no longer support it. Instead, with his friend Asimov, and others like Damon Knight, Judith Merril, Cyril Kornbluth, and James Blish, Pohl became a founding member of the Futurians, a New York–based fan group and writer's network.

According to his official Web site, "Frederik Pohl has been about everything that it is possible to be in the field of science fiction, from consecrated fan and struggling poet to critic, literary agent, teacher, book and magazine editor and, above all, writer."

Over sixty-five years, Pohl has produced over 100 books and many, many stories, alone and in collaboration. In the early decades of his writing career he wrote, alone and with others, under a bewildering array of pen names. (The Futurians, as a group, for example, had a "house name," "Paul Dennis Lavond.") Appropriately for such a long career, there are "eras" in Pohl's work that reflect his interests at the time he was writing, his regular writing partners, and the time he had available, given his other professional activities.

Pohl's early work was relatively optimistic. In the 1950s and 1960s, for example, he wrote near-future stories of the all-too-possible absurdities that could easily arise from our culture, often with Cyril Kornbluth (who died suddenly in 1958, at the age of thirty-three). These slickly ironic tales include *The Space Merchants* (1953), a dystopian satire of a world ruled by advertising agencies, and "The Tunnel Under the World" (1955), in which an entire community is held captive by advertising researchers.

From the late 1950s until 1969 Pohl served as editor of *Galaxy* and *if* magazines. Under his editorship, *if* won the Hugo Award for Best Professional Magazine in 1966, 1967, and 1968. He continued to write, finishing stories and ideas that had been left unfinished by the death of Kornbluth, and working with Jack Williamson on space operas and juveniles that, according to *The Encyclopedia of Science Fiction* (1999), combined "Williamson's flair with [Pohl's] economy of style." In the mid-1970s, as science fiction editor for Bantam Books, he was able to publish a number of great SF writers, such as Samuel R. Delany and Joanna Russ, as "Frederik Pohl Selections." During the 1970s Pohl also began his Heechee series, in which humankind makes a living among the stars by picking up the lost gadgets and artifacts of a superior alien race, and wrote various other well-received, stand-alone novels such as *JEM: The Making of a Utopia* (1979) and *Man Plus* (1976). Pohl played a major part in the professionalization of SF, the introduction of a new generation of writers, and the transformation of the genre from the realm of disregarded pulps to serious literature. "I write what interests me, in the hope that it will interest others" (Author Comment, *St. James Guide* 1996).

Frederik Pohl has hardly been idle in recent years—although he admits that "when I turned 80, I decided I no longer have to do four pages a day. For me, it's like retiring" ("Chasing Science" 2000). Novels keep coming, and a new story, "Generations," was published in September 2005. He is in great demand as a public speaker, on science fiction and on his favorite causes and issues, such as the Democratic Party and world peace. His interests are not limited to SF alone: for a time he was the official authority for the *Encyclopedia Britannica* on the subject of Roman Emperor Tiberius. He has been married five times; his former wives include the Canadian SF writer and editor Judith Merril (they divorced in 1952) and Carol M. Ulf Stanton (they divorced in 1983), with whom he collaborated on several books. He is also the father of five children, including Frederik Pohl IV, with whom he has also collaborated.

Frederik Pohl lives in the suburbs of Chicago with his wife, SF editor and scholar Dr. Elizabeth Anne Hull. He is "a star among stars. He has shaped and seasoned the literature of science fiction as almost no one else has" (Wilcox 1996).

Awards

Edward E. Smith Memorial Award for Imaginative Fiction ("Skylark award") (1966)
SFWA Grand Master (1993)
Milford Award for lifetime achievement in SF publishing and editing (1995)
Science Fiction Hall of Fame (1998)
Prix Utopia (2000)

Novels

Man Plus (1976) **Nebula**
Gateway (1977) **Campbell Memorial, Hugo, Locus Poll, Nebula**

Short Fiction

"The Meeting" (1972, with C. M. Kornbluth) **Hugo**
"The Gold at the Starbow's End" (1972) **Locus Poll**
"Fermi and Frost" (1985) **Hugo**

Collections

The Years of the City (1984) **Campbell Memorial**

As Editor

if (1966, 1967, 1968) **Hugo**

Nonfiction

The Way the Future Was (1978) **Locus Poll**

 ## Works by the Author

Preferred Risk (1955, with Lester Del Rey)
Slave Ship (1956)
Drunkard's Walk (1960)
A Plague of Pythons (1964; aka Demon in the Skull)
The Age of the Pussyfoot (1965)
Syzygy (1981)
Starburst (1982)
Outnumbering the Dead (1991)
JEM: The Making of a Utopia (1979)
The Cool War (1981)
The Merchants' War (1984)
Black Star Rising (1985)

The Coming of the Quantum Cats (1986)
Terror (1986)
Chernobyl (1987)
The Day the Martians Came (1988)
Narabedla Ltd. (1988)
Homegoing (1989)
The World at the End of Time (1990)
Outnumbering the Dead (1990)
Stopping at Slowyear (1991)
Mining the Oort (1992)
The Voices of Heaven (1994)
O Pioneer! (1998)
The Last Theorem (2008, with Arthur C. Clarke)

Eschaton trilogy

The Other End of Time (1996)
The Siege of Eternity (1997)
The Far Shore of Time (1999)

The Heechee

Gateway (1977)
Beyond the Blue Event Horizon (1980)
Heechee Rendezvous (1984)
The Annals of the Heechee (1987)
The Gateway Trip (1990)
The Boy Who Would Live Forever: A Novel of Gateway (2004)

Mars

Man Plus (1976)
Mars Plus (1994, with Thomas T. Thomas)

With C. M. Kornbluth

The Space Merchants (1953)
Search the Sky (1954)
Gladiator at Law (1955)
Wolfbane (1957)
Presidential Year (1958)
Critical Mass (1977)

With Jack Williamson

Land's End (1988)
The Singers of Time (1991)

Undersea Eden Trilogy

Undersea Quest (1954)
Undersea Fleet (1955)
Undersea City (1958)

Starchild Trilogy

The Reefs of Space (1964)
Starchild (1965)
Rogue Star (1969)

Saga of Cuckoo

Farthest Star (1975)
Wall Around a Star (1983)

Other Notable Short Fiction

"The Tunnel Under the World" (1955)
"The Merchants of Venus" (1972)
"Shaffery Among the Immortals" (1972)
"We Purchased People" (1974)
"Growing Up in Edge City" (1975)
"The Mother Trip" (1975)
"Swanilda's Song" (1978)
"Mars Masked" (1979)
"Servant of the People" (1983)
"The Greening of Bed-Stuy" (1984)
"The Kindly Isle" (1984)
"Stopping at Slowyear" (1992)

Collections

Alternating Currents (1956)
The Case Against Tomorrow (1957)
Tomorrow Times Seven (1959)
The Man Who Ate the World (1960)
Turn Left At Thursday (1961)
The Wonder Effect (1962, with Cyril M. Kornbluth)
The Abominable Earthman (1963)
Digits and Dastards (1966)

The Frederik Pohl Omnibus (1966)
Day Million (1970)
The Best of Frederik Pohl (1975)
In the Problem Pit (1976)
The Early Pohl (1976)
Survival Kit (1979)
This Is My Best (1981)
Planets Three (1982, as James MacCreigh)
Midas World (1983)
Pohlstars (1984)
The Years of the City (1984)
Venus, Inc. (1985)
BiPohl (1987)
Our Best: The Best of Frederik Pohl and C. M. Kornbluth (1987)
The Gateway Trip: Tales and Vignettes of the Heechee. (1990)
Pohlstars (1990)
The Undersea Trilogy (1992)
Platinum Pohl (2001)
Confounding SF (2008)

As Editor

Super Science Stories (1940)
Astonishing Stories (1940)
Super Science Stories (1941)
Astonishing Stories (1941)
Star Science Fiction Magazine (1958)
The Best Science Fiction from if (1964)
The Best Science Fiction from Worlds of Tomorrow (1964)
International Science Fiction (1967)
International Science Fiction (1968)

Magazines

Galaxy Science Fiction (1961–1969)
if (1962–1969)
Worlds of Tomorrow (1963–1967)

In Other Media

The Clone Master. Paramount Television, 1978. Directed by Don Medford; starring Art Hindle and Stacy Keach Sr.; based on an idea by Pohl.
The Space Merchants was produced for radio in 1953.

In Europe, a number of his stories have been televised by the BBC and German television, and "The Tunnel Under the World," was made into a feature film in Italy. *Man Plus* and *Gateway* are currently in development.

Gateway has also been made into computer games by Legend Entertainment, under the titles "Frederik Pohl's Gateway" and "Gateway II: The Home World."

Nonfiction Books

Tiberius (1960, as "Ernst Mason")
Practical Politics: 1972 (1971)
The Way the Future Was: A Memoir (1978)
Science Fiction Studies in Film (1981, with Frederik Pohl IV)
Our Angry Earth (1991, with Isaac Asimov)
Chasing Science: Science as Spectator Sport (2000)
Science Fiction in the Classroom (2000, videocassette, with Elizabeth A. Hull)

Articles and Essays

"Creating Tomorrow Today: SF's Special Effects Wizards." In *Omni's Screen Flights/Screen Fantasies: The Future According to Science Fiction Cinema*, ed. Danny Peary, 214–23. Garden City, NY: Doubleday, 1984.

"Edgar Rice Burroughs and the Development of Science Fiction." *Burroughs Bulletin* (April 1992): 8–14.

"Pohlemic: Mail Call." *Science Fiction Chronicle* (May 1992).

"The Politics of Prophecy." in *Political Science Fiction,* Ed. Donald M. Hassler and Clyde Wilcox, 7–17. Columbia: University of South Carolina Press, 1997.

"The Publishing of Science Fiction." In *Science Fiction, Today and Tomorrow: A Discursive Symposium,* ed. Reginald Bretnor, 17–45. New York: Harper & Row, 1974.

"Ragged Claws." In *Hell's Cartographers,* ed. Brian W. Aldiss and Harry Harrison, 144–72. New York: Harper & Row, 1975.

"Science Fiction: Stepchild of Science." *Technology Review* 97, no. 7 (1994): 57–61.

"The Science Fiction Professional." In *Science Fiction Writers of America Handbook,* ed. Kristine K. Rusch, 7–25. Eugene, OR: Writer's Notebook, 1990.

"The Study of Science Fiction: A Modest Proposal." *Science Fiction Studies* 24 (1997): 11–16.

Bibliographies

Stephensen-Payne, Phil, and Gordon R. Benson Jr. *Frederik Pohl: Merchant of Excellence, A Working Bibliography*. Albuquerque, NM: Galactic Central, 1989.

For Further Information

Official Web site: http://www.frederikpohl.com/

Frederick Pohl Papers. Syracuse University: http://library.syr.edu/digital/guides/p/pohl_f.htm

"Chasing Science." *Locus* (October 2000). http://www.locusmag.com/2000/Issues/10/Pohl.html

Clareson, Thomas. *Frederik Pohl*. Mercer Island, WA: Starmont, 1987.

Hassler, Donald M. "A Platinum Moment for Frederik Pohl: From Golden Pulp to Steely." *Extrapolation* 47 (2006): 148–52.

———. "Swift, Pohl, and Kornbluth: Publicists Anatomize Newness." In *Political Science Fiction,* ed. Donald M. Hassler and Clyde Wilcox, 18–25. Columbia: University of South Carolina Press, 1997.

McCarty, Michael. "The Man Who Sees Tomorrow: Frederik Pohl." In *Modern Mythmaker*. Jefferson, NC: McFarland, 2008.

Samuelson, David N. "Critical Mass: The Science Fiction of Frederik Pohl." In *Voices for the Future, Vol. 3,* ed. Thomas D. Clareson, 106–26. Bowling Green: Bowling Green University Popular Press, 1984.

Wilcox, Robert H. "Frederik Pohl" (and Author Comment). In *St. James Guide to Science Fiction Writers,* ed. Jay Pedersen. Detroit, MI: St. James, 1996.

Wilson, Connie C., and Michael McCarty. "Frederik Pohl Is Both the Boy Who Will Live Forever and the Man Who Sees Tomorrow." *Science Fiction Weekly,* May 29, 2006.

Mike Resnick

Myth and Legend; Space Opera

Benchmark Title:
Kirinyaga: A Fable of Utopia (1998)

b. 1942 (Chicago, Illinois)

Photo credit: Lezli Robyn.
Permission of Mike Resnick.

[W]hat kind of myths or stories will they tell in the future? "Will high deeds be told in poetry, or only in computer code?" And I ... decided that somebody should try to find out. I've been spending a third of my career ever since then creating myths of the future.

—Nelson, "An Interview with Mike Resnick,"
Daily Dragon Online (2008)

About the Author and the Author's Writing

Michael Diamond Resnick has been a professional writer since he graduated from college in the early 1960s. He edited seven newspapers and a trio of men's magazines. He produced a weekly column on horse racing for more than a decade, and for eleven years wrote a monthly column on purebred collies. (Mike and Carol Resnick bred and exhibited champion collies; today, Resnick is still an AKC-licensed collie judge.) Between 1964 and 1976 he wrote more than 200 novels, under various pseudonyms. And until 1981, only two of them were science fiction.

Mike Resnick was born in Chicago, Illinois. He attended the University of Chicago, where he won three letters on the college fencing team, and met, and eventually married, his wife Carol. An early shared interest of the young couple—besides collies—was science fiction. Mike and Carol discovered fandom in 1962, the same year their daughter Laura was born, and they attended their first Worldcon in 1963. The Resnicks were true enthusiasts; they appeared in five Worldcon "masquerades" in the 1970s, in costumes that Carol created, and they won four of them. Having worked hard to build up their dog breeding and grooming business, by 1980 Mike turned the day-to-day running of the enterprise over to staff and returned to his first career, writing, and his first love, science fiction. *The Soul Eater,* the first novel in what would become the series <u>The Birthright Universe</u>, was published in 1981.

Some Mike Resnick bottom lines:

- 100 novels

- Translated into two dozen languages (including Korean, Bulgarian, Hebrew, Castilian, and Chinese, as well as major European languages)

- 40 anthologies edited

- 150 published short stories

- 44 collaborations, working with 41 different writers on short fiction, and 3 on novels

- 5 Hugos (Resnick is now the leading award winner for short fiction among all science fiction writers, living or dead.)

There are several notable trends running through Mike Resnick's science fiction. There is his love of fable and legend: Mike Resnick clearly sees himself as not a processor or "reteller" of myth and legend, but as a sort of bard, who is making entirely new myth and legend suitable for the Modern Age. Of novels as distinctive as the Kirinyaga stories, *The Dark Lady: A Romance of the Far Future* (1987), and *Ivory* (1988), Resnick writes that "I'm not at all sure that I write honest-to-God, true-blue science fiction. What I write are morality plays" (Author Comments, *St. James Guide* 1996).

Resnick is also interested in exactly how the process of legend making happens, and it is not uncommon for his stories to feature a bard who either is the voice of the truth at the heart of the tale or openly and unapologetically exaggerates and edits his accounts as he goes along, to given them more staying power, more "*pizzazz.*" Resnick's legends and Resnick's bards abide by the wisdom of the filmmaker John Ford in his classic film, *The Man Who Shot Liberty Valance*: "When the legend becomes fact, print the legend."

In Resnick's work there are even further striking resemblances to the conventions of the classic Western. Many of his stories, such as the Birthright series and *Santiago: A Myth of the Far Future* (1986), are set in frontier worlds, where his characters are compelled to fight to "earn their spurs" or are using the vast open spaces of the frontier to create their own hard-won reality. Resnick's stories also commonly feature larger-than-life, archetypal characters with colorful names like "The Widowmaker," Lucifer Jones, "The Forever Kid," and Catastrophe Baker, and idiosyncratic outcasts and ne'er-do-wells like the circus performers of the Tales of the Galactic Midway, or the courtesans of the orbiting brothel of the Tales of the Velvet Comet, the sort of characters who have been a staple of Westerns from time immemorial.

Finally—and perhaps most interesting, given all of these aspects of his stories—Resnick's SF career reflects a long-standing and thoughtful fascination with Africa and African culture, traditionalism, and colonialism and its repercussions on individuals and societies. Some of Resnick's stories are allegories of African history and politics. Others are actually set in Africa, or about futuristic attempts to recapture the ways of Africa on colony planets or orbiting habitats. Stories such as "For I Have Touched the Sky" (1989) and "The Manamouki" (1990) are "controversial and thought-provoking stories of the conflict between Western values and those of Africa"

(D'Ammassa 1996). Resnick has visited Africa many times, and he draws on this experience skillfully in his work.

Mike Resnick's writing output is impressive. In addition to his fiction, he frequently contributes articles to fanzines; he is executive editor of the online fantasy and science fiction magazine *Jim Baen's Universe* and a regular contributor. He has expanded into screenwriting and the possibility of bringing some of his books to the screen. He has always credited Carol as his "behind the scenes" collaborator and line editor, but she is listed officially as co-writer on two scripts in development—*Santiago* and *The Widowmaker*. Their daughter Laura has joined the family industry and is a writer herself, the winner of two awards for her romance novels, as well as the 1993 Campbell Award for Best New Science Fiction Writer. Recently Resnick donated his papers, consisting of at least 125 boxes, to the Special Collections Library of the University of South Florida in Tampa.

Awards

Edward E. Smith Memorial Award for Imaginative Fiction ("Skylark award") (1995)

Short Fiction

"Kirinyaga" (1988) **Hugo**
"The Manamouki" (1990) **Hugo**
"Seven Views of Olduvai Gorge" (1994) **Hugo, Nebula**
"When the Old Gods Die" (1995) **Locus Poll**
"The 43 Antarean Dynasties" (1997) **Hugo**
"Travels with My Cats" (2004) **Hugo**

Works by the Author

The Goddess of Ganymede (1967)
Pursuit on Ganymede (1968)
Redbeard (1969)
Battlestar Galactica No. 5: Galactica Discovers Earth (1980)
The Branch (1984)
Second Contact (1990)
The Red Tape War (1991, with Jack L. Chalker and George Alec Effinger)
Dragon America: Revolution (2005)
Lady with an Alien (YA: 2005)

The Birthright Universe

The Soul Eater (1981)
Birthright: The Book of Man (1982)
Walpurgis III (1982)

Ivory: A Legend of Past and Future (1988)
A Miracle of Rare Design (1994)
A Hunger in the Soul (1998)
The Outpost (2001)

Chronicles of Different Worlds

Paradise (1989)
Purgatory (1992)
Inferno (1993)

Lucifer Jones

Adventures (1985)
Exploits (1992)
Encounters (1993)
Hazards (2009)

Oracle

Soothsayer (1991)
Oracle (1992)
Prophet (1993)

Santiago

Santiago: A Myth of the Far Future (1986)
The Dark Lady: A Romance of the Far Future (1987)
The Return of Santiago (2003)

Starship *Teddy R*

Starship: Mutiny (2005)
Starship: Pirate (2006)
Starship: Mercenary (2007)
Starship: Rebel (2008)
Starship: Flagship (2009)

Tales of the Galactic Midway

Sideshow (1982)
The Three-Legged Hootch Dancer (1983)
The Wild Alien Tamer (1983)
The Best Rootin' Tootin' Shootin' Gunslinger in the Whole Damned Galaxy (1983)

Tales of the Velvet Comet

Eros Ascending (1984)

Eros at Zenith (1984)
Eros Descending (1985)
Eros at Nadir (1986)

Widowmaker

The Widowmaker (1996)
The Widowmaker Reborn (1997)
The Widowmaker Unleashed (1998)
A Gathering of Widowmakers (2005)

Other Notable Genre Fiction

Lara Croft, Tomb Raider: The Amulet of Power (2003)
The World Behind the Door (YA: 2007)

John Justin Mallory fantasy detective series

Stalking the Unicorn (1987)
Stalking the Vampire (2008)
Stalking the Dragon (2009)

Notable Short Fiction

"For I Have Touched the Sky" (1989)
"Bully!" (1990)
"One Perfect Morning, with Jackals" (1991)
"Winter Solstice" (1991)
"The Lotus and the Spear" (1992)
"Song of a Dry River" (1992)
"Mwalimu in the Squared Circle" (1993)
"Barnaby in Exile" (1994)
"A Little Knowledge" (1994)
"Bibi" (1995, with Susan Shwartz)
"The Land of Nod" (1996)
"Hothouse Flowers" (1999)
"The Elephants on Neptune" (2000)
"Redchapel" (2000)
"Old MacDonald Had a Farm" (2001)
"Robots Don't Cry" (2003)
"A Princess of Earth" (2004)
"Travels with My Cats" (2004). http://www.asimovs.com/_issue_0501/travelswithmycats.shtml
"Down Memory Lane" (2005)
"All the Things You Are" (2006)

"Distant Replay" (2007). http://www.asimovs.com/_issue_0805/Distantreplay.shtml
"Alastair Baffle's Emporium of Wonders" (2008)
"Article of Faith" (2008)
"Idle Roomer" (2008, with Lezli Robyn). http://clarkesworldmagazine.com/resnick_11_08/.

A complete list of Mick Resnick's stories available online (with the author's permission) is at http://www.freesfonline.de/authors/Mike_Resnick.html (text) and http://www.sffaudio.com/?page_id=2388 (audio podcast).

Collections

Unauthorized Autobiographies (1984)
Through Darkest Resnick with Gun and Camera (1990)
Stalking the Wild Resnick (1991)
Pink Elephants and Hairy Toads (1991)
The Alien Heart (1991)
Will the Last Person to Leave the Planet Please Shut Off the Sun? (1992)
A Safari of the Mind (1995)
Solo Flights Through Shared Worlds (1996)
Magic Feathers: The Mike and Nick Show (2000, with Nick DiChario)
In Space No One Can Hear You Laugh (2000)
Hunting the Snark and Other Stories (2002)
With a Little Help from My Friends (2002). Twenty-six stories, each a collaboration with a different author.
New Dreams for Old (2006)
The Other Teddy Roosevelts (2008)
Dreamwish Beasts and Snarks (2009)

Kirinyaga

An Alien Land (1998)
Kirinyaga: A Fable of Utopia (1998)
Kilimanjaro (2008)

As Editor

Shaggy B.E.M. Stories (1988)
Inside the Funhouse (1992)
Aladdin: Master of the Lamp (1992, with Martin H. Greenberg)
Whatdunits (1992)
More Whatdunits (1993)
Future Earths: By Any Other Fame (1993)
Christmas Ghosts (1993)
The Passage of the Light: The Recursive Fiction of Barry N. Malzberg (1994, with Anthony R. Lewis)

Deals with the Devil (1994, coedited with Loren D. Estelman)
Sherlock Holmes in Orbit (1996)
Girls for the Slime God (1997)
Return of the Dinosaurs (1997)
Dimensions of Sheckley (2002)
Women Writing Science Fiction as Men (2003)
Men Writing Science Fiction as Women (2003)
Stars: Original Stories Based on the Songs of Janis Ian (2003)
New Voices in Science Fiction (2003)
I, Alien (2005)
Down These Dark Spaceways (2005)
Worldcon Guest of Honor Speeches (2006, with Joe Siclari)
Space Cadets (2006)
This Is My Funniest (2006)
Nebula Awards Showcase, 2007 (2007)
Alien Crimes (2007)
The Dragon Done It (2008, with Eric Flint)
This Is My Funniest 2 (2007)
History Revisited (2008)
The Best of Jim Baen's Universe 2 (2008, with Eric Flint)
When Diplomacy Fails (2008, with Eric Flint)

Fantastic anthologies

Dinosaur Fantastic (1993, with Martin H. Greenberg)
Witch Fantastic (1995)

Future Earths anthologies, with Gardner Dozois

Under South American Suns (1993)
Under African Skies (1993)

Alternate Anthologies

Alternate Presidents (1992)
Alternate Kennedys (1992)
Alternate Warriors (1993)
Alternate Outlaws (1994)
Alternate Worldcons (1994)
Again, Alternate Worldcons (1996)
Alternate Tyrants (1997)
Alternate Skiffy (1997, with Patrick Nielsen Hayden)

Other Series

Library of African Adventure

Resnick Library of African Adventure
Resnick Library of Worldwide Adventure

Nonfiction Books

The Official Guide to Fantastic Literature (1976)
Putting It Together: Turning Sow's Ear Drafts into Silk Purse Stories (2000)
I Have This Nifty Idea . . . Now What Do I Do with It? (2001)
Once a Fan . . . (2002)
The Science Fiction Professional (2002)
Resnick at Large (2003)
. . . Always a Fan (2009)

Articles and Essays

"The Matrix and the Star Maker." In *Exploring the Matrix: Visions of the Cyber Present,* ed. Karen Haber, 112–21. New York: St. Martin's, 2003.

"The Tiniest Assassins." In *The War of the Worlds: Fresh Perspectives on the H.G. Wells Classic,* ed. Glenn Yeffeth. Dallas, TX: BenBella, 2005

Me and Lucifer. Subterranean Press, 2007. http://subterraneanpress.com/index.php/magazine/spring2007/column-me-and-lucifer-by-mike-resnick/

Bibliographies

Kelleghan, Fiona, and Ralph Roberts. *Mike Resnick: An Annotated Bibliography and Guide to His Work.* Alexander, NC: Farthest Star, 2000.

For Further Information

Official Web site: http://www.fortunecity.com/tattooine/farmer/2/

Huddleston, Kathie. "Award Winning Author Mike Resnick Tells Tall Sci-Fi Tales. *SciFi.com* (February 2003).

Jamneck, Lynne. Interview. *Strange Horizons* (May 2004). http://www.strangehorizons.com/2004/20040517/resnick.shtml

"Mike Resnick." In *Authors & Artists for Young Adults, Volume 38,* 127–36. Farmington Hills, MI: Gale Group, 2001.

Nelson, Bobbie. "An Interview with Mike Resnick." *Daily Dragon Online,* September 3, 2008. http://dailydragon.dragoncon.org/2008/mike-resnick/

Rosenman, John. "Kirinyaga and Beyond: Mike Resnick's African Diaspora in Space." *Internet Review of Science Fiction* (March 2006). http://www.iroSF.com/q/zine/article/10259

Swanwick, Michael. "Singular Interviews: Mike Resnick." *New York Review of Science Fiction* 18, no. 4 (2005).

Kim Stanley Robinson

Hard SF; Near Future

Benchmark Title: *Red Mars* (1992)

b. 1952 (Waukegan, Illinois)

I think of science fiction as being about the histories that we cannot know—future, alternative, deep past. These are all historical fictions. So every time you write one you sketch out a kind of theory of how history happens.
—"Kim Stanley Robinson," *Locus* (2002)

Photo credit: Beth Gwinn

About the Author and the Author's Work

Kim Stanley Robinson's work, whether he is dealing with a possible, and very plausible, middle-distance future on Mars or the immediate dangers that may result from our poor stewardship of the one planet we occupy now, is a satisfying example of Brian Aldiss's observation in *Billion Year Spree* that "the greatest successes of SF are those which deal with man in relation to his changing surroundings and abilities: what might loosely be called *environmental fiction*" (Chapter 1). When Aldiss wrote those words in 1973, the term *environmental fiction* probably did not have the same resonance that it carries today. Before Hurricane Katrina, before the relentless disintegration of the polar ice caps, before rising seas threatened low-lying nations and even washed inhabited islands off the face of the earth, the environment was just something that surrounded us. Its changes were a challenge to humankind, but not necessarily a threat to its very survival.

From his very earliest work, Kim Stanley Robinson's work has challenged readers to reconsider environment, to think of if as something more than setting, but almost as another character in the story. His fiction is "both didactic and entertaining, and . . . fully utilizes the potential of SF to overcome the despair of man's current situation and glory in the potential of the future worlds we can help create" (Fratz 1996). A recurring theme in all of Robinson's novels is the struggle to survive in a hostile, alien environment—whether that is the virgin canvas of the planet Mars or the polluted biosphere of the planet Earth. In his Mars Trilogy, beginning with the journey of a hand-picked group of pioneers, we watch the Martian landscape being transformed, as Robinson traces the social, political, and even philosophical impact of the choices that the colonists make over a 200-year period. In his more recent novels of the Capital Code series, the planet being "terraformed" is Earth, as politicians and scientists are forced to confront the impact of global warming and try to undo the damage that has been done. As he said in an interview in the *Guardian* (UK) in 2005: "It seems so easy on Mars, and looks so hard on Earth, which is kind of ironic. It's infinitely more difficult when there's already an established ecology. There's no room for error. And also, alas, there are some mistakes that we simply don't have the power to correct." Ironically for one who is identified as a voice of liberal, even radical, SF, Robinson's work often portrays the worlds he imagines as having distinctive similarities to the mythologized frontier of the American West, and the respect his novels demand for the environment is often tempered with a sentimental affection for the freedom that a wild frontier territory (such as Mars or Antarctica) offers.

Robinson's work has been identified with the "Mundane Movement," a group of SF writers who have foresworn shiny rockets, faster-than-light drives, and galactic empires in favor of fictional futures that may more closely resemble what actually awaits us in the immediate future, here on Earth. Although Robinson is the first to admit that his stories of marginal ecologies, sustainable technologies, and survival in extreme environments are very much in the spirit of the "Mundane," he firmly denies the label, saying that he dislikes the idea of literary groups, and the connotations of "boring" or "tedious" that could accompany the word "mundane" are unfortunate (Adams 2007). But Robinson is not afraid to be identified as a utopian; like Ursula K. Le Guin, whom he admires, he writes stories in which an intelligent, well-informed individual can make a difference, changing society along ecological, egalitarian, and democratic lines. "I do consider my books to be a political work. It seems to me that the more stories out there that encourage these kinds of actions, then the better off people would be" (Smith 2002).

Kim Stanley Robinson was born in Waukegan, Illinois, the birthplace of Ray Bradbury, although he spent most of his childhood in Southern California. He studied English literature at the University of California, San Diego, and received an MA from Boston University. He returned to San Diego to do his PhD, doing research on Philip K. Dick, and in 1984, his doctoral thesis was published as *The Novels of Philip K. Dick*. Before becoming a full-time writer in 1985, he worked as a bookstore clerk and a teacher. Robinson became interested in SF as a college student and began writing stories inspired by his favorite authors, H. G. Wells, Clifford Simak, and Ursula K. Le Guin.

He was the first science fiction writer to win a National Science Foundation grant to study Antarctica, as research for his 1997 book set on the southern continent. It was an experience that he likens to the environment that future space pioneers will find, which deeply influenced his subsequent work, especially the Science in the Capital series. He is an enthusiastic mountain climber, and mountain climbing appears in several of his works, most notably *Antarctica*, the novellas in the collection *Escape from Kathmandu*, and *Forty Signs of Rain*. Robinson is married to Lisa Howland Nowell, an environmental chemist, and they have two sons. He and his family currently live in a sustainable community in Davis, California, that boasts solar water heating, natural cooling systems, and a drainage system that also irrigates eight cooperatively cultivated orchards and a vineyard; its energy consumption is one-third to one-half that of other neighborhoods in Davis. Kim Stanley Robinson has been intensively involved in the local governing of his neighborhood, a place that "strangely echoed what I had already written in my utopian novel *Pacific Edge*, so that I felt I was coming home in a way" (Smith 2002).

Awards

Novels

The Wild Shore (1984) **Locus Poll**
Pacific Edge (1990) **Campbell**
Red Mars (1992) **BSF, Nebula**
Green Mars (1993) **Hugo, Locus Poll**
Blue Mars (1995) **Hugo, Locus Poll**
The Years of Rice and Salt (2002) **Locus Poll**

Short Fiction

"The Blind Geometer" (1986) **Nebula**
"A Short, Sharp Shock" (1990) **Locus Poll**

Collections

The Martians (1999) **Locus Poll**

Works by the Author

Icehenge (1984)
The Memory of Whiteness (1985)
A Short, Sharp Shock (1990)
Antarctica (1997)
The Years of Rice and Salt (2002)

The Mars Trilogy

Red Mars (1992)
Green Mars (1993)
Blue Mars (1995)

The Orange County Trilogy, or the Three Californias

The Wild Shore (1984)
The Gold Coast (1988)
Pacific Edge (1990)

The Science in the Capital series

Forty Signs of Rain (2004)
Fifty Degrees Below (2005)
Sixty Days and Counting (2007)

Notable Short Fiction

"On the North Pole of Pluto" (1981)
"Venice Drowned" (1981)
"To Leave a Mark" (1982)
"Black Air" (1983)
"The Lucky Strike" (1984)
"Ridge Running" (1984)
"Down and Out in the Year 2000" (1986)
"Escape from Kathmandu" (1986)
"Mother Goddess of the World" (1987)
"Glacier" (1988)
"Remaking History" (1988)
"Before I Wake" (1989)
"The True Nature of Shangri-La" (1989)
"A History of the Twentieth Century, with Illustrations" (1991). http://www.infinityplus.co.uk/stories/history.htm
"Vinland the Dream" (1991)
"A Martian Childhood" (1994)
"Arthur Sternbach Brings the Curveball to Mars" (1999)
"A Martian Romance" (1999)
"Sexual Dimorphism" (1999)

Collections

The Planet on the Table (1986)
Escape from Kathmandu (1989)
Remaking History and Other Stories (1994)
The Martians (1999). Includes supplementary material relating to the Mars Trilogy, such as the early novella version of "Green Mars" (1985)
Vinland the Dream and Other Stories (2002)

As Editor

Future Primitive: The New Ecotopias (1994)
Nebula Awards Showcase (2002)

Nonfiction Books

The Novels of Philip K. Dick (1984)

Articles and Essays

"Pentalude: Science Fiction as Fantasy." In *Imaginative Futures,* ed. Milton T. Wolf and Daryl F. Mallett, 353–56. San Bernardino, CA: Borgo, 1995.

"The Psychic Landscape." In *Paragons: Twelve Master Science Fiction Writers Ply Their Craft,* 164–68. Robin Wilson. New York: St. Martin's, 1996.

"Science in the Third Millennium." In *Envisioning the Future: Science Fiction and the Next Millennium,* ed. Marleen S. Barr, 199–201. Middletown: Wesleyan University Press, 2003.

Bibliographies

Stephens, Christopher P., and Tom Joyce. *A Checklist of Kim Stanley Robinson.* Rev. ed. Hastings-on-Hudson, NY: Ultramarine, 1991.

For Further Information

Adams, John Joseph. Interview. *Science Fiction Weekly* (March 2007).

Buhle, Paul. "Kim Stanley Robinson, Science Fiction Socialist." *Monthly Review: An Independent Socialist Magazine* 54, no. 3 (2002): 87–90.

Crown, Sarah. "Future Tense." *Guardian Online,* September 14, 2005. http://www.guardian.co.uk/books/2005/sep/14/sciencefictionfantasyandhorror.sarahcrown

Fratz, D. Douglas. "Kim Stanley Robinson." In *St. James Guide to Science Fiction Writers,* ed. Jay Pedersen. Detroit, MI: St. James, 1996.

Gunn, Moira. "Tech Nation: Audio Interview." *ITConversations* (January 2006). GigaVox Media Channel. http://www.itconversations.com/shows/detail935.html

James, Warren W. "Interview: Kim Stanley Robinson." *Mike Hodel's Hour 25: Science Fiction Radio for Southern California* (June 2001 and August 2004). http://www.hour25online.com/

Jamneck, Lynne. Interview. *Strange Horizons*, August 15, 2005. http://www.strangehorizons.com/2005/20050815/robinson-int-a.shtml

"Kim Stanley Robinson: The Years of Rice and Salt." *Locus* (January 2002). http://www.locusmag.com/2002/Issue01/KSR.html

Lawrie, Duncan. "This Is Year One: Kim Stanley Robinson." *Zone-SF.com* (November 2005). Pigasus Press. http://www.zone-sf.com/ksrobinson.html

Manaugh, Geoff. "Comparative Planetology: An Interview with Kim Stanley Robinson." *Bldgblog,* December 19, 2007. http://bldgblog.blogspot.com/2007/12/comparative-planetology-interview-with.html

Neilson, Robert. "Axes of Evil: Interview." *Albedo One,* July 27, 2006. http://www.albedo1.com/html/kim_s_robinson.html

Rohn, Jennifer. Interview. *Lablit: The Culture of Science in Fiction & Fact,* February 4, 2007. http://www.lablit.com/article/208/

Smith, Jeremy. "The Ambiguous Utopian." *January Magazine* (July 2002). http://www.januarymagazine.com/profiles/ksrobinson.html

Snider, John C. Podcast Interview. *SciFi Dimensions,* April 10, 2008. http://www.scifidimensions.com/main/2008/04/15/the-scifidimensions-podcast-5/

Swidorski, Carl. "Kim Stanley Robinson's Martian Vision." In *The Utopian Fantastic,* ed. Martha-Bartter, 43–56. Westport, CT: Praeger, 2004.

Spider Robinson

Humor and Satire; Space Opera

Benchmark Title:
Callahan's Crosstime Saloon (1977)

b. 1948 (The Bronx, New York)

Photo credit: Greg McKinnon. Permission of Spider and Jeanne Robinson.

We do not need artists to tell us Life Sucks. We knew that already. . . . Certainly, artists should express their inner pain—but if they cannot find some way to live with it, some trick to cope with it, some perspective from which to transcend it, then they should do so in private, with the door closed, and wash their hands afterwards.
—Aragão, "Cheering People," *Intempol* (2008)

About the Author and the Author's Writing

The popular SF author Spider Robinson, and his wife Jeanne, live on an island off the coast of British Columbia, where they raise, and exhibit, hopes.

Is it possible *not* to love that little joke, taken from Spider's Official Web site Biography (and repeated the length and breadth of the Internet)? And, like the very best jokes, it has at its heart a diamond core of truth: it seems that everyone loves Spider Robinson. Readers love him; fellow writers love him; critics love him; the estate of Robert A. Heinlein loves him. (And it is entirely possible that the Great Man himself, in whatever Valhalla is reserved for the Writers of Classic SF, loves him, too.) Everyone loves Spider Robinson because of his optimism, his belief in happy endings, his terrible puns, and his willingness to *play*—to play with the convention of storytelling, as well as the conventions of SF itself.

At Callahan's Crosstime Saloon, the regulars are time travelers, cybernetic aliens, and telepaths; the Saloon itself is the wayside inn where stories are told, wisdom is dispensed, and adventures begin—think the Inn of the Prancing Pony, the White Hart Inn, the Mos Eisley Cantina, Ten Forward, *Cheers*, and the favorite watering holes of any of the great gumshoes of classic detective fiction. The gruff but friendly barkeep Callahan, and eventually his bartender and protégé Jake Stonebender, aided by the outcasts and the oddballs, save humanity, and occasionally the universe itself, again and again, with nothing more than "human initiative and technological advancement" (Brennan 1996). The episodic quality of Robinson's <u>Callahan</u> stories, his fondness for atrocious puns, the song parodies, and snickering SF in-jokes, are deliberate links to an old tradition, in which it took a village to tell a tale. "Robinson tells stories . . . that rocket along on greased rails, moving so fast that you hardly even notice when the author slides in all kinds of grace-notes, tidbits about politics, spycraft and the oversimplification of the mythology of the 1960s" (Doctorow 2008). John P. Brennan, in the *St. James Guide to Science Fiction*, even sees a serious purpose in the puns, which (he says) "call into question the ability of language to express any external reality." Perhaps.

Spider Robinson ("Spider" is the name on his passport, driver's license, and marriage certificate) was born on November 24, 1948, in the Bronx, New York. In some versions of his biography, he claims that he was born over three successive days because "they had to handle him in sections" (Author Profile 2003). He holds a BA in English from the State University of New York and was a regular book reviewer for *Galaxy*, *Analog*, and *New Destinies* magazines for some years. Robinson met his wife Jeanne in the woods of Nova Scotia in the early 1970s, and they have been married, and lived in Canada, for the past thirty years.

The Robinson marriage is a collaborative enterprise: Jeanne Robinson is a writer and choreographer; in the 1980s she was scheduled to be a civilian astronaut on the space shuttle, where she would fulfill her ambition to choreograph a dance in zero gravity. Unfortunately the *Challenger* disaster put an end to the Civilian in Space program, but together Spider and Jeanne coauthored The Stardance Trilogy, in which a crippled dancer is a central figure in first contact with an alien race that holds the key to humanity's transcendence to the next level of consciousness. Over the past few years Jeanne Robinson has been producing, writing, and choreographing a feature film based on the novels and her ideas about dance in zero-G.

In 2004 Robinson was approached by the estate of the late Robert A. Heinlein to write a novel based on a lengthy 1955 outline of a Heinlein story. *Variable Star*, which is billed as a collaboration between Heinlein and Robinson, was published in 2006 and seems to have confirmed Gerald Jonas's 1982 estimation in the *New York Times*, of Robinson as Heinlein's logical heir: "I'd nominate Spider Robinson as the new Robert Heinlein. Like Mr. Heinlein in his prime, Mr. Robinson writes in a crisp, tightly controlled prose about a future that is recognizably descended from today's world, yet provocatively altered."

In 2008 Robinson was awarded the Robert A. Heinlein Award for Lifetime Excellence in Literature. His short work has appeared in magazines from *OMNI* and *Analog* to the Moscow SF magazine *Xhurnal Izobretatel i Rationalizator*. He is recognized in the industry as a skilled audiobook reader, of his own work and that of others; he has won the Earphones Award and been a finalist for the "Audie." On his podcast *Spider on the Web*—perhaps serious for once—he lists his "employment other than writing" as folk singing, and in 2001 he recorded a CD of original music (*Belaboring the Obvious*) accompanied by guitar legend Amos Garrett. He has also performed and written songs in collaboration with music greats such as David Crosby and Todd Butler.

In the summer of 2009, Jeanne and Spider Robinson welcomed the arrival of their first grandchild, Marisa Alegria. But in autumn 2009, following a year of worrying symptoms and surgery, Jeanne Robinson was diagnosed with stage 4 biliary cancer. Friends and fans rallied around the Robinsons, offering moral support and practical measures, such as fund-raising concerts and auctions, as she was about to start chemotherapy. "Shared joy is increased, shared pain is lessened—thus do we refute entropy"

(*Callahan and Company*). In the face of entropy, that most fragile of virtues, hope, continues to hang on in the Pacific Northwest.

Awards

Edward E. Smith Memorial Award for Imaginative Fiction ("Skylark award") (1978)
Campbell New Writer Award (1974)
Robert A. Heinlein Award (2008)

Short Fiction

"By Any Other Name" (1976) **Hugo**
"Stardance" (1977, with Jeanne Robinson) **Hugo, Locus Poll, Nebula**
"Melancholy Elephants" (1982) **Hugo**

Critic

1977, **Locus Poll**

Works by the Author

Telempath (1976)
Night of Power (1985)
The Free Lunch (2001)
Variable Star (2006, with Robert A. Heinlein)

The Callahan's Series: Callahan's Place

Callahan's Crosstime Saloon (1977)
Callahan's Secret (1986)
The Callahan Touch (1993)
Callahan's Legacy (1996)
Callahan's Key (2000)
Callahan's Con (2003)

The Callahan's Series: Lady Sally's

Callahan's Lady (1989)
Lady Slings the Booze (1992)

The Deathkiller Trilogy

Mindkiller (1982)
Time Pressure (1987)
Lifehouse (1997)

SF Mysteries

Very Bad Deaths (2004)
Very Hard Choices (2008)

The Stardance Trilogy, with Jeanne Robinson

Stardance (1979)
Starseed (1991)
Starmind (1995)

Other Notable Short Fiction

"Dog Day Evening" (1977)
"Have You Heard the One . . .?" (1980)
"Serpent's Teeth" (1981)
"Melancholy Elephants" (1982). http://www.baen.com/chapters/W200011/0671319744___1.htm
"The Mick of Time" (1986)

Collections

Antinomy (1980)
Time Travelers Strictly Cash (1981)
Melancholy Elephants (1984)
Callahan and Company: The Compleat Chronicles of the Crosstime Saloon (1987)
True Minds (1990)
Off the Wall at Callahan's (1994)
User Friendly (1998)
By Any Other Name (2001)
God Is an Iron and Other Stories (2002)

As Editor

The Best of All Possible Worlds (1980)

Nonfiction Books

The Crazy Years: Reflections of a Science Fiction Original (2004)

Articles and Essays

"Rah, Rah, R.A.H.!" *Destinies* (Summer 1980) (reprinted in *Time Travelers Strictly Cash*) http://www.heinleinsociety.org/rah/works/articles/rahrahrah.html

For Further Information

Official Web site: http://www.spiderrobinson.com/

Aragão, Octavio. "Cheering People: Interview with Spider Robinson." *Intempol,* July 7, 2008. http://intemblog.blogspot.com/2008/07/cheering-people-interview-with-spider.html

Author Profile. *BC Bookworld* (Winter 2003). http://www.abcbookworld.com/view_author.php?id=3120

Bova, Ben. "Spider Robinson: The SF Writer as Empath" (Introduction). In *Callahan's Crosstime Saloon.* New York: Tor, 1999 (orig. pub. 1977).

Brennan, John P. "Spider Robinson." In *St. James Guide to Science Fiction Writers,* ed. Jay Pedersen. Detroit, MI: St. James, 1996.

Doctorow, Cory. "Spider Robinson's *Very Hard Choices*—Rigorous, Science Fictional Look at Telepathy's Problems." *BoingBoing,* November 4, 2008. http://boingboing.net/2008/11/04/spider-robinsons-ver.html

Interview. Audio Broadcast. *The Future and You,* August 1, 2006. http://www.thefutureandyou.libsyn.com/?search_string=spider&Submit=Search&search=1

Jonas, Gerald. "Imaginary People." *The New York Times,* August 29, 1982.

Richards, Linda. "Spider Robinson Talks about Everything." *January Magazine* (September 2000). http://januarymagazine.com/profiles/spiderrobinson.html

Schellenberg, James, and David M. Switzer. Interview. *Challenging Destiny* (December 2007). http://www.challengingdestiny.com/interviews/robinson.htm

Snider, John C. Interview. *SciFiDimensions* (September 2006). http://www.scifidimensions.com/Sep06/spiderrobinson.htm

"Spider Robinson." In *Authors & Artists for Young Adults, Volume 35,* 113–20. Farmington Hills, MI: Gale Group, 2000.

"Spider Robinson: Laugh When It Hurts." *Locus* (February 2004). http://www.locusmag.com/2004/Issues/02Robinson.html

Joanna Russ

Feminist SF; New Wave; Science Fantasy

Benchmark Title: *The Female Man* (1975)

b. 1937 (The Bronx, New York)

> [Y]ou must look at very, very big things until they seem small, and then you must look at very, very small things until they seem big.
> —Delany, Interview in *Broad Universe* (2007)

About the Author and the Author's Work

Samuel Delany has said of Joanne Russ that feminism works for her "the way Marxism works for the great German writer Bertolt Brecht. It is something innate to the concerns, not something that can be dismissed" (Delany 2007). Although her earliest work has been described as feminist "only obliquely" (Snyder 1996), the subtext was always there; her early story "Nor Custom Stale" (1959) depicts a conventional marriage that is sheltered from reality—and its own monotony—by the high-tech house the couple occupies. In "Mr. Wilde's Second Chance," the dead poet and playwright Oscar Wilde—famous victim of his era's attitudes to homosexuality—decides to pass on an opportunity to live a more conventional life. Her "Alyx" tales of the late 1960s, (collected and re-released in 1985 as *The Adventures of Alyx*) were remarkable for their time: on the surface, traditional action-adventure, with a thin veneer of SF and a protagonist who is a time-traveling mercenary, "whose daring and cunning issue from her womanly strength. . . . [H]er unromantic heroics are designed to satirize the 'he-man ethos' of Sword and Sorcery" (Snyder 1996). If Russ had stopped there, we would still have good reason to remember her Alyx as the "mother" of strong female characters like Ripley in *Alien* and Starbuck, the cigar-smoking space jockey of *Battlestar Galactica*.

Russ's work of the 1970s moved on to much more sophisticated ways to consider the issues of gender and sexuality, visions of an emancipated future that were only implied by her earlier work. "When It Changed" (1972) was one of her first stories set in Whileaway, using an old SF device—the world without men—to consider how truly emancipated women might live: it might be possible to call Whileaway a "utopia" except for the fact that Russ is sophisticated enough to recognize that, even with the best of intentions, "life remains unpredictably anguishing and rewarding" (Snyder 1996). *The Female Man* (1975), which also features Whileaway, uses the device of four parallel worlds, whose four protagonists share identical genes but have developed into different women. Thirty years after its first publication, *The Female Man* remains a provocative—and readable—example of the feminist SF of the 1970s; Russ "boldly challenges all preconceptions about gender and the 'natural' relationships between the sexes" (Andrews and Rennison 2006).

Born Joanna Ruth Russis, her parents were teachers, and she grew up in the Bronx, New York. As a senior in high school she was a winner of the Westinghouse Science Talent Search, with an experiment on the effect of light on *Aspergillis janus* fungus. ("By the time I finished I thought it was terribly boring") (Delany 2007). She attended Cornell University, followed by an MFA in drama from Yale, and since then has taught at various universities, including Cornell, State University of New York at Binghamton, and the University of Washington. For some time she was an active participant in Kirk/Spock "slash" fanfiction, the first to deem the phenomenon worthy of academic attention; she wrote about it in her essay "Pornography by Women for Women, with Love," which appears in her 1985 essay collection *Magic Mommas, Trembling Sisters, Puritans & Perverts*. She has been nominated for all of the major SF awards, and in the 1990s three of her works were awarded retrospective or "classic" Tiptree Awards in recognition of their place in the history of fiction that "expands or explores our understanding of gender." Her work has been translated into many languages, including Japanese, Danish, Catalán, and Finnish.

Joanna Russ currently lives in Tucson, Arizona. Since the late 1980s she has suffered from chronic fatigue syndrome; she has only produced one short story ("Invasion," 1996) and the occasional critical piece, because, as she explained in her 2006 interview with Samuel Delany, "writing takes an enormous amount of energy. It takes concentration, and this is a physical thing.... If you're writing a novel, you're keeping stuff in the back of your head for a year or two, and it's very difficult to find suddenly you can't do that. It took about—oh let's see —eight or nine years for me to live with that comfortably."

Awards

Science Fiction Research Association Pilgrim Award (1988)

Novels

The Female Man (1975) **Retro Tiptree 1996**

Short Fiction

"When It Changed" (1972) **Nebula, Retro Tiptree 1996**
"Souls" (1982) **Hugo, Locus Poll**

Works by the Author

Picnic on Paradise (1968)
And Chaos Died (1970)
The Female Man (1975)
We Who Are About To (1977)
The Two of Them (1978)
On Strike Against God (1980)

Notable Short Fiction

"Nor Custom Stale" (1959)
"The Second Inquisition" (1970)
"Poor Man, Beggar Man" (1971)
"The Extraordinary Voyages of Amelie Bertrand" (1979)
"The Mystery of the Young Gentleman" (1982)
"Invasion" (1996)

Collections

The Adventure of Alyx (1976)
The Zanzibar Cat (1983)
(Extra)ordinary People (1985)
The Hidden Side of the Moon (1987)

Nonfiction Books

How to Suppress Women's Writing (1983)

Magic Mommas, Trembling Sisters, Puritans, and Perverts: Essays on Sex and Pornography (1985)

To Write Like a Woman: Essays in Feminism and Science Fiction (1995). Includes essays such as "*Amor Vincit Foeminam,* The Battle of the Sexes in SF" (1980) and "On Mary Wollstonecraft Shelley" (1995).

The Country You Have Never Seen: Essays and Reviews (2005)

Articles and Essays

"Alien Monsters." In *Turning Points: Essays on the Art of Science Fiction,* ed. Damon Knight, 132–43.. New York: Harper & Row, 1977.

"*A Boy and His Dog:* The Final Solution." *Frontiers: A Journal of Women's Studies* 1, no. 1 (1975).

"The Image of Women in Science Fiction." *Vertex* (February 1974): 32+.

"On Setting." In *Those Who Can: A Science Fiction Reader,* ed. Robin Scott Wilson, 149–54. New York: St. Martin's, 1996.

"Recent Feminist Utopias." In *Future Females: A Critical Anthology,* ed. Marleen S. Barr, 71–85. Bowling Green, OH: Popular University Press, 1981.

"SF and Technology as Mystification." *Science Fiction Studies* 5 (1976): 250–60. http://www.depauw.edu/SFs/backissues/16/russ16.htm

"Towards an Aesthetic of Science Fiction." *Science Fiction Studies* 2 (1975): 112–19. http://www.depauw.edu/SFs/backissues/6/russ6art.htm

For Further Information

Cortiel, Jeanne. *Demand My Writing: Joanna Russ, Feminism, Science Fiction.* Liverpool, UK: Liverpool University Press, 1999.

Delany, Samuel. Interview. *Broad Universe* (2007). http://www.broaduniverse.org/broadsheet/0702jrsrd.html

———. "Joanna Russ and D. W. Griffith." *PMLA* 119 (May 2004) 500–508.

———. "Orders of Chaos: The Science Fiction of Joanna Russ." In *Women Worldwalkers: New Dimensions of Science Fiction and Fantasy,* ed. Jane Branham Weedman, 195–124.. Lubbock: Texas Tech, 1985.

"Joanna Russ." *Feminist Science Fiction, Fantasy and Utopia,* May 28, 1996. http://feministSF.org/reviews/russ.j.html

Johnson, Charles. "A Dialogue: Samuel Delany and Joanna Russ on Science Fiction." *Callaloo: A Journal of African American and African Arts and Letters* 7, no. 3 (1984): 27–35.

Lefanu, Sarah. "The Reader as Subject: Joanna Russ." In *In the Chinks of the World Machine: Feminism and Science Fiction,* 173–98. London: Women's, 1988.

McCaffery, Larry. Interview. In *Across the Wounded Galaxies;* 176–210. Urbana: University of Illinois Press, 1990.

Mendlesohn, Farah. *On Joanna Russ.* Middletown, CT: Wesleyan University Press, 2009.

Perry, Donna. "Joanna Russ." In *Backtalk: Women Writers Speak Out,* 287–311. New Brunswick, NJ: Rutgers University Press, 1993.

Snyder, Carol L. "Joanna Russ." In *St. James Guide to Science Fiction Writers,* ed. Jay Pedersen. Detroit, MI: St. James, 1996.

Teslenko, Tatiana. *Feminist Utopian Novels of the 1970s: Joanna Russ & Dorothy Bryant.* New York: Routledge, 2003

Willmer, J. Caissa. "Joanna Russ (1937–)." In *Contemporary Lesbian Writers of the United States: A Bio-Bibliographical Critical Sourcebook,* ed. Sandra Pollack and Denise D. Knight, 481–89. Westport, CT: Greenwood, 1993.

Pamela Sargent

Feminist SF; Hard SF

Benchmark Title: *Venus of Dreams* (1986)

b. 1948 (Ithaca, New York)

But science fiction, at its core, is not about 'freeing the imagination of all technological restrictions,'... In genuine science fiction, even in tales some might class as borderline, the limits of what is known and what is possible are respected.
—"A SciFi Case History" (1997)

Photo credit: © Jerry Bauer.
Courtesy of Pamela Sargent.

About the Author and the Author's Work

Pamela Sargent was born in Ithaca, New York. Her mother was a chemistry teacher, a pianist, and an administrator; her father was a Marine Corps officer until he was invalided out due to a heart attack and injuries in combat. From her accounts in interviews conducted with Jill Engel of *Nova* magazine, her parents were interesting but complicated people, and Sargent's childhood was difficult—the kind that is fascinating to look back upon, and surviving it provides all sorts of material for a writer, but must have been very difficult for a sensitive child. "They had their share of bad luck, when my father's health problems caught up with him and he was unable to work. I was the oldest, so I looked after my younger brothers and sister. I became a buffer between them and my parents' problems, and that caught up with me later" (Engel 1991).

When she was fourteen, this "catching up" resulted in a crisis, and Sargent spent some time, as she puts it in the Engel interview, "committed to a horrendous institution." It was during this terrible time in her young life that she discovered SF, and she found that it was "escapist" reading in more ways than one. "I read *The Stars My Destination* in a very unsophisticated way.... In a weird way, the book gave me some sense of a possible future, because I'd try to imagine myself leaping past that experience and looking back from a time when I'd finally escaped it" (Engel 1991).

And "leap past" she did. Pamela Sargent sold her first published story during her senior year in college at the State University of New York/Binghamton University, where she earned a BA and MA in philosophy and also studied ancient history and Greek. There, too, she met Jack Dann and George Zebrowski, two future writers of SF who would become lifelong friends and important influences on her career as an SF writer. Meanwhile, however, Sargent had a number of "day jobs"—the worst, she relates, as solderer on an assembly line; the best, "receptionist for a paper company—I had plenty of supplies for my writing" (Engel 1991).

During the early 1970s Sargent's short stories began to be published in magazines such as *Fantasy and Science Fiction*, but her first important impact on SF was in the role of editor, when she persuaded a publisher to produce a volume of SF by women, about women. The resulting volume, *Women of Wonder* (1975)—which was followed by two more volumes on the theme in the 1970s—established Sargent's credentials as a serious critic and advocate of feminist SF. Each volume has received, retrospectively, the James Tiptree Jr. Classic Award for its contribution to fiction that expands or explores our understanding of gender.

Sargent's first novel, *Cloned Lives*, was published in 1976, and in her own fiction she demonstrates that same insight into gender, relationships, and individuals' roles in their societies. The three volumes of her Venus terraforming series, in which the personal dramas of real men and women are played out against the background of reshaping the face of a whole planet, are exciting and entertaining, but also reflect her repeated insistence that hard SF should be, as she put it in her afterword to *Venus of Shadows* (1988), the second volume of the trilogy, "as demanding in its depictions of characters and attention to literary values as it is with ideas." Her 1986 novel *The Shore of Women* is a refreshing twist on the conventional SF tale of a post-holocaust Earth where women rule, and men are banished and subjugated. Sargent's original take on the traditional scenario is that power would corrupt the women as it once had the men who brought the world to this pass. Thomas J. Morrissey, in the *St. James Guide*, calls *The Shore of Women* "a classic of intelligent SF."

Sargent lives near Albany in upstate New York, with her partner and former classmate at SUNY Binghamton, George Zebrowski, author of *Macrolife A Mobile Utopia* (1979), *Stranger Suns* (1991), and the recent horror-noir novel, *Empties* (2009). Together Sargent and Zebrowski have collaborated on several Star Trek novels, which are widely acknowledged to be among the best and most thoughtful of the many novels developed from the Trek Universe. Sargent has written a novel about the Plains Indians, *Climb the Wind* (1998), an alternative history about how Native Americans might have developed a nation of their own following the Civil War. She has also written a mainstream historical novel, *Ruler of the Sky* (1993), which examines the life of Genghis Khan through the eyes of the women who were closest to him: not SF, but with themes familiar to any reader of SF, as "[Khan's] unimaginable conquests changed the lives of the Mongols as much as technology is changing ours " (Morrissey 1996). *Thumbprints,* a new collection of Sargent's most recent short fiction with an introduction by James Morrow, was released in 2004, and includes a mixture of SF and her "Mongolian" stories. Pamela Sargent lectures on science fiction, historical fiction, and science fiction by women at high schools and colleges all over the world; for over thirty years, as writer, editor, anthologist, and teacher, Pamela Sargent has been a pioneer and a force for good in SF.

Awards

Service to Science Fiction and Fantasy Writers of America Award, with George Zebrowski (2000)

Short Fiction

"Danny Goes to Mars" (1992) **Nebula, Locus Poll**

 ## Works by the Author

Cloned Lives (1976)
Sudden Star (1979)
The Golden Space (1982)
The Alien Upstairs (1983)
The Shore of Women (1986)
Alien Child (1988)
Climb the Wind (1998)

The Seed series

Earthseed (1983)
Farseed (2007)

The Venus Trilogy

Venus of Dreams (1986)
Venus of Shadows (1988)
Child of Venus (2001)

The Watchstar Trilogy

Watchstar (1980)
Eye of the Comet (1984)
Homesmind (1984)

With George Zebrowski

Classic Trek

Heart of the Sun (1997)
Across the Universe (1999)
Garth of Izar (2003)

Star Trek: The Next Generation

A Fury Scorned (1996)

Other Mainstream and Genre Fiction

Ruler of the Sky (1993)

Other Notable Short Fiction

"Gather Blue Roses" (1972)
"Father" (1974)
"The Renewal" (1978)
"Fears" (1984)
"Hillary Orbits Venus" (1999)
"Venus Flowers at Night" (2004)
"Utmost Bones" (2005)

Collections

Starshadows (1977)
The Golden Space (1983)
The Best of Pamela Sargent (1987) (foreword by Michael Bishop)
Behind the Eyes of Dreamers and Other Short Novels (2002)
The Mountain Cage and Other Stories (2002)
Thumbprints (2004) (introduction by James Morrow)

As Editor

Women of Wonder (1975)
More Women of Wonder (1976)
Bio-Futures (1976)
The New Women of Wonder (1978)
Afterlives (1986, with Ian Watson)
Nebula Awards 29 (1995)
Nebula Awards 30 (1996)
Women of Wonder: The Classic Years (1996)
Women of Wonder: The Contemporary Years (1996)
Nebula Awards 31 (1997)
Conqueror Fantastic (2004)

In Other Media

"The Shrine," *Tales from the Darkside* (1986). Directed by Christopher T. Welch; starring Lorna Luft.

Articles and Essays

Guest of Honor Speech. Wiscon, March 2, 1991. http://www.wiscon.info/downloads/sargent.pdf
"The Historical Novelist and History." *Para*doxa* 1 (1995): 363–74.
"Jewish Enough" *Femspec* 4, no. 2 (2004): 83–89.

"The Martians Among Us." In *The War of the Worlds: Fresh Perspectives on the H.G. Wells Classic,* ed. Glenn Yeffeth. Dallas, TX: BenBella, 2005.

"A SciFi Case History." *Science Fiction Studies* 24 (1997). http://www.depauw.edu/SFs/review_essays/sargent7.htm

"Women in Science Fiction." In *Women of Wonder: The Contemporary Years,* ed. Pamela Sargent. San Diego: Harcourt Brace, 1995.

"The Writer as Nomad." In *The Profession of Science Fiction: SF Writers on Their Craft and Ideas,* ed. Maxim Jakubowski and Edward James, 111–19. New York: St. Martin's, 1992.

Bibliographies

Elliot, Jeffrey M., and Boden Clarke. *The Work of Pamela Sargent: An Annotated Bibliography & Literary Guide.* 2nd ed. San Bernardino, CA: Borgo, 1996.

Bibliography. Official Web site. Ed. Jill Engel-Cox. September 2005. http://www.pamelasargent.com/bibliography.html

For Further Information

Official Web site: http://www.pamelasargent.com/

Engel, Jill. "Letters from Upstate New York: A Correspondence with Pamela Sargent." *Nova Express* (Winter 1991). http://www.pamelasargent.com/nova_express_interview.html

———. "Pamela Sargent: The Millennium Interview." December 2000-April 2001. http://www.pamelasargent.com/the_millennium_interview.html

Melloy, Kilian. "Woman of Wonder: Pamela Sargent Has Left Her Thumbprints Across the Face of Modern SF." *Science Fiction Weekly,* November 8, 2004.

Morrissey, Thomas J. "Pamela Sargent." In *St. James Guide to Science Fiction Writers,* ed. Jay Pedersen. Detroit, MI: St. James, 1996.

———. "Pamela Sargent's SF for Young Adults: Celebrations of Change." *Science Fiction Studies* 16 (1989): 184–90.

Reid, Suzanne Elizabeth. "Feminism and Science Fiction: Pamela Sargent." In *Presenting Young Adult Science Fiction,* 101–19. New York: Twayne, 1998.

Wilson, Alyce. Interview. *Wild Violet* (Winter 2005). http://www.wildviolet.net/heavenhell/pamela_sargent.html

Robert J. Sawyer

Hard SF; Time Travel

Benchmark Title: *Flashforward* (1999)

b. 1960 (Canada: Ottawa)

My job is to carve away the jargon and leave behind the awe.
—Butler, "Nothing But Blue Skies,"
Quill & Quire (2007)

Photo credit: Carolyn Clink.
Permission of Robert J. Sawyer.

About the Author and the Author's Writing

In 1999 Robert J. Sawyer was described by *The Ottawa Citizen* as the dean of Canadian SF; in *Science Fiction Quarterly* in 2008, the interviewer referred to him as a "publishing machine." But the road to this distinguished career—seventeen titles in as many years, multiple awards, and respect throughout the SF field—was not Teflon-smooth. When Orson Scott Card declared Sawyer's first published novel, *Golden Fleece*, to be the best SF novel of 1990, in his year-end column in *The Magazine of Fantasy and Science Fiction*, it was a few days after Sawyer was dropped by his first publisher for poor sales. His agent had to arrange a bidding war for Sawyer's next two books, but then a third—*The Terminal Experiment* (1995)—was rejected when Sawyer refused to "dumb it down" and remove references to the issue of abortion and the difficult question of when life actually begins.

> I've never known the SF readership to shy away from anything I wanted to do, including discussing racism, evolution vs. creationism, the abortion debate, the biology of rape, and so on, but genre editors sometimes self-impose strictures that I do find frustrating. Me, I just ignore them and write what I want to write. (Wright 2008)

Sawyer's insistence that his stories actually *mean* something, even when he is writing about sentient dinosaurs, is something he has been passionate about from his very first book. The interstellar murder mystery of *Golden Fleece* was rooted in a recognition of the unreliability of computer systems. His publisher (the same one who rejected *The Terminal Experiment*) insisted that he remove references to U.S. President Ronald Reagan and his "Star Wars" missile-defense system. *Far-Seer*, the first volume of the Quintaglio Ascension (the sentient dinosaurs) is a veiled consideration of the implications of the Catholic Church's stance on birth control. "On the one hand, I had grown up reading far-future off-Earth spaceships-and-aliens SF. On the other hand, *The Terminal Experiment* had succeeded precisely because it was none of those things" ("Autobiographical Essay" 2004).

Robert James Sawyer was born in Ottawa, Canada. He grew up the middle child of three boys in Toronto, where his father and mother were university lecturers in economics and statistics. Sawyer was an intelligent, bookish child, not "sporty," fascinated by museums, inclined to seek out the other smart, well-behaved boys (and girls) in his class who were aiming to become scientists or had an interest in SF. In 1968 the movie *2001: A Space Odyssey*, then mint-new and Sawyer's first introduction to the work of Arthur C. Clarke, made a great impression on him. Part of the fascination, as he reflects in his "Autobiographical Profile," is the date in the title—that he could look forward to a time in his own life when the wonders of giant space stations and cities on the moon and independent-minded computers would be a reality.

Sawyer graduated with a bachelor's degree in radio and television arts from Ryerson University in 1982. He has been a professional writer all his life—he admits only two forays into the world of nonwriting employment: a stint at Ryerson, teaching television studio production techniques to undergraduates, and (an SF writer's dream) a spell as a clerk at Bakka, Toronto's famous SF specialty bookstore. (As any self-respecting SF reader or writer would, Sawyer confesses that, "I really didn't end up making any money at Bakka.... I spent almost my entire earnings buying books.") Before devoting himself to fiction writing, he wrote more than 200 feature articles for magazines such as *Sky & Telescope* and *Archaeology*. In 1988 he made the decision to write fiction full-time.

Among other international writing and SF awards, Robert J. Sawyer is a five-time winner of the Canadian SF award Aurora (1991, 1995, 1996, 1999, and 2005), a three-time winner of the international *Premio UPC de Ciencia Ficción*, and a recipient of the Seiun (Japan), *Le Grand Prix de l'Imaginaire* (France), and, in 2007, the Galaxy Award (China) for "Most Popular Foreign Author." On June 2, 2007, Sawyer received an honorary doctorate (Doctor of Letters, *honoris causa*) from Laurentian University in Sudbury, Ontario. In autumn 2009 a television series based on Sawyer's 1999 novel *Flashforward* premiered on ABC, developed by Brendan Braga (whose credits include the *Star Trek: The Next Generation* and *Deep Space Nine*). In a September 2009 interview with *symmetry* (the in-house magazine of Fermilab and the SLAC National Accelerator Laboratory), Sawyer said:

> The TV series based on my novel is a fairly liberal adaptation.... I was thrilled to find how many of the actors... had chosen to read the novel.... It was fun talking with them about the philosophical notions from the novel—the central questions of fate vs. free will and of the nature of time and consciousness" ("*Flashforward* Author" 2009)

Sawyer has also written an upcoming episode of the series.

In 1984 Robert Sawyer married Carolyn Clink, his high school sweetheart and fellow alum of SF clubs with names like the Northview Association for Science Fiction Addicts and the Society for Speculative Thinking. Sawyer and Clink have made the decision to remain child-free; he acknowledges the irony of this decision for a writer whose work explores evolution and the forces that might impel organisms to pass their essence on to the future. "I guess that means I'm more interested in the survival of my memes than my genes—'meme' being evolutionist Richard Dawkins's term for a persistent idea" ("Autobiography"). Sawyer and his wife, Carolyn Clink, live in Mississauga, Ontario, just outside Toronto, where he writes, and strives, as he puts it in his autobiography, "to combine the intimately human with the grandly cosmic."

Awards

Novels

The Terminal Experiment (1995) **Nebula**
Hominids (2003) **Hugo**
Mindscan (2005) **Campbell Memorial**

Works by the Author

Golden Fleece (1990)
End of an Era (1994)
The Terminal Experiment (1995; aka *Hobson's Choice*)
Starplex (1996)
Frameshift (1997)
Illegal Alien (1997)
Factoring Humanity (1998)
Flashforward (1999)
Calculating God (2000)
Mindscan (2005)
Rollback (2007)

The Neanderthal Parallax

Hominids (2002)
Humans (2003)
Hybrids (2003)

The Quintaglio Ascension

Far-Seer (1992)
Fossil Hunter (1993)
Foreigner (1994)

WWW Trilogy (in progress)

Wake (2009)

Notable Short Fiction

"Just Like Old Times" (1993)
"Lost in the Mail" (1995)
"You See But You Do Not Observe" (1995)
"Above It All" (1996)

"Helix" (1996)
"Peking Man" (1996)
"The Hand You're Dealt" (1997)
"Psychospace" (1997)
"Block Universe" (1997)
"Stream of Consciousness" (1998)
"Ineluctable" (2002)
"Shed Skin" (2004)
"Identity Theft" (2005)
"Biding Time" (2006)

Collections

Iterations (2002)
Relativity (2004)
Identity Theft and Other Stories (2008)

As Editor

Tesseracts 6 (1997, with Carolyn Clink)

Boarding the Enterprise: Transporters, Tribbles, and the Vulcan Death Grip in Gene Rodenberry's Star Trek (2006, with David Gerrold)

In Other Media

Flashforward. HBO Entertainment and ABC Studios, 2009. Produced by Brannon Braga and David S. Goyer; starring Joseph Fiennes, Sonya Walger, John Cho, Jack Davenport, and Dominic Monaghan. Many articles about the conception and production of the TV series are featured on RJS's official Web site.

Articles and Essays

Autobiographical Essay. In *Contemporary Authors Volume 212*. Detroit, MI: Gale, 2004. http://www.SFwriter.com/gale.htm

Big Ideas (lecture on the history of SF). TVOntario, February 2, 2008. http://www.SFwriter.com/2008/02/rob-sawyer-SF-lecture-on-tvontario.html

For Further Information

Official Web site: http://www.SFwriter.com/index.htm

Adams, John Joseph. Interview. *SciFi Weekly*, April 2, 2007.

Anders, Charlie Jane. "Robert J. Sawyer Gives Us a Glimpse of Our Televisual Future." *IO9*, March 10, 2009. http://io9.com/5167679/robert-j-sawyer-gives-us-a-glimpse-of-our-televisual-future

Butler, Gary. "Nothing But Blue Skies (Profile)." *Quill and Quire* (May 2007). http://www.quillandquire.com/authors/profile.cfm?article_id=7745

D'Ammassa, Don. "Robert J. Sawyer." In *St. James Guide to Science Fiction Writers,* ed. Jay Pedersen. Detroit, MI: St. James, 1996.

DeForest, Roger. "Interview: Robert J. Sawyer Confronts Our Damn Life Clocks in *Rollback.*" *Hard SF.com,* April 3, 2007. http://www.hardsciencefiction.rogerdeforest.com/?mode=8&id=6

"*Flashforward* Author Robert J. Sawyer on the LHC, Higgs, and Hollywood." *symmetry,* September 22, 2009. http://www.symmetrymagazine.org/breaking/2009/09/22/flashforward-author-robert-j-sawyer-on-the-lhc-higgs-and-hollywood/

Humphrey, Stephen. Interview. *Strange Horizons,* September 8, 2003. http://www.strangehorizons.com/2003/20030908/sawyer.shtml

Menegon, Katia. "Robert J. Sawyer on The Future." *Forbes,* October 15, 2007. http://www.forbes.com/2007/10/13/robert-sawyer-prediction-tech-future07-cx_1015sawyer.html

Palmer, James. "A Conversation with Robert J. Sawyer." *Internet Review of Science Fiction* (December 2005). http://www.iroSF.com/q/zine/article/10218

Pollard, Kent. Interview. *McNally-Robinson.com,* January 29, 2008. http://www.mcnallyrobinson.com/editorial-662/Robert-J.-Sawyer,-an-Interview

"Robert J. Sawyer: Quantum Metaphysics." *Locus* (February 2003). http://www.locusmag.com/2003/Issue02/Sawyer.html

Silver, Stephen H. "A Conversation with Robert J. Sawyer." *SF Site* (July 2002). http://www.SFsite.com/09a/rsa135.htm

van Belkom, Edo. "Robert J. Sawyer." In *Northern Dreamers: Interviews with Famous Science Fiction, Fantasy and Horror Writers,* 197–209. Kingston, ON: Quarry Press, 1998.

Willmetts, Geoff. "Mindscanned: An Interview with Robert J. Sawyer." *SF Crowsnest,* July 1, 2008. http://www.SFcrowsnest.com/

Wright, Glover. Interview. *SF Quarterly,* February 26, 2008. http://www.SFquarterly.net/

Robert Sheckley

Humor and Satire; Science Fantasy; Space Opera

Benchmark Title: *Immortality, Inc.* (1958)

b. 1928 (Brooklyn, New York); d. 2005 (Poughkeepsie, New York)

> *I've been called "the first SF absurdist." I don't know if it's true, but it's certainly a title I love.*
> —"Robert Sheckley: Still Laughing," Locus (2003)

About the Author and the Author's Work

In his obituary for Robert Sheckley, which appeared in the British newspaper *The Guardian* on December 20, 2005, SF author Christopher Priest wrote, "In a just world, Sheckley would be recognised as one of the most important American short story writers of the 20th century but, as anyone who has read him knows, while justice might in theory be available, it is not for everyone - and then only with a catch." What's the catch? The catch is that, as a writer of SF and fantasy, Sheckley's work would never get the unbiased consideration required to get his due recognition among American writers in general. And although Sheckley was undoubtedly a master of the *science fiction* short form, and the short story is respected as a subgenre of SF, the fact is that short stories, in and of themselves, just don't sell. The respect and even adulation of critics doesn't pay the utility bills. The adulation of fans does not save a writer with a complicated personal life, and delicate health. The sad fact is that, although we admired Robert Sheckley, our admiration did not support him, and he had to work very hard all his life to get by.

Sheckley's genius—for he *was* a genius—was for plausible madness, the sort of crazy humor in which the reader recognizes the unsettling grain of truth within the laugh. Some of his most "outlandish" ideas—such as the TV game show in which the contestants win big cash prizes for evading competitors who are trying to kill them ("The Prize of Peril," 1958)—have almost seen reality catch up with them. His first novel, *Immortality Inc.* (1952), in which scientists have discovered a genuine afterlife, with real ghosts, and business has already worked out a way to market it, was nominated for a Hugo award in 1953. "His heroes, innocents abroad, were ... ingenious, resourceful, capable of action and always able to utter plain common sense in a galaxy full of conmen, unscrupulous advertisers and inscrutable aliens" (Priest 2005).

But Sheckley was always too far out of the mainstream—whatever that stream might happen to be—to be natural prize-winning, best-seller material. In 2000, when the Science Fiction Writers Association belatedly awarded him a Special Nebula, it named him as the oddly disappointing and halfhearted "Author Emeritus." "I knew they were trying to recognize me for something. I didn't think highly of it because 'emeritus' sounds like retirement. So I didn't like that. Because I've always been active, in fact I'm writing more now than I have in some years" (Urell 2003).

Sheckley's personal life could have been a pitch for one of his novels. He was married five times, and the father of four children from his first three marriages. During the 1970s and 1980s he lived for a while on the island of Ibiza, off the coast of Spain, followed by an unsettled period when he "wandered"—the Florida Everglades, New York, Paris, France, Ibiza again, Connecticut, Portland, Oregon, and Red Hook, New York. This had a marked affect on his writing style—for better, some would say, although possibly in terms of his home market, for worse. As he told *Locus* magazine in 2003, "When I traveled around, I became awfully interested in certain European models among French, Italian, and Russian writers. For the US, that's also a dead end. For some years I was very big in France. I sell well now in Russia."

He also suffered badly from writer's block during this time, probably (as he admitted himself) because of the disruption. However, by the standards of most writers, he kept up a steady stream of work (including tie-in novels for *Babylon V*, *Star Trek*, *Deep Space Nine*, and *Alien*, and a number of science fantasy collaborations with Harry Harrison, Roger Zelazny, and David Hartwell in the 1990s). Even when he was writing for the money—which had to be true much of the time—Sheckley's work was always better than it needed to be and full of interesting twists on the serious questions, such as metaphysics and the nature of reality, the "self."

Robert Sheckley was born in Brooklyn, New York, and grew up in New Jersey. After serving in the U.S. Army and attending New York University, he began to sell stories to SF magazines. Over the course of his career, he was the author of several hundred short stories and fifteen novels; during his most prolific period, "magazine editors insisted he publish some stories under pseudonyms to avoid having his byline appear more than once in an issue" (Jonas 2005). Sheckley's work has been translated into many languages, including Greek, Romanian, Finnish, and Lithuanian. And he *was* very popular in Eastern Europe; always welcomed with open arms at cons and readings in the former Soviet Union, in April 2005 he was a guest at such an event in Kiev, Ukraine, when he became very ill and had to be hospitalized. He appeared to be slowly recovering (Kiev newspapers called him "the unkillable Robert Sheckley"), but on his return to upstate New York he required open heart surgery. On December 9, 2005, following further complications and surgery for a brain aneurysm, Robert Sheckley died in a Poughkeepsie hospital.

Awards

Science Fiction and Fantasy Writers of America Author Emeritus (2001)

 Works by the Author

Immortality, Inc. (1958; orig. *Time Killer*)
The Status Civilization (1960)
Journey Beyond Tomorrow (1962; aka *The Journey of Joenes)*
Mindswap (1966)

Dimension of Miracles (1968)
Options (1975)
Crompton Divided (1978)
Futuropolis (1978)
Dramocles (1983)
Bill, the Galactic Hero on the Planet of Bottled Brains (1990, with Harry Harrison)
Star Trek, Deep Space Nine: The Laertian Gamble (1995)
Aliens: Alien Harvest (1995)
Babylon 5: A Call to Arms (1999)

Hunter/Victim novels

The 10th Victim (1966)
Victim Prime (1987)
Hunter/Victim (1988)

Other Notable Genre Fiction

The Game of X (1965)
Godshome (1999, with David G. Hartwell)

Hob Draconian series

The Alternative Detective (1993)
Draconian New York (1996)
Soma Blues (1997)

Millennial Contest series, with Roger Zelazny

Bring Me the Head of Prince Charming (1991)
If at Faust You Don't Succeed (1993)
A Farce to Be Reckoned With (1995, with Roger Zelazny)

Stephen Dain series

Calibre .50 (1961)
Dead Run (1961)
Live Gold (1962)
White Death (1963)
Time Limit (1967)

Notable Short Fiction

"The Demons" (1953). http://www.lesekost.de/HHL139D.htm
"Seventh Victim" (1953)
"The Prize of Peril" (1958)

"Shall We Have a Little Talk?" (1965)
"Zirn Left Unguarded, the Jenghik Palace in Flames, John Westerley Dead" (1972)
"A Suppliant in Space" (1973)
"The Day the Aliens Came" (1995)
"The Quijote Robot" (2001)
"Reborn Again" (2004). http://www.infinitematrix.net/stories/index.html

Collections

Untouched by Human Hands (1954)
Citizen in Space (1955)
Pilgrimage to Earth (1957)
Notions: Unlimited (1960)
Store of Infinity (1960)
Shards of Space (1962)
The People Trap (1968)
Can You Feel Anything When I Do This? (1971; aka *The Same to You Doubled and Other Stories*)
The Wonderful World of Robert Sheckley (1979)
The Robot Who Looked Like Me (1982)
Is That What People Do? (1984)
Feast of Sheckley: Short Stories (1989)
The Collected Short Fiction of Robert Sheckley: *Vols. 1–5* (1992)
Dimensions of Sheckley (2002)
The Masque of Mañana (2005)

As Editor

After the Fall (1980)

In Other Media

Captain Video and His Video Rangers. TV series, 1949–1955. Sheckley contributed an unidentified number of episodes.

La Decima vittima. Compagnia Cinematografica Champion, 1965. Directed by Elio Petri; starring Marcello Mastroianni and Ursula Andress in an Italian production based on Sheckley's 1966 novel *The 10th Victim*.

"The People Trap," *ABC Stage 67* (1966). TV play based on a story by Sheckley; starring Vera Miles and Connie Stevens.

Condorman. Walt Disney Productions, 1981. Directed by Charles Jarrott; starring Michael Crawford and Oliver Reed; based on Sheckley's 1965 novel *The Game of X*.

Freejack. Morgan Creek Productions, 1992. Directed by Geoff Murphy; starring Emilio Estevez and Mick Jagger; based on the 1958 novel *Immortality Inc*.

"Watchbird," *Masters of Science Fiction* (2007). TV play based on Sheckley's story of the same name; starring James Cromwell and Sean Astin.

Robert Sheckley's In a Land of Clear Colours. Brian Eno and Pete Sinfield. Release date 1993. Limited edition book/CD package of a story by Sheckley, recorded in 1979. The story is read by Sinfield (lyricist and founding member of the band King Crimson), with synthesizer interludes by Eno.

Articles and Essays

"Introduction." In *Pane Burro e Paradossina,* by Roberto Quaglia. October 1996. http://www.robertoquaglia.com/rs_intro.html

"Philosophy & Science Fiction: A View of a Personal Reality." *Greenwich Village Gazette* (March 2000). http://www.nycny.com/columns/sheckley/SHECKLEY3-00.html

"The Search for the Marvellous." In *Science Fiction at Large: A Collection of Essays, By Various Hands, About the Interface Between Science Fiction and Reality,* ed. Peter Nicholls, 185–98. London: Gollancz, 1976.

Bibliographies

Willick, George C. "Bibliography." *Spacelight* (June 2006). http://www.gcwillick.com/Spacelight/sheckley.html

For Further Information

Official Web site: http://www.sheckley.com/frames.html

Aldiss, Brian W. "Why They Left Zirn Unguarded: The Stories of Robert Sheckley." In *This World and Nearer Ones,* 59–63. Kent, OH: Kent State University Press, 1981.

Dunn, Thomas P. "Existential Pilgrims and Comic Catastrophe in the Fiction of Robert Sheckley." *Extrapolation* 26 (1985): 56+.

Faber, Michel. "Close Encounters." *Guardian Online,* February 1, 2003. http://www.guardian.co.uk/books/2003/feb/01/featuresreviews.guardianreview35

Horwich, David. "Irony and Misunderstanding in the Stories of Robert Sheckley." *Strange Horizons,* September 25, 2000. http://www.strangehorizons.com/2000/20000925/Article_Sheckley_Horwich.shtml

Jonas, Gerald. Obituary. *New York Times,* December 10, 2005. http://www.sheckley.com/

Nicholls, Stan "Robert Sheckley Is a Dreaming Boy." In *Wordsmiths of Wonder: Fifty Interviews with Writers of the Fantastic,* 25–32. London: Orbit, 1993.

Priest, Christopher. Obituary. *Guardian,* December 20, 2005. http://www.guardian.co.uk/news/2005/dec/20/guardianobituaries.booksobituaries1

"Robert Sheckley: Still Laughing." *Locus* (September 2003). http://www.locusmag.com/2003/Issue09/Sheckley.html

Rusch, Kristine Kathryn. Obituary. *Internet Review of Science Fiction* (June 2006). http://www.iroSF.com/q/zine/article/10277

Sallis, James. "Revisiting Sci-fi's Neglected Hero and Others." *Boston Globe,* December 12, 2005. http://www.grasslimb.com/sallis/GlobeColumns/globe.11.sheckley.html

Stephenson, Gregory. In *Comic Inferno: The Satirical Work of Robert Sheckley.* San Bernardino, CA: Borgo, 1997.

Urell, Bob. "Other Dimensions: An Afternoon with Robert Sheckley." *Singularity* (2003). http://members.tripod.com/~sheckley/intsing.htm

White, Fred. D. "Robert Sheckley." In *St. James Guide to Science Fiction Writers,* ed. Jay Pedersen. Detroit, MI: St. James, 1996.

Wingrove, David. " 'I Am a Bill Collector Disguised as a Tree, Said the Bill Collector Disguised as a Tree': An Interview with Robert Sheckley." *Vector* 89 (1978): 10–20. http://members.tripod.com/~sheckley/intv78a.htm

Mary Wollstonecraft Shelley

Early SF; SF Horror

Benchmark Title: *Frankenstein* (1818)

b. 1797 (England: Somers Town, London); d. 1851 (England: Westminster, London)

> *Dream that my little baby came to life again; that it had only been cold, and that we rubbed it before the fire and it lived. Awake and find no baby. I think about the little thing all day. Not in good spirits.*
> —*Mary Shelley's Journal*, entry dated March 19, 1815 (1947)

About the Author and the Author's Work

She was nineteen years old.

Her mother—notorious feminist and author of *The Vindication of the Rights of Women*—died ten days after her birth; her father—fond of her, but feckless and self-centered—remarried a woman who despised her and tried to cut her off from her birthright. At age sixteen she ran away with a married man, who—brilliant, exciting, but feckless and self-centered—was immediately cut off by his wealthy family, leaving the young couple to roam Europe, dodging debt collectors and cadging off wealthy friends. The child who died, a few weeks old—her first baby—haunted her. And then, in the course of an after-dinner challenge to write a ghost story, Mary Wollstonecraft Shelley—who was actually several weeks short of her nineteenth birthday—created two of the most powerful and enduring archetypes of SF and of the modern age: the monster created by the man of science and the "creator" who pays the ultimate price for refusing to take responsibility for his actions.

> I saw the pale student of the unhallowed arts kneeling beside the thing he had put together. I saw the hideous phantasm of a man stretched out, and then, on the working of some powerful engine, show signs of life, and stir with an uneasy, half vital motion. (1831 Introduction, *Frankenstein*)

The genesis of *Frankenstein*, the novel, is probably about as famous as the genesis of Dr. Victor Frankenstein's monster itself. The story, as Shelley wrote it, has been distorted by subsequent film and stage versions, by sequels and homages, reworkings and retellings, right down to the simple mistake that most people, when they hear the word "Frankenstein," think "monster" and not the scientist who creates the monster. But in a way, that is only further testament to the power of Shelley's story and the lasting impact that it has had on the popular imagination since its anonymous publication in 1818. If Percy Bysshe Shelly, Lord Byron, and Doctor Polidori were men of honor, then young Mary was the hands-down winner of whatever wagers were made at Lake

Geneva that cold, damp summer. (In her own account of the challenge in the 1817 Preface to the first edition, Shelley notes—with some satisfaction, perhaps?—"The following tale is the only one which has been completed." This is a little unfair: Dr. Polidori's contribution to the fun was published, without his permission, and attributed to Byron, by a London magazine in 1919. *The Vampyre*, coincidentally, laid the foundation for all future vampire stories. It was quite a party.)

Brian Aldiss calls *Frankenstein* "the first real novel of science fiction." Other critics and historians of SF (such as Thomas M. Disch, who was a firm champion of Edgar Allan Poe's claim to that label) may disagree, but Aldiss makes a strong case, citing the deep complications of the story as Shelley told it, the richness of the sources it draws upon, and the way it resonates with the consequences of love, death, and free will.

After the death by drowning of her husband Percy Bysshe Shelley in 1822, Mary Shelley supported herself and her sole surviving child, Percy Florence, with her writing. This included a number of short stories with recognizable SF themes, and *The Last Man* (1826), a novel about the single human survivor of a worldwide plague. When she died at the young age of fifty-three of a brain tumor, she had the dual satisfaction of knowing that her son had been accepted by his father's family as the heir to his baronetcy and that her *other* child, the one she had stitched together from bits and pieces of her tragedies and her imagination, had achieved a permanent place in popular culture. "Time is no more, for I have stepped within the threshold of eternity" (*The Last Man*, 1826).

Awards

Science Fiction Hall of Fame (2004, posthumous)

Works by the Author

Frankenstein (1818)
The Last Man (1826)

Notable Mainstream and Other Genre Fiction

Mathilda (1819)
Valperga; or, The Life and Adventures of Castruccio, Prince of Lucca (1823)
The Fortunes of Perkin Warbeck (1830)
Lodore (1835)
Falkner (1837)

Notable Short Fiction

"Valerius: The Reanimated Roman" (1819)
"The Mortal Immortal" (1833)
"Roger Dodsworth: The Reanimated Englishman" (1863)

Collections

Tales and Stories (1891)

The Mary Shelley Reader (1990, edited by Betty T. Bennett and Charles E. Robinson)

The Mortal Immortal: The Complete Supernatural Short Fiction of Mary Shelley (1996)

Transformation (2004). Three stories with a supernatural theme: "The Mortal Immortal," "The Transformation" (1830), and "The Evil Eye" (1830).

As Editor

Posthumous Poems of Percy Bysshe Shelley (1824)

Adventures of a Younger Son, by Edward John Trelawny (1831)

Transfusion; or, The Orphan of Unwalden, by William Godwin Jr. (1835)

The Poetical Works of Percy Bysshe Shelley (1839)

Essays, Letters from Abroad, Translations and Fragments, by Percy Bysshe Shelley (1840)

In Other Media

The International Movie Database (IMDb) lists almost fifty movies and TV episodes that credit Mary Shelley's *Frankenstein* as their inspiration. These range from the sublime to the ridiculous: *Abbott and Costello Meet Frankenstein* (1948), *Mr. Magoo's Doctor Frankenstein* (1965), and *Alvin and the Chipmunks Meet Frankenstein* (1999), to name but a few.

Following are some of the most notable works based on the writing of Mary Shelley:

Frankenstein. Edison Manufacturing Company. 1910. Directed by J. Searle Dawley.

Frankenstein. Universal Pictures, 1931. Directed by James Whale; starring Boris Karloff.

The Bride of Frankenstein. Universal Pictures, 1935. Directed by James Whale; starring Boris Karloff and Elsa Lanchester.

The Curse of Frankenstein. Hammer Film Productions, 1957. Directed by Terence Fisher; starring Peter Cushing and Christopher Lee.

Young Frankenstein. Gruskoff/Venture Films, 1974. Directed by Mel Brooks; starring Gene Wilder and Peter Boyle.

Frankenstein. American Zoetrope, 1994. Directed by and starring Kenneth Branagh; also starring Robert de Niro and Helena Bonham Carter.

Nonfiction Books

History of Six Weeks' Tour through a Part of France, Switzerland, Germany, and Holland, with Letters Descriptive of a Sail round the Lake of Geneva, and of the Glaciers of Chamouni (1817)

Rambles in Germany and Italy in 1840, 1842, and 1843 (1844)

The Letters of Mary Wollstonecraft Shelley (1980) (edited by Betty T. Bennett)

Mary Shelley's Journal (1947) (edited by Frederick L. Jones)

Articles and Essays

"Author's Preface." *Frankenstein* (1818)

"Author's Introduction." *Frankenstein* (1831). Reprinted in the 1992 Penguin edition, pp. 5–10.

Bibliograpies

Garrett, Martin. *A Mary Shelley Chronology*. New York: Palgrave, 2002.

Lawson, Shannon. "Mary Wollstonecraft Shelley Chronology & Resource Site." *Romantic Circles* (June 1999). University of Maryland. http://www.rc.umd.edu/reference/chronologies/mschronology/mws.html

Voller, Jack G. "Mary Shelley." *The Literary Gothic,* February 3, 2007. http://www.litgothic.com/Authors/mshelley.html

For Further Information

Mary Wollstonecraft Shelley: http://people.brandeis.edu/~teuber/shelleybio.html

Aldiss, Brian. "Science Fiction's Mother Figure." In *The Detached Retina: Aspects of SF and Fantasy,* 52–86. Syracuse, NY: Syracuse University Press, 1995.

Aldiss, Brian, with David Wingrove. "On the Origin of Species: Mary Shelley." In *Speculations on Speculation: Theories of Science Fiction,* ed. James Gunn and Matthew Candelaria, 163–204. Lanham, MD: Scarecrow, 2005.

Badalamenti, Anthony F. "Why Did Mary Shelley Write *Frankenstein*?" *Journal of Religion & Health* 45 (2006): 419–39.

Bennett, Betty T. *Mary Wollstonecraft Shelley: An Introduction.* Baltimore, MD: Johns Hopkins University Press, 1998.

Bennett, Betty T., and Stuart Curran, eds. *Mary Shelley in Her Times.* Baltimore, MD: Johns Hopkins University Press, 2000.

Mellor, Anne K. *Mary Shelley: Her Life, Her Fiction, Her Monsters.* New York: Routledge, 1988.

Morrison, Lucy, et al. *A Mary Shelley Encyclopedia.* Westport, CT: Greenwood, 2003.

Nichols, Joan K. *Mary Shelley, Frankenstein's Creator: First Science Fiction Writer.* Berkeley, CA: Conari, 1998.

Purinton, Marjean D. "Mary Shelley's Science Fiction Short Stories and the Legacy of Wollstonecraft's Feminism." *Women's Studies* 30 (2001): 147–75.

Russ, Joanna. "On Mary Wollstonecraft Shelley." In *To Write Like a Woman: Essays in Feminism and Science Fiction*, 120–32. Bloomington: Indiana University Press, 1995.

Seymour, Miranda. *Mary Shelley*. New York: Grove, 2001.

Spark, Muriel. *Mary Shelley: A Biography*. New York: Dutton, 1987.

Williams, John. *Mary Shelley: A Literary Life.* New York, London: Macmillan, 2000.

Lucius Shepard

Military SF; Myth and Legend; Slipstream

Benchmark Title:
Life During Wartime (1987)

b. 1947 (Lynchburg, Virginia)

Writing fiction is like taking a rubbing of your brain. All the bulges and convolutions and fissures will show up in your work whether you want them to or not.
—"God Is in the Details" (1996)

Photo credit: Beth Gwinn

About the Author and the Author's Work

Lucius Shepard had done many things prior to 1980. He ran away from home at age fifteen, traveling to Ireland aboard a freighter and then working his way around Europe, North Africa, and Asia. While enrolled at the University of North Carolina, he traveled some more, to south Central America and Southeast Asia, at a time when these places were not obvious tourist destinations; he "ended his academic career as a tenth-semester sophomore with a heightened political sensibility, a fairly extensive knowledge of Latin American culture, and some pleasant memories" (luciusshepard.com/). He met and married his wife, Joy Wolf, and set off with her to California. To pay for urgent auto repairs after a breakdown on their way, he joined a rock 'n' roll band in Detroit, and for the remainder of the 1970s, when he wasn't traveling some more or taking odd jobs, he toured the Midwest with various bands. He and his wife had a son, Gullivar (now an architect in New York City).

Prior to 1980, the one thing that Lucius Shepard was *not* was a published author. But then, with encouragement from his wife—interviewed by *Locus* in 2001, he said, "I think she was trying to get me out of the house!"—he attended a Clarion Writers' Workshop at Michigan State University. He sold his first story in 1981; his first novel followed in 1984. In 1985 Lucius Shepard won the John W. Campbell Best New Author award. Since that late start, he has written a dozen novels; he has had half a dozen collections of his stories published and written enough short stories to fill many more.

Lucius Taylor Shepard was born in Lynchburg, Virginia, and "raised up hard" (Dunn 2001), as he has put it, by an abusive and demanding father in Daytona Beach, Florida. The young man took the earliest opportunity that presented itself to get away, and set off on the travels that led him to that Clarion workshop and his career as a writer. His fiction reflects the sometimes difficult and varied life he has led; for example, his affinity for Central and South American settings dates from the days when he visited Cuba, Mexico, and Guatemala with his mother, a teacher of Spanish. Shepard's stories tend to be set in the marginal and put-upon territories of the world, places that have been at the sharp end of the ambitions of bigger, more powerful nations. In stories such as *Life During Wartime* and "Salvador," Central America is the new Vietnam, where surgically altered and drugged troops replay a nightmare version of a conflict with no obvious exit strategy. *Green Eyes* (1984) is set in the bayous of Louisiana, a "dark universe of perversion, murder and voodoo" (Levy 1996).

Shepard writes, not about "heroes," but about people "who live on the fringes of society and find themselves caught up in impossible situations" (Matthews 2004). He is a "genre-bender": as the *Encyclopedia of Science Fiction* puts it, he "embeds SF elements" into his stories—the alien planet he is writing about is often called "Earth," but "hoboes ride trains that take them to other worlds, drug addicted soldiers fight guerilla warfare in the near future, and a man can share spiritual communion with iguanas. The line between reality and fantasy can be very thin" (Matthews 2004). As the author has said about his recent, most mainstream work, "It's mainstream, I guess, but it's weird" ("Banging Nails" 2004).

Lucius Shepard has also written nonfiction pieces on sports, particularly boxing, and during a prolonged trip to Central America in 1981–1982 he worked as a freelance journalist, reporting on the civil war in El Salvador. He is also a regular film reviewer for *The Magazine of Fantasy & Science Fiction* and *electricstory.com*. He currently lives in Vancouver, Washington.

Awards

Campbell New Writer Award (1985)

Novels

The Golden (1993) **Locus Poll**

Short Fiction

"Salvador" (1984) **Locus Poll**
"R & R" (1986) **Locus Poll, Nebula**
"The Scalehunter's Beautiful Daughter" (1988) **Locus Poll**
"The Father of Stones" (1989) **Locus Poll**
"Barnacle Bill the Spacer" (1992) **Hugo, Locus Poll**
"Radiant Green Star" (2000) **Locus Poll**
"Over Yonder" (2002) **Sturgeon**

Collections
The Jaguar Hunter (1987) **Locus Poll**

Works by the Author
Green Eyes (1984)
Life During Wartime (1987)
The Golden (1993)
Viator (2004)
Softspoken (2007)

Other Notable Mainstream and Genre Fiction
Valentine (2002)
Louisiana Breakdown (2003)
Colonel Rutherford's Colt (2003)
Floater (2003)
Liar's House (2004)
A Handbook of American Prayer (2004)
Trujillo (2004)

Other Notable Short Fiction
"Solitario's Eyes" (1983)
"The Man Who Painted the Dragon Griaule" (1984)
"A Traveler's Tale" (1984)
"The Night of White Bhairab" (1984). http://www.electricstory.com/stories/story.aspx?title=bhairab/bhairab
"The Jaguar Hunter" (1985). http://www.infinityplus.co.uk/stories/jaguarhunter.htm
"Aymara" (1986)
"Delta Sly Honey" (1987)
"Shades" (1987)
"The Sun Spider (1987)
"Youthful Folly" (1988)
"The All-Consuming" (1990, with Robert Frazier)
"Kalimantan" (1990)
"Beast of the Heartland" (1992)
"Crocodile Rock" (1999)
"AZTECHS" (2001)
"Jailwise" (2003)
"Only Partly Here" (2003)
"Stars Seen Through Stone" (2007)
"Vacancy" (2007)

Collections

The Jaguar Hunter (1987)
The Ends of the Earth (1991)
Beast of the Heartland and Other Stories (1999; UK: *Barnacle Bill the Spacer and Other Stories*)
Two Trains Running (2004)
Eternity and Other Stories (2005)
Dagger Key and Other Stories (2007)
The Best of Lucius Shepard (2008)

Nonfiction Books

Sports & Music (1994)
Weapons of Mass Seduction (2005, movie reviews)

Articles and Essays

"God Is in the Details." In *Paragons: Twelve Master Science Fiction Writers Ply Their Craft,* ed. Robin Wilson, 195–205. New York: St. Martin's, 1996.
"Introduction." In *Brighten to Incandescence,* by Michael Bishop. Urbana, IL: Golden Gryphon, 2003.

Bibliographies

Contento, William G. "Lucius Shepard: A Bibliography." *Magazine of Fantasy and Science Fiction* 100, no. 3 (2001): 85–88.
Stephens, Christopher P., and Tom Joyce. *A Checklist of Lucius Shepard.* Rev. ed. Hastings-on-Hudson, NY: Ultramarine, 1991.

For Further Information

Official Web site: http://lucius-shepard.com/

"Banging Nails." *Locus* (November 2001). http://www.locusmag.com/2001/Issue11/Shepard.html
Blaschke, Jayme L. "Interview: Lucius Shepard." *Strange Horizons,* January 5, 2004. http://www.strangehorizons.com/2004/20040105/shepard.shtml
Dunn, Katherine. "An Introduction to Lucius Shepard." *Magazine of Fantasy and Science Fiction* 100, no. 3 (2001): 4–10.
Gevers, Nick. Interview. *SciFi.com* (April 2003).
Kelly, James Patrick. "How to Talk to Lucius Shepard." In *Essays/Appreciations*. 1995. At Jim Kelly.com. http://www.jimkelly.net/index.php?option=com_content&task=view&id=51&Itemid=49
Levy, Michael M. "Lucius Shepard." In *St. James Guide to Science Fiction Writers,* ed. Jay Pedersen. Detroit, MI: St. James, 1996.

Martini, Adrienne. "An Interview with Lucius Shepard." *Bookslut.com* (December 2004). http://www.bookslut.com/features/2004_12_003799.php

Matthews, Aaron. "Lucius Shepard: Borges, Influence and References." In *Jorge Luis Borges: The Garden of Forking Paths*. The Modern Word, January 2004. http://www.themodernword.com/borges/borges_infl_shepard.html

Vander Meer, Jeff. "Prolofic and Prodigious." *Rain Taxi* (Winter 2004). http://vanderworld.blogspot.com/2005/07/lucius-shepard.html

West, Jen. Interview. *Nebula Awards*, November 3, 2008. http://www.nebulaawards.com/index.php/interview/lucius_shepard/

Robert Silverberg

Hard SF; Science Fantasy

Benchmark Title: *Dying Inside* (1972)

b. 1935 (Brooklyn, NY)

And I do wonder, even though I understand what 50 years is, 'How the hell did you write all that?' Well, you do it one word at a time.
—"One Word at a Time," *Locus* (2004)

Photo credit: Beth Gwinn

About the Author and the Author's Work

Robert Silverberg has been a professional writer since he was twenty years old. "Have never had a day job, or, for that matter, any sort of job at all. Writing has been my sole means of livelihood" (Hunt 2002). In 1956 he was awarded a Nebula as "Most Promising New Author," the youngest recipient of the award. By 1959 he had seen eleven novels and more than 200 of his short works published, often under a pen name so magazine readers didn't see the name "Silverberg" again and again in the table of contents. By the time Robert Silverberg received the Damon Knight Memorial Grand Master Award, in April 2004, he had published more than 400 stories and approximately eighty novels—and that is his SF alone.

Robert Silverberg was born in Brooklyn, New York, an only child who found companionship in SF and fantasy. He graduated from Columbia University with a BA in English literature in 1956; his first novel was published while he was there. By his own count, during the 1950s he wrote a million words a year; when the market for science fiction collapsed at the end of that decade, he turned to other genres—history, popular science, anthropology, and erotica (again, written under an assumed name). Silverberg's SF career can be roughly divided into three "eras"—his early apprenticeship, in which he wrote a staggering amount of workmanlike, "good, old-fashioned" genre stories; the period from the mid-1960s to the mid-1970s, when he took advantage of changing tastes to write stories that paid far more attention to depth of character and social background, stories with ambiguous or even negative conclusions, that experimented with form and content, and harkened back to the modernist literature he had studied at Columbia—in effect, his own personal "New Wave"; and finally, in the early 1980s, short fiction that *Locus* describes as "formally inventive, psychologically astute, and idea-rich," such as "Our Lady of the Sauropods" (1980), "Sailing to Byzantium" (1985), and "The Secret Sharer" (1988—a "SF-ization" of Joseph Conrad's story of the same title).

Robert Silverberg remains the youngest writer ever to win a Nebula; he has also won major awards in six consecutive decades (from the 1950s through the 2000s): "My goal now is to become the oldest to win one, but Jack Williamson, who won a Hugo at the age of 91 or so a few years back, has made that a very difficult challenge" (Hunt 2002). Given the length of his career and the breadth and quality of his output, it is almost impossible to say *this* is Silverberg at his best, or *that* is "typical Silverberg." In the course of his career, Silverberg has probably tackled each and every trope and twist of SF—alien invasion and occupation, the exploitation of indigenous alien species, the personal cost of extraordinary power (personal and political), time travel, overpopulation and its impact on society, eco-futurism, SF horror—a list like this merely scratches the surface. A common thread that runs through Silverberg's novels and stories is *redemption*—whether it is the repentant colonial administrator who takes a leap of faith to cleanse his conscience regarding the alien race he patronized and exploited (*Downward to the Earth*), or the telepath who must come to terms with losing the powers he once considered a curse (*Dying Inside*). Even *Lord Valentine's Castle*, the opening novel of what would become the Majipoor series of jolly heroic fantasies, has the serious subtext of a man who awakens to the fact that he is not who he seems—and perhaps he doesn't much like the man he once was.

Robert Silverberg continues to write, to encourage young, upcoming writers, and to delight his fans. When he is *not* writing, he collects artifacts, ancient and modern, and travels widely. He lives with his wife Karen Haber, who is also a writer and a scholar of science fiction, in Oakland, California.

Awards

Most Promising New Author (1956) **Hugo**
Milford Award for lifetime achievement in SF publishing and editing (1981)
Edward E. Smith Memorial Award for Imaginative Fiction ("Skylark award") (1984)
SF Hall of Fame (1999)
Retro Hugo—Fan Writer, 1950 (2001)
Prix Utopia (2002)
SFWA Damon Knight Memorial Grand Master (2004)

Novels

Nightwings (1969) **Hugo**
A Time of Changes (1971) **Nebula**
Dying Inside (1972) **Campbell, Special Award**
Lord Valentine's Castle (1980) **Locus Poll**

Short Fiction

"Passengers" (1968) **Nebula**

"Good News from the Vatican" (1971) **Nebula**
"Born with the Dead" (1974) **Locus Poll, Nebula**
"Sailing to Byzantium" (1985) **Nebula**
"Gilgamesh in the Outback" **Hugo**
"Secret Sharer" (1987) **Locus Poll**
"Enter a Soldier. Later, Enter Another" (1989) **Hugo**

Collections

The Collected Stories of Robert Silverberg, Volume 1: Secret Sharers (1992) **Locus Poll**

As Editor

The Science Fiction Hall of Fame Volume 1 (1970) **Locus Poll**
Epoch (1975, with Roger Elwood) **Locus Poll**
The Avram Davidson Treasury (1998, with Grania Davis) **Locus Poll**
Legends (1998) **Locus Poll**
Far Horizons (1999) **Locus Poll**

Works by the Author

Revolt on Alpha C (1955)
The Thirteenth Immortal (1956)
Master of Life and Death (1957)
The Shrouded Planet (1957, with Randall Garrett, as "Robert Randall")
Aliens from Space (1958, as "David Osborne")
Collision Course (1958)
Invaders from Earth (1958)
Invisible Barriers (1958, as "David Osborne")
Lest We Forget You, Earth (1958, as "Calvin M. Knox")
Starman's Quest (1958)
The Dawning Light (1959, with Randall Garrett, as "Robert Randall")
The Planet Killers (1959)
Lost Race of Mars (1960)
The Seed of Earth (1962)
Recalled to Life (1962)
The Silent Invaders (1963)
Time of the Great Freeze (1963)
Regan's Planet (1964)
Conquerors from the Darkness (1965)
The Gate of Worlds (1967)
Planet of Death (1967)

Thorns (1967)
Those Who Watch (1967)
The Time Hoppers (1967)
To Open the Sky (1967)
Hawksbill Station (1968)
The Man in the Maze (1968)
The Masks of Time (1968)
World's Fair 1992 (1968)
Across a Billion Years (1969)
Nightwings (1969)
Three Survived (1969)
To Live Again (1969)
Up the Line (1969)
Downward to the Earth (1970)
Tower of Glass (1970)
Son of Man (1971)
The Second Trip (1971)
A Time of Changes (1971)
The World Inside (1971)
The Book of Skulls (1972)
Dying Inside (1972)
The Stochastic Man (1975)
Shadrach in the Furnace (1976)
Tom O'Bedlam (1985)
Star of Gypsies (1986)
The Mutant Season (1989, with Karen Haber)
Nightfall (1990, with Isaac Asimov)
To the Land of the Living (1990)
Thebes of the Hundred Gates (1991)
The Face of the Waters (1991)
Kingdoms of the Wall (1992)
The Positronic Man (1992, with Isaac Asimov)
The Ugly Little Boy (1992, with Isaac Asimov)
Hot Sky at Midnight (1994)
Starborne (1996)
The Alien Years (1998)
The Longest Way Home (2002)
Roma Eterna (2003)
Seventh Shrine (2004, with Andres Finer)

Majipoor series

Lord Valentine's Castle (1980)
Majipoor Chronicles (1982)
Valentine Pontifex (1983)
The Mountains of Majipoor (1995)

Majipoor: The Prestimion Trilogy

Sorcerers of Majipoor (1997)
Lord Prestimion (1999)
The King of Dreams (2001)

New Springtime

At Winter's End (1988)
The New Springtime (1990; aka *The Queen of Springtime*)

Other Notable Genre Fiction

Lord of Darkness (1983)
Gilgamesh the King (1984)

Notable Short Fiction

"Hawksbill Station" (1967)
"Sundance" (1969)
"To Jorslem" (1969)
"Caught in the Organ Draft" (1972)
"When We Went to See the End of the World" (1972)
"The Feast of St. Dionysus" (1973)
"Ms. Found in an Abandoned Time Machine" (1973)
"Schwartz Between the Galaxies" (1974)
"The Desert of Stolen Dreams" (1981)
"The Pope of the Chimps" (1982)
"Thesme and the Ghayrog" (1982)
"Homefaring" (1983)
"Looking for the Fountain" (1992)
"Via Roma" (1994)
"The Mountains of Majipoor" (1995)
"Sorcerers of Majipoor" (1996)
"On the Inside" (1997)
"The Colonel in Autumn" (1998)
"With Caesar in the Underworld" (2002)
"The Emperor and the Maula" (2007)

Collections

Needle in a Timestack (1966)
The Calibrated Alligator (1969)
Dimension Thirteen (1969)
The Cube Root of Uncertainty (1970)
Moonferns & Starsongs (1971)
Valley Beyond Time (1972)
The Reality Trip and Other Implausibilities (1972)
Unfamiliar Territory (1973)
Sunrise on Mercury (1975)
The Shores of Tomorrow (1976)
The Best of Robert Silverberg (1976)
Next Stop the Stars (1977)
Capricorn Games (1979)
World of a Thousand Colors (1982)
The Conglomeroid Cocktail Party (1984)
Sailing to Byzantium (2000)
Phases of the Moon: Stories from Six Decades (2004)
To Be Continued: The Collected Stories of Robert Silverberg (2006)
In the Beginning (2006)
To the Dark Star: The Collected Stories Volume 2 (2007)
Something Wild Is Loose: The Collected Stories Volume 3 (2008)

The Collected Stories of Robert Silverberg

Beyond the Safe Zone (1986)
Pluto in the Morning Light (1992)
Secret Sharers (1992),
The Road to Nightfall (1996)
Ringing the Changes (1997)
Lion Time in Timbuctoo (2000)

As Editor

According to the International Science Fiction Database (ISFDb), Robert Silverberg is the editor, alone or in collaboration, of over 80 anthologies. The following is a selection of award-winning and nominated volumes from across his career.

Great Short Novels of Science Fiction (1970)
The Science Fiction Hall of Fame Volume 1 (1970)
The Nebula Awards No. 18 (1983)
Robert Silverberg's Worlds of Wonder (1987)
Far Horizons: The Great Worlds of Science Fiction (1999)
Nebula Awards Showcase (2001)

Fantasy: The Best of 2001 (2001, with Karen Haber)
Science Fiction 101: Where to Start Reading and Writing Science Fiction (2001)
The Great SF Stories: 1964 (2002, with Martin H. Greenberg)
Science Fiction: The Best of 2002 (2002, with Karen Haber)
Between Worlds (2004)
Chains of the Sea (1974)
Threads of Time (1974)
Epoch (1975, with Roger Elwood)
The New Atlantis (1975)
The Crystal Ship (1976)
The Edge of Space (1979)
A Century of Science Fiction, 1950–1959 (1997)
The Avram Davidson Treasury (1998, with Grania Davis)
Alpha series (1970–1978)
The Arbor House Treasuries (1980, 1983, with Martin H. Greenberg)
Legends series (1998–2004)
New Dimensions series (1971–1981)
Universe (1990, 1992, 1994, with Karen Haber)

In Other Media

Amanda and the Alien. IRS Media, 1995. Directed by Jon Kroll; starring Nicole Eggert, Michael Dorn, and Stacey Keach. Based on a short story by Silverberg.

Bicentennial Man. 1492 Pictures, 1999. Directed by Chris Columbus; starring Robin Williams and Sam Neill. Based on the novel *The Positronic Man* (1992), which Silverberg cowrote with Isaac Asimov.

Nonfiction Books

First American into Space (1961)
Lost Cities and Vanished Civilizations (1962)
Men Against Time: Salvage Archaeology in the United States (1967)
Drug Themes in Science Fiction (1974)
The Realm of Prester John (1996)
Reflections and Refractions: Thoughts on Science-Fiction, Science, and Other Matters (1997)

Articles and Essays

Introduction to "Sundance." In *Those Who Can: A Science Fiction Reader*, ed. Robin Scott Wilson, 149–54. New York: St. Martin's, 1996 (orig. pub. 1973).

"Introduction." In *Virtual Unrealities: The Short Fiction of Alfred Bester,* ed. Robert Silverberg, Byron Preiss, and Keith R. A. DeCandido. New York: Vintage Books, 1997.

"Introduction." In *The War of the Worlds: Fresh Perspectives on the H.G. Wells Classic,* ed. Glenn Yeffeth. Dallas, TX: BenBella, 2005.

"Reflections: The Conquest of Space." *Asimov's Science Fiction* (April 2003). Dell Magazines. http://www.asimovs.com/_issue_0304/ref.shtml

"Sounding Brass, Tinkling Cymbal." In *Hell's Cartographers: Some Personal Histories of Science Fiction Writers,* ed. Brian W. Aldiss and Harry Harrison. London, 7–45. Weidenfeld, 1975. This volume also includes Silverberg's contribution to "How We Work" (pp. 213–17).

Bibliographies

Clareson, Thomas D. *Robert Silverberg: A Primary and Secondary Bibliography*. Boston: G. K. Hall, 1983.

Bibliography. *Majipoor: The Quasi-Official Robert Silverberg Website,* ed. Jon Davis. http://www.majipoor.com/

For Further Information

The Quasi-Official Robert Silverberg Website, ed. Jon Davis: http://www.majipoor.com/

Chapman, Edgar L. *The Road to Castle Mount: The Science Fiction of Robert Silverberg*. Westport, CT: Greenwood, 1999.

Clareson, Thomas D. "Robert Silverberg." In *Voices for the Future: Essays on Major Science Fiction Writers Vol. 1,* ed. Thomas D. Clareson, 1–33. Bowling Green: Bowling Green University Popular Press, 1977.

Elkins, Charles L., and Martin Harry Greenberg, eds. *Robert Silverberg's Many Trapdoors: Critical Essays on His Science Fiction*. Westport, CT: Greenwood, 1992.

Freund, Jim. Interview. *Hour of the Wolf,* September 7, 1997. WBAI New York. http://www.hourwolf.com/chats/silverberg.html

Horwich, David. "Interview: Robert Silverberg." *Strange Horizons,* December 11, 2000. http://www.strangehorizons.com/2000/20001211/silverberg.shtml

Huddleston, Kathie. Interview. *Science Fiction Weekly,* August 5, 2002.

Hunt, Stephen. "Hot Spice and Majipoor." *SF Crowsnest* (July 2002). http://www.sfcrowsnest.com

Lalumière, Claude. "A Brief History of Robert Silverberg." *Locus Online,* October 13, 2004. http://www.locusmag.com/2004/Reviews/10_LalumiereOnSilverberg.html

"One Word at a Time." *Locus* (March 2004). http://www.locusmag.com/2004/Issues/03Silverberg.html

Stableford, Brian M. In "The Metamorphosis of Robert Silverberg." *Outside the Human Aquarium: Masters of Science Fiction,* 37–48. San Bernardino, CA: Borgo, 1995.

Dan Simmons

Myth and Legend; SF Horror

Benchmark Title: *Hyperion* (1989)

b. 1948 (Peoria, Illinois)

It's a pleasure to shift from one genre-skin to another . . . just as a break from the concentrated effort of levitating a certain kind of novel into being, of focusing on a certain bent of vocabulary or tech-think for too long.
—Lilley, Interview in *SFRevu* (2003)

Photo credit: Cliff Grassmick.
Permission of Dan Simmons.

About the Author and the Author's Work

Hyperion, by Dan Simmons, is what might have resulted if Chaucer's pilgrims had been on the road to deep space, instead of Canterbury, or the young *aristos* of Boccaccio's *Decameron* had taken refuge on a spaceship instead of an Italian country villa. It is the story of seven strangers who have been summoned to the planet Hyperion by the terrible Shrike, the guardian of the Time Tombs. The travelers all have secrets; they all carry burdens from the past. The *Encyclopedia of Science Fiction* (1999) calls it "a space opera about the end of things . . . the displacement of the old gods, the victory of a new pantheon."

Dan Simmons uses allusions to classic—some might even say, unlikely—writers to enhance the depth and substance of his narratives. The first two volumes of the <u>Hyperion Cantos</u> take their titles, and some of their rich mythic texture, from poems by Keats; Simmons's very first, prize-winning story had the *Cantos* of Ezra Pound at the very heart of the narrative. Other stories and novels have used Gerard Manley Hopkins, Dante's *Divine Comedy*, T. S. Eliot, and Vladimir Nabokov. More recently, Simmons has been looking to history for his inspiration: in *Ilium* (2003), a race of meta-humans on Mars decide to call themselves gods and re-create the Trojan War with reconstituted Greeks and Trojans. His 2007 novel *The Terror* is based on the ill-fated Franklin expedition to the Canadian Arctic to find the Northwest Passage. Although not SF, like all of Simmons's other genre and mainstream works, it uses fantastic elements—in this case, Inuit legend—to conjecture about the mystery of the fate of Franklin and his crew. *Drood* (2009), Simmons's most recent and highly regarded novel, is based on the final years of the life of Charles Dickens.

Simmons was born in Peoria, Illinois, and grew up in the Midwest. He has a BA in English from Wabash College in Indiana, and a master's in education from Washington University in St. Louis, Missouri. For eighteen years he wrote in his spare time while teaching elementary school in Missouri, Buffalo, New York, and Colorado. By all accounts he was a devoted and inspirational teacher, winning various teaching awards and developing programs for encouraging gifted students and for improved writing skills for all ages and achievement levels; the classroom results of his "Write Well" curriculum led to a position as a national language arts consultant.

Meanwhile, there was his own writing. His first published story, "The River Styx Runs Upstream," won first prize in a *Twilight Zone Magazine* story competition and appeared in that magazine in February 1982, on the very day his daughter, Jane Kathryn, was born. That coincidence, as Simmons says on his Web site, helps him to keep "things in perspective when it comes to the relative importance of writing and life."

Simmons's earliest work could be described as horror with SF underpinnings: "He mixes SF-style telekinetics with horrific set pieces straight out of Dante's *Inferno*" (Shindler 2002). He is unafraid of mixing styles and genres—detective fiction, historical romance, and dark comedy horror; what Darmon Schindler, in a profile in *Salon*, describes as "Jamesian spookiness and Alfred Hitchcock thrills." Simmons has never lost his passion for improving the art of writing; he has lectured at various universities across the United States and taught in New Hampshire's Odyssey writing program for adults. In 1995 Wabash College awarded him an honorary doctorate for his contributions to education and writing.

Dan Simmons lives with his wife and daughter along the Front Range of the Colorado Rocky Mountains and does much of his writing at Windwalker, the family's mountain retreat at the base of the Continental Divide just south of Rocky Mountain National Park. An eight-foot-tall sculpture of *Hyperion*'s Shrike—a gift from a former student—stands guard near the isolated cabin.

Awards

Novels

Hyperion (1989) **Hugo, Locus Poll**

Carrion Comfort (1989) **Locus Poll**

The Fall of Hyperion (1990) **BSF, Locus Poll**

Summer of Night (1991) **Locus Poll**

Children of the Night (1992) **Locus Poll**

Fires of Eden (1994) **Locus Poll**

The Rise of Endymion (1997) **Locus Poll**

Ilium (2003) **Locus Poll**

Short Fiction

"Entropy's Bed at Midnight" (1990) **Locus Poll**

"All Dracula's Children" (1991) **Locus Poll**

"This Year's Class Picture" (1992) **Sturgeon**

"Death in Bangkok" (1993) **Locus Poll**
"Orphans of the Helix" (1999) **Locus Poll**

Collections

Prayers to Broken Stones (1990) **Bram Stoker**

Works by the Author

Phases of Gravity (1989)
Ilium (2003)
Olympos (2005)

The Hyperion Cantos

Hyperion (1989)
The Fall of Hyperion (1990)
Endymion (1995)
The Rise of Endymion (1997)

Other Genre Fiction

Song of Kali (1985)
Carrion Comfort (1989)
Summer of Night (1991)
Children of the Night (1992)
The Hollow Man (1992)
Fires of Eden (1994)
The Crook Factory (1999)
Darwin's Blade (2000)
A Winter Haunting (2002)
The Terror (2007)
Drood (2009)

Joe Kurtz

Hardcase (2001)
Hard Freeze (2002)
Hard as Nails (2003)

Other Notable Short Fiction

"The River Styx Flows Upstream" (1982)
"Remembering Siri" (1983)
"Metastasis" (1988)
"Flashback" (1993)

"The Great Lover (*Le Grand Amant*)" (1993)
"Looking for Kelly Dahl" (1995)
"The End of Gravity" (2002)
"On K2 with Kanakaredes" (2002)
"Muse of Fire" (2007)

Collections

Prayers to Broken Stones (1990)
LoveDeath (1993)
Worlds Enough and Time: Five Tales of Speculative Fiction (2002)

Nonfiction Books

Going After the Rubber Chicken, Three Guest of Honor Speeches (1991)
Summer Sketches (1992)
Writing Well. Dan Simmons Official Web site. 2006–2009. http://www.dansimmons.com/writing_welll/archive/writing_index.htm

For Further Information

Official Web site: http://www.dansimmons.com/

Interview. *SF World.com,* February 6, 2007. http://www.SFfworld.com/mul/218p0.html

Lilley, Ernest. Interview. *SFRevu* (July 2003). http://www.sfrevu.com/ISSUES/2003/0307/Dan%20Simmons%20Interview/Review.htm

Schweitzer, Darrell, ed. "Dan Simmons Interview." In *Speaking of the Fantastic,* 158–71. Holicong, PA: Wildside, 2002.

Sheehan, Bill. "The Void and the Word: Dan Simmons' Complete Hyperion Cantos." *Nova Express* 5, no. 1 (1998). http://home.roadrunner.com/~lperson1/hyperion.html

Shindler, Dorman T. "The Outsider." *Salon,* February 27, 2002. http://dir.salon.com/story/books/int/2002/02/27/simmons/index.html

Silver, Steven H. "A Conversation with Dan Simmons." *SF Site* (July 2003). http://www.SFsite.com/09b/ds160.htm

Cordwainer Smith
[Paul Linebarger]

Myth and Legend; Post-human SF

Benchmark Title: "Scanners Live in Vain" (1950)

b. 1913 (Milwaukee, Wisconsin); d. 1966 (Baltimore, Maryland)

Photo credit: Courtesy of The Estate of Cordwainer Smith

[I]t is tough to be modern; the difficulty of being modern makes it easy for individuals to be restless and anxious; restlessness and anxiety lead to fear; fear converts freely into hate; hate very easily takes on political form; political hate assists in the creation of real threats such as the atomic bomb and guided missiles, which are not imaginary threats at all.
—*Psychological Warfare* (1948)

About the Author and the Author's Work

However strange the creations of golden age SF writer Cordwainer Smith may seem, they can hardly be more strange and impressive than the story of the man who created the author with the action hero name, the true source of the tales of Norstrilia, Scanners and Habermans, Underpeople, and The Instrumentality. Paul Linebarger—otherwise known as "Cordwainer Smith"—was a godson of Sun Yat-sen, the man who ended 4,000 years of imperial rule and invented modern China; he was a friend and advisor of Chiang Kai-shek, the military leader who saved China from the Japanese but lost it to Mao Tse-Tung and the Chinese Communist Party. He was a major in the U.S. Army during World War II who was recalled to active service in the 1950s and 1960s to act as a "visitor to small wars" and freelance intelligence officer for the CIA; he was an advisor to President John F. Kennedy. Fluent in six languages and author of serious volumes on the history and political development of China, a pioneer of the science of psychological warfare, as "Cordwainer Smith" Linebarger wrote novels about a nightmarish far-future in which 100-ton sheep are milked for an immortality drug; animals, genetically modified into human form and intelligence, are enslaved; and criminals are punished, like Prometheus, by having their organs harvested for transplant and regrown, endlessly. Paul Linebarger was not the most prolific of SF writers—the other demands on his time were too varied, and his life was cut off at a point when he might have been able to give his imaginary worlds more of his attention. But the impact of his vision on the ideas and style of writers who have followed him, means that his importance is out of all proportion to his output.

Paul Myron Anthony Linebarger was born in Milwaukee, Wisconsin, but spent his childhood moving around Asia and Europe as his father, a lawyer and political activist with close ties to Sun Yat-Sen, advocated for the aims of the Chinese revolution of 1911. Cordwainer Smith scholar Alan C. Elms puts the strangeness of this childhood into context in his essay "The Creation of Cordwainer Smith," comparing it to "a modern-day conservative American judge in the Panama Canal Zone retiring and going down to join the *Sandanistas*." His godfather, Sun Yat-sen, took an affectionate interest in him throughout his life: he gave young Paul the Chinese name Lin Bai-lo, which roughly translates as "Forest of Incandescent Bliss." Paul Linebarger honored this connection by using the occasional pen name "Felix C. Forrest" and, later in life, wearing a tie embroidered with the Chinese characters for his name (Patterson 2005).

Linebarger was blinded in his right eye in a childhood accident, and the vision in his remaining eye was impaired by infection, but despite these setbacks, by age twenty-three he had earned a PhD in political science from Johns Hopkins University. During World War II he was involved in the development of military intelligence, the army's first psychological warfare section, and was sent to China to coordinate military intelligence operations there. Science fiction biographer George C. Willick (2006) imagines the scene:

> [H]e looked like a spy. Linebarger was hawk featured, slight, wore the gray fedora hat, and had tinted glasses because of his visual problems (may even have been unable to resist wearing a patch occasionally). While his appearance may have made the Devil break stride, his toothy, winning grin worked for him and coupled with his brilliant mind, allowed him to survive.

Linebarger published a total of thirty-two SF stories and three novels, interconnected episodes in the "Instrumentality of Mankind." Strange, stylized stories such as "The Ballad of Lost C'mell," "The Dead Lady of Clown Town," and "The Game of Rat and Dragon" blend sociology and flamboyant pseudo-science; the style and substance reflect his easy familiarity with philosophy and mythology, particularly of the East. His history of the Instrumentality and the Underpeople who serve it reflects a keen political awareness that the downtrodden don't stay trodden down forever. His stories randomly cover the full extent of Instrumentality history, from its earliest days ("Scanners Live in Vain") to the "Rediscovery of Man," a point in the distant future when Underpeople have taken their place in society ("Alphs Ralpha Boulevard," *Quest for Three Worlds*).

Toward the end of his life Paul Linebarger became a devout Episcopalian and began to include layers of religious allegory in his tales of the Instrumentality. He most certainly had more to say and would have found ever more interesting ways to say it, but he died suddenly of a heart attack in 1966, in Baltimore, Maryland. He is buried beside his wife, Genevieve, in Arlington National Cemetery in Washington DC.

Works by the Author

The Planet Buyer (1964)
The Underpeople (1968)
Norstrilia (1975)

Other Notable Genre Fiction

Ria (1947, as "Felix C. Forrest")
Carola (1948, as "Felix C. Forrest")
Atomsk: A Novel of Suspense (1949, as "Carmichael Smith")

Notable Short Fiction

"Scanners Live in Vain" (1950)
"The Game of Rat and Dragon" (1955)
"No, No, Not Rogov!" (1959)
"Alpha Ralpha Boulevard" (1961)
"Mother Hitton's Littul Kittons" (1961)
"A Planet Named Shayol" (1961)
"The Ballad of Lost C'mell" (1962)
"Think Blue, Count Two" (1963)
"The Dead Lady of Clown Town" (1964)
"On the Storm Planet" (1965)
"Under Old Earth" (1966)
"Down to a Sunless Sea" (1975)

Collections

You Will Never Be the Same (1963)
Space Lords (1965)
Quest of the Three Worlds (1966)
Under Old Earth and Other Explorations (1970)
Stardreamer (1971)
The Instrumentality of Mankind (1979)
The Best of Cordwainer Smith (1975, edited by John J. Pierce)
The Rediscovery of Man: The Complete Short Science Fiction of Cordwainer Smith (1993)
We the Underpeople (2006)
When the People Fell (2007)

Nonfiction Books

The Political Doctrines of Sun Yat-Sen: An Exposition of San Min Chu I (1937)

Government in Republican China (1938)

The China of K'ai-shek: A Political Study (1941)

Psychological Warfare (1948)

Articles and Essays

"Prologue and Epilogue." In *Space Lords* (1965)

Bibliographies

Bennett, Mike. *A Cordwainer Smith Checklist*. Polk City: Chris Drumm, 1991.

Willick, George C. "Bibliography." *Spacelight* (June 2006). http://www.gcwillick.com/Spacelight/smith_c.html

For Further Information

The Remarkable Science Fiction of Cordwainer Smith. Ed. Rosana Linebarger Hart. Hartworks: http://www.cordwainersmith.com

Elms, Alan C., ed. "Between Mottile and Ambiloxi: Cordwainer Smith as a Southern Writer." *Extrapolation* 42 (2001): 124–36.

———. *Cordwainer Smith Unofficial Biography Page*. March 2007. http://www.ulmus.net/ace/menus/ace_s5_c7_b0_d0_x.html

———. "The Creation of Cordwainer Smith." *Science Fiction Studies* 11 (1984): 264–83. Although this is an older article and may be difficult to find, it contains a very thorough (and even amusing) narrative of Linebarger's early life—well worth reading.

Hellekson, Karen L. *The Science Fiction of Cordwainer Smith*. Jefferson, NC: McFarland, 2001.

Le Guin, Ursula. "Thinking About Cordwainer Smith." In *The Wave in the Mind: Talks and Essays on the Writer, the Reader, and the Imagination*. Boston: Shambhala, 2004.

Lewis, Anthony R. *Concordance to Cordwainer Smith*. Cambridge: New England Science Fiction Association, 2000.

McGuirk, Carol. "The Rediscovery of Cordwainer Smith." *Science Fiction Studies* 28 (2001): 161–200.

Patterson, Michael Robert. Biography. *Arlington National Cemetary Website*. November 2005. http://www.arlingtoncemetery.net/linebarg.htm

Porter, Andrew, John Foyster, and John Bangsund, eds. *Exploring Cordwainer Smith*. New York: Algol, 1975.

E. E. "Doc" Smith

Early SF; Space Opera

Benchmark Title: *The Skylark of Space* (1928)

b. 1890 (Sheboygan, Wisconsin); d. 1965 (Seaside, Oregon)

[My] characters get away from me and do exactly as they damn please.
—"The Epic of Space" (1947)

About the Author and the Author's Work

One evening in 1915, at a dinner party in Washington, D.C., two young couples rounded off a pleasant evening together by chatting about space travel. The hostess, Mrs. Lee Hawkins Garby, suggested that one of her guests, Dr. E. E. Smith, write a story set in outer space, which he agreed to do, if Mrs. Garby would handle the romance and the dialogue. Mrs. Garby gradually lost interest, but Dr. Smith kept doggedly at it, finishing *The Skylark of Space* in 1920. It was eight years before he found a publisher, and *Amazing Stories* serialized it, beginning in the August 1928 issue (Hugo Gernsback insisted on keeping the "PhD" after Smith's name, as it sounded classy). Smith estimated that he spent far more on postage to publishers and magazines than the princely $125 he received for his work, but no matter: E. E. "Doc" Smith, whose thesis in food science dealt with "*the effect of bleaching with oxides of nitrogen upon the baking quality and commercial value of wheat flour,*" whose day job involved developing flour mixes for doughnuts, had invented "space opera."

Edward Elmer Smith was born in Sheboygan, Wisconsin. His father was a sailor, born in Maine; his mother was a teacher from Michigan. When he was twelve, the family moved to Seneaquoteen, near the Pend d'Oreille River in Idaho, where his father farmed. Smith graduated from The University of Idaho in 1914 with two degrees in chemistry (in 1984 he was installed in the University of Idaho Alumni Hall of Fame). After graduation he worked for some time as a chemist for the National Bureau of Standards in Washington, D.C., developing standards for butter and oysters. Meanwhile, he was working on his master's degree at George Washington University, which he received in 1917, and a doctorate in chemical engineering, which followed a year later. In spite of the heady success of *Skylark* and subsequent volumes—for *Skylark Three* he was paid an unheard of three-quarters of a cent per word—Smith never gave up his "day job." Except for an interlude during World War II, when war-time rationing cut back the production of "luxury" cereal food like doughnuts, and he worked as a chemist for the U.S. Army, Smith worked as a food technologist for various companies until he retired. SF fans are enchanted by the claim that Smith's food technology research led to the process that binds powdered sugar to donuts. Sadly, this has never been substantiated—but it makes a wonderful story.

"Doc" Smith painted his interstellar adventures on a big canvas, with broad brushstrokes. Dialogue was not his strong point (one of the "feminine" touches that Mrs. Garby had been enlisted to supply). As a scientist he was conscious of scientific plausibility—for the series that followed *The Skylark of Space*, Spacehounds of the IPC, he aimed for a higher degree of scientific rigor, "not, like the Skylarks, pseudo-science" (Sheridan 1977). But it did not go over well—readers complained that he had cramped his style by limiting the action to the solar system, and they had to be reassured that in his next story, the first in his Lensman series, "scientific detail would not be bothered about, and . . . his imagination would run riot" (Warner 1939). He never made that mistake again: according to the *Encyclopedia of Science Fiction*, "Doc" Smith's great contribution to modern SF was to "define its essential territory, galactic space."

Dr. Smith retired from food technology in 1957 and devoted himself to his second career. He had always been an enthusiastic supporter of SF fandom—as guest of honor at the second World Science Fiction Convention in Chicago in 1940, his keynote speech "What Does This Convention Mean?" addressed the importance of fans to the genre. But once he retired, he was able to step up his involvement a notch—he and Mrs. Smith would spend several weeks of the summer and early autumn each year driving from their home in Seaside, Oregon, to their winter home in Clearwater, Florida, and back again, crisscrossing the country and stopping at SF cons along the route. "Doc" Smith died suddenly, in Seaside, on August 31, 1965, as he and Mrs. Smith were preparing to return to Florida.

But his legacy lives on, honored in various ways by the SF community. The New England Science Fiction Association named its annual Boskone convention after the evil empire in the Lensman series. And each year, in his honor, NESFA presents the Edward E. Smith Memorial Award—the "Skylark award"—to one who is deemed to have contributed significantly to science fiction. Like other SF notables such as H. G. Wells and Philip K. Dick, "Doc" has had a lively literary afterlife—he features in the novel *The Chinatown Death Cloud Peril* (2006) by Paul Malmont, a pulp mystery pastiche based very loosely on popular authors of the 1930s, and he was immortalized by Robert A, Heinlein as "Lensman Ted Smith" in his 1980 novel *The Number of the Beast*. E. E. "Doc" Smith is the spiritual father of Buck Rogers, of *Star Trek* and *Star Wars*, of the Hainish and the Culture, and of the new space opera that appeared on bookstore shelves yesterday.

Awards

SF Hall of Fame (2004, posthumous)

Works by the Author

The dates given are for the original periodical publication of the stories—all of Smith's stories were later revised and reissued as single volumes and volumes in series. Consult one of the bibliographies listed below for subsequent publication details.

Spacehounds of IPC (1931)

The Galaxy Primes (1959)

Subspace Explorers (1965)
The Clockwork Traitor (1976)
Imperial Stars (1976)
Masters of Space (1976, with E. Everett Evans)

The Lensman series

Triplanetary: A Tale of Cosmic Adventure (1934)
Galactic Patrol (1937)
Gray Lensman (1939)
Second Stage Lensman (1941)
The Vortex Blaster (1941; aka *Masters of the Vortex*)
Children of the Lens (1947)
First Lensman (1950)

The Skylark series

The Skylark of Space (1928, with Mrs. Lee Hawkins Garby)
Skylark Three (1930)
Skylark of Valeron (1934)
Skylark DuQuesne (1965)

Lord Tedric (with Gordon Eklund)

Lord Tedric (1978)
The Space Pirates (1979)
Black Knight of the Iron Sphere (1979)
Alien Realms (1980)

Other Genre Fiction

Have Trenchcoat—Will Travel. Ed. Lloyd Arthur Eshbach (2001). Detective stories, Westerns, and motorcycle adventures.

Collections

The Best of E. E. "Doc" Smith (1975)
Chronicles of the Lensmen (1998; the Lensman series, Volumes 1 and 2)
The Skylark of Space (2007)

In Other Media

Shinseiki Lensman (1985) and *Lensman: Kozûmosu no daisensô* (1987). MK Company. Japanese children's cartoons based on the Lensman stories.

Lensman: Power of the Lens. Fuji Television Network, 2000. Another Japanese animation based on the Lensman series.

Barrett, Sean. *GURPS Lensman.* Steve Jackson Games, 1994 (revised 2002).

Articles and Essays

"Catastrophe." *Astounding Science Fiction* (May 1938).

"The Epic of Space." In *Of Worlds Beyond: The Science of Science Fiction Writing,* ed. Lloyd Arthur Eshbach. Fantasy, 1947.

"Introduction." In *Man of Many Minds,* by E. Everett Evans. Fantasy, 1953.

"Worldcon Guest of Honor Speech. Chicon I, September 1, 1940." In *Worldcon Guest of Honor Speeches,* ed. Mike Resnick and Joe Siclari., ISFiC, 2006.

Bibliographies

Lucchetti, Stephen C. *"Doc"—First Galactic Roamer: A Complete Bibliography and Publishing Checklist of Works By and About E.E. "Doc" Smith.* Framington, MA: New England Science Fiction Association, 2004.

Willick, George C. "SF Bibliography." *Spacelight* (May 2006). http://www.gcwillick.com/Spacelight/smith_ee.html

For Further Information

Ellik, Ron, and Bill Evans. *The Universes of E. E. Smith.* Chicago: Advent, 1966.

Fleicsher, Ethan. *Z9M9Z: A Lensman Website.* Pariah Press, April 2007. http://www.ethanfleischer.com/lensman/main.htm

Heinlein, Robert A. "Larger Than Life: A Memoir in Tribute to Dr. Edward E. Smith." In *Expanded Universe.* New York: Ace, 1982.

King, Larry. "The Lensmen: FAQ." In *Space Monkey Science Fiction Timeline Site,* November 27, 1994. http://www.chronology.org/noframes/lens/

Pohl, Frederik. "Ode to a Skylark." *if Magazine* (May 1964). Reprinted in Lucchetti, *"Doc"—First Galactic Roamer.*

Sanders, Joseph. *E.E. "Doc" Smith.* Mercer Island, WA: Starmont House, 1986.

Sheridan, Thomas. Interview. *Fantasy Review* (1948). Republished as *E.E. "Doc" Smith, Father of Star Wars.* Necronomicon Press, 1977.

Warner, Harry. "Edward E. Smith—A Biography." Spaceways (June 1939). http://fanac.org/fanzines/Spaceways/Spaceways1-06.html

Neal Stephenson

Cyberpunk; TechnoThriller

Benchmark Title: *Snow Crash* (1992)

b. 1959 (Fort Meade, Maryland)

I like the rhythm of being a writer. People leave you alone for a few years. When the book comes out, there is a big burst of attention. Then it's over and I can concentrate on another project.
—Asaro, "Conversation with Neal Stephenson," *SF Site* (1999)

Photo credit: Courtesy of the author

About the Author and the Author's Work

According to the biography that appears on the 2003 novel *Quicksilver*, the author "issueth from a Clan of yeomen, itinerant Parsons, ingenieurs, and Natural Philosophers that hath long dwelt in bucolick marches and rural Shires of his native Land." He was born in Fort Meade, Maryland, and grew up in Ames, Iowa. He attended Boston University, first as a physics major and then, when he found that it would allow him to spend more time on the university mainframe, as a geography major. His interest in the narrative possibilities of virtual reality, personal physical enhancements, and a bleakly technology-dependent society firmly establishes his pedigree as a successor to the cyberpunks. But his ironic tone, as well as his keen interest in the history of science as a new narrative territory worthy of consideration by SF, marks him as one of a new breed—post-cyberpunk, if you will. "Giving his central character a name like 'Hiro Protagonist' also tends to suggest that Stephenson is intending something other than realism" (Kincaid 1996).

With some authors, it is not always easy to say that this novel or that story represents their breakthough into popular awareness and critical acclaim. Some authors work quietly in the background for several years, or even many books, doing solid work, accumulating a devoted cadre of fans and good word-of-mouth, until one day something tips the balance, and both established fans and newcomers can point to one particular novel and say, *I told you he was good*. On the other hand, there is Neal Stephenson. His breakthough novel is *Snow Crash*, no ifs, ands or buts. Prior to *Snow Crash*, he had written a couple of almost-SF eco-thrillers and a couple of mainstream-with-computers thrillers, as Stephen Bury, with his uncle, J. Frederick George, but nothing to set the world on fire, nothing to indicate what was to come.

Snow Crash was obviously something different. Perhaps it is because Neal Stephenson, unlike most of the original 1980s cyberpunks, grew up in the new techno-culture and, with a hacker's background, knows how it really works. Perhaps a decade of dark, angst-ridden cyberpunk had made us all ready for someone who could see the joke—the crazy possibilities of computer chips with everything, a world that has no privacy and few morals, and the unlimited technical prowess to achieve just about any harebrained scheme. "The Deliverator belongs to an elite order, a hallowed subcategory. He's got esprit up to here. Right now, he is preparing to carry out his third mission of the night. His uniform is black as activated charcoal, filtering the very light out of the air" (*Snow Crash*, 1).

In *Snow Crash*, Hiro Protagonist, The Deliverator, is a pizza delivery guy. Pizza delivery is an entrepreneurial enclave controlled by the mafia and Asian gangsters. The United States no longer exists, having dissolved into a sort of anarcho-capitalism run amok. Mercenary armies compete for national defense contracts, while those who have the wherewithal live in "burbclaves," sovereign, gated suburbs, guarded by trigger-happy private contractors. Hiro Protagonist's pursuit of the mystery of "snow crash," a deadly designer drug that is wreaking havoc with the hackers of this brave new world, takes the reader on a roller-coaster ride through arcane elements of history, linguistics, anthropology, archaeology, religion, computer science, politics, cryptography, philosophy, and pizza delivery.

The novels that followed *Snow Crash* visited very similar themes, but from greatly varying angles. *The Diamond Age* (1995) is a far-future Dickensian tale about extreme privilege and extreme deprivation that considers the importance of education and the role that modern technologies can play in the divide between the haves and the have-nots. *Cryptonomicon* (1999) is a cyber-thriller, which uses the Allies' top-secret efforts to break the Nazi Enigma code as the launching point for secret conspiracies that extend over time and space. And Stephenson's Baroque Cycle—*Quicksilver* (2003), *The Confusion* (2004), and *The System of the World* (2004)—revisits the early days of modern science. This may seem more like a historical novel, but Stephenson himself insists that the work is science fiction, in the tradition of alternate history and works that use fiction to examine the impact of science and technology. In an interview with *Rason* magazine online, he points out that "people who know and love science fiction will recognize these books as coming out of that tradition. . . . The earlier books like *Snow Crash* and *The Diamond Age* actually had a lot of historical content in them" (Godwin 2005).

When time allows, Neal Stephenson writes non-fiction articles about technology for publications such as *Wired*, and he works as an occasional advisor for 'Blue Origin,' a company funded by Jeff Bezos to develop a manned suborbital launch system. He also serves on the advisory board of the Science Fiction Museum in Seattle. He lives near Seattle, Washington.

Awards

Novels

The Diamond Age (1995) **Hugo, Locus Poll**

Cryptonomicon (1999) **Locus Poll**

Quicksilver (2003), **ACC**

The Baroque Cycle: *The Confusion* (2004) and *The System of the World* (2004) **Locus Poll**

The System of the World (2004) **Prometheus**

Works by the Author

Snow Crash (1992)

The Diamond Age: or a Young Lady's Illustrated Primer (1995)

Cryptonomicon (1999)

Anathem (2008) Author reading: http://www.longnow.org/projects/seminars/

The Baroque Cycle

Quicksilver (2003)

The Confusion (2004)

The System of the World (2004)

Other Genre Fiction

The Big U (1984)

Zodiac (1988)

As "Stephen Bury," with J. Frederick George

Interface (1994)

Cobweb (1996)

Notable Short Fiction

"Spew" (1994) http://www.wired.com/wired/archive/2.10/spew.html

"The Great Simoleon Caper" (1995) http://kuoi.asui.uidaho.edu/~kamikaze/Text/simoleon.html

"Jipi and the Paranoid Chip" (1997) http://www.vanemden.com/books/neals/jipi.html

Nonfiction Books

In the Beginning . . . Was the Command Line (1999). http://www.cryptonomicon.com/beginning.html

Articles and Essays

"Communication Prosthetics: Threat, or Menace?" *Whole Earth Review* (Summer 2001). http://www.wholeearth.com/issue/2105/article/108/communication.prosthetics.threat.or.menace

"Global Neighborhood Watch." *Wired* (November 16, 1998). http://www.wired.com/wired/scenarios/global.html

"In the Kingdom of Mao Bell." *Wired* (February 1994). http://www.wired.com/wired/archive/2.02/mao.bell.html

"It's All Geek to Me." *New York Times,* March 18, 2007 (op-ed piece on the movie *300* and geek culture).

"Mother Earth Mother Board." *Wired* (December 1996). http://www.wired.com/wired/archive/4.12/ffglass.html

"Smiley's People." *The New Republic,* September 13, 1993.

"Turn On, Tune In, Veg Out." *New York Times,* June 17, 2005 (op-ed piece on *Star Wars*).

For Further Information

Official Web site, *Neal Stephenson*: www.nealstephenson.com

Asaro, Catherine. "A Conversation with Neal Stephenson." *SF Site* (September 1999). http://www.SFsite.com/10b/ns67.htm

Godwin, Mike. "Neal Stephenson's Past, Present and Future." *Reason* 36, no. 9 (2005): 38–45. http://www.reason.com/news/show/36481.html

Kendrick, Michelle. "Space, Technology and Neal Stephenson's Science Fiction." In *Lost in Space: Geographies of Science Fiction,* ed. Rob Kitchin and James Kneale, 57–73. London: Continuum, 2002.

Kincaid, Paul. "Neal Stephenson." In *St. James Guide to Science Fiction Writers,* ed. Jay Pedersen. Detroit, MI: St. James, 1996.

Leonard, Andrew. "The Summit of Mount Stephenson." *Salon,* September 22, 2004. http://dir.salon.com/story/tech/books/2004/09/22/system/index.html

———. "Philosophy! Theology! Global Catastrophe! Adventure!" *Salon,* September 11, 2008. http://www.salon.com/books/review/2008/09/11/Stephenson/

Levine, Robert. "Neal Stephenson Rewrites History." *Wired* (September 2003). http://www.wired.com/wired/archive/11.09/history.html

McClellan, Jim. "Neal Stephenson, the Interview." *The Guardian,* November 4, 2004. http://www.guardian.co.uk/technology/2004/nov/04/onlinesupplement

Miller, Laura. "Neal Stephenson: The Salon Interview." *Salon,* April 21, 2004. http://dir.salon.com/story/books/int/2004/04/21/stephenson/index.html/

Miller, Robin. "Neal Stephenson Responds with Wit and Humor." *Slashdot,* October 20, 2004. Open Source Technology Group. http://interviews.slashdot.org/article.pl?sid=04/10/20/1518217

Bruce Sterling

Cyberpunk; Post-human SF; Technothriller

Benchmark Title: *Schismatrix* (1985)

b. 1954 (Brownsville, Texas)

Photo credit: Beth Gwinn

Consider the repulsive ghastliness of the SF category's Lovecraftian inbreeding. . . . Shared-world anthologies. Braided meganovels. Role-playing tie-ins. Sharecropping books written by pip-squeaks under the blazoned name of established authors. Sequels of sequels, trilogy sequels of yet-earlier trilogies . . .. What's the common thread here? The belittlement of individual creativity, and the triumph of anonymous product.

—"Slipstream," *SF Eye* (1989)

About the Author and the Author's Work

In September 2008 Bruce Sterling addressed a convention of game designers in Austin, Texas on the subject "Computer Entertainment Thirty-Five Years from Today." *Or did he?* The gentleman standing at the front of the room claimed to be a graduate student, and announced "The reason Bruce Sterling couldn't make it is because, in the year 2043, Bruce Sterling is 89 years old. Dr. Sterling is a little too frail to get in a time machine and travel into the past to talk to game developers." The "grad student," who seemed a little underwhelmed by his near-past experience, went on to explain the sophistications of computer entertainment in the year 2043, demonstrated the dazzling games hardware and nanotechnology that will be available in thirty-five years' time (a cloth napkin and a salt shaker), and explained the amazing scientific rationales behind them.

Sterling (for of course it was he) has been described as "big thinker in residence" by the organizers of an annual conference that explores the social implications of new technologies, and it is as a "big thinker" that he has made a lasting impact on science fiction. Michael Bruce Sterling was born in 1954 in Brownsville, Texas. His grandfather was a rancher, his father an engineer. He spent several years in India, an experience that he has described as "profoundly transformative" (Neves 2003), and which left him with a soft spot for Bollywood films. In 1976 he graduated from the University of Texas at Austin with a degree in journalism—and sold his first SF story. Since

1983 he has supported himself with his writing, lecturing, and international wandering as the voice of the future.

Bruce Sterling's name will always be linked, with chains of carbon nanotubes, to cyberpunk, the movement he defined in his introduction to his definitive 1986 anthology *Mirrorshades* as "an unholy alliance of the technical world of organized dissent—the underground world of pop culture, visionary fluidity and street-level anarchy." Novels like *The Artificial Kid* (1980), about a young street fighter who continuously films himself using remote controlled cameras, and *Islands in the Net* (1988), a thriller involving data piracy, marked him as one of the pioneers who (with writers like William Gibson, Rudy Rucker, and Pat Cadigan) defined the boundaries of the movement. But from a cursory glance at Sterling's career, it's obvious that he "covered far more territory" (Godwin 2004). *The Difference Engine* (1990), written with William Gibson, is a "steampunk" alternative history, which imagines the impact on humanity and history if "difference engines" (steam-driven computers) had brought on the Information Revolution 100 years early Sterling's Shaper/Mechanist universe is set in a far future in which two warring factions battle over the future of humankind. Like all the best internecine wars (think Swift's Lilliputian big-endians and little-endians), the conflict between the Shapers and the Mechanists is based on a distinction that isn't much of a difference: the Mechanists believe in improving the human body and mind using computer-based, mechanical technologies, whereas the Shapers enhance their stock by using intensive genetic engineering. His books "range so widely in settings and characters that it's hard to talk about them collectively. What they have in common is their author's willingness to stare uncomfortable truths in the face" (Godwin 2004).

Sterling's output and energy are enormous. He writes fiction and nonfiction *The Hacker Crackdown: Law and Disorder on the Electronic Frontier*, 1990; *Tomorrow Now: Envisioning the Next Fifty Years,* 2002); his essays and reviews appear regularly in *The New York Times*, *Newsday*, *Whole Earth Review*, the Web site *Boing Boing*, and the online magazine *Wired*. He teaches, and in 2003 he was appointed professor at the European Graduate School, teaching intensive summer courses on media and design. The Art Center College of Design in Pasadena, California, and the Sandberg Instituut in Amsterdam have named him "visionary in residence."

Sterling describes himself as a techno-green and firmly believes that technology can save the planet. In the late 1990s he launched the Viridian Greens to encourage ideas on how industrial design could respond to global climate change. Sterling is fond of coining neologisms when the language fails the future concepts he is describing: "spime" (a device that can track its own history of use and interact with the world), "buckyjunk" (difficult-to-recycle consumer waste made of carbon nanotubes), "Wexelblat disaster" (a natural disaster that triggers a secondary, and more damaging, failure of human technology), and "slipstream"—in his July 1989 column in *SF Eye* magazine, Sterling proposed this term to describe a new type of speculative fiction, "Novels of Postmodern Sensibility," which "simply make you feel very strange; the way that living in the late twentieth century makes you feel, if you are a person of a certain sensibility."

Sterling has two daughters by his first wife. He lives in Turin, Italy, with his second wife, Serbian author and filmmaker Jasmina Tesanovic.

Awards

Novels
Islands in the Net (1988) **Campbell**
Distraction (1998) **ACC**

Short Fiction
"Bicycle Repairman" (1996) **Hugo**
"Maneki Neko" (1998) **Locus Poll**
"Taklamakan" (1998) **Hugo, Locus Poll**

Nonfiction
Tomorrow Now: Envisioning the Next Fifty Years (2003) **Locus Poll**

Works by the Author

Involution Ocean (1977)
The Artificial Kid (1980)
Schismatrix (1985)
Islands in the Net (1988)
The Difference Engine (1990, with William Gibson)
Heavy Weather (1994)
Holy Fire (1996)
Distraction (1998)
Zeitgeist (2000)
The Zenith Angle (2004)
The Caryatids (2009)

Other Notable Short Fiction
"Spider Rose" (1982)
"Swarm (1982)
"Cicada Queen" (1983)
"Sunken Gardens" (1984)
"Dinner in Audoghast" (1985)
"Green Days in Brunei" (1985)
"Storming the Cosmos" (1985, with Rudy Rucker)
"Flowers of Edo" (1987)
"Our Neural Chernobyl" (1988)
"Dori Bangs" (1989)
"Deep Eddy" (1993)
"The Blemmye's Stratagem" (2005)
"Kiosk" (2007)

Collections

Crystal Express (1989)
Semi No Jo-o (1989)
Globalhead (1992)
A Good Old-fashioned Future (1999)
Visionary in Residence (2006)
Schismatrix Plus (1996)
Ascendancies: The Best of Bruce Sterling (2007)

As Editor

Mirrorshades: A Cyberpunk Anthology (1986). The defining cyberpunk short story collection. Introduction by Sterling.

Nonfiction Books

The Hacker Crackdown : Law and Disorder on the Electronic Frontier (1992)
Tomorrow Now: Envisioning the Next Fifty Years (2002)
Shaping Things (2005)

Articles and Essays

Boing Boing: *A Directory of Wonderful Things.* http://boingboing.net/

"Slipstream." *Catscan* (online archive). Electronic Frontier Foundation, March 13, 2003. http://w2.eff.org/Misc/Publications/Bruce_Sterling/. This is an online archive of columns by Sterling published in the late 1980s and 1990s by *SF Eye* magazine. This particular essay categorized a new subgenre for the twenty-first century.

"Computer Entertainment Thirty-Five Years from Today: A Solo Spoken Word Performance." Keynote Address at the Game Developers Conference, Austin, Texas, September 16, 2008. http://www.flurb.net/6/6sterling.htm

"Free as Air, Free as Water, Free as Knowledge." Speech to the Library Information Technology Association, San Francisco, CA, June 1992. http://www.cni.org/pub/LITA/Think/Sterling.html

"Mobiles and the Urban Poor." *Lift France 09*, September 4, 2008. http://liftconference.com/parallel-financial-system-come

"Science or Fiction." Presented at the American Center for Design "Living Surfaces" Conference, San Francisco, CA, October 1994. http://www.cscs.umich.edu/~crshalizi/Sterling/science-or-fiction.html

"Spimes and the Future of Artifacts." *Lift France 09*, February 2, 2006.

"State of the World 2008." *Inkwell: Authors and Artists,* December 21, 2007. Topic 289. The Well. http://www.well.com/conf/inkwell.vue/topics/317/Bruce-Sterling-State-of-the-Worl-page01.html. Bruce Sterling and Jon Lebkowsky discuss the events of the previous year in the spirit of highly informed speculation. Previous years' discussions can be found by searching The Well, a *Salon.com* online discussion group.

Veridian Design.org. http://www.viridiandesign.org/. Words of wisdom from the Viridian "Pope-Emperor" himself. Includes links to the Sterling essay "Can Technology Save the Planet?" (*Sierra*, 2005); "Embracing the Decay," the 2003 interactive, Web-based project for the Museum of Contemporary Art, Los Angeles; and various blogs.

"The Wonderful Power of Storytelling." Presented at the Computer Game Developers Conference, San Jose, CA, March 1991. http://w2.eff.org/Misc/Publications/Bruce_Sterling/comp_game_designers.article

Bibliographies

Bruce Sterling Archive. Electronic Frontier Foundation, March 13, 2003: http://w2.eff.org/Misc/Publications/Bruce_Sterling/

For Further Information

Beyond the Beyond. Author's blog: http://blog.wired.com/sterling/

de Beer, David. Interview. *Nebula Awards*, October 7, 2008. http://www.nebulaawards.com/index.php/interview/bruce_sterling/

"Bruce Sterling." In *Edge*. Edge Foundation, Inc. August 28, 2008. http://www.edge.org/3rd_culture/bios/sterling.html

Godwin, Mike. "Cybergreen: Bruce Sterling on Media, Design, Fiction, and the Future." *Reason* (January 2004). http://www.reason.com/news/show/29002.html

Interview [in French]. *ActuSF* (August 2004). http://www.actuSF.com/spip/?article3042

McNett, Gavin. "The Ambivalent Cyberpunk." *Salon.com,* October 30, 2000. http://archive.salon.com/books/feature/2000/10/30/sterling/index.html

Neves, José Carlos. "*Entrevista* (Interview): 'Cyber-Guru' Bruce Sterling." *Alan Moore:* Senhor do Caos/*Lord of Chaos,* November 1, 2003. http://www.alanmooresenhordocaos.hpg.ig.com.br/entrevistas81.htm. Brazilian Alan Moore fan site, featuring an English-language interview with Sterling that clears up some biographical details.

Sanders, Joe. "Bruce Sterling." In *St. James Guide to Science Fiction Writers,* ed. Jay Pedersen. Detroit, MI: St. James, 1996.

"The Singularity: Your Future as a Black Hole" (seminar). *The Long Now Foundation,* June 11, 2004. http://www.longnow.org/projects/seminars/

Charles Stross

Science Fantasy; Space Opera; Post-human SF

Benchmark Title: *Singularity Sky* (2003)

b. 1964 (England: Leeds, West Yorkshire)

    GTW/CS/L/MD d— s:+ a? C++++$
UL++++$ UC++$ US+++$ P++++$ L+++$
E——— W+++$ N+++ o+ K+++ !w——— O-
M+ V- PS+++ PE Y++ PGP+ !t 5? X— !R(+++)
tv— b+++ DI++++/++ !D G+ e+++
h++/-/——— r++ z?

—"Who Am I?" (in "geek code"*),
The Charles Stross FAQ (2007)

Photo credit: Beth Gwinn

About the Author and the Author's Work

    Charles David George Stross was born in Leeds, in West Yorkshire, England. He took his undergraduate degree at King's College, London, and qualified as a pharmacist in 1987. In an interview with John Scalzi in 2006, he confessed that he began to have second thoughts about his choice of career when, more than once, the pharmacy where he worked had to be staked out by undercover police because it was being targeted by armed robbers. (In the same interview he also helpfully advised against pharmacology as a career "if you can't cope with the idea that you might occasionally poison or kill someone entirely by accident.") In addition, Stross had rapidly realized that "puttering around in CP/M was *much* more interesting than learning the minutiae of pharmaceutical law and ethics" (Lilley 2005), so he went to Bradford University for a further degree in computer science. He worked as a technical author and programmer until the dot-com crash in 2000.
    Stross sold his first story, "The Boys," to *Interzone* in 1987, and during the 1990s his stories appeared regularly in anthologies like *New Worlds* and *The Weerde,* and in magazines like *Interzone* and *Asimov's Science Fiction.* Although Stross turned to writing nonficiton and op-ed pieces for computer magazines after the dot-com bubble burst, his novels, like *Singularity Sky* (2003), emerged as a logical extension of his own experience and his earlier fiction, as well as his response to the ideas of SF authors and futurists like Vernor Vinge, whose fiction had opened up conjecture about how humankind would cope with extreme technological and political change. "[Stross's] book is filled with trippy ideas: . . . the planet gets pushed through the technological

singularity in a few months; . . . [and] the clash of tech levels when the encounter finally happens" (Rawdon 2005).

Accelerando (2005) brought together a number of Stross's 1990s short stories into a single narrative, including the story "Lobsters" (2001), which he had written to try to capture the pressure and excitement of the world in which he had been working in the 1990s. Like a number of British SF writers of the late 1990s and afterward, Stross's fiction has a "genre-bending" quality: his SF has distinct elements of fantasy and Lovecraftian horror; his fantasy and horror contain distinct nods to SF. In 2004 he published *The Family Trade*, first in the Merchant Princes science fantasy series, which combines fantasy romance with the modern gangster story, noir-ish attitudes, and high-tech possibilities with medieval trappings.

Charles Stross has been a full-time writer since 2003, and since 2000 he has been nominated for every major SF award, winning the Hugo Award for best novella in 2005. He regularly works with fellow post-cyberpunk and slipstream writer Cory Doctorow. He also has yet another claim to immortality. In the 1970s and 1980s he published a number of articles about role-playing games for Advanced Dungeons & Dragons, and some of his creatures, such as the death knight, *githzerai* (extraplanar humanoid creatures that reside on the Plane of Limbo), and *slaad* (a chaotic race notable for its rigid caste system), were later immortalized in the *Fiend Folio* monster compendium. He lives in Edinburgh, Scotland, with his wife Feòrag NicBhride.

> Charles Stross's "Who Am I?" translates as follows: Geek of Technical Writing, Computer Science, Literature and Medicine, who is a punk dresser and a little taller, and rounder than most people. Claims to be immortal. And he'll be the first in line to get the new cybernetic interface installed into his skull. He is very computer-savvy, extremely liberal in his politics, and distrustful of government. Unimpressed by *Star Trek*, but very fond of role-playing games, devoted to the comic strip *Dilbert*, and *Doom*. [For a complete translation, see http://www.geekcode.com/geek.html#type.]

Awards

Edward E. Smith Memorial Award for Imaginative Fiction ("Skylark award") (2008)

Novels

Accelerando (2005) **Locus Poll**
Glasshouse (2006) **Prometheus**

Short Fiction

"The Concrete Jungle" (2004) **Hugo**
"Missile Gap" (2006) **Locus Poll**

 Works by the Author

Scratch Monkey (1993). Unpublished, but available online at Charles Stross's official Web site, http://www.antipope.org/charlie/fiction/monkey/index.html.

Singularity Sky (2003)
Iron Sunrise (2004)
Accelerando (2005)
Glasshouse (2006)
Halting State (2007)
Saturn's Children (2008)

Merchant Princes series

The Family Trade (2004)
The Hidden Family (2005)
The Clan Corporate (2006)
The Merchants' War (2007)
The Revolution Business (2009)

Notable Short Fiction

"A Colder War" (2002). http://www.infinityplus.co.uk/stories/colderwar.htm
"Rogue Farm" (2003)
"The Concrete Jungle" (2004). http://www.goldengryphon.com/Stross-Concrete.html
"Unwirer" (2004, with Cory Doctorow). http://craphound.com/unwirer/archives/000006.html
"Down on the Farm" (2008). http://www.tor.com/index.php?option=com_content&view=story&id=61

Collections

Toast: And Other Rusted Futures (2002)
Wireless (2009)

The Laundry Organization stories

The Atrocity Archives (2004)
The Jennifer Morgue (2006)
On Her Majesty's Occult Service (2006)

In Other Media

Rogue Farm. New Found Land, 2004. Short film, funded by Scottis TV and Grampian TV; based on Stross's short story of the same name, which appeared in the 2003 anthology *Live Without a Net*, edited by Lou Anders.

Nonfiction Books

The Web Architect's Handbook (1996)

Articles and Essays

"Civil Liberties in Cyberspace." *Computer Shopper* (July 1995). (UK: pub. by Dennis Publishing Ltd.). http://www.antipope.org/charlie/journo/civil-lib.html

For Further Information

Official Web site: http://www.antipope.org/charlie/

Anders, Lou. "New Directions: Decoding the Imagination of Charles Stross." *RevolutionSF,* April 19, 2002. http://www.revolutionSF.com/article.php?id=1096

DeForest, Roger. "Charles Stross Uploads His Mind To HardSF.net." *Hard Science Fiction* (June 28, 2006). http://www.hardsciencefiction.rogerdeforest.com/?mode=6

"du Flippi, Poali." "Charles Stross Attains Posthuman Status." *Locus,* April 1, 2005. http://www.locusmag.com/2005/Features/0401_Stross.html. An announcement to the effect that "author Charles Stross ceased his existence as a baseline human being and entered an unknowable posthuman condition." The date should be the reader's first clue that this is not an entirely serious article.

"Fast Forward." *Locus* (January 2005). http://www.locusmag.com/2005/Issues/01Stross.html

Kemble, Gary. "Charles Stross: Keeping Life Interesting." *Articulate*, July 31, 2006. Australian Broadcasting Company. http://www.abc.net.au/news/arts/articulate/200607/s1700770.htm

Lilley, Ernest. "Interview with Charles Stross." *SFRevu,* April 7, 2005. http://sfrevu.com/Review-id.php?id=2715

Lohr, Michael. "Searching for Scottish Ghosts, Stardust and Causality Violations: An Interview with Charles Stross." *Internet Review of Science Fiction* (March 2006). http://www.iroSF.com/q/zine/article/10260

Scalzi, John M. Interview. *By the Way . . . ,* December 6, 2006 (cached; interview reproduced at http://wagner.typepad.com/wagner/2006/12/page/3/).

The Brothers Strugatsky

Humor and Satire; Science Fantasy; Space Opera

Benchmark Title: *Roadside Picnic* (1972)

Arkady: b. 1925 (USSR: Georgia); d. 1991 (USSR: Moscow)

Boris: b. 1931 (USSR Leningrad)

> *SF is capable of most fully embodying the problems that worry us—and that trouble our fellow citizens as well. Of course there are people writing SF now who . . . think that it's enough just to fantasize a bit more, and more sensationally. But SF is heavy artillery—you don't use it for shooting sparrows.*
> —Gopman, "Science Fiction Teaches the Civic Virtues," *Science Fiction Studies* (1991)

About the Author and the Author's Work

The Brothers Strugatsky are the best known, most widely translated Russian SF authors in the world. They managed to crash through the language barrier with their humor, ingenuity, and ability to use the tropes of SF to zero in on the big targets. In their fiction they render the absurdity of life in a crumbling, paranoid Soviet Union in cosmic terms, in such a way that readers anywhere can relate to the universal experience of the "little man" struggling for survival, meaning, and dignity against overwhelming forces.

Arkady Natanovich Strugatsky and Boris Natanovich Strugatsky were born in the Soviet Union, Arkady in the Georgian city of Batumi, on the Black Sea, and Boris six years later in Leningrad. Their father was a bibliographer, their mother a teacher. The family suffered terribly during the siege of Leningrad during World War II: their father died of starvation, and ten-year-old Boris and their mother barely survived. The teenage Arkady, who had served in the civil defense building fortifications and worked at a grenade factory, was evacuated from the city in 1942 and then called up for military service. He was trained as an interpreter in English and Japanese. Until he was demobilized in 1955 he worked as an interpreter in the Far East and trained interpreters for the Soviet Army. When he was released from military service, he moved to Moscow and became an editor and magazine writer. After the war Boris completed his studies in astronomy at Leningrad State University and became a computer mathematician at the Pulkovo Observatory there. The brothers began to write together in the late-1950s, beginning with unchallenging space operas that stayed close to the party line for futuristic fiction—*Country of the Crimson Clouds* (1959) depicted a Soviet universe in which capitalism had withered away, right on schedule, and good Communist heroes were conquering the stars in the name of Marxist-Leninism.

But in the Soviet Union, writing SF like this could in itself be seen as a challenge to the system, however mild the opening salvos might seem. In an interview in 1991 Arkady recalled that "an SF writer who dared to write about the cosmos would be accused of cosmopolitanism, of being cut off from life, and of ideologically straying in interplanetary spaces" (Gopman). The system had good reason to be concerned; as the *Encyclopedia of Science Fiction* puts it, the Strugatsky's "utopian hopefulness did not survive unscathed." Subsequent Strugatsky works, such as *Monday Begins on a Saturday* (1965), *Tale of a Troika* (1968), and *Roadside Picnic* (1972), used allegory, social satire, and the conventions of Russian folktales to express their disillusionment with the Soviet system and concern for the future of their country.

The writing partnership of the Brothers Strugatsky ended in October 1991 when Arkady Strugatsky died of a chronic heart condition. He had at least lived to see the arrival of a Russia in which their works were freely available and the pair could say what they liked without fear of censorship or prosecution. This is not to suggest that the brothers had no more to say; in an interview shortly before his death, Arkady said "We used to write about the world as we would like it to be, now we write about the world as we are afraid it is becoming" (Howell 1994).

Since the death of his brother, Boris Strugatsky has continued to write SF, under the name "S. Vititsky." His 1994 novel *Search for Designation* includes the novella *A Happy Boy*, about the desperate days of his childhood, and survival, in wartime Leningrad. The Strugatsky brothers are the recipients of numerous Russian and foreign awards for their writing, and they were guests of honor at the 1987 World Science Fiction Convention, in Brighton, England (their first trip abroad). An asteroid discovered in 1977 was named after them (1977 RE7 STRUGATSKIA).

Works by the Author

The following Strugatsky titles have been published in English translation, but most are currently out of print. (*Roadside Picnic* is available on Amazon.co.uk in an Orion SF Masterworks edition, published in February 2007.)

Three Strugatsky Brothers novels and one novella are available as a download at http://www.ruSF.ru/abs/english/index.htm. They can also be found in libraries and used bookstores. For a more detailed list of their works, together and individually, with titles in Russian, see the bibliographies listed below.

Monday Begins on Saturday (1965)

The Snail on the Slope (1965)

Tale of the Troika (1968). An excerpt can be found in *Politicizing Magic: An Anthology of Russian and Soviet Fairy Tales,* ed. Marina Balina et al., 316–44. Evanston, IL: Northwestern University Press, 2005.

The Second Martian Invasion (1968)

Roadside Picnic (1972)

Definitely Maybe: A Manuscript Discovered Under Unusual Circumstances (1977)

Noon Universe stories

Noon: 22nd Century (1962)
Escape Attempt (1962)
Far Rainbow (1963)
Hard to Be a God (1964)
Prisoners of Power (1971; aka *The Inhabited Island*)
Beetle in the Anthill (1980)
The Time Wanderers (1986)

In Other Media

Stalker. Directed by Andrei Tarkovsky; performed by Aleksandr Kajdanovsky and Alisa Frejndlikh. MoSFilm, 1979. The screenplay of *Stalker*, written with Andrei Tarkovsky can be found in *Collected Screenplays*, translated by William Powell and Natasha Synessios (London: Faber, 1999). Based on *Roadside Picnic*.

Notable Short Fiction

"Destination: *Amaltheia*" (1960, trans. Leonid Kolesnikov). http://www.kuzbass.ru/moshkow/koi/STRUGACKIE/engl_amal.txt

"The Gigantic Fluctuation." (1962, trans. Gladys Evans). http://www.lib.ru/STRUGACKIE/r_fluct_engl.txt

"The Visitors" (1979) (in *Aliens, Travelers, and Other Strangers,* trans. Roger DeGaris, London: Macmillan, 1984)

Articles and Essays

Strugatsky, Boris N. "Working for Tarkovsky." *Science Fiction Studies* 31, no. 3 (November 2004): 418–20.

Strugatsky, Arkady. "Working with Andrei [Tarkovsky] on the Script of *Stalker.*" In *About Andrei Tarkovsky, Memoirs and Biographies*, trans. Sergei Sossinsky. Moscow: Progress, 1990. http://www.acs.ucalgary.ca/~tstronds/nostalghia.com/TheTopics/Stalker/strugatsky.html

Bibliographies

Borisov, V. "English Language Bibliography (Primary and Secondary Sources)." In *The Brothers Strugatsky,* ed. Alexandr Usov. http://www.rusf.ru/abs/english/index.htm

Sofka, Mike. Bibliography. February 2004. Rensselaer Polytechnic Institute. http://www.rpi.edu/~sofkam/lem/abs.html

For Further Information

The Brothers Strugatsky. Ed. Alexandr Usov: http://www.rusf.ru/abs/english/index.htm

Gopman, Vladimir. "Science Fiction Teaches the Civic Virtues: An Interview with Arkadii Strugatsky." *Science Fiction Studies* 18 (1991): 1–10 http://www.depauw.edu/SFs/interviews/Gopman53interview.htm

Howell, Yvonne. *Apocalyptic Realism: The Science Fiction of Arkady and Boris Strugatsky*. New York: Peter Lang, 1994.

Ivanova, Vera, and Mikhail Manykin. "Stalkers of Russian Science Fiction—the Strugatsky Brothers." *Russian InfoCenter,* August 16, 2006. Moscow State University. http://www.russia-ic.com/culture_art/literature/230/

Potts, Stephen W. *The Second Marxian Invasion: The Fiction of the Strugatsky Brothers*. San Bernardino, CA: Borgo, 1991.

Simon, Erik. "The Strugatskys in Political Context." *Science Fiction Studies* 31 (2004): 378–406.

Slusser, George Edgar. *Stalkers of the Infinite: The Science Fiction of Arkady and Boris Strugatsky: A Collection of Essays*. Riverside, CA: Xenos, 1991.

Somov, Yuri. "Sci-Fi under Soviet Eyes: Arkady Strugatsky Dies." *Guardian,* October 18, 1991, 39.

Vishnevsky, Boris. "Boris Strugatsky: "We Cannot Do It Any Other Way Yet." *The Moscow News* (August 2004). http://www.eng.yabloko.ru/Publ/2004/PAPERS/06/040604_mn.html

Theodore Sturgeon

Post-human SF

Benchmark Title: *More Than Human* (1953)

b. 1918 (Staten Island, New York);
 d. 1985 (Eugene, Oregon)

But I don't write down! I can't, and sell stories. Be proud of my doing the impossible. I have sold thirty-two stories and a poem in a year of writing.... I have made a living out of writing.... I'm no uplifter, I'm a craftsman.
—Letter to his mother, 1940, in *Complete Short Stories of Theodore Sturgeon*, vol. 1, *The Ultimate Egoist* (1994)

Photo credit: Beth Gwinn

About the Author and the Author's Work

Theodore Sturgeon's long-ago letter to his mother catches some of the key dynamics, both good and bad, in the career of a man whom the *Encyclopedia of Science Fiction* calls "a powerful and generally liberating influence in post-WWII US SF." There is the driven quality here: the thirty-two stories and (most touchingly) a poem, churned out by the young man who is desperate to be a professional writer, to be respected, *and* to make a living wage. Sturgeon would not be able—for better or for worse—to keep up that pace over the course of his long career, because of financial pressures; the complications of five wives and seven children; and occasional bouts of deep, soul-destroying writer's block. But there is no need to lament the stories he didn't write; a list of the stories that he *did* produce scrolls on and on, and there are many gems on that list. Sturgeon's letter to his mother also reveals his quiet pride in what he is doing, tempered by a down to earth awareness that he is a craftsman—that even when he was writing about rocket science, it was *not rocket science*. Sturgeon's career was a patchwork of contradictions, but his legacy to SF is a genuine and abiding one.

Born Edward Hamilton Waldo on Staten Island, New York, he was renamed "Sturgeon" when he was adopted by his stepfather in 1929. Later he changed his first name to fit his nickname, "Ted." It appears that the family's circumstances were not happy: Sturgeon's stepfather was austere and demanding—in later life Sturgeon told how he watched in impotent rage as his stepfather destroyed his collection of SF magazines, which he considered little better than pornography. Sturgeon was a promising gymnast in high school and wanted to become a circus acrobat, but his ambitions were crushed by rheumatic fever. At age seventeen he ran away and joined the Merchant

Marines. During three years at sea he began to write, churning out mainstream adventure and romance stories for McClure's Syndicate and *Argosy Magazine* and, in 1939, making his first SF sale to *Astounding Science Fiction*. Sturgeon's massive output at this time was such that he would use pen names, particularly "E. Waldo Hunter," as camouflage when two of his stories ran in the same issue of *Astounding*.

Regardless of what he said, Sturgeon was a craftsman *and* an artist: his worst hack work is readable, enjoyable, and workmanlike; his best writing has depth and substance. His stories are peopled with "outcast" characters (such as in the superhuman gestalt in *More Than Human*); his heroes are youngsters whose powers and talents are underestimated and reviled, young men and women who need to discover themselves—and others like them—before they triumph over a repressive world. As his career matured, Sturgeon wrote of sexual diversity, one of the first SF authors to deal matter-of-factly with homosexual love ("The World Well Lost," 1953). One way or another, his stories were about acceptance and resolution, and love.

At the height of his popularity in the 1950s Theodore Sturgeon was the most anthologized author alive. By the 1960s he was able to earn a living as a writer, even if it meant writing for television, for such series as *The Invaders*, *The Wild, Wild West*, and *Star Trek*. One of his *Star Trek* episodes, "Amok Time" (1967), is fondly remembered by fans for his invention of the *pon farr*, the Vulcan mating ritual. Another script, although it was never produced, was notable for introducing the "Prime Directive" into the Trek canon.

Later in life his involvement with science fiction seminars (most notably at the University of Kansas) brought him into contact with young and upcoming SF writers such as Ray Bradbury, Brian Aldiss, and Norman Spinrad, who remember him as a selfless and affectionate mentor, ever accepting of those who were different. Kurt Vonnegut based his character Kilgore Trout on Theodore Sturgeon. During his final years he lived in Springfield, Oregon. A chain smoker all of his life, Sturgeon suffered from lung problems for a decade before he died of pneumonia on May 8, 1985, in Eugene, Oregon. In 1987 the Theodore Sturgeon Memorial Award for short fiction was created in his honor.

Awards

SF Hall of Fame (2000, posthumous)

Short Fiction

"Slow Sculpture" (1970) **Hugo, Nebula**

Works by the Author

The Dreaming Jewels (1950; aka *The Synthetic Man*)
More Than Human (1953)
The Cosmic Rape (1958)
Venus Plus X (1960)
Voyage to the Bottom of the Sea (1961; movie novelization)
Godbody (1986)

Notable Genre Fiction

I, Libertine (1956, as "Frederick R. Ewing")
The King and Four Queens (1956; movie novelization)
Some of Your Blood (1961)
The Player on The Other Side (1963, uncredited, with Ellery Queen)
The Rare Breed (1966; movie novelization)

Other Notable Short Fiction

"It" (1940)
"Microcosmic God" (1941)
"Killdozer!" (1944)
"Bianca's Hands" (1947)
"The World Well Lost" (1953)
"And Now the News . . ." (1956)
"The Man Who Lost the Sea" (1959)
"Need" (1960)
"When You Care, When You Love" (1962)
"If All Men Were Brothers, Would You Let One Marry Your Sister?" (1967)
"The Man Who Learned Loving" (1969)
"Case and the Dreamer" (1973)

Collections

The Complete Short Stories of Theodore Sturgeon (1994)

The Ultimate Egoist (1937 to 1940) (foreword by Ray Bradbury)
Microcosmic God (1940 to 1941)
Killdozer! (1941 to 1946)
Thunder and Roses (1946 to 1948)
The Perfect Host (1948 to 1950)
Baby Is Three (1950 to 1952)
A Saucer of Loneliness (1953) (foreword by Kurt Vonnegut)
Bright Segment (1953 to 1955)
And Now the News . . . (1955 to 1957)
The Man Who Lost the Sea (late 1950s and early 1960s)
The Nail and the Oracle (mid- to late 1960s)

Nonfiction Books

Argyll: A Memoir (1993)

In Other Media

Killdozer. Universal TV, 1974. Directed by Jerry London; starring Clint Walker and Neville Brand.

The Other Celia. Brookstreet Pictures, 2005. Directed by Jon Knautz.

"Ordeal in Space," *Out There* (1951). Teleplay, as "Edward Waldo," based on a story by Robert A. Heinlein; starring Rod Steiger. "Mewhu's Jet" *Out There* (1951); starring Eileen Heckart.

"Shore Leave," *Star Trek* (1966); directed by Robert Sparr; "Amok Time" *Star Trek* (1967); directed by Joseph Pevney; starring Leonard Nimoy and William Shatner.

Articles and Essays

"Introduction." In *Roadside Picnic* and *Tale of the Troika,* by the Strugatsky Brothers. New York: Macmillan, 1977.

"Science Fiction, Morals, and Religion." In *Science Fiction, Today and Tomorrow; A Discursive Symposium,* ed. Reginald Bretnor, 98–115. New York: Harper & Row, 1974.

"Theodore Sturgeon on Philip Dick." In *Philip K. Dick: The Dream Connection,* ed. D. Scott Apel, 288–89. San Jose, CA: Permanent, 1987.

"Why So Much Syzygy?" In *Turning Points: Essays on the Art of Science Fiction,* ed. Damon Knight, 269–72. New York: Harper & Row, 1977.

Bibliographies

Stephensen-Payne, Phil, and Gordon R. Benson Jr. *Theodore Sturgeon: Sculptor of Love and Hate, A Working Bibliography.* Albuquerque, NM: Galactic Central, 1989.

Willick, G. C. "Bibliography." *Spacelight* (June 2006). http://www.gcwillick.com/Spacelight/sturgeon.html

For Further Information

The Theodore Sturgeon Page. Ed. Eric Weeks: http://www.physics.emory.edu/~weeks/misc/sturgeon.html

Aldiss, Brian. "Sturgeon—The Cruelty of the Gods" (Obituary). In *The Detached Retina: Aspects of SF and Fantasy,* 87–91. Syracuse, NY: Syracuse University Press, 1995.

Delany, Samuel. "Sturgeon." In *Starboard Wine: More Notes on the Language of Science Fiction.* Pleasantville, NY: Dragon, 1984.

Klass, Philip. "Sturgeon: The Improbable Man." In *Bright Segment: Volume VIII, The Complete Stories of Theodore Sturgeon,* ed. Paul Williams, ix–xiv. Berkeley: North Atlantic, 2002.

Menger, Lucy. *Theodore Sturgeon (Recognitions).* New York: Frederick Ungar, 1981.

Merril, Judith. "A [Real?] Writer — Homage to Ted Sturgeon." *Fantasy & Science Fiction* (October/November 1999).

Rapp, Rodger. "E. Pluribus Unicorn: Theodore Sturgeon: 1918–1985." *Bloomsbury Review* 6, no. 3 (1986): 23.

Sackmary, Regina. "An Ideal of Three: The Art of Theodore Sturgeon." In *Critical Encounters: Writers and Themes in Science Fiction,* ed. Dick Riley, 132–43. New York: Frederick Ungar, 1979.

Sharenov, Evelyn. Interview. *Pulpsmith* 3, no. 2 (1983): 5–13.

Spinrad, Norman. "Sturgeon, Vonnegut and Trout." In *Science Fiction in the Real World,* 167–81. Carbondale: Southern Illinois University Press, 1990.

Westfahl, Gary. "Sturgeon's Fallacy." *Extrapolation* 38 (1991): 255–77.

Michael Swanwick

Myth and Legend; Slipstream; Time Travel

Benchmark Title: *Stations of the Tide* (1991)

b. 1950 (Schenectady, New York)

Photo credit: Beth Gwinn.
Courtesy of Michael Swanwick.

So I always tell my students: You are the next big thing. Those qualities and insights that you as a writer have and nobody else does are exactly what the editors are looking for. They want to be amazed and astounded. They want to see something new.

—Smith, "The Periodic Prime of Michael Swanwick," *Crescent Blues* (2003)

About the Author and the Author's Writing

Michael Swanwick's autobiographical essay on his official Web site begins with his arrival in Philadelphia in 1973, with "a suitcase full of clothes, seventy dollars in traveler's checks, a friend who was willing to put me up on his couch for a few weeks, and the absolute conviction that science fiction was the highest form of literature and that I could teach myself to write it." As he describes it, it was a rough ride: he wound up living across the street from a flophouse, sold his blood, ghosted term papers, and has vivid memories of a dead youth, who had unsuccessfully tried to mug a salesman, being carried in a body-bag from his front door. During the first winter in the City of Brotherly Love, he "lost forty pounds for lack of food." Six novels and over forty stories later, however, his youthful ambition and self-confidence have been amply proven; Swanwick is a multiple award-winning author, who is widely considered "one of American SF's most stylish and subversive writers, bringing to his intense, finely wrought stories and novels a sardonic intelligence that has few literary peers" (Gevers 2007). He writes steadily, but not quickly, averaging about one novel every three years, as well as short stories and extended writing projects, such as his ambitious "Periodic Table of Science Fiction," which appeared in the "Sci Fiction" section of *SciFi.com*, between 2001 and 2003. It's a collection of 118 very short stories, each named after an element in the periodic table, including the as-yet-undiscovered "ununseptium":

> I began, of course, simply hoping I could come up with something—anything!—on each element.... But as the series progressed, the attempt to keep the stories varied and unpredictable imposed a sort of overall shape on the series. I now picture the totality as being a sort of crazy-quilt portrait of the science fiction genre. (Smith 2003)

A crazy quilt of the SF genre is probably a decent way to describe Swanwick's *oeuvre* as a whole. Pinning him down to an SF category or subgenre is, as editor and friend Gardner Dozois said in his foreword to the 2000 collection *Moon Dogs*, "rather like trying to catch fog in a net." As Swanwick himself put it in his Author Comments in the *St. James Guide*, his stories range from "hard science fiction to stone fantasy, with stops at all stations in between, and are written at whatever length is best." An example of the "stone fantasy" is *The Iron Dragon's Daughter* (1993), with elves in Armani suits and dragons as jet fighters; the hard SF, Hugo-winning 1998 story, "The Very Pulse of the Machine," was written "just to prove to the world and myself that I could. When you're perceived as a 'literary' writer, it's assumed you can't do the science" (Jamneck 2003). His 1997 novel *Jack Faust* is a retelling of the Faust legend with modern science and technology, something he appears to have had ambitions to try from his very earliest days as a writer:

> I was a science kid growing up, so I identified with Faust's ambition, but since I was a Roman Catholic his willingness to sell his soul for knowledge was literally terrifying to me. Most non-Catholics don't take Hell very seriously, possibly because they don't have nuns drawing verbal pictures of it daily in extremely graphic Grand Guignol terms. (Smith 2003)

His 1980 story "Ginungagap" is considered by many to be a forerunner of what is now known as cyberpunk. *Stations of the Tide* is a wonderful novel, impossible to categorize, a potent blend of SF and magic. And *Bones of the Earth* (2002) is about *dinosaurs.*

As Swanwick puts it on his Web site, he has "lost something like twenty major awards, and won five"; those five Hugos for fiction were received in five out of six years—a unique record among SF writers. (Most recently, his 2008 story "From Babel's Fall'n Glory We Fled" was nominated for a 2009 Hugo.)

Michael Swanwick was born in Schenectady, New York, where his father was an engineer; according to his Author Comments in the *St. James Guide*, "in the normal course of things, I probably would have become one as well. But I was lured away from the engineering by science, and then lured away from science by literature. Science fiction allows me to keep faith with my past as well as my future." He received a BA from The College of William and Mary in Williamsburg, Virginia. He and his wife, Marianne Porter (whom he sometimes acknowledges in his books as "the M.C. Porter Endowment for the Arts") have been married since 1980, and he has been a full-time writer since 1983. The Swanwicks lives in Philadelphia with their son Sean, who recently started college. As Swanwick says on his Web site, "The important stuff of life keeps on happening."

Awards

Novels

Stations of the Tide (1991) **Nebula**

Short Fiction

"The Edge of the World (1989) **Sturgeon**
"The Very Pulse of the Machine" (1998) **Hugo**

"Scherzo with Tyrannosaur" (1999) **Hugo**
"The Dog Said Bow-Wow" (2001) **Hugo**
"Slow Life" (2002) **Hugo**
"Legions in Time" (2003) **Hugo**
"A Small Room in Koboldtown" **Locus Poll**

Collections

Tales of Old Earth (2000) **Locus Poll**

Nonfiction

Being Gardner Dozois (2001) **Locus Poll**

Works by the Author

In the Drift (1984)
Vacuum Flowers (1987)
Stations of the Tide (1991)
Jack Faust (1997)
Bones of the Earth (2002)
The Dragons of Babel (2008)

Other Notable Genre Fiction

The Iron Dragon's Daughter (1993)

Other Notable Short Fiction

"The Feast of Saint Janis" (1980)
"Ginungagap" (1980)
"Mummer Kiss" (1981)
"Marrow Death" (1984)
"Trojan Horse" (1984)
"Dogfight" (1985, with William Gibson)
"The Gods of Mars" (1985, with Gardner Dozois and Jack Dann)
"A Midwinter's Tale" (1988)
"Griffin's Egg" (1991)
"Cold Iron" (1993)
"Radio Waves" (1995)
"Walking Out" (1995)
"The Dead" (1996)
"Archaic Planets: Nine Excerpts from the Encyclopedia Galactica" (1998, with Sean Swanwick)
"Radiant Doors" (1998)

"Wild Minds" (1998)
"Ancient Engines" (1999)
"'Hello,' Said the Stick" (2002)
"The Little Cat Laughed to See Such Sport" (2002)
"Coyote at the End of History" (2003)
"Lord Weary's Empire" (2006)
"From Babel's Fall'n Glory We Fled" (2008)

Collections

Gravity's Angels (1991)
A Geography of Unknown Lands (1997)
Moon Dogs (2000, edited by Ann A. Broomhead and Timothy P. Szczesuil)
Puck Aleshire's Abecedary (2000)
Tales of Old Earth (2000)
Cigar-Box Faust and Other Miniatures (2003)
Michael Swanwick's Field Guide to the Mesozoic Megafauna (2004)
The Periodic Table of Science Fiction (2005)
The Dog Said Bow-Wow (2007)
The Best of Michael Swanwick (2008)
Poem du Jour. April–December 2008. http://poemdujour.blogspot.com/. One hundred e-mails, originally sent to his sons and college friends, "to show . . . how simple appreciating poetry can be."
The Sleep of Reason. With illustrations by Francisco José de Goya y Lucientes. May 2005. http://www.infinitematrix.net/stories/swanwick/sleep_of_reason.html. A series of very short stories by Michael Swanwick based on *Los Caprichos*, a series of etchings by Francisco Goya.

Nonfiction Books

The Postmodern Archipelago (1997)
Being Gardner Dozois: An Interview by Michael Swanwick (2001)
What Can Be Saved from the Wreckage?: James Branch Cabell in the Twenty-First Century (2007) (preface by Barry Humphries)

Articles and Essays

"Growing Up in the Future" (Disclave GOH speech, 1996). In *Moon Dogs* (2004) http://www.michaelswanwick.com/nonfic/future.html
"The Lady Who Wrote *Lud-in-the-Mist*." *Infinity Plus* (July 2007). http://www.infinityplus.co.uk/introduces/mirrlees.htm
"Scribbledehobbledehoydenii: Autobiographical Essay." *Tangent* 19 (Summer 1997). http://www.michaelswanwick.com/auth/hobbled.html

For Further Information

Official Web site: http://www.michaelswanwick.com/
Author's Blogs. *Flogging Babel:* http://floggingbabel.blogspot.com/

Anders, Lou. "Conversations with a Dark God: An Interview with Michael Swanwick." *SF Site* (June 2002). http://www.SFsite.com/07b/ms132.htm

Cox, F. Brett. "A User's Guide to Michael Swanwick." *New York Review of Science Fiction* 147, no. 1 (November 2000): 4+.

Dozois, Gardner. "Michael Swanwick: The Chameleon Eludes the Net (Foreword)." In *Moon Dogs,* by Michael Swanwick. http://www.michaelswanwick.com/auth/chamelon.html

Gevers, Nick. "The Literary Alchemist: An Interview with Michael Swanwick." *Infinity Plus* (July 2007). http://www.infinityplus.co.uk/nonfiction/intms.htm

Jamneck, Lynne. "Michael Swanwick: Twenty Questions. *Strange Horizons,* November 17, 2003. http://www.strangehorizons.com/2003/20031117/swanwick.shtml

Matveev, Andrew. "Walking the City with an American Writer." *The New York Review of Science Fiction* 197, no. 5 (January 17, 2005): 1, 8–9.

"Michael Swanwick: God Reached Down and Flicked a Switch." *Locus* (March 2009). http://www.locusmag.com/2009/Issue03_Swanwick.html

Moher, Aidan. "The Theoretical Man: Michael Swanwick Interviewed." *SF Crowsnest,* May 1, 2008. http://www.sfcrowsnest.com

Nicholls, Stan. "Michael Swanwick Has Strange Notions." In *Wordsmiths of Wonder: Fifty Interviews with Writers of the Fantastic*, 92–98. London: Orbit, 1993.

Rambo, Cat. "Call Me Prolific: An Interview with Michael Swanwick." *Suite 101.com,* August 10, 2006. http://scififantasyfiction.suite101.com/article.cfm/call_me_prolific#ixzz0D3oaghhO&B

Santala, Ismo. "Interview." *The Modern Word,* September 26, 2003. http://www.themodernword.com/features/interview_swanwick.html

Shepard, Lucius. "An Interview with Michael Swanwick." *The New York Review of Science Fiction* 236, no. 8 (April 20, 2008): 1, 4–6.

Smith, Stephen. "The Periodic Prime of Michael Swanwick." *Crescent Blues* (June 2003). http://www.crescentblues.com/6_6issue/int_swanwick.shtml

Sheri S. Tepper

Apocalyptic SF; Science Fantasy

Benchmark Title:
The Gate to Women's Country (1988)

b. 1929 (Littleton, Colorado)

In my reviews, I'm accused of being a writer who preaches. Actually, I'm a preacher who writes!
—Szpatura, "Of Preachers and Storytellers," *Strange Horizons* (2008)

Photo credit: Beth Gwinn

About the Author and the Author's Work

The *Encyclopedia of Science Fiction* describes Sheri S. Tepper as the "kindly spellbinder, who tells romantic tales around the campfire, [but] has jaws that bite and claws that snatch." These biting jaws and prickly claws take a number of narrative forms: rather than trying to shoe-horn Sheri Tepper in to "scifi" or fantasy, it might be more constructive to think of her as the Mistress of *All Is Not What It Seems*, whether she is writing about a society that has rebuilt itself along strictly gender-segregated lines, or the seemingly magical powers of a realm of shape-shifters, necromancers, and giants, who play a chesslike game that holds their entire world under the thrall of disastrous petty wars and arbitrary vendettas. There are always enough elements of the fantastic in a Tepper novel "to bemuse reviewers" ("Speaking to the Universe" 1998), and when the fantasy turns out to have a firm backbone or some surprising insights about religion, politics, and familial relationships up its wide, wizard sleeves, that which appears to be pure whimsy usually achieves the unexpected.

Her first novels, the nine volumes of the <u>Land of True Game</u> "trilogy of trilogies" are set in what seems like obvious fantasy territory: a boy named Peter, a trainee games-player whose special power has not manifested itself yet, is forced to begin a quest by a mystery that threatens his life and the lives of the few individuals he loves and trusts. His world is a place where the gamesmen and -women mercilessly use their extraordinary powers to torment and dominate each other and to wreak havoc on the lives of those who are not "magically enabled." Tepper's imaginary world is well worth the journey for the wonders that she reveals on the way. In the Land of the True Game, you can be Prince or Sorcerer, Demon or Doyen, and bonedancers raise up armies of the dead. At the end of the first trilogy, a good SF rationale to all of these goings-on is revealed, but as in so many things, Tepper was ahead of her time, anticipating by decades the genre-bending that has become commonplace, particularly in British SF, over the last ten years.

Sheri Stewart Tepper was born Shirley Stewart Douglas near Littleton, Colorado. She was married at age twenty, but her marriage ended a few years later; of that time of her life, she says "I became a single mother of two kids, and spent ten years on my own, working all kinds of different jobs" ("Speaking to the Universe" 1998). For twenty years she worked for Rocky Mountain Planned Parenthood, eventually becoming its executive director. In the late 1960s she married Gene Tepper, and in the mid-1980s the couple moved to New Mexico.

As early as 1963 Tepper—as "Sheri S. Eberhart"—wrote poetry and children's stories (including, in 1963, a poem called "Lullaby 1990," which appeared in the SF magazine *Galaxy*). Her writing career took off in earnest upon her move to New Mexico, with a burst of creativity that included the True Game series, the Marianne fantasy trilogy, and *The Gate to Women's Country* (1988), Tepper's take on a popular SF convention of that period, the postapocalyptic Earth in which men and women have gone their separate ways. It was a beautifully written, provocative novel, which was immediately recognized as one of the great feminist SF classics:

> [H]er own anger is aroused by what is, at root, fundamentally a *theological* category: pride.... It is pride that treats the environment as merely a resource to be exploited, and pride (mostly in male form) that threatens humanity (mostly in the form of women and children) in the post-holocaust world of *The Gate to Women's Country.* (Roberts 2005)

Whether she decides to dress up her favorite themes in the motley of fantasy or the futurism of SF, anything written by Sheri S. Tepper is worth reading. Since *The Gate to Women's Country*, she has kept up a steady stream of inventive and challenging novels that confront the issues that trouble her: cruelty, the abuse of power, and the exploitation of nature. And in her opinion, expressed in a forthright interview in *Strange Horizons* online magazine in 2008, in speculative fiction she has found the genre that allows her to handle those horrors as she sees fit:

> Fairy tales and myths almost always come out right. The bad things are beaten, the good things are elevated. Even ordinary stories about children are often fairy tales, because it is rare for them to end in tragedy. Children cling to fairy tales and myths as they cling to a loved parent because they represent security. Everything will be okay. Really. It really will. (Szpatura 2008)

Sheri S. Tepper also writes well-received horror novels (as E. E. Horlak), and detective stories (under various pseudonyms, but particularly as A. J. Orde and B. J. Oliphant); she and her husband still live in New Mexico and operate a guest ranch near Santa Fe.

Awards

Novels

Beauty (1991) **Locus Poll**

Works by the Author

The Revenants (1984)
After Long Silence (1987; UK: *The Enigma Score*)
The Gate to Women's Country (1988)
Beauty (1991)
A Plague of Angels (1993)
Shadow's End (1994)
Gibbon's Decline & Fall (1996)
Family Tree (1997)
Six Moon Dance (1998)
Singer from the Sea (1999)
The Fresco (2000)
The Visitor (2002)
The Companions (2003)
The Margarets (2007)

The Arbai Trilogy

Grass (1989)
Raising the Stones (1990)
Sideshow (1992)

The Awakeners

NorthShore (1987)
SouthShore (1987)

The Land of True Game

Peter

King's Blood Four (1983)
Necromancer's Nine (1983)
Wizard's Eleven (1984)

Mavin Manyshaped

The Song of Mavin Manyshaped (1985)
The Flight of Mavin Manyshaped (1985)
The Search for Mavin Manyshaped (1985)

Jinian (The End of the Game)

Jinian Footseer (1985)
Dervish Daughter (1986)
Jinian Star-Eye (1986)

Other Genre Fiction

Still Life (1989, as "E. E. Horlak")
Dead on Sunday (1994, as "A. J. Orde")
The Shirley McClintock Mysteries (as "B. J. Oliphant")
The Jason Lynx Mysteries (as "A. J. Orde")

Ettison Duo

Blood Heritage (1986)
The Bones (1987)

The Marianne Trilogy

Marianne, the Magus, and the Manticore (1985)
Marianne, the Madame, and the Momentary Gods (1988)
Marianne, the Matchbox, and the Malachite Mouse (1989)

Notable Short Fiction

"The Gardener" (1988; aka "The Bone Yard," with F. Paul Wilson and Ray Garton)
"Someone Like You" (1990)

The "Crazy" Carol Stories

"The Gazebo" (1990)
"Raccoon Music" (1991)
"The Gourmet" (1991)

Collections

The True Game (1985; single-volume edition of the Peter trilogy)
The Awakeners (1989; single-volume edition of *NorthShore*, 1987, and *SouthShore*, 1987)

Nonfiction Books

The People Know (1968)

Articles and Essays

"Extraterrestrial Trilogue." *Galaxy* (August 1961, as Sheri S. Eberhart)
"The Power of Art." *SFfworld.com* (2002). http://www.SFfworld.com/authors/t/tepper_sheri/articles/powerofart.html

Bibliographies

Novel Reflections. n.d. http://www.novelreflections.com/authors/sheri-tepper/bibliography.php

For Further Information

Sheri S. Tepper. Ed. Atlant and Jan Schmidt. http://www.sheri-s-tepper.com

Audio Interview. *Fresh Air from WHYY,* April 24, 2002. National Public Radio. http://www.npr.org/templates/story/story.php?storyId=1142218

D'Ammassa, Don. "Sheri Tepper." In *St. James Guide to Science Fiction Writers,* ed. Jay Pedersen. Detroit, MI: St. James, 1996.

Roberts, Adam. *The History of Science Fiction.* London: Palgrave Macmillan, 2005.

"Speaking to the Universe." *Locus* (September 1998). http://www.locusmag.com/1998/Issues/09/Tepper.html

Szpatura, Neal. "Of Preachers and Storytellers: An Interview with Sheri S. Tepper." *Strange Horizons*, July 21, 2008. http://www.stran_gehorizons.com/2008/20080721/szpatura-a.shtml

James P. Tiptree Jr.
[Alice Hastings Bradley Sheldon]

Feminist SF; New Wave

Benchmark Title: "The Girl Who Was Plugged In" (1973)

b. 1915 (Chicago, Illinois); d. 1987 (McLean, Virginia)

A male name seemed like good camouflage. I had the feeling that a man would slip by less observed. I've had too many experiences in my life of being the first woman in some damned occupation.

—Profile in *Isaac Asimov's SF Magazine* (1983)

About the Author and the Author's Work

In the late 1960s, a man of mystery appeared in the pages of SF magazines. It was widely known that the name "James P. Tiptree Jr." was a pseudonym; just to add piquancy to the mystery, it was rumored that the subterfuge was necessary to protect his identity as of a member of the U.S. intelligence community. And, as if it couldn't get any better, "Tiptree's" stories were marvels of dark irony, featuring provocative sexuality, challenging ideas about identity and male/female relations, and unusual attitudes to life in general, and death in particular. Stories like "The Women Men Don't See" (1973); "Love Is the Plan, the Plan Is Death" (1973); and "Houston, Houston, Do You Read?" (1976) are "fraught with mystery of all kinds—disguised motives, muffled, sinister conversations, depths of fear, regret and remorse, and an overall atmospheric gloom an uniformly developed and as finely crafted as the best writing of Edgar Allan Poe" (Dunn 1996).

One of Tiptree's earliest stories, "The Last Flight of Doctor Ain" (1969), concerns a biology researcher who, convinced that humankind is destroying the earth, develops an incurable virus and sets off on a murderous mission to spread it throughout the world. This deceptively simple story is remarkable for the dark devotion of its central character—and the sense, upon reading it forty years after it was written, that Tiptree saw and understood the grim possibilities waiting for us.

But the mystery surrounding the author's identity resulted in all sorts of wild ideas, including (can you believe it!) that Jim Tiptree was a *woman*. Robert Silverberg, in his introduction to Tiptree's 1975 collection *Warm Worlds and Otherwise,* did his best to knock this notion right on the head:

> [F]or there is to me something ineluctably masculine about Tiptree's writing. I don't think the novels of Jane Austen could have been written by a man nor the

stories of Ernest Hemingway by a woman, and in the same way I believe the author of the James Tiptree stories is male.

Oh, dear. But he was not alone: Harlan Ellison, in the introduction to his *Again, Dangerous Visions* anthology, stated firmly that "Tiptree is the man to beat this year." And after all, wasn't James Tiptree a World War II veteran, a retired Air Force officer? Hadn't *he* helped set up the Photo Intelligence Department of the CIA? Wasn't *he* a successful businessman, didn't he hunt and fish and travel boldly all over the globe? Didn't he have a PhD in clinical psychology? Weren't his letters to admirers and fellow writers full of manly jokes about his conquests with the ladies, and didn't he even conduct a mild epistolary flirtation with Ursula K. Le Guin?

And all the same, wasn't "he" Alice Hastings Bradley Sheldon? All of the details —the hunting and the fishing, the war-time service, the PhD, and the flirtations—were accurate and unembellished, but belonged to a woman who had begun writing in earnest in her mid-fifties and was in her mid-sixties when she was "exposed." In her life as well as her fiction, Tiptree "called into question the entire notion of what is masculine or feminine in fiction," as Robert Silverberg graciously put it when her true identity was revealed.

Alice Hastings Bradley (her first identity, among the several to follow) was born in Chicago and spent much of her childhood trailing around Africa and India with her author/adventurer parents. To escape her mother's debutante ambitions for her, she married (disastrously) very young. She was divorced by the time she joined the U.S. Army Air Intelligence as a photo interpreter, shortly after the United States entered World War II. While she was serving in Europe, she met her second husband, Huntingdon Sheldon; together, after the war ended they were enlisted in the development of the CIA. After retiring from military service in the late 1950s, Bradley acquired a PhD in experimental psychology, researching the responses of animals to novel stimuli in various environments. She began writing science fiction as she was finishing her thesis, as "light relief." Although she had published stories under her own name as early as 1946, when she adopted the pseudonym "James P. Tiptree Jr." in 1967 (a name acquired, with the help of her husband "Ting," from a jar of marmalade), she embarked upon a period of sustained and concentrated creativity. For ten years she used the skills she had acquired in her intelligence work to fool everyone, until an off-hand remark about the death of her mother in 1977 prompted sharp-eyed readers to discover her mother's obituary and the secret identity of her writer-daughter.

Tiptree is recognized as a master of the short story form, and her work demonstrates that SF can "square" various circles—"hard" technology and "soft" psychology, the masculine and feminine; reconciling the style and spirit of space opera with the darker, deeper alienation of the New Wave. In his obituary for her in *Locus*, Gardner Dozois commented that, "[h]er footprints are all over cyberpunk turf." Tiptree's greatest period of creativity was between 1970 and 1977; some critics conjecture that losing her cover "persona" robbed Sheldon of an important distancing device that allowed her to do her best work. But there may be a sadder, more mundane explanation: after James Tiptree was "outed," both Sheldon and her husband suffered from increasingly poor health. Ting, her senior by more than a decade, was quite frail and nearly blind after a series of strokes, although there is a possibility that she exaggerated the extent of his incapacity as she chafed at her own problems: heart attacks, bleeding ulcers, and severe depressions. She had always told anyone who would listen that she would not outlive her husband, but neither would she sit back and watch herself fade away. In 1987, true to her word, she shot and killed Ting, and then herself, in their home in McLean, Virginia.

Robert Silverberg, in that 1975 introduction to *Warm Worlds and Otherwise*, made many true and wise statements about the talent of James Tiptree. Among them, he said that in her stories, "we wander in a brave, desperate, but only occasionally successful quest for answers." And surprisingly often, with Tiptree and Alice Sheldon, as with Dr. Ain, the answer is death.

Awards

The James Tiptree Jr. Award was established in her honor. Every year since 1992 it has recognized a work of science fiction or fantasy that explores and expands the roles of women and men and our understanding of gender.

Short Fiction

"The Girl Who Was Plugged In" (1973) **Hugo**
"Love Is the Plan, the Plan Is Death" (1973) **Nebula**
"Houston, Houston, Do You Read?" (1976) **Hugo, Nebula**
"The Screwfly Solution" (1977) **Nebula**
"Beyond the Dead Reef" (1983) **Locus Poll**
"The Only Neat Thing to Do" (1985) **Locus Poll**

Works by the Author

Up the Walls of the World (1978)
Brightness Falls from the Air (1985)
The Starry Rift (1986; linked stories)

Other Notable Short Fiction

"The Last Flight of Dr. Ain" (1969)
"Your Haploid Heart" (1969)
"And I Awoke and Found Me Here on the Cold Hill Side" (1972)
"Painwise" (1972)
"The Women Men Don't See" (1973)
"A Momentary Taste of Being" (1975)
"The Psychologist Who Wouldn't Do Awful Things to Rats" (1976)
"Time-Sharing Angel" (1977)
"Lirios: A Tale of the Quintana Roo" (1981)
"Out of the Everywhere" (1981)
"With Delicate Mad Hands" (1981)
"The Boy Who Waterskied to Forever" (1982)

"The Color of Neanderthal Eyes" (1988)
"Come Live with Me" (1988)

Collections

Ten Thousand Light-Years from Home (1973)
Warm Worlds and Otherwise (1975) (introduction by Robert Silverberg)
Star Songs of an Old Primate (1978) (introduction by Ursula K. LeGuin)
Out of the Everywhere and Other Extraordinary Visions (1981)
Byte Beautiful: Eight Science Fiction Stories (1985)
Tales of the Quintana Roo (1986)
Crown of Stars (1988)
Her Smoke Rose Up Forever (2004)

In Other Media

"Houston, Houston, Do You Read?" National Public Radio, 1990. Radio drama for the series *Sci-Fi Radio*.
"Yanqui Doodle." National Public Radio, 1990. Radio drama for the series *Sci-Fi Radio*.
"The Girl Who Was Plugged In," *Welcome to Paradox* (1998). TV adaptation, directed by Jorge Montesi.
Weird Romance (1992). Off-Broadway musical by Alan Menken, based in part on "The Girl Who Was Plugged In."
"The Screwfly Solution," *Masters of Horror* (2006). TV adaptation, directed by Joe Dante; starring Jason Priestley and Kerry Norton.

Nonfiction Books

Meet Me at Infinity: The Uncollected Tiptree (2000) Thirty-five essays and articles, including: "Everything But the Signature Is Me" (1979), "Review of Ursula K. Le Guin's *The Lathe of Heaven*" (1975), "With Tiptree Through the Great Sex Muddle" (1975), "A Woman Writing Science Fiction and Fantasy" (1988), "Do You Like It Twice?" (1972, as Alice Sheldon) and "The Lucky Ones" (1946, as Alice Bradley).
Neat Sheets: The Poetry of James Tiptree, Jr. (1996)

Articles and Essays

"Dear Starbear: Letters between Ursula K. Le Guin and James Tiptree Jr." *Fantasy & Science Fiction* 111, no. 3 (2006): 77–115.
Profile. *Isaac Asimov's Science Fiction Magazine* (April 1983).

Bibliographies

Stephensen-Payne, Phil, and Gordon Benson Jr. *James Tiptree Jr., a Lady of Letters: A Working Bibliography.* Polk City, IA: Galactic Central, 1988.

Willick, George C., "Biography and Bibliography." *Spacelight* (May 3, 2006). http://www.gcwillick.com/Spacelight/tiptree.html

For Further Information

James Tiptree, Jr World Wide Website. Edited by David Lavery. http://davidlavery.net/Tiptree/

Bishop, Michael. "James Tiptree, Jr. Is Raccoona Sheldon Is Alice B. Sheldon Is Alli Is . . . ." In *A Reverie for Mister Ray: Reflections on Life, Death, and Speculative Fiction,* ed. Michael H. Hutchins. Hornsea, UK: PS, 2005 (orig. pub. 1992).

Dozois, Gardner. *The Fiction of James Tiptree, Jr.* New York: Algol Press, 1977.

Dunn, Thomas P. "James Tiptree Jr." In *St. James Guide to Science Fiction Writers,* ed. Jay Pedersen. Detroit, MI: St. James, 1996.

Elms, Alan C. "The Psychologist Who Empathized with Rats: James Tiptree, Jr. as Alice B. Sheldon, PhD." *Science Fiction Studies* 31 (2004): 81–96.

Felts, Susannah J. "Alice in Genderland." *Chicago Reader,* November 3, 2006. http://www.chicagoreader.com/chicago/alice-in-genderland/content?oid=923514

Itzkoff, Dave. "Alice's Alias." *New York Times Book Review,* August 20, 2006: 1+.

Le Guin, Ursula. "Introduction to *Star Sounds of an Old Primate.*" In *Language of the Night.* New York: Putnam, 1979.

Lefanu, Sarah, "Who Is Tiptree, What Is She?" In *In the Chinks of the World Machine: Feminism and Science Fiction,* 105–29. London: Women's Press, 1988.

Philips, Julie. *James Tiptree, Jr.: The Double Life of Alice B. Sheldon.* New York: St. Martin's, 2006.

Ross, Jean W. "Interview with James Tiptree, Jr." In *Contemporary Authors*, vol. 18. Detroit: Gale, 1983, 444–50. Reprinted in *Meet Me at Infinity* (2000).

Siegel, Mark. *James Tiptree Jr.* Starmont Reader's Guide 22. San Bernardino, CA: Borgo, 1984.

———. "Love Was the Plan, the Plan Was . . . A True Story about James Tiptree, Jr." *Foundation* (Winter 1988/1989). http://davidlavery.net/Tiptree/siegellwtptpw.htm

Silverberg, Robert. "Introduction: Who Is Tiptree? What Is He?" In *Warm Worlds and Otherwise,* by James P. Tiptree Jr. New York: Ballantine, 1975.

A. E. Van Vogt

Post-human SF; Space Opera

Benchmark Title: *The World of Null-A* (1945)

b. 1912 (Canada: Manitoba); d. 2000 (Los Angeles, California)

> *I fell out of a second-storey window when I was age two and a half, and was unconscious for three days, near death. . . . I discovered that unconsciousness has in it endless hallucinations. The normal part of my brain has probably spent a lifetime trying to rationalize the consequent fantasies and images. This could explain a lot about my bent for science fiction.*
>
> —"Introduction," in *SF Voices No. 3* (1980)

About the Author and the Author's Work

Alfred Elton van Vogt grew up on a farm in a Mennonite community in Manitoba, Canada. An avid reader, one of his great pleasures was Hugo Gernsback's *Amazing Stories*. During the Great Depression, while he worked on farms, as a truck driver, and as a statistical clerk at the Canadian Department of National Defence, he dreamed of making his name and fortune by writing and approached the craft very methodically. Based on the advice in various "how to" books, he taught himself to break the narrative down into segments, build in a plot twist or resolution every 800 words or so, and hold the reader's attention with frequent little obscurities or mysteries (or "hang ups") . He had some success with the "true story" magazine market and writing plays for Canadian radio, which enabled him to develop his own unique system for storytelling and to gain an understanding of the publishing business.

During the 1940s van Vogt wrote a vast number of science fiction short stories, which he later patched together into novels such as *Slan* (1946) and *The Voyage of the Space Beagle* (1950). He called this process a "fix-up," a term that is widely used in SF to this day. During this period he also began his Null-A novels, which combined his favorite theme of the "superman" who triumphs due to his superior mental powers—in this case, his ability to use intuitive reasoning (that is, non-Aristotelian or "null-A" logic) rather than deductive logic. In the 1950s he became involved briefly with L. Ron Hubbard and Dianetics (the forerunner of Scientology), a form of psychoanalysis that offered to unleash the individual's potential to become the very sort of superman that van Vogt's *Slan* and *Null-A* novels depicted. When they fell out and went their separate ways, Van Vogt's writing more or less stopped for a time.

There is a real split in opinion about van Vogt, his style, his methods, and his quirks. "In the stories of A.E. Van Vogt all things are possible, for saying makes them so" (Pierce 1996). Damon Knight, in "Cosmic Jerrybuilder," an essay expanded from

Knight's classic fanzine review of 1945, memorably described Van Vogt as "not a giant as [is] often maintained. He's only a pygmy using a giant typewriter." But Philip K. Dick admired him greatly, and Van Vogt's disjointed, dreamlike style may have been an influence on his work. Other SF authors and critics have paid him generous tributes:

> Van Vogt knew precisely what he was doing in all areas of his fiction writing. There's hardly a wasted word.... His plots are marvels of interlocking pieces, often ending in real surprises and shocks, genuine paradigm shifts, which are among the hardest conceptions to depict.... Each tale contains a new angle, a unique slant, that makes it stand out (DiFilippo 2003).

Van Vogt's many stories, and fix-ups of those stories, include telepathy, teleportation, shape-shifters, elements of space opera, investigations of inner space, and "technological wonders beyond count" (Pierce 1996). In 1980 he was named the inaugural winner of Canada's top honor for science fiction writers, the Aurora Award, and in the mid-1990s he was named Grand Master by the Science Fiction and Fantasy Writers of America and one of its first four inductees into the Science Fiction and Fantasy Hall of Fame.

At the end of his life A. E. van Vogt suffered from Alzheimer's disease, although he continued writing and reworking old material. On January 26, 2000, he died of pneumonia in Los Angeles. But he is not forgotten; in 2007 the Planetary Society arranged with NASA to send a "specialized silica-glass DVD" with the Phoenix mission to Mars. Among eighty classic Martian-themed stories, art, and radio productions—by H. G. Wells, Ray Bradbury, and Kim Stanley Robinson—was "Enchanted Village" by A. E. van Vogt. In an ultimate tribute, the story of a dreamer from Manitoba was part of "the first library on Mars."

Awards

SFWA Grand Master (1996)
Science Fiction Hall of Fame (1996)
Worldcon Special Convention Award (1996)
Aurora Lifetime Achievement (1980)

Novels

The Weapon Shops of Isher (1951) **Prometheus Hall of Fame 2005**

Works by the Author

Slan (1946)
The Book of Ptath (1947)
The Weapon Makers (1947)
The Voyage of the Space Beagle (1950)
The Weapon Shops of Isher (1951)
The Mixed Men (1952)
Empire of the Atom (1957)

The Mind Cage (1957)
Rogue Ship (1965)
The Silkie (1969)
Children of Tomorrow (1970)
The Battle of Forever (1971)

Null-A series

The World of Null-A (1945)
The Pawns of Null-A (1956; aka *The Players of Null-A,* 1966)
Null-A Three (1985; aka *Null A-3*)

Notable Short Fiction

"Black Destroyer" (1939)
"Discord in Scarlet" (1939)
"The Weapon Shop" (1942)
"The Mixed Men" (1945)
"Hand of the Gods" (1946)
"The Twisted Men" (1950; aka "Rogue Ship")
"Research Alpha" (1965, with James Schmitz)
"The Human Operators" (1971, with Harlan Ellison)

Collections

Out of the Unknown (1948, with Edna Mayne Hull)
Masters of Time (1950)
Away and Beyond (1952)
The Mixed Men (1952; aka *Mission to the Stars*)
Destination: Universe! (1952)
The Far-Out Worlds of A. E. van Vogt (1956)
Monsters (1965)
The Sea Thing and Other Stories (1970)
M33 in Andromeda (1971)
The Proxy Intelligence and Other Mind Benders (1971, with Edna Mayne Hull; rev. version *The Gryb,* 1976)
The Book of Van Vogt (1972; aka *Lost: Fifty Suns*)
Far Out Worlds of Van Vogt (1973)
The Three Eyes of Evil Including Earth's Last Fortress (1973)
Pendulum (1978)
Futures Past: The Best Short Fiction of A. E. van Vogt (1999) (introduction by Harlan Ellison)

Transfinite: The Essential A. E. van Vogt (2003)

Transgalactic (2006, edited by Eric Flint and David Drake)

In Other Media

"Since Aunt Ada Came to Stay," *Rod Serling's Night Gallery.* 1971. Directed by William Hale; starring Jeanette Nolan and James Farentino.

"The Human Factor," *The Outer Limits* (2002). Directed by Steve Aspis and Robert Habros; starring Robert Duncan McNeill.

Nonfiction Books

The Hypnotism Handbook (1956; with Charles Edward Cooke)

The Money Personality (1972; aka *Unlock Your Money Personality*)

Reflections of A. E. Van Vogt: The Autobiography of a Science Fiction Giant with a Complete Bibliography (1975)

Articles and Essays

"Complication in the Science Fiction Story." In *Of Worlds Beyond,* ed. Lloyd Arthur Eshbach. Reading, PA: Fantasy Press, 1947.

"Introduction." In *SF Voices No. 3,* ed. Jeffrey M. Elliot, 3–7. San Bernardino, CA: Borgo, 1980.

"My Life Was My Best Science Fiction Story." In *Fantastic Lives*, ed. Martin H. Greenberg, 175–215. Carbondale: Southern Illinois University Press, 1981.

"Tomorrow on the March: The Text of a speech Delivered July 4, 1946 at the Pacificon by the guest of Honor, A.E. Van Vogt" (1946).

Bibliographies

Stephensen-Payne, Phil, and Ian Covell. *A. E. van Vogt: Master of Null-A, A Working Bibliography*. Leeds, UK: Galactic Central, 1997.

Willick, George C. "Bibliography." *Spacelight* (June 2006). http://www.gcwillick.com/Spacelight/biblio/vanvogtbib.html

For Further Information

Icshi: The A. E. Van Vogt Information Site: http://www.home.earthlink.net/~icshi/

Appreciations and Obituary (Anderson, Bradbury, Clarke, Ellison, et al.). *Locus* (January 2000): 66–68.

Axelsson, Magnus, ed. *The Weird Worlds of A.E. Van Vogt.* January 2007. http://vanvogt.www4.mmedia.is/index.htm

Bloom, Harold. "A. E. Van Vogt." In *Science Fiction Writers of the Golden Age,* 188–203. New York: Chelsea House, 1995.

DiFilippo, Paul. "Transfinite: The Essential A. E. van Vogt." *SciFi.com,* July 21, 2003.

Drake, H. L. *A.E. van Vogt: Science Fantasy's Icon*. Lancaster, PA: H. L. Drake 2002.

Elliot, Jeffrey M. "A. E. Van Vogt: A Writer with a Winning Formula." In *SF Voices No. 3,* 30–40. San Bernardino, CA: Borgo, 1980. http://vanvogt.www4.mmedia.is/jeff.htm

———. Interview. *Science Fiction Review* (1977). http://www.angelfire.com/art/megathink/vanvogt/vanvogt_interview.html

Knight, Damon. "Cosmic Jerrybuilder: A.E. Van Vogt." In *In Search of Wonder: Essays on Modern Science Fiction.* 3rd ed. Framingham, MA: NESFA Press, 1996.

Obituary. *Guardian Online.* February 1, 2000. http://books.guardian.co.uk/news/articles/0,,131148,00.html

Panshin, Alexei, and Cory Panshin. "Man Beyond Man: The Early Stories of A. E. Van Vogt." In *The World Beyond the Hill.* Los Angeles: J.P. Tarcher, 1989. http://www.enter.net/~torve/articles/vanvogt/vanvogt1.html

Pierce, Hazel. "A.E. Van Vogt." In *St. James Guide to Science Fiction Writers,* ed. Jay Pedersen. Detroit, MI: St. James, 1996.

Platt, Charles. "A. E. van Vogt." In *Dream Makers: The Uncommon People Who Write Science Fiction,* 133–44. New York: Berkley, 1980. http://vanvogt.www4.mmedia.is/Plattprofile.htm

von Puttkamer, Jesco. "The Childlike Enthusiasm and Unmatched Imagination of A.E. van Vogt." *Space.com,* January 28, 2000. http://www.space.com/sciencefiction/books/van_vogt_tribute_000128.html

Walters, Trent. "Oh, the Humanity of A.E. van Vogt's Monsters: Reorienting Critics and Readers to the van Vogt Method." In *The Zone Online.* Pigasus Press, November 2005. http://www.zone-sf.com/vanvogtmethod.html

Weinberg, Robert. "An Astounding Interview with A. E. Van Vogt." Unpublished interview for *Astounding* magazine (1980). Published on *Ischi: The A. E. Van Vogt Information Site*, March 31, 2008. http://www.home.earthlink.net/~icshi/Interviews/Weinberg-1980.html

John Varley

Post-human SF

Benchmark Title:
The Ophiuchi Hotline (1977)

b. 1947 (Austin, Texas)

Photo credit: Lee Emmett. Permission of Lee Emmett and John Varley.

I've never been a logger or shipped out on a tramp steamer or spent a year on the Greek islands. I have only one hobby, which I don't pursue with a lot of ardor. I'm not an authority on cooking or history or anything. I like to read and writer and travel when I can. It's a pretty dull life, but it suits me.

—"About the Author," in *Millennium* (1983)

About the Author and the Author's Work

John Varley was one of the most exciting new writers of the 1970s, and many of the variations on old SF tropes that he worked effortlessly into his earliest fiction quickly became standard—the gritty, survive-at-all-costs interplanetary refugees of *The Ophiuchi Hotline* (1977); the strong female protagonists of the Gaia Trilogy and the 1976 short story "Air Raid" (written as "Herb Boehm," and later expanded into the 1983 novel *Millennium*); and the gender-bending, free-for-all cloning of almost all of his work. Before long everyone was doing it, and it is easy to forget that Varley did it first.

Varley has a fondness for gadgets, dark scenarios, and alienated characters that might qualify him as a an immediate forerunner of cyberpunk. But on the other hand, his action-fueled plots and unconventional attitudes to diverse sexualities suggest the sort of thing that might have been written by Robert A. Heinlein, had RAH been granted another lifetime. In fact, Varley acknowledges the influence of Heinlein, "because I've read everything he's ever written and he was the very first science fiction writer I read" ("John Varley: The Wonderful Alarming Future" 2004). It's easier to say that John Varley is a one-off than to try to pin his work to any one SF style or subgenre.

John Herbert Varley was born in Austin, Texas, and grew up in Nederland, near Port Arthur, on the Gulf Coast. He was awarded a National Merit scholarship and decided to use it to attend Michigan State University, on the grounds that it was as far as he could get from the "hellish humidity" of Texas and its killer mosquitoes. He discovered, however, that higher education was not to his taste, and dropped out. He spent six years traveling around, from love-ins in San Francisco, to Woodstock, to Tucson and back to San Francisco again, with no visible means of support ("and still can't recall how he did that," according to notes on his official Web site). In 1973 he decided that the only thing this checkered career had prepared him to do, and the only thing he wanted to be, was a science fiction writer. His first published short story, "Picnic on Nearside," appeared in *Fantasy and Science Fiction* in 1974. His willingness to "take risks with his plots, characters, [and] inventive views of the future" (Barth 1996) in novels like *The Ophiuchi Hotline* (1977) and the many excellent and entertaining short stories in his collections *In the Hall of the Martian Kings* (1978) and *The Persistence of Vision* (1978) gained Varley immediate critical and fan recognition. Many of these stories were part of his Eight Worlds sequence, elements of a complicated (and sometimes contradictory) narrative of a time when humanity has been exiled from Earth by mysterious invaders. It appeared that John Varley was on an unstoppable upward trajectory.

But then there was a long period, during the 1980s, when almost no new Varley books or stories appeared, time he spent in Hollywood working on scripts for various movie projects. "You might say I wasted a lot of time in Hollywood over the past 20 years. I've probably been trying to put most of it out of my mind" ("John Varley: The Wonderful Alarming Future" 2004). The only tangible result of this was the film *Millennium*, based on that novel of the same name and the short story "Air Raid," a script he ended up rewriting six times, for four different directors; it was, as he admitted in his 2005 *Locus* interview "not very good"—a heartbreaking result from so much effort and a fine story. John Varley has since returned to writing fiction, and although not at the white-hot pace that he set himself in the 1970s, he has added two novels, *Steel Beach* (1992) and *The Golden Globe* (1998), to the Eight Worlds sequence. His more recent novels, *Red Thunder* (2003), *Red Lightning* (2006), and *Rolling Thunder* (2008), are exuberant tributes to the Heinlein juvenile novels of his youth, space opera-esque adventure, with uncensored images of disaster, potential disaster, and paranoia that fit all too well with the changed circumstances of the first decade of the twenty-first century.

Until recently, John Varley divided his time between Portland, Oregon, and an RV parked fifty yards from the beach along California's central coast, shared with his partner Lee Emmett who has also become his first editor because "[s]he's good at it and full of useful suggestions" (official Web site). Varley and Emmett now live in East Hollywood in a neighborhood called Thai Town or Little Armenia, "depending on who you ask."

Awards

Novels

Titan (1979) **Locus Poll**

The Golden Globe (1998) **Prometheus**

Short Fiction

"The Barbie Murders" (1978) **Locus Poll**

"The Persistence of Vision" (1978) **Hugo, Locus Poll, Nebula**

"Blue Champagne" (1981) **Locus Poll**

"The Pusher" (1981) **Hugo, Locus Poll, Nebula**
"Press ENTER []" (1984) **Hugo, Locus Poll, Nebula**

Collections

The Persistence of Vision (1978) **Locus Poll**
The Barbie Murders (1980) **Locus Poll**
Blue Champagne (1986) **Locus Poll**
The John Varley Reader (2004) **Locus Poll**

Works by the Author

Millennium (1983)
Red Thunder (2003)
Mammoth (2005)
Red Lightning (2006)
Rolling Thunder (2008)

Eight Worlds

The Ophiuchi Hotline (1977)
Steel Beach (1992)
The Golden Globe (1998)

The Gaea Trilogy

Titan (1979)
Wizard (1980)
Demon (1984)

Other Notable Short Fiction

"Picnic on Nearside" (1974)
"In the Bowl" (1975)
"Retrograde Summer" (1975)
"Gotta Sing, Gotta Dance" (1976)
"Overdrawn at the Memory Bank" (1976)
"The Phantom of Kansas" (1976)
"Air Raid" (1977, as Herb Boehm)
"In the Hall of the Martian Kings" (1977)
"Options" (1979)
"Beatnik Bayou" (1980)
"Tango Charlie and Foxtrot Romeo" (1986)
"The Bellman" (2003)

Collections

In the Hall of the Martian Kings (1978)
The Persistence of Vision (1978)
The Barbie Murders (1980; reissued in 1984 as *Picnic on Nearside*)
Blue Champagne (1986)
The John Varley Reader (2004)

As Editor

Superheroes (1995, with Ricia Mainhardt)

In Other Media

Overdrawn at the Memory Bank. WNET Channel 13 New York, 1983. Directed by Douglas Williams; starring Raul Julia. Mesmerizingly awful, but it does have Raul Julia.

Millennium. First Millenium Partnership, 1989. Directed by Michael Anderson; starring Cheryl Ladd and Kris Kristofferson. Based on the short story "Air Raid" and the novel *Millennium.*

Articles and Essays

"About the Author." In *Millennium.* Camp Hill, PA: Berkley/SFBC, 1983. 214+.

"Introduction." In *Superheroes*, ed. John Varley and Ricia Mainhardt, 1–12. New York: Ace, 1995.

For Further Information

Official Web site: http://www.varley.net/

Barth, Melissa E. "John Varley." In *St. James Guide to Science Fiction Writers,* ed. Jay Pedersen. Detroit, MI: St. James, 1996.

Bolhafner, J. Stephen. "Science-Fiction Writer Wilted In Hollywood." *St. Louis Post-Dispatch,* July 20, 1992.

Budrys, Algis. "Introduction." In *The Persistence of Vision.* New York: Dial Press, 1978.

Farrell, Shaun. Interview. *Shaun's Quadrant* (July 2005). Far Sector.com. http://www.farsector.com/quadrant/interview-johnvarley.htm

Interview. *Xero Magazine* 1, no. 4 (1996). http://www.xeromag.com/varley.html

"John Varley: The Wonderful Alarming Future." *Locus* (October 2004). http://www.locusmag.com/2004/Issues/10Varley.html

Lilley, Ernest. Interview. *SFRevu* (May 2003). http://www.sfrevu.com/ISSUES/2003/0305/Feature%20-%20John%20Varley/Interview.htm

Jules Verne

Early SF; Hard SF

Benchmark Title: *From the Earth to the Moon* (1865)

b. 1828 (France: Nantes); d. 1905 (France: Amiens)

> *[V]ery curious, and, I will add, very English. But I do not see the possibility of comparison between [H. G. Wells's] work and mine. . . . his stories do not repose on very scientific bases. No, there is no rapport between his work and mine. I make use of physics. He invents.*
> —Sherard, "Jules Verne Re-Visited," *T.P.'s Weekly* (1903)

About the Author and the Author's Work

According to the *Index Translationum*, a worldwide record of books in translation kept by UNESCO, Verne is the third most translated author in the world (after the Disney Corporation and Agatha Christie, and immediately before Vladimir Ilyich Lenin). He has not always been served well by his translators—thanks to their crude efforts, and ad hoc editing, he is sometimes dismissed as a writer of clumsy pulp, simple adventures, and children's stories. But although the great majority of Jules Verne's *Voyages Extraordinaires* might have seemed like utterly conventional adventures, excuses to send his characters to exotic corners of our familiar world, he "created an imaginative space into which the exploring urge could move itself . . . grounded at all times in contemporary discourses of 'the possible' and 'the known'" (Roberts 2006). Just as H. G. Wells gave us the SF novel of ideas, disguised as adventure stories, Jules Verne gave us the technological adventure.

Jules Gabriel Verne was born in the *prefecture* of the Loire region of France, in Nantes, a bustling harbor city in Brittany. He was the son of an attorney. At the age of eleven he tried to run away to sea as a cabin boy, only to be rescued at the last minute by his father. Standing there, shamefaced, on the dock, perhaps with his father's hand firmly on his collar, watching the ship he had planned to use for his great adventure sail away, he is supposed to have promised: *"Je ne voyagerai plus qu'en rêve"* ("I will no longer travel except in my dreams") (Roberts 2006).

After that episode of youthful wanderlust, Verne's rebellion was confined to passing up the opportunity to follow in his father's footsteps and practice law; he spent some years as a genteel failure in Paris, writing (largely unstaged) plays; mild adventure stories; and ponderous, "serious" historical novels. He did not set the world on fire and was all but ready to give up and go home to Nantes, when he met publisher P. J. Stahl, of the publishing house Hetzel. Stahl cannily noticed that Verne's adventures really came to life when he was writing about geography and science. In 1863 Hetzel began to publish Verne's *Voyages Extraordinaires* (*Fantastic Voyages*), beginning with *Cinq semaines en ballon* (*Five Weeks in a Balloon*). It was an immediate success; in the course of his career, Verne wrote more than sixty "scientific romances," drawing upon his fascination with geography and technology. *The Encyclopedia of Science Fiction* (1999) sums up his enduring appeal thus: "[T]he Vernean thrill [contains] a congenial admixture of 19th century moral clarity, the safety of numbers . . . and a sense of coming very close but never toppling over the edge of the known."

Verne's final years were clouded by ill-health—he suffered from chronic diabetes and, in 1886, he was shot in the leg by his mentally ill nephew, which left him with a painful limp for the rest of his life. There was also some bitterness that he did not receive the recognition that he felt he deserved from the French literary establishment. But he never lost his spark and the sense that he was doing something worth remembering. In 1903, when an interviewer dared to compare his writing to that of his young upstart British rival, H.G. Wells, the reader can feel the temperature drop a few degrees in Verne's comfortable sitting room a hundred years after the event.

On March 24, 1905, Jules Verne died at his home in Amiens, on the Boulevard Longueville. Today, it is Boulevard Jules-Verne. The *Voyages Extraordinaires* continued churning out, as if from the grave, for several years, but it is now recognized that most of the posthumous "Verne" output was drastically edited, if not actually written, by his son, Michel. Verne is buried in the Amiens Madeleine cemetery, beneath a splendid tomb that depicts him, bare-chested, bursting out of the grave and reaching for the heavens. The title of the sculpture is *Vers l'Immortalite et l'Eternelle jeunesse* ("Toward Immortality and Eternal Youth").

Awards

SF Hall of Fame (1999, posthumous)

Works by the Author

Jules Verne's works are out of copyright, and therefore there are a great number of editions available, of widely varying quality. To get a true sense of Verne's quality as a writer, it would always be more satisfactory to find one of the excellent modern translations that are available, rather than the cheap facsimile versions of early translations.

Titles are given in English only, unless the spirit of the title in French differs greatly from the title English language readers know and love. Many of Verne's titles are available on Project Gutenberg, in French, English, and other languages (http://www.gutenberg.org/browse/authors/v#a60).

The *Voyages Extraordinaires*

A Journey to the Centre of the Earth (1864). The Bantam edition of 2006, translated by Lowell Blair, has an introduction by Kim Stanley Robinson.

From the Earth to the Moon (1865)

Twenty Thousand Leagues Under the Sea (1869)

From the Earth to the Moon . . . and a Trip Around It (1870)

Around the World in Eighty Days (1873). The Penguin edition of 2004, translated by Michael Glencross, has an introduction by Brian Aldiss.

The Mysterious Island (1874). The Modern Library edition of 2004, translated by Jordan Stump, has an introduction by Caleb Carr.

Off on a Comet (*Hector Servadac, voyages et aventures à travers le monde solaire*, 1877)

The Begum's Five Hundred Million (1879)

The Clipper of the Clouds (*Robur le Conquerant*, 1886)

Floating Island (*L'Île à hélice*, 1895; aka *Propeller Island*)

Facing the Flag (1896)

An Antarctic Mystery, or The Sphinx of the Ice-fields (1897). A sequel to Edgar Allan Poe's *The Narrative of Arthur Gordon Pym*.

The Village in the Treetops (1901)

The Sea Serpent (1901)

Master of the World (1904)

Invasion of the Sea (1905)

Published Posthumously

Paris in the Twentieth Century (1863)

The Chase of the Golden Meteor (1908)

Other Notable Genre Fiction

Five Weeks in a Balloon (1863)

The English at the North Pole (*Voyages et aventures du capitaine Hatteras*, 1866)

In Search of the Castaways (*Les enfants du capitaine Grant*, 1868)

Michael Strogoff (1876)

The Survivors of The Chancellor (1875)

North against South (1887)

Two Years' Vacation (1888)

Carpathian Castle (1892)

Collections

Doctor Ox and Other Stories (1872). Contains early stories, with some of SF interest, such as "A Drama in the Air" (1851) and "Master Zacharius, or The Clockmaker Who Lost His Soul" (1854)

Yesterday and Tomorrow (*Hier et demain*, 1910). Includes *La Journée d'un journaliste américain en 2890* ("In the Year 2890," 1889) and "The Eternal Adam" (1910), which was probably written by Verne's son Michel after his death.

In Other Media

The International Movie Database (IMDb) lists 130 movies for which Jules Verne is credited as writer. Following are just a few of the highlights of that long list:

Le voyage dans la lune. Edison Manufacturing Company, 1902. Directed by Georges Méliès; drawing on (un-credited) elements of both *From the Earth to the Moon* and H. G. Wells's *The First Men on the Moon.*

20,000 Leagues Under the Sea. Universal Film Manufacturing Company, 1916. Directed by Stuart Paton; starring Allen Holubar as Captain Nemo.

Around the World in Eighty Days. Michael Todd Company, 1956. Directed by Michael Anderson; starring David Niven and Cantinflas. In addition, this film is credited as the first to use the "celebrity cameo"; there are brief appearances by stars such as Buster Keaton, Frank Sinatra, and Marlene Dietrich, among many others.

In Search of the Castaways. Walt Disney Productions, 1962. Directed by Robert Stevenson; starring Maurice Chevalier and Hayley Mills.

Rocket to the Moon. Jules Verne Films Ltd., 1967. Directed by Don Sharp; starring Burl Ives (as Phineas T. Barnum) and Troy Donahue.

Around the World in Eighty Days. Walt Disney Pictures, 2004. Directed by Frank Coraci; starring Steven Coogan and Jackie Chan.

Mysterious Island. Larry Levinson Productions, 2005. Directed by Russell Mulcahy; starring Kyle MacLachlan, with Patrick Stewart as Captain Nemo.

Journey to the Center of the Earth. New Line Cinema, 2008. Directed by Eric Brevig; starring Brendan Frasier.

Nonfiction Books

La Decouverte de la Terre (*The Discovery of the Earth*, 1878)

Articles and Essays

"Edgard Poë [sic] et ses oeuvres." *Musée des Familles* (April 1864). Highly edited English version, "The Bizarre Genius of Edgar Poe." In *The Jules Verne Companion,* ed. Peter Haining, 26–30. London: Pictorial, 1978. Translated by I. O. Evans.

And Inspired . . .

Rick Wakeman. *Journey to the Centre of the Earth* (1974). Concept album, loosely based on the novel, by the composer and songwriter best known as the keyboardist for the progressive rock group Yes.

Michael Palin. *Around the World in 80 Days.* BBC TV series. British Broadcasting Corporation, 1989. Former member of Monty Python's Flying Circus attempts to re-create the journey of Phileas Fogg.

Bibliographies

Dehs, Volker, Jean-Michel Margot, and Zvi Har'El. "The Complete Jules Verne Bibliography." In *Zvi Har'El's Jules Verne Collection*. June 2007. http://jv.gilead.org.il/biblio/

Evans, Arthur B. "A Bibliography of Jules Verne's English Translations." *Science Fiction Studies* 32 (2005): 105–41.

Kytasaari, Dennis. "*Les Voyages Extraordinaires*: The Works of Jules Gabriel Verne, 8 Feb 1828 to 24 Mar 1905." Jules Verne—Links of Interest, July 13, 2006. http://epguides.com/djk/JulesVerne/works.shtml

Willick, George C. "SF Bibliography." *Spacelight* (June 2006). http://www.gcwillick.com/Spacelight/verne.html

For Further Information

The North American Jules Verne Society. Ed. Andrew Nash. March 2007. http://www.najvs.org/

Belloc, Marie A. "Jules Verne at Home." *Strand Magazine* (February 1895): 207–13.

Brown, Eric. *The Extraordinary Voyage of Jules Verne*. Hornsea, UK: PS, 2005.

Butcher, William. *Jules Verne: The Definitive Biography*. New York: Thunder's Mouth, 2006.

Chesneaux, Jean. *The Political and Social Ideas of Jules Verne*. London: Thames, 1972.

Derbyshire, John. "Jules Verne, Father of Science Fiction." *New Atlantis* (Spring 2006). http://www.thenewatlantis.com/archive/12/derbyshire.htm

Evans, Arthur B. "Introduction to the Jules Verne Centenary Issue." *Science Fiction Studies* 32 (2005): 1–4.

Morrow, Laurie. "Prophet-Poet of Technology." *World and I Online* (December 2002).

Renzi, Thomas C. *Jules Verne on Film: A Filmography of the Cinematic Adaptations of His Works, 1902 through 1997*. Rev. ed. Jefferson, NC: McFarland, 2004.

Roberts, Adam. "Jules Verne." In *The History of Science Fiction*. Basingstoke, UK: Palgrave Macmillan, 2006.

Sherard, Robert H. "Jules Verne at Home." *McClure's Magazine* (January 1894): 115–24.

———. "Jules Verne Re-Visited." *T.P.'s Weekly,* October 9, 1903. http://jv.gilead.org.il/sherard2.html

Smyth, Edmund J., ed. *Jules Verne: Narratives of Modernity*. Liverpool, UK: Liverpool University Press, 2000.

Stover, Leon. "Verne and Wells." In *Science Fiction from Well to Heinlein*. Jefferson, NC: McFarland, 2002. 47-94

Taves, Brian, et al. *The Jules Verne Encyclopedia*. Lanham, MD: Scarecrow, 1996.

Teeters, Peggy. *Jules Verne: The Man Who Invented Tomorrow*. New York: Walker, 1992.

Unwin, Timothy. *Jules Verne: Journeys in Writing*. Liverpool, UK: Liverpool University Press, 2005.

Verne, Jean Jules. *Jules Verne: A Biography*. Trans. and abr. Roger Greaves. New York: Taplinger, 1976. Written by Verne's grandson.

Vernor Vinge

Hard SF;
Post-human SF

Benchmark Title:
A Fire Upon the Deep (1992)

b. 1944 (Waukesha, Wisconsin)

Photo credit: Courtesy of Beth Gwinn.

Within thirty years, we will have the technological means to create superhuman intelligence. Shortly after, the human era will be ended.

—"The Coming Technological Singularity" (1993)

About the Author and the Author's Work

When Vernor Vinge's story "True Names" (1981)—widely credited with establishing the concept of cyberspace and making cyberpunk possible—was first published, a friend told him the story was "too far out." However, when the same friend reread the story *just four years later*, she described it as "really too conventional" (Leonard 1999). Today, "True Names" reads like slightly over-enthusiastic creative nonfiction, rather than SF—a reader who doesn't get out much might mistake this story of a group of computer geeks who, their identities hidden by imaginative and somewhat flattering avatars, gather at an exotic virtual location to save the world, as a contemporary advertisement for Second Life. But, no: Vernor Vinge wrote "True Names" when the Internet itself was hardly more than a twinkle in Tim Berners-Lee's eye. According to *Salon* magazine, "William Gibson may get all the glory for defining the word 'cyberspace,' but Vinge actually nailed the details" (Leonard 1999).

If current SF has a difficult time keeping *ahead* of ideas and developments in modern science and culture, it is thanks to authors like Vinge, who are using their fiction to push at the boundaries of what we can expect next. From his earliest stories and novels, Vinge has risen to the challenge by structuring his narratives around the clash between different levels of intelligence and technological advancement—clashes that mimic the gulf that he believes will exist after Singularity. In his first novel, *Grimm's World* (1969), the population of a colony planet that is held back technologically due to a metals-poor environment is exploited and enslaved. In his short story "Bookworm, Run!" (1966), lab chimps' intelligence is chemically enhanced. The universe of *A Fire Upon the Deep* and *A Deepness in the Sky* is divided into "Zones" which neatly ration progress and power to their inhabitants: the Unthinking Depths, the Transcend, the Beyond—and the Slow Zone, where Earth is located. In the near-future of "Fast

Times at Fairmont High" (2001), teenagers can only watch as they are overtaken in skills and ability by youngsters a few years younger than themselves, thirteen-year-olds who are sharing direct mind-links. In a fast-forward nightmare of senility and obsolescence, the older teens find themselves "less adaptive, unable to specialise anew from day to day, plain out of touch" (Hind 2002).

In 1993, having established his reputation as "an author who would explore ideas to their logical conclusions in particularly inventive ways" (Hind 2002), Vinge took his thinking about the future one step further, in a paper at a symposium sponsored by NASA, in which he defined The Singularity as "the imminent creation by technology of entities with greater than human intelligence" ("The Coming Technological Singularity" 1993). This is the moment, Vinge predicts, when smarter-than-human entities—whether they are sentient computers, computer/human interfaces, or the biologically enhanced members of the human race—will accelerate technological progress beyond the capability of ordinary, unenhanced human beings to participate meaningfully. "So as a scientist and mathematician he sees this singularity as a point beyond which meaningful prediction (and fiction) becomes impossible, yet nevertheless he is a science-fiction writer who tries to do that. 'Call me inconsistent—what the heck'" (Hind 2002).

Vernor Steffen Vinge was born in Waukesha, Wisconsin. He attended Michigan State University as an undergraduate and received his PhD in mathematics from the University of California at San Diego. From 1972 he was professor of mathematics at San Diego State University. During the 1970s he was married for a time to Joan D. Vinge, author of space fantasies such as *The Snow Queen* and the "Cat" young adult space opera series.

Vernor Vinge is the recipient of various major awards, including two Prometheus awards for promoting libertarian ideals in science fiction. In 2002 he retired from teaching to devote himself full-time to his writing. He is on record as saying that he is a little disappointed that, as he now has four times as much time to write, he hasn't done four times as much writing.

Awards

Novels

Marooned in Realtime (1986) **Prometheus**

A Fire Upon the Deep (1992) **Hugo**

A Deepness in the Sky (1999) **Campbell, Hugo, Prometheus**

Rainbow's End (2006) **Hugo, Locus Poll**

Short Fiction

"True Names" (1981) **Prometheus Hall of Fame 2008**

"The Ungoverned" (1985) **Prometheus Hall of Fame 2004**

"Fast Times at Fairmont High" (2001) **Hugo**

"The Cookie Monster" (2003) **Hugo, Locus Poll**

Works by the Author

Grimm's World (1969; rev. *Tatja Grimm's World*, 1987)
The Witling (1976)
The Peace War (1984)
Marooned in Realtime (1986)
A Fire Upon the Deep (1992)
A Deepness in the Sky (1999)
Rainbow's End (2006)

Other Notable Short Fiction

"Bookworm, Run!" (1966)

"The Peddler's Apprentice" (1975, with Joan D. Vinge)

"The Ungoverned" (1985). http://www.webscription.net/chapters/1416520724/1416520724_4.htm

"The Barbarian Princess" (1986)

"The Cookie Monster" (2003). http://www.analogsf.com/0310/cookie.shtml

"Synthetic Serendipity" (2004). http://www.spectrum.ieee.org/archive/1552

Collections

True Names . . . and Other Dangers (1987)
Threats . . . and Other Promises (1988)
Across Realtime (1991)
The Collected Stories of Vernor Vinge (2001)

Articles and Essays

"The Coming Technological Singularity: How to Survive in the Post-Human Era." VISION-21 Symposium (NASA Lewis Research Center and the Ohio Aerospace Institute), March 30–31, 1993. A slightly changed version appeared in *Whole Earth Review* (Winter 1993).

"Introduction." In *Skylark of Space,* by E. E. "Doc" Smith. Lincoln: University of Nebraska Press, 2007.

"Introduction." In *True Names . . . And the Opening of the Cyberspace Frontier,* ed. James Frenkel. New York: Tor, 2001.

"The Singularity." Talk to VISION-21 Symposium (NASA Lewis Research Center and the Ohio Aerospace Institute), March 30-31, 1993. http://hem.passagen.se/replikant/vernor_vinge_singularity.htm

"Technological Singularity." *Whole Earth Review* 81 (1993): 88–95. A slightly revised version of the above talk.

"A Universe of One's Own." *New Scientist,* October 26, 1996, 43.

"What If the Singularity Does NOT Happen?" Seminar (The Long Now Foundation), February 15, 2007. http://www.longnow.org/projects/seminars/

For Further Information

"Accelerating Change 2005." *IT Conversations* (audio interview), September 17, 2005. Giga Vox Media. http://www.itconversations.com/shows/detail711.html

Blaschke, Jayme Lynn. Interview. *Strange Horizons*, September 15, 2003. http://www.strangehorizons.com/2003/20030915/vinge.shtml

Farrell, Shaun. "Countdown to Singularity: A Conversation with Vernor Vinge." *Clarkesworld Magazine* (January 2008). http://clarkesworldmagazine.com/farrell_01_08/

———. Interview. *Far Sector.com* (April 2006). http://www.farsector.com/quadrant/ interview-vinge.htm

Frenkel, James, ed. *True Names . . . And the Opening of the Cyberspace Frontier*. New York: Tor, 2001. The short story "True Names" plus eleven essays that spell out Vinge's impact on fact and fiction.

Hind, John. Interview. *The Observer* (London), December 29, 2002. http://observer.guardian.co.uk/magazine/story/0,11913,865638,00.html

Leonard, Andrew. "Vernor Vinge: Online Prophet." *Salon.com*, April 5, 1999. http://www.salon.com/tech/feature/1999/04/05/vinge/

Means, Loren. Interview. *YLEM Journal*, 23, no. 4 (2003): 4–7. http://www.ylem.org/Journal/2003Iss04vol23.pdf

Singular Vernor Vinge Fan Page. http://mindstalk.net/vinge/

Tierney, John. "Technology That Outthinks Us: A Partner or a Master?" (Interview). *New York Times*, August 25, 2008. http://www.nytimes.com/2008/08/26/science/26tier.html?_r=1

Kurt Vonnegut

Humor and Satire; Time Travel

Benchmark Title:
Slaughterhouse-Five (1969)

b. 1922 (Indianapolis, Indiana);
d. 2007 (New York City)

Photo credit: Zach Fine. Permission of *The Daily*, University of Washington.

> [T]he single idea that lies at the core of my life work so far.... "Love may fail, but courtesy will prevail." This seems true to me—and complete.... I needn't have bothered to write several books. A seven-word telegram would have done the job. Seriously.
>
> —Prologue, *Jailbird* (1979)

About the Author and the Author's Work

And so it goes...

Billy Pilgrim is unstuck in time. As a young soldier, he survived the firebombing of Dresden by sheltering with his fellow American POWs and their Nazi guards in the underground meat locker of a slaughterhouse—*Schlachthof Fünf*, or Slaughterhouse Five—as above their heads a beautiful medieval city and all of its inhabitants burned. Now Billy Pilgrim is unstuck in time. As Vonnegut explains in the subtitle of the novel *Slaughterhouse Five*, his story is

> a Duty-Dance with Death, by Kurt Vonnegut, Jr., a Fourth-Generation German-American Now Living in Easy Circumstances on Cape Cod (and Smoking Too Much) Who, as an American Infantry Scout Hors de Combat, as a Prisoner of War, Witnessed the Fire-Bombing of Dresden, Germany, the Florence of the Elbe, a Long Time Ago, and Survived to Tell the Tale: This Is a Novel Somewhat in the Telegraphic Schizophrenic Manner of Tales of the Planet Tralfamadore, Where the Flying Saucers Come From.

Kurt Vonnegut Jr. was born in Indianapolis in 1922, the son of a successful architect. (He became "Kurt Vonnegut" when his father died in 1973.) He attended Cornell University, majoring in chemistry and biology, working on the student newspaper and pledging with his father's fraternity, Delta Upsilon. But it was not a happy time for him, and in 1942 he enlisted in the U.S. Army. On a scouting mission as a private with the 106th Infantry Division late in 1944, Vonnegut was cut off from his battalion and captured by Wehrmacht troops. He was imprisoned with other POWs in the city of Dresden, and in February 1945 he survived the firebombing of that city with a handful of other U.S. POWs. They emerged to a scene of unbelievable carnage and destruction. In *Slaughterhouse-Five*, he recalls that the remains of the once-beautiful city resembled the surface of the moon. The POWs were set to work clearing bodies, burning them on great pyres when the task became too much. They were liberated by the Russian army and repatriated in May 1945. He learned that a year before his ordeal, his mother had killed herself.

Following the war Vonnegut studied anthropology at the University of Chicago. (He was awarded his MA in 1971, when the university accepted his novel *Cat's Cradle* as his master's thesis on the basis of its anthropological content.) He worked as a crime reporter, publicist, and car salesman while trying to establish a writing career. His first novel, *Player Piano*, was published in 1952, but by the early 1960s he was on the verge of abandoning writing when he was offered a teaching job at the University of Iowa Writers' Workshop. While there he began *Slaughterhouse-Five*, now considered one of the classic twentieth-century American novels.

In his work Vonnegut makes extensive use of comfortable old SF conventions—time travel, visiting aliens, automated dystopias, misguided inventions, and fake religions—but also struggles to avoid being pigeon-holed. His unique role in twentieth-century American literature was, perhaps, to demonstrate that the familiar tropes of pulp SF had an important part to play in expressing the inexpressible—the deaths of 135,000 civilian in a firestorm, the danger to people and the planet posed by human pride, and humankind's tricky relationship with God the Utterly Indifferent. But at the same time, Vonnegut made it very clear that the tricks of postmodern mainstream literature—experimental narrative structure, characters who drift from one volume to another, and robust interventions by the authorial voice—had a place in good SF.

Kurt Vonnegut died at the age of eighty-four on April 11, 2007, in New York City after a fall at his East Side Manhattan home. Just a year before he had visited The Ohio State University—the site, he was delighted to point out, of his very first campus reading many, many years before, and now, as he put it, his "last speech for money" (Wasserman 2006). He clearly enjoyed the neat symmetry; the 2,000 students and faculty who had braved the long lines, and the dull, rainy evening were treated to vintage Vonnegut—slightly frail, but having lost none of the peppery wit and the dry wisdom. "Answering questions written in by students, he explains the meaning of life. 'We should be kind to each other. Be civil. And appreciate the good moments by saying, *If this isn't nice, what is?*'" (Wasserman 2006).

Shortly after his death, his son, Mark Vonnegut, appeared on his behalf at a lecture in Indianapolis, where 2007 had been proclaimed "The Year of Kurt Vonnegut." Mark Vonnegut delivered the speech that his father had written for the event, which is reproduced on his official Web site. Reportedly the last thing he wrote, it ended with the words, "I thank you for your attention, and I'm outta here."

The asteroid 25399 Vonnegut is named in his honor.

Works by the Author

Kurt Vonnegut's fiction, nonfiction, and general musings could fill many, many pages. Listed below are the merest highlights, with particular emphasis on SF and writing in general. An extensive list of fiction, nonfiction, interviews, and secondary sources can be found at *The Vonnegut Web* (Ed. Chris Huber. http://www.vonnegutweb.com/).

Player Piano (1952)
The Sirens of Titan (1959)
Cat's Cradle (1963)
Slaughterhouse-Five; or, *The Children's Crusade: A Duty-Dance with Death* (1969)
Breakfast of Champions; or, *Goodbye Blue Monday!* (1973)
Slapstick; or, Lonesome No More (1976)
Galápagos: A Novel (1985)
Timequake (1997)

Notable Mainstream and Other Genre Fiction

Mother Night (1961)
God Bless You, Mr. Rosewater; or, Pearls before Swine (1965)
Jailbird (1979)
Deadeye Dick (1982)
Bluebeard (1987)
Hocus Pocus (1990)

Notable Short Fiction

"Report on the Barnhouse Effect" (1950)
"Tomorrow and Tomorrow and Tomorrow" (1953)
"Harrison Bergeron" (1961)
"2BR02B" (1962)
"Welcome to the Monkey House" (1968)

Collections

Canary in a Cathouse (1961)
Welcome to the Monkey House: A Collection of Short Works (1968)
Bagombo Snuff Box: Uncollected Short Fiction (1999)
Armageddon in Retrospect (2008, posthumous)

In Other Media

Between Time and Timbuktu: A Space Fantasy. National Educational Television Network, 1972. Directed by Fred Barsyk; starring Kevin McCarthy and Hurd Hatfield.

Slaughterhouse-Five. Universal Pictures, 1972. Directed by George Roy Hill; starring Michael Sachs and Valerie Perrine.

Mother Night. New Line Cinema, 1996. Directed by Keith Gordon; starring Nick Nolte and Sheryl Lee.

Harrison Bergeron. Atlantic Films Ltd., 1995. Directed by Bruce Pittman; starring Sean Astin, Buck Henry, and Christopher Plummer.

Breakfast of Champions. Flying Hearts Films, 1999. Directed by Alan Rudolf; starring Bruce Willis and Albert Finney.

2081. Moving Picture Institute, 2009 (in production). A feature film based on the short story "Harrison Bergeron"; directed by Chandler Tuttle; starring Patricia Clarkson and Armei Hammer.

Nonfiction Books

Wampeters, Foma and Granfalloons (Opinions) (1974)

Palm Sunday (1981)

Fates Worse Than Death: An Autobiographical Collage of the 1980s (1991)

God Bless You, Dr. Kevorkian (1999)

A Man Without a Country (2005)

Articles and Essays

"Custodians of Chaos." *Guardian Online*, January 21, 2006. http://www.guardian. co.uk/books/2006/jan/21/kurtvonnegut

"Heinlein Gets the Last Word." *New York Times*, December 9, 1990.

In These Times. Newspaper columns and interviews for newsmagazine committed to political and economic democracy. http://www.inthesetimes.com/. Includes "Kurt Vonnegut vs. the !&#*!@" (Interview, 2003), "Cold Turkey" (2004), and "Requiem for a Dreamer" (Vonnegut Interviews Kilgore Trout) (2004)

"On Science Fiction." *The New York Times*, September 5, 1965. http://www.vonnegutweb.com/archives/arc_scifi.html

Bibliographies

"Complete Writing." In *The Vonnegut Web,* ed. Chris Huber. February 4, 2005. http://www.vonnegutweb.com/vonnegutia/biblio.html

For Further Information

The Vonnegut Web. Ed. Chris Huber. http://www.vonnegutweb.com/

Allen, Rodney, ed. *Conversations with Kurt Vonnegut.* Jackson: University Press of Mississippi, 1988.

Boon, Kevin A., ed. *At Millennium's End: New Essays on the Work of Kurt Vonnegut.* Albany: State University of New York Press, 2001.

Brinkley, Douglas. "Vonnegut's Apocalypse." *Rolling Stone*, August 24, 2006, 77–110. http://www.rollingstone.com/politics/story/11123162/kurt_vonnegut_says_this_is_the_end_of_the_world

Davis, Todd F. *Kurt Vonnegut's Crusade or, How a Postmodern Harlequin Preached a New Kind of Humanism.* Albany: State University of New York Press, 2006.

Hayman, David et al. "Kurt Vonnegut: The Art of Fiction No. 64." *The Paris Review* (Spring 1977). http://www.theparisreview.org/viewinterview.php/prmMID/3605

"The Infinite Mind Interview with Kurt Vonnegut Live from Second Life" (and other video clips). *Video.Google,* September 22, 2006. http://video.google.com/videoplay?docid=-2140455044291565033

Klinkowitz, Jerome. *The Vonnegut Effect.* Columbia: University of South Carolina Press, 2004.

"Kurt Vonnegut." *NOW,* October 7, 2007. Public Broadcasting System. http://www.pbs.org/now/arts/vonnegut.html

"Kurt Vonnegut Judges Modern Society." *The Long View,* January 23, 2006. National Public Radio. http://www.npr.org/templates/story/story.php?storyId=5165342

Leeds, Marc. *The Vonnegut Encyclopedia: An Authorized Compendium.* Westport, CT: Greenwood, 1995.

Leeds, Marc, and Peter J. Reed. *Kurt Vonnegut: Images and Representations* Westport, CT: Greenwood, 2000.

Lessing, Doris. "Vonnegut's Responsibility." *New York Times,* February 4, 1973.

Marvin, Thomas F. *Kurt Vonnegut: A Critical Companion.* Westport, CT: Greenwood, 2002.

Morse, Donald E. *The Novels of Kurt Vonnegut: Imagining Being an American.* Westport, CT: Praeger, 2003.

Reed, Peter J., and Marc Leeds. *The Vonnegut Chronicles: Interviews and Essays.* Westport, CT: Greenwood, 1996.

Wasserman, Harvey. "Kurt Vonnegut's 'Stardust Memory.'" *Columbus Free Press* (Ohio), March 5, 2006. http://www.commondreams.org/views06/0305-27.htm

David Weber

Military SF; Space Opera

Benchmark Title: *On Basilisk Station* (1993)

b. 1952 (Cleveland, Ohio)

Photo credit: Beth Gwinn

In the most fundamental sense, almost all of my stories are about choices. I believe that the best measure of anyone's character is to be found in the decisions they make in the face of adversity. . . . In my books, the heroes are almost always the responsibility-takers, the ones who step up when a problem has to be confronted.

—Adams, Interview at *SciFi.com* (2007)

About the Author and the Author's Work

On his new official Web site, David Weber modestly begins, "I don't really do 'biography' very well." His fans will surely forgive him, because what he undoubtedly does do very well indeed is spirited, modern-minded military SF, in the tradition of the classic naval adventures of C. S. Forester's Horatio Hornblower and Patrick O'Brian, stories that take men (and, in Weber's case particularly, women) of great courage and honor and then make them the only thing that stands between humanity and extinction. Like Forester and O'Brian, Weber showcases the fine art of military strategy, and his characters embody values such as leadership, justice, and loyalty.

David Mark Weber was born in Cleveland, Ohio, in 1952. His family moved to South Carolina when he was a baby: one of his earliest memories, as a preschooler, is of "helping" his father clear the site of the house the family later built, just outside Simpsonville, South Carolina. Weber earned an MA in history at Appalachian State University in Boone, North Carolina; it was his ambition to carry on and complete a PhD in the subject, until he realized the limited prospects that awaited young, untenured history professors. This resulted in an adjustment in his ambitions, and Weber returned to Greenville, South Carolina, to run the advertising agency founded by his mother, writing copy for radio, television, national print magazines, and newspapers. "All of these are (or should be) excellent training for any professional writer. None of them are the sort of writing which will tolerate the concept of 'writer's block,' and all of them are deadline intensive" (davidweber.com).

Meanwhile, Weber found an outlet for his interest in history and his love of military history in particular—war game design. He worked on the development of the StarFire gaming series from Task Force Games of Amarillo, Texas, becoming "the person who developed the campaign and strategic rules which allowed players to build entire empires and expand them" (davidweber.com). This led directly to Weber's first published novel, *Insurrection*, written with fellow gamer Steve White. And the publication of *Insurrection* led directly to Weber's involvement with Jim Baen of Baen Books, who recognized Weber's talent for involved, challenging series and set about channeling it.

David Weber has little time for agonizing over that talent: "I have to admit the term 'artistic' bothers me sometimes. I think of what I do as my craft, not as my 'art.' I don't think of myself as an 'artist' at all, really" (Hoover 2009). His stories are old-fashioned in style and structure, and they spotlight the old-fashioned virtues of loyalty and courage. But it is undeniable that aspects of his novels are decidedly forward looking: the gender-neutral military service that exists in his futures and the strong, resourceful women in what have traditionally been male roles. And neither is this window dressing or exploiting the possible titillation value of having a pretty girl wielding the broadsword. The women in Weber's novels are soldiers, and they are professionals, and although Weber's future may talk the talk of gender neutrality, Weber is canny enough to build into his tales the challenges faced by women like Honor Harrington in a power structure of any time and any place.

Weber is an enthusiastic collaborative writer; he has worked productively with other authors, from his first novel based on the Starfire games, with Steve White, to more recent collaborations with stars of military SF Eric Flint and John Ringo. He is a popular guest at SF conventions, and he has said that he makes an effort to accept as many invitations as he can, because he finds them great opportunities for direct feedback from his readers. He has an endearing habit of embedding fans and friends (or at least borrow their names) in his novels. In 2008 he donated his writing archive to the department of Rare Books and Special Collections at Northern Illinois University.

Interviews with Weber suggest a man who is bubbling with ideas, ideas with which even his amazing output of "the equivalent of about three quarter-million-word novels a year" (Hoover 2009) cannot keep pace. His work ranges from novels dramatizing war game scenarios, to epic fantasy (*Oath of Swords*, *The War God's Own*), to space opera (*Path of the Fury*, *The Armageddon Inheritance*), to rewriting history (the very popular 1632 series, written with Eric Flint). But in anybody's universe, it's Honor Harrington who is the rock star: to date, over three million copies in print, thirteen novels and four shared-universe anthologies, and thirteen of those titles featured on *The New York Times* Best Seller list. And—if his fans have any say in the matter—Honor Harrington and her saga of life in the Royal Manticoran Navy looks set fair for many, many more adventures. David Weber currently makes his home in South Carolina, where he is a Methodist lay preacher, with his wife Sharon, their three children, and, according to his Web site, "a passel of dogs."

Works by the Author

The Apocalypse Troll (1999)
The Excalibur Alternative (2002)
Bolo! (2005)
Old Soldiers (2005)
In Fury Born (2006, rev. version of *Path of the Fury*, 1992)

Dahak series

Mutineers' Moon (1991)
The Armageddon Inheritance (1993)
Heirs of Empire (1996)

Empire of Man series, with John Ringo

March Upcountry (2001)
March to the Sea (2001)
March to the Stars (2003)
We Few (2005)

Honor Harrington series

On Basilisk Station (1993)
The Honor of the Queen (1993)
The Short Victorious War (1994)
Field of Dishonor (1994)
Flag in Exile (1995)
Honor Among Enemies (1996)
In Enemy Hands (1997)
Echoes of Honor (1998)
Ashes of Victory (2000)
War of Honor (2002)
At All Costs (2005)

Honorverse: Saganami

The Shadow of Saganami (2004)
Storm from the Shadows (2009)

Honorverse: Wages of Sin

Crown of Slaves (2003)
Torch of Freedom (2009)

Safehold series

Off Armageddon Reef (2007)
By Schism Rent Asunder (2008)
By Heresies Distressed (2009)

Starfire series (with Steve White, based on the Starfire games)

Insurrection (1990)
Crusade (1992)
In Death Ground (1997)
The Shiva Option (2002)

1632 series, with Eric Flint

1633 (2002)
1634: The Baltic War (2007)

Multiverse series, with Linda Evans

Hell's Gate (2006)
Hell Hath No Fury (2007)

Other Notable Genre Fiction

War God series

Oath of Swords (1995)
The War God's Own (1999)
Wind Rider's Oath (2004)

Other Notable Short Fiction

"A Beautiful Friendship" (1998)
"What Price Dreams?" (1999)
"The Hard Way Home" (1999)
"Ms. Midshipwoman Harrington" (2001)
"Changer of Worlds" (2001)
"Nightfall" (2001)
"Sir George and the Dragon" (2001)
"The Service of the Sword" (2003)
"In the Navy" (2004)

Collections

More Than Honor (1998). Includes a novella by S. M. Stirling, *A Whiff of Grapeshot* (1998), set in the Honorverse.
Worlds of Honor (1999)
Changer of Worlds (2001). Includes a novella by Eric Flint, *From the Highlands* (2001), set in the Honorverse.
The Service of the Sword (2003)
Worlds of Weber: Ms. Midshipwoman Harrington and Other Stories (2008)

Nonfiction Books

Jayne's Intelligence Review: The Royal Manticoran Navy (2006, with Ken Burnside and Thomas Pope)

Jayne's Intelligence Review No. 2: The People's Navy (2007, with Ken Burnside and Thomas Pope)

Articles and Essays

"Pearls of Weber." Edited by Cynthia Gonsalves. December 2001. http://infodump.thefifthimperium.com/. A collection of posts by David Weber containing background information for his stories.

"Who Is Honor Harrington?" *BaenBooks.com,* September 20, 2002. http://www.baen.com/hh_essay.htm

For Further Information

Official Homepage. http://www.davidweber.net/

Adams, John Joseph. Interview. *SciFi.com*, May 7, 2007.

Hoover, Kenneth Mark. "Wordcraft and War Fiction: An Interview with David Weber." *Strange Horizons*, August 10, 2009. http://strangehorizons.com/2009/20090810/hoover-a.shtml.

Hunt, Stephen. "In Honor I Gained Them: Interview." SF *Crowsnest* (July 2002). http://www.sfcrowsnest.com/

"An Interview with David Weber, Parts 1–7." *Blackfive Media* (Video), October 20, 2008. http://www.blackfive.net/main/2008/10/an-interview—7.html

Mallozzi, Joseph. "Author David Weber Answers Yours Questions." *Josephmallozzi's Weblog,* January 17, 2009. http://josephmallozzi.wordpress.com/2009/01/17/january-17-2009-author-david-weber-answers-yours-questions/

Wilson, Alyce. Interview. *Wild Violet* (Spring 2007). http://www.wildviolet.net/live_steel/david_weber.html

H. G. Wells

Early SF; Utopian SF

Benchmark Title: *The Time Machine* (1895)

b. 1866 (England: Bromley, Kent); d. 1946 (England: London)

> [S]ome of the Utopias are among the most enduring gems in the literary treasure house. They throw down no such self-destructive challenge as the futurist writer does, when he says, "This is the way things are going—and this what is coming about." The Utopian says merely, "If only," and escapes from time, death and judgment.
> —"Utopias" (1939)

About the Author and the Author's Work

During World War II, H. G. Wells refused to let the Blitz drive him out of London. While friends worried about him and tried to tempt him away to safer locations, Wells stayed in his house in Regent's Park throughout the war, watching bombs rain down all around him; some nights, watching London burn. He might have been forgiven for thinking, like his nameless Narrator in *The War of the Worlds*, that it was the end of the world; but unlike his Narrator, Wells would not have observed the beginnings of the conflict in the comfortable complacency—the denial—that meets the Martian invasion of his great 1898 novel. H.G. Wells would have known exactly what to expect from the "total war" that was raining down on the people of Europe—he had, after all, invented the future in which it was happening.

Herbert George Wells was born in Bromley, the son of working-class parents whose lives were a constant struggle to climb up into middle class respectability. Young Wells endured a series of unhappy apprenticeships and dead-end jobs meant to consolidate this upwardly mobile scenario, and escaped them through education: he won a scholarship to the Normal School of Science (later the Royal College of Science, and today part of Imperial College London). There, he studied biology under T. H. Huxley, famous champion of Charles Darwin and the theory of evolution, scientific humanist and, like Wells, a self-made man; in 1905, Wells recalled that time as "beyond all question the most educational year [of my life] . . . at the end of that time I had acquired a fairly clear and complete and ordered view of the ostensibly real universe" (*Modern Utopia* 1905).

Wells completed his degree in 1890 and, while teaching with the University Correspondence College, wrote textbooks and science articles aimed at a popular audience, increasingly using the techniques of fiction to illustrate dry concepts like natural selection, the solar system, and the possibilities of alien life-forms.

While he was at college Wells had begun a series called The Chronic Argonauts for the undergraduate magazine *Science Schools Journal*, to test the idea that fiction might be a suitable way to convey complex scientific ideas. He was so dissatisfied with the three installments that appeared in 1888 that in later years he attempted to buy up all existing copies of the offending issues. By 1895 Wells had worked on it long enough to get it spectacularly right, and his apprenticeship as a writer ended with the publication of *The Time Machine*. This was rapidly followed by *The Island of Dr. Moreau* (1896), *The Invisible Man* (1897), and *The War of the Worlds* (1898). These four novels staked the boundaries of the genre that, in the next century, would come to be called "science fiction." They all, one after the other, sum up the themes that would run like a bright thread throughout his work, and indeed his entire life: faith in the literal possibilities of Darwin's evolutionary theory, an abiding hatred of arrogance, and a passionate desire to eradicate the injustices and hypocrisies of his world. However famous—indeed notorious—and influential Wells would become, however challenging his ideals and his ego, there was part of him that always remained that scholarship boy, listening to Professor Huxley offer the possibility that humankind, and society, can change, but it is up to us to decide what form those changes may take. "Wells's great achievement was to use the apparatus of science to take a long, bleak view of the human condition; to show how tiny we appear through the reversed telescope of eternity, dwarfed by the grandeur of a purely materialistic universe" (Langford 2005).

Following his great burst of SF creativity in the late 1890s and early twentieth century, Wells's fiction tended to be more utopian—prescriptive of the future as he thought it could be, or should be. He took the fullest advantage of his fame and his popular image as spokesman for the future. He traveled extensively, meeting and speaking to ordinary people and the leaders of the day, stating his views forthrightly to U.S. presidents Theodore Roosevelt and Franklin Delano Roosevelt and Soviet leaders Stalin, Trotsky, and Lenin (who, according to Wells biographer Michael Foot, exclaimed "What a little *bourgeois*! What a philistine," after their meeting, because Wells asked too many awkward questions). He wrote shrewd, readable social comedies, about charming, fiercely intelligent young men, who escape from dead-end apprenticeships to follow their bliss, and young women who shake off the sexual and social repressions of society to lead full and happy lives (usually arm-in-arm with the charming, fiercely intelligent young men).

By the start of World War II, some of Wells's utopianism could seem naïve; his fiercely egalitarian attitudes and faith in evolution seemed like blindness in the face of the brutal facts. But it was impossible to shake off the awareness that he had done something special with those four prescient novels, written as one century turned into another, very different century. In 1941 George Orwell—another author with a clear-eyed view of what the future might throw at us—wrote in his otherwise sharply critical essay "Wells, Hitler and the World State": "The minds of all of us, and therefore the physical world, would be perceptibly different if Wells had never existed."

H. G. Wells died in London on August 13, 1946. Craters on both the moon and the planet Mars have been named after him. It is impossible to imagine science fiction without him.

Awards

Science Fiction Hall of Fame (1997, posthumous)

Works by the Author

H. G. Wells was a prolific writer of both fiction and nonfiction, with a writing career that spanned more than sixty years. An extensive list of his novels is available online at Project Gutenberg (http://www.gutenberg.org/) and the Online Library of the University of Adelaide, Australia (http://etext.library.adelaide.edu.au/w/wells/hg/).

The Time Machine (1895)
The Invisible Man (1897)
The Island of Doctor Moreau (1896)
War of the Worlds (1898)
When the Sleeper Wakes (1899; rev. *The Sleeper Awakes*, 1910)
The First Men on the Moon (1901)
The Food of the Gods and How It Came to Earth (1904)
A Modern Utopia (1905)
In the Days of the Comet (1906)
The War in the Air (1908)
Tono-Bungay (1909)
The World Set Free (1914)
Men Like Gods (1923)
The Shape of Things to Come (1933)
Star Begotten (1937)

Notable Mainstream and Other Genre Fiction

The Wonderful Visit (1895)
The Wheels of Chance (1896)
Kipps (1905)
Ann Veronica (1909)
The History of Mr. Polly (1910)

Notable Short Fiction

"The Chronic Argonauts" (1888) http://www.colemanzone.com/Time_Machine_Project/chronic.htm
"The Star" (1897)
"The Crystal Egg" (1899) http://etext.lib.virginia.edu/toc/modeng/public/WelCrys.html
"The Land Ironclads" (1903) http://www.zeitcom.com/majgen/60w-1_landironclads.html
"The Truth About Pyecraft" (1903)

"The Country of the Blind" (1904)
"The Door in the Wall" (1906)

Collections

H. G. Wells: Early Writings in Science and Science Fiction (1975, edited by Robert M. Philmus and David Y. Hughes)

H.G. Wells's Literary Criticism (1980, edited by Patrick Parrinder and Robert M. Philmus)

The Complete Short Stories of H. G. Wells (2001, edited by John Hammond)

Selected Stories of H.G. Wells (2004, edited by Ursula K. Le Guin)

The Country of the Blind and Other Stories. (2007, edited by Patrick Parrinder and Andy Sawyer)

In Other Media

The International Movie Database (IMDb) lists eighty-three movies and television programs for which H. G. Wells is credited as writer. Following are just a few of the highlights of that long list:

Le voyage dans la lune. Edison Manufacturing Company, 1902. Directed by Georges Méliès; drawing on (uncredited) elements of both *The First Men on the Moon* and Jules Verne's *From the Earth to the Moon*.

Island of Lost Souls. Paramount Pictures, 1932. Directed by Erle C. Kenton; starring Charles Laughton and Bela Lugosi.

The Invisible Man. Universal Pictures, 1933. Directed by James Whale; starring Claude Rains.

Things to Come. London Film Productions, 1936. Directed by William Cameron Menzies; starring Raymond Massey.

The War of the Worlds. Paramount Pictures, 1953. Directed by Byron Haskin; starring Gene Barry and Ann Robinson.

The Time Machine. George Pal Productions, 1960. Directed by George Pal; starring Rod Taylor and Yvette Mimieux.

The Food of the Gods. American International Pictures (AIP), 1976. Directed by Bert I. Gordon; starring Ida Lupino and Marjoe Gortner.

The Island of Dr. Moreau. New Line Cinema, 1996. Directed by John Frankenheimer, starring Marlon Brando and David Thewlis.

The Time Machine. DreamWorks SKG, 2002. Directed by Simon Wells (the great-grandson of Herbert George); starring Guy Pearce.

War of the Worlds. DreamWorks SKG, 2005. Directed by Steven Spielberg; starring Tom Cruise and Dakota Fanning.

The History of Mr, Polly. Granada Television, 2007. Directed by Gillies MacKinnon; starring Lee Evans and Anne-Marie Duff.

Nonfiction Books

Mankind in the Making (1903)
First and Last Things (1908)
New Worlds for Old (1913)
The Outline of History (1920)
Experiment in Autobiography: Discoveries and Conclusions of a Very Ordinary Brain since 1866 (1934)
The New World Order (1940)

Articles and Essays

"Utopias." The Australian Broadcasting Company, January 19, 1939. *Science Fiction Studies* 9 (1982): 117–21. http://www.depauw.edu/sfs/documents/wells1.htm

"Woman and Primitive Culture." *Science Fiction Studies* 8 (1981): 35–37. http://www.depauw.edu/sfs/documents/wells2.htm (orig. pub. 1895).

Bibliographies

"An H.G. Wells Bibliography." *The H.G. Wells Society of the Americas* (July 2004). http://www.hgwellsusa.50megs.com/bibliography.html

For Further Information

The H.G. Wells Society: http://www.hgwellsusa.50megs.com/
The Wellsian: http://www.hgwellsusa.50megs.com/UK/wellsian.html

Austin, Mary. "An Appreciation of H. G. Wells, Novelist." *American Magazine* 72 (1911). http://etext.lib.virginia.edu/toc/modeng/public/AusWell.html

Beresford, J. D. *H.G. Wells: A Critical Study*. Rockville, MD: Wildside, 2005.

Chesterton, G. K. "Mr. H. G. Wells and the Giants." In *Heretics,* 1905. Charlotte: Saint Benedict, 2006. http://www.cse.dmu.ac.uk/~mward/gkc/books/heretics/ch5.html

Coren, Michael. *The Invisible Man: The Life and Liberties of H. G. Wells*. London: Bloomsbury, 1992.

Creek, Dave. "H.G. Wells: Creature of the Twilight." *Internet Review of Science Fiction* (July 2005). http://www.irosf.com/q/zine/article/10167

Crossley, Robert. "The Grandeur of H.G. Wells." In *A Companion to Science Fiction*, ed. David Seed, 353–63. Malden: Blackwell, 2005.

Foot, Michael. *H. G.: The History of Mr. Wells*. Washington DC: Counterpoint, 1995.

Gunn, James. "H.G. Wells: The Man Who Invented Tomorrow." In *The Science of Science-Fiction Writing*, 117–37. Lanham, MD: Scarecrow, 2000.

Hammond, J. R. *A Preface to H. G. Wells*. New York: Longman, 2001.

Langford, David. "The History of Mr. Wells." *Fortean Times* 199 (2005). http://www.ansible.co.uk/writing/ft-wells.html

Obituary. *The New York Times*, August 14, 1946. http://www.gcwillick.com/Spacelight/obit/hgwellso.html

Orwell, George. "Wells, Hitler and the World State." *Horizon* (August 1941). http://orwell.ru/library/reviews/wells/english/e_whws

Parrinder, Patrick. *Shadows of the Future: H.G. Wells, Science Fiction, and Prophecy*. Liverpool, UK: Liverpool University Press, 1995.

Smith, Don G. *H.G. Wells on Film: The Utopian Nightmare*. Jefferson, NC: McFarland, 2003.

Stover, Leon. "Verne and Wells." In *Science Fiction from Wells to Heinlein*, 47–94. Jefferson, NC: McFarland, 2002.

Wagar, W. Warren. *H.G. Wells: Traversing Time*. Middletown, NH: Wesleyan University Press, 2004.

Wells, G.P., ed. *H. G. Wells in Love: Postscript to an Experiment in Autobiography*. Boston: Little, Brown, 1984.

West, Anthony. *H. G. Wells: Aspects of a Life*. New York: Random House, 1984. Anthony West (1914–1987) was Wells's son by Rebecca West. Also see his radio interview with Don Swaim for *Wired for Books* (June 26, 1984; WOUB Online, http://wiredforbooks.org/anthonywest/).

Zamyatin, Yevgeny. "H.G. Wells." In *A Soviet Heretic: Essays by Yevgeny Zamyatin,* ed. and trans. Mirra Ginsburg, 259–90. Chicago: University of Chicago Press, 1970.

Kate Wilhelm

Apocalyptic SF; Feminist SF

Benchmark Title:
Where Late the Sweet Birds Sang (1976)

b. 1928 (Toledo, Ohio)

The problem with labels is that they all too quickly become eroded; they cannot cope with borderline cases.

—The Infinity Box (1975)

Photo credit: Richard Wilhelm. Courtesy of Kate Wilhelm.

About the Author and the Author's Work

Kate Wilhelm was born Kate Gertrude Meredith in Toledo, Ohio. In high school she took an employment aptitude test that told her she was meant to be an architect, and she has proved to be an architect of a long list of well-constructed stories and novels in various genres, *and* of writing lives. She and her late husband, the writer and critic Damon Knight, helped to found the Clarion Writers Workshop and hosted the first Milford Writer's Conferences at their home in Milford, Pennsylvania, as get-togethers for their friends in the world of SF. Over the years Wilhelm and Knight ran hundreds of workshops, and thousands of writers benefited from her "ability to analyze a story and gently but firmly bring out the weaknesses in a constructive manner" (Van Gelder 2001). In the year 2000, all four winners of the Nebula Awards for fiction were former students of Kate Wilhelm.

Kate Meredith grew up with her brothers and sister in Kentucky. She married young, divorced, and raised her two young sons by working variously as an insurance underwriter, a long-distance telephone operator, and a professional model. According to the author biography on her first novel, *More Bitter Than Death* (1962), she wrote it "between the hours of 9 P.M. and midnight, when her two children were in bed" (Van Gelder 2001).

Wilhelm's fiction is firmly rooted in real life: while some of her stories stray off on other planets (*The Killer Thing*, 1967) or deal with the arrival of invading aliens (*Let the Fire Fall*, 1969), usually her wonders are found in deceptively ordinary "heartland" locations such as Ohio, the Shenandoah Valley, and Oregon, and her horrors happen in familiar laboratories and family kitchens, where, as the *The Encyclopedia of Science Fiction* (1999), puts it "chillingly, the fragility of our social worlds can be discerned." Most notable of her SF novels is *Where Late the Sweet Birds Sang*

(1976), winner of a Nebula and a Locus Poll Award, in which the members of a wealthy family "survive" a worldwide eco-catastrophe by cloning themselves, but in the process their "descendants" lose the individuality that makes them human.

Wilhelm is particularly notable for short fiction and novels that deal effectively with scientists at work, such as *The Clewiston Test* (1976), in which the central character's personal dilemmas, and isolation as a woman, are symbolized by her work on a project testing behavior-controlling drugs. Other stories hinge on the life-changing personal or social implications of scientific discoveries, such as serums that stop aging (*Welcome, Chaos*, 1983) or promise immortality ("April Fool's Day Forever," 1970). As noted SF writer and critic Pamela Sargent said in her essay on Wilhelm's work in the *St. James Guide*, "Wilhelm's work gains much of its strength by showing us life as it is lived, as so many works of science fiction do not."

Since the mid-1980s Wilhelm has been concentrating on thrillers and detective fiction, although in 1990 she blended these two genres in the commercially successful *Death Qualified*, a legal thriller in which the victim is mixed up in a top-secret experiment to use chaos theory to change the observer's perception of the universe. Since the death of her husband in 2002, Kate Wilhelm continues to write and to support writers and the cause of good writing. She lives in Eugene, Oregon.

Awards

Science Fiction Hall of Fame (2003)

Novels

Where Late the Sweet Birds Sang (1976) **Hugo, Locus Poll**

Short Fiction

"The Planners" (1968) **Nebula**
"The Girl Who Fell into the Sky" (1986) **Nebula**
"Forever Yours, Anna" (1987) **Nebula**

Nonfiction

Storyteller: Writing Lessons and More from 27 Years of the Clarion Writers' Workshop (2005) **Hugo, Locus Poll**

Works by the Author

The Clone (1965, with Theodore L. Thomas)
The Nevermore Affair (1966)
The Killer Thing (1967)
Let the Fire Fall (1969)
The Year of the Cloud (1970, with Theodore L. Thomas)
Margaret and I (1971)
City of Cain (1974)

Where Late the Sweet Birds Sang (1976)
The Clewiston Test (1976)
Juniper Time (1979)
The Winter Beach (1981)
Welcome, Chaos (1983)
Huysman's Pets (1985)
Crazy Time (1988)

Other Notable Genre Fiction

More Bitter Than Death (1962)
Fault Lines (1977)
A Sense of Shadow (1981)
Crazy Time (1988)
Cambio Bay (1990)
Justice for Some (1993)
The Good Children (1998)
The Deepest Water (2000)
Skeletons: A Novel of Suspense (2002)
MoonGate (2003)

Constance and Charlie

The Hamlet Trap (1987)
Seven Kinds of Death (1992)
A Flush of Shadows (1995)
The Casebook of Constance and Charlie Volumes 1 and 2 (1999)

Barbara Holloway Novels

The Best Defense (1994)
Death Qualified: A Mystery of Chaos (1991)
Cold Case (2009)

Other Notable Short Fiction

"Baby, You Were Great" (1967)
"April Fool's Day Forever" (1970)
"A Cold Dark Night with Snow" (1970)
"The Encounter" (1970)
"The Plastic Abyss" (1971)
"The Funeral" (1972)
"A Brother to Dragons, a Companion of Owls" (1974)
"A Winter Beach" (1981)
"With Thimbles, With Forks and Hope" (1981)
"The Mind of Medea" (1983)

"The Gorgon Field" (1985)
"Naming the Flowers" (1992)
"I Know What You're Thinking" (1994)
"Yesterday's Tomorrows" (2001)

Collections

The Mile-Long Spaceship (1963; aka *Andover and the Android*)
The Downstairs Room, and Other Speculative Fiction (1968)
Abyss: Two Novellas (1971)
The Infinity Box: A Collection of Speculative Fiction (1975)
Somerset Dreams and Other Fictions (1978)
Listen, Listen (1981)
Children of the Wind: Five Novellas (1989)
State of Grace (1991)
And the Angels Sing (1992)
Better Than One (1980, with Damon Knight)

As Editor

Nebula Award Stories Nine (1974)
Clarion SF (1977)

In Other Media

The Lookalike. Gallo Entertainment Inc., 1990. Directed by Gary Nelson; starring Melissa Gilbert and Diane Ladd. Based on a short story by Kate Wilhelm.

Nonfiction Books

The Hills Are Dancing (1986, with Richard Wilhelm)
Storyteller: Writing Lessons and More from 27 Years of the Clarion Writers' Workshop (2005)

Articles and Essays

"My Silent Partner" (excerpt from *Storyteller*). 2005. http://www.sfsite.com/01b/sp216.htm
"On Point of View." In *Those Who Can: A Science Fiction Reader,* ed. Robin Scott Wilson, 149–54. New York: St. Martin's, 1996.

Bibliographies

Contento, William G. "Kate Wilhelm Bibliography." *Fantasy & Science Fiction,* 101, no. 3 (2001): 74+.

For Further Information

Official Web site: http://www.katewilhelm.com/

Cramer, Kathryn. "The Planners." In *The Ascent of Wonder,* ed. David G. Hartwell and Kathryn Cramer. New York: Tor, 1994. http://ebbs.english.vt.edu/exper/kcramer/anth/Planners.html

Hopkinson, Nalo. "If All Birds Were of a Feather, Would You Let One Marry Your Sister?" (Review of Kate Wilhelm's *Where Late the Sweet Bird Sang*). *Scifi.com,* October 5, 1998.

Sargent, Pamela. "Kate Wilhelm." In *St. James Guide to Science Fiction Writers,* ed. Jay Pedersen. Detroit, MI: St. James, 1996.

Thielemans, Johan. "Interview with Damon Knight and Kate Wilhelm." In *Just the Other Day: Essays on the Suture of the Future,* ed. Luk de Vos, 395–97. Antwerp: EXA, 1985.

Van Gelder, Gordon. "Kate Wilhelm: An Appreciation" *Fantasy & Science Fiction* 101, no. 3 (2001): 66+. http://www.sfsite.com/fsf/2001/gvg0109.htm

Wood, Susan. "Kate Wilhelm Is a Writer" (Introduction). In *The Mile-Long Spaceship,* by Kate Wilhelm. Boston: Gregg, 1980.

Connie Willis

Humor and Satire; Time Travel

Benchmark Title: *Doomsday Book* (1992)

b. 1945 (Denver, Colorado)

I find that looking at things obliquely, through the disguise of other places, other times, cuts through not only the reader's prejudices and defenses but my own and makes it possible to look clearly at our own world, our own faces.

—Kelleghan, Profile in *Contemporary Novelists vol. 18* (1999)

Photo credit: Beth Gwinn

About the Author and the Author's Work

Connie Willis writes widely loved and admired novels about, among other things, time travel, in which the travelers must learn that "history is not a matter of textbook statistics but of living people, laboring side by side to save what they love, with their many species of courage and weakness" (Kelleghan 1999). Willis has been called the P. G. Wodehouse of SF but, for all their wit, stories like "Fire Watch" (1982) and *Doomsday Book* (1992), based on the misadventures of historians from a near-future Oxford, resonate with the sadness at the very core of the concept of time travel: that no matter what happens, or what the protagonists *do*, the past is dead and gone, and nothing can be done about *that*.

Constance Elaine Trimmer Willis was born in Denver, Colorado. When she was twelve years old, her mother died in childbirth. As Willis told *Locus* magazine in an interview in 2003, it was "an astonishing, totally unexpected death. She went to the hospital to have a baby and died that night. Like Katherine Anne Porter says in *Pale Horse, Pale Rider*, it was 'a knife that cut across my life and chopped it in two.' Everything changed."

In interview after interview, Willis testifies to the impact that this terrible event had on her, as a person and as a writer: it is the wellspring of the emotion and understanding that she brings to her subjects, the source of the insight beneath the satirical humor and the light, breezy tone. It also created the circumstances that led to her love of fiction in general, and SF in particular. "What saved me was the books I had read and the books I went back to read" ("Connie Willis: The Facts of Death" 2003). Robert Heinlein was a great favorite at this time. And when she came to write for herself, the conventions of SF gave her the means to say what she wanted about the "big themes" of life and death, without being oversentimental or patronizing.

Willis has a BA in English and education from the University of Northern Colorado. During the late 1960s she married and taught in elementary school and junior high school for some years. Like many would-be writers, she assumed that the arrival of her first child would give her "free time" and open up an opportunity to write—an excuse to give up the day job and get down to writing as the baby sleeps. What happened, of course, was writing in snatched moments and an "apprenticeship" of ten years' or so duration: getting some SF short stories and what she describes as "tawdry true confession" romance stories written and accepted and writing two light SF romance novels in collaboration with her friend Cynthia Felice.

And then, in 1983, her short story "Fire Watch" appeared in *Asimov's* and won both the Nebula and Hugo awards; the world of SF was on notice that a special talent had arrived. Her first solo novel, *Lincoln's Dreams*, won the John W. Campbell Memorial award in 1988. Her reputation was sealed with *Doomsday Book* (1992), a time travel thriller that darts to and fro between a near-future Oxford that is struggling in the grip of a worldwide pandemic and the plight of a temporal researcher who is marooned in a medieval village suffering the first signs of the Black Death. But Willis's work has not been limited to time travel; in her fiction she has dealt with quantum theory ("At the Rialto") and black holes ("Schwarzschild Radius"), and even some of the most traditional conventions of SF—aliens, space stations, and the exploration of strange planets ("All Seated on the Ground," "D.A.," "Spice Pogrom," and "Uncharted Territory"). Her 1983 story, "The Sidon in the Mirror," is set on the surface of a dying star. Her real strength, according to Michael Levy in Barron's *Anatomy of Wonder* (2004), is "her ability to impart warmth and intimacy into classic SF themes." Her most recent novel, *Passage*, is a very personal blending of the themes that have been important to her throughout her career—the impact that time and history have on our attitudes, our sense of ourselves, and what happens when we die. "I wanted to make sure some reader who had just had somebody die, instead of wanting to slap me, would say, 'Thank you for telling the truth and trying to help me understand this whole process.' I tried to be as honest as I could" ("Connie Willis: The Facts of Death" 2003).

She is the first author to win Nebulas in all four fiction categories (novelette, novella, short story, and novel), and, as of 2007, she has won, among many other awards, nine Hugos and six Nebulas. Connie Willis lives in Greeley, Colorado, with her husband, a professor of physics, and their daughter Cordelia. She is one of the great positive personalities of SF, and a welcome participant in cons and workshops all over the world. "After all these years, I still come to science fiction with that same shock of joy and recognition that I did at thirteen" (Kelleghan 1999).

Awards

Novels

Lincoln's Dreams (1987) **Campbell**

Doomsday Book (1992) **Hugo, Locus Poll, Nebula**

Remake (1994) **Locus Poll**;

Bellwether (1996) **Locus Poll**

To Say Nothing of the Dog (1997) **Hugo, Locus Poll**

Passage (2001) **Locus Poll**

Short Fiction

"Fire Watch" (1982) **Hugo, Nebula**
"A Letter from the Clearys" (1982) **Nebula**
"The Last of the Winnebagos" (1988) **Hugo, Nebula**
"At the Rialto" (1989) **Nebula**
"Even the Queen" (1992) **Hugo, Locus Poll, Nebula**
"Close Encounter" (1993) **Locus Poll**
"Death on the Nile" (1993) **Hugo**
"The Soul Selects Her Own Society: Invasion and Repulsion: A Chronological Reinterpretation of Two of Emily Dickinson's Poems: A Wellsian Perspective" (1996) **Hugo**
"Newsletter" (1997) **Locus Poll**
"The Winds of Marble Arch" (1999) **Hugo**
"Inside Job" (2005) **Hugo**
"All Seated on the Ground" (2007) **Hugo**

Collections

Impossible Things (1993) **Locus Poll**
The Winds of Marble Arch and Other Stories (2007) **Locus Poll**

Works by the Author

Water Witch (1982, with Cynthia Felice)
Berserker Base: A Collaborative Novel (1984, with Poul Anderson, Larry Niven, Roger Zelazny, et al.)
Lincoln's Dreams (1987)
Light Raid (1989, with Cynthia Felice)
Doomsday Book (1992)
Uncharted Territory (1994)
Remake (1994)
Bellwether (1996)
Promised Land (1997, with Cynthia Felice)
To Say Nothing of the Dog (1997)
Passage (2001)
D.A. (2007, YA)
Blackout (forthcoming, 2010)

Other Notable Short Fiction

"Daisy, in the Sun" (1979)
"The Sidon in the Mirror" (1983)

"Blued Moon" (1984)
"Chance" (1986)
"Spice Pogrom" (1986)
"Schwarzschild Radius" (1987)
"Time-Out" (1989)
"Cibola" (1990)
"In the Late Cretaceous" (1991)
"Jack" (1991)
"Miracle" (1991)
"Inn" (1993)
"Why the World Didn't End Last Tuesday" (1994)
"Nonstop to Portales" (1996)
"deck.halls@boughs/holly" (2001)
"Just Like the Ones We Used to Know" (2003)

Collections

Fire Watch (1984)
Impossible Things (1993)
Even the Queen: And Other Short Stories (1998)
Miracle and Other Christmas Stories (1999)
The Winds of Marble Arch and Other Stories (2007)

As Editor

Nebula Awards 33 (1999)
The New Hugo Winners: Volume III (1994, with Martin H. Greenberg)
A Woman's Liberation: A Choice of Futures By and About Women (2001, with Sheila Williams)

In Other Media

Snow Wonder. Warner Bros. Television, 2005. Directed by Peter Werner; starring Mary Tyler Moore, Jason Priestley, and Jennifer Esposito. Based on Willis's short story "Just Like the Ones We Used to Know."

Articles and Essays

"Learning to Write Comedy or Why It's Impossible and How to Do It." In *Writing Science Fiction & Fantasy*. The Staff of *Analog & Isaac Asimov's Science Fiction Magazine,* 76–90. New York: St. Martin's Griffin, 1993.

"Science in Science Fiction: A Writer's Perspective." In *Chemistry and Science Fiction,* ed. Jack H. Stocker, 21–34. Washington, DC: American Chemical Society, 1998.

"2006 Worldcon Guest of Honor Speech." *SFRevu,* September 1, 2006. http://sfrevu.com/Review-id.php?id=4426

"The Women SF Doesn't See." *Asimov's Science Fiction Magazine* 16, no. 11 (1992): 4–8.

For Further Information

Connie Willis.net: http://www.sftv.org/cw/

"Connie Willis: The Facts of Death." *Locus* (January 2003). http://www.locusmag.com/2003/Issue01/Willis.html

Duval, Linda. "Transcending Genres: Connie Willis." *Writer* 117, no. 11 (2004): 24–27.

Fortis, A., and Tad Mack. Interview. *SF Crowsnest,* December 1, 2007. http://www.sfcrowsnest.com

Freund, Jim. Interview Transcript. *Hour of the Wolf,* December 4, 1997. http://www.hourwolf.com/chats/willis.html

Hennessey-DeRose, Christopher, and Michael McCarty. "Connie Willis—*To Say Nothing of the Dog.*" *The Zone Online,* November 24, 2005. http://www.zone-sf.com/conniewillis.html

Kellaghan, Fiona. Profile. In *Contemporary Novelists Volume 18.* 1999. http://biography.jrank.org/pages/4839/Willis-Connie.html

McCarty, Michael. "Connie Willis." In *Giants of the Genre: Interviews with Science Fiction, Fantasy and Horror's Greatest Talents,* 121–27. Holicong, PA: Wildside, 2003.

Shindler, Dorman T. "Connie Willis: The Truths of Science Fiction." *Publishers Weekly,* May 21, 2001.

Slonczewski, Joan. "Bells and Time." In *Imaginative Futures,* ed. Milton T. Wolf and Daryl F. Mallett, 161–66. San Bernardino, CA: Borgo, 1995.

Gene Wolfe

Apocalyptic SF; Myth and Legend; Science Fantasy

Benchmark Title:
The Fifth Head of Cerberus (1972)

b. 1931 (Brooklyn, New York)

Photo credit: Beth Gwinn

"Things could be different," says fantasy. "They could be very, very different just over that hill. Have hope."
"They may be better," says SF, "or they may be worse. But they will not be like this."

—De Beer, Interview in *Nebula Awards* (2008)

About the Author and the Author's Work

Gene Wolfe never lies. He said so in a joint interview, conducted with his friend and protégé Neil Gaiman in 2002 ("The Wolfe & Gaiman Show."). Reviewers and interviewers say so, all the time: "Gene Wolfe will tell you the truth, in conversation and in fiction, whether you want to hear it or not" (Person 1998). In his rich and allusive fiction—*The Fifth Head of Cerberus* and the dozen or so books and various stories comprising the Urth universe, beginning with *The Shadow of the Torturer* (1980, first volume of The Book of the New Sun) and concluding (at least for now) with *Return to the Whorl* (2001, final volume of The Book of the Short Sun)—Wolfe may not tell you what you *think* you want to know. But in everything he writes, he gives you what you *need to know*, to work it out for yourself. "What would I do that I don't do, if I were being user-friendly? . . . Phooey! I don't want to write that kind of thing. Rats! I don't like it and it would bore me to write it" ("The Wolfe & Gaiman Show" 2002).

In a heady mixture of myth, history, religion and gorgeous imagery—"mazes, giantism, gates, caves, roses, claws, cannibalism and suns"—Wolfe transforms his coming-of-age stories and far-future allegories about the "End of All Things" to a "densely imagined work of Christian symbolism . . . characterized by complexity and ambiguity, and by their meticulously crafted and luminously metaphorical prose style" (Gordon 1996).

Gene Rodman Wolfe considers himself a Texan, and he spent the better part of his childhood in a suburb of Houston, which he considers "my home town, the place I was 'from'" (Edwards 1973), but he was born in Brooklyn, New York. His parents "moved and moved": New Jersey, Massachusetts, Peoria, Illinois, Des Moines, Iowa, and Logan, Ohio (his father's hometown). They eventually settled in Houston, where Wolfe attended Edgar Allan Poe Elementary School (this, remember, is true); an only child, he kept himself busy with his model airplanes (which would one day feature in his stories "Against the Lafayette Escadrille," 1972, and "Continuing Westward," 1973), the family dog, Boots, and odd neighbors, one of whom, like a good cartoon mad scientist, blew up his private chemistry lab over the garage across the street. And only five blocks away, in the sweltering Houston heat, was "Richmond Pharmacy, where a boy willing to crouch immobile behind the candy case could cram *Planet Stories, Thrilling Wonder Stories,* or (my favorite) *Famous Fantastic Mysteries* while the druggist compounded prescriptions" (Edwards 1973). Some of these details of his early life may be helpful in explaining the recurring themes in his work,". . . isolation, memory, faith, and the search for self and human identity" (Gordon 1996).

After high school, Wolfe attended Texas A&M University, an all-male land-grant college specializing in animal husbandry and engineering, and officially sanctioned violence toward underclassmen ("The Wolfe & Gaiman Show" 2002); not, from his various reminiscences and interviews, a happy time: "Only Dickens could have done justice to A&M as I knew it, and he would not have been believed" (Edwards 1973).

But his first stories were published in the campus literary magazine, where he remembers an editor, an upperclassman, who kept after him to edit and rewrite his work, tormenting him with a blue pencil instead of physical violence. "I learned more from [him] than I have ever learned from any other editor" ("The Wolfe & Gaiman Show." 2002). Wolfe dropped out during his junior year, lost his student draft deferment, and was sent to Korea. He served in the Seventh Infantry Division and was awarded the Combat Infantry Badge. *Letters Home* (1991), a collection of the letters he wrote while in Korea, is an account of his experiences. With the assistance of the GI Bill, Wolfe finished his college degree at the University of Houston and took a job in engineering development at Procter & Gamble in Cincinnati; he then met and married his wife, Rosemary Dietsch. As a young husband, Wolfe was writing in whatever free time he could find. His first sale was the short story "The Dead Man," to *Sir* magazine, in 1965. For many years he worked in that field, developing industrial processes (such as the one used to produce Pringle potato chips) and then as editor of a professional engineering journal before he became a full-time writer in 1984, an engineer who "transmuted himself into an alchemist" (Andre-Driussi 2007).

Wolfe is a "writer's writer"—widely admired by his fellow SF writers and anyone who cares about writing. It is surprising how often, in interviews with other great SF and fantasy writers, the subject turns to Gene Wolfe—and the talk is full of nothing but admiration and marvel at the man's art. Gaiman said in their shared 2002 *Locus* interview, "if he said 'Here There Be Dragons,' by God, you knew that was where the dragons were." In an interview in 2003, Michael Swanwick said "there is nobody who can even approach Gene Wolfe for brilliance of prose, clarity of thought, and depth in meaning" (Santala 2003). Patrick O'Leary says, with simple directness, "Gene Wolfe is the Best Writer Alive."

Wolfe converted to Roman Catholicism when he married Rosemary, and his writing is suffused with the moral attitudes and quandaries derived from his faith. He is forthright in his opinions—"I am a conservative. I certainly read William F. Buckley, Jr. with delight. . . . I think he mellowed a little too much at the end. . . . Perhaps the same thing will happen to me. But that doesn't mean that it's good" (Miller 2009). He has been nominated for Nebulas eight times and has repeatedly won the other major SF awards, U.S. and international. In 1996 he was awarded the World Fantasy Award for Lifetime Achievement.

Gene Wolfe never lies—when the interviewer for *Clarkesworld Magazine* observed that "his fantasy seems truer to reality, truer to what we humans experience in this life," he replied, "Fantasy is nearer the truth, that's all. . . . Realistic fiction leaves out far, far too much" (Jones 2008).

He currently lives in Barrington, Illinois, a suburb of Chicago, with his wife Rosemary, surrounded by their children and grandchildren.

Awards

SF Hall of Fame (2007)

Edward E. Smith Memorial Award for Imaginative Fiction ("Skylark award") (1988)

Novels

The Shadow of the Torturer (1980) **BSF**

The Claw of the Conciliator (1981) **Locus Poll, Nebula**

The Sword of the Lictor (1982) **Locus Poll**

The Citadel of the Autarch (1983) **Campbell**

Soldier of the Mist (1986) **Locus Poll**

Short Fiction

"The Death of Doctor Island" (1973) **Locus Poll, Nebula**

"Golden City Far" (2004) **Locus Poll**

 ## Works by the Author

Operation Ares (1970)

The Fifth Head of Cerberus (1972)

Peace (1975)

The Devil in a Forest (1976)

Free Live Free (1984)

There Are Doors (1988)

The Briah Cycle

The Shadow of the Torturer (1980)

The Claw of the Conciliator (1981)

The Sword of the Lictor (1982)

The Citadel of the Autarch (1983)

Book of the Long Sun

Nightside the Long Sun (1993)
Lake of the Long Sun (1994)
Caldé of the Long Sun (1994)
Exodus From the Long Sun (1996)

Book of the Short Sun

On Blue's Waters (1999)
In Green's Jungles (2000)
Return to the Whorl (2001)

Other Notable Genre Fiction

Castleview (1990)
Pandora by Holly Hollander (1990)
A Walking Tour of the Shambles (2002, with Neil Gaiman)
Pirate Freedom (2007)
An Evil Guest (2008)

The Soldier series

Soldier of the Mist (1986)
Soldier of Arete (1989)
Soldier of Sidon (2006)

The Wizard Knight

The Knight (2004)
The Wizard (2004)

Other Notable Short Fiction

"The Island of Doctor Death and Other Stories" (1970)
"Against the Lafayette Escadrille" (1972)
"How I Lost the Second World War and Helped Turn Back the German Invasion" (1973)
"The Eyeflash Miracles" (1976)
"The Computer Iterates the Greater Trumps" (1977)
"The Doctor of Death Island" (1978)
"War Beneath the Tree" (1979)
"The Woman the Unicorn Loved" (1981)
"A Cabin on the Coast" (1984)
"The Arimaspian Legacy" (1987). http://www.infinityplus.co.uk/stories/arimaspian.htm
"Counting Cats in Zanzibar" (1996)

"No Planets Strike" (1997)
"Under Hill" (2002). http://www.infinitematrix.net/stories/shorts/under_hill.html
"Pulp Cover" (2004)
"Sob in the Silence" (2006)
"Memorare" (2007)

Collections

The Island of Doctor Death and Other Stories and Other Stories (1980)
Gene Wolfe's Book of Days (1981)
The Wolfe Archipelago (1983)
Plan(e)t Engineering (1984)
Bibliomen (1984)
Storeys from the Old Hotel (1988)
Endangered Species (1989)
Castle of Days (1992)
The Young Wolfe (1992)
Strange Travelers (2000)
Innocents Aboard (2004)
Starwater Strains (2005)
The Best of Gene Wolfe (2009)

Nonfiction Books

The Castle of the Otter (1982)
Letters Home (1991)
A Wolfe Family Album (1991)
Shadows of the New Sun: Wolfe on Writing, Writers on Wolfe (2007)

Articles and Essays

"The Best Introduction to the Mountains." *Interzone*. December 2001. http://home.clara.net/andywrobertson/wolfemountains.html

"Foreword." In *Other Voices, Other Doors*. By Patrick O'Leary. Bonney Lake, WA: Fairwood, 2001.

"Introduction." In *Sandman: Fables and Reflections,* by Neil Gaiman. Vertigo DC Comics, 1993.

"The Profession of Science Fiction." In *The Profession of Science Fiction: SF Writers on Their Craft and Ideas,* ed. Maxim Jakubowski and Edward James, 131–39. New York: St. Martin's, 1992.

Bibliographies

Stewart, Perrin. "Master of the House of Pens: Bibliography." February 1997. Clemson University. http://hubcap.clemson.edu/~sparks/wolfpage.html

For Further Information

Map of the Whorl: Elucidations of the Suns. March 2006. http://www.urth.org/whorlmap/

Andre-Driussi, Michael. "Gene Wolfe: The Man and His Work." *Fantasy & Science Fiction* (April 2007). http://www.sfsite.com/fsf/toc0704.htm

Borski, Robert. *The Long and Short of It: More Essays on the Fiction of Gene Wolfe.* New York: iUniverse, 2006.

De Beer, David. Interview. *Nebula Awards,* December 30, 2008. http://www.nebulaawards.com/index.php/interview/gene_wolfe/

Duggan, Paul, ed. Gene Wolfe Fan Site. March 2007. http://members.bellatlantic.net/~vze2tmhh/wolfe.html

Edwards, Malcolm. "Interview." In *Shadows of the New Sun: Wolfe on Writing, Writers on Wolfe,* ed. Peter Wright. Liverpool (UK): Liverpool University Press, 2007. First appeared in *Vector* (May–June 1973).

Gaiman, Neil. "How to Read Gene Wolfe." *Fantasy & Science Fiction* (April 2007). http://www.sfsite.com/fsf/toc0704.htm

Gevers, Nick, Michael Andre-Driussi, and James Jordan. "Some Moments with the Magus: An Interview with Gene Wolfe." *Infinity Plus* (December 2003). http://www.infinityplus.co.uk/nonfiction/intgw.htm

———. "A Magus of Many Suns: An Interview with Gene Wolfe." *SF Site* (January 2002). http://www.sfsite.com/03b/gw124.htm

Gordon, Joan L. *Gene Wolfe.* Mercer Island, WA: Starmont, 1986.

———. "Gene Wolfe." In *St. James Guide to Science Fiction Writers,* ed. Jay Pedersen. Detroit, MI: St. James, 1996.

Jones, Jeremy L. C. Interview. *Clarkesworld Magazine* (August 2008). http://clarkesworldmagazine.com/wolfe_interview/

Laidlow, Jonathan, and Nigel Price, eds. *Ultan's Library: A Journal of the Study of Gene Wolfe.* March 2007. http://www.ultan.org.uk/

Miller, John J. "Gene Wolfe on *The Best of Gene Wolfe* (Audio Interview)." *National Review Online,* March 26, 2009. http://radio.nationalreview.com/betweenthecovers/post/?q=MmQ2ZjA2OGE4ZWNmZjBkMGQ1MjRjYjlhOTA4YmU2OWE=

O'Leary, Patrick. "If Ever a Wiz There Was—The Ineffable Art of Gene Wolfe." In *Other Voices, Other Doors.* Bonney Lake, WA: Fairwood, 2001. http://web.mac.com/paddybon/Site/a_tribute_to_Gene_Wolfe.html

Person, Lawrence. "Suns New, Long, and Short: An Interview with Gene Wolfe." *Nova Express* 5, no. 1 (Fall/Winter 1998). http://home.roadrunner.com/~lperson1/wolfe.html

Santala, Ismo. Interview with Michael Swanwick. *The Modern Word,* September 26, 2003. http://www.themodernword.com/features/interview_swanwick.html

"The Wolfe & Gaiman Show." *Locus* (September 2002). http://www.locusmag.com/2002/Issue09/GaimanWolfe.html

Wright, Peter. *Attending Daedalus: Gene Wolfe, Artifice and the Reader.* Liverpool, UK: Liverpool University Press, 2003.

Wright, Peter, ed. *Shadows of the New Sun: Wolfe on Writing, Writers on Wolfe.* Liverpook (UK): Liverpool University Press, 2007.

John Wyndham [John Wyndham Parkes Lucas Beynon Harris]

Apocalypstic SF; Near Future; SF Horror

Benchmark Title: *The Day of the Triffids* (1951)

b. 1903 (England: Edgbaston, Birmingham); d. 1969 (England: Petersfield, Hampshire)

> *The moving vegetable would be a real menace. . . . Once when I was younger, before the war, when I was trying to write ghost stories, I used to frighten myself pallid . . . These aren't frightening, I think, no.*
> —BBC, "The Lost Decade" (1960)

About the Author and the Author's Work

John Wyndham's literary reputation suffered badly at the hands of New Wave SF writers of the 1960 and 1970s—Christopher Priest once described him as the "the master of the middle-class catastrophe," while Brian Aldiss dismissed him as writing "cozy disasters." But Wyndham's signature themes—ecological disasters, alien invasion, genetic mutations, and nuclear war, all brought on or made worse by a potent combination of humankind's blindness and hubris—would seem to be just about right for the fraught opening years of the twenty-first century. Combine this with current research on his life that connects these themes with the childhood trauma caused by the very messy, public breakup of the marriage of his parents, and Wyndham's popularity—as a writer, and as a source of creepy, evocative SF horror movies and television dramas—is not surprising.

John Wyndham Parkes Lucas Beynon Harris spent his childhood in Edgbaston, near Birmingham, an exclusive enclave of the Victorian middle class in the midst of England's industrial heartlands. His father practiced law. His mother was the daughter of a local industrialist. When John was eight years old, his parents' marriage ended in acrimony, and his father, George Harris, brought legal action against his father-in-law and other members of his wife's family for alienating her affection toward him. This turned out to be a terrible, if understandable, mistake: Harris lost the case after a four-day trial in which his in-laws saw to it that he was dragged through the mud as a gold-digger who molested female domestic staff, abused his wife, and could not be trusted with the care of his two young sons. And perhaps he was. After a hundred years, it is hard to be sure of anything in the case—except that an eight-year-old boy never saw his father again.

After the divorce, John Benyon Harris spent many unhappy years shuttling from one boarding school to another. (He would not become "John Wyndham" until after World War II; prior to that, Harris used a number of permutations on the embarrassment of riches he had been christened with, to serve as pen names.) After school he considered several careers, including farming, law, commercial art, and advertising; he eventually tried writing. His first story was a pure-pulp space opera published in 1931, and throughout the 1930s he wrote steadily—space stories with titles like "Stowaway to Mars," juveniles, ghost, and detective fiction. During World War II John Harris joined the Royal Corps of Signals.

Following the war there was a radical change in both his style and subject matter. John Benyon Harris became "John Wyndham," and *The Day of the Triffids* was published in 1951. In *Triffids*, humankind is hit by a double apocalypse: most people are blinded by a rain of meteors, and the shocked and blinded population then finds itself at the mercy of experimental plants, the triffids, that escape from the labs where they have been cultured. They turn out to be extremely mobile, vicious, and carnivorous. Like his subsequent world-in-peril novels, *The Day of the Triffids* was unusual for SF, and remains striking today, because catastrophe doesn't happen to stalwart scientists and chisel-jawed heroes, but to ordinary people, very like the people who were reading about it. Wyndham was also ahead of his time in recognizing and drawing plausible horror scenarios from the complicated threads that hold our modern world together. It was just bad luck for humankind to be struck blind by a rogue meteorite shower, but it has no one but itself to blame for the genetically modified, killer plants roaming the streets.

Other catastrophes that Wyndham inflicted on humankind in his subsequent fiction were invaders from space, who attempt to make the world a better place for themselves by melting the polar ice-caps (*The Kraken Wakes*) and invaders from space who use otherworldly children to establish dominance over Earth and its inhabitants (*The Midwich Cuckoos*). Wyndham's final novel, *Chocky* (1968), also centers on a child—a boy whose imaginary friend may actually be an alien intelligence who is using him to learn about Earth.

For some years Wyndham lived in London, in a small room at the Penn Club, on Bedford Place in London, a private members club associated with the Quakers. In 1963 he married Grace Wilson, who had lived in a nearby room at the club for more than twenty years. The couple moved to a cottage in Hampshire, just outside the grounds of Bedales School, the one place Wyndham had been happy after the collapse of his family. He died on March 12, 1969.

Works by the Author

Planet Plane (1936; aka *Stowaway to Mars*)
The Day of the Triffids (1951)
The Kraken Wakes (1953)
The Chrysalids (1955)
The Midwych Cuckoos (1957)
The Outward Urge (1959). Published as cowritten by John Wyndham and "Lucas Parkes," but these were both Harris's pen names.

Trouble with Lichen (1960)
Chocky (1968)
Web (1979, published posthumously)

Other Notable Genre Fiction

As "John Benyon"
Foul Play Suspected (1935)
The Secret People (1935)

Collections
Jizzle (1954)
The Seeds of Time (1956)
Tales of Gooseflesh and Laughter (1956)
The Infinite Moment (1961)
Consider Her Ways and Others (1961)
The John Wyndham Omnibus (1965)
The Best of John Wyndham (1973)
Sleepers of Mars (1973)
Wanderers of Time (1973)
The Man from Beyond and Other Stories (1975)
Exiles on Asperus (1979)
No Place Like Earth (2003)

In Other Media
Village of the Damned. Metro-Goldwyn-Mayer British Studios, 1960. Directed by Wolf Rilla; starring George Sanders; based on *The Midwych Cuckoos*.
The Day of the Triffids. Security Pictures Ltd., 1962. Directed by Steve Sekely; starring Howard Keel.
"Consider Her Ways," *The Alfred Hitchcock Hour* (1964). Directed by Robert Stevens; starring Gladys Cooper and Barbara Barrie.
The Day of the Triffids. British Broadcasting Corporation (BBC), 1981. TV serialization, directed by Ken Hannam; starring John Duttine.
Chocky. Thames Television, 1984. TV serialization; starring James Hazeldine and Carol Drinkwater.
Village of the Damned. Alphaville Films, 1995. Directed by John Carpenter; starring Christopher Reeve and Kirstie Alley.
Random Quest. British Broadcasting Corporation (BBC), 2006. Directed by Luke Watson; starring Samuel West and Kate Ashfield; based on Wyndham's 1961 short story.

Nonfiction

"Introduction." In *The Best from New Worlds Science Fiction*. London: John Carnell, 1955.

"The Pattern of Science Fiction." *Science Fantasy* 3, no. 7 (1954).

Bibliographies

Stephensen-Payne, Phil. *John Wyndham: Creator of the Cozy Catastrophe*. 3rd ed. Leeds, UK: Galactic Central, 2001.

Willick, George C. "SF Bibliography." *Spacelight* (June 2006). http://www.gcwillick.com/Spacelight/biblio/wyndhambib.html

For Further Information

Bleiler, E. F. "Luncheon with John Wyndham." *Extrapolation* 25 (1984): 314–17.

British Broadcasting Company. "The Lost Decade—1945–1955 (People)" (TV Interview). 1960. Posted on BBC Four, January 2007. http://www.bbc.co.uk/bbcfour/lostdecade/

Davies, Sue. "The Long and Wyndham Road." *SF Crowsnest.com* (2003). http://www.computercrowsnest.com/

Ketterer, David. "John Wyndham: The Facts of Life Sextet." In *A Companion to Science Fiction*, ed. David Seed, 375–88. Malden, UK: Blackwell, 2005.

———. "John Wyndham and the Sins of His Father: Damaging Disclosures in Court." *Extrapolation* 46 (2005): 163–88.

———. "'A Part of the Family' (?): John Wyndham's *The Midwich Cuckoos* as Estranged Autobiography." In *Learning from Other Worlds: Estrangement, Cognition, and the Politics of Science Fiction and Utopia*, ed. Patrick Parrinder, 146–77. Durham: Duke University Press, 2001.

Obituary. *Times* (London), March 12, 1969. http://www.gcwillick.com/Spacelight/obit/wyndhamo.html

Sawyer, Andy. "The John Wyndham Archive." In SF *Hub for Science Fiction Research*. University of Liverpool, 2005. http://www.sfhub.ac.uk/Wyndham.htm

———. "A Stiff Upper Lip and a Trembling Lower One: John Wyndham on Screen." In *British Science Fiction Cinema*, ed. I.Q. Hunter, 75–87. New York: Routledge, 1999.

Roger Zelazny

Mythology and Legend; Science Fantasy

Benchmark Title: *This Immortal* (1965)

b. 1937 (Cleveland, Ohio); d. 1995 (Santa Fe, New Mexico)

I like to keep my writing apart from my personal life. I make my living displaying pieces of my soul in some distorted form or other. The rest is my own.
—Walker, Interview in *Speaking of Science Fiction* (1987)

About the Author and the Author's Work

Although he was a devoted reader and writer of science fiction from an early age, getting paid for his first published story when he was only about sixteen, Roger Zelazny did not immediately see himself becoming a professional SF writer. This is hardly surprising, given the lyricism and depth of even the least of his enormous output; Zelazny's first interest was poetry. However, common sense, and the realities of the market, prevailed, and he decided to devote that lyricism and depth to a genre that paid a bit more and was on the cusp of a remarkable change of direction. A genre, in other words, that was ready for a writer like Roger Zelazny

Roger Joseph Zelazny was born in Euclid, Ohio, near Cleveland. He earned a BA in English from Western Reserve University (now Case Western Reserve University) and, in 1962, an MA from Columbia University, where he specialized in Elizabethan and Jacobean drama. Having decided that he would write SF, Zelazny's publication strategy was nothing if not methodical: "What I'd do was send my story out to the best paying magazine and if they didn't want it, then I'd send it out the second best paying and so on, until I'd gone through the entire list. . . . That first year I sold seventeen stories, all short. I didn't get rich that year" (Robson 1995).

However, in the end, method and talent prevailed: the following year his novelette, *A Rose for Ecclesiastes*, was nominated for a Hugo Award. Although it didn't win, it was a portent of success, and greatness, to come. On the advice of Robert Silverberg, Zelazny discarded his carpet-bombing approach to story marketing and acquired a good agent.

Roger Zelazny is recognized as a leading figure of the American New Wave. Prior to 1960, with a few notable exceptions, the style and technique of SF was, in contrast to its out-of-this-world plots and ideas, mundane and somewhat artless, what Zelazny himself, in a 1981 interview, called "mostly nuts-and-bolts prose." Zelazny was one of a number of young authors who broke that nuts-and-bolts mold: his work is sometimes allusive and lyrical, and sometimes makes wise-cracking references to classical and pop culture. He experimented with elements of mainstream fiction, borrowing from many traditions such as Greek, Egyptian, Hindu, and Native American mythology, and making unapologetic references to classic prose and poetry of the late nineteenth and early twentieth centuries. *A Rose for Ecclesiastes* and *The Doors of His Face, the Lamps of His Mouth*—two novellas whose settings make fond references to the unscientific, mythic Mars and Venus of 1930s pulp SF—effectively use the Old Testament and *Moby Dick* to enhance narrative and imagery. Today, Zelazny is probably better known for the two linked fantasy series that make up his Amber sequence. But his SF novels, like *This Immortal* and *Lord of Light,* as well as his shorter works, remain stunning examples of the pyrotechnics that SF is capable of in the hands of a master.

In 1975 Zelazny found that he was earning enough from his writing that he could give up his job with the Social Security Administration in Baltimore and write full-time. With a young family, and a job that allowed him to work anywhere, he decided to relocate to a smaller, family-friendly city, and moved to Santa Fe, New Mexico. There, while valuing his low profile and his privacy, he was a welcome part of the local arts scene, giving talks and readings, indulging local journalists with occasional interviews, and teaching the martial art of Aikido. Throughout his career he was a popular and friendly participant in the SF convention circuit.

Roger Zelazny died in 1995, in Santa Fe, of kidney failure due to lung cancer. The reaction to his death in the SF writing and reading community was shock and surprise; as with all the other important moments in his life, Zelazny had kept his illness very private, and he was giving interviews, attending conferences (as far away as England), and charming fans up to a few weeks before his death. Asked in one of these final interviews how he would like to be remembered, he said "that's a hell of a question—I don't tend to look at my stuff that way. I just look at it a book at a time" (Interview 1994).

Fortunately for his fans, and new readers alike, the novels and stories of Roger Zelazny are still there, waiting to enthrall us, one book at a time.

Awards

Novels

This Immortal (1965) **Hugo**
Lord of Light (1967) **Hugo**
Trumps of Doom (1985) **Locus Poll**

Short Fiction

"The Doors of His Face, The Lamps of His Mouth." (1965) **Nebula**
"He Who Shapes" (1965) **Nebula**
"Home Is the Hangman" (1975) **Hugo, Nebula**
"Unicorn Variation" (1981) **Hugo**
"24 Views of Mt. Fuji, by Hokusai" (1985) **Hugo**
"Permafrost" (1986) **Hugo**

Collections

Unicorn Variations (1983) **Locus Poll**

Works by the Author

This Immortal (1965; originally *. . . And Call Me Conrad*)
The Dream Master (1966)
Lord of Light (1967)
Creatures of Light and Darkness (1969)
Isle of the Dead (1969)
Jack of Shadows (1971)
Today We Choose Faces (1973)
To Die in Italbar (1973)
Deus Irae (1976, with Philip K. Dick)
Doorways in the Sand (1976)
Roadmarks (1979)
Coils (1982, with Fred Saberhagen)
Eye of Cat (1982)
The Black Throne (1990, with Fred Saberhagen)
Psychoshop (1998, with Alfred Bester). A doubly posthumous novel, it was finished by Zelazny after Bester's death, and published after Zelazny's death.

Other Notable Genre Fiction

Changeling (1980)
Madwand (1981)
The Changing Land (1981)
Dilvish, the Damned (1982)
A Night in the Lonesome October (1993, illustrated by Gahan Wilson)
The Dead Man's Brother (1971, published posthumously in 2009)

The Chronicles of Amber

Nine Princes in Amber (1970)
The Guns of Avalon (1972)
Sign of the Unicorn (1975)
The Hand of Oberon (1976)
The Courts of Chaos (1978)
Trumps of Doom (1985)
Blood of Amber (1986)
Sign of Chaos (1987)
Knight of Shadows (1989)
Prince of Chaos (1991)

The Millennial Contest series (with Robert Sheckley)

Bring Me the Head of Prince Charming (1991)
If at Faust You Don't Succeed (1993)
A Farce to Be Reckoned With (1995)

Other Notable Short Fiction

"A Rose for Ecclesiastes" (1963)
"Devil Car" (1965)
"Comes Now the Power" (1966)
"For a Breath I Tarry" (1966)
"The Keys to December" (1966)
"This Moment of the Storm" (1966)
"Damnation Alley" (1967)
"This Mortal Mountain" (1967)
"'Kjwalll'kje'k'koothailll'kje'k" (1973)
"The Engine at Heartspring's Center" (1974)
"Come Back to the Killing Ground, Alice, My Love" (1992)
"The Three Descents of Jeremy Baker" (1995)

Collections

Four for Tomorrow (1967)
A Rose for Ecclesiastes (1969; UK: *Four for Tomorrow*)
The Doors of His Face, The Lamp of His Mouth, and Other Stories (1971)
My Name Is Legion (1976)
The Illustrated Roger Zelazny (1979)
The Last Defender of Camelot (1981)
Unicorn Variations (1983)
Frost & Fire (1989)
The Graveyard Heart/Elegy for Angels and Dogs (1992)
Manna from Heaven (2003)
The Collected Stories of Roger Zelazny (2009)
    Volume 1: Threshold
    Volume 2: Power & Light
    Volume 3: This Mortal Mountain
    Volume 4: Last Exit to Babylon
    Volume 5: Nine Black Doves
    Volume 6: The Road to Amber

As Editor

Nebula Award Stories 3 (1968)
Forever After (1995)
Warriors of Blood and Dream (1995, with Martin H. Greenberg)
Wheel of Fortune (1995)
The Williamson Effect (1996)

In Other Media

Damnation Alley. Twentieth Century-Fox Film Corporation, 1977. Directed by Jack Smight; starring Jan-Michael Vincent and George Peppard.

"The Last Defender of Camelot," *The Twilight Zone* (1986). Starring Richard Kiley and Jenny Agutter.

Chronomaster. 1996. Adventure game developed by DreamForge Intertainment, published by IntraCorp. Designed by Zelazny and Jane Lindskold (who finished it after his death). Features the voices of Ron Perlman and Brent Spiner.

Nonfiction Books

Wilderness (1994, with Gerald Hausman)

Articles and Essays

"Fantasy and Science Fiction: A Writer's View." In *Intersections: Fantasy and Science Fiction,* ed. George E. Slusser and Eric S. Rabkin, 55–60. Carbondale: Southern Illinois University Press, 1987.

"Stand on Zanzibar: The Novel as Film." In *SF: The Other Side of Realism,* ed. Thomas D. Clareson, 181–85. Bowling Green, OH: Bowling Green University Popular Press, 1971.

Bibliographies

Stephens, Christopher P. *A Checklist of Roger Zelazny*. Hastings-on-Hudson, NY: Ultramarine, 1993.

Stephensen-Payne, Phil. *Roger Zelazny: Master of Amber; A Working Bibliography*. Albuquerque, NM: Galactic Central, 1991.

Willick, George C. "Science Fantasy Bibliography." *Spacelight* (June 2006). http://www.gcwillick.com/Spacelight/biblio/zelaznybib.html

For Further Information

Bisson, Terry. "Roger Zelazny: An Appreciation." In *1996 World Fantasy Program Book*. http://www.sff.net/people/TBisson/zelazny.html

Dowling, Terry, and Keith Curtis. "A Conversation with Roger Zelazny." *Science Fiction: A Review of Speculative Literature* 1, no. 2 (1978): 11–23.

Heatley, Alez. "An Interview with Roger Zelazny." *Phlogiston Forty-four* (1995). http://www.roger-zelazny.com/repository/phlogiston_interview.html

Interview. *Absolute Magnitude* 11 (Fall/Winter 1994). http://www.roger-zelazny.com/repository/absmag.html

Lindskold, Jane M. *Roger Zelazny.* New York: Twayne, 1993.

Martin, George R. R. "In Memoriam: Roger Zelazny, Lord of Light." *GRRM—The Official Website of George R. R. Martin.* June 1995. http://www.georgerrmartin.com/musings-roger.html

Robson, Alan. "The Lesser Spotted Science Fiction Writer, Part 7: Roger Zelazny." *Phlogiston Forty-Two* (1995). http://homepages.paradise.net.nz/triffid/trimmings/volume2/08_The_Lesser_Spotted_Roger_Zelazny.htm

Thomlinson, Norris, ed. *Zelazny.Corrupt.net,* August 4, 2007. http://web.archive.org/web/*/http://zelazny.corrupt.net/zelazny.html. This Web site is now defunct, but all content has been archived by date.

Walker, Paul. Interview. In *Speaking of Science Fiction.* Oradell, NJ: Luna Publications, 1987.

Wilgus, Neal. "Lord of the Shadows, Jack of Light." In *Seven by Seven: Interviews with American Science Fiction Writers of the West and Southwest,* 93–107. San Bernardino, CA: Borgo; 1996.

Yoke, C. B. *Roger Zelazny.* Mercer Island, WA: Starmont, 1979.

Zelazny & Amber. January 12, 2009. http://www.roger-zelazny.com/. Site primarily devoted to the Amber sequence, but also contains links to interviews and bibliographies.

References

Frequently Cited Sources

Andrews and Rennison: Stephen E. Andrews and Nick Rennison. 2006. *100 Must-Read Science Fiction Novels.* London: A. & C. Black.

Barron: Neil Barron. 2004. *Anatomy of Wonder.* 5th ed. Westport, CT: Libraries Unlimited.

***ESF*:** John Clute and Peter Nicholls, eds. 1999. *The Encyclopedia of Science Fiction.* Rev. ed. New York: Orbit.

Cited by the name of authors of individual essays: 1996. *St. James Guide to Science Fiction Writers,* ed. Jay Pedersen. Detroit, MI: St. James.

Roberts: Adam Roberts. 2005. *The History of Science Fiction.* London: Palgrave Macmillan.

Other Text Sources

Bloom, Harold, ed. 1995. *Classic Science Fiction Writers.* New York: Chelsea House.

Magill, Frank N., ed. 1979. *Survey of Science Fiction Literature.* Englewood Cliffs, NJ: Salem.

Nicholls, Stan. 1993. *Wordsmiths of Wonder: Fifty Interviews with Writers of the Fantastic.* London: Orbit.

Perret, Patti. 1984. *The Faces of Science Fiction.* New York: Bluejay.

Platt, Charles. 1980. *Dream Makers: The Uncommon People Who Write Science Fiction,* 183–92. New York: Berkley, 1980. A list of authors Platt has interviewed, as well as active links to two full interviews, at http://www.davidpascal.com/charlesplatt/interviews.html.

Seed, David, ed. 2005. *A Companion to Science Fiction.* Malden, UK: Blackwell.

Stover, Leon. 2002. *Science Fiction from Wells to Heinlein.* Jefferson, NC: McFarland.

Westfahl. Gary, ed. 2005. *The Greenwood Encyclopedia of Science Fiction and Fantasy: Themes, Works, and Wonders.* Westport, CT: Greenwood.

Westfahl. Gary, ed. 2005. *Science Fiction Quotations: From the Inner Mind to the Outer Limits.* New Haven, CT: Yale University Press.

Whissen, Thomas Reed. 1992. *Classic Cult Fiction: A Companion to Popular Cult Literature.* New York: Greenwood.

Web Sites

URLs cited in this volume were checked during October 2009.

Best Science Fiction Stories. June 21, 2009. http://bestsciencefictionstories.com/. Fan site that offers synopses and reviews of science fiction short stories, written by fans. Also gives links for finding the stories in anthologies or online.

Books and Writers: Authors' Calendar. August 2007. Petri Liukkonen and Ari Pesonen. Pegasos. http://www.kirjasto.sci.fi/calendar.htm. Finnish literary Web site, organized by author's birthdates, with detailed biographical entries and selected bibliographies.

Contemporary Writers.com. British Arts Council. http://www.contemporarywriters.com/. Up-to-date profiles of some of the UK's and the Commonwealth's most important living writers: biographies, bibliographies, critical reviews, prizes, and photographs.

Fantastic Fiction. April 2008. http://www.fantasticfiction.co.uk/. Bibliographies of more than 4,000 British and American authors, including SF authors. Some entries include portraits and biographical statements. Bibliographies include titles and images of book jackets of selected primary works (books and stories written by the author). Generally reliable, but has occasional glitches (for instance, in many cases, short story collections are listed as "novels") .

Internet Speculative Fiction Database. April 2008. The Cushing Library Science Fiction and Fantasy Research Collection. Texas A&M University. http://www.isfdb.org/. Open-content collaborative bibliographic database for science fiction, fantasy, and horror. Bibliographic data, award listings, magazine, anthology and collection content listings, and forthcoming books.

Literature Resource Center. Thomson Gale. Links through library home pages. Incorporates materials from the Dictionary of Literary Biography series, as well as other printed reference series published by Gale. Available online by subscription; check your local library for availability

Modern Language Association International Bibliography. Modern Language Association. http://www.mla.org/bibliography. Indexes scholarly articles on English- and non-English-language literature, film, cultural studies, folklore, and linguistics. Published in print and online. Available in print and online by subscription; check your local library for availability.

Science Fiction and Fantasy Research Database. October 2007. Hal W. Hall. Texas A & M University. http://library.tamu.edu/cushing/sffrd/default.asp. Online index to historical and critical items about science fiction, fantasy, and horror. Encompasses and updates Hal W. Hall's classic Science Fiction and Fantasy Reference Index series.

SciFan.com. March 2008. Olivier Travers and Sophie Bellais. http://www.scifan.com/. Comprehensive bibliographic database of SF and fantasy writers, focused on organizing the author data into series and themes. Links to relevant Web sites.

Spacelight. March 2008. George C. Willick. http://www.gcwillick.com/Spacelight/index.html. "Vital statistics and personal data for the golden age writers of pulp magazine stories and paperback books." Includes much interesting information not available elsewhere, such as original obituaries.

Templeton Gate. Galen Strickland. http://templetongate.tripod.com/mainpage.htm. Professional fan Web site, collecting essays on various SF writers.

Additional Valuable Resources

Bleiler, Everett Franklin. 1982. *Science Fiction Writers.* New York: Scribner. Critical studies of the major authors from the early nineteenth century to the early 1980s.

Contemporary Authors. 1981– . Detroit, MI: Gale Research. Also available online; check availability with your school or library.

Contemporary Authors. Autobiography Series. 1984–1999. Detroit, MI: Gale Research. Thirty volumes, each containing about twenty autobiographical essays written exclusively for the series.

Contemporary Authors, New Revision Series. 1981– . Detroit, MI: Gale Research.

Harris-Fain, Darren, ed. 1997. *British Fantasy and Science-Fiction Writers before World War I.* Dictionary of Literary Biography 178. Detroit, MI: Gale.

Harris-Fain, Darren, ed. 2002. *British Fantasy and Science-Fiction Writers, 1918-1960.* Dictionary of Literary Biography 255. Detroit, MI: Gale.

Harris-Fain, Darren, ed. 2002. *British Fantasy and Science-Fiction Writers Since 1960.* Dictionary of Literary Biography 261. Detroit, MI: Gale.

Sabella, Robert. 2000. *Who Shaped Science Fiction?* Commack, NY: Kroshka.

Tixier, Diana, ed. 1999. *Strictly Science Fiction.* Englewood, CO: Libraries Unlimited.

Web Sites

Access My Library. April 2008. The Gale Group. http://www.accessmylibrary.com/. Free access to millions of articles in Thomson Gale databases for patrons of public and school libraries. Available online with a library card; check whether your local library is registered.

Alpha Ralpha Boulevard. September 2006. http://www.catch22.com/SF/ARB/. Bibliographic Web site, with links.

Archive of Science Fiction. December 2001. CyberSpace Spinner. http://www.hycyber.com/SF/. Not a pretty site, and seems to be dormant since 2001, but extremely useful: comprehensive bibliographies, list of authors' pseudonyms, and cinema archive.

Feminist Science Fiction, Fantasy and Utopia. June 2007. Laura Quilter. http://feministsf.org/. Complex bibliography that lists, cites, and describes SF and critical works from a feminist perspective. Includes a wiki of author information.

SFF Audio. March 29, 2009. Edited by Scott Danielson and Jesse Willis. http://www.sffaudio.com/. A comprehensive guide to SF audio: radio drama, audiobooks, podcasts, MP3, and just about every other imaginable aural version of great SF literature.

Themes/Genres in Science Fiction: An Idiosyncratic and Woefully Incomplete List. June 2002. Edited by Kathleen L. Fowler. http://phobos.ramapo.edu/~kfowler/sfthemes.html. Extremely knowledgeable; a wide range of reading possibilities. Unfortunately (as the subtitle warns us), work on the list appears to have been abandoned, and the final few links are not active. (And they would have been interesting ones!)

Uchronia: The Alternative History List. April 2008. Robert B. Schmunk. http://www.uchronia.net/. A bibliography of over 2,800 novels, stories, essays, and other printed material involving "allohistory," or the "what ifs" of history.

The Ultimate Science Fiction Web Guide. February 2004. Edited by Jonathan Vos Post. Magic Dragon Multimedia. http://www.magicdragon.com/UltimateSF/thisthat.html. An extensive list of themes, with titles ranging from the earliest "proto-SF" to the late 1990s.

Organizations and Conventions

The New England Science Fiction Association (NESFA). http://www.nesfa.org/. Founded in 1967, one of the oldest science fiction clubs in New England. Organizes the long-running, annual Boskone convention, and runs NESFA Press.

Science Fiction Oral History Association. http://www.sfoha.org/. Founded in 1975, this nonprofit organization maintains an archive of audio and video recordings of historic people and events related to science fiction and fantasy. Archive Catalog online.

Science Fiction Research Association. http://www.sfra.org/. "The oldest professional organization for the study of science fiction and fantasy literature and film."

Science Fiction and Fantasy Writers of America, Inc. http://www.sfwa.org/. The Science Fiction and Fantasy Writers of America sponsors the yearly Nebula Awards. Its Web site includes a variety of resources for writers, as well as readers. Obituary Archive. http://www.sfwa.org/News/obits.htm

The Speculative Literature Foundation. http://www.speclit.org/index.php. Volunteer- run, nonprofit organization dedicated to promoting the interests of readers, writers, editors, and publishers in the speculative literature community.

World Science Fiction Society/World Science Fiction Convention. http://www.worldcon.org/. The World Science Fiction Society sponsors the yearly Hugo Awards, as well as the yearly World Science Fiction Convention.

Portals and Home Pages

Locus Online. http://www.locusmag.com/Links/Portal.html. Links to any and all Web sites the SF and fantasy fan could possibly wish for: "zines, blogs, forums, authors' websites.... If it is on the web, it is here, and if it isn't here, there are links to half-a dozen other link collection websites." Includes a section for closed or dormant magazine Web sites, and "fun."

SF Site. http://www.sfsite.com/home.htm. The home page for science fiction and fantasy. Includes author interviews (extensive index), articles, and reviews. Index of reviews.

SciFiPedia. http://scifipedia.scifi.com/index.php/Main_Page. Wiki encyclopedia.

Science Fiction Citations. January 2008. Edited by Jesse Sheidlower, Jeff Prucher, and Malcolm Farmer. http://www.jessesword.com/sf/home. Fascinating site maintained by the editor at large of the *Oxford English Dictionary*, which aims to provide accurate definitions and first-known use dates for science fiction terms. The project grew out of regular work that was being done for the OED's reading programs; each entry supplies a basic definition, the history of this project's research on the term, and quotes supporting the earliest known use, gathered for OED.

Science Fiction-Related Materials. October 2006. Paul Brians. Washington State University. http://www.wsu.edu/~brians/science_fiction/. Study guides for various SF novels, bibliographies, and other links.

Syfy.com. http://www.syfy.com/. It is difficult to work up enthusiasm for this new incarnation of the SciFi Channel, which appears to have dropped most, if not all, of the author interviews, reviews, and articles about fantasy and science fiction literature and media that made it really useful to the SF reader. Sources formerly found on scifi.com have been listed in this text, in the hopes that they can be found in cached versions or have been reproduced on other Web sites.

Author/Title Index

The names of authors who are the subjects of this book are in boldface type.

I. See *Slant*

A.D., 107
A.I.: Artificial Intelligence, 9
Abba Abba, 107
"ABCs in Zero G," 300
"Abduction of Bunny Steiner, or A Shameless Lie, The," 163
Abominable Earthman, The, 335
About the Size of It, 163
About Time, 187
About Writing: Seven Essays, Four Letters and Five Interviews, 152
"Above It All," 368
Absolute Ronin, 293
Abyss, The (Card), 125
Abyss: Two Novellas (Wilhelm), 482
Accelerando, 416, 417
Acceptable Time, An, 263
Accidental Time Machine, The, 203
Achilles' Choice, 319
Acorna series, 277, 279, 280
Across a Billion Years, 389
Across Realtime, 460
Across the Universe, 363
"Active in Time and History," 329
"Acts of God," 73
"Adam and No Eve," 58
Adams, Douglas, 1-4, 259
Adding a Dimension, 28
"Adjustment Bureau, The," 158
"Adrift Just Off the Islets of Langerhans: Latitude 38° 54' N, Longitude 77° 00' 13,' W," 173
Adulthood Rites, 116
Adventure of Alyx, The, 357, 359
"Adventure of the Field Theorems, The," 289
Adventures, 342
Adventures of Bill, the Galactic Hero, 208, 209
Adventures of the Peerless Peer, The, 182
Adventures of the Stainless Steel Rat, The, 211
"Advice to New Writers," 91

"Advocates," 131
Affairs at Hampden Ferrers, 8
After Doomsday, 14
"After King Kong Fell," 182
After Long Silence, 435
After Many a Summer, 238, 239
After Such Knowledge, 67
After the Fall, 374
Afterlives, 364
Aftermath, The (Bova), 72
"Aftermaths" (Bujold), 102, 103
Again, Alternate Worldcons, 345
Again, Dangerous Visions, 172, 173, 175
Against a Dark Background, 43, 44
Against the Fall of Night, 144
"Against the Lafayette Escadrille," 489, 491
Against the Odds, 301
Age Like This, 1920–1940, An, 324
Age of Exploration, 135
Age of Miracles, 99
Age of the Pussyfoot, The, 333
Age, An, 7
Agent of the Terran Empire, 16
Ages in Chaos: James Hutton and the Discovery of Deep Time (Baxter), 50
Ages of Chaos (Bradley), 90
Agrippa (A Book of the Dead), 192
Ahmed and the Oblivion Machine, 83
"Air Raid," 448, 450
Airs of Earth, The, 8
Alan Moore: Wild Worlds, 313
Alan Moore's Shocking Futures, 313
Alan Moore's Twisted Times, 313
Alan Moore's Writing for Comics, 314
"Alastair Baffle's Emporium of Wonders," 344
Alchemist's Question, The, 305
Alchemy & Academe, 280
Alder Tree, 244
Aldiss, Brian W., 5-11, 59, 69, 198, 208, 211, 240, 298, 337, 347, 375, 378, 380, 393, 424, 426, 454, 495
Aldous Huxley: The Gravity of Light, 239
Aleutian Trilogy, 243, 244

Alfred Bester Redemolished, 58
Alfred the Great, 162
Algebraist, The, 43, 44
Alias Grace, 32
Alien Child, 363
Alien Crimes, 345
Alien Harvest, 373
Alien Heart, The, 344
Alien Heat, An, 305
Alien Land, An, 344
"Alien Monsters," 359
Alien Realms, 404
Alien Upstairs, 363
Alien Within, The, 73
Alien Years, The, 389
Aliens, 74
Aliens from Space, 388
"Aliens Have Taken the Place of Angels," 30, 31, 32
Alight in the Void, 17
All Art Is Propaganda: Critical Essays, 324
"All Dracula's Children," 395
All My Sins Remembered, 203, 204
All One Universe, 17
"All Seated on the Ground," 484, 485
"All the Colors of the Rainbow," 78
"All the Lies That are My Life," 174
All the Myriad Ways, 319, 320
"All the Robots and Isaac Asimov," 54
"All the Things You Are," 343
All the Weyrs of Pern, 279
All Tomorrow's Parties, 191
"All You Zombies—," 221
"All-Consuming, The," 383
Alley God, The, 182
Alliance Space, 137
<u>Alliance-Union Universe</u>, 135
Ally, Ally, Aster, 244
Alpha, 19, 20
Alpha Centauri or Die!, 78
"Alpha Ralpha Boulevard," 399, 400
<u>Alpha series</u> (Silverberg), 392
Altar on Asconel, The, 99
Alternate Asimovs, The, 27
"Alternate History" (McHugh), 284
Alternate Kennedys, 119, 345
Alternate Outlaws, 345
Alternate Presidents, 345
Alternate Realities, 137
Alternate Skiffy, 345
Alternate Tyrants, 345
Alternate Warriors, 345

Alternate Worldcons, 345
Alternating Currents, 335
Alternative Detective, The, 373
Alvin Journeyman, 126
. . . Always a Fan, 346
Always Coming Home, 255
"Amanda and the Alien," 392
Amaryllis Night and Day, 231
"American Dead, The," 210
Amnesia, 161, 163
Amnesia Moon, 269
"Amnesty," 116
"Amok Time," 426
"Among Strangers," 121
"*Amor Vincit Foeminam,* The Battle of the Sexes in SF," 359
Analog anthologies, 74
Anathem, 408
"Ancestor Money," 284
"Ancient Engines," 431
Ancient of Days, 61, 62
"Ancient Shadows," 306
. . . And All the Stars a Stage, 67
. . . And Call Me Conrad, 501
And Chaos Died, 358
"—And He Built a Crooked House," 221
"And I Awoke and Found Me Here on the Cold Hill Side," 440
". . . And Now You Don't," 26
And Now the News . . . , 425
And Strange at Ecbatan the Trees, 61, 62
And the Angels Sing, 482
. . . And the Lurid Glare of the Comet, 10
Anderson, Poul, 12–18, 52, 318, 485
Andover and the Android, 482
"Android and the Human, The," 158
"Angel," 120
"Angel in the Darkness, The," 36
"Angel of Light," 204
Angel with the Sword, 135
"Angels and You Dogs," 196
"Angouleme," 162
Angry Candy, 173, 175
Animal Farm, 323, 324
Ann Veronica, 474
Annals of the Heechee, The, 334
"Anniversary Project," 204
"Another Story or A Fisherman of the Inland Sea," 255
Antarctic Mystery, An, or The Sphinx of the Ice-fields, 454
Antarctica, 348, 349

Antic Hay, 237, 239
Anti-Ice, 48
"Anti-Muffins, The," 264
Antinomy, 355
"Anti-SF Novel, The," 284
Anvil of Stars, 53
Anvil of the World, The 35, 36
Anywhen, 67
"Apartheid, Superstrings and Mordecai Thubana, The," 63
"Ape and Essence," 238, 239
Apocalypse Troll, The, 468
"Appeals Court," 168
Approaching Oblivion, 175
"April Fool's Day Forever," 479, 481
Arbai Trilogy, 435
Arbor House Treasuries, 392
"Archaic Planets: Nine Excerpts from the Encyclopedia Galactica," 430
Argyll: A Memoir, 425
"Arimaspian Legacy, The," 491
Ark of Mars, The, 78
Arm of the Starfish, The, 263
Armageddon in Retrospect, 464
Armageddon Inheritance, The, 468, 469
Aronsdale series, 21
Around the World in Eighty Days, 454, 455
Art after Apogee, 10
Art of Blessing the Day, The, 329
Art of Playboy, The, 85
Art of Seeing, The, 239
Art of Sin City, The, 294
"Arthur Sternbach Brings the Curveball to Mars," 350
"Article of Faith," 344
Artificial Kid, The, 411, 412
As I Please, 1943–1945, 324
As on a Darkling Plain, 71
As She Climbed Across the Table, 269
Asaro, Catherine, 19–22, 409
Ascendancies: The Best of Bruce Sterling, 413
Ascendant Sun, 21
Ascension Factor, The, 226
Ascent to Orbit: A Scientific Autobiography, 146
"Ash Circus, The," 215
Ashes of Victory, 469
"Asian Shore, The," 162
Asimov, Isaac, xiv, xv, **23–29**, 52, 54, 63, 65, 94, 208, 331, 337, 389, 392
"Aslan's Kin: Interfaith Fantasy and Science Fiction," 264

"Assassination of John F. Kennedy Considered as a Downhill Motor Race, The," 39
Assault on a Queen, 185, 187, 187
Assured Survival: Putting the Star Wars Defense in Perspective, 74
Asteroid Wars, 72
Astonishing Stories, 336
Astounding: The John W. Campbell Memorial Anthology, 209
Astounding Days: A Science Fictional Autobiography, 146
Astral Mirror, The, 73
At All Costs, 469
"At Lightspeed, Slowing," 168
At the City Limits of Fate, 63
At the Earth's Core, 111, 112
At the Edge of Space, 137
"At the Rialto," 485
At Winter's End, 390
Atheling, William. *See* Blish, James
Atlantic Abomination, The, 99
Atlantis: Three Tales, 151
Atomsk: A Novel of Suspense, 400
Atrocity Archives, The, 417
Atrocity Exhibition, The, 37, 38, 39
Attar's Revenge, 203
Atwood, Margaret, xiv, **30–33**
Aurora: Beyond Equality, 289
"Aurora in Four Voices," 21
Austin Family Stories, 264
Autism: Past, Present, Future, Speculative," 302
Autumn People, The, 83
Avatar (Cadigan), 120
Avatar, The (Anderson), 15
Avram Davidson Treasury, The, 388, 392
Awakeners, The, 435, 436
Awards Showcase 2008, 74
Away and Beyond, 445
"Aye, and Gomorrah," 150, 151
Aye, and Gomorrah, and Other Stories, 151
"Aymara," 383
Azazel, 27
"Aztechs" (McIntyre), 288
"AZTECHS" (Shepard), 383

Babel-17, 148, 150
Baby Is Three, 425
"Baby, You Were Great," 481
Babylon 5: A Call to Arms, 373
Back to the Stone Age, 111

Bad Moon Rising, 163
Bagombo Snuff Box: Uncollected Short Fiction, 464
Baker, Kage, 34–36
"Balinese Dancer," 245
"Ballad of Beta-2, The," 151
"Ballad of Lost C'mell, The," 399, 400
Ballard, J. G., xiv, **37–41**, 198
Band of Gypsies, 244
Bandit of Hell's Bend, The, 111
Bane of the Black Sword, The, 306
Banks, Iain M., xvii, **42–45**, 214
Barbara Holloway Novels, 481
"Barbarian Princess, The," 460
Barbarians of Mars, 305
Barbary, 288
Barbie Murders, The, 449, 451
Barefoot in the Head, 7
"Barnaby in Exile," 343
"Barnacle Bill the Spacer," 382
Barnacle Bill the Spacer and Other Stories, 384
Barnstormer in Oz, A, 182
Baroque Cycle, 407, 408
Barrayar, 102, 103, 104
"barry westphall crashes the singularity," 249
Barsoom, 35, 76, 79, 109, 110, 319,
"Barsoom and Myself," 79
Barsoom Project, The, 319
"Basilisk," 173
Batman, 291, 292, 293
Batman: Year One, 293
Battle of Forever, The, 445
Battle Station, 73
Battlestar Galactica No. 5: Galactica Discovers Earth, 341
Baxter, Stephen, 46–50, 145
Bear, Greg, 13, **51–55**, 94
"Bears Discover Smut," 63
Bear's Fantasies: Six Stories in Old Paradigms, 54
"Beast from 20,000 Fathoms, The," 83
Beast Must Die, The, 68
"Beast of the Heartland," 383
Beast of the Heartland and Other Stories, 384
Beast That Shouted Love at the Heart of the World, The, 173, 175
"Beatnik Bayou," 450
"Beautiful Friendship, A," 470
Beauty, 434, 435
"Beauty and the Opera or the Phantom Beast," 131

"Becalmed in Hell," 319
Beds in the East, 107
Bedtime for Frances, 231
"Beep," 67
Beetle in the Anthill, 421
Before Armageddon, 308
"Before I Wake," 350
Before the Golden Age, 25, 27
"Beginning of the Affair, The," 211
Beginning Place, The, 255
Beguilement, 103
Begum's Five Hundred Million, The, 454
Behind the Eyes of Dreamers and Other Short Novels, 364
Behind the Walls of Terra, 181
Behold the Man, 304, 305
Being Gardner Dozois: An Interview by Michael Swanwick, 430, 431
Believeniks!: 2005: The Year We Wrote a Book About the Mets, 269
"Bellman, The," 450
Bellwether, 484, 485
Beneath the Shattered Moons, 61
Benyon, John. *See* Wyndham, John
Beowulf's Children, 319
"Bernardo's House," 249
Berserker Base: A Collaborative Novel, 318, 485
Best Defense, The, 481
"Best Introduction to the Mountains, The," 492
Best Military Science Fiction of the 20th Century, 205
Best of All Possible Worlds, The, 355
Best of Edmond Hamilton, The, 79
Best of Jim Baen's Universe, The, 341, 345
Best of Omni Science Fiction, The, 74
Best of Planet Stories No. 1, The, 79
Best Rootin' Tootin' Shootin' Gunslinger in the Whole Damned Galaxy, The, 342
Best SF series, 211
Bester, Alfred, **56–59**, 190
Betrayal, The, 135
Better Than One, 482
Between Planets, 220
Between the Wars series, 306
Between Time and Timbuktu: A Space Fantasy, 465
Between Worlds, 392
Beyond Armageddon, 296, 298
"Beyond Between," 280
Beyond Heaven's River, 53

Beyond 1984: A Remembrance of Things Future, 83
Beyond the Blue Event Horizon, 334
"Beyond the Dead Reef," 440
Beyond the Fall of Night, 145
"Beyond the Farthest Star," 112
Beyond the Safe Zone, 391
Beyond the Stars, 27
"Beyond Thirty," 112
Beyond This Horizon, 220
"Bianca's Hands," 425
"Bibi," 343
Bibliomen, 492
"Bicentennial Man, The," 25, 28
Bicentennial Man, 392
Bicentennial Man and Other Stories, The, 27
"Bicycle Repairman," 412
"Biding Time," 369
"Big Hunger, The," 297
"Big Ideas," 369
Big Jump, The, 77
Big U, The, 408
Bill, the Galactic Hero on the Planet of Bottled Brains, 209, 373
Bill, the Galactic Hero series, 207, 209
"Bill, the Galactic Hero's Happy Holiday," 210
"Billenium," 39
Billion Year Spree, 5, 7, 10, 347
Bio-Futures, 364
"Biological Century and the Future of Science Fiction, The," 196
BiPohl, 336
Bird, Cordwainer. *See* Ellison, Harlan
"Birth of a Writer," 116
Birthday of the World, The, 254, 256
Birthright: The Book of Man, 339, 341
Bishop, Michael, 60–64, 364, 384, 442
"Bizarre Genius of Edgar Poe," 455
"Black Air," 350
Black Alice, 162
"Black Amazon of Mars," 78
Black Corridor, The, 305
"Black Destroyer," 445
Black Dossier, 313
Black Easter: Or Faust Aleph-Null, 67
Black Horses for the King, 280
Black Knight of the Iron Sphere, 404
Black Mist and Other Japanese Futures, 127
Black Projects, White Knights: The Company Dossiers, 36
Black Star Rising, 333

Black Throne, The, 501
Blackout, 485
Blade Runner, 157
Blades of Mars, 305
Blair, Eric Arthur. *See* Orwell, George
"Blemmye's Stratagem, The," 412
Blind Assassin, The, 30, 31
"Blind Geometer, The," 349
Blish, James, 10, 13, 18, **65–69,** 331
"Block Universe," 369
Blood: A Southern Fantasy, 306
Blood Heritage, 436
Blood Music, 51, 53
Blood of Amber, 501
Blood Red Game, The, 305
"Blood Sisters," 204
Bloodchild and Other Stories, 116
Blooded on Archane, 62, 63
Bloody Sun, The, 89
Blown: Or Sketches Among the Ruins of My Mind, 180, 181
Blue Champagne, 449, 451
Blue Kansas Sky, 63
Blue Mars, 349
Bluebeard, 464
"Blued Moon," 486
Boarding the Enterprise 369
Boat of a Million Years, The, 12, 15
Bodily Harm, 32
Body Armor: 2000, 205
Body of Glass, 328, 329
Body Snatchers, 188. *See also Invasion of the Body Snatchers*
Bojeffries Saga, The, 312
Bold As Love, 243, 244
Bolo!, 468
"Bone Yard, The," 436
Bones, The, 436
"Bones of the Earth, The" (Le Guin), 254, 255
Bones of the Earth (Swanwick), 429, 430
Bones of Time, The, 195, 196
"Boobs," 130
"Book of Martha, The," 116
Book of Ptath, 444
Book of Skaith, The, 78
Book of Skulls, The, 389,
Book of the Long Sun, 491
Book of the New Sun, 488, 490
Book of the Short Sun, 488, 491
Book of Van Vogt, The, 445
"Bookworm, Run!," 458, 460
"Boot Hill," 21

Booze, Broads, & Bullets, 294
"Borderland of Sol, The," 317, 318
Borders of Infinity, The, 104
"Born with the Dead," 388
Bova, Ben, 35, **70–75**, 174, 356
Bow Down to Nul, 7
Boy and His Dog, A (Ellison), 172, 173, 175
Boy and His Dog, A: The Final Solution" (Russ), 359
"Boy Who Waterskied to Forever, The," 440
Boy Who Would Live Forever, The: A Novel of Gateway, 334
"Boys, The," 415
Brackett, Leigh, 76–80, 81, 82, 87, 88, 109, 308
Bradbury, Ray, xiii, 78, **81–86,** 109, 348, 424, 425, 444, 446
Bradbury Speaks: Too Soon from the Cave, Too Far from the Stars, 85
Bradley, Marion Zimmer, 87–92, 300
Brain & Brawn Ships, 277, 278
Brain Wave, 14
Branch, The, 341
Brave Little Toaster, The, 160, 162, 163
Brave New World, 237, 239, 322
Brave New World Revisited, 239
"Brave New Worlds: A Few Rules for Predicting the Future," 116
Brave to Be a King, 16
Bread and Jam for Frances, 231
Breakfast in the Ruins, 305
Breakfast of Champions; or, Goodbye Blue Monday!, 464, 465
Briah Cycle, 490
Bride, The, 288
"Bride of Elvis," 196
Bride of Frankenstein, The, 379
Bridge, The (Banks), 42, 44
Bridge of Lost Desire, The, 151
Bridge Trilogy (Gibson), 191
Bridging the Galaxies, 320
"Brigantia's Angels," 49
Bright Segment, 425
Brighten to Incandescence, 63
Brightfount Diaries, The, 8
Brightness Falls from the Air, 440
Brightness Reef, 95
"Brillo," 73, 174
Brin, David, 52, 54, **93–96**
Bring Me the Head of Prince Charming, 373, 502

"Bringing It All Back Home," 63
Brittle Innings, 61, 62
"Broken Axiom, The," 56
Broken Sword, The, 14
Bronze King, The, 131
Brothel in Rosenstrasse, The, 306
"Brother to Dragons, a Companion of Owls, A," 481
Brothers, 72
Brothers in Arms, 103
Brothers of Earth, 134, 135
"Brothers of the Head," 7, 9
Brown Girl in the Ring, 233, 234, 235
Brunner, John, 97–100, 157, 202
Brunner, Kilian Houston. *See* Brunner, John
Budet Laskovyy Dozhd, 84
Buffalo Gals, and Other Animal Presences, 256
"Buffalo Gals, Won't You Come Out Tonight," 254
Building Harlequin's Moon, 318
Bujold, Lois McMaster, 101–4
"Bully!," 343
Buonarotti Quartet, The, 245
Burgess, Anthony, 105–8
Burmese Days, 322, 324
"Burn," 248, 249
Burning Chrome, 191, 192
Burning City, The, 319
Burning Tower, The, 319
Burning World, The, 39
Burroughs, Edgar Rice, xiv, 35, 76, **109–13**
Bury My Heart at W. H. Smith's, 10
Bury, Stephen. *See* Stephenson, Neal
Businessman, The: A Tale of Terror, 161, 162
"But Who Can Replace a Man?," 8, 9
Butler, O. E. *See* Butler, Octavia E.
Butler, Octavia E., 114–18
Buy Jupiter and Other Stories, 27
Buying Time, 203
By Any Other Name, 354, 355
By Heresies Distressed, 469
"By His Bootstraps," 221
By Schism Rent Asunder, 469
By Space Possessed: Essays on the Exploration of Space, 146
"By the Falls," 210
Byte Beautiful (Bishop), 63
Byte Beautiful: Eight Science Fiction Stories (Tiptree), 441
Byworlder, The, 14
Byzantium Endures, 306

"Cabin on the Coast, A," 491
Cache, The, 180
Cache from Outer Space, 180
Cadigan, Pat, 119–22, 411
"Cairene Purse, The," 307
Calculating God, 368
Caldé of the Long Sun, 491
Calibrated Alligator, The, 391
Calibre, 50, 373
California Voodoo Game, The, 319
Call of Earth, The, 126
Callahan and Company: The Compleat Chronicles of the Crosstime Saloon, 254, 355
Callahan's [Crosstime Saloon], 57, 254, 352, 354, 355
Callahan's Crosstime Saloon: Lady Sally's, 354
Cambio Bay, 481
Camilla, 264
Camilla Dickinson, 264
Camouflage, 203
Camp Concentration, 160, 161, 162
"Can Technology Save the Planet?," 414
Can You Feel Anything When I Do This?, 374
Can You Hear Me, Think Tank Two?, 163
Canal Dreams, 44
Canary in a Cathouse, 464
Canticle for Leibowitz, A, 296, 297
Capitol, 125
Capital Code, 347, 349
Capricorn Games, 391
Captain Video and His Video Rangers, 374
Captive Universe, 208, 209
Captives of the Flame, 150
Card, Orson Scott, 123–28, 366
Cardography, 127
Carola, 400
Carpathian Castle, 454
Carradyne Touch, The, 279
Carrion Comfort, 395, 396
Carson of Venus, 111
Caryatids, The, 412
"Casablanca" (Disch), 162
Casablanca (Moorcock), 307
Case Against Tomorrow, The, 335
"Case and the Dreamer," 425
Case of Conscience, A, 65, 66, 67
Casebook of Constance and Charlie, The, 481
Caspak, 111
"Cassandra," 135
Cassini Division, The, 275

Castaways' World, 99
Castle of Days, 492
Castle of Indolence, The, 161, 164
Castle of Perseverance, The, 161, 164
Castle of the Otter, The, 492
Castles Made of Sand, 244
Castleview, 491
Cat Who Walks Through Walls, The, 221
Catacomb Years, 61, 62
"Catastrophe," 405
Catch a Falling Star, 98
Catch the Lightning, 21
Caterpillar's Question, The, 181
"Cathedrals in Space," 68
Cat's Cradle, 463, 464
Cat's Eye, 32
Catteni, The, 278
"Caught in the Organ Draft" (Silverberg), 390
Caught in the Organ Draft: Biology in Science Fiction (Asimov), 27
Cave Girl, The, 111
Caves of Steel, The, 25
Celestial Blueprint, The: And Other Stories, 182
Cellular, 120
Centauri Device, The, 213, 215
Century, The, 305
Century of Science Fiction, 1950–1959, A, 392
Cetaganda, 103
Chacal, 119, 121
"Chain of Chance, The," *260*
Chain of Logic, 14
Chains of the Sea, 392
Chalion Universe, 102, 103
Challenge of the Sea, The, 146
Challenge of the Spaceship, The, 146
Challenges, 73
"Chance," 486
Change of Command, 301
Changed Man, The, 127
Changeling, (Zelazny), 501
Changelings (McCaffrey), 280
Changer of Worlds, 470
Changes, 63
Changing Land, The, 501
Changing Planes, 254, 256
Chanur series, 135, 137
Chapterhouse: Dune, 226
Character and Viewpoint: Elements of Writing, 127
"Charles Dickens," 322, 325

Charmed Sphere, The, 21
Charnas, Suzy McKee, 129–32
Chase of the Golden Meteor, The, 454
Chasing Science: Science as Spectator Sport, 337
"Chatting with Anubis," 174
"Cheering for the Rockets," 307
"Chemical Persuasion," 240
Chernevog, 137
Chernobyl, 334
Cherry, Caroline Janice. *See* Cherryh, C. J
Cherryh, C. J., 133–38
Chessmen of Mars, The, 110
Chiang, Ted, 139–41
Child of Time, 25
Child of Venus, 363
Childhood's End, 142, 143, 144
Children of Dune, 226, 227
Children of the Company, The, 35
Children of the Lens, 404
Children of the Mind, 125
Children of the Night, 396
Children of the State, The, 320
Children of the Streets, 174
Children of the Wind: Five Novellas, 482
"Children of Time, The," 49
Children of Tomorrow, 445
China Mountain Zhang, 282, 283, 284
China of K'ai-shek, The, 401
"Chinese Perspective, A," 8
Chocky, 496, 497
Christmas Ghosts, 344
"Chronic Argonauts, The," 473, 474
Chronic City, 269
Chronicles of Amber, 500, 501
Chronicles of Different Worlds, 342
Chronicles of Pern, The: First Fall, 280
Chronicles of the Lensmen, 404
Chronomaster, 503
Chronopolis and Other Stories, 40
Chrysalids, The, 496
"Cibola," 486
"Cicada Queen," 412
Cigar-Box Faust and Other Miniatures, 431
Circle of Quiet, A, 265
Circus of Dr. Lao and Other Improbable Stories, The, 83
Circus of Hells, A, 16
Citadel of the Autarch, The, 490
Cities and Stones—A Traveller's Yugoslavia, 10

Cities in Flight, 65–66, 67, 68
"Cities of the Future?," 196
Citizen in Space, 374
Citizen of the Galaxy, 221
City and the Stars, The, 144
City at the End of Time, 53
City Beyond Play, The, 180
City in the Autumn Stars, The, 306
City of a Thousand Suns, 150
City of Cain, 480
"City of Cries, The," 21
City of Darkness, 72
City of Darkness, City of Light, 328, 329
City of Illusions, 255
City of Sorcery, 89
"City on the Edge of Forever, The," 172, 173, 175
Civil Campaign, A, 102, 103
"Civil Liberties in Cyberspace," 418
Clan Corporate, The, 417
Clans of the Alphane Moon, 156
Clara Reeve, 161, 162
Clarion SF, 482
Clarke, Arthur C. (Sir), xiv, xv, 46, 47, 48, 57, 71, 95, **142–47,** 219, 316, 334, 367
Clash of Cymbals, A, 67
Classical Elements, 39
Claw of the Conciliator, The, 490
Clay's Ark, 115, 116
Clergyman's Daughter, A, 324
Clewiston Test, The, 479, 481
Climb the Wind, 362, 363
Climbers, 214, 215
"Clink," 323
Clipper of the Clouds, The, 454
Clock of Time, The, 187
Clockwork Orange, A, 105, 106, 107
Clockwork Testament, The, or Enderby's End, 107
Clockwork Traitor, The, 404
Clone, The, 480
"Clone Alone," 216
Clone Master, The, 336
Cloned Lives, 362, 363
"Close Encounter," 485
Close Encounters with the Deity: Stories, 63
Closeup: New Worlds, 74
Cloud's Rider, 136
Coalescent, 48
Coast of Coral, The, 146
Cobweb, 408

Cocaine Nights, 39
Coelura, The, 278
Coils, 501
"Coin Collector, The," 187
Cold Case, 481
"Cold Dark Night with Snow, A," 481
"Cold Iron," 430
"Cold Turkey," 465
Cold Victory, 15
"Colder War, A," 417
"Coldest Place," 316
Collision Course, 388
"Colonel in Autumn, The," 390
Colonel Rutherford's Colt, 383
Colony, 72
"Color of Neanderthal Eyes, The," 441
Colors of Space, The, 89
"Come Back to the Killing Ground, Alice, My Love," 502
"Come Live with Me," 441
"Come to Venus Melancholy," 162
"Comes Now the Power," 502
Comic Inferno, The, 9
Coming, The, 203
"Coming of Age in Karhide," 255
Coming of the Quantum Cats, The, 334
Coming of the Space Age, The, 146
Coming of the Terrans, The, 78
"Coming Technological Singularity," 458, 459, 460
Coming Up for Air, 324
Command Decision, 301
Committed Men, The, 213, 215
Common Clay: 20-Odd Stories, 9
"Communication Prosthetics: Threat, or Menace?," 408
Companions, The, 435
Company, The (Baker), 34, 35
Company Wars, 135
Compass Rose, The, 254, 256
Compleat Traveller in Black, The, 98, 99
Complete Frank Miller Spider-Man, 294
Complete Idiot's Guide to Publishing Science Fiction, The, 169
Complete Robot, The, 27
"Complex Speeds and Special Relativity," 20
"Complication in the Science Fiction Story," 446
Complicity, 42, 44
Computer Connection, The, 58
"Computer Entertainment Thirty-Five Years from Today," 410, 413
"Computer Iterates the Greater Trumps, The," 491
Concrete Island, 39
"Concrete Jungle, The," 416, 417
Condition of Muzak, The, 304, 305
Conditionally Human and Other Stories, 298
Condorman, 374
Confessions of a Crap Artist, 155,
"Confessions of a Space Junkie," 204
Confusion, The, 407, 408
Conglomeroid Cocktail Party, The, 391,
Conqueror, 49
Conqueror Fantastic, 364
Conqueror's Child, The, 130
Conquerors from the Darkness, 388
"Consciousness, Literature, and Science Fiction," 196
ConSentiency, 226
"ConSentiency and How It Got That Way, The," 227
Consider Her Ways and Others, 497
"Consider Her Ways," 497
Consider Phlebas, 42, 44
Conspirator, 136
Constance and Charlie, 481
Constantine, 313
Contacting Aliens: An Illustrated Guide to David Brin's Uplift Universe, 96
Content: Selected Essays on Technology, Creativity, Copyright, and the Future of the Future, 169
"Continuing Westward," 489
Convergent Series, 318, 320
"Cookie Monster, The," 459, 460
Cooking Out of This World, 280
Cool War, The, 333
Cordelia's Honor, 104
Cornelius Chronicles, The, 307
Cornelius Quartet, The, 307
Corona, 53
Corridors of Time, The, 14
Corum: The Coming of Chaos, 307
Corum: The Prince With the Silver Hand, 308
Cosmic Carnival of Stanislaw Lem, The, 260
Cosmic Critiques: How & Why Ten Science Fiction Stories Work, 28
Cosmic Laughter, 205
Cosmic Puppets, The, 156
Cosmic Rape, The, 424
Cosmonaut Keep, 272, 275
"Cost to Be Wise, The," 284
Count Brass, 308

Count Geiger's Blues, 62
"Count the Clock That Tells the Time," 173
Count Zero, 191
Counter-Clock World, 156
"Counting Cats in Zanzibar," 491
Counting the Eons, 28
Country of the Blind and Other Stories, The, 475
Country of the Crimson Clouds, 419
Country of the Mind, 53
Country You Have Never Seen, The, 359
Course of the Heart, The, 215
Courts of Chaos, The, 501
"Coyote at the End of History," 431
Crack in Space, The, 156
Cradle, 145
Craft of Writing Science Fiction That Sells, The, 74
"Craphound," 168
Crash, 38, 39
Crashlander, 320
Crazy Carol Stories, 436
Crazy Time, 481
Crazy Years, The: Reflections of a Science Fiction Original, 355
"Creating and Using Near Future Settings," 284
"Creating Tomorrow Today: SF's Special Effects Wizards," 337
"Creation of Imaginary Worlds, The," 18
Creatures of Light and Darkness, 501
Crescent City Rhapsody, 195, 196
Cretan Teat, The, 6, 8
"Cri de Coeur," 63
Crisis on Doona, 278
Critical Mass, 334
"Croatoan," 173
"Crocodile Rock," 383
Crome Yellow, 237, 239
Crompton Divided, 373
Crook Factory, The, 396
Crooked Inheritance, The: Poems, 329
Cross of Centuries, A 63
"Crossing Into Cambodia," 306
Crosswicks Journals, 264
Crow Road, The, 42, 44
Crown of Slaves, 469
Crown of Stars, 441
"Crucifixus Etiam," 297
Crusade, 469
Cryptonomicon, 407, 408
Cryptozoic!, 7

Crystal City, The, 126
"Crystal Egg, The," 474
Crystal Express, 413
Crystal Line, 278
Crystal Ship, The, 392
Crystal Singer, 277, 278
"Crystal Spheres, The," 94, 95
Crystal Star, The, 288
Crystal World, The, 39
Cube Root of Uncertainty, The, 391
Cuckoo's Egg, 135
Cultural Breaks, 9
"Culture and the Individual," 240
Culture, The, 42–43, 44, 403
Cure for Cancer, A, 305
Curious Pursuits—Occasional Writing 1970–2005, 32
Currents of Space, The, 26
Curse of Chalion, The, 103
Curse of Frankenstein, The, 379
"Custodians of Chaos," 465
Cyberbooks, 72
Cyberiad, The: Fables for the Cybernetic Age, 260
"Cydonia (THE WEB)," 275
Cyrano de Bergerac, 107
Cyteen, 134, 135

D.A., 484, 485
Dagger Key and Other Stories, 384
Dahak series, 469
"Daisy, in the Sun," 485
Daleth Effect, The, 209
Damia, 279
Damia's Children, 279
Damnation Alley, 502, 503
"Dance in Blue," 21
Dance the Eagle to Sleep, 329
Dancer from Atlantis, The, 15
Dancers at the End of Time, The, 304, 307
Dancing at the Edge of the World, 256
Dandelion Wine, 81, 82, 83
Dangerous Visions, 172, 173, 175
"Danny Goes to Mars," 363
Dare, 180
Dare to Be Creative! A Lecture Presented at the Library of Congress, 264
Daredevil, 291, 292, 293, 294
Daredevil: The Man without Fear, 293
Daredevil Visionaries, 293
"Darfsteller, The," 297
Darfsteller and Other Stories, The, 298

Dark Benediction, 298
Dark Between the Stars, The, 17
Dark Carnival, 83
Dark Design, The, 181
Dark Heart of Time, The, 182
Dark Intruder and Other Stories, The, 90
Dark Is the Sun, 180
Dark Knight Returns, The, 291, 292, 293
Dark Knight Strikes Again, The, 293
Dark Lady, The: A Romance of the Far Future, 340, 342
Dark Light, 275
Dark Light Years, The, 7
Dark Mondays, 36
Dark Reflections, 149, 150
Dark Side of the Earth, The, 58
Dark Verses & Light, 163
Dark Void, The, 27
Dark-Haired Girl, The, 158
<u>Darkover</u>, 87–92
Darkover: First Contact, 90
Darkover Landfall, 89
"Darkover Retrospective, A," 88, 91
Darwin's Blade, 396
Darwin's Children, 53
Darwin's Radio, 52, 53
Datableed, 120
David Starr, Space Ranger, 26
Dawn, 115, 116
Dawn Star, The, 21
Dawning Light, The, 388,
Day After Judgement, The, 67
"Day Before the Revolution, The," 254
Day It Rained Forever, The, 83
Day Million, 336
Day of Creation, The, 38, 39
Day of Forever, The, 40
"Day of the Great Shout," 182
Day of the Star Cities, The, 99
Day of the Triffids, The, 495, 496, 497
Day of Their Return, The, 16
"Day the Aliens Came, The," 374
"Day the Dam Broke, The," 196
Day the Martians Came, The, 334
Daybreak on a Different Mountain, 199
Daymaker, The, 244
<u>Dayworld, Trilogy</u>, 181
DC Universe: The Stories of Alan Moore, 313
"Dea Ex Machina," 249
"Dead, The," 430
"Dead Air," 44
"Dead Lady of Clown Town, The," 399, 400

Dead Lines, 54
"Dead Man, The," 489
Dead Man in Deptford, A, 107
Dead Man's Brother, The, 501
Dead on Sunday, 436
"Dead Run" (Bear), 54
Dead Run (Sheckley), 373
Deadeye Dick, 464
Deadly Streets, The, 174
Dealing in Futures, 204
Deals With the Devil, 345
"Death and Designation among the Asadi," 62
Death by Ecstasy: Illustrated Adaptation of the Larry Niven Novella, 320
Death Dealers, The, 26
Death Dream, 72
"Death from Exposure," 120
"Death in Bangkok," 396
Death Is a Lonely Business, 83
"Death of Doctor Island, The," 490
Death of Sleep, The, 301
"Death on the Nile," 485
Death Qualified: A Mystery of Chaos, 479, 481
Deathbird Stories, 173, 175
<u>Deathkiller Trilogy</u>, 354
<u>Deathworld Trilogy</u>, 209
<u>Decade series</u>, 9, 211
Deceivers, The, 57, 58
Decision at Doona, 278
"deck.halls@boughs/holly," 486
"Deconstructing Divine Endurance—Chosen Among The Beautiful," 242, 245
Deconstructing the Starships, 245
Deep Beyond, The, 137
"Deep Eddy," 412
Deep Fix, The, 307
Deep Future, 50
Deep Range, The, 144
Deepest Water, The, 481
Deepness in the Sky, A, 458, 459, 460
Defender, 136
"Defending the Searchers," 269
"Defenseless Dead, The," 320
Definitely Maybe: A Manuscript Discovered Under Unusual Circumstances, 420
Delany, Samuel R., 148–53, 163, 164, 193, 234, 235, 257, 332, 357, 358, 360, 426
"Delany's Mad Man: The Dark Side of Human Desire," 235
Deliverer, 136
"Delta Sly Honey," 383

Deluge, 280
Demolished Man, The, 56–57, 58
Demon, 450
Demon in the Skull, 333
Demon of Scattery, The, 15
"Demon with a Glass Hand," 175
"Demons, The," 373
Deputy Sheriff of Comanche County, The, 111
Dervish Daughter, 435
Dervish Is Digital, 119, 120
Descent of Anasi, The, 319
"Desert of Stolen Dreams, The," 390
Destination Moon, 220, 222
"Destination: Amaltheia," 421
Destination: Universe!, 445
Destination: Void, 225, 226
Destiny's Children, 48
Destiny's Road, 318
Destroyer (Cherryh), 136
"Destroyers" (Bear), 51
Detached Retina: Aspects of SF and Fantasy, The, 10
Deus Irae, 157, 501
"Devil Car," 502
Devil Girl from Mars: Why I Write Science Fiction," 117
Devil in a Forest, The, 490
Devil to the Belt, 137
Devils, The, 239
Devil's Day, The, 68
Devil's Game, The, 15
Devils of Loudun, The, 240
Dhalgren, 150
"Dial F for Frankenstein," 142
Dialogue with Darkness, 17
Diamond Age, The: or a Young Lady's Illustrated Primer, 407, 408
Diamond Star, The, 20, 21
"Diatribe against Science Fiction, A," 59
Dick, Philip K., xviii, 46, 57, 62, **154–59**, 161, 164, 267, 268, 270, 348, 350, 403, 426, 444, 501
Difference Engine, The, 190, 191, 411, 412
Dig, The, 127
Digits and Dastards, 335
Dilvish, the Damned, 501
Dimension of Miracles, 373
Dimension Thirteen, 391
Dimensions of Sheckley, 345, 374
"Dinner in Audoghast," 412
Dinosaur Fantastic, 345

Dinosaur Junction, 244
Dinosaur Planet, 277, 278, 301
Dinosaur Planet Survivors, 278, 301
Dinosaur Summer, 53
Dinosaur Tales, 83
Diplomatic Immunity, 103
Direct Descent, 226
Dirk Gently's Holistic Detective Agency, 3
Dirty Work, 121
Disappointment Artist, The, 269
Disaster Area, The, 40
Disch, Thomas, 63, 155, **160–65**, 378,
"Discord in Scarlet," 445
Discovery of the Earth, The, 455
"Disneyland with the Death Penalty," 192
"Dispatches from the Revolution," 121
Dispossessed, The: An Ambiguous Utopia, 254, 255
"Distant Replay," 344
Distant Stars, 151
Distraction, 412
Divided Allegiance, 302
Divine Endurance, 242, 243
Divine Invasion, The, 157
Divine Right, 138
"Division by Zero," 139, 141
"Djinn, No Chaser," 173
Do Androids Dream of Electric Sheep?, 155, 156
"Do You Like It Twice?," 441
Doc Savage: His Apocalyptic Life, 182
Doctor Mirabilis, 67
"Doctor of Death Island, The," 491
Doctor Ox and Other Stories, 454
Doctorow, Cory 166–70, 353, 356, 416, 417
"Doctors of the Mind: Effective Mental Therapy and Its Implications," 54
"Does Science Fiction Have to Be About the Present?," 275
"Dog Day Evening," 355
Dog Said Bow-Wow, The, 430, 431
"Dog Star Girl," 192
"Dogfight," 191, 430
"Dogs' Lives," 62
"Dogwalker," 125, 126
Dolphin Island, 144
Dolphins of Pern, The, 279
Domains of Darkover, 90
Don't Open Your Eyes, 244
"Don't Stop," 248, 249
Doomsday Book, 483, 484, 485

"Doomsday Machine, The," 162
Doomsman, 174
Doona series, 277, 278
"Door Gunner, The," 63
"Door in the Wall, The," 475
Door into Summer, The, 221
Door through Space, The, 89
"Doors of His Face, The Lamps of His Mouth, The," 500
Doors of His Face, The Lamp of His Mouth, and Other Stories, The, 502
Doors of Perception, The, 239
Doorways in the Sand, 501
"Dori Bangs," 412
Dorothea Dreams, 130
Dosadi Experiment, The, 226
Double Persephone, 30
Double Star, 220, 221
"Double Timer, The," 160
Down and Out in Paris and London, 323, 324
Down and Out in the Magic Kingdom, 168
"Down and Out in the Year 2000," 350
Down in the Black Gang, 182
"Down Memory Lane," 343
"Down on the Farm," 417
Down These Dark Spaceways, 345
"Down to a Sunless Sea," 400
Downbelow Station, 134, 135
"Downloadable Boy, The," 275
Downstairs Room, and Other Speculative Fiction, The, 482
Downward to the Earth, 387, 389
"Dowser," 126
Dr. Bloodmoney: Or, How We Got Along After the Bomb, 156
Dr. Franklin's Island, 244
Dr. Futurity, 156
Draco Tavern, The, 317, 320
Draconian New York, 373
Dracula Unbound, 6, 8
Dragon America: Revolution, 341
Dragon Done It, The, 345
Dragon Harper, 279
Dragon in the Sea, The, 224, 226
Dragondrums, 279
Dragonflight, 276, 278
"Dragonfly," 255
Dragonheart, 279
Dragonlover's Guide to Pern, The, 281
Dragonquest, 278
"Dragonrider," 278
Dragonriders of Pern, 276, 277, 278, 280

Dragon's Kin, 279
Dragons of Babel, The, 430
Dragons of Darkness, 127
Dragons of Heorot, The, 319
Dragons of Light, 127
Dragonsdawn, 279
Dragonseye, 279
Dragonsinger, 278
Dragonsong, 278
"Drama in the Air, A," 454
"Dramatic Mission," 280
Dramocles, 373
"Dread Empire," 99
Dream Jumbo: Working the Absolutes, 192
Dream Master, The, 501
Dream Park, 319
Dreaming Jewels, The, 424
Dreams Our Stuff Is Made Of, The, 162, 164
Dreams with Sharp Teeth: A Film about Harlan Ellison, 176
Dreamsnake, 286, 287, 288
Dreamstone, The, 136
Dreamthief's Daughter, The, 306
Dreamweaver's Dilemma: Short Stories and Essays, 104
Dreamwish Beasts and Snarks, 344
Driftglass/Starshards, 151
Driving Blind, 83
Drood, 394, 396
"Dropping Science: Black Science Fiction in the 90's," 235
"Drowned Giant, The," 39
Drowned World, The, 39
Drug Themes in Science Fiction, 392
Drunkard's Walk, 333
Dueling Machine, The, 73
Dune, 224, 225, 226
"Dune Genesis," 227
Dune Messiah, 226
Duplicated Man, The, 66
Dusk of Idols, A, 68
"Dust Enclosed Here, The," 36
Duty, Honor, Redemption, 289
"Dying Fall, The," 39
Dying for Tomorrow, 307
Dying Inside, 386, 387, 389

Ealdwood, 136
Earl Aubec and Other Stories, 308
Early Asimov, The, 27
Early Grrrl: The Early Poems of Marge Piercy, 329

Early Harvest, 54
Earth, 93, 94, 95
Earth Book of Stormgate, The, 16
Earth Is Room Enough, 26
Earthborn, 126
Earthfall, 126
Earthlight, 144
Earthly Powers, 107
Earthman, Come Home, 66, 67
Earthman, Go Home! (Anderson), 16
Earthman, Go Home! (Ellison), 174
Earthman's Burden, 15
Earthsea, 255
Earthseed (Butler), 116
Earthseed (Sargent), 363
Earthworks, 7
"East, The," 215
Eastern Standard Tribe, 168
"Ebooks: Neither E Nor Books," 169
Ecco the Dolphin: Defender of the Future, 95
Echo Round His Bones, 162
Echoes of Honor, 469
"Ecstasy of Influence, The: A Plagiarism," 270
Eden (Lem), 260
Eden Trilogy (Harrison), 208, 210
"Edgar Rice Burroughs and the Development of Science Fiction," 337
"Edgard Poë [sic] et ses oeuvres," 455
Edge in My Voice, An, 176
Edge of Space, The, 392,
"Edge of the World, The," 429
Edges, 256
Edible Woman, The, 32
Efficiency Expert, The, 111
Egg Thoughts and Other Frances Songs, 231
"Egnaro," 215
"Eidolons," 173
Eight Worlds, 449, 450
"Eight-Legged Story," 284
80 Minute Hour, The, 7
Einstein Intersection, The, 150
Election Day 2084: Science Fiction Stories About the Future of Politics, 27
Elektra, 293, 294
Elektra Lives Again, 293
"Elephants on Neptune, The," 343
Ellison Wonderland, 174
Ellison, Harlan, 57, 73, 74, 114, 167, **171–77**, 183, 294, 295, 438, 439, 445, 446
Elric: Song of the Black Sword, 307
Elric: The Stealer of Souls, 303, 307
Elric at the End of Time, 306, 307
Elric in the Dream Realms, 306
Elric of Melniboné, 306
"Embarrassments of Science Fiction, The," 164
"Embracing the Decay," 414
Emmet Otter's Jug-Band Christmas, 231
Emperor, 49
"Emperor and the Maula, The," 390
Emphatically Not SF, Almost, 63
Empire (Card), 125
Empire (Delany) 50
Empire Builders, 72
Empire Novels, The, 26
Empire of Dreams & Miracles, 127
Empire of Man, 469
Empire of the Atom, 444
Empire of the Sun, 37, 39
Empire Star, 150
Empire Strikes Back, The, 77, 79
Empress of Mars, The (Baker), 35, 36
Empress of Mars, The (Brackett), 77
Empties, 362
"Enchanted Village," 444
Enchantment, 126
"Enchantress of Venus," 76, 78
"Encounter, The" (Wilhelm), 481
Encounters (Resnick), 342
End of All Songs, The, 305
End of an Era, 368
End of Eternity, The, 25
End of Exile, 72
"End of Gravity, The," 397
End of the World News, The, 106
Endangered Species, 492
Ender's Game, 123, 124, 125, 126
Ender's Shadow, 125
Enderby Quartet, 107
Endgame, 138
Ends of the Earth, The, 384
Endymion, 396
"Enemies of the System," 8
Enemy in the Blanket, The, 107
Enemy Stars, The, 14
Engaging the Enemy, 301
"Engine at Heartspring's Center, The," 502
Engine City, 275
Engines of Light Trilogy, 274
England Invaded, 308
"England Your England," 325
English Assassin, The, 305

English at the North Pole, The, 454
Enigma Score, The, 435
"Enormous Space, The," 40
Ensign Flandry, 16
"Enter a Soldier. Later, Enter Another," 388
Enterprise: The First Adventure, 288
Entropy Effect, The, 287, 288
Entropy Exhibition, The, 198, 200, 304
Entropy Tango, The, 305
"Entropy's Bed at Midnight," 395
Eon, 52, 53
"Epic of Space, The," 402, 405
Epoch, 388, 392
Equator, 7
Equinox, 150
Eric John Stark, Outlaw of Mars, 78
Eros Ascending, 342
Eros at Nadir, 343
Eros at Zenith, 343
Eros Descending, 343
Escape!, 71
Escape Attempt, 421
Escape from Hell, 319
Escape from Kathmandu, 348, 350
Escape from Loki, 182
Escape on Venus, 111
Escape Plans, 243
Escape Plus, 73
Escape to Verna, 188
Eschaton trilogy, 334
ESPer, 66
Essential Blogging: Selecting and Using Weblog Tools, 169
Essential Ellison, The, 175
"Et in Arcadia Ego," 162
"Eternal Adam, The," 454
Eternal Champion, The, 307
"Eternal Lover, The," 111
Eternity (Bear), 53
Eternity and Other Stories (Shepard), 384
Ethan of Athos, 103
Ettison Duo, 436
"Even the Queen," 485
Even the Queen: And Other Short Stories, 486
  "Evening and the Morning and the Night, The," 116
"Evening at Home, An," 307
"Everything But the Signature Is Me," 441
Evil Earths, 9
"Evil Eye, The," 379
Evil Guest, An, 491
"Evil Stepmother, The," 283, 284

Evolution, 47, 48
Excalibur Alternative, The, 468
Excession, 43, 44
Exchange, The, 244
Exchange of Gifts, An, 280
Execution Channel, The, 274
"Exhalation," 140
Exile Waiting, The, 287, 288
Exiled from Earth, 72
Exiles, 72, 74
Exile's Gate, 136
Exiles on Asperus, 497
Exile's Song, 90
Exodus from the Long Sun, 491
Expanded Universe, 222
"Expanding Universe, The," 265
Expedition to Earth, 145
Experiment, The, 120
Experiment in Autobiography: Discoveries and Conclusions of a Very Ordinary Brain since 1866, 476
"Experiment Perilous: The Art and Science of Anguish in Science Fiction," 91
Exploits, 342
Exploration of Space, The, 142, 146
Exploration of the Moon, The, 146
Explorer, 136
(Extra)ordinary People, 359
"Extraordinary Voyages of Amelie Bertrand, The," 359
Extraterrestrial Civilization, 96
"Extraterrestrial Relays," 142
"Extraterrestrial Trilogue," 436
Extro, 58
Exultant, 48
Eye, 227
Eye for an Eye, An (Brackett), 78
"Eye for Eye" (Card), 125, 126
Eye in the Sky, 156
Eye of Cat, 501
Eye of the Comet, 363
Eye of the Heron, 255
Eye of the Sibyl and Other Classic Stories, The, 157
"Eyeflash Miracles, The," 491
Eyeless in Gaza, 239
"Eyes Do More Than See," 26
Eyes of Fire, 62
Eyes of Heisenberg, The, 226

Fabulous Harbours, 306
Fabulous Riverboat, The, 181

Face in the Photo, The, 187
Face of the Waters, The, 389,
"Faces," 204
Facing the Flag, 454
Facing Unpleasant Facts: Narrative Essays, 324
Fact and Fancy, 28
Factoring Humanity, 368
<u>Faded Sun Trilogy</u>, 134, 136, 137
Faery in Shadow, 136
Fahrenheit 451, 81, 82, 83, 85
Faint Echoes, Distant Stars: The Science and Politics of Finding Life Beyond Earth, 75
"Faith of Our Fathers," 157
Falkner, 378
Fall of Hyperion, The, 395, 396,
Fall of Moondust, A, 144
Fall of the Towers, The, 150, 151
<u>Fall Revolution series</u>, 272, 274
Fallen Angels, 318, 319
Fallen Star, 67
Falling Free, 102, 103
<u>Familias Regnant</u>, 300, 301
Family Trade, The, 416, 417
Family Tree, 435
Family Values, 294
"Fandon: Its Value to the Professional," 91
Fantastic Voyage, 25
Fantasy: The 100 Best Books, 308
Fantasy: The Best of 2001, 392
"Fantasy and Science Fiction: A Writer's View," 503
"Fantasy and the Believing Reader," 128
Far as Human Eye Could See, 28
Far Horizons: The Great Worlds of Science Fiction, 388, 391
Far Rainbow, 421
Far Shore of Time, The, 334
Farce to Be Reckoned With, A, 373, 502
Farewell Fantastic Venus, 9, 211
Farewell Summer, 81, 83
Farmer in the Sky, The, 220
Farmer, Philip José, 178–84
Farnham's Freehold, 221
Farseed, 363
Far-Seer, 366, 368
Farthest Star, 335
"Fast Times at Fairmont High," 459
"Fatal Fulfillment, The," 16
Fates Worse Than Death: An Autobiographical Collage of the 1980s, 465

Father Carmody stories, 182
"Father of Stones, The," 382
Father to the Stars, 182,
"Father" (Sargent), 364
"Father" (Farmer), 182
Fault Lines, 481
Fawcett on Rock, 216
Fear Man, The, 244
Fear No Evil, 78
"Fears," 364
"Feast of Saint Janis, The," 430
Feast of Sheckley: Short Stories, 374
"Feast of St. Dionysus, The," 390
Feast Unknown, A, 181
"Feedback," 204
"Feel the Zaz," 249
Feeling Very Strange: The Slipstream Anthology, 249
Feersum Endjinn, 43, 44
Female Man, The, 357, 358
"Feminine Equivalents of Greek Love in Modern Fiction," 91
"Fermi and Frost," 333
Festival Moon, 137
Fever Season, 138
"Few Notes on the Culture, A," 44
Fiasco, 260
Fiction, 200
Field of Dishonor, 469
"'Field' and the 'Wave', The," 200
Fifth Head of Cerberus, The, 488, 490
Fifty Degrees Below, 349
50 in 50: Fifty Stories for Fifty Years!, 211
Fifty Short Science Fiction Tales, 27
Fighting Man of Mars, A, 110
Final Key, The, 21
Final Programme, The, 303, 305, 308
"Finder, The," 254
Finding Helen, 199
Finity's End, 135
Finney, Jack, 185–88
Fire and the Night, 181
Fire Opal, The, 21
Fire Time, 15
Fire Upon the Deep, A, 458, 459, 460
Fire Watch, 483, 484, 485, 486
Fireclown, The, 305
"Fireflood," 288
Fireflood and Other Stories, 289
Fires of Azeroth, 136
Fires of Eden, 395, 396
"Firing the Cathedral," 307

First American into Space, 392
First and Last Things, 476
"First Annual Performance Arts Festival at the Slaughter Rock Battlefield, The," 163
First Lensman, 404
First Men on the Moon, The, 455, 474, 475
"First Person Shooter," 192
"First Sale" (Goonan), 196
"First Sales" (Lethem), 270
"First to the Moon," 49
Firstborn, 48, 145
Fisherman of the Inland Sea, A, 256
Five against the House, 185, 187
Five Weeks in a Balloon, 453, 454
Flag in Exile, 469
Flagship, 342
Flandry, 16
Flandry of Terra, 16
"Flare Time," 320
"Flashback," 396
Flashforward, 366, 367, 368, 369
Flatlander: The Collected Tales of Gil "the Arm," Hamilton, 319, 320
Fledgling, The, 116
Fleet of Stars, The, 15
Flesh, 180
"Flesh Circle, The," 215
Flight from Nevèrÿon, 151
"Flight into Fancy," 245
Flight of Exiles, 72
Flight of Mavin Manyshaped, The, 435
Flight of the Horse, The, 320
Flight to Opar, 182
Floater, 383
Floating Gods, The, 215
Floating Island, 454
Flood, 48
Flood Tide (Cherryh), 138
"Floodtide" (Bova), 73
Flow My Tears, the Policeman Said, 156, 157
"Flowers from Alice," 168
"Flowers of Edo," 412
Flush of Shadows, A, 481
Flux, 48
"Fly-by-Night," 320
Flying Sorcerers, The, 318
"Fog Horn, The," 83
Folk of the Fringe, The, 124, 125, 127
Follow the Free Wind, 78
"Fondly Fahrenheit," 58
Food of the Gods and How It Came to Earth, The, 474, 475

"Fool to Believe," 121
Fools, 120
Footfall, 319
"For a Breath I Tarry," 502
"For God and Gilead," 32
"For I Have Touched the Sky," 340, 343
For Love and Glory, 15
"For the Lady of a Physicist," 61
"For White Hill," 204
Forbidden Circle, 90
Forbidden Tower, 89
Foreigner (Cherryh), 136
Foreigner (Sawyer), 368
Forever After, 503
Forever Free, 202, 203
Forever Peace, 202, 203
Forever War, The, 201, 202, 203
"Forever Yours, Anna," 479
Forge of God, The, 52, 53
Forge of Heaven, 136
Forgiveness, 95
"Forgiveness Day," 254
Forgotten Life, 8
Forgotten News: The Crime of the Century and Other Lost Stories, 188
Forgotten Tales of Love and Murder, 112
Forrest, Felix C. *See* Smith, Cordwainer
Fortress in the Eye of Time, 137
Fortress of Dragons, 137
Fortress of Eagles, 137
Fortress of Ice, 137
Fortress of Owls, 137
Fortress of Solitude, The, 269
Fortress of the Pearl, The, 306
Fortunes of Perkin Warbeck, The, 378
Forty Signs of Rain, 348, 349
Forty Thousand in Gehenna, 135
"43 Antarean Dynasties, The," 341
Forward in Time, 73
Forward the Foundation, 25
Fossil Hunter, 368
Foul Play Suspected, 497
<u>Foundation</u>, 23, 25, 52, 53, 94, 95
"Founding Father," 26
Fountains of Paradise, The, 144
Four for Tomorrow, 502
"Four Hour Fugue, The," 58
Four Moons of Darkover, 90
Four Novels of the 1960s (Dick), 154, 157
Four Ways to Forgiveness, 254, 256
Four-Dimensional Nightmare, The, 39
"Fourth Profession, The," 320

Fourth State of Matter, The, 74
Frameshift, 368
Frank Miller's Robocop, 293
Frankenstein, 51, 377, 378
Frankenstein (movies), 379
Frankenstein Unbound, 7, 9
Free Amazons of Darkover, 90
"Free as Air, Free as Water, Free as Knowledge," 413
"Free Floaters," 320
Free Live Free, 490
Free Lunch, The, 354
Freedom Beach, 247, 249
Freedom's Challenge, 278
Freedom's Choice, 278
Freedom's Landing, 278
Freedom's Ransom, 278
Freejack, 374
Freelance Writer's Handbook, The, 200
Fremder, 230
French, Paul. *See* Asimov, Isaac
Fresco, The, 435
Friday, 221
"Fringe, The," 126
"From A to Z, in the Chocolate Alphabet," 174
"From Babel's Fall'n Glory We Fled," 429, 431
From Earth to Heaven, 28
From Hell, 312, 313
From the Dust Returned, 83
From the Earth to the Moon, 452, 453, 455, 475
From the Earth to the Moon . . . and a Trip Around It, 453
"From the Highlands," 470
From the Land of Fear, 174
From Time to Time, 186, 187
Frost & Fire, 502
Frozen Year, The, 66
"Full House, A: An Austin Family Christmas," 264
"Fun with Your New Head," 162
"Function of Dream Sleep, The," 173
Fundamental Disch, 163
"Funeral, The," 481
Funeral for the Eyes of Fire, A, 60–61, 62
Furies, The, 130
Fury Scorned, A, 363
Future Crime, 73
Future Earth, 344, 345
Future History, 220, 221

Future Imperfect, 107
"Future of Warfare, The," 104
Future on Fire, 127
Future on Ice, 127
Future Primitive: The New Ecotopias, 350
Future Quartet: Earth in the Year 2042: A Four-Part Invention, 74
"Future Shock," 148, 149, 152
Future Weapons of War, 205
Futures Past: The Best Short Fiction of A. E. van Vogt, 445
Futurological Congress, The: From the Memoirs of Ijon Tichy, 260
Futuropolis, 373

Gaea Trilogy, 448, 450
"Gaia, Freedom, and Human Nature," 96
Galactic Breed, The, 77
Galactic Cluster, 67
Galactic Dreams, 211
Galactic Empires, 9
Galactic Patrol, 404
Galactic Pot-Healer, 156
Galactic Storm, 97, 99
Galápagos: A Novel, 464
Galaxies like Grains of Sand, 8
Galaxy Primes, The, 403,
Galaxy Science Fiction, 336
Game of Empire, The, 16
"Game of Rat and Dragon, The," 399, 400
Game of X, 373
Game-Players of Titan, The, 156
Ganymede Takeover, The, 156
Garden of Rama, The, 145
"Gardener, The," 436
Garth of Izar, 363
Gate of Ivrel, 134, 136
Gate of Time, The, 180
Gate of Worlds, The, 388
Gate to Women's Country, The, 433, 434, 435
Gates of Creation, The, 181
Gates of Hell, 137
Gateway, 331, 333, 334
Gateway Trip, The, 334, 336
"Gather Blue Roses," 364
Gathering of Widowmakers, A, 343
"Gazebo, The," 436
Gene Wars, 136
Gene Wolfe's Book of Days, 492
Generation Warriors, 301
"Generations," 332
Genesis, 14, 15

Genius and the Goddess, The, 239
Genocides, The, 162
Gentleman Junkie and Other Stories of the Hung-Up Generation, 174
Geography of Unknown Lands, A, 431
George Orwell's Library, 325
George Orwell's 1984, 324
"Gernsback Continuum, The," 191
"Gert Fram," 123
"Gestation of Genres, The," 152
Get Off the Unicorn, 280
Getting into Death and Other Stories, 163
Getting Lost, 127
Ghost from the Grand Banks, The, 145
"Ghost Pit, The," 49
"Giaconda Smile, The," 240
Giant Lizards from Another Star, 275
Gibbon's Decline & Fall, 435
Gibraltar Falls, 16
Gibson, William, 57, **189–93,** 411, 412, 430
Gift of Dragons, A, 280
"Gigantic Fluctuation, The," 421
"Gilgamesh in the Outback," 388
Gilgamesh the King, 390
Ginger Star, The, 78
"Ginungagap," 429, 430
Girl from Hollywood, The, 111
Girl in Landscape, 269
"Girl Who Fell into the Sky, The," 479
Girl Who Heard Dragons, The, 280
"Girl Who Was Plugged In, The," 438, 440, 441
Girls for the Slime God, 345
Give Me Liberty, 294
"Giving Plague, The," 95
"Glacier," 350
Gladiator at Law, 334
Glass and Amber, 137
"Glass Bottle Trick, The," 235
"Glass Cloud," 249
"Glass Forest: An Attempt at Autobiography, The," 5, 10
Glass of Darkness, A, 156
Glass Teat, The, 176
"Glasses, The," 269
Glasshouse, 416, 417
Glide Path, 144
Global Disaster Quartet, 37, 39
"Global Neighborhood Watch," 408
Globalhead, 413
Gloriana, 304, 306
Glory Road, 221

Glory Season, 95
"Goat Song," 14
Goblin Mirror, The, 136
God Bless You, Dr. Kevorkian, 465
God Bless You, Mr. Rosewater; or, Pearls before Swine, 464
God Emperor of Dune, 226
God Is an Iron and Other Stories, 355
"God Is in the Details," 381, 384
Godbody, 424
Goddess of Ganymede, The, 341
Godmakers, The, 226
Gods and Pawns, 36
"God's Little Toys," 192
Gods of Mars, The (Burroughs), 110
"Gods of Mars, The" (Swanwick), 430
Gods of Riverworld, 181
Gods Themselves, The, 25
Godshome, 373
Going After the Rubber Chicken, Three Guest of Honor Speeches, 397
Going for Infinity, 17
"Gold," 25
Gold: The Final Science Fiction Collection, 27
"Gold at the Starbow's End, The," 70, 333
Gold Coast, The, 349
Golden, The, 382, 383
Golden Apples of the Sun and Other Stories, The, 83
Golden Cat, The, 215
"Golden City Far," 490
Golden Fleece, 366, 368
Golden Globe, The, 449, 450
"Golden Man, The," 154, 158
Golden Road, 319
Golden Space, The, 363, 364
Golden Thread, The, 131
"Golden Years of the Stainless Steel Rat, The," 210
Golem^{100}, 58
Gone to Soldiers, 329
"Good Bad Books," 324
Good Children, The, 481
Good Neighbor Sam, 185, 187, 187
"Good News from the Vatican," 388
Good Old-fashioned Future, A, 413
"Goodbye Star Wars, Hello Alley-Oop," 138
"Goodbye to All That," 174, 176
Goonan, Kathleen Ann, 194–97
"Gorgon Field, The," 482
"Gospel According to Gamaliel Crucis, The," 63

"Gotta Sing, Gotta Dance," 450
"Gourmet, The," 436
"Gourmet Dining in Outer Space," 59
Government in Republican China, 401
Grand Adventure, The, 182
<u>Grand Tour of the Universe</u>, 72
Grass, 435
"Grass Princess, The," 244
"Graves," 203
Graveyard for Lunatics, A, 83
Graveyard Game, The, 35
Graveyard Heart, The/Elegy for Angels and Dogs, 502
"Gravity Mine, The," 49
Gravity's Angels, 431
Gravity's Rainbow, 294
Gray Lensman, 404
Grazing the Long Acre, 245
Great Balls of Fire! A History of Sex in Science Fiction, 211
"Great Lover, The (*Le Grand Amant*)," 397
"Great Moon Hoax, The, or A Princess of Mars," 73
Great Rock 'n' Roll Swindle, The, 305
Great SF Stories, The: 1964, 392
Great Short Novels of Science Fiction, 391
"Great Simoleon Caper, The," 408
Greatheart Silver, 181
"Greedy Choke Puppy," 235
Green Brain, The, 226
"Green Days in Brunei," 412
Green Eyes, 382, 383
"Green Hills of Earth, The," 221
Green Lantern: Ganthet's Tale, 320
Green Mars, 349, 350
Green Odyssey, The, 179, 180
Green Shadows, White Whale, 83, 85
Green Trap, The, 72
"Greening of Bed-Stuy, The," 335
Greenland, Colin, 198–200
Greetings, Carbon-Based Bipeds! Collected Essays, 1934–1998, 147
Gremlins, Go Home!, 72
Grey Eminence, 240
Greybeard, 7
Greyhaven, 90
"Griffin's Egg," 430
Grimm's World, 458, 460
Gripping Hand, The, 319
"Growing Up in Edge City," 335
"Growing Up in the Future," 431
Grumbles from the Grave, 220, 222

Gryb, The, 445
Guardian, 203
Guardians of Time, The, 17
Gulliverzone, 49
Gun with Occasional Music, 269
Guns of Avalon, The, 501
GURPS Lensman, 404

"H.G. Wells's Enduring Mythos of Mars," 50
Hacker Crackdown, The, 413
Hackers, 119
Hadon of Ancient Opar, 182
<u>Hainish sequence</u>, 255, 403
Halam Ann. *See* Jones, Gwyneth
Haldeman, Joe, 70, 97, 99, **201–6**
Half the Day Is Night, 282, 284
Halfling and Other Stories, The, 78
Hallowed Hunt, The, 103
Halloween Tree, The, 83, 85
Hallucination Orbit: Psychology in Science Fiction, 27
Halting State, 417
Hamlet Trap, The, 481
Hammer of God, The, 145
Hammerfall, 136
Hand of Oberon, The, 501
"Hand of the Gods," 445
"Hand You're Dealt, The," 369
Handbook of American Prayer, A, 383
Handmaid's Tale, The, 30, 31, 32, 33
Hand-Reared Boy, The, 5, 8
"Hanging, A," 322, 325
"Happy Boy, A," 420
"Happy Man, The," 269
Hard as Nails, 396,
Hard Freeze, 396
Hard to Be a God, 421
"Hard Way Home, The," 470
Hardboiled, 293
Hardcase, 396
Hardfought/Cascade Point, 54
"Hardfought," 53
Hargrave, Leonie. *See* Thomas M. Disch
Harlan Ellison Hornbook, The, 176
Harlan Ellison's Dream Corridor, 176
Harlan Ellison's The City on the Edge of Forever, 175
Harlan Ellison's Watching, 176
HARM, 8
Harm's Way, 198, 199
Harris, John Beynon. *See* Wyndham, John
Harrison Bergeron, 464, 465

Harrison, Harry, 207–12, 373
Harrison, M. John, 213–17
Hart's Hope, 126
Harvest of Stars, 15
Harvest the Fire, 15
"Hatrack River," 126
Haunting of Jessica Raven, The, 244
Have Space Suit—Will Travel, 221
Have Trenchcoat—Will Travel, 404
"Have You Heard the One . . . ?," 355
Hawkmistress, 89
Hawkmoon, 307
Hawksbill Station, 389, 390
Hawkwind: The Chronicle of the Black Sword, 308
Hazards, 342
H-Bomb Girl, The, 49
"H-Bombs' Thunder, The," 98
He, She And It, 328, 329
"He Who Shapes," 500
Heads, 53, 54
Heart of the Comet, 94
Heart of the Sun, 363
Heart Stars, 67
Heartfire, 126
Heaven and Hell, 239
Heaven Makers, The, 226
Heaven's Reach, 95
Heavenly Breakfast: An Essay on the Winter of Love, 151
Heavy Time, 135
Heavy Weather, 412
Hector Servadac, voyages et aventures à travers le monde solaire, 454
Heechee, 332, 334
Heechee Rendezvous, 334
Hegira, 51, 53
Heinlein, Robert A., xiv, xv, xviii, xix, 12, 23, 46, 93, 102, 157, 161, 208, **218–23**, 316, 352, 353, 354, 355, 403, 405, 426, 448, 449, 465, 483
"Heinlein Gets the Last Word," 465
Heirs of Empire, 469
Heirs of Hammerfell, 89
"Helix," 369
Hell Hath No Fury, 470
"Hell Is the Absence of God," 139, 140
Hell's Cartographers, 9, 211
Hell's Gate, 470
Hellblazer, 311
Hellburner, 135
Helliconia Spring, 5, 7, 8

Helliconia Summer, 7, 8
Helliconia Winter, 7, 8
Hello America, 39
"'Hello,' Said the Stick," 431
Hellstrom's Hive, 226
"Helping Hand, The," 16
"Hemingway Hoax, The," 203
"Her Habiline Husband," 62
Her Name Was Lola, 231
Her Smoke Rose Up Forever, 441
Herald Childe trilogy, 181
Herbert, Frank, 224–28
Heretics of Dune, 226
Heritage and Exile, 90
Heritage of Hastur, The, 87, 88, 89
"Hero," 70, 204
Heroes in Hell, 137
"Heroics," 249
Heroines, 249
Hestia, 135
"Hibernators, The," 8
Hidden Family, The, 417
Hidden Ones, The, 244
Hidden Side of the Moon, The, 359
Hiding Place, The, 16
Hier et demain, 454
High Crusade, The, 14
High Road, The, 74
Highcastle: A Remembrance, 260
High-Rise, 39
Highway Men, The, 274, 275
"Hillary Orbits Venus," 364
Hills Are Dancing, The, 482
His Master's Voice, 260
"Historical Novel and History, The," 364
"History in SF: What (Hasn't Yet) Happened in History," 275
History of Mr. Polly, The, 474, 475
History of Six Weeks' Tour through a Part of France, Switzerland, Germany, and Holland . . . , 379
"History of the Twentieth Century, with Illustrations, A," 350
History Revisited, 345
"Hitch Your Dragon to a Star: Romance and Glamour in Science Fiction," 277, 281
Hitchhiker's Guide to the Galaxy, The, 1, 2, 3, 4
"Hitchhiking in Nevada Is Illegal," 270
Hitting the Skids in Pixeltown, 127
Hob Draconian series, 373
Hoban, Russell, 229–32

Hobson's Choice 368
Hocus Pocus, 464
Hogg, 149, 150
Hoka!, 15
Hoka! Hoka! Hoka!, 17
Hokas Pokas!, 17
Holdfast, 129, 130
Hole in Space, A, 320
"Hole Man, The," 317, 318
Holistic Detective, 3, 313
Hollow Lands, The, 305
Hollow Man, The, 396
Holy Fire, 412
Holy Terror, Batman!, 293
Homage to Catalonia, 324
Homage to QWERT YUIOP: Essays, 107
Home, 40
Home by the Sea, 121
"Home Is the Hangman," 500
Homebody, 126
Homecoming (Card), 124, 126
"Homecoming" (Chiang), 137
"Homefaring," 390
Homegoing, 334
Homesmind, 363
Homeworld, 210
Hominids, 368
Honor Among Enemies, 469
Honor Harrington series, 469
Honor of the Queen, The, 469
Hopkinson, Nalo, 233–36, 482
Horatio Stubbs Trilogy, 6
Horizon, 103
Horlak, E. E. *See* Tepper, Sheri S.
Hot Sky at Midnight, 389
Hot Sleep 125
Hothouse, 6, 7
"Hothouse Flowers," 343
Hounds of Skaith, The, 78
Hour of the Thin Ox, The, 198, 199
House of Numbers, The, 187
House of the Stag, The, 36
House That Fear Built, The, 162
"Houston, Houston, Do You Read?," 438, 440
"How Beautiful with Banners," 63, 67
"How I Lost the Second World War and Helped Turn Back the German Invasion," 491
"How I Write," 216
"How I Wrote the Tarzan Books," 109, 112
How the World Was One: Beyond the Global Village, 146

"How to Build a Planet," 18
How to Suppress Women's Writing, 359
How to Write Science Fiction and Fantasy, 125, 127
How We Got Insipid, 269
"How We Work," 393
"Huddle, The," 47
"Human Factor, The," 446
"Human Front, The," 275
"Human Operators, The," 174, 175, 445
"Human Race Straining the Ecosystem," 75
"Human Readable," 168
Humans, 368
Hunger in the Soul, A, 342
Hunter of Worlds, 134, 135
Hunter, E. Waldo. *See* Sturgeon, Theodore
Hunter/Victim, 373
"Hunter's Moon," 14
Hunters of Dune, 225
Hunters of Pangaea, The, 49
Hunting Party, 299, 301
Hunting the Snark and Other Stories, 344
Huxley, Aldous, 237–41, 322
Huxley and God: Essays, 239
Huysman's Pets, 481
Hybrids, 368
Hyperion, 394, 395, 396
Hyperland, 3
Hypnotism Handbook, The, 446
"Hypothetical Lizard, A," 313

I, Alien, 345
I Am Legend—Awakening, Story 3, 127
I, Asimov: A Memoir, 25, 28
"I Did It," 215
"I, Dreamer," 297
I Have No Mouth, and I Must Scream, 172, 173, 174
I Have This Nifty Idea . . . Now What Do I Do with It?, 346
"I Know What You're Thinking," 482
I, Libertine, 425
I Love Bees, 283, 284
I Love Galesburg in the Springtime, 187
"I Love Paree," 168
"I of Newton," 205
I Owe for the Flesh, 178
I, Robot, (Asimov), 27
"I, robot" (Doctorow), 168
"I, Row-Boat," 168
I Sing the Body Electric!, 83
I Will Fear No Evil, 221

Icarus Montgolfier Wright, 85
Ice Monkey & Other Stories, The, 216
Ice Schooner, The, 305
Icebones, 49
Icehenge, 349
"Icons of Science Fiction, The," 245
Identifying the Object, 245
Identity Theft and Other Stories, 369
"Idle Roomer," 344
Idoru, 191
if (anthologies), 333, 336
"If a Flower Could Eclipse," 62
"If All Men Were Brothers, Would You Let One Marry Your Sister?," 425
If at Faust You Don't Succeed, 373, 502
If Wishes Were Horses, 280
Ilium, 394, 395, 396
Illegal Alien, 368
Illustrated Man, The, 83, 85
"I'm Looking for Kadak," 174
"I'm Scared," 187
Image of the Beast, The, 180, 181
"Image of Women in Science Fiction," 359
"Images," 204
"Images of *Nineteen Eighty-Four*: Fiction and Prediction," 200
Imagination/Space, 245
Imago, 116
Immortality, 75
Immortality Factor, The, 72
Immortality, Inc. 371, 372
Imperial Earth, 144
Imperial Stars, 404
Impossible Man, The, 40
Impossible Smile, The, 7
Impossible Things, 485, 486
"Imprint of Chaos," 99
In a Land of Clear Colours, 375
In Death Ground, 469
"In Defense of the Novel," 324
In Enemy Hands, 469
In Front of Your Nose, 1945–1950, 324
In Fury Born, 468
In Green's Jungles, 491
In Joy Still Felt, 25, 28
In Memory Yet Green, 23, 28
In Our Hands the Stars, 209
In Pursuit of VALIS, 158
In Quest of Quasars, 74
In Search of the Castaways, 454, 455
In Space No One Can Hear You Laugh, 344
In the Beginning (Silverberg), 391

In the Beginning . . . Was the Command Line (Stephenson), 408
"In the Bowl," 450
In the Days of the Comet, 474
In the Drift, 430
In the Garden of Iden, 34, 35
In the Hall of the Martian Kings, 449, 450, 451
"In the Kingdom of Mao Bell," 409
"In the Late Cretaceous," 486
"In the Navy," 470
In the Problem Pit, 336
"In the Year 2890," 454
In These Times, 465
In This World, or Another, 68
In Viriconium, 213, 215
In War Times, 195, 196
"In Your Name," 329
"Incognita, Inc.," 174
Inconstant Moon, 318, 320, 321
"Ineluctable," 369
"Infamy: The New Fame," 176
Inferno (Niven), 319
Inferno (Resnick), 342
Infinite Dreams, 204
Infinite Moment, The, 497
Infinity Box, The: A Collection of Speculative Fiction, 478, 482
Infinity Concerto, The, 54
Infinity's Shore, 95
Influence of Ironwood, The, 244
Inhabited Island, The, 421
Inheritor, 136
Inheritors of Earth 15
"Inn," 486
Inner Landscape, The, 308
Innocents Aboard, 492
"Inside Job," 485
Inside Mr. Enderby, 107
Inside Outside, 181
Inside the Funhouse, 344
Inside the Whale and Other Essays, 324
"Insipid Profession of Jonathan Horneboom, The," 269
"Inspiration," 73
Instrumentality of Mankind, The, 399, 400
Insurrection, 467, 469
Intangibles, Inc. and Other Stories, 9
Integral Trees, The, 318
Interface (Stephenson), 408
Interfaces, (Le Guin), 256
"Interim Report: An Autobiographical Ramble," 201, 205

International Science Fiction, 336
"Internet: The Last Battleground of the 20th Century, The," 3
Interplanetary Flight, 146
Interpreter, The, 7
<u>Interstellar Empire</u>, 97, 99
Interzone: The 1st Anthology, 200
Introducing Science Fiction, 9
"Introducing the Future: the Dawn of Science-Fiction Criticism," 211
Invader, 136
Invaders from Earth, 388
"Invasion," 358
Invasion: Earth, 209
Invasion of the Body Snatchers, 186, 187, 188
Invasion of the Sea, 454
Invasive Procedures, 126
Inversions, 44
Investigation, The, 260
Invincible, The, 260
Invisible Barriers 388
Invisible Man, The, 473, 474, 475
Involution Ocean, 412
Iron Dragon's Daughter, The, 429, 430
Iron Sunrise, 417
Ironcastle, 181
Irrational Season, The, 265
Irresistible Forces, 21
Is That What People Do?, 374
Is There Life on Other Worlds?, 18
Isaac Asimov Presents the Best Science Fiction of the 19th Century, 27
Island, 239
"Island of Doctor Death and Other Stories, The," 491
Island of Doctor Death and Other Stories and Other Stories, The, 492
Island of Doctor Moreau, The, 473, 474, 475
Island of Lost Souls, 475
Islands in the Net, 412
Islands in the Sky, 144
Isle of the Dead, 501
"Isobel Avens Returns to Stepney in the Spring," 215
Issue at Hand, The, 68
"It," 425
It Came from Outer Space, 85
"It's All Geek to Me," 409
It's Been a Good Life, 29
Iterations, 369
"Itsy Bitsy Spider," 248

Ivory: A Legend of Past and Future, 342
"Jack," 486
Jack Faust, 429, 430
Jack of Eagles, 66
Jack of Shadows, 501
Jagged Orbit, The, 98, 99
Jaguar Hunter, The, 383, 384
Jailbird, 462, 464
"Jailwise," 383
Jamie and Other Stories, 90
"Jamie's Hair," 63
Jane Eyre, 238
<u>Jason Lynx Mysteries</u>, 436
Jason X, 119, 120
Jayne's Intelligence Review: The Royal Manticoran Navy, 470
Jayne's Intelligence Review No. 2: The People's Navy, 470
"Jeffty Is Five," 173
JEM: The Making of a Utopia, 332, 333
Jennifer Morgue, The, 417
<u>Jerry Cornelius Multiverse</u>, 214, 304, 305
Jerry Cornell's Comic Capers, 307
Jerusalem Commands, 306
Jesting Pilate, 240
"Jesus Christ, Reanimator," 275
Jesus Incident, The, 226
Jesus of Nazareth 107
Jesus on Mars, 180
"Jewel of Bas, The," 78
Jewel-Hinged Jaw, The, 151
Jewels of Aptor, The, 149, 150
"Jewish Enough," 364
"Jigsaw Man, The," 319
Jinian Footseer, 435
Jinian Star-Eye, 435
"Jipi and the Paranoid Chip," 408
Jizzle, 497
"Joanna Russ," 329
Job: A Comedy of Justice, 220, 221
Jocasta, 6, 8
<u>Joe Kurtz Thrillers</u>, 396
John Brunner Presents Kipling's Science Fiction, 100
John Carter, Warlord of Mars, 291
John Carter's Chronicles of Mars, 112
Johnny Mnemonic, 191, 192
Johnny Mnemonic: The Screenplay and the Story 191
Jones, Gwyneth, 242–46
Journey Beyond Tomorrow, 372
Journey of Joenes, The, 372

"Journey, The [as the Revelation of the Unknown]," 183
Journey to the Centre of the Earth, A, 453, 455
Jugular Wine: A Vampire Odyssey, 294
"Juice from a Clockwork Orange," 108
Jungle Girl, 111
Juniper Time, 481
Jupiter, 72
Jupiter Plague, The, 209
"Jury Service," 168
"Just Like Old Times," 368
"Just Like the Ones We Used to Know," 486
Justice for Some, 481
Juvies, The, 174

Kafka Americana, 269
Kairos, 244
"Kairos: The Enchanted Loom," 245
"Kalimantan," 383
"Kamehameha's Bones," 196
Kane of Old Mars, 307
Keep the Aspidistra Flying, 324, 325
Keeper of Dreams, 127
Keeper's Price, The, 90
Kelly, James Patrick, 247–51, 269, 384,
Kesrith, 134, 136
Key Word and Other Mysteries, The, 26
"Keys to December, The," 502
Kif Strike Back, The, 135
Kilimanjaro, 344
"Kill Switch," 192
Killashandra, 278
Killdozer!, 425, 426
Killdozer!, 425
Killer Thing, The, 478, 480
"Kil'n People," 95
Kilternan Legacy, The, 279
"Kindly Isle, The," 335
Kindness of Women, The, 38, 39
Kindred, 115, 116
King, Gabriel. *See* Harrison, M. John
King and Four Queens, The, 425
King Kong Is Back!, 95
King of Dreams, The, 390
King of Kings, 85
King of the City, 306
"King of the Elves," 158
Kingdom Come 39
Kingdom of Kevin Malone, The, 131
Kingdoms of the Wall, 389
"Kings," 200

King's Blood Four, 435
King's Death's Garden, 244
Kings in Hell, 137
Kinship with the Stars, 17
Kinsman Saga, The, 72
"Kiosk," 412
Kipps, 474
Kirinyaga: A Fable of Utopia, 344
"Kirinyaga," 339, 341
"Kjwalll'kje'k'koothailll'kje'k," 502
Knight, The, 491
Knight of Ghosts and Shadows, A, 16
Knight of Shadows, 501
Knot Garden, The, 215
Komarr, 103
Kraken Wakes, The, 496
"Kurt Vonnegut vs. the !&#*!@," 465
Kutath, 136
"Kyrie," 16

"L Alone at the Movies," 270
"La Cenerentola," 243
La Decima vittima, 374
La Decouverte de la Terre, 455
La Journée d'un journaliste américain en 2890, 454
"Labyrinth," 103
Lady, The, 279
"Lady of the Winds, The," 16
Lady Oracle, 32
Lady Slings the Booze, 354
"Lady Who Wrote *Lud-in-the-Mist,* The," 431
Lady with an Alien, 341
Laertian Gamble, The, 373
"Lake of the Gone Forever, The," 76, 78
Lake of the Long Sun, 491
"Lamia Mutable," 215
"Land Ironclads, The," 474
Land Leviathan, The, 305
"Land of Nod, The," 343
Land of Terror, 111
Land of True Game, 433, 434, 435
Land That Time Forgot, The, 111, 112
Land That Time Forgot, The (movie), 308
Land's End, 335
Language of the Night, The, 256
Lara Croft, Tomb Raider: The Amulet of Power, 343
Last Call Poker, 284
Last Chance to See, 3
"Last Contact," 49
Last Defender of Camelot, The, 502, 503

Last Exit to Babylon, 502
"Last Flight of Dr. Ain, The," 438, 440
Last Hawk, The 21
"Last Lonely Man, The," 99
Last Man, The, 378
"Last of the Winnebagos, The," 485
Last Orders and Other Stories, 9
Last Theorem, The, 145, 334
Last White Class, The, 328
"Lateral Genius and the Persistence of Neuromancer," 121
Lathe of Heaven, The, 254, 255, 256
"Laugh Track," 174
Laughing Space, 27
Laughter of Carthage, The, 306
Laundry Organization, 417
Lavalite World, The, 181
Lavinia, 255
Lazarus Effect, The, 226
Le Guin, Ursula K., xiv, xv, 88, 155, 159, 247, **252–57,** 289, 330, 348, 401, 439, 441, 442, 475
Le voyage dans la lune, 455, 475
League of Extraordinary Gentlemen, The, 31,, 313
Learning the World: A Novel of First Contact, 273, 274
"Learning to Write Comedy or Why It's Impossible and How to Do It," 486
"Leaving His Cares Behind," 35
Left Hand of Darkness, The, xv, 88, 252, 253, 254, 255
Left Hand of the Electron, The, 28
Legacy (Bear), 53
Legacy (Bujold), 103
Legacy of Gird, 301
Legacy of Heorot, The, 319
Legends, 388, 392
Legends from the End of Time, 308
"Legions in Time," 430
Legions of Hell, 137
Lem, Stanislaw, 155, 159, 161, **258–61**, 267
L'Engle, Madeleine, 262–66
Lensman, 403, 404
Lensman: Kozûmosu no daisensô, 404
Lensman: Power of the Lens, 404
Leroni of Darkover, 90
Les enfants du capitaine Grant, 454
Lest We Forget You, Earth, 388
Let the Fire Fall, 478, 480
Let the Spacemen Beware, 16
Lethem, Jonathan, 157, 249, **267–71**

Let's All Kill Constance, 83
"Letter from the Clearys, A," 485
Letters from Hollywood, 308
Letters from Home, 119, 121
Letters Home, 489, 492
Letters of Aldous Huxley, 237, 240
Letters of Mary Wollstonecraft Shelley, The, 308
"Letterspace: In the Chinks Between Published Fiction and Published Criticism," 104
Liar's House, 383
Liar's Oath, 301
"Liberation Spectrum," 168
"Libertarianism, the Looney Left and the Secrets of the Illuminati," 275
Library of African Adventure, 345
Library of Worldwide Adventure, 346
Lies, Inc., 156
Life, 243, 244
Life and Death of a Satellite, The, 59
Life and Times of Martha Washington in The Twenty-First Century, 293
Life Before Man, 32
Life During Wartime, 381, 382, 383
Life Eaters, The, 95
Life for the Stars, A, 67
Life in the West, 8
"Life of Prose and Poetry: An Inspiring Combination," 329
Life of the World to Come, The, 35
"Life of Your Time, The," 16
Life, the Universe and Everything, 2
Lifeboat, 209
Lifehouse, 354
"Life-Line," 221
"Lifeloop," 126
Lifeship, 209
Light, 214, 215
"Light and Shadow," 21
Light Fantastic, The, 58
Light Music, 195, 196
Light of Other Days, The, 48, 145
Light Raid, 485
Light Years and Dark, 62, 63
"Lighting Out," 273
"Liking What You See: A Documentary," 139, 140, 141
L'Île à hélice, 454
Lillith's Brood, 116
Limits, 320
"Lincoln Train, The," 283

Lincoln's Dreams, 484, 485
Linebarger, Paul. *See* Smith, Cordwainer
"Lines of Power," 151
"Lion and the Unicorn, The: Socialism and the English Genius," 325
Lion of Boaz-Jachin and Jachin-Boaz, The, 230, 231
Lion Time in Timbuctoo, 391
"Lirios: A Tale of the Quintana Roo," 440
Listen, Listen, 482
"Listening to Brahms," 131
"Listening to the Left Hand," 227
Literature and Science, 239
"Literature of Comfort, A," 216
Little Brother, 168
"Little Cat Laughed to See Such Sport, The," 431
"Little Faces," 289
Little Knowledge, A, (Bester) 61, 62
"Little Knowledge, A" (Resnick), 343
"Little Something for Us Tempunauts, A," 157
Little Wilson and Big God, 107
Live Coal in the Sea, A, 264
Live Gold, 373
Lives and Times of Jerry Cornelius, The: Stories of the Comic Apocalypse, 307
Llana of Gathol, 110
"Lobsters," 416
"Locusts, The," 320
Lodore, 378
Lois & Clark: A Superman Novel, 136
London Bone, 307
Long After Midnight and Other Stories, 83
Long Afternoon of Earth, The, 7
Long Day Wanes, The, 107
Long Goodbye, The, 77, 79
Long Habit of Living, The, 203
Long Night, The 16, 17
Long Tomorrow, The, 77
Long Way Home, The, 14
Long, Dark Tea-Time of the Soul, The, 1, 3
Longest Voyage, The, 14, 15
Longest Way Home, The, 389
Longings of Women, The, 328
Longtusk, 49
Look into the Sun, 249
Look to Windward, 44
Lookalike, The, 482
"Looking for Clues," 235
"Looking for Kelly Dahl," 397
"Looking for the Fountain," 390

"Loophole," 145
Lord of Darkness, 390
Lord of Light, 500, 501
Lord of the Trees, 181
Lord Prestimion, 390
Lord Tedric, 404
Lord Tyger, 181
Lord Valentine's Castle, 387, 390
"Lord Weary's Empire," 431
"Lorelei of the Red Mist," 76, 78
Lorelei of the Red Mist: Planetary Romances, 79
Losing David 199
"Lost Boys," 125, 126
Lost Cities and Vanished Civilizations, 392
"Lost Continent, The" (Burroughs), 111
Lost Continent series (Asaro), 19, 21
Lost in Space—Promised Land, 119, 120
"Lost in the Mail," 368
Lost on Venus, 111
Lost Race of Mars, 388
Lost Souls, 53
Lost Worlds of 2001, The, 146
Lost: Fifty Suns, 445
"Lotus and the Spear, The," 343
Louder: We Can't Hear You (Yet!): The Political Poems of Marge Piercy, 329
Louisiana Breakdown, 383
Love Ain't Nothing But Sex Misspelled, 175
"Love and Sex in the Year 3000," 330
"Love Is the Plan, the Plan Is Death," 438, 440
Love Letter, The, 188
Love Song, 180
LoveDeath, 397
Lovelock, 125
Lovers, The, 178, 180
Low-Flying Aircraft and Other Stories, 40
Lucifer Jones, 342
Lucifer's Hammer, 319
Luck in the Head, The, 215
"Lucky Ones, The," 441
Lucky Starr series, 26
"Lucky Strike, The," 350
"Lullaby 1990," 434
"Luminous Future, A," 22
Lunar Activity, 302
"Lunching at the Eschaton: Douglas Adams and the End of the Universe in Science 'Fiction'," 50
Lunching with the Antichrist, 307
Lyon's Pride, 279
Lythande, 90

M.D., The: A Horror Story, 162
Machine in Shaft Ten & Other Stories, The, 216
Machine's Child, The, 35
Machineries of Joy, The, 83
Machines That Think: The Best Science Fiction Stories about Robots and Computers, 27
MacLeod, Ken, 272–75
Macrolife A Mobile Utopia, 362
Mad Goblin, The, 181
Mad King, The, 111
Mad Man, The, 150
Madeleine L'Engle: Star*Gazer, 264
Madeleine L'Engle Herself: Reflections on a Writing Life, 264
Madwand, 501
Maelstrom, 280
Magic, 27
Magic Feathers: The Mike and Nick Show, 344
Magic Goes Away, The, 317, 319
Magic Labyrinth, The, 181
Magic May Return, The, 319
Magic Mommas, Trembling Sisters, Puritans, and Perverts, 358, 359
Magic Street, 126
Majipoor Chronicles, 390
Make Room! Make Room!, 208, 209
"Makeover," 284
Maker of Universes, The, 181
Makeshift Rocket, The, 14
"Making Monsters," 250
Making of a Moon, The, 146
Making of Lost in Space, The, 121
Malacia Tapestry, The, 6, 8
Malafrena, 255
Malayan Trilogy, 107
Mammoth (Baxter), 49
Mammoth (Varley), 450
Man and Space, 146
"Man Android, and Machine," 158
Man from Beyond and Other Stories, The, 497
"Man from the Big Dark, The," 99
"Man in His Time," 8
Man in the High Castle, The, 154, 155, 156
Man in the Maze, The, 389,
"Man of Steel, Woman of Kleenex," 321
"Man of the People, A," 255
Man of Two Worlds, 226
Man Plus, 332, 333, 334
Man Who Ate the World, The, 335

"Man Who Came Early, The," 16
Man Who Counts, The, 16
Man Who Had No Idea, The, 163
Man Who Japed, The, 156
"Man Who Learned Loving, The," 425
Man Who Lost the Sea, The, 425
"Man Who Lost the Sea, The," 425
"Man Who Painted the Dragon Griaule, The," 383
"Man Who Rowed Christopher Columbus Ashore, The," 174
"Man Who Sold the Moon, The," 220, 221
"Man Who Was Heavily into Revenge, The," 174
Man with Nine Lives, The, 174
Man Without a Country, A, 465
"Manamouki, The," 340, 341
Man-Eater, The, 111
"Maneki Neko," 412
Manifold: Origin, 48
Manifold: Space, 48
Manifold: Time, 48
Mankind in the Making, 476
Mankind under the Leash, 162
Man-Kzin Wars, 317, 320
Manna from Heaven, 502
"Many Dimensions of Rod Serling, The," 270
Many Waters, 263
Many Worlds of Science Fiction, The, 74
Maps in a Mirror 125, 127
March to the Sea, 469
March to the Stars, 469
March Upcountry, 469
Margaret and I, 480
Margarets, The, 435
Marianne, the Madame, and the Momentary Gods, 436
Marianne, the Magus, and the Manticore, 436
Marianne, the Matchbox, and the Malachite Mouse, 436
Marianne Trilogy, 434
Marion Zimmer Bradley's Fantasy Magazine, 88, 90
Marion's Wall, 187, 188'
"Mark of Batman, The: An Introduction," 295
Mark of Merlin, The, 279
Marooned in Realtime, 459, 460
"Marooned Off Vesta," 23, 25, 26
"Marque and Reprisal" (Anderson), 16
Marque and Reprisal (Moon), 301
"Marrow Death," 430

Mars (Bova) 70, 72
"Mars Girl, The," 204
"Mars Is Heaven!," 83
Mars Life 73
"Mars Masked," 335
Mars Plus, 334
Mars Trilogy, 347, 349
Marsbound, 203
Martha Washington Dies, 293
"Martian Childhood, A," 350
Martian Chronicles, The, 81, 82, 83
Martian Quest: The Early Brackett, 78, 79
"Martian Romance, A," 350
Martian Tales of Edgar Rice Burroughs, 112
Martian Time-Slip, 156
Martian Way and Other Stories, The, 26
Martians, The, 349, 350
"Martians among Us, The," 365
Marvelman, 312
Mary Shelley's Journal, 380
Marzipan Pig, The, 231
Masks of Time, The 389,
Masque of Mañana, The, 374
Master Mind of Mars, The, 110
Master of Life and Death, 388
Master of the World, 454
"Master Zacharius, or The Clockmaker Who Lost His Soul," 454
Masterharper of Pern, The, 279
Masterpieces: The Best Science Fiction of the Twentieth Century, 127
Masters of Space, 404
Masters of the Vortex, 404
Masters of Time, 445
Match to Flame: The Fictional Paths to Fahrenheit 451, 85
Mathilda, 378
"*Matrix* and the Star Maker, *The,*" 346
"*Matrix* as Sci-Fi, *The,*" 205
Matter, 44
"Matter of Seggri, The," 254
Maurai and Kith, 17
Mavin Manyshaped, 435
Maxie, 188
"Maxwell the Magic Cat," 311
Maxwell's Demons, 73
"Mayflower II," 47, 49
Maze of Death, A, 156
Maze of Stars, A, 99
McCaffrey, Anne, 88, **276–81,** 301,
McHugh, Maureen F., 282–85
McIntyre, Vonda N., xv, 90, 257, **286–90**

"Me and Lucifer," 346
Mecca\Mettle, 164
Medea: Harlan's World, 173, 175
Medicine for Melancholy, A, 83
"Meditation on the Singular Matrix," 250
Medusa Frequency, The, 231
Meet Me at Infinity: The Uncollected Tiptree, 441
Meet the Austins, 264
"Meeting, The," 333
"Meeting with Medusa, A," 144
"Mefisto in Onyx," 173, 294
Melancholy Elephants, 354, 355
Memoirs Found in a Bathtub, 260
Memoirs of a Space Traveler: Further Reminiscences of Ijon Tichy, 260
"Memorare," 492
Memories of the Space Age, 40
Memory, 103
Memory of Earth, The, 126
Memory of Murder, A, 83
Memory of Whiteness, The, 349
Memos from Purgatory, 176
Men Against Time: Salvage Archaeology in the United States, 392
Men and Cartoons, 269
"Men Are Trouble," 247, 249
Men from P.I.G. & R.O.B.O.T., The, 211
Men Like Gods, 474
"Men on Other Planets," 227
"Men Who Murdered Mohammed, The," 58
Men Writing Science Fiction as Women, 345
Mendoza in Hollywood, 35
Mercenaries of Tomorrow 17
Mercenary, 342
Merchant and the Alchemist's Gate, The, 139, 140
Merchant Princes, 416, 417
Merchanter's Luck, 135
"Merchants of Venus, The," 335
Merchants' War, The (Pohl), 333
Merchants' War, The (Stross), 417
Mercury, 72
Merovingen Nights Anthologies, 137
Metaphase, 288
"Metastasis," 396
Metatemporal Detective, The, 307
"Metempsychosis of the Machine," 245
Methuselah's Children, 220, 221
"Mewhu's Jet," 426
Miami Vice, 164
Michael Moorcock: Death Is No Obstacle, 200

"Michael Moorcock Speaks," 309
Michael Moorcock's Multiverse, 308
Michael Strogoff, 454
Michael Swanwick's Field Guide to the Mesozoic Megafauna, 431
"Mick of Time, The," 355
Microcosmic God, The, 425
"Microcosmic God, The," 425
Microworlds: Writings on Science Fiction and Fantasy, 261
Midas World, 336
Midnight Lamp, 244
Midnight Robber, 235
"Midnight Swordsman," 295
Midsummer Century, 67
"Midwinter's Tale, A," 430
Midwych Cuckoos, The, 496, 497
Mile-Long Spaceship, The, 482
Miles Errant 104,
Miles in Love, 104
Miles, Mutants and Microbes, 104
Miles, Mystery, and Mayhem, 104
Milky Way Galaxy, The, 74
<u>Millennial Contest</u>, 373, 502
Millennium (Bova), 72
Millennium (Varley), 448, 450, 451
Millennium People, 39
Miller, Frank, xv, **291–95**
Miller, Walter M., 296–98
Mind Cage, The, 445
Mind Fields, 175
"Mind of Medea, The," 481
Mind of My Mind, 116
Mindbridge, 203
Mindkiller, 354
Mindplayers, 120
Mindscan, 368
Mindswap, 372
Mining the Oort, 334
"Minnesota Gothic," 162
Minority Report, 156
"Miracle," 486
Miracle and Other Christmas Stories, 486
Miracle of Rare Design, A, 342
Miracles of Life: Shanghai to Shepperton, an Autobiography, 40
Mirkheim, 16
Mirror Dance, 102, 103
Mirrorshades: A Cyberpunk Anthology, 248, 411, 413
"Miss Otis Regrets," 199
"Missile Gap," 416

"Missing Hours," 164
"Missing Mass, The," 318
Mission Child, 284
Mission to the Heart Stars, 67
Mission to the Stars, 445
Mississippi Blues, 195, 196
Misted Cliffs, The, 21
Mists of Avalon, The, 89, 91
Mixed Men, The, 444, 445
Moat Around Murcheson's Eye, The, 319
"Mobiles and the Urban Poor," 413
Moby Dick, 81, 85, 500
"Modern Boys and Mobile Girls," 192
Modern Utopia, A, 472, 474
Mojo: Conjure Stories, 235
Moment of Eclipse, The, 7, 9
"Momentary Taste of Being, A," 440
Mona Lisa Overdrive, 191
Monday Begins on Saturday, 420
Money Personality, The, 446
Monkey Sonatas, 127
"Monophobic Response, The," 117
Monsters (Van Vogt), 445
"Monsters" (Kelly), 249
Moon and the Sun, The, 287, 288
Moon by Night, The, 264
Moon Dogs, 429, 431
Moon Flights 302
Moon Is a Harsh Mistress, The, 220, 221
Moon Is Always Female, The, 329
Moon Maid, The, 111
"Moon Six," 49
Moon, Elizabeth, 277, **299–302**
Moon's Shadow, The, 21
Moonferns & Starsongs, 391
MoonGate, 481
Moonrise, 72
Moonseed, 46, 47, 48
Moonstone and Tiger-Eye, 131
Moonwar, 72
Moorcock, Michael, 41, 80, 109, 112, 161, 165, 198, 200, 214, 216, **303–10**
Moorcock's Book of Martyrs, 307
Moore, Alan, xv, 304, **311–15**, 414
"Morality in Videogames," 128
More Bitter Than Death, 478, 481
More Issues at Hand, 68
More Magic, 319
More Tales of Pirx the Pilot, 260
More Tales of the Black Widowers, 26
More Than Fire, 181
More Than Honor, 470

More Than Human, 423, 424
More Than One Universe, 146
"More Than the Sum of His Parts," 204
"More Than You'll Ever Know: Down the Rabbit Hole of *The Matrix*," 196
More Whatdunits, 344
Moreau's Other Island, 7
Moreta: Dragonlady of Pern, 279
Morgaine Saga, The, 136, 137
Mortal Engines, 260
"Mortal Immortal, The," 378, 379
Mostly Harmless, 2
Mote in God's Eye, The, 319
"Moth and Rust," 180
"Mothballed Spaceship, The," 210
"Mother," 182
Mother Ægypt and Other Stories, 36
"Mother Earth Mother Board," 409
"Mother Goddess of the World," 350
"Mother Hitton's Littul Kittons," 400
Mother London, 304, 306
Mother Night, 464, 465
Mother of Kings, 15
Mother of Plenty, 199
"Mother Trip, The," 335
Mother Was a Lovely Beast, 182
Motherless Brooklyn, 269
Motherlines, 130
Mothers and Other Monsters, 283, 284
Motion of Light in Water, The, 148, 149, 150, 151
Mountain Cage and Other Stories, The, 364
"Mountain Ways," 254
Mountains of Majipoor, The, 390,
"Mountains of Mourning, The," 102
"Mountains of Sunset, the Mountains of Dawn, The," 288
Mouse and His Child, The, 231
Mouthful of Air, A, 107
Moving Mars 52, 53
Moving Target, 301
"Mr. Boy," 247, 249
Mr. Rinyo-Clacton's Offer, 231
"Mr. Spock's Dad," 289
"Mr. Wilde's Second Chance," 357
"Ms. Found in an Abandoned Time Machine," 390
"Ms. Midshipwoman Harrington," 470
M33 in Andromeda, 445
"Mule, The," 25
Multiple Man, The 71
"Mummer Kiss," 430
Murder at the ABA, 26

Murder Bound, 14
Murder in Black Letter, 14
"Murder Your Darlings," 250
"Muse of Fire," 397
Music of the Night, 131
Muskrat Courage, 62
Mutant Season, The, 389,
Mutineers' Moon, 469
Mutiny, 342
"Mwalimu in the Squared Circle," 343
"My Affair with Science Fiction," 59
"My Country Right or Left," 325
My Experiences in the Third World War 307
My Father's Ghost 131
"My Life in Science Fiction/Ma Vie et la Science-Fiction," 31, 32
"My Life Was My Best Science Fiction Story," 446
"My Marvel Years," 270
My Mother's Body, 329
My Name Is Legion, 502
"My Own Private Tokyo," 192
"My Silent Partner," 482
"My Sister's Brother," 182
My Tango with Barbara Strozzi, 230, 231
Mysterious Island, The, 454, 455
Mysterious Universe, 143
Mysterious World, 143
"Mystery of the Young Gentleman, The," 359
Myths for the Modern Age: Philip José Farmer's Wold Newton Universe, 182
Myths of the Near Future, 39, 40

Nail and the Oracle, The, 425
Naked Came the Farmer, 181
Naked Sun, The, 26
"Naming the Flowers," 482
<u>Nanotech Cycle</u>, 194, 196
Narabedla Ltd., 334
Narrative of Arthur Gordon Pym, The, 454
<u>NASA Trilogy</u>, 48
"Nash Circuit, The," 215
"Natural History & Extinction of the People of the Sea, The," 289
Nature of the Catastrophe, The, 308
Nautilus, 288
Navigator, 49
<u>Neanderthal Parallax</u>, 368
Neanderthal Planet, 9
Neat Sheets: The Poetry of James Tiptree, Jr., 441
Nebula Awards anthologies, 17, 63, 74, 151, 205, 211, 227, 256, 289, 345, 350, 364, 391, 482, 486, 503

Necessity for Beauty, The: Robert W. Chambers & the Romantic Tradition, 91
"Necessity of Tomorrows, The," 149, 152
Necromancer's Nine, 435
"Need," 425
Needle in a Timestack, 391
Negotiating with the Dead: A Writer on Writing, 32
Neighboring Lives, 162
Nekropolis, 283, 284
Nemesis, 25
Nemesis from Terra, The, 77
"Neon Heart Murders, The," 215
Nerilka's Story, 279
Neuromancer, 189, 190, 191
"Neuroscience of Cyberspace, The," 245
Neutron Star, 318, 320
Nevermore Affair, The, 480
Nevèrÿon series, 149, 151
Nevèrÿona, 151
New America, 15
New Arrivals, Old Encounters, 9
New Atlantis, The (Silverberg), 392,
"New Atlantis, The" (Le Guin), 254
"New Communications Technologies and the Developing World," 147
New Constellations, 163
New Dimensions, 392
New Dreams for Old, 344
New Dreams This Morning, 68
New Hugo Winners: Volume III, 486
New Improved Sun, The, 163
New Legends, 54
"New Literature for the Space Age, A," 309
New Moon's Arms, The, 234, 235
New Rose Hotel, 192
New Springtime, The, 390,
New Voices in Science Fiction 345
New Women of Wonder, The, 364
New World or No World, 227
New World Order, The, 476
New Worlds anthologies, 303, 308
New Worlds for Old, 476
"Newsletter," 484, 485
Newton's Wake: A Space Opera, 274
Next, 158
Next Stop the Stars, 391
Night Bird, The, 21
Night Face, The, 16
Night Face & Other Stories, The, 17
Night Fantastic, The, 17
Night in the Lonesome October, A, 501

Night of Light, 180
Night of Power, 354
"Night of White Bhairab, The," 383
Night People, The, 187
Night Sessions, The, 272, 274
Night Shapes, The, 67
"Nightfall" (Asimov), 24, 25, 26, 27
Nightfall (Silverberg), 389
"Nightfall" (Weber), 470
Nighthorse, 136
Nightside the Long Sun, 491
Nightwings, 387, 389
"Nimby and the Dimension Hoppers," 168
Nimisha's Ship, 278
Nine Billion Names of God, The, 144, 145
Nine Black Doves, 502
"Nine Failures of the Imagination," 270
"Nine Lives," 255
Nine Princes in Amber, 501
Nine Tomorrows, 26
1985, 106
1984 (Delany), 149, 151
1984 (movie), 324. See also Nineteen Eighty-Four
1984: Spring, A Choice of Futures (Clarke), 146
Nineteen Eighty-Four, 237, 322, 323, 324
1968, 204
"Ninety Percent of Everything," 249, 269
Ninety-Nine Novels: The Best in English Since 1939: A Personal Choice, 107
Niven, Larry, 316–21, 485
Niven's Laws, 320
No Doors, No Windows, 175
No Enemy But Time, 60, 61, 62
No Good from a Corpse, 78
No Maps for These Territories, 192
"No, No, Not Rogov!," 400
No One Noticed the Cat, 280
No Place Like Earth, 497
"No Planets Strike," 491
"No Prisoners," 121
"No Such Thing as Tearing Down Just a Little," 131
"No Truce with Kings," 14,
No World of Their Own, 14
"Noble Mold," 36
Nomad of the Time Streams, A, 307
None So Blind, 203, 204
Nonesuch, 215
Non-Stop, 6, 7
"Nonstop to Portales," 486

Noon: 22nd Century, 421
"Nor Custom Stale," 357
Norby Chronicles, 26
Norstrilia, 400
North against South, 454
North Wind, 244
NorthShore, 435
Norton Book of Science Fiction, The: North American SF, 1960–1990, 256
"Not Being There," 204
"Not Long Before the End," 320
Notebooks of Lazarus Long, 221
Notes to a Science Fiction Writer, 74
Nothing Burns in Hell, 180
Nothing Like the Sun: A Story of Shakespeare's Love Life, 107
"Nothing Special," 200
Notions: Unlimited, 374
Nova (Delany), 150,
Nova series (Harrison), 211
Nova Swing, 214, 215
Novel Now, The, 107
Novella: 3, 74
Novels of Philip K. Dick, The, 348, 350
Now and Forever: Somewhere a Band Is Playing & Leviathan '99, 83
Now Wait for Last Year, 156
N-Space, 321
Null-A series, 443, 445
Number of the Beast, The, 219, 221, 403

"O Brave New (Virtual) World," 75
O Pioneer!, 334
Oath of Fealty, 319
Oath of Gold, 302
Oath of Swords, 468, 470
Odyssey File, The, 146
Of Matters Great and Small, 28
"Of Men, Halflings, and Hero Worship," 91
Of Missing Persons, 187, 188
"Of Mist, Grass and Sand," 287
Of Time and Space and Other Things, 28
Of Time and Stars, 145
"Of Time and Third Avenue," 58
Off Armageddon Reef, 469
Off on a Comet, 454
Off the Main Sequence, 222
Off the Wall at Callahan's, 355
Official Guide to Fantastic Literature, The, 346
O'Keefe Family Trilogy, 263
"Old MacDonald Had a Farm," 343

"Old Music and the Slave Women," 255
Old Soldiers, 468
Old Twentieth, 203
Oliphant, B. J. *See* Tepper, Sheri S.
Olympos, 396
Omegatropic: Non-Fiction & Fiction, 48, 49
"Ommatidium Miniatures, The," 63
"On *A Clockwork Orange,*" 107
On Basilisk Station, 467, 469
On Blue's Waters, 491
On Her Majesty's Occult Service, 417
"On K2 with Kanakaredes," 397
"On Mary Wollstonecraft Shelley," 359
"On Point of View" (Wilhelm), 482
"On Reviewing and Being Reviewed," 60, 61
"On Science Fiction Criticism," 68
"On Science Fiction," 465
"On Self-Transcendence," 240
"On Setting," 359
On SF, 164
On Strike Against God, 358
"On the Inside," 390
On the Margin, 239
"On the Net," 248, 250
"On the North Pole of Pluto," 350
"On the Orion Line," 49
"On the Storm Planet," 400
"On the Writing of Speculative Fiction," 222
"On Thud and Blunder," 18
On Wings of Song, 161, 162
Once a Fan . . . , 346
Once a Hero, 301
"102 H-Bombs," 162
"One Hundred and Two H-Bombs, 163
100th Millennium, The, 98
One Man's Chorus, 107
One More for the Road, 83
"One Perfect Morning, with Jackals," 343
One Step from Earth, 211
One Winter in Eden, 63
"One Woman's Experience in Science Fiction," 91
"Ones Who Walk Away from Omelas, The," 254
"Only Death in the City, The," 137
"Only Neat Thing to Do, The," 440
"Only Partly Here," 383
Open to Me, My Sister, 182
Operation Ares, 490
Operation Plowshare, 156
Ophiuchi Hotline, The, 448, 449, 450
Opium General, The, 307

Options (Sheckley), 373
"Options" (Varley), 450
Opus series, 27
Or Else My Lady Keeps the Key, 35, 36
Oracle, 342
Orange County Trilogy, 349
Orbit Unlimited, 14, 17
Orde, A. J. *See* Tepper, Sheri S.
"Ordeal in Space, The," 426
Ordering of Love, The: The New and Collected Poems of Madeleine L'Engle, 264
"Orders of Chaos: The Science Fiction of Joanna Russ," 152
Original Hitchhiker Radio Scripts, The, 3
Orion, 73
Orion among the Stars, 73
Orion and the Conqueror, 73
Orion in the Dying Time, 73
Orion Shall Rise, 15
Ornery American, The, 124, 128
"Orphans of the Helix," 396
Orphans of the Sky, 221
Orsinian Tales, 252, 255
Orson Scott Card's InterGalactic Medicine Show, 127
Orwell, George, 192, 238, **322–26,** 473
Oryx and Crake, 30, 31
Oswald Bastable series, 305
Other Celia, The, 426
Other End of Time, The, 334
Other Glass Teat, The, 176
Other in the Mirror, The, 183
Other Log of Phileas Fogg, The, 182
"Other People, The," 78
Other Side of the Mirror, The, 90
Other Side of the Sky, The, 145
Other Teddy Roosevelts, The, 344
Other Voices, 198, 199
Otherness, 94, 95
"Où Suis-Je? Or, Where Am I?," 235
Our Angry Earth, 28, 337
"Our Favorite Cliché: A World Filled with Idiots . . . ," 96
Our Friends from Frolix 8, 156
"Our Lady of the Sauropods," 387
"Our Neural Chernobyl," 412
Out of the Dead City, 150
Out of the Everywhere (Asimov), 28
"Out of the Everywhere" (Tiptree), 440
Out of the Everywhere and Other Extraordinary Visions (Tiptree), 441

Out of the Sun, 71
Out of the Unknown, 445
Out of Time's Abyss, 111
Outlaw of Torn, The, 111
Outline of History, The, 476
Outnumbering the Dead, 333, 334
Outpost, The, 342
Outward Urge, The, 496
Over the Edge, 175
"Over Yonder," 382
Overclocked: Stories of the Future Present, 169
Overdrawn at the Memory Bank, 450, 451
Overloaded Man, The, 40
Owl in Daylight, The, 158

Pacific Edge, 348, 349
Paingod and Other Delusions, 174
"Painwise," 440
Paksenarrion, 300, 302
Paladin, The, 136
Paladin of Souls, 102, 103
"Paladin of the Lost Hour," 173, 174
"Pale Roses," 306
Pale Shadow of Science, The, 10
Palm Sunday, 465
Pandora by Holly Hollander, 491
Parable of the Sower, 116
Parable of the Talents, 115, 116
Paradise, 342
"Paradises Lost," 255
Parietal Games, 216
"Paris in June," 121
Paris in the Twentieth Century, 454
"Parrots, the Universe and Everything," 3
Partners in Wonder 175
Passage (Bujold), 103
Passage (Willis), 484, 485
Passage of the Light, The, 344
"Passengers," 387
Passing for Human, 63
"Passion for Lord Pierrot, A," 199
Passport to Eternity, 39
Past Through Tomorrow, The, 222
Past Times, 17
Pastel City, The, 213, 215
Pastwatch: The Redemption of Christopher Columbus, 126
"Patchwork Girl, The," 320
Path of the Fury, 468, 469
"Pathways of Desire, The," 255
"Pattern of Science Fiction, The," 497

Pattern Recognition, 190, 191
Patternist series, 115, 116
Patternmaster, 114, 116
Patterns, 120, 121
Pawns of Null-A, The, 445
Paycheck, 158
Peace, 490
Peace on Earth, 260
Peace War, The, 460
Peacekeepers, The, 72
Pearls from Peoria, 182
"Pearls of Weber," 471
Pebble in the Sky, 26
"Peddler's Apprentice, The," 460
Pegasus in Flight, 279
Pegasus in Space, 279
"Peking Junction, The," 306
"Peking Man," 369
Pellucidar, 110, 111
Pendulum, 445
Penelopiad, The, 32
Penguin anthologies, 9
"Pentalude: Science Fiction as Fantasy," 350
Penultimate Truth, The, 156
People Know, The, 436
People of Pern, 281
People of the Talisman, 78
People of the Wind, The, 16
People That Time Forgot, The, 111, 112
People Trap, The 374
Peregrine, The, 15
Perennial Philosophy, The, 239
Perfect Host, The, 425
Perilous Planets, 9
Periodic Table of Science Fiction, The, 428, 431
Perish by the Sword, 14
"Permafrost," 500
Pern, 276, 277, 279
Persistence of Vision, The, 449, 451
"Perspectives in SF," 137
Pesach for the Rest of Us: Making the Passover Seder Your Own, 329
Petaybee series, 280
"Petra," 54
"Phantom of Kansas, The," 450
Phase Space: Stories from the Manifold and Elsewhere, 49
Phases, 302
Phases of Gravity, 396
Phases of the Moon: Stories from Six Decades, 391

"Phil in the Marketplace," 269
Philip K. Dick Is Dead, Alas, 62
"Philosophy & Science Fiction: A View of a Personal Reality," 375
Phoenix Café, 244
Phoenix Code, The, 20
"Photographs and Memories," 204
"Pi Man, The," 58
Picnic on Nearside, 450, 451
Picnic on Paradise, 358
Piercy, Marge, 327–30
Pilgermann, 230, 231
Pilgrimage to Earth, 374
Pink Elephants and Hairy Toads, 344
Pirate, 342
Pirate Freedom, 491
Pirates of Venus, 111
"Pitfalls of Writing Science Fiction & Fantasy," 289
Place So Foreign and Eight More, A, 169
Plague from Space, 209
Plague of Angels, A, 435
Plague of Pythons, A, 333
Plan(e)t Engineering, 492
Planet Buyer, The, 400,
Planet Called Treason, A, 125
Planet Killers, The, 388
"Planet Named Shayol, A," 400
Planet of Death, 388
Planet of Exile, 255
Planet of Judgment, 203
Planet of No Return, 14
Planet of the Damned, 209
Planet of Whispers, 247, 249
Planet on the Table, The, 350
Planet Pirates, 301
Planet Plane, 496
Planet Savers, 87, 88, 89
Planet Story, 209
Planet That Wasn't, The, 28
Planets Three, 336
"Planners, The," 479
"Plastic Abyss, The," 481
Platinum Pohl, 336,
Player of Games, The, 4, 44
Player on The Other Side, The, 425
Player Piano, 463, 464
Players of Null-A, The, 445
Playgrounds of the Mind, 316, 321
Plenty Principle, The, 200
Pluto in the Morning Light, 391
Podkayne of Mars, 221

546 Author/Title Index

Poe, Edgar Allan, 378, 438, 454, 455, 459
Poem du Jour, 431
Pohl, Frederik, 28, 65, 70, 74, 113, 145, 316, **331–38**, 405
Pohlstars, 336
Point Counter Point, 239
"Point of View," 205
Polesotechnic League, 16
Political Doctrines of Sun Yat-Sen, The, 400,
"Politics and Science Fiction," 275
"Politics and the English Language," 325
"Politics of Prophecy, The," 337
"Poor Man, Beggar Man," 359
"Pope of the Chimps, The," 390
"Pornography by Women for Women with Love," 358
Port Eternity, 135
Positronic Man, The, 389,
Positronic Robot stories, 27
Postman, The, 94, 96
Postmodern Archipelago, The, 431
Power & Light, 502
"Power and the Passion, The," 121
Power Lines, 280
"Power of Art, The," 436
Power Play, 280
Powers That Be, 280
Powersat, 73
Practical Politics: 1972, 337
Practice Effect, The, 94
Prayers to Broken Stones, 396, 397
Precipice, The, 72
Precursor, 136
Preferred Risk, 333
Prelude to Foundation, 25
Prelude to Space, 144
Prentice Alvin, 126
"Presence," 284
Preserving Machine, The, 158
Presidential Year, 334
"Presidents, Experts, and Asteroids," 147
"Press ENTER []," 450
Prestimion Trilogy, 390
Pretender, 136
"Pretty Boy Crossover," 121
"Pretty Maggie Moneyeyes," 174
Pride and Prejudice, 238
Pride of Chanur, The, 135
Priest, The: A Gothic Romance, 162
Priests of Psi, The, 227
Primal Urge, The, 7
Primary Inversion, 19, 21

Prime Number, 211
Prince of Chaos, 501
"Princess of Earth, A," 343
Princess of Mars, A, 109, 110
"Prismatica," 151
"Prisoner of Chillon, The," 249
Prisoner, The, 162
Prisoners of Power, 421
"Privacy," 95
Private Cosmos, A, 181
Privateers, 72
"Prize of Peril, The," 371, 373
"Profession of Fiction, The," 216
"Profession of Science Fiction, The," 492
Profiles of the Future, 146
Project Moon Base, 222
Project Solar Sail, 95
Promethea, 313
Prometheans, 73
Promise of Space, The, 146
Promised Land, 485
"Propagation of Light in a Vacuum, The," 249
Propeller Island, 454
Prophet, 342
"Protection," 284
Proxy Intelligence and Other Mind Benders, The, 445
"Psychic Landscape, The," 351
Psychlone, 53
Psychological Warfare, 398, 401
"Psychologist Who Wouldn't Do Awful Things to Rats, The," 440
Psychoshop, 58, 501
"Psychospace," 369
Psychotechnic League, 15
"Publishing of Science Fiction, The," 337
Puck Aleshire's Abecedary, 431
"Pulp Cover," 492
Puppet Masters, The, 220, 222
Puppies of Terra, The, 162
Purgatory, 342
Purple Book, The, 182
Pursuit on Ganymede, 341
"Pusher, The," 450
"Putting a Tag on It," 309
Putting It Together: Turning Sow's Ear Drafts into Silk Purse Stories, 346
"Pyramid of Amirah, The," 250

Quantico, 52, 53
Quantum Rose, The, 19, 20, 21
Quasar, Quasar, Burning Bright, 28

Queen City Jazz, 194, 195, 196
"Queen of Air and Darkness, The," 14
Queen of Angels, 52, 53
Queen of Springtime, The, 390
"Queen of the Martian Catacombs," 76, 78
"Queen of the Martian Mysteries: An Appreciation of Leigh Brackett," 309
"Queer Ones, The," 78
Quest of the Three Worlds, 399, 400
Question and Answer, 14
"Quickening, The," 62
Quicker Than the Eye, 83
Quicksilver, 406, 407, 408
"Quijote Robot, The," 374
Quincunx of Time, The, 67
Quintaglio Ascension, 366, 368

"R & R," 382
R Is for Rocket, 83, 84
"Raccoon Music," 436
Rachel and Leah, 126
"Racism and Science Fiction," 152
"Radiant Doors," 430
"Radiant Green Star," 382
Radiant Seas, The, 21
Radiant War Aftermath, 21
Radio Free Albemuth, 157
"Radio Waves," 430
Raft, 48
"Ragged Claws," 337
Ragnarok, 313
"Rah, Rah, R.A.H.!," 355
Rainbow Bridge, 244
Rainbow Mars, 318
Rainbow's End, 459, 460
Raising the Stones, 435
Rama II, 145
Rama Revealed, 145
Rambles in Germany and Italy in 1840, 1842, and 1843, 379
Random Quest, 498
Rare Breed, The, 425
"Rat," 249
Rat Race, The, 58
Raw Spirit: In Search of the Perfect Dram, 44
"Ray Bradbury: The Illustrated Spaceman," 85
Ray Bradbury Theater, The, 85
Reach for Tomorrow, 145
"Real Matrix, The," 50
"Real Weather, Small Towns, and Science Fiction," 302

"Reality Check," 95
Reality Dust, 48
Reality Trip and Other Implausibilities, The, 391,
Realm of Prester John, The, 392,
Reavers of Skaith, The, 78
Rebekah, 126
Rebel, 342
Rebel in Time, A, 209
Rebel Worlds, The, 16
"Reborn Again," 374
Recalled to Life, 388
"Receding Horizon," 269
"Recent Feminist Utopias," 359
Red Lightning, 449, 450
Red Mars, 347, 349
Red Orc's Rage, 181
Red Planet, 220
Red Prophet, 126
"Red Sonja and Lessingham in Dreamland," 244
Red Star Rising: Second Chronicles of Pern, 279
"Red Star, Winter Orbit," 191
Red Sun of Darkover, 90
Red Tape War, The, 341
Red Thunder, 449, 450
Redbeard, 341
"Redchapel," 343
Rediscovery, 90
Rediscovery of Man, The, 400
Reefs of Space, The, 335
Reengineering Information Technology: Success Through Empowerment, 49
"Reflections: The Conquest of Space," 393
Reflections and Refractions 392
Reflections of A. E. Van Vogt, 446
Regan's Planet, 388
Regenesis, 135
"Region Between, The," 173
Relativity, 369
Relativity of Wrong, The, 28
"Relic of Empire, A," 319
Remake, 484, 485
Remaking History and Other Stories, 350
"Remembering Siri," 396
Remembrance Day, 8
Remnant Population, 300, 301
"Render Unto Caesar," 284
Rendezvous with Rama, 143, 144
Renegades of Pern, The, 280
"Renewal, The," 364

Renunciates of Darkover, 90
Repairmen of Cyclops, The, 99
"'Repent, Harlequin!' Said the Ticktockman," 171, 173
Report on Planet Three and Other Speculations, 146
Report on Probability A, 7
"Report on the Barnhouse Effect," 464
"Requiem for a Dreamer," 465
"Requiem," 220
"Rescue Party," 145
"Rescue Run," 280
Research Alpha," 445
Resnick at Large, 346
Resnick, Mike, 21, **339–46**, 405
Resplendent, 48
"Responsibilities and Temptations of Women Science Fiction Writers," 91
Rest of the Robots, The, 27
Restaurant at the End of the Universe, The, 2
Restoration Game, The, 274
Restoree, 277, 278
Resurrecting the Mummy, 119, 121
"Resurrection of Jimber-Jaw, The," 112
Rethinking Theory, 260
Retreat from Liberty, The: The Erosion of Democracy in Today's Britain, 308
"Retrograde Summer," 450
Return from the Stars, 260
Return of Santiago, The, 342
Return of Swamp Thing, The, 313
Return of the Dinosaurs, 345
"Return of William Proxmire, The," 320
Return to Eden, 210
Return to Mars (Bova) 72
Return to Mars (Burroughs), 112
Return to the Whorl, 488, 491
Revenants, The, 435
Revenge of the Rose, The, 306
Reverie for Mister Ray, A, 61, 63
Revolt on Alpha C, 388
Revolution Business, The, 417
Revolutions in the Earth: James Hutton and the True Age of the World, 50
Rewired: The New Cyberpunk Anthology, 249
Ria, 400
Richter 10, 145
"Riddles in the Dark," 245
Riddley Walker, 229, 230
Rider at the Gate, 136
Riders of the Purple Wage, 179, 180, 182
"Ridge Running," 350

Riding the Rock, 48
Rimrunners, 134, 135
Ring, 48
Ring of Endless Light, A, 264
Ring of Fear, 279
Ringing the Changes, 391
Ringworld, 316, 317, 318
Ringworld Engineers, The, 318
Ringworld Throne, The, 318
Ringworld's Children, 318
Rio Bravo, 77, 79
Rise of Endymion, The, 395, 396
Rites of Ohe, The, 99
Rituals of Infinity, The, 305
River of Eternity, 181
River of Time, 95
"River Styx Runs Upstream, The," 395
Riverworld, 179, 181, 182, 183
Riverworld and Other Stories, 182
Riverworld War: The Suppressed Fiction of Philip José Farmer, 182
Road to Amber, The, 502
Road to Dune, The, 227
"Road to Heaven, The," 164
Road to Infinity, The, 28
Road to Nightfall, The, 391"
"Road to Oceania, The," 192
Road to Wigan Pier, The, 324
Roadmarks, 501
Roads Between the Worlds, The, 307
"Roads Must Roll, The," 221
Roadside Picnic, 419, 420
Robber Bride, The, 32
"Robbie," 26
Robert Silverberg's Worlds of Wonder, 391
Robinson, Kim Stanley, 35, **347–51**, 444
Robinson, Spider, 57, 219, 221, **352–56**
RoboCop, 294
Robot Dreams, 25, 26, 27
Robot Visions, 27
Robot Who Looked Like Me, The, 374
Robots and Empire 26
"Robots Don't Cry," 343
Robots of Dawn, The, 26
Robur le Conquerant, 454
Rocannon's World, 255
"Rock Diver," 210
Rock Rats, The, 72
Rock That Is Higher, The: Story as Truth, 264
Rockabilly, 174
"Rocket Man, The," 83
"Rocket Radio," 191

Rocket Ship Galileo, 220, 222
Rocket to the Moon, 455
"Roger Dodsworth: The Reanimated Englishman," 378
Rogue Farm, 417
Rogue Planet, 53
Rogue Ship, 445
Rogue Star, 335
"Rogue Tomato," 62
"Role of Science Fiction, The," 75
Rollback, 368
Rolling Stones, The, 221
Rolling Thunder, 449, 450
Roma Eterna, 389
Romance of the Equator, A, 9
"Romantic/Science Fiction: The Oldest Form of Literature," 137
Ronin, 292
Rose for Ecclesiastes, A, 499, 500, 502
Rowan, The, 279
Ruby Dice, The, 21
Ruby Tear, The, 131
Rude Awakening, A, 8
"Rude Mechanicals," 36
Ruins of Earth, The, 163
Ruler of the Sky, 363
Rules of Engagement, 301
Rumble, 172
"Run for the Stars," 174,
"Runaround," 24, 25, 26
"Runesmith," 174
"Running Down," 215
"Running Wild," 39
Rusalka, 137
Rushing to Paradise, 39
Russ, Joanna, 332, **357–60**

S Is for Space, 83
Safari of the Mind, A, 344
Safehold series, 469
Saga of Cuckoo, 335
Saga of the Renunciates, The, 90
Saga of the Skolian Empire, 19, 21
"Sailing to Byzantium," 387, 388
Sailing to Byzantium, 391
Sailing to Utopia, 307
Sailor on the Seas of Fate, The, 306
Saint Leibowitz and the Wild Horse Woman, 297
"Saint Theresa of the Aliens," 249
Saints, 126
"Saliva Tree, The," 7

Saliva Tree, and Other Strange Growths, The, 9
Salmon of Doubt: Hitchhiking the Galaxy One Last Time, The, 3
Salt Roads, The, 235
"Salvador," 382
Sam Gunn Omnibus, The, 73
Same to You Doubled and Other Stories, The, 374
"Samurai and the Willows, The," 62
Sanctuary in the Sky, 99
Sands of Mars, 144
Sandworms of Dune, 225
Sanity and the Lady, 8,
Santaroga Barrier, The, 226
Santiago: A Myth of the Far Future, 340, 341, 342
Sarah, 126
Sargent, Pamela, 100, **361–65**, 479, 482
Sassinak, 301
Satan's World, 16
Saturn, 72
Saturn Game, The, 14, 15
Saturn's Children, 417
Saturn's Race, 319
Saucer of Loneliness, A, 425
Saul's Death and Other Poems, 204
Savage Pellucidar, 111
Sawyer, Robert J., **366–70**
"Scalehunter's Beautiful Daughter, The," 382
Scanner Darkly, A, 156, 157, 158
"Scanners Live in Vain," 398, 399, 400,"Scapegoat, The," 137
Scatterbrain, 321
"Scherzo with Tyrannosaur," 430
Schism, 21
Schismatrix, 410, 412
Schismatrix Plus, 413
"Schwartz Between the Galaxies," 390
"Schwarzschild Radius," 484, 486
"Science and Fiction: Escape from the Laws of Physics," 44
"Science Fiction: Its Nature, Faults and Virtues," 222
"Science Fiction: Stepchild of Science," 337
Science Fiction: The Best of 2002, 392
Science Fiction A to Z, 27
"Science Fiction after the Future Went Away," 275
"Science Fiction and a World in Crisis," 227
"Science Fiction and All That Jazz," 194, 196

"Science Fiction and 'Literature'—or, The Conscience of the King," 152
"Science Fiction and Mrs. Brown," 256
"Science Fiction and the Larger Lunacy," 100
"Science Fiction and the Renaissance Man," 59
Science Fiction Art, 10
Science Fiction Box, The, 74
"Science Fiction Can Teach Us Something If We Stop to Learn," 75
Science Fiction Hall of Fame, The, 388, 391
Science Fiction Hall of Fame anthologies 74
Science Fiction in the Classroom, 337
Science Fiction Masterpieces, 27
Science Fiction Omnibus, A, 9
Science Fiction 101: Where to Start Reading and Writing Science Fiction, 392
"Science Fiction Professional, The" (Pohl), 337
Science Fiction Professional, The (Resnick), 346
Science Fiction Stories 256
Science Fiction Studies in Film, 337
"Science Fiction, Morals, and Religion," 426
"Science in Science Fiction, The" (Blish) 65, 68
"Science in Science Fiction: A Writer's Perspective" (Willis), 486
Science in the Capital, 349
"Science in the Third Millennium," 351
"Science, Language and Magic," 141
Science, Numbers, and I, 28
"Science or Fiction," 413
"Scientists Revolt, The," 112
Sci-Fi Buzz, 171, 175
"SciFi Case History, A," 361, 365
"Scorched Supper on New Niger," 131
Scratch Monkey 416
Screamers, 157
"Screwfly Solution, The," 440, 441
"Scribbledehobbledehoydenii: Autobiographical Essay," 431
Sea Serpent, The, 454
Sea Thing and Other Stories, The, 445
Sea-Kings of Mars and Otherworldly Stories, 77, 79
Search for Designation 420
Search for Mavin Manyshaped, The, 435
Search for Spock, The, 288
"Search for the Marvellous, The," 375
Search the Sky, 334
Searoad, 256

Seasons in Flight, 9
Seasons of Plenty, 199
"Seasons of the Ansarac, The," 255
'Second Comings—Reasonable Rates," 121
Second Contact, 341
Second Ether sequence, 306
Second Foundation, 25
"Second Inquisition, The," 359
Second Martian Invasion, The, 420
Second Stage Lensman, 404
Second Trip, The, 389,
Second Variety, 157, 158
Second Words: Selected Critical Prose, 32
Secret Agent of Terra, 99
Secret Ascension, The, 62
"Secret Characters: The Interaction of Narrative and Technology," 245
"Secret of Holman Hunt and the Crude Death Rate, The," 8
Secret of Monkey Island, The, 127
Secret of Sinharat, The, 78
Secret of the Universe, The, 28
Secret of This Book, The, 9,
Secret People, The, 497
"Secret Sharer," 387, 388
Secret Sharers: The Collected Stories Volume 1, 388, 391
Seed of Earth, The, 388
"Seed to Harvest," 116
"Seeding Program," 67
Seedling Stars, The, 66, 67
Seeds of Time, The, 497
Selected Letters (Huxley), 240
Selected Letters of Philip K. Dick 1980–82, The, 158
"Self-World of Depression, The," 283, 284
Semi No Jo-o, 413
Sense of Obligation, A, 209
Sense of Shadow, A, 481
Sentinel, The, 143, 145, 146
Separate War and Other Stories, A, 204
Sermonettes, 164
Serpent Mage, The, 54
Serpent's Reach, 135
"Serpent's Teeth," 355
"Servant of the People," 335
Serve It Forth—Cooking with Anne McCaffrey, 280
Service of the Sword, The, 470
Seven from the Stars, 89
Seven Kinds of Death, 481
Seven Tales and a Fable, 245

"Seven Views of Olduvai Gorge," 341
Seventh Shrine, 389
Seventh Son, 126
"Seventh Victim," 373
"Seventy-Two Letters," 140, 141
Severed Wasp, A, 264
Sex Gang, 174
Sex Wars, 329
"Sexual Dimorphism," 350,
<u>SF: Authors' Choice series</u>, 211
SF and Technology as Mystification," 359
SF Reprise, 308
"Shades," 383
Shadow Matrix, The, 90
Shadow of Saganami, The, 469
Shadow of the Giant, 125
Shadow of the Hegemon, 125
Shadow of the Torturer, The, 488, 490
Shadow Over Mars, 77
Shadow Puppets, 125
"Shadowed Heart, The," 21
Shadow's End, 435
Shadows of the New Sun: Wolfe on Writing, Writers on Wolfe, 492
Shadrach in the Furnace, 389
"Shaffery Among the Immortals," 335
Shaggy B.E.M. Stories, 344
"Shall We Have a Little Talk?," 374
"Shaman's View, A," 96
Shape of Further Things, The, 10
Shape of Space, The, 320
Shape of Things to Come, The, 474
<u>Shaper/Mechanist Universe</u>, 411
Shaping Things, 413
Shards of Honor, 103
Shards of Space, 374
<u>Sharing Knife</u>, 102, 103
"Sharing of Flesh, The," 14
Sharra's Exile, 89
Shatterday, 171, 174, 175
Shattered Chain, 89
"Shattered Like a Glass Goblin," 174
Shayol, 119, 121
"She Unnames Them," 255
Sheckley, Robert, 2, 93, 208, 209, 345, **371–76**, 502
"Shed Skin," 369
"Sheena 5," 49
Sheep Look Up, The, 98, 99
Sheepfarmer's Daughter, 300, 302
Sheldon, Alice Hastings Bradley. *See* Tiptree, James P., Jr.

Shelley, Mary Wollstonecraft, 377–80
"Shelter," 127
Shepard, Lucius, 63, 297, **381–85,** 432
Sherlock Holmes in Orbit, 345
Shield, 14
Shield of Time, The, 16, 17
Shifting Realities of Philip K. Dick, The, 158
Shinseiki Lensman, 404
Ship Who Sang, The, 278, 280
Ships of Earth, The, 126
<u>Shirley McClintock Mysteries</u>, 436
Shiva Option, The, 469
"Shobies' Story, The," 255
Shockwave Rider, The, 98, 99
Shon'Jir, 136
"Shooting an Elephant," 322, 325
"Shore Leave," 426
Shore of Women, The, 362, 363
Shores of Death, The, 305
Shores of Tomorrow, The, 391
Short Happy Life of the Brown Oxford, The, 157
Short, Sharp Shock, A, 349
Short Victorious War, The, 469
Shorter Views: Queer Thoughts & the Politics of the Paraliterary, 151
"Shrine, The," 364
Shrouded Planet, The, 388,
Siberia, 244
Sideshow (Resnick), 342
Sideshow (Tepper), 435
"Sidon in the Mirror, The," 484, 485
Siege of Eternity, The, 334
Sign of Chaos, 501
Sign of the Unicorn, 501
Signs of Life, 215
Silent Interviews: On Language, Race, Sex, Science Fiction, and Some Comics, 149, 151
Silent Invaders, The, 388
Silent Partner, 78
Silent War, The, 72
Silkie, The, 445
Silver Glove, The, 131
Silverberg, Robert, 25, 58, 98, **386–93**, 438, 439, 440, 441, 442, 499
Silverhair, 49
Silverheart, 306
Simmons, Dan, 394–97
Simulacra, The, 156
Sin City, 292, 294
"Since Aunt Ada Came to Stay," 446

"Since 1948," 189, 192
Singer from the Sea, 435
Singers of Time, The, 335
"Singularities and Nightmares," 96
"Singularity, The," 460
Singularity Sky, 415, 417
Sir Arthur C. Clarke, 146
"Sir George and the Dragon," 470
Sirens of Titan, The, 464
"Sisters," 54
Six Moon Dance, 435
1634: The Baltic War, 470
1633, 470
<u>1632 series</u>, 468, 470
Sixth Column, 220
Sixty Days and Counting, 349
<u>Skaith novels</u>, 77, 78, 88
Skeletons: A Novel of Suspense, 481
"Sketches Among the Ruins of My Mind," 182
Skies of Pern, The, 279
Skin Folk, 235
Skrayling Tree, The, 306
Sky Coyote, 35
Sky Horizon: Colony High, Book One, **95**
Sky Road, The, 273, 275
"Sky's No Limit, The," 10
Skybreaker, The, 244
Skyfall, (Harrison), 209
Skyfall (Asaro), 21
Skylark DuQuesne, 404
Skylark of Space, The, 402, 403, 404
Skylark of Valeron, 404
Skylark Three, 402, 404
Slan, 443, 444
Slant, 52, 53.
Slapstick; or, Lonesome No More, 464
Slaughterhouse-Five; or, The Children's Crusade: A Duty-Dance with Death, 462, 464, 465
Slave and the Free, The, 131
Slave Ship, 333
Sleep of Reason, The, 431
Sleeper Awakes, The, 474
Sleepers of Mars, 497
Sleeping Sorceress, The, 306
Sleeping with Cats: A Memoir, 327, 329
Sleepless Nights in the Procrustean Bed: Essays, 173, 176
Sleepside: The Collected Fantasies, 54
"Sliced-Crosswise Only-on-Tuesday World, The," 182

Slippage: Previously Uncollected, Precariously Poised Stories, 173, 175
"Slipstream" (Kelly), 250
"Slipstream" (Sterling), 410, 413
"Slow Cold Chick," 235
"Slow Life," 430
"Slow Saturday Night at the Surrealist Sporting Club, A," 307
"Slow Sculpture," 424
"Slowboat to the Stars!," 75
Small Assassin, The, 83
Small Changes, 329
"Small Room in Koboldtown, A," 430
"Smile on the Face, The," 235
"Smiley's People," 409
Smith, Cordwainer, xv, xvii, xviii, 190, 267, **398–401**
Smith, E. E. ("Doc"), xiv, **402–5**, 460
Smoke Ring, The, 318
Smugglers Gold, 138
Snail on the Slope, The, 420
Snow Crash, 406, 407, 408
Snow Queen, The, 459
Snow Wonder, 486
Snows of Darkover, 90
Snows of Ganymede, The, 15
Snows of Olympus, The, 147
So Close to Home, 67
So Long, and Thanks for All the Fish, 2
So Long Been Dreaming, 235
So You Want to Write: How to Master the Craft of Writing Fiction and Memoir, 329
"Sob in the Silence," 492
"Social Science Fiction," 29
Softspoken, 383
Sojan, 307
Solar Lottery, 156
Solar System and Back, The, 28
Solaris, 260
"Soldier," 174, 175
Soldier Erect, A, 8
Soldier of Arete, 491
Soldier of Sidon, 491
Soldier of the Mist, 490, 491
"Solitario's Eyes," 383
"Solitude," 254
Solo Flights Through Shared Worlds, 344
"Solstice," 248, 249
Soma Blues, 373
Some of Your Blood, 425

"Some Presumptuous Approaches to Science Fiction," 152
Someone Comes to Town, Someone Leaves Town, 168
"Someone Like You," 436
Somerset Dreams and Other Fictions, 482
"Something to Hitch Meat To," 235
Something Wicked This Way Comes, 81, 83, 85
Something Wild Is Loose: The Collected Stories Volume 3, 391
Somewhere East of Life, 7, 8,
"Son of Dr. Strangelove," 147
Son of Man, 389
"Song of a Dry River," 343
Song of Kali, 396
Song of Mavin Manyshaped, The, 435
"Songhouse," 126
Songmaster, 125
Songs of Distant Earth, The, 144
<u>Songs of Earth and Power</u>, 54
Songs of Muad'Dib, 227
Sons of Heaven, The, 35
Soothsayer, 342
Sorcerers of Majipoor, 390
"Sorceress in Spite of Herself, The," 121
<u>Sorcery Hall</u>, 130, 131
"Soul Case," 235
Soul Catcher, 226
Soul Eater, The, 339, 341
"Soul of Light," 21
"Soul Selects Her Own Society, The: Invasion and Repulsion," 485
"Souls," 358
Sound of a Scythe, The, 174
Sound of Thunder and Other Stories, A, 83
"Sounding Brass, Tinkling Cymbal," 393
SouthShore, 435
Soylent Green, 208, 209, 211
Space and Time, 294
Space Cadet (Heinlein), 220
Space Cadets (Resnick), 345
Space Folk, 17
Space Lords, 400
Space Merchants, The, 332, 334
Space Opera (Aldiss), 9
Space Opera (McCaffrey), 280
Space Pirates, The, 404
Space Travel: Science Fiction Writing Series, 75
Space Wars, 17
Space, Time and Nathaniel, 8
Spacecraft in Fact and Fiction, 211

Spacefighters, 205
Spacehounds of IPC, 403
Spaceship Medic, 209
Space-Time Juggler, The, 99
"Space-Time Pool, The," 20
Spawn: Batman, 293
Speaker for the Dead, 124, 125
"Speech Sounds," 116
Speed of Dark, The, 300, 301
"Speed, Speed the Cable," 36
Spell Sword, The, 89,
"Spencer Inheritance, The," 307
"Spew," 408
Spherical Harmonic, 21
Sphinx at Dawn, The: Two Stories, 264
"Spice Pogrom," 484, 486
Spider Kiss, 174
"Spider Rose," 412
<u>Spiderman</u>, 291, 294
"Spimes and the Future of Artifacts," 413
"Spirals," 320
Spirit: or The Princess of Bois Dormant (Jones), 244
Spirit, The (Miller, F.), 291, 294
Spirit Ring, The, 103
Spiritfeather, 199
Spock Must Die, 66, 67
Spook Country, 191
Sporting Chance, 301
Sports & Music, 384
"Squandered Promise of Science Fiction, The," 270
<u>Squire Quartet</u>, 6, 8
Stagestruck Vampires: And Other Phantasms, 131
<u>Stainless Steel Rat, The</u>, 207, 208, 210, 211
Stalker, 421
Stalking the Dragon, 343
Stalking the Nightmare, 175
Stalking the Unicorn, 343
Stalking the Vampire, 343
Stalking the Wild Resnick, 344
Stand on Zanzibar, 97, 98, 99
"Stand on Zanzibar: The Novel as Film," 503
Stanislaw Lem Reader, A, 261
Star Beast, The, 221
Star Begotten, 474
Star Brothers, 73
Star Conquerors, The, 70, 73
Star Dwellers, The, 67
Star Fox, The, 13, 14
Star Fraction, The, 272, 273, 275

Star Light, Star Bright, 58
Star of Danger, 89,
Star of Gypsies, 389
"Star of the Sea," 16
Star Peace, 74
"Star Pit, The," 151
Star Prince Charlie, 15
Star Science Fiction Magazine, 336
Star Smashers of the Galaxy Rangers, 209
Star Songs of an Old Primate 441
Star Trek (TV series), xiii, 66, 110, 172, 173, 175, 286, 287, 372, 403, 416, 424, 426
Star Trek (book series), xv, 66, 203, 287, 288, 362, 363
Star Trek Readers, 68
Star Trek: The Next Generation (TV series), 95, 367
Star Trek: The Next Generation (book series), 363
Star Trek Universe, 53
Star Trek, Deep Space Nine (TV series), 372, 373
Star Wars (book series), 288
Star Wars (movies), 77, 110, 403
Star Wars on Trial, 95
Star Wars Universe, 53
Star Wars Weekly, 311
Star Watchman, 73
Star Ways, 15
"Star, The" (Clarke), 144
"Star, The" (Wells), 474
Starboard Wine: More Notes on the Language of Science Fiction, 151
Starborne, 389
Starburst, 58, 333
Starchild, 335
Starcrossed, The, 72
Stardance, 353, 354, 355
Stardreamer, 400
Starfarers (Anderson), 15
Starfarers (McIntyre), 288
Starfire series, 467, 469
Stark and the Star Kings, 79
Stark series, 77
Starlight: The Great Short Fiction of Alfred Bester, 58
Starlost, The, 74, 174, 175
Starman Jones, 221
Starman's Quest, 388
Starmen of Llyrdis, The, 77
Starmen, The, 77
Starmind, 355

Starplex, 368
Starry Rift, The, 440
Stars: Original Stories Based on the Songs of Janis Ian, 345
Stars Are Also Fire, The, 14, 15
Stars in My Pocket Like Grains of Sand, 149, 150
Stars in Their Courses, The, 28
Stars, Like Dust, The 26
Stars My Destination, The, 56, 57, 58, 361
"Stars Seen Through Stone," 383
Starseed, 355
Starshadows, 364
Starship (Aldiss), 6
Starship (Anderson), 15
"Starship Stormtroopers," 309
Starship *Teddy R,* 342
Starship Titanic, 3
Starship Troopers, 161, 208, 219, 220, 221, 222
Starswarm, 9
Startide Rising, 93, 94, 95
Starwater Strains, 492
Starworld, 210
State of Grace, 482
State of the Art, The, 42, 44
"State of the World 2008," 414
Stations of the Nightmare, 180, 182
Stations of the Tide, 428, 429, 430
Status Civilization, The, 372
Stealer of Souls, The, 306
Steel Beach, 449, 450
Steel Tsar, The, 305
"Steelcollar Worker," 288
Steep Approach to Garbadale, The, 42, 44
Steering the Craft, 256
Stephenson, Neal, xviii, **406–9**
Sterling, Bruce, 190, 191, **410–14**
Still Life, 436
Stitch in Snow, 279
Stolen Faces, 61, 62
Stone Canal, The, 273, 275
Stone God Awakens, The, 180
Stone in Heaven, A, 16
Stone Tables, 126
Stonehenge: Where Atlantis Died, 210
"Stones of Significance," 95
Stopping at Slowyear, 334, 335
Store of Infinity, 374
Storeys from the Old Hotel, 492
Stories of Your Life, and Others, 139, 140, 141

Storm from the Shadows, 469
Storm of Wings, A, 215
Storm Tide, 328, 329
Storm Warnings: Science Fiction Confronts the Future, 200
Stormbringer, 306
"Storming the Cosmos," 412
Stormqueen, 89
"Story of Your Life," 140
Storyteller: Writing Lessons and More from 27 Years of the Clarion Writers' Workshop, 482
Storyteller in Zion, A, 127
Stowaway to Mars, 496
Strange But Not a Stranger, 249
Strange Powers, 143
Strange Relations, 182
Strange Seas, 131
Strange Things: The Malevolent North in Canadian Literature, 32
Strange Travelers, 492
Strange Wine, 175
Strangeness: A Collection of Curious Tales, 163
Stranger at Home, 78
Stranger in a Strange Land, 218, 219, 220, 221
Stranger Suns, 362
"Stream of Consciousness," 369
Strength of Stones, 53
"String, The" (Goonan), 196
"Strings" (McHugh), 284
"Strong vs. Weak Characters," 138
Stross, Charles, 168, **415–18**
Strugatsky Brothers, 419–22, 426
Strugatsky, Arkady. *See* Strugatsky Brothers
Strugatsky, Boris. *See* Strugatsky Brothers
"Study of Science Fiction, The: A Modest Proposal," 337
Study War No More, 205
Sturgeon, Theodore, 172, 174, 208, **423–27**
Sub, The: A Study in Witchcraft, 162
Subatomic Monster, The, 28
Subspace Explorers, 404
"Such Interesting Neighbors," 187
"Such, Such Were the Joys," 325
Sudden Star, 363
"Suicide Coast," 215
Summa Technologiae, 261
Summer Morning, Summer Night, 83
Summer of Night, 395, 396
Summer of the Great-grandmother, The, 265
Summer People, 328
Summer Sketches, 397
Sun Shines Bright, The, 28
"Sun Spider, The," 383
"Sundance," 390
Sundered Worlds, The, 305
Sundiver, 95
Sunfall, 137
"Sunflowers," 196
"Sunjammer," 145
"Sunken Gardens," 412
Sunrise Alley, 19, 20
Sunrise on Mercury, 391
Sunstorm, 48, 145
"Super Goat Man," 269,
Super Science Stories, 336
Super-Cannes, 39
Superheroes, 451
Superluminal, 288
Super-State, 7
Supertanks, 205
Super-Toys Last All Summer Long and Other Stories of Future Time, 8, 9
"Suppliant in Space, A," 374
"Sur," 254
"Surface Tension," 66, 67
Surfacing, 32
"Surprise Party," 249
Surrender None, 301
Survival: A Thematic Guide to Canadian Literature, 32
Survival Kit, 336
"Survival of the Cunning, The," 224
Survivor, 116
Survivors of The Chancellor, *The*, 454
"Susan," 174
Swamp Thing, 313
"Swanilda's Song," 335
Swanwick, Michael, 191, 346, **428–32**, 489, 493,
"Swarm," 412
Swiftly Tilting Planet, A, 263
Sword of Aldones, 87, 88, 89
Sword of Chaos, 90
Sword of Rhiannon, The, 76, 77
Sword of the Lictor, The, 490
Swords of Mars, 110
Synners, 119, 120
Synthetic Man, The, 424
Synthetic Men of Mars, 110
"Synthetic Serendipity," 460
System of the World, The, 407, 408
Syzygy, 333

Tabitha Jute Trilogy, 199
Taint, 234
Take Back Plenty 198, 199
Take Back Your Government, 222
"Taklamakan," 412
"Tale of Gorgik, The," 151
"Tale of Rumor and Desire, The," 151
Tale of the Eternal Champion, 304, 307
Tale of the Troika, 420
Tale That Wags the God, The, 68
Talent series, 279
Tales and Stories (Shelley), 379
Tales from Planet Earth, 146
Tales from the Texas Woods, 307
Tales from the White Hart, 145
Tales of Alvin Maker, 124, 126
Tales of Gooseflesh and Laughter, 497
Tales of Known Space, 316, 317, 320
Tales of Nevèrÿon, 151
Tales of Old Earth, 430, 431
Tales of Pirx the Pilot, 260
Tales of Ten Worlds, 145
Tales of the Galactic Midway, 340, 342
Tales of the Grand Tour, 73
Tales of the Quintana Roo, 441
Tales of the Velvet Comet, 340, 342
Tanar of Pellucidar, 111
Tangents, 53, 54
"Tango Charlie and Foxtrot Romeo," 450
Tarzan Alive: A Definitive Biography of Lord Greystoke, 182
Tarzan at the Earth's Core, 111
Tarzan of the Apes, The, 109, 110, 111
Tatja Grimm's World, 460
Tau Zero 12, 14
Taylor Five: The Story of a Clone Girl, 244
Tea from an Empty Cup, 119, 120
Technic History, 13, 15
Technicolor Time Machine, The, 208, 209
Technological Singularity, The," 460
Tehanu: The Last Book of Earthsea, 255
Telebugs, 245
Telempath, 354
Telepathist, 99
Teleportress of Alpha C, 78
"Tell Me a Story," 265
Telling, The, 254, 255
"Ten SF/Fantasy/Genre Films That Should Not Have Been Made," 121
"10^{16} to 1," 247
Ten Thousand Light-Years from Home, 441

"Ten Years After," 121
Tender Loving Rage, 58
10th Victim, The, 373
Tepper, Sheri S., 433–37
Terminal Beach, The, 39, 40
Terminal Experiment, The, 366, 367, 368
Terran Empire, 15
Terror (Pohl), 334
Terror, The (Simmons), 394, 396
Terrorists of Tomorrow, 17
Terrornauts, The, 100
Tesseracts anthologies 169, 234, 235, 369
Test of Fire, 72
"That Thou Art Mindful of Him!," 26
Thebes of the Hundred Gates, 389
Themepunks, 168
Thendara House, 89
"Theodore Sturgeon on Philip Dick," 426
There Are Doors, 490
There Is No Darkness, 204
"There Shall Be No Darkness," 67, 68
There Will Be Time, 14, 15
"There Will Come Soft Rains," 82, 83
"There's a Great Big Beautiful Tomorrow/Now Is the Best Time of Your Life," 169
"Thesme and the Ghayrog," 390
They Fly at Çiron, The, 149, 150
They Shall Have Stars, 67
"Thing at the Top of the Stairs, The," 83
"Things That Are Gods, The," 99
Things That Never Happen, 216
Things to Come, 475
"Think Blue, Count Two," 400
"Think Like a Dinosaur," 247, 249, 250
Think Like a Dinosaur and Other Stories, 249
Third Level, The, 187
"Thirteen to Centaurus," 40
Thirteenth Immortal, The, 388
This Immortal, 499, 500, 501
This Is My Best, 336
This Is My Funniest, 345
"This Moment of the Storm," 502
This Mortal Mountain, 502
"This Shape We're In," 269
"This Space for Rent," 204
This World and Nearer Ones, 10
"This Year's Class Picture," 395
"Thor Meets Captain America," 94
Thorns, 389
Those Who Watch, 389

"Thought Experiments: When the Singularity Is More Than a Literary Device," 169
Threads of Time, 392
"'Threat' of Creationism, The," 29
Threats . . . and Other Promises, 460
Three by . . . (novellas), 74
Three Californias, 349
"Three Descents of Jeremy Baker, The," 502
Three Eyes of Evil Including Earth's Last Fortress, The, 445
300 (movie), 292, 294
334, 162
Three Martian Novels, 112
Three Stigmata of Palmer Eldritch, The, 156
Three Survived, 389
3001: The Final Odyssey, 145
Three Women, 329
Three Worlds to Conquer, 14
Three-Legged Hootch Dancer, The, 342
Threshold (Le Guin), 255
Threshold (Zelazny), 502
Threshold: The Blue Angels Experience, 227
Threshold of Eternity, 99
Through a Glass, Clearly, 26
Through Darkest Resnick with Gun and Camera, 344
Through Eyes of Wonder, 74
"Through the Apple," 22
"Through the Shaving Mirror . . . or, How We Abolished the Future," 307
Thumbprints, 362, 364
Thunder and Roses, The, 425
Thuvia, Maid of Mars, 110
THX 1138, 71
Tiberius, 337
"Tides of Kithrup, The," 95
Tides of Lust, 150
Tiger Among Us, The, 78
Tiger, Tiger, 58
Tillers, The, 225
Time and Again, 185, 187
Time and Stars, 17
"Time Considered as a Helix of Semi-Precious Stones," 150, 151
Time Dweller, The, 307
Time Enough for Love, 218, 220, 221
Time Fantasy, 263
Time for a Tiger, 107
Time for the Stars, 221
Time Has No Boundaries, 187
Time Hoppers, The, 389,

"Time Is Just a Place," 187
"Time Is the Traitor," 58
Time Killer, 372
Time Limit, 373
Time Machine, The, 47, 472, 473, 474, 475
"Time Machine Cuba," 192
Time Odyssey, 48
Time of Changes, A, 387, 389
Time of the Great Freeze, 388
Time of the Warlock, The, 319
Time out of Joint, 156
Time Patrol, 12, 16, 17
Time Pieces, 63
Time Pressure, 354
Time Quartet, 263
Time Ships, The, 47, 48
"Time to Survive, A," 67
Time Travel: Science Fiction Writing Series, 75
Time Travelers Strictly Cash, 355
Time Wanderers, The, 421
Time Wars, 17
Timeless Stories for Today and Tomorrow, 83
Timelike Infinity, 48
"Time-Out," 486
Timequake, 464
Time's Eye, 48, 145
Time's Last Gift, 182
Times Square Red, Times Square Blue, 149, 152
Time's Tapestry, 49
"Time-Sharing Angel," 440
"Tiniest Assassins , The," 346
Tiptree, James P., Jr., xv, xvi, 57, 58, 63, 64, 190, 257, **438–42**
Titan (Baxter), 48
Titan (Bova) 71, 73
Titan (Varley), 449, 450
Titan's Daughter, 67
To Be Continued: The Collected Stories of Robert Silverberg, 391
To Conquer Chaos, 99
To Die in Italbar, 501
"To Jorslem," 390
"To Leave a Mark," 350
To Live Again, 389
To Open the Sky, 389
To Outlive Eternity and Other Stories, 17
To Ride Pegasus, 279
To Sail Beyond the Sunset, 221
To Save a World, 90

To Say Nothing of the Dog, 484, 485
To the Dark Star: The Collected Stories Volume 2, 391
To the Land of the Living, 389
To the Stars, 210, 211
To Write Like a Woman: Essays in Feminism and Science Fiction, 359
To Your Scattered Bodies Go, 178, 179, 180, 181
Toast: And Other Rusted Futures, 417
Today We Choose Faces, 501
Tom O'Bedlam, 389
"Tomb Wife, The," 245
"Tomorrow and Tomorrow and Tomorrow," 464
"Tomorrow Calling," 192
Tomorrow Happens, 95
"Tomorrow May Be Different," 96
Tomorrow May Be Even Worse: An Alphabet of Science Fiction Cliches, 100
Tomorrow Midnight, 83
Tomorrow Now: Envisioning the Next Fifty Years, 412, 413
"Tomorrow on the March," 446
Tomorrow Stories, 313
Tomorrow Times Seven, 335
Tomorrow's Children, (Anderson), 14
Tomorrow's Children (Asimov), 27
Tomorrow's Warfare, 205
Tongues of the Moon, 180
Tono-Bungay, 474
Tool of the Trade, 204
"Top Five Depressed Superheroes," 270
Torch of Freedom, 469
Torrent of Faces, A, 67
"Total Environment," 8
Total Recall, 157
"Totally Rich, The," 99
Touch of Infinity, A, 174
"Tourism," 215
"Toward and Aesthetic of Science Fiction," 359
Tower and the Hive, The, 279
"Tower of Babylon," 139
Tower of Glass, 389
Towers of Darkover, 90
Towers of Toron, The, 150
Toynbee Convector, The, 83
Traces, 49
"Trademarks," 169
Trader to the Stars, 14, 16
Trading in Danger, 301

Tragedy of the Moon, The, 28
Trailing Clouds of Glory: Spiritual Values in Children's Literature, 264
Traitor to the Living, 181
Traitor's Sun, 90,
Tramp Royale, 222
Transatlantic Tunnel, Hurrah!, A, 209
Transcendent, 48
Transfigurations, 62
Transfinite: The Essential A. E. van Vogt, 446
"Transformation, The" (Shelley), 379
Transformation of Miss Mavis Ming, The, 305'
Transformations, The (Jones), 244
Transgalactic, 446
"Transit," 288
Transition, 288
Transmigration of Timothy Archer, The, 157
"Transparency Means Nothing Without Justice," 169
Transparent Society, The, 96
Trantorian Empire, 26
Traps of Time, The, 308
Travel Arrangements, 216
"Traveler's Tale, A," 383
"Traveling into Darkness," 330
"Travels with My Cats," 341, 343
Treason, 125
Treasure Box, 126
Treasure of the Great Reef, The, 146
Treaty at Doona, 278
Tree of Swords and Jewels, The, 136
"Trends," 23, 25
Triangle, 26
"Tricentennial," 203
Trigger, The, 145
Trikon Deception, The, 72
Trillion Year Spree, 5, 7, 10
Triplanetary: A Tale of Cosmic Adventure, 404
Tripoint, 135
Triton, 149, 150
Triumph, 72
"Triumph of the City," 309
Triumph of Time, The, 67
"Trojan Horse," 430
Trouble on Triton, 149, 150
Trouble Twisters, The, 16
Trouble with Lichen, 497
Troubled Waters, 138
Troublemakers: Stories by Harlan Ellison, 175
Troubling a Star, 264

Trout, Kilgore. *See* Farmer, Philip José
"True Faces," 121
True Game, The, 436
True Minds, 355
"True Names," 169, 458, 459
True Names . . . and Other Dangers, 460
"True Nature of Shangri-La, The," 350
Trujillo, 383
Trumps of Doom, 500, 501
"Truncat," 168
"Truth About Pyecraft, The," 474
Tunnel in the Sky, 221
Tunnel Through the Deeps, 209
"Tunnel Under the World, The," 332, 336
Tupolev too Far, A, 9
Turing Option, The, 209
Turn Left At Thursday, 335
"Turn On, Tune In, Veg Out," 409
Turtle Diary, 230, 231
"Tweener, The," 78
20,000 Leagues Under the Sea, (movie), 455
Twenty Thousand Leagues Under the Sea, 453
"Twenty-four Days Before Christmas, The," 264
"24 Views of Mt. Fuji, by Hokusai," 500
Twice Seven, 73
Twilight Man, The, 305
Twilight World, 14
Twilight Zone—Upgrade/Sensuous Cindy, 119, 120
Twinkling of an Eye: My Life as an Englishman, The, 7, 10
"Twisted Men, The," 445
"Two," 121
"2BR02B," 464
Two Hawks from Earth, 180
Two of Them, The, 358
Two Tales and Eight Tomorrows, 211
2081, 465
2001: A Space Odyssey, 143, 144, 145, 146, 367
"2001 and All That (or, Life Before and After the End of History)," 275
2061: Odyssey Three, 145
2010: Odyssey Two, 144, 145, 146
"Two Thousand Words," 246
Two to Conquer, 89
Two Trains Running, 384
Two Years' Vacation, 454
Two-Part Invention: The Story of a Marriage, 265
Ubik, 156

Ugly Little Boy, The, 25, 26, 389
Ultimate Cyberpunk, The, 121
Ultimate Egoist, The, 423, 425
"Ultimate Revolution," 240
Unaccompanied Sonata and Other Stories, 127
Unauthorized Autobiographies, 344
Uncharted Territory, 484, 485
Under African Skies, 345
Under Compulsion, 163
Under Heaven's Bridge, 62
"Under Hill," 492
Under Old Earth and Other Explorations, 400
Under Pressure, 224, 226
Under South American Suns, 345
"Under the Moons of Mars,"
Underpeople, The, 400,
<u>Undersea Trilogy</u>, 335, 336
"Understand," 141
"Understanding Human Behavior," 163
"Undone," 247, 249
Unfamiliar Territory, 391
"Ungoverned, The," 459, 460
Unicorn Mountain, 62
"Unicorn Tapestry, The," 130
Unicorn Trade, The, 17
"Unicorn Variation," 500
Unicorn Variations, 502
Union Club Mysteries, The, 26
<u>Universe</u>, 392
"Universe of One's Own, A," 460
"Universe of Things, The," 246
Unknown Worlds of Science Fiction, 320
Unlimited Dream Company, The, 38, 39
Unlock Your Money Personality, 446
Unlocking the Air and Other Stories, 256
Un-Man and Other Novellas, 17
Unreasoning Mask, The, 180
"Unsettling the World," 200
Unteleported Man, The, 156
Untouched by Human Hands, 374
"Unwirer," 417
Up from the Bottomless Pit, 180
Up from the Bottomless Pit and Other Stories, 183
Up the Line, 389
Up the Walls of the World, 440
<u>Uplift Universe</u>, 93, 94, 95
<u>Urban Nucleus</u>, 61, 62
<u>Urth</u>, 488
"Use of Archaeology in Worldbuilding, The," 137
Use of Weapons, 44

User Friendly, 355
User's Guide to the Millennium, A, 40
"Utmost Bones," 364
"Utopias," 472, 476

V for Vendetta, 312
"Vacancy," 383
Vacuum Diagrams, 47, 48
Vacuum Flowers, 430
Valentine, 383
Valentine Pontifex, 390
"Valerius: The Reanimated Roman," 378
Valis, 155, 157
Valley Beyond Time, 391
Valperga; or, The Life and Adventures of Castruccio, Prince of Lucca, 378
Vampire Tapestry, The, 130
Vampire's Ghost, The 79
Vampyre, The, 377
Van Vogt, A. E. 174, 175, **443–47**
Vanguard from Alpha, 7
"Vanilla Dunk," 269
Vanished Jet, The, 67
Vanishing Tower, The, 306
Variable Star, 221, 353, 354
Varley, John, 448–51
"Vaster Than Empires and More Slow," 255
Vatta's War, 299, 300, 301
Vault of the Ages, 14
"Veil of Astellar, The," 78
Veiled Web, The, 20
Vendetta for the Saint, 210
Vengeance of Orion, 73
Vengeance of Rome, The, 306
Venging, The, 54
"Venice Drowned," 350
Venus, (Bova) 72
"Venus Flowers at Night," 364
Venus Hunters, The, 40
Venus of Dreams, 361, 363
Venus of Shadows, 362, 363
Venus on the Half-Shell, 180
Venus on the Half-Shell and Others, 183
Venus Plus X, 424
Venus stories (Burroughs), 110, 111
Venus Trilogy (Sargent), 362
Venus, Inc., 336
Vermilion Sands, 39
"Vernalfest Morning," 63
Verne, Jules, xiv, 82, **452–57**, 475, 477
Very Bad Deaths, 355
Very Hard Choices, 355

"Very Pulse of the Machine, The," 429,
"Via Roma," 390
Viator, 383
Victim Prime, 373
Victims of the Nova, The, 99
Victory Conditions, 301
Vida, 329
Vietnam and Other Alien Worlds, 204
View from a Height, 28
View from Serendip, The, 146
View from the Stars, The, 298
Viewpoint, 74
Village in the Treetops, The, 454
Village of the Damned, 497
"Vinegar Peace," 63
Vinge, Vernor, 167, 189, 190, 415, **458–61**
Vinland the Dream and Other Stories, 350
Virconium, 213, 214, 215
Virgin Planet, 15
Viriconium Nights, 216
Virtual Light, 191
"Virtual Love," 284
Virtual Unrealities, 58
Visible Light, 137
"Visible Men, The," 307
Vision of the Future: The Art of Robert McCall, 74
Visionary in Residence, 413
"Visit the Sins," 168
Visitor, The (Tepper), 435
"Visitors, The" (Strugatsky Brothers), 421
Vitals, 53
Vititsky, S. *See* Strugatsky Brothers
Voice Across the Sea, 146
Voices from the Sky—Previews of the Coming Space Age, 146
Voices of Heaven, The, 334
Voices of Time and Other Stories, The, 39, 40
Von Bek, 307
Vonnegut, Kurt, 2, 179, 259, 424, 425, 427, **462–66**
Voodoo Game, The, 319
VOR (Blish) 67
Vor Game, The (Bujold), 102, 103
Vorkosigan's Game, 104
Vortex Blaster, The, 404
Voyage, 47, 48
Voyage Home, The, 288
Voyage of the Space Beagle, The, 443, 444
Voyage to the Bottom of the Sea, 424
Voyager in Night, 135
Voyagers, 73

Voyages et aventures du capitaine Hatteras, 454
<u>Voyages Extraordinaires</u>, 452, 453
Vulcan's Hammer, 156

Wake, 368
Waldo and Magic, Inc., 221
Walk to the End of the World, 129, 130
Walking on Glass, 44
Walking on Water: Reflections on Faith and Art, 264
"Walking Out," 430
Walking Tour of the Shambles, A, 491
Wall Around a Star, 335
Wall of America, The, 163
Wall of the Sky, the Wall of the Eye, The, 269
Walpurgis III, 341
Wampeters, Foma and Granfalloons (Opinions), 465
Wanderers of Time, 497
Wanting Seed, The, 105, 106
Wanton of Argus 99
War Amongst the Angels, The, 306
"War Beneath the Tree," 491
"War Birds, The," 47
War Chief, The, 111
War Fever, 40
War God's Own, The, 468, 470
War Hound and the World's Pain, The, 306
War in the Air, The, 474
War of Honor, 469
War of Nerves, 203
War of the Gods, 15
War of the Wing-Men, 16,
War of the Worlds, 51, 472, 473, 474, 475
War of Two Worlds, 14
War Stories, 204
War with the Robots, 210
War Year, 204
Warlord of Mars, The, 110
Warlord of the Air, The, 305
Warm Worlds and Otherwise, 438, 440, 441
Warrior's Apprentice, The, 101, 102, 103
Warriors of Blood and Dream, 503
Warriors of Day, The, 66
Warriors of Mars, 305
Wasp Factory, The, 42, 44
"Watchbird," 375
Watchmen (Moore), 311, 312, 313
<u>Watchmen Trilogy</u> (Bova), 73
Watchstar, 363
Water in the Air, 244

Water Witch, 485
Wave in the Mind, The, 254, 256
Wave Without a Shore, 135
Way the Future Was, The: A Memoir 333, 337
"Ways of Love, The," 16
"We All Die Naked," 67
We Can Build You, 156
We Can Remember It for You Wholesale, 157
We Claim These Stars, 15
We Few, 469
We Have Fed Our Sea, 14
"We Purchased People," 335
We the Underpeople, 400
We Who Are About To, 358
"We, in Some Strange Power's Employ, Move on a Rigorous Line," 151
Weapon Makers, The, 444
"Weapon Shop, The," 445
Weapon Shops of Isher, The, 444
"Weapon Too Dreadful to Use, The," 23, 25
Weapons of Mass Seduction 384
Weathermakers, The 71
"Weatherman," 103
Weaver, 49
Web (Wyndham), 497
Web 2028, The (Cadigan), 119, 120
Web Architect's Handbook, The, 417
Web of the City, 172
Webcrash, 49
Weber, David, 467–71
Weird Romance 441
Welcome to Mars!, 67
Welcome to Moonbase, 74
Welcome to the Monkey House: A Collection of Short Works, 464
Welcome, Chaos, 479, 481
Well of Shiuan, 136
Wells, H. G., xiv, xviii, 47, 50, 57, 82, 143, 190, 237, 324, 346, 348, 365, 393, 403, 444, 452, 453, 455, 457, **472–77,** 485
"Wells, Hitler and the World State," 324, 473
<u>West of Eden Trilogy</u>, 208, 210
"Weyr Search," 278
What Can Be Saved from the Wreckage, 431
"What Continues, What Fails . . . ," 95
"What Does This Convention Mean?," 403
"What Good Is a Glass Dagger?," 320
"What I Tell Librarians," 321
What If Our World Is Their Heaven? The Final Conversations of Philip K. Dick, 158
"What If the Singularity Does NOT Happen?," 461

"What It Might Be Like to Live in Viriconium," 216
"What Price Dreams?," 470
Whatdunits, 344
Wheel of Fortune, 503
Wheels of Chance, The, 474
Wheelworld, 210
When Dinosaurs Ruled the Earth, 40
When Diplomacy Fails, 345
"When It Changed," 357, 358
When the Feast Is Finished, 10
"When the Old Gods Die," 341
When the People Fell, 400
When the Sky Burned, 72
When the Sleeper Wakes, 474
"When We Went to See the End of the World," 390
"When You Care, When You Love," 425
"Where Do I Get My Crazy Ideas?," 321
Where Do We Go from Here?, 27
"Where I Get My Other Ideas From," 275
Where Late the Sweet Birds Sang, 478, 479, 481
"Where the Cluetts Are," 187
"Which Way to Inner Space?," 38, 40
"Whiff of Grapeshot, A," 470
Whipping Star, 225, 226
Whispers from the Cotton Tree Root, 235
White Death, 373
White Dragon, The, 279
"White Fang Goes Dingo," 162
White Fang Goes Dingo and Other Funny SF Stories, 163
White Mars Or, The Mind Set Free, 7
"White Otters of Childhood, The," 62
White Plague, The, 225, 226
White Queen, 243, 244
"White Whales, Raintrees, Flying Saucers, . . . ," 178, 183
White Wolf's Son, The, 306
Who He?, 58
"Who Is Honor Harrington?," 471
Who Made Stevie Crye?, 62
"Who's Afraid of Wolf 359?," 275
Whole Man, The, 99
"Why and How I Became Kilgore Trout," 183
"Why I Am Not Post-Modern," 282, 284
"Why I Write," 323, 325
"Why So Much Syzygy?," 426
"Why the Bridge Stopped Singing," 249
"Why the World Didn't End Last Tuesday," 486

"Why We Need Science Fiction," 30, 31, 32
Widowmaker series, 341, 343
"Wikipedia: A Genuine H2G2—Minus the Editors," 169
Wild Alien Tamer, The, 342
"Wild Girls, The," 254
"Wild Minds," 431
Wild Road, The, 215
Wild Seed, 115, 116
Wild Shore, The, 349
WildC.A.T.S, 313
Wilderness, 503
Wildlife, 249
Wilhelm, Kate, 478–82
"Will the Atomic Bomb Ever Be Perfected, and If So What Will Become of Robert Heinlein?," 155, 157
Will the Last Person to Leave the Planet Please Shut Off the Sun?, 344
Williamson Effect, The, 503
Willis, Connie, 483–87
Wilson, John Anthony Burgess. *See* Burgess, Anthony
Wind from a Burning Woman, The, 54
Wind from Nowhere, The, 39
Wind from the Sun, The, 146
Wind in the Door, A, 263
Wind Rider's Oath, 470
Wind Whales of Ishmael, The, 180
Windows & Mirrors, 63
Winds of Altair, The, 72
Winds of Change and Other Stories, The, 27
Winds of Darkover, 89
Winds of Limbo, The, 305
Winds of Marble Arch and Other Stories, The, 485, 486
Wind's Twelve Quarters, The, 254, 256
"Wings," 288
Winners 17
Winning Colors, 301
Winter Beach, The, 481
Winter Haunting, A, 396
Winter in Eden, 210
Winter Journey, 163
"Winter Market, The," 191
Winter of the World, The, 15
"Winter Solstice," 343
"Winter's King," 255
"Winterfair Gifts," 103
"Wire Continuum, The," 145
Wireless, 417
Witch Fantastic, 345

With a Little Help from My Friends, 344
"With Caesar in the Underworld," 390
"With Delicate Mad Hands," 440
"With Thimbles, with Forks and Hope," 481
"With Tiptree Through the Great Sex Muddle," 441
"With Virgil Oddum at the East Pole," 173
Without Me, You're Nothing, 227
Witling, The, 460
Wizard (Varley), 450
Wizard, The (Wolfe), 491
Wizard of Earthsea, A, 255
Wizardry and Wild Romance: A Study of Epic Fantasy, 308
Wizard's Eleven, 435
Wold Newton Family, 179, 181
Wolfbane, 334
Wolfe, Gene, 189, **488–94**
Wolfe Archipelago, The, 492
Wolfe Family Album, A, 492
Wolverine, 294
Woman a Day, A, or The Day of Timestop, 180
"Woman and Primitive Culture," 476
"Woman Appeared, A," 131
Woman of Destiny, 124, 126
Woman on the Edge of Time, 327, 328, 329
"Woman the Unicorn Loved, The," 491
"Woman Writing Science Fiction and Fantasy, A," 441
"Woman's Liberation, A" (Le Guin), 255
Woman's Liberation, A: A Choice of Futures by and About Women (Willis), 486
Woman's Vengeance, A, 239
"Women in Science Fiction" 365
"Women Men Don't See, The," 438, 440
Women of Genesis, 126
Women of Wonder anthologies, 362, 364
"Women SF Doesn't See, The," 487
Women Writing Science Fiction as Men, 345
Wonder Effect, The, 335
"Wonderful Power of Storytelling, The," 414
Wonderful Visit, The, 474
Woodrow Wilson Dime, The, 187
"Word for World Is Forest, The," 254
Word of God, The, 161, 162
Work of Art and Other Stories. A, 68
World at the End of Time, The, 334
World Behind the Door, The, 343
World Divided, A, 90
World Inside, The, 389,
World Jones Made, The, 156

World Named Cleopatra, A, 17
World of a Thousand Colors, 391
World of Chance, 156
World of Null-A, The, 443, 445
World of Tiers, 181
World Out of Time, A, 318, 320
World Set Free, The, 474
World Swappers, The, 99
"World Watch," 124, 128
"World Well Lost, The," 424, 425
World Without End, 203
"World without Racism, A," 117
World without Stars, 14
World Wreckers, 88, 89
World's Fair 1992, 389
"Worlds Beside Worlds," 212
Worlds Enough and Time: Five Tales of Speculative Fiction, 397
Worlds of Honor, 470
Worlds of Tomorrow anthologies, 336
Worlds of Weber: Ms. Midshipwoman Harrington and Other Stories, 470
Worlds, The, 204
WorShip series, 226
Worthing Chronicle, The, 125
Would It Kill You to Smile?, 62
Wrath of Khan, The, 288
Wreck of the Godspeed and Other Stories, The, 249
Wrecks of Time, The, 305
Wrinkle in Time, A, 263, 264
"Writer as Nomad, The," 365
Writer's Talk: Michael Moorcock with Colin Greenland, 200, 308
"Writer's Workshops," 250
"Writerisms and Other Sins: A Writer's Shortcut to Stronger Writing," 138
"Writing and the Demolished Man," 59
"Writing Science Fiction as If It Mattered: A Self-Interview," 64
"Writing Star Trek Novels, or, Why Don't You Get a Morally Acceptable Job?," 289
Writing Well, 397
"Wrong-Way Street," 319
W3: Women in Deep Time, 54
WWW Trilogy, 368
Wyndham, John, 216, **495–98**
Wyrms, 125

X Stands for Unknown, 28
Xeelee Sequence, 48, 49
Xenocide, 125

Xenogenesis, 115, 116
X-Files, The, 190, 192
X-Men, 291, 294

"Yanqui Doodle," 441
Year before Yesterday, The, 7
Year of the Cloud, The, 480
Year of the Flood, The, 30, 31
"Year of the Jackpot, The," 221
Year of the Lucy, The, 279
Year of the Ransom, The, 16
Year 2018!, 67
Year Zero, 283, 284
Years of Rice and Salt, The, 349
Years of the City, The, 333, 336
Yes, Let's: New and Selected Poems, 163
Yesterday and Tomorrow, 454
"Yesterday's Tomorrows," 482
Yestermorrow: Obvious Answers to Impossible Futures, 85
"You and Your Characters," 250
You Can Be the Stainless Steel Rat, 210
"You Don't Know Dick," 270
You Don't Love Me Yet, 269
"You See But You Do Not Observe," 368
You Will Never Be the Same, 400
Young Frankenstein 379
"Young Man's Journey to Viriconium, A," 215
Young Miles, 104
Young Unicorns, The, 263, 264
Young Wolfe, The, 492
"Your Appointment Will Be Yesterday," 157
"Your Haploid Heart," 440
Yours, Isaac Asimov: A Life in Letters, 23, 28
"Youthful Folly," 383
You've Had Your Time, 105, 107
Yvgenie, 137

Zanne series, 244
Zanzibar Cat, The, 359
Zap Gun, The, 156
Zarathustra Refugee Planets, 97, 99
Zeitgeist, 412
Zelazny, Roger, 58, 61, 157, 193, 318, 372, 373, 485, **499–504**
Zen in the Art of Writing: Essays on Creativity, 85
Zenith Angle, The, 412
"0wnz0red," 168
"Zirn Left Unguarded, the Jenghik Palace in Flames, John Westerley Dead," 374
Zodiac, 408

Subject Index

Apocalyptic SF, 37, 46, 160, 194, 229, 286, 296, 433, 478, 488, 495

Cyberpunk, 119, 189, 406, 410

Dystopias, 97, 105, 129, 237, 322

Early SF, 377, 402, 452, 472

Feminist SF, 30, 87, 129, 252, 286, 327, 357, 361, 438, 478

Graphic novels, 207, 291, 311

Hard SF, 12, 19, 23, 46, 51, 70, 93, 142, 201, 218, 258, 316, 347, 366, 386, 448, 452, 458

Humor and satire, 1, 81, 101, 154, 166, 178, 207, 237, 258, 331, 352, 371, 419, 462, 483

Military SF, 201, 299, 381, 467

Myth and legend, 5, 12, 114, 123, 139, 171, 198, 229, 233, 242, 258, 286, 327, 339, 381, 394, 398, 428, 488, 499

Near future, 30, 37, 97, 105, 154, 160, 166, 189, 233, 242, 247, 282, 347, 495

New Wave, 5, 37, 148, 160, 171, 213, 252, 303, 357, 361, 438

Post-human SF, 51, 56, 65, 93, 194, 224, 398, 410, 415, 423, 443, 448, 458

Science fantasy, 1, 60, 76, 81, 87, 109, 123, 133, 178, 185, 198, 213, 233, 262, 276, 303, 357, 361, 371, 386, 415, 419, 433, 488, 499

Sense of wonder, 23, 46, 65, 123, 142, 194, 262

SF horror, 377, 394, 495

SF romance, 19, 34, 87, 101, 276

Slipstream, 139, 247, 267, 371, 381, 428

Space opera, 23, 42, 56, 76, 97, 101, 133, 148, 198, 207, 224, 272, 299, 316, 331, 339, 352, 402, 415, 419, 443, 467

Technothrillers, 119, 166, 189, 406, 410

Time travel, 12, 34, 60, 185, 303, 327, 366, 428, 462, 483

Utopias, 42, 114, 237, 252, 327, 472

About the Author

Maura Heaphy is the author of *Science Fiction Authors: A Research Guide* (Libraries Unlimited, 2008) and a Senior Lecturer at The Ohio State University. She has a BA from Marymount Manhattan College, in New York, and an MA in politics from Lancaster University in the United Kingdom. She is married to the long-suffering Richard Dutton, and they have two patient and understanding daughters, Kate and Claire.